T

Magda Sweetland was born in Edinburgh where she was educated, and now lives in the South of England.

Her first novel, *Eightsome Reel*, published in 1985, received a Scottish Arts Council Publication grant and won the Authors' Club First Novel Award. *The Connoisseur*, 1986, has received recognition as a small masterpiece.

Also by Magda Sweetland in Pan Books

Eightsome Reel
The Connoisseur

MAGDA SWEETLAND

THE HERMITAGE

PAN BOOKS
in association with Macmillan

First published in Great Britain in 1988 by Macmillan London Ltd
This edition published in 1989 by Pan Books Ltd,
Cavaye Place, London SW10 9PG
in association with Macmillan London Ltd
9 8 7 6 5 4 3 2 1
© Magda Sweetland 1988
ISBN 0 330 30672 3

Printed and bound in Great Britain by
Richard Clay Ltd, Bungay, Suffolk

I

1

The map of Edinburgh is complex, defined by two contrary forms
of logic, geography and history, the practical versus the emotive.
Fact and sentiment run through the pattern of the streets
sometimes in concurrence, sometimes at loggerheads. The castle
dominates the outline, combining both forms of necessity, a rock
with a well that makes it impregnable to climatic as well as the
human foe. But the roads that run down from it are incompatible:
regular to the north, random behind, squares and circles which
adapt to the lie of the land in a way that acknowledges the power of
accident over systems of geometry. Seven hills and four rivers
combine in a formula that is not likely to be bettered for town
planning, stones and water balanced so that the city flows like a
vast deltaic deposit of sandstone into the sea.

Among its natives, none was more strictly factualist than Fergus
Petrie.

He came out of the room at the top of the house in George Square
where he was in the final stages of checking the statistics on his
thesis, by using the computer of the University department to
which he was attached, and headed up the Middle Meadow Walk
towards Lauriston Place. He counted his minutes carefully and
wasn't over-pleased to be distracted along his route. James Geddes, the Professor of Jurisprudence, stopped him near the bollards
that kept the traffic in the square pedestrian.

"Good day to you, Fergus. Knocking off?"

For the professor, this was a pleasantry which Fergus misinter-
preted. "No. I'm not going home."

"Ah, the library, of course. How is your doctorate coming
along?"

"Should be ready by the end of next week, all being well."

"I hear the department of Artificial Intelligence is interested in
your research material."

3

"Yes. Some of it was published in a mathematical journal. They happened to have been working on the same problems, from the other end. The semantic considerations of nonmonotonic logic."

"Not my area at all," said the professor, "though I wish you every success with it." He was benevolent but not indulgent. He turned in the direction of George Square which, caught in the cross-reference of architecture and convenience, was already a hybrid of classical and concrete. "Do come and see us sometime when you're free. Irene often asks after you. And Matthew complained all Easter that he needed a tennis partner."

The young man said, "I've stopped playing competitive tennis for the season. There was a major tournament at Mortonhall this evening I'd like to have entered. But I thought Harris was my stand-in."

"Ah, Harris." The professor's tone was severe. "We see rather too much of your brother for my liking."

Fergus wasn't inclined to delve into the habits, sporting or unsporting, of his brother and made to move off. He nodded and parted from his friend and one-time neighbour, who had made a predictable enough assumption about where Fergus was going. If the eldest Petrie wasn't going home, he must be heading towards the library on George IV Bridge, probably going to consult some esoteric reference on computing. There were only two places in Fergus' hemisphere, home and work.

But the professor was wrong in his deduction.

Fergus was less than half a mile from his destination and didn't deviate from the straight path although it was a half mile in the ancient quarter of the city that intersected many arcs of interest, from the Meadows to the High Street, places of history and study and prayer which were drawn inside a small circumference. On his left rose the turrets of George Heriot's School where he had been a distinguished scholar. He had learned to be grateful for the endowment left by the philanthropic Jingling Geordie, goldsmith and moneylender to his extravagant monarch, James VI and I. Like Christ's Hospital in London, the school was endowed 'for the education, nursing and upbringing of youth, being puir orphans and fatherless children of decayet burgesses and freemen of the said burgh, destitute and left without means'. Fergus was thankful for his education, but not to the point of being sentimental. He

4

found 'Distribute Cheerfulle' a specious motto and never went back. He was not interested in history, even his own.

He passed the statue of Greyfriars' Bobby, a dog cast in bronze on top of a fountain, memorial to loyalty. He remembered that he too was thirsty but didn't stop to drink, sensing that he was already late for the proceedings. He pressed on up George IV Bridge, past the doors of the public library as well as the National Library of Scotland opposite, and headed towards the High Street, where he turned right towards St Giles Cathedral. His feet crossed the stones of the Mercat Cross which were said to mark the Heart of Midlothian. Gradually, his options diminished until he came into the cul-de-sac of Parliament Square, a misnomer deriving from the time when the courtyard housed the Scottish Assembly in the seventeenth century before it united with the English one at Westminster, but from then devolved into its secondary function as the ancillary of government. It was the home of the Scottish Law Courts, enforcing legislation instead of passing it. Fergus walked along the colonnade as far as the Great Hall of Parliament and, pushing open the door, went inside.

Fergus was a man of practical dimension, maybe unimaginative, but he briefly found himself daunted by the associations of place. The stained glass windows and the alternating chequers of the floor reminded him of the cathedral fifty yards away. The Great Hall was as hushed as a church cloister, with only a lawyer or two crossing the squared floor to chambers or ward rooms reminding him of the real function of the place, which was temporal not divine justice, but even they were priest-like in their robes, black, fluttering, tonsured with wig. It was a historic place, this seat of law. Fergus was impressed by the respect due first to its antiquity, then to religion and finally to learning, for the Great Hall emanated a solemnity that derived from all of these adjuncts and he was awed by its formal airs.

An usher spoke to him. "Can I be of assistance, sir?" The young man was formal himself, the usher thought, taking him for a research student in Government and Constitution, or maybe intended for the bar and come to take notes.

"I wondered if a case had been called today. The Crown versus Petrie."

Fergus said the name in a murmur, letting the sentence fall, so that the sound missed the usher's ear and he had to ask again, "Versus who?"

"Petrie."

The man consulted a printed list of the day's business and found the number of the court which had been allocated to the case. "It's just a routine fraud. You don't want to go into that one. There's a murder in the High Court and armed robbery in six." Hardened to visitors' tastes, he offered the extreme.

"No. The Petrie case. It has started?"

"Just. It's been pushed down the order. They won't get much in this afternoon but it's likely to be a longish one anyway. Outside and along on your right. It's the Justiciary Court. You're an observer, are you, not a witness?" he asked, alerted to the possibility that the young man was not a casual visitor after all.

"No. I'm an observer."

But as Fergus made this disclaimer, he felt his perjury had the weight of Peter's denial. He walked along to where the usher had indicated and found a varnished door leading to the ante-chamber of the court. He said to the policeman on duty, "An observer."

"Through this door and it's on your left."

Doors opened and closed in rapid succession until Fergus found himself mounting a few wooden steps in a narrow staircase and suddenly emerged with the scene of the courtroom in full view below him, laid out like a stage set. Compared with the panelling of the Great Hall and the shaded colonnade, this chamber was light and airy. In the middle of an April afternoon the sun streamed through the high domed windows and was diffused across the pale oak fitments, so that he was temporarily unsighted and groped his way to a seat which the sergeant indicated, unable to focus clearly on either the room or its occupants.

Gradually, his vision re-adjusted. He looked about more calmly and took in the separate elements of the court room. A dozen pews lined the raised dais he sat on, separated down the middle by a wooden bar. He was the only person on the left, while on the right there were several rows of men, some of whom he recognised, and one elderly woman, chief among the plaintiffs. Below him, to his left, sat the jury in stalls which looked only marginally more comfortable than his own, while the lawyers and clerks grouped themselves round an oval table in the centre of the floor space. The

6

judge sat alone on his bench, a curved arc running the full width of the room. He wore the saltire cross on his shoulder, symbol of suffering, and the front of his gown was bordered in red on which sat ermine flecks. This provided almost the only colour in a scene composed of neutrals, the pale wood predominating.

Above the judge's head, Fergus noticed a large coat of arms bearing the insignia of the Great Seal of Scotland. The scroll of heraldry focused his attention with its powerful motto, Dieu et mon Droit. In this moment of uncertainty, it read as a huge statement of faith and large enough to fix his hopes on. The incantations of his childhood came back to him after a decade of half-hearted observance. Thy kingdom come, thy will be done on earth as it is in heaven. Though his version became confused with the language of his mother church and concurrently the words Fiat voluntas tua . . . in saecula saeculorum . . . Amen ran in his head. The symbols of the seal were vivid, the scrollwork making a frame to a shield which was supported by two sparring animals, the unicorn of Scotland and the lion rampant of England, face on in combat. Stylisation had not entirely removed the aggressiveness from their postures, an analogue to the drama of the court.

Fergus had arrived at a moment of indecision. A contentious jury in the morning had held this case over and, though it had been introduced, the judge consulted his watch to consider if he had had enough for one day but, finding counsel zealous, decreed that they should proceed to open the examination of the defendant.

"Call Michael Petrie."

Fergus looked round, expecting to see the accused come out of a side door. Instead, a tall man stood up from the lowest row of benches where he had been sitting flanked by two policemen and walked across the open area of the court to the witness box. Fergus noticed how loose the jacket was that he wore, hanging in two deep creases from his shoulder blades. Its folds accentuated a stoop that made the man look prematurely aged. Fergus was able to gauge by the circumference of cloth how the man had lost girth and stature since it had been cut to fit him.

All the same, he commanded attention. The judge and the scribe to his right looked up and took cognisance of the accused as he walked up the half dozen steps to the witness box. At a glance, one would have placed him as an art dealer, or an academic, conforming to standards of refinement both in his physique and in his mannerisms which were slow and studied.

"You are Michael Petrie?" began the counsel for the prosecution once his witness had been sworn in.

The man in the witness box hesitated and appeared to cogitate so that his questioner asked more insistently, "You *are* Michael Petrie, aren't you?" and a titter went round the room that any man should have to reflect on the most elemental fact about himself, his name.

"No. I am really Mihail Petrovitch." His accent, which was broad and slanted in its vowels, thickened when he spoke the foreign name as it would be pronounced in his native Russian.

The titters ceased.

Counsel consulted his notes. "Not Michael Petrie as appears on the charge."

"Michael Petrie is the name I use."

"You changed your name by deed poll?" The legal man sounded as though he were trying to be helpful, but somehow the effect was contrary.

"No. I simply used it for convenience."

"I see. You use a name you are not entitled to."

The man, whatever his name was, suddenly looked tired. Tired of waiting for his case to be called that day, tired of the protracted processes of law which had brought him to this place after almost two years of delay through the circuitous collection and sifting of evidence. Nor was this the end. Standing at the point of crisis, he could see it was only a culmination of one part of the procedure. It gave him an elevation from which he could anticipate a week of such specific questions and oblique answers, all of them futile because they did not ask why he had done such and such a thing, and motive was to him the single factor worth establishing. Next would come a verdict, a sentence possibly, its enactment and the aftermath, whatever these might be. His trial was no end. It was the start. Seeing how long a road he had to travel, he was daunted, Pilgrim calling from his den, 'What shall I do?'

"It is what other people called me. It seemed wise to call myself that too."

"May we not dispense with nomenclature?" asked the judge, eying the clock.

"Very good, my lord." Counsel was quick to avoid antagonism.

Accuracy was a point he was prepared to waive. "And you are a British subject?" He turned again.

"No. I kept my Russian nationality."

"And you live at. . ." he consulted his papers as he spoke and read out an address.

This was unfortunate. The man had changed address since the charge sheet was made out, and so this information too he had to amend. There was a restiveness let loose in the chamber which was not boredom, shifting in seats, but suspicion making itself manifest. He was a foreigner. He changed name and address with a disregard to the permanence each implied, betokening respect-ability. He looked a dubious character, a little sly in his answers, a little shifty.

Fergus caught this rumour in the air and was dismayed by the implications of prejudice. Nor was the prosecuting counsel blind to his advantage. "Let us see if we can establish the true location of your business premises. . . at least." It was unfair that sarcasm could be used to barb a question, that tiny throwaway remarks could create a climate of opinion in the jury's mind against which unimaginative facts were feeble. The professional could impute the other's honesty, to which the accused had no right of reply.

Fergus listened to the rise and fall of the two voices, the orotund Englishness of the barrister as against the nasal reediness of his witness, one loudly confident, the other faltering both in its command of language and of the situation. The man in the dock was doubly disadvantaged.

Fergus had perhaps expected a gentle dissertation on the rules of law, or kindly questioning in order to arrive at a generally agreed conclusion. Not so. The two sides took every opportunity to score points which often to his way of thinking sounded trivial or base, concerning the form of words rather than the essential matter which they should elucidate. He was alerted early on to the difference in language between lawyer and layman, one technical and precise, the other vague and so less effective. The counsel, and particularly that for the prosecution, had a scalpel-like refinement with his whetted tongue. He cast over all defence witnesses a putative colouring. 'It has been suggested that. . . are you quite clear. . . are you telling the truth about that?' Occasionally, he met his match in a man who answered obdurately, I can't estimate that or I couldn't tell you or I don't want to answer that question.

Michael wasn't one of these. He faltered throughout the questioning, simply forgetful or confused. And indeed the plurality of bits of paper and statements and counter-statements was confusing. The jargon of the courts compounded this with diligences and arrestment and poinding so that it was impossible for Fergus to say, after hearing maybe two hours of the evidence, how that session had gone. He knew the facts but couldn't guess the emphasis which the proceedings had placed on them. He knew that insolvency per se was not an offence. The problem lay in whether by the disposition of his assets to 'conjunct and confident persons', the bankrupt had incurred the charge of fraud, demonstrating a willingness to deprive his prior creditors. What sums were transferred to which accounts, what record was kept of the transaction? That the enormity of guilt might reside in nothing more than muddle-headedness was not lost on Fergus.

As the dialogue proceeded, defining the place and nature of the business that had become insolvent, Fergus found he couldn't bear to watch the gestures and facial changes that accompanied the drama. It made it too vivid, to see as well as hear. He put his head down, unconsciously adopting the attitudes of prayer. He put his hands between his knees and fixed his eyes on the floor while his lips moved in a repeated sequence akin to a Paternoster or Hail Mary. The words which he formulated were less coherent than they. "Oh please. . . oh please," but still comprised the essential prayer. A plea for mercy, justice, intervention, that men might be more equal before God than the law.

Fergus heard the thick accent and the hesitancy which struck a note between pedantry and obstruction while the prosecutor, who was skilled in the manipulation of a question, asked the same thing over and over again, knowing that in the shorthand transcript this would read as a wilful evasion of the point, and that was what the judge would infer at the summing-up. Fergus heard an appalling thing – his father reduced to the incoherence of a child, worse than an infant because he was overcome with nerves, stumbled over words, repeated himself, made untypical errors in fact and language. Fergus knew this weakness, having conquered it. He had got the better of a stammer as a child and now spoke with great deliberation so as not to trip himself, but this slowness of speech sometimes allowed his enemies in. Words flew away from him and were not his friends.

There was a change. The prosecution stopped abruptly and with the words, "Request to recall the witness at a future date", sat down. It was over for the day and would be resumed, like any other business, at opening time. The court emptied, witnesses filtering back through the stalls as policemen waited to check the empty premises for security and lock up afterwards.

Fergus and Michael Petrie found themselves outside on the cobbles of the square, carried along by the crowd which headed up or down the High Street. A mean wind blew and the man shivered, thinly vulnerable.

"Do you want to borrow my coat? I forgot. I could have brought yours with me."

"The weather's turned," was all Michael said and then, as they graduated to the upper and more exposed levels at the top of the Mound, added, "So. She didn't come." None of them had come to support him with their interest, if not their love. Not his wife, not Harris and not his daughter Alison. Only the faithful Fergus.

"No, she didn't come today."

Fergus put the best interpretation on the absence, implying she might come another day, but did not fundamentally believe his mother would undergo a change of heart. This caring about the woman's state of mind highlighted a corresponding negligence towards his own. He wanted Michael to say, 'Thank you for coming. I'm sorry you had to leave your work when time's so precious now. What else happened to you today?' But the man was alone in the cell of himself and could not feel for the agony of another.

A number 23 bus took them along the thoroughfares of the city, Tollcross, Holy Corner and Church Hill, where shops and banks and housing alternated with the greenery of open spaces. People went putting on the links at Bruntsfield, in among the shadows cast by the trees that bordered the terraces. Children flew kites. Lovers loved, ignorant of the incipient dew on grass stems. Old men sat on benches watching the progress and all of them were happy in what they did. The men and women who joined or left the bus had faces that connected with each other, displaying interest in their purchases or their clothes or whether it would be fine over the weekend – the sum of normality. The Petries saf apart. Michael didn't lift his eyes from the ground or, if he did, they were unseeing. Fergus was the more unfortunate for he was aware both of the nature of the everyday, and their own distance from it. Percipience underscored the rift between them and their fellows, proving his inability to alleviate the man's despair.

They got off at the end of Canaan Lane, below the clock at Morningside, and walked silently between the buildings that pressed on the street until they reached their block of flats. It was, in the idiom of the tenements, a main door flat. It was reached by a door no one else in the stair used and had a private patch of soil in front as well as sharing rights in the drying green which the block enclosed. The advantage of the flat was diminished by two conditions: first, that it was north facing and secondly that the little sunlight which filtered between the solid stone walls of the street was reduced by the time it reached ground level, so that the apartment was almost permanently in a gloom thickened by the net curtains which proximity to the street made compulsory.

An envelope lay on the mat together with a free newspaper and, quickly, Fergus bent and picked them up, hiding them under his coat.

"Any letters?" asked Michael automatically, following on behind.

"No. Just advertising leaflets." Fergus went into his room and dropped the coat and missives on the bed.

In the living room, Michael sat rubbing his temples the way he did, in a circular motion and, without a word, Fergus fetched a glass of water and the tablets the man took, three at a time, for migraine. He stood over him and watched as he swallowed them down.

"Are you hungry?"

"Not really. A sandwich perhaps."

So Fergus went and cut sandwiches in the corner cupboard that served as a kitchen, buttering and spreading to the edge in the hope that what he produced would be appetising and tempt a palate like an invalid's, fastidious to the point where starvation was as enjoyable as eating. He put only one on Michael's plate and left the rest out of sight on the table, bringing plate and cup and saucer to his armchair.

They did not speak. There was no point. There was no word which could mitigate catastrophe while incursions into trivia were demeaning to them both.

The shadows in the room slowly softened as the evening sun withdrew round a corner, leaving them in half-light, but it wasn't one that enhanced the surrounding objects. An ugly three-piece suite, a table and four chairs, a rug, a fireplace of beige tiles without date or distinction. The basics. There wasn't a picture or an ornament in sight, while the books and the few personal items ranged on a dresser were patent additions. The two men who found themselves in this setting were at odds with it. The suit that hung from the elder was still, in its decline, cashmere and silk. Fergus was untraceable; with deliberate studied speech, wearing ancient gabardine and tweed, he was the casual classicist to whom guesses did not apply. They each had overtones of gentility, elongated features, reflective eyes, so that they were incongruous in the ugly room like players passing across a stage on their way to another set. It did not vitalise them, or they it.

The silence between them became constrained and Fergus, knowing what interminable pensiveness they could inhabit together, broke it before the tension told on him. "I must look at some work tonight." He would have liked to go and stretch his legs, play tennis up at Mortonhall but didn't dare to leave the man alone.

"Yes. I think I'll go to lie down for a while. Maybe I'll get some sleep."

They knew he wouldn't sleep. He would get up and walk the room, rolling cigarettes between thin fingers, side to side, side to side. Previewing another such shared night, in opposite rooms, they were both exhausted.

In his own bedroom, Fergus went to hang his coat up and found the envelope which he'd forgotten. He didn't like the look of this for he'd grown accustomed to these brown envelopes with the address typed across the shorter side. They smacked of legal matters. Addressed to Mr Michael Petrie. What else could they find to throw at him? Trembling a little at his audacity in tampering with the sacrosanct mail, Fergus sat down on the edge of the bed and pulled open the flap. He read through the sheets hurriedly but thinking they related to the insolvency, couldn't make sense of them. Then he saw his mother's name, Mrs Muriel Petrie, in among the typescript and began again, turning pale as he read from anger and final comprehension.

It was so perfectly timed that she must have planned it. She was instituting divorce proceedings on the actual day that he was brought to trial. No wonder she hadn't dared to show her face. What was her cause? The irretrievable breakdown of the marriage? He read the phrase with scorn. Mental cruelty she cited, but by whom on whom? She'd waited for this moment on purpose, knowing that as long as she was Michael's wife the law couldn't compel her to give evidence against her husband. She did this less out of consideration for the man than to guard her own neutrality, to hide behind the screen of spouse as long as it could give her some protection from the charge of fraud.

He put the papers back in their envelope and thought, I'll have to break this to him sometime, but couldn't imagine how. Perhaps seal it up and pretend it arrived the next day. What was one day more or less?

Fergus opened his books and tried to work but at the end of an hour he had achieved only a few rough jottings. He was going through the motions.

He watched the evening creep along the enclosed space of the drying green. Flowerless and functional, it had no elements of beauty. Embedded in the grass there were a dozen metal poles with spikes welded near the top, like truncated signposts. In the morning, women passed a foot from his window ledge as they heaved wet washing onto ropes. Rotas prevailed, in which he did not participate, for a prime drying position, for the weekly cutting of the grass, washing of the stairs, but the communality of these chores was alien to him in concept. He remembered privacy and elevation, his own lawn to look out on and a gardener, who had called him Master Petrie once upon a time, tending it two days a week.

Gone. All gone. Sunlight expired. The last corner of the green was cast in shadow. In a little while darkness would follow and the night dews. Fergus realised it was only nine o'clock and that elsewhere young men of his age were out and doing. He suddenly remembered that at Mortonhall the tournament would be drawing to a close, points fought against the light. He wondered who would make the final, his friend Matthew Geddes perhaps and Harris. The irk that he would in all probability have displaced his brother was unendurable. He recalled the new tennis racquet Harris had shown off to him the last time they'd met in the club, taking a perverse delight in making him hold it, telling him how good it was and how expensive, the latest model, large head, steel frame, that made other racquets redundant overnight, from the top range at Lillywhite's. His brother was a boaster, the brag of childhood. But all along Fergus knew he was rejoicing that he had elected for the winning side in the parental separation, while his foolish elder brother opted for the losing one. Money was his, position, power. As he put his head down to his reading, Fergus found himself hoping that, in spite of the new racquet and the weakened opposition, Harris had lost his match.

2

A woman passenger on the same number 23 bus as Michael and Fergus Petrie saw them board it at the High Street and moved upstairs to avoid speaking to them. She knew where they'd been and although she felt compassionate towards the man, considering him a victim of bungling both personal and legal, she didn't see eye to eye with his son and preferred to avoid even casual social contact.

She stayed on the bus until a stop before the terminus, reading the notes she'd made in the library during the afternoon. She spent some part of every day in the public library, reading the newspapers. She didn't have her own delivered. Where was the sense in that, when the lending library had them all for free? She sat unconcerned among the tramps and dossers, knowing she was upholding the intellectual tradition embodied by Karl Marx and the penniless young Shaw who had turned the facilities of the British Museum to such good use.

Like these researchers, what she extracted from her studies was two-fold. Warmth first of all. The municipal libraries, of which she did the rounds, supplied free heat as well as newspapers, the chairs and tables to read them on, accommodation more ample than her own. Information second. She hunted down all sorts of information on the two subjects which were her passion, tenuously linked in politics. She was a Scottish Nationalist of long standing, her father having been one of the founder members of the Scottish Party before its amalgamation with the nationalists. She had grown up parallel to the national movement, inspired by its evolution and checked by its reverses. The first men of the party, Sir Alexander McEwan, John MacCormick, Douglas Young and R. D. MacIntyre, were callers at their house and, when other young women went out to parties and dressed their hair in ringlets or in chignons, she sat at the feet of politicians and wrangled with them over the issue of devolution from England. She was an out-

and-out separatist, had no truck with moderates and detested all things English, their Parliamentary parties, their royal house, the social patterns of class rather than clan, the cold, derivative language they imposed on the warm pulse of Scots. There was nothing sly or mean about her hatred of the south. It was a broad and generous detestation.

She was a self-appointed watchdog of the Edinburgh Corporation. She made it her business to challenge wasteful spending on civic amenities in an outpouring of letters to her local councillor or, when Professor James Geddes grew tired of answering her questions, detailed in numbered points, directly to the secretary of the council chambers. She thought it a poor week if one or other of the Scottish dailies carried no letter of protest by her. Nor was her opinion scorned as freakish. The arduous sessions in the public library removed any accusation that her opinions were misinformed or emotional. She assured herself of fact before she put pen to paper, and wasn't often wrong. A vocal minority, an ombudswoman, a champion of losing causes, a tartan maniac – the view of her activities depended on the stance of the observer, but no one north or south of the nationalist line dismissed them lightly.

Fergus saw her sweep upstairs to avoid him, and was resigned to it. It was less of a slight than cutting each other dead in adjacent seats. He was amused that she should imagine she was invisible when hers was one of the most distinctive public faces in the city, and she was the last person who could pass as anonymous. Ellice Barr, so called. Barr she was born with. Ellice she was not. She had re-christened herself, dissatisfied with a floral feminine name that was a relic of nineteenth-century posies, and chose a neutral tone or one not readily identifiable. It became titular, ousting Miss or Mrs with their harping on the married status, and was her own.

Ellice Barr looked a strong woman bodily, although it was mental strength that was implicit in her disregard of the female standards of the day. She was a woman who went out intrepidly at night alone, out without a man, out on a mission. She was thin and sinewy and a head taller than the average of her sex. By April, Fergus noticed in passing, she was brown and weather-beaten, the skin of her face and hands tanned by exposure. It was the windburn of gardeners and mountaineers and other active, out-door folk who despised ritual sunseekers and went out rain or shine to meet the elements. She was a weariless walker. Even the tinge of her skin was mannish and her hair and face had nothing like conventional femininity. Grey and wiry, her hair was cut into the shape of a helmet while her complexion was unpampered by make-up. Soap and water was her cosmetic treatment for clear skin and bright eyes. Cold water splashed on in the mornings, and she wouldn't have balked at breaking ice.

Fergus had first encountered her when he was a boy and she delivered leaflets through his letter box, knocking on doors, criss-crossing the tree-lined avenue where he lived. He watched her over wet evenings, knocking, delivering, discoursing while he was dry indoors, and saw that she was indomitable. He thought that she was probably a worker for one of the smaller and more evangelical sects, Plymouth Brethren or Jehovah's Witnesses, a colporteur or conversion seeker. Only later, when he was able to read them, did he realise that the leaflets were political. The woman did have the look of a missionary sporting odd, sombre clothes which were, even to a boy's eye, out of date. She struck him as somewhere between the picture of Emmeline Pankhurst in his history book and Katharine Hepburn, who was photographed on the front cover of his copy of *The African Queen*. For him, she carried all the elements of witching, fearsome and fascinating together.

Ellice Barr wouldn't have been offended by the comparison he made with Emmeline Pankhurst or Katharine Hepburn, these being two of the brightest stars in her firmament of remarkable women, which included Beatrice Webb and Vera Brittain as well as the writers who had done other things than merely write, Virginia Woolf, Vita Sackville-West and the other West, Rebecca out of Ibsen. She admired the publisher and critic, the gardener and the socialist before she admired the storyteller in these women. There were no men in this firmament, though George Orwell was admitted as a benevolent uncle, Shaw as a wicked one.

A casual glance registered that Ellice Barr was man-resistant. Not many suitors could have defied the withering looks she gave them. Man in search of sexual union was the human type she most despised. Fergus ran through the catalogue of sexual deviance to find a term that fitted her. Lesbian? Hermaphrodite? No, neuter.

18

She simply wasn't interested in the sex of individuals, her own or other people's.

Perhaps the most surprising, then, out of the list of her eccentricities was the fact that she was a mother. This motherhood was a deliberate act. Towards the end of her fertile life, nearer fifty than forty, she looked down a long vista of empty years and thought they were dismal. She took a mate, choosing him with the same care as if she sifted through the coding of a sperm bank for the messages his body carried, height, looks, intellect and damn his morals. Those weren't recorded on anybody's pedigree. The visiting lecturer in Anthropology went home after his semester and she kept his child a secret. It was a girl child. Ellice Barr avoided the ineptitude of fond parents who called the dark-haired Blanche, the homely Belle, knowing how hard it was to live up to such a name. She looked closely at the infant before she chose the appellation. She saw that the child was tawny and fierce-hearted and called her Leonie.

A cub. A ball of hair and fire. A roamer, difficult to pin down or contain. A child who was precious beyond the medical definition of one especially wanted. This child ran counter to all the conventions, defying both sexual inclination and economic good sense and was the exceptional investment. Ellice Barr was never better entertained in her life than by this energetic product of selective breeding, a Shavian paradigm.

Ellice Barr went to the supermarket at Morningside when she got off the bus. She liked the anonymous self-service and browsed as good-humouredly along the shelves, picking up and turning over, as in the public library. Tins or books, she read them all. Her trolley filled very slowly. The standards for inclusion in her diet were complex, relating only partially to what she liked to eat. She didn't like to eat much, and would have lived happily off porridge and herring and Baxter's Royal Game Soup, and had done so in times of privation, for weeks on end.

She didn't buy the phoney. It must be good, uncontaminated by synthetic additive. A printed list of chemical ingredients put a tin back pronto on the shelf. It must also be cheap and preferably reduced. Once inside, her first stop was the tray of damaged goods because she was impervious to sell-by dates, knowing that the

19

human stomach was adapted to ingest everything the tongue or nose would pass. She was no picker. She shopped at the end of the day for bargains, unsold bread, squashed butter packets – who cared, anyway, when it was patted in a crock? She scoured out the best buys not only in terms of price per unit or calorific value, which were subsidiary criteria, but to find which packets and brands ran the best competitions. Or she bought so that she could save the coupons to validate her entry for them and kept a back stock of these in a drawer, alongside special offer discounts against future purchases.

Entering these competitions was Ellice's livelihood. She made her income by her pen and by her wits, even if it was in a less illustrious fashion than her mentors, Shaw and Marx. Ranking a list of qualities in order of merit was straightforward enough. The test came in the slogan. When it came down to saying in ten or twenty words why this product was superior, she came up with a pithy sentence time after time. She had a natural epigrammatic wit, a fine way with assonance and the pun, and could roll up a sentence into a cannonball. She was a winner. Her neighbours grew tired of taking in the prizes delivered when she was out, often hideous and certainly unwanted, but tradeable or saleable. This income was all found and, moreover, it was a gratuity that was free of the encumbrance of taxation, which in any case was a subsidy to English government at Westminster. Money was an exchequer through which she did not feel it necessary to pass. She had no income and paid no revenue, a subtle anarchist.

She had revealed this industry to Fergus bit by bit. He was taken by its cunning, legitimate and successful. She lived one crumb above the bread line. So? She lived. It was the perfect socialist answer to the economics of the entrepreneur, which she abhorred. It made her the chameleon, living off air, or exemplified the mental scavenging at which she was adept, turning over a ragbag of ideas and objects and people to sustain herself.

A single bulb burned in a single lamp. The six o'clock news, relayed by wireless, played into the room as it historically did on evenings when she was at home. The table was covered with an Indian rug that trailed to the floor, a detail from Vermeer. She used it like this not because it was too good to walk on but because it was

20

too frail. Besides, it hid the blemishes of the table on which she wrote and ironed indiscriminately. The miracle was that her and her page and her blouse emerged pristine, avoiding acci clashes with each other en route. The rooms to which she returned were as bizarre as the meal she ate, and for the same reason. Free choice entered neither.

She lived alone again with Leonie coming back only between engagements and reverted to the occupations that had absorbed her before the interregnum of motherhood. She cleared her meal away and set to work, writing a letter to a landowner near Penicuik about a right of way he had infringed with gates, then drew up the agenda of the next committee meeting of the local party and made notes for a speech she was to give that Saturday to a women's group, on the economic future of Scotland as an independent state. Soroptimists she thought it was this week, or maybe the Townswomen's Guild. She turned to her diary to check.

The pages flicked over. Every day was filled. Some inscriptions were small, some large. Attendance at the open sessions of the city council, evening leafletting for the local elections that spring entered according to the specific area covered, a turn on rotas as receptionist at a family planning clinic. The names of people hardly ever appeared but there were many abbreviations. WEA, SNT, Amnesty – she supported them all and in her mind made no absolute distinction between education, conservation and prisoners of conscience. They all fell into the category of public service, of living for others than oneself.

And Fergus, finding that he had a tendency to smile at her for her ugly flat and her mad lack of foresight when it came to the practicalities of life, stopped himself and thought, just what did he do to express the smallest degree of social conscience? It wasn't work as he understood it, but it was achievement none the less. And he felt a moment of affection for her. Leonie's mother. Chin high, courage bright, plated with eccentricity.

3

At the end of Prime Minister's question time, at which his question had not been called due to a welter of detailed supplementaries, Quercus got to his feet and left the chamber. He bowed to the Speaker and went through the swing doors, joining the stream of exodus. He was a little disappointed at the fate of his question, a good question neatly worded, and he had a stinging follow-up prepared. But it had fallen in twelfth place. Not a good position, twelve, for like twelfth man it implied the reserve status becoming to a player who was useful in an emergency but not worthy of inclusion on his own merits. A depressing accuracy of placement, he considered, rolling up the order paper into a tube and throwing it away.

He stood for a few moments on the tiled floor of the Lobby while the other members filtered past him in twos and threes, making for somewhere: Annie's Bar, the Smoking Room in search of quenching tea, their offices to clear the correspondence before Friday's return to the constituency. He didn't feel inclined towards any of these outlets. He felt like doing something entirely different. It was the first of May. Outside Westminster, the sun broke the sky over London into its astonishing components, air and cloud and light, encouraging truancy.

He recalled he hadn't seen Watson Moncrieffe in the chamber that afternoon, or indeed for a day or two. He noticed his own pleasant reaction to the name. Well, that was what he was after, an entertainment, a lightening of mood and didn't think he disparaged his friend by making him into a diversion. So he walked along the corridor and pushed open succeeding doors, saying to those members he passed, "Have you seen Moncrieffe?"

"He was on the terrace a little while ago, I think, with a constituent."

But the terrace was almost empty. A cool breeze mixed with the sunlight and the river was choppy and dark. Quercus held good his intention not to be deterred.

"Have you seen Moncrieffe?" he asked the steward.

"Not for an hour, sir. Had a guest with him."

Moncrieffe and his manifold guests! He held court at Wes~~ter~~ ter like a paladin. "Gentleman or lady?" That might give a clue to what he'd done afterwards.

"Gentleman, sir. Friend of his uncle's."

Waiters were useful for more than serving drinks.

"No idea where he's gone, I suppose?"

The steward considered a moment. "Someone said his uncle's due to speak this afternoon."

Quercus nodded. Foolish of him to have forgotten. Lord Moncrieffe was bitterly opposed to a clause in a bill on fisheries and made it an occasion for a rare denouncement from the cross-benches. Almost certainly the member for Ross, Cromarty and Skye would be present to hear his uncle's peroration, but he hesitated to interrupt either of them. He crossed the Central Lobby where visitors sat waiting for their MP to come and listen to their problem, as ancient a ritual as litigants at the office of the Lord Chancellor pressing their case, and headed towards the Lords. He found an usher who confirmed that the younger Moncrieffe was indeed listening to the older. Quercus scribbled a message and let the usher take it in to the MP standing at the Lords Bar, while he retired to Moncrieffe's office in Normanshaw North, without much hope of making an escape in tandem.

Within half an hour, however, he heard the footsteps of the younger man come along the corridor to his room. He knew at twenty paces it was Moncrieffe.

The face of the young man who entered wasn't young. It had been called many things from heavy through to strong, but both adjectives implied a weightiness normally attendant on maturity. It wasn't corpulence, mere fleshiness, but the set of his face that was emblocked. He didn't have a single good feature – overcast eyes, a nose that was Grecian in length but not width, frankly splayed, and a mouth that was too distinctive to be a norm of excellence. It was the collocation that was interesting. He had a double lower lip, or a pronounced roll under the rim so that the mouth was either full or severely drawn according to mood. These two phases denoted the extremes of his character. He was moody, difficult, unpredictable – but bursting with mental as well as physical energy which Quercus, who had sat in the House for over thirty years, recognised as the potential of a major politician, once it was harnessed, directed, or made old.

"Good afternoon, Watson. Lord Moncrieffe has had his say?"

"With surprising brevity. But fiery. Very fiery today. Nothing quite like fish quotas to make him seethe." His voice too burst. It came straight from the lungs, powerful and aspirate, without dwelling too long in the articulators of speech.

"I've dragged you away from your guest."

"No. I was only a stand-by. He was Charlie's guest. I was glad to excuse myself. What can I do for you?"

Moncrieffe was lucky enough to have an office to himself, and so the two men sat on opposite sides of the same desk, glad not to have to share the room with a second or even a third resident in the way of eavesdropper. The desk wasn't tidy. A dozen newspapers were spread over it, on top of files of work and correspondence, incoming and outgoing, making up a traffic of congestion in so small a space.

"Catching up on your reputation?" Quercus signalled to the columns of the press.

"Too late for that," said the younger man. "It's catching up with me."

This was true. Moncrieffe's name was found more frequently among the gossip columns than in the lines of political analysts. This was a form of publicity wished on him rather than sought, and obscured the serious elements of his tenure at Westminster. Sometimes he read the newspapers to reassure himself that these did exist.

Quercus lifted the topmost paper and said, "Have you noticed the date?"

"May, isn't it?"

"The inauguratory first. We ought to celebrate."

"Well, it's too late to wash our faces in the morning dew. What do you suggest?"

"Something equally bardic. There's a remarkable occurrence taking place at Oxford."

Quercus thumbed through the pages of the entertainments guide looking for a notice while Moncrieffe thought it was going to be a rather esoteric happening. A revivalist meeting would qualify in the other's terms of reference; or a Latin verse-speaking competition where some undergraduate had a fine declamatory style with Horace.

Eheu, fugaces, Postume, Postume, labuntur anni.

Something exhausting to the brain however uplifting to the spirit. He began to compose excuses.

"Ah, at last." Quercus found the place. "There's a young woman in Oxford who is turning heads."

"A commonplace, surely, even in Oxford."

"But these are unusual heads she's turning, even academic ones, like the critic of *The Times* who's blasted every other performance for the last six months. Now he rapturises her. This is worth seeing."

He turned the page towards Moncrieffe who read that at the Oxford Playhouse, a performance of *Twelfth Night* was to be given, with Leonie Barr appearing in the part of Viola. "Leonie Barr. Leonie Barr," Watson repeated as though he ought to know the name.

"You should," said Quercus, "she's your countrywoman."

"A Scottish actress. Well I should know it, but I don't." He measured the temptation laid before him. A fellow national, a success, not in Stratford or the West End, although it was a success that softened the drama critic of the Thunderer into a zephyrous mood. But in *Twelfth Night?* He thought his Shakespeare days were over, sitting in the middle of school children who'd come to hear it live and ladies' outings from the shires, straining eagerly after textual accuracy. A not irresistible temptation. What did sway him, however, was the weight Quercus attached to the event. Quercus had a gift for what was going on, attuned to listening rather than speaking. It was the gift that made him a wily whip in his day, if no more. Not an instigator himself, he stopped at sifting ideas which had their origin elsewhere. Commentator and analyst, he was still an accurate barometer for change, so if he said there was a remarkable occurrence at Oxford, Moncrieffe was predisposed to believe him. He looked at his watch, which was a disclaimer to apparent indifference because he was working out how long it would take to drive to Oxford. "Seven thirty curtain up? Well, I said I might dine with Uncle Charlie but I won't be missed in all that crowd. I'll give the usher my apology."

"Shall we all go?" asked Quercus. "Make an evening of it?"

Moncrieffe was struck by the format of this question. Its absolute normality was apparent. Two men decide that instead of going to the theatre and taking supper afterwards with each other, they will go as a foursome. But not with their wives. Wives were a negative commodity with both men. They considered travelling to Oxford with their friends, a group of four men displacing the current social unit. Moncrieffe felt that in the small distinction of the evening lay the potential for an enormous one, which for the time being he resisted.

"I think we must go alone. We've hardly time to get hold of them. You reserve the tickets and I'll see Uncle Charlie right." He pulled out a card from the stationery rack and inked the words 'An Oxford happening. My apologies to you and the Savoy. W.'

Meantime Quercus had confirmed that the only accommodation left in the theatre was in the upper circle.

"Must be doing well for a Thursday evening. Upper circle it is. And shall we have evening dress to live up to our surroundings?"

"What a popinjay you are."

"Popinjay," the young man considered. "Are you the last person in the world to use that word?"

Moncrieffe drove. He took the road past Hyde Park Corner to join the M40 at Paddington. He drove at a speed others might consider foolhardy but Quercus had been chauffeured by the young man for so long that he had lost his nervousness.

They reviewed the week together, reading straws for the political fortunes of others. Their own were easily told. If the general election were to fall that year, and Quercus agreed the leader of his party was more likely to have the date forced on him than to choose it, especially if the local elections in a week's time were unfavourable, they would both be returned. They each had a huge majority in their seat, a hump which they could live off for some time ahead. The uncertainty was, would the government? Moncrieffe thought not; Quercus felt it would but without a large overall majority which would make the next session of the House a troublesome one. The topic lasted all the way to Oxford, for they had the psephologist's delight in swings and counter-checks, detailing which out of some six hundred and thirty members would be in

26

danger of peremptory dismissal by the electorate.

They arrived at dusk, an hour that settled well on Oxford. The streets merged into a dusty heat at the end of the working day, and they were glad to park the car and saunter under the walls of All Souls and Queen's, until they came to the boundary of Magdalen Bridge and turned through the grounds of the college, reviewing their association with the place. Some undergraduates came out of an alleyway in evening dress and livened up the grey cloisters on their way to a birthday celebration. The men found themselves both charmed and wistful at the sight of the ephemera of evening, gowns of net and gauze. The expedition had appealed indirectly because it revitalised their own days in the University precincts but this first of May was a real anniversary, measuring a connection with the original event less than it measured the intervening states of change. Youth observed but not experienced. For Moncrieffe, who was thirty-five years closer to his fellowship than Quercus, the circuit was more poignant. He recalled with great sharpness his early years at Christ Church and the aspirations came back hauntingly to mock him with the unfulfilled potential of his alumnus. A first. The first of many such accolades, which became a series without climax. And then it was true, they walked side by side like monks down a sombre quadrangle while, all round them, men of a different generation were accompanied by the colourful sex. Moncrieffe felt himself slipping towards frustration, middle age and, worst of all, a dour celibacy of spirit which a decade at Westminster did nothing to dispel.

In this mood, *Twelfth Night* ought to have been a frippery. Reading the print of the glossy programme, while some recorded music played the curtain up, Watson did feel a twinge of displacement. He remembered the plot too clearly, people like clockwork models fully wound but heading in the wrong direction until the hand of the playwright re-routed them with a change of heart or sex. Did it matter which? Romantic comedy was the lowest form of art and he turned his attention to it with a heavy heart. Dinner at the Savoy with a dozen men of Uncle Charlie's generation would have been the stuff of social interchange. Talk political and masculine, to the point.

He thought he was being a most ungracious guest. He owed it to his host to be receptive to the play and so he resigned himself to music being the food of love, thinking that in the interval in all probability there would be some mutual friends in the audience to make up a party for supper, so that he could imitate the entertainment he had missed.

But the play was thoughtfully set. Illyria had the charm of the Western Isles, and indeed he could have sworn his uncle's house at Torrisaig was used as the model for the Duke's palace where the waters had an Atlantic roar about them. Storm-tossed sailors, Edwardian gentlemen and ladies languid in Edwardian morning rooms. He knew them, at least by reputation, and he began to enjoy the fantasy, putting the tests of scepticism to one side.

Then Viola entered and the audience, who were quicker to respond than he was, grew tense. A ripple of expectancy went through the body of the hall like a waft of established fame, although her reputation was far from widespread or was still being made by such moments.

Moncrieffe looked across the span of the dress circle, well placed for reading faces. He noticed, as the speeches unrolled, that the atmosphere wasn't the standard concentration given to serious drama – respectful, attentive, a little ponderous – and this was because, contrary to the make-up of most audiences, men were in the majority. There were twice as many men as women. Was the play a set text, he asked himself? Was its performance a variation on private study that evening because it was examinable? No. The mood of the auditorium wasn't academic; it had more of the night club or the striptease, costume on then off and who was what underneath it? It was charged with a physical tension as every evening five hundred men came to see Leonie Barr change from being a woman to a man and back again.

He looked at the actress who had this knack of updating the bard. She had an unusual appearance, good for the theatre, but not necessarily a comfortable one in everyday life. She was a tall woman, at least as tall as the men on the stage and her height was given emphasis by a mass of hair. In crowded scenes, the eye caught against her and came to a stop. Why? Beauty? No, she wasn't conventionally beautiful. Changeable maybe. She had distinctive colouring, the fashionable Tudor tones of dull gold hair, grey eyes and pale skin that harmonised the rest. Neutrality, although, as he defined it, the colour shifted again like a base tint subtle enough to let all the others in. He started to wait for these shifts of emphasis, finding the voice, the face, the physique so elusive that they were paradoxical. Temptress to pageboy, tearaway demure. Was it only the text or was it herself?

Quercus noticed that his guest hadn't moved for half an hour, arms crossed, head set attentively. The feel of the language started to invade them both, a nostalgia in itself which harked back to the instruction of the classroom. Little by little, they abandoned themselves to its harmonies, ignoring the implausibility of comic stage convention.

In the interval, when they did come across more than one friend and made plans for supper, Moncrieffe said to a master of one of the colleges, "How much freedom did women have in Shakespeare's day? I'd forgotten how emancipated the heroines of the comedies were. Portia, Rosalind, Petruchio's Kate – what a sterling bunch of women. Not the regulation stay-at-homes. They can't all have been modelled on Elizabeth?"

But to his disappointment, the man weighed him down with a solemn answer, tracing the education of women down through Roger Ascham to the concept of chivalry at the court of Eleanor of Aquitaine, Froissart's *Roman de la Rose* and the Christian Madonna. Through nods, Moncrieffe's mind flew back to the reality. A real woman, pulsing with wit that was her own, now, here, a hundred yards from where he stood. He wasn't late at the bell.

During the second half, he made up his mind to go to the dressing room and . . . what? He could leave his calling card, pay his respects in some foolish gesture of admiration. He did not know what to do. Thirty-five and he didn't know what was appropriate. He thought a concrete expression was the standard. He could send flowers in the morning but at the moment he felt stripped of anything in the way of personal assets and saw himself in true perspective, an unknown man demonstrating by his presence only the power of hers.

"Go on," said Quercus while he hesitated over curtain calls. "But don't forget we're spoken for at supper."

Moncrieffe arrived at her dressing room before she had taken the final curtain and had time to appreciate that flowers, cut or potted, were superfluous. The room was banked with them and he flipped the cards over, pre-empted by 'With my warmest appreciation' and 'A hothouse of violets would not do justice to one Viola'. So there were idiots at large besides himself. He tempered the excess of his enthusiasm seeing how, written or spoken, it might be absurd if she happened not to reciprocate it.

"How do you do," the actress said, coming in suddenly and addressing him over his shoulder. "You beat me to it, I see. Didn't you bother to wait out the last act?" She sat down at the dressing table and looked neither at herself in the mirror, nor at him.

"Oh yes, I waited to the very end."

Several things about her confounded the response he had prepared; the lack of formality in her greeting, the accent in which she spoke for it had a different metre from Shakespeare's, the height which he had become accustomed to on stage but was troublesome close up, demanding a second adjustment. Perhaps because of this, he fell back on male assurances and to introduce himself he produced a printed card, like a business card, from his wallet and gave it to her.

She looked at him before she looked at it. She had grown, not bored precisely, but tolerant with these nightly admirers. Their admiration was essential to keep the theatre running but her acceptance of it was mitigated by sadness that they had no one more immediate to admire. These men knew everything about Viola but nothing of Leonie and were very disappointed to discover the two were not the same. This look of tedium at having to resolve the confusion of identities crossed her face, and then she read the slip of card. Two addresses were printed in either corner, a London address and an Edinburgh one, right and left-handed, and the name, Watson Abercrombie Moncrieffe.

She looked away from it and from him. The tedium had gone and a visible anxiety succeeded it. She stood up and came forward to shake him by the hand, saying with warmth, "I am so pleased to meet you," as if she meant it and among the formalities of English salutation, this was not a stock response.

But then the room filled in a gust of bodies. Friends came and other actors. People stood between them. Orsino said, "Look here, Leonie, give me a straight answer. Are you coming on to this party? You don't even need to change."

Nor she did. The dress she wore was maybe chosen, like the flowers of her well-wishers, for its appropriateness to her rôle that evening. It was a demure shade, becoming to a Brontë governess, but the cut was not demure. It plunged. It plunged so far it was impossible the thing supported its own weight. Deep waisted, almost severed from its sleeves, it was a work of marvellous complexity, the tissue of erotica.

A call boy came in and put a yellow envelope in her hand.

"Late in the day for telegrams," said Orsino.

But no one paid much attention while she opened it because there had been so many. Watson began to feel redundant. She was spending the remainder of the evening with her friends, and he with his. He had done what he came to do, make himself known, but the hiatus made him look more foolish than admiring; so he worked his way towards the door hoping to say the last word, 'Goodnight', quietly before he left. He was only a foot or so from her chair when she read the message on the telegram and he was compelled by the crush in the room to read it too. An odd message and certainly not one of congratulation.

GUILTY FERGUS

That was all.

He watched the make-up of the stage become a mask as its colour grew more distant from her own. He could see she was shocked by whatever the telegram meant. For several moments, the room and its throng were a dinning in her ears, while the others went on planning their evening without realising her willingness to share in it might have altered.

The door opened again and the director came in to make his own stake in events. "Alan," she called him before anone else in the hum of the dressing room could divert his attention. "Alan," and passed him the piece of paper.

"So what do you want to do?"

"I'll have to go."

"But you can't go now. Friday and two performances on Saturday. You can't cry off."

"I'm not fit for anything while this is on my mind."

Watson envied the other man his knowledge of what the

message meant. Whatever the cause, he took it seriously but not as seriously as she did.

"For heaven's sake, Leonie, you can't do a thing about it."

"I couldn't do anything about a death, but that wouldn't stop me going to the funeral."

Alan Mills and his leading lady were held in suspended disagreement on the point.

"The understudy's fine, and I promise to be back by Monday."

"Where's the sense, Leonie? It'll take you all day tomorrow to get up there, and all day Sunday to travel back. For twenty-four hours in Edinburgh."

Listening, Watson perceived the crystal of her plan and intervened. "Are you going up to Edinburgh?" he asked. "I can drive you, starting now if you like. I will just have to tell a friend who came with me this evening."

Leonie gave him gratitude with her eyes, the director damnation. Quercus was more moderate than either when he heard the explanation.

"Skirting disaster – again," was his comment.

"But it does concentrate the mind so wonderfully," Moncrieffe excused his second exeat of the day.

This quip produced a long silence in the older man while diverse thoughts rose to the surface and fell again without being spoken. The quotation reminded him of a definition of hanging and the death sentence; dying as one of Shakespeare's images for the sexual act; a reference to the judge in *The Weir of Hermiston* who considered no one was worse off for a hanging. Stray ideas which proved him to be what he was most often, a collator who was too complex for easy communication. So he said in the end, "Go carefully. I'll be fine. Someone will be driving back to London or I may stay with the master at Magdalen. Don't worry."

As Watson disappeared backstage again to collect his impromptu passenger, the older man underwent misgivings about the expedition he had mounted, the doubts of go-between and match-maker. A strange form of celebration it had turned out to be, to end with a long drive over the border and he himself cast up in the halls of youth, a relic of nostalgia for what was essentially unreachable.

4

They drove in silence for a long time, as far as Manchester. Leonie hadn't changed but hurried out of the theatre in her final costume. A fichu was added at the neck but instead of modesty, it brought an emphasis of nudity as her skin asserted its allure beneath the lace. She sat in thought. Hours of thought she expended on those two words of her telegram and Watson was equally puzzled, hoping that if nothing else the drive would unravel the meaning of 'Guilty' and 'Fergus'.

She started to enjoy the journey. It was a powerful car, a silver-grey Daimler which was less fashionable than elegant. Although he used the shuttle flights back and forwards each weekend from Heathrow to Inverness, he enjoyed fast driving out of London. Leonie was a novice in these matters. It might have power brakes and power steering, but irrespective of nuances it denoted power. She was grateful for the energy that rolled them through the night as well as the comfort in which it was achieved.

The headlights made the evening come alive, in the same way that stage lights did. The rolling scenery of the motorway, which she knew to be barren in daylight, was transformed by the beam he projected onto it. Hills became an important backdrop, midnight blue, the arc panning the horizon picked up a village in the distance so that she was continually entertained by the depth or foreshortening made by the vehicle in the slipstream of the dark.

Seeing that she wasn't likely to begin a discussion, he said, "I came to Oxford this evening with a friend who thought I ought to know your name."

"But you didn't?"

"No. But it does have a familiar ring about it."

She gave him a long look and he granted her this privilege of staring at him. He didn't hurry to curtail it by glancing from the road they travelled. It was flattering to have her extend as much attention to his profile as he had to hers three hours before. He felt there were many answers she could give, as many as he would have given himself to the circumscription of his fame. Chide him, inform him of how and where she had scored successes, or be falsely modest. 'No reason on earth why you should have heard of me.' He had done each of these things at one time but she did none. He was entirely taken by surprise when she replied, "It's my mother you're thinking of. She's quite well known in Edinburgh politics."

"Of course. I remember now. Ellice Barr."

The height. The suggestion of masculinity in the appearance. It started to fall into place. The precise details of his knowledge made a space between them, and one that Leonie was familiar with. It was the silence that greeted mention of her mother. She hesitated to say, What do you know about Ellice Barr that keeps you quiet, in precisely the same way that he hesitated to ask, Who is this Fergus? They wanted to probe beyond common civility, but were restrained by their reasons for wanting to establish the intelligence of the other. I want to know what it is you know, was a discourtesy between strangers.

"How are the Nationalists doing in Edinburgh?" he asked, hoping she would refresh his memory about their eccentric lady champion and make it less obvious that it was her eccentricity that was general knowledge.

"Oh well, they have high hopes but Pentlands won't return an SNP candidate, now or ever."

"What did they get at the last general election?"

"About ten per cent. A swing of six."

"That's not bad," he said appreciatively.

Not bad, but she remembered the work that went into every one of those marked ballot papers, and not enough was her verdict.

Watson was rummaging in his brain for facts about the well known Ellice Barr but none had stuck beyond her aura of strangeness. He had a suspicion that Ellice was a pseudonym, but he couldn't remember why she abandoned her own name. Where did they live? Apparently in the Pentlands constituency, but it was infuriatingly nebulous material to build a conversation on, far less a friendship. Above all, who was this Fergus who sent telegrams of such dramatic urgency that just one word and his name could summon her at night and out of the context of her work, his claim

34

being the stronger? A brother? A husband? She wore neither the rings of marriage nor betrothal.

To confound him further she said without warning, "I know you a good deal better than you know me."

His eyes moved from the roadway and looked at hers. There was that shadow of anxiety in them again and he thought, My God, I have met her before and forgotten. How embarrassing.

Most eerily, she read his mind and made remarks that sprang from his thinking which was enacted for her perusal as clearly as a mime. "No. I've never met you. But things stuck, over the years. Tell me," she went on, "are you a real Independent?"

"What qualifies as real?" he wondered.

"I mean, you're not an Independent Conservative?"

"No, I am a true, deep-dyed, authentic, one and only Independent."

"But I thought that was impossible."

"It is. I am a patent anachronism. Independents went out of fashion in 1948 when the Universities lost their franchise. There were quite a few before that, and some good ones too, like A. P. Herbert."

"But then," she persevered, "how did you make it?"

"Nepotism. Literally," he said to her face which had grown sceptical, thinking he meant a bought office. "My uncle is a mix of squire and landlord and figurehead in Wester Ross, almost a surrogate king. And he takes his duties in the Lords quite seriously, so he carries a degree of political weight. He's a cross-bencher." He smiled to himself. "We always did run against the grain. The Moncrieffes were almost the only family in the Highlands to keep their titles and land intact although they went with the Jacobites. I was elected on that family ticket, out of perverse loyalty."

"So you're really a nationalist?"

He smiled, having resisted more devious attempts to categorise his affiliations. "Independence *is* a kind of nationalism in the north. But for the Highlander, don't forget, it's independence from Edinburgh as much as London. Free thinkers, you know. They've got a wilful streak that likes running anti-clockwise and that's the nearest I can get to a manifesto."

She knew this wasn't all. Reared on the minutiae of politics, she knew no one stood wholly altruistically. "I thought you supported electoral reform?"

"I do."

"So why don't you join the Liberals?"

"I must have been asked that at least a thousand times, and my answer's different every time. Vanity's the simplest." This sounded probable to her, given the fact that he was one of only two men in evening dress at the Oxford Playhouse that evening. "I wonder how you know, about electoral reform."

"My mother made me read the articles you wrote in *The Times*."

"Made you read?"

"She wanted someone to disagree with."

"For or against?"

"She was against. She can't see anything beyond devolution."

"PR would be good for Scottish Nationalists. And how about you?"

"I don't know."

"That's a spoiled paper, not to know. You've got to go one way or the other."

She wondered at a sadness in his insistence, not knowing how often the injunction was given and ignored. "It's an option that doesn't apply to me."

"You're wrong there," he admonished. "It applies."

To distract him from the pursuit of her own political faith, she asked, "Didn't you stand for Pentlands at one time?"

"That's well remembered," he said admiringly. "Almost nobody remembers that."

"I think my mother kept you out. She threw her weight behind the Labour candidate and he just scraped home."

"Ah well," he said without rancour, "she did me a favour really. Suburban Edinburgh and I would have fallen out before long. I'd have spoken my mind just once too often for their liking. Anyway, I did a rather foolish thing, for a Parliamentary candidate. It went against me. You can never tell how things will go. If they succeed, everyone says 'Brilliant' and if they don't, then it was just a stunt."

She knew the incident he referred to. It was a talking point for a long time afterwards and made him a cult hero in the student community, if nowhere else. After a torchlit procession, to inaugurate Rag Week, he and two others had hung a banner from the

Napoleonic monument on Calton Hill. It made an eye-catching photograph on the front of Scottish dailies, but for the wrong reason. With unusual wit it was captioned 'Edinburgh's Disgrace', his first brush with journalistic freedoms. It was the press who kept him out of Pentlands. She tried to remember the slogan, draped inside its banner, but could not. As far as Edinburgh was concerned, it might as well have been a plea for free love as for free votes. He was stigmatised libertarian after that, and in truth one of the reasons he didn't join a political party was that nobody wanted him.

It was he who had begun the game of reputations and found he was impaled by his own victory. He had his fame but, as always, it tipped over into notoriety. Here she was, intelligent, informed, maybe even sympathetic, but all she knew of him was the sensational, the stuff of headlines and gossip columns. What he actually supported and why, was a dull pulp in comparison. He despaired at the difficulty of getting over one sensible idea to the electorate, one that wasn't charged with the personality of its adherent.

She could see that she had depressed him by her reference, or sunk him into a searching review of old mistakes, and so to cheer him she asked, "Do you still live at Inveresk?" hoping to imply not all she knew about his background was dubious. "I visited the house once, a long time ago."

"That's not my house," he corrected. How well she knew him! "My grandmother lives there, because really it's the dower house of Lord Moncrieffe. She holds it as a grace and favour residence."

"Yes," she agreed. "I thought it a graced and favoured residence."

"Do you know my family?" he wondered.

"No, I don't know your family. There was an appeal for funds, I think, to re-roof the church in the village. Most of the big houses were open to the public."

"That's some time ago," he reflected.

"Ten years."

It came back with precision. That was the year that he was married, in the church of St Michael that she referred to, under a leaky roof.

The house had made a profound impression on her and she was

able to record it accurately as he listened. A Georgian house, with famous gates which were reprieved from addition to the metal stock in the second world war because they had some historical significance. She thought they had a crest on them, but he did not correct her misuse of 'crest'. They bore the family shield, a chevron, two lions rampant and a crescent. She had admired the furniture and he told her, without boast, that it was famous furniture, important enough to be catalogued in a cabinet maker's inventory which was kept in the archives of the Museum of Antiquities in Queen Street. He saw it through her eyes, through the perspective of visitor. He previewed his own arrival at Inveresk in a few hours' time. His grandmother undemonstrative, the antithesis of shrill, a woman as refined as the furniture of which she was custodian. There were only half a dozen things that she might say to him when he walked in, unannounced, at sunrise on a Friday morning and none of them would reveal an unpreparedness.

He listened, almost disbelieving, while Leonie Barr described the actual room in which he would sleep that night, with a meticulous eye to detail. A set, disposed just so. She remembered it professionally. This bed, this cover made of silk lozenges, worn, the wadding showing through, a wallpaper they were making modern copies of, maps of mountain ranges on the wall and cricket teams. It hadn't changed. Nothing had changed from her description and he found himself deeply perturbed by her insights into what he considered private. Behind her recital, he caught glimpses of something he couldn't define but which hinted at why the place had made such a deep impression on her. Envy? Gratitude that it had survived virtually undisturbed for two hundred years? Perhaps a nationalistic pride. There were few Scottish Blenheims. Neither wealth nor social tranquillity encouraged private palaces north of the border, but Inveresk and Torrisaig did represent one strand of continuity in the national heritage. Was that it?

She stopped suddenly, mid-monologue. The recollection highlighted their divergent pasts, his historical, familial, hers entirely her own. It reminded her of the moment when she was fifteen and had done something she was deeply ashamed of, and regarded as one of her closest secrets. Because the emotion of that visit had been so intense, and sharing some of it with its originator

38

impelled her to share more, Leonie admitted to him almost involuntarily, "I took something from that room."

"Took?" he asked sharply, alerted by the transparent euphemism. However good the cause, he always warned against the opening of the house to the public, and to intending pilferers. "Do you mean stole?"

"Yes. I stole something. It was valueless."

"Then why was it worth stealing?" The soundness of his logic won many arguments and few friends.

"It wasn't really. It was very childish of me, but I was a child. I just wanted to have something that would remind me of that room."

"Have you kept it?" He was stern, corrective, utterly unamused by such a trifle because he did not know how little she had purloined.

"Yes I have. I'll give it back to you if you like. I promise I will pay it back with interest."

He was bemused by her confession. He wondered what she could have taken. It was another drawback of public reputation, which turned the famous into a magnet for scroungers and thieves. He hated them, people who assumed that what his family owned was easily come by and wouldn't be missed. What could she have taken? He searched back mentally over the room, like a man feeling his back pocket for his wallet, checking the silver photograph frames, the boxes and ornaments, whatever was small and portable but he could think of nothing that was missing at the time. Nothing noticeable. How puerile to steal, and even more puerile to confess it. It aroused two quite contrary reactions: to condemn the act in defence of his own property, and very painfully to examine his own thefts which couldn't be exposed so glibly because they were larger and more reprehensible. She troubled him by her example and they each fell into a baffled silence.

He thought that at the outset of the evening he had meant to seduce her. During Act One, he foresaw a dinner, not necessarily that evening but some evening, leading to a conquest. She deviated from this by the sudden acquiescence to make the drive with him and to trust herself entirely to his direction. Perhaps his name and MP printed on a card inspired this confidence or it might have had its source long ago when she took whatever she did take from

39

his room. Either way, she had ceased to be seducible. She demanded more from him. He found he had to defer to the exigencies of her character, and wanted to, so that he was prepared to show what there was of himself and let her choose. That is, he acknowledged the need for a conventional courtship, which was the last thing he had envisaged.

Leonie wished she hadn't said it. It had been a form of reparation, but now that the words were spoken and that the secret of her indefensible action was out, even to one person, she knew that it had become unforgivable – or unforgettable. She never had understood the difference between the two. It made a huge debt because it admitted a predilection on her side which she would rather have disguised and she was afraid he would put the wrong interpretation on it. Yes, she had followed his career avidly through newspaper cuttings, making him an idol. Or the right one, ten years out of date. It made her forward when she should more wisely have been reticent.

The night had darkened and was quite clear. All the distracting minor lights had been extinguished by three in the morning and their own movement forward had a compulsive intensity about it as if they were obeying the force of gravity or a drift of migration or were magnetized to the surface of the roadway and were drawn along it helplessly. They came to the end of the motorway and the landscape reduced in scale as their speed underwent a corresponding diminution. Walls and beech hedges sprang out of the darkness to block their passage, and were superseded by an avenue of trees that touched overhead, or a barren stretch of moor running into the valley of the Lammermuirs, or a village glimpsed in stone too hurriedly to visualise as houses.

Leonie did not want it to end. She told herself she was high on a night's performance at the end of a long season. The telegram excited her brain so that she raced ahead to what was waiting for her at the end of the journey, but the intervening episode of travel, of suspended activity while she moved between two peaks, was in fact the most exhilarating span of all. The night fell and broke and was reformed in every minute. They were magical, moving when others were asleep and charged with occupation of the landscape. They made their own energy and their own light, hurtling at high velocity through darkness and space that parted to accommodate

40

them, a spark of meteoric brilliance illuminating the hemisphere.

Dawn found them on the edge of the city which rose like Mecca from a mass of turrets and spires, unusually gilded and clear in the first light. Watson arrived pragmatically. He would drop her off, wherever she was headed, and go on to Inveresk for breakfast. He was not sure of the composition of the day. This evening his agent expected him in Inverness, but he would phone and cancel the long-standing arrangement to pick him up at the airport. He might drive up early on Saturday morning and make his calls round the constituency in the Daimler. There was a morning surgery in Dingwall, ten till twelve, opening a Garden Party at a country house in the afternoon. Dinner with friends on Skye before a political gathering in Portree to air the fishing quotas that absorbed Lord Moncrieffe himself at Westminster. The last ferry to Kyle of Lochalsh and a night in yet another bed at Torrisaig. A mad gallop it was, and a mad way to live. And then the car itself would have to be driven back to London on Sunday. No, he couldn't face another all-night drive. On Monday morning he might get up at five in Wester Ross and do it before midday. If he went like the wind, he might just do it.

The forced mental activity he went through to re-arrange his schedule, together with a passing consideration of its varying pleasures and antipathies, did not disturb his composure. His was not the longest journey from Westminster, or the most difficult. Someone travelling to Brecon and Radnor or south Devon had a worse time of it than he did. The weekly journey during sessions of the House did for him what it did for Leonie; it made a break between two forms of emotional expenditure and was a vacuum he could fill with work, or reading, or even mindlessness. He commuted like most of London's workers, but over a wider range, and he didn't accord it more significance than the man who stepped on a tube from Victoria to Wimbledon.

Travel inside the constituency: that was another matter.

"Not so fast," said Leonie. "I'll get out beside the clock at Morningside."

"Let me take you to your door."

She hesitated, then dismissed the awkwardness of revealing just where it was she lived. Why be proud? "On the left. Then the second block of flats."

41

He switched the engine off and looked. A tenement of great solidity and no pretensions. Even with the enhancement of early morning light, it was bereft of charm. It had a double aspect, a disused railway line in front and a cemetery behind.

"Top flat," she said, glancing up. "It's such a climb."

"What will you do today?" he asked, realising it was the end of their passage together and he was none the wiser.

"See people."

Ditto, he thought, ditto. And admired the laconic trait. Some proposition formulated itself to meet her during the course of the day he had purloined out of his schedules, or even to offer to drive her back to Oxford on Monday if he delayed the return that long; but the route was of such complexity that he hesitated to make another detour. Besides, he waited for an effusion of gratitude to bring out a second magnanimity.

Her mind was already absorbed in the present. Its difficulties were pressing and though she said her 'Thank you', it was perfunctory. He got out of the car and opened her door and walked her the last steps to the block of flats. The sun made a pocket of heat in which they lingered, and the paper boy who came round the corner at that moment on his delivery round was taken aback. A lady in a ballgown, a man in evening dress. Mauve and black and white, like a streaked iris which blossomed fulsomely in the thin soil of the city terraces. He eyed them with caution, thinking they were paranormal, a hallucination of the sunrise.

"Till later," Watson could not stop himself from hoping.

She nodded and disappeared into the well of the stairs.

A politician's fault, he thought as he drove away, expecting gratitude.

42

5

Leonie walked into the flat at Canaan Lane without warning, using her own latch key and Fergus stood up to greet her, his height, his age, his equal. They drew the curtains and made love in the daylight, the way they'd always done. Darkness was a luxury that hadn't extended to their student days, though that didn't inhibit the welcome of his body or of hers. The cretonne of the curtains threw a ripple of colour over the room and their skin, flowers made vibrant by the sunlight.

This was the picture she carried of Fergus, undressing by daylight modestly, not fully. Nakedness was a later exploration, when underwear was like caution tossed aside. Nakedness under cover. Flesh to flesh, he said, and she hadn't resisted the fleshing of their contact. It was stupid to pretend she was a dimity maid and didn't have, of whatever element made him passionate, an equal share. When she was bored, during long rehearsals or journeys, she brought out these images of undressing and love-making and caressed them, working herself into a state of dilation, the way other people might have reiterated favourite lines of poetry or played patience. She entertained herself with the erotic additions of man to woman, a more subtle and absorbing pastime.

They made love throughout the afternoon, falling asleep briefly, waking and making love again, with more intensity than diversity.

"You're brown already," she complained and traced the points at which the tan ended near his body hair. Fergus became two people when he was undressed, carrying the extremities of the public, decent body round the torso of the pale, intimate and private one. He was an unusually perfect human specimen, unusual perhaps because he was unconscious of effect. His physique of extreme leanness, he weighed not much more than Leonie, was exaggerated by a strong head and longer hair than convention allowed. He could have had a following, this young man, if he had thought to cultivate it.

"Ah, that was the tennis."

"How on earth do you find the time?"

"I don't. Not any more. Things are far too hectic."

She sat up, her body falling into the disposition of the sedentary. She had learned not to question Fergus' allocation of time. He suffered from monomania when he was under stress, and cut all the pleasure out of his life so that he could work, work, work relentlessly. If he could have eaten vitamin capsules and drunk plain tap water to stay alive, he would have done it for the sake of economy in time and money. This obsession was a worry to her. She liked to live expansively, packing in more and more and more when she was pressurised, living to the limits of experience which were defined only by exhaustion. He liked frugality, favouring the method of the stylite who stripped away the non-essential and lived in a purity of dedication on top of his column, reduced to minimalism.

Except for making love. He indulged himself in that and she wondered if her own tastes had developed as the one certain means of retaining a modicum of his attention.

She turned to the hybrid body, dark exposed, pale under-exposed.

"Addenda," she denoted, "and pudenda."

"Hooray for a classical education."

Leonie Barr walking up and down the cobbles of George Square, learning lines by recitation. Head in a book, not his books, but head in a book. Leonie dressed in throwouts which smacked of the green room, theatrical and exaggerated. Her clothes had elements of period costume – her favourite a black and white ensemble that made her look like the solemn Prince of Denmark. This vision stalking Middle Meadow Walk or Chambers Street had a remarkable effect on passers-by. She grew used to men and children staring at her in the street. The women were more discreet and looked out of the side of their eyes, less prone to being amazed or covetous.

He saw her once in a crowd of friends who teased her; the hair like pelage and her light eyes induced the taunt of Marmalade cat, an insult she didn't take too seriously. But when they accused her of crimping her hair, she was indignant. She stood beside

44

Greyfriars' Bobby and emptied a cup of water from the fountain over her head.

"See, it curls," she said, "it curls all by itself."

Leonie standing for the student council, handing out leaflets at a street corner. Fergus went to listen to her address at the Union where the voting took place, and was embarrassed by an image of her different from the picturesque. Swift with hecklers, rude, hovering somewhere near coarseness in layers of language he hadn't known about in her, a dangerous alter ego that disturbed him. The oil in shale when it was compressed. Surely a degree in Government and Politics needn't be carried into practice. He sighed and wished she had the restraint to stay a theorist like him.

They made love among the books at Baxendales and Thins and John Menzies. They pretended they might buy something though they never did pass anything in exchange but kisses. Whole days were spent in a kind of dizziness of rapture, parting and meeting and parting again. Work and love: there was nothing else. Work the effort, love the reward, though sometimes they tipped the proportion in favour of the sweets and skimped the plain fare of drudgery at books.

Leonie taking the theatre in Adam House by storm. St Joan – the only woman on the stage and a man for most of the performance. She alternated between the Shavian dilemmas, nationalism and protestantism, in a way that was personal to her, Scotland not France being subjugated to the oppressor England. The portrayal expressed a mood that was popular, and she became well known, in their one square mile of influence. She said all acting was political and all politics was acting. He didn't understand that, but allowed she was a heterogeneous being.

Leonie spread that morning's copy of the *Scotsman* on the floor and read it kneeling. In a bottom corner, compressed into a two-inch square, she came across the headline

CITY FINANCIER GUILTY OF FRAUD

Put that way, it was an incontrovertible assertion.

"Do you think he was really guilty?"

"What's really guilty?" asked Fergus. "That he set out to

defraud? No, I don't think that. But he committed acts that could have a fraudulent interpretation put on them, yes. What does it matter anyway, whether he was or wasn't, if that's the verdict."

"It wasn't unanimous."

"Seven dissenters out of fifteen in the jury. The smallest guilty you can have. The judge accepted their verdict rather than have a retrial."

"It might have been the lesser evil," she considered. "Going through all that again would be such torture."

For someone who hadn't been present, she guessed well at the nature of a trial – torture, an autopsy on the living membrane, skull-breaking, nail-pulling, sleep-denied torture – or did she recall the experience of Joan, examined for heresy by tricksters with the law? If so, she'd forgotten the wider implication of admitting guilt and the reason for Joan's retraction of her forced confession. "Once you're guilty, you're never anything else. Michael may discharge his bankruptcy in time, or pay his debt to society, if that's something different, but nothing can take away that word 'guilty'."

Fergus was so uncompromising himself that it was hard for her to mitigate the effects of the judgment by saying it was only more or less true. She admired this unwavering quality because of the other affirmatives it brought in its train, loyalty and steadfastness. His religion underscored this staunchness of outlook. Guilt wasn't a simple stigma, attached by the judiciary or public comment. It was a sin, mortal or venial, but a sin. A moral stain had been attached to his father and it was irremovable. She sighed, not so much at the verdict as at his intransigence, the unwillingness to compromise with reality.

"The judge was fair. He was even-handed in his summing-up and didn't direct the jury. Fraud is so hard to prove, apparently, so we looked to have better than fifty-fifty odds. But the defence was a shambles." He rubbed his face and eyes. "The most damning evidence was the accountant's. It just looked what it was, a botch."

He got up and started to dress. The talk of accounts and organisation reminded him of his own work and how he neglected it. His deadlines were always imminent.

"Have you seen your mother yet?" Leonie asked the fond question. She often tried to normalise situations round him because that made her feel less isolated too.

46

"No. Why should I?"

She shook her head. An attempt to put his mother's point of view would bring her into disrepute with him, so she put her head down and went on reading the columns in the newspaper until, at the end of the account, she came to the names of the counsel, prosecuting and defending and the major pursuers among whom was specified Lady Frances Moncrieffe of Inveresk. Leonie's shock was hardly less than on opening the telegram. A verdict and its engineers; the two inseparable, cause and effect. This was the mother of Lord Moncrieffe and grandmother of the MP whose lift she had in all innocence accepted the night before. Leonie felt stricken with guilt, as if she'd consorted with an enemy. She was glad now that she'd said nothing to Watson about the sources of her telegram, or to Fergus about the means of transport that brought her so swiftly to his door. She'd kept the two sides separate, prosecution and defence, but they warred silently in her conscience.

She thought of the day evolving in the big house at Inveresk. A discussion might ensue from this account in the newpaper, much like theirs. Watson saying, 'Only two years. It's a disgrace when you think he's lost tens of thousands for investors.' The capitalist instinct would be hard to quell. Her own theft grew, adding to the sum of deficit so that the judgment also devolved on her. Knowing the complainant made a difference when simple cash became converted into more tangible forms of loss. It mattered more.

"I'll walk you home," said Fergus. "Then I must get back to work." He looked down at the sheets of figures waiting for him and started to regret how much time he had wasted with her, debiting.

"Have you decided yet?" he asked when they reached the end of Canaan Lane and joined the main thoroughfare of Morningside.

She knew this question was inevitable and realised that her sudden arrival in Edinburgh could be read as an encouragement to ask it again. "No, I haven't given it much thought."

"I think we should get married." He said this so emphatically, it was hard to realise it was only an opinion.

"Perhaps, but not necessarily to each other."

Fergus was baffled by her defiance on this point. Men tradition-ally offered and women traditionally refused, but it was a pedantry to go on refusing time after time when they were lovers and would have lived together if their lives had happened to concur. This state of fixed uncertainty had held sway for so long that they both came to think of it as normal, though Fergus knew they had traversed the middle ground of courtship and was determined on an outcome, yea or nay. In his pocket was a marriage licence, applied for ahead of the event in the hope of accelerating it.

It was by now almost dark and on either hand the lights from houses sprang up, Colinton, Cluny, Church Hill to the rear. They outlined the suburban enclaves to which he felt drawn. Stone houses, solid and secure, defining one's position both in territory and in rank. He yearned to escalate, even in his own esteem, and marriage was the first move towards acquiring the unshakeable edifice of respectability.

"What would we live on?" she pressed. "Your sponsorship has hardly covered living expenses these last three years and I don't save more than the cost of a ticket home."

He had waited for her to arrive at this well-worn objection, which was the best prelude to his disclosure. "I've been offered a lectureship in computing, in the Maths department, starting in October. I think they'll set up a new unit in Machine Intelligence shortly and I'll be well placed for promotion in that."

Her practicalities were forestalled, and she was generous in defeat. "That's marvellous for you. Has your thesis been accepted?"

"As good as. And I'm in the hat for the research prize. Down to the last three. I have my viva in June."

She ran her arm through his, and they walked on under the light from street lamps, relishing a success for which they'd both made sacrifices. Doctor Petrie. Doctor Fergus Petrie. A title doubly earned.

"It makes a difference, an income."

She couldn't disagree but cast her eyes over the city streets and their unitary housing. Two public, two bedrooms. All services. Low rates. What was desirable to him was anathema to her, being closeted in four walls with some bits of furniture. She was very happy with the contents of her suitcase when she was mentally in transit as much as physically. Her clothes were borrowed from the wardrobe, and returned. The necessities of life were supplied by

48

props. A chair, a book, a stage. That was all she needed. Property was a burden, and the acquisition of it a middle-class tendency she didn't understand, like marriage itself. The idea of settlement was odious.

He went on, pursuing his independent thoughts. "I would enjoy putting a home together. We live like tinkers, you and I, in rented rooms. It's time we settled down. I swear I don't expect you to stop working."

"You say that, but you don't know what it means, being on tour for three months at a time. Up and away. Up and away." She hesitated to say he didn't care for the people that she mixed with, didn't even enjoy going to the theatre when this could be taken as an impertinent criticism of his standards, and of him.

"We can write our own marriage contract, you know. It doesn't need to be like everyone else's. Freedom of movement," he promised, "and freedom of association. All your civil liberties intact."

Seeing that he wanted it so much and that her own behaviour in catapulting herself northwards to be with him in a crisis was evidently quirky or misleading, if she didn't mean to marry him sometime, she gave in.

"I have the marriage notice forms. If we submit them tomorrow, we can marry the next time you are up. That will give us fifteen days."

Leonie was beguiled by his grasp of events. Round about the clock at Morningside she finally said yes.

6

The flat to which Leonie had ascended at daybreak might be ugly and inconvenient as far as the externals went, but that was no discouragement to the visitors who were welcome to drop in at any time, and did. Ellice Barr kept irregular hours. She kept irregular everything, so her friends came by after the theatre or a concert at the Usher Hall when other entertainments were closed. They weren't theatre-goers, however, but the players who came groping up the stairway to her door, so that the rooms were littered with the strange belongings which her callers brought with them, costumes or scenery on their way to repair, or a cello would appear in a corner beside its cellist. People lent each other things. There was a pile of lace blouses for someone to try on, apropos of fancy dress, and a box of books she'd hand-picked from the charity shop in case a visiting antiquarian thought they were worth having. It was a house of transference; people and objects and ideas met briefly and often left in different company from the one they came in. During the course of an evening the flat took on the air of ante-room, filled with props and actors waiting to begin.

Stuart Ainslie pressed the doorbell with his free hand. In the other was a bottle of whisky, in his pocket one of milk. It was a double tactfulness. Ellice Barr took the first neat and added the second to something she termed coffee for her abstemious guests.

His welcome was complete. She opened the door herself, letting out into the hallway a waft of sound and heat and music that was as unmistakable as incense; a crowd. A busy crowd. A crowd of talkers.

She greeted him from six feet and opened the door wider to accommodate him. Of a good build, strong-faced and dressed in clothes which a tailor would have recognised as well made, if not cut in the latest style, Stuart Ainslie was nevertheless so tousled, unkempt, besmirched and dribbled on that his entire appearance was a mess, the dry cleaner's nightmare. Sometimes even Ellice had to rebuke him for dishevelment, for she was as neat as a pin.

"You don't mind if I bring a friend, do you, Ellice? We met in Rose Street this evening and I said you wouldn't notice another body."

"In a tavern?"

"Where else?"

"Could have been a house of ill fame."

She looked his companion up and down quite blatantly as she said this and Moncrieffe thought, Another errant fact about me lodged. She gave him a frontal stare that left him little to hide behind. His face, his name, his purpose; she knew them all. "Welcome to you, Mr Moncrieffe. You've not been here before. Different sides of the political fence." Her expression and voice played with several suggestions, chief among them being, So what brings you now? His motive was so obvious that Watson was abashed by it. Stuart Ainslie was a heaven-sent introduction to the flat which had appeared impenetrable, but standing on its doorstep he felt as gauche and presumptuous as a gangling boy. Naturally, she would know of his service to her daughter and he realised he looked a chancer. On the make, oh God, was he really on the make?

The hostess in Ellice prevailed over the mother and she gestured them in accommodatingly. Watson found himself guided by noise into a room filled with maybe forty people, an unpremeditated party that formulated itself on several evenings of the week. The politician stepped over the coffee and whisky drinkers who sat about on chairs or cushions on the floor and the air thickened with talk and smoke together, a heady mix. He knew a dozen faces in the room and his own name came back at him more than once, so that the embarrassment of his arrival was replaced by something warmer, not welcome, but recognition.

Quickly, he cast his eye about the room and saw that Leonie wasn't there. He relaxed and was disappointed in equal measure. Stuart and he found places by the fire and sank almost at once into a conversational oblivion. Stuart was tired after a day rehearsing a new play at the Lyceum. He came only because it was somewhere comfortable to be, a bolt hole out of the Edinburgh night, no questions asked, and because Watson told him Leonie was back and he himself was anxious to speak to her. The exhaustion of talk

51

was too much for him. He was content to watch the antics of the room. He rested his back on one of the pilasters of the fireplace and, from time to time, peeled the bark and moss from the silver birch logs which were piled up beside him, drying out before they reached the fire.

Watson sat by the other pilaster and felt uncomfortable for many reasons. The floor was hard. The wall was harder still. One needed to be a student to enjoy such unreceptive surfaces. He was queasy about his own motives in coming, using the public venue as a cover for private interests, less pressing as long as the cause herself was absent. He stilled his conscience by saying he might never be found out but this induced a more subtle frenzy, that she might not come and witness his devotion.

He was most uncomfortable because of the décor of the flat which jarred on him. Décor? Well, décor implied intention. Surely nobody could have chosen these objects, or not with the idea of putting them together and living in the middle. Most of them looked new, not bric-à-brac from second hand shops. Maybe they were goods on which a hire purchaser had defaulted or bankrupt stock, sold off in a church hall. There was a perspex coffee table. A three-tier drinks trolley in blue enamel with gold legs. And then suddenly something good. A Charles Rennie Mackintosh sideboard stood like an elder statesman, stiff against a wall.

The rooms which Ellice had put together in her curious way ought to have been as anonymous as the frontage of a junk shop, for the aesthetics were as abysmal as those that put tartan on the Chippendale at Balmoral. But Watson, glancing round the room, was almost charmed by its bizarre quality. It achieved the aim of more sophisticated salons. It was unique. Who else had gone in for sepia walls to camouflage the smoke?

He remembered how Leonie had been able to recall each of the features of his home with almost loving accuracy and that he had said, glibly, it was famous furniture. It had a history. With hindsight, he wouldn't have been quite so patrician and he wondered if her lack of confidentiality arose from arrogance on his part which she found unsympathetic, hostile even. This place was actually a denial of acquisition. It put goods into their proper perspective as functionaries. What was wrong with the drinks trolley after all?

The door opened and Leonie herself came in. The fresh air that she admitted caught the fire draught so that the flames burned more brightly for a moment, raising the level of illumination. Her eyes took a while to adjust to the fireglow and so she stood still while her pupils dilated, making them larger and darker by absorption.

The room disturbed itself to accommodate her. The two men at the fireplace watched the way she crossed a floor compulsively. Stuart watched her moves and gestures in analysis, as if she were following stage directions and he projected a play about her. Barbara Undershaft perhaps, attending the hangers-on at the Salvation Army depot. No, at this moment something more evocative than Shaw, something more glowing. He drifted mentally towards Chekhov in trying to place her. The Russians accorded women such central power on the stage while English dramatists subordinated them to men. She would hold the centre well.

She crossed the room towards the fire where her mother occupied an armchair, stopping among the company to pass a word here and there. Stuart admired this ability to live in the public eye. She wasn't put out to find her living room inhabited by forty – he looked about him – bohemians, odd-balls, weirdos, the flip side of suburbia, intellectual drop-outs. He disparaged them because he liked achievement, not talk which was the vacuum of activity. Leonie didn't talk excessively, but rested on doing. Unshy and unflappable, the assets of profession carried over.

Leonie came and sat in front of the fire. As she passed Watson, her eye picked him out of the shadows with some surprise but all she said was, "So you are here."

This might have struck him as an unremarkable greeting if it hadn't been the exact form of words used by his grandmother as she came downstairs at Inveresk that morning in her dressing gown. Women without excess. Like Ainslie, he admired the lean frame of the mind.

"And how is Viola?" the director distracted her.

"Rather tired of comic glibness."

"When does she run out of repartee?"

"Another three weeks, alternating with Lady Windermere's daughter."

"Then what?"

"I'm doing a couple of modern plays in rep at Bristol. End of June finish. How about you?"

"I've got a new play in rehearsal then a Shaw season that I want to take through to the Festival. Though the RSC will oust me from the Lyceum for that."

"Shaw. Well." She made a gesture with the flat of her hand to imply this was a dubious undertaking.

"In modern dress. The political plays."

She adjusted her hand to palm, admitting maybe.

"Are you interested?"

"Me? Of course." A Shavian interlude at the Lyceum. A settled start to marriage. She leaped at it but only mentally, not allowing the personal to cloud her judgment of the professional rôles he offered her.

"I'll hold off casting for another two weeks till you've finished this run at Oxford. I haven't decided finally which plays but almost certainly *Major Barbara* and *Man and Superman* and maybe *The Apple Cart*."

"Barbara," she murmured appreciatively.

"You won't even need to wear a girdle. What bliss."

She raised her eyes and caught the humour in his. So he knew that much, how she had to wear a girdle for men's roles to flatten her breasts. "Bliss indeed."

"You've played so many men in your time, it must almost come as a novelty to act the woman." He teased with words, like little flicks behind the ear.

Hearing this, Ellice intervened. "Leonie's a better man than most."

Stuart nodded, agreeing to her primary suggestion that Leonie played men better than other women, if not to her secondary one that general imposture by one of the other was preferable to the differentiation of the sexes. He thought privately that such performances, however good, did smack of pantomime. Sarah Bernhardt as Hamlet? Preposterous.

"How tall are you, Leonie?" he asked with professional interest.

This was a sensitive point and so she answered it by analogy. "The same height as Mary, Queen of Scots."

"And what height is that?" he persevered.

54

"Five foot eleven and a half inches," she defined for him.

A half inch short of masculine ideals, for themselves, but not for women. "Too tall," he said. "Too tall. It makes it so hard to find the right leading man, you know." He said this, knowing full well that he was riling each of his immediate neighbours in the room, Leonie, her mother and Moncrieffe. The long-standing relationship with Fergus Petrie, for which Ellice had scant tolerance, wasn't likely to be produced as a rebuttal nor was the tardy suitor going to voice his willingness to understudy for the part.

Leonie separated the intimate from the theatrical. "You always did think I was going to be stuck with Hermia."

The director looked serious. "A painted maypole? No, I felt someone might risk you as Titania, provided you played it sitting down."

They laughed and Ellice, catching drifts of their dialogue between the crackling of the fire and the general rumour that swelled and thinned in pauses round about them, thought that they did well together. She felt a little ousted by their compatibility which was exclusive of third parties, and alienated most of all by a flirtation which might be mental or professional in emphasis but also had elements of the sexual. One side of her wanted to keep them strenuously apart, in case, having fallen for the seduction of the stage through Stuart's agency, Leonie also fell for his through it. The woman distrusted both forms of allure, finding the glamour of sex as false as the glamour of theatricality. She sent her daughter to elocution lessons for public speaking, the noble art of oratory, not for the trivialising stage, and was repeatedly disappointed by Leonie's chosen profession. Mere play acting. But on the other hand . . . she rather liked the young director who'd hung around her door for ten years, admired the name he'd built up for himself and his company at the Lyceum with some interesting new plays and unorthodox versions of the classics. His Shaw in modern dress would reinstate the political revolutionary. She listened sympathetically to his thoughts about a Scottish National Theatre. Orchestra, Ballet, Opera, why not the theatre graced with capitals? It was a cherished dream of hers as much as his, the national scene, and when he talked about a theatre workshop where Scottish actors as well as playwrights and craftsmen would find a collective purpose instead of joining the inevitable drift south, she was fired too.

But giving her daughter to the cause, that was another matter.

The room shifted. In the hallway, the cellist started to play part of the Bach suite which made a dulcet backdrop to the ensemble. The woman who was borrowing Edwardian blouses went in and out, displaying different modes for general approval. The man who was interested in the box of old books thumbed through them and read passages aloud which seemed as musty as the covers.

A group by the door spilled over from the hall noisily. The four were interrupted and, looking up, saw that they were young people who talked above the pitch of the room. One of the girls caught a glimpse of Leonie and they nodded significantly to each other, communicating knowledge.

"Alison Petrie," answered Stuart to his companion by the fire.

"A friend of Leonie's?" Watson wanted to know specifically, anxious to establish the geography of her relationships.

"Almost a relative," said Stuart with his fondness for stirring people into a brew. "Almost".

This was a handsome girl, better looking than the actress, with a burnish on dark hair and skin that was the outcome of regular attention. Not preening. Her appearance was wholesome and natural, but resulted from regular meals and a regular lifestyle. The stresses Alison Petrie underwent were self-imposed. She was intense, this girl, her voice soaring high above the conversational level so that Watson could hear her say, "I've just come back from Aldermaston. I can't tell you how wonderful it was, thousands of us on the march, like Jarrow. A crusade. It really was a peace crusade." She said this with such zionist fervour that several people in the room nodded in agreement. The newpapers had been full of an anniversary Aldermaston over Easter. The two men didn't nod. Her reference to Jarrow and to real hardship rather than an ideological adventure struck them as shallow.

"But what did you achieve, Alison," mocked Stuart, "beyond some blisters?"

"Oh you," she retorted to an old tormentor. "A principle. Peaceful demonstration in support of peace." When she spoke of these abstracts of faith Alison's eyes flooded with emotion which was either moving or ridiculous according to the stance of her observers. Watson knew a hundred times more about defence procurement than she did and the tangible threat of knock-out nuclear warfare, so he was one of the latter. But he held his silence, not wishing to appear too polemic in this company.

"Think of all the petty crime committed in the inner cities while the police force was absent marshalling you. Did you actually bring about some arms reduction, by the by?"

"It'll come. CND will make the superpowers re-think. Ban the Bomb."

"I see you've been very well programmed. Did you go on an indoctrination course first to have your brains washed out? Bunch of lefties," Stuart said, goading her. "Probably funded by the KGB to counteract the American arms race."

"That's a lie." She could have cried with anger at his lack of conviction, and her own failure to change him.

"Alison, hush," called Ellice "Come and tell me all about it. You're the first person I've met who was there."

Leonie, moving to make space on the floor, gravitated towards the politician.

"Is Fergus well?" asked Stuart, raising a spectre. "I presume you saw him today."

"Yes, I saw him."

"Fergus is Alison's brother," the director amplified for his guest, to whom the relationships began to make one composite, from which he was excluded by fact and by association. "It was bad news about Michael. I couldn't believe it when I read the verdict in today's paper." He dropped his bantering tone. "Bad news for all of you."

"Aldermaston is maybe more important," Leonie said shrugging.

"Allow her some youthful idiocies," Stuart interceded.

"Nobody went," she added. "Nobody went to a single day of the trial except Fergus."

Stuart did raise his eyebrows at the callousness but in him this expressed resignation. It was his custom to highlight drama, not to shape it, and so he relapsed into observer, merely entertained to have two such young women as Alison and Leonie within watching distance.

57

Watson leaned forwards to capture Leonie's attention. "Is this the case of Michael Petrie, the financier who was sentenced for fraud?"

She nodded. In both their faces there was the consciousness of the people external to themselves who might find their juxtaposition strange and even repugnant.

"I'm sorry. I'm so sorry about the way it happened and that my family has been involved."

"Our loyalties are on different sides. You must rejoice at a conviction."

His expression was inimical, remembering that both of them had cause to be exasperated at the confusions of rôle-playing. Professional and personal; do not mix the two. "The law is cruel. I only hope it was a just verdict."

"However just, it wasn't deserved."

Watson was dismissive of intermediary interests. "This needn't apply to us."

Perhaps he was impertinent to use the plural pronoun. As far as Leonie was concerned there was no 'us' and so she answered with some hauteur, having the position of advantage in this debate, "It applies."

He was determined to know the answer to the question that had dogged him for the last twenty-four hours. "Fergus is . . ."

"My fiancé."

Stuart heard, with a glee at the improbability of such an announcement, now, here, of all times. "Are you engaged, Leonie?"

"Yes, we are engaged." The words were firm. The delivery was not, and elided the facts of the marriage licence. One thing at a time, thought Leonie, shy of the real reason for her reticence which was her own uncertainty.

"Not a bad day's work then. Worth coming all the way from Oxford. Do you hear that, Ellice? Leonie and Fergus have gone and done it."

The broadcast cut through other dialogues. People came to congratulate her, first among them Alison, and to embrace. "But where is the ring, Leonie? And where is Fergus?"

"Busy with more important things," supplied Stuart savagely. "Make sure you bring him to the wedding."

Watson was crestfallen. The festivity released into the room was painful to him for it was reminiscent of his own betrothal, the absolute regularity of which made this announcement, which he himself had forced, feel almost accidental. No ring and no man. What kind of marriage was it going to be?

Ellice was no better pleased. Marriage. Good heavens, a conventional marriage and to a man. Herself as stock figure of mother-in-law. She recanted on the thought she'd had half an hour before. She'd rather be linked to the acerbic Ainslie than the pious mathematician. Or Moncrieffe, sitting in the corner, even he. Her old opponent was her ally in this. Someone to expand her daughter's potential, not contract it. She despaired at the slowness and inequality of all three-legged races. She did not add her congratulations to the general but sat mulling on her double disappointment, neither the vocation nor the husband her daughter had chosen being to her liking.

It was two in the morning. They each remembered Saturday and drifted away for a few hours' sleep before its chores fell due. The men left as they had come, together. Going down the stone steps, clanging, cold, Watson heard a murmuring overhead and looked back up the elliptical well of the stairs. On the top landing, Leonie and her future sister-in-law stood talking, arms leaning on the wooden banister. The curving rail made a frame of baroque asymmetry round their heads and the light in a wall bracket behind focused them in chiaroscuro depth. Sculptured women. Goddesses flying over his head, like a Tiepolo ceiling.

"Goodnight, Leonie," he could not stop himself from calling up three flights of steps.

She leaned further out and caught sight of him, craned upwards.

"Goodnight, Watson," she replied.

The words dropped like coins into a well, carrying unspoken wishes.

Alone at last after two days of crowding, Leonie went to her own bedroom. Here her tastes reigned, spartan and quiet. The violet gown hung on the back of the door, like a corsage preserved after a ball, a reminder which was inappropriate to its setting. The rest was cell-like. An iron bedstead, a painted chest, a wicker chair. It was a place of stern neutrality, similar to Fergus' room but for different reasons. He refused to domesticate the ugly; Leonie didn't think about it. Plainness was an act of self-denial to the young man, amounting to a conscious abstinence from beauty or even a flagellation of the spirit into a pain caused by the unaesthetic. To Leonie, plainness was beauty. She lived in action, not in objects. Wild grasses in a jam jar, where the water magnified the stems and grains of pollen fell onto the painted surface of the chest: that was the essence for her, the real transported indoors.

There were only five drawers in the chest and the bottom one was reserved as a file where important letters and documents were kept, ranked in order. She was almost obsessively tidy, and knew where to put her hand on the piece of paper she was looking for. It was folded in quarters, good thick paper with slight ridges on the writing surface. The name and address which were printed on it hadn't faded in ten years. Meeting the man whose name flowed like a banner over the heading raised their lettering in high relief. That was all she had taken, one sheet of printed stationery from his desk. Not much, but culpable. It turned her into a common tourist as well as a common thief, breaking off masonry to remember a building by. Stupid.

What did she say her party's representation was? Ten per cent, a swing of six brought about after four years of effort by her mother and twenty other workers locally. But it would take more than that to bridge the gap between Moncrieffe and herself. She felt the stupendous political effort counted for nothing when it couldn't change the shape of one constituency or that of national representation, far less redefine the boundaries between people. Rich and poor, landed and unentitled, winner and loser; these were the immutable classes. Casting herself into the lower order, Leonie found herself little content with the subsidiary role and a surge of determination ran through her to be as good as any principal. She saw that the limitation of her birth did endow her with a useful anonymity. No one. Nobody. That was a blank page on which anything might be written whereas Watson Abercrombie Moncrieffe with his established name was always and indelibly just that.

7

Fergus didn't go back to Canaan Lane after he left Leonie but walked on in the direction they'd followed, going south. He took the left fork from the clock at Morningside and rose slowly with the terrain. The invitation which the professor had extended to him in George Square was a reminder of how unfairly he'd boycotted his old friends, not because of who they were but because of where they lived.

He turned from Braid Road into Hermitage Drive. He hadn't come along this stretch of road in the two years of the pending law suit and so he was separated from his own antecedence by a span of personal development far in excess of simple chronology; a compound one perhaps, age and experience escalating like a graph line out of sight. He wanted to come, and dreaded it. He'd spent his whole life in one house and the sale of it to meet the debts of bankruptcy was a personal disaster which didn't fade. It was social, economic, professional collapse. The house at the Hermitage was a talisman of stability which was access to childhood, or innocence, and irretrievably lost.

It was a broad avenue with trees running along a high rill and then dipping towards Blackford Pond. The better side was south where the houses backed onto the Hermitage of Braid, a wooded dell and its Palladian mansion, now devolved into a municipal parkland, which gave its name to the surrounding district. Some properties had a private gate leading into the park, a privilege which the Petrie children had exercised daily, making the Hermitage into their playground. The houses, in variegated styles, were built of stone and had settled into a maturity of placement behind walls or iron railings or hedges of luxuriant thickness. The avenue was so broad that the two sides were disconnected from each other and each unit was its own environment. Exclusive: it was. It excluded him.

He drew alongside the Geddes' house, his neighbours', which was highlighted by an ornamental lamp-post that broke the rhythm of other standard provisions along the street. One for town councillor; two for provost if the professor ever rose that high. Fergus tried not to look at his own house, thinking it was a ghoulish revisiting, but he couldn't help himself. It magnetised his mind. He went warily to the end of the driveway and looked up, with an insistent preference for pain which made rubbing a bruise or pressing an abscess feel remedial. He scourged himself with looking.

In the dim light, a bank of daffodil and mixed narcissus suddenly loomed out at him, planted in a sweep of the lawn, and further on a magnolia held up its candelabrum flowers. Soon the rhododendrons. He stood still and listened to the incessant noise of woodland nearby, squirrels, a ruffling of birds and a heavier brushing perhaps of an urban fox trailing through the undergrowth.

Locked out, he was locked out all round. The house changed hands. Other people used the asphalt tennis court and the back gate or let them become overgrown, having no use for the land beyond the cultivated. There was no major change but through the sustained evolution of the house he could trace his own disconnection from it. The beech hedge was thicker, the cypresses wider by a margin of so much growth. He felt incalculable resentment at the organic pattern that flourished even in his absence. By rights, the garden should have withered and died making a barren spot on the top crest of the Hermitage, blighted by some spores of destruction that were ineradicable. Flowers in a border, nodding, were a mockery. He glanced up to his left and could pick out, through the foliage, the lights in the window of the turret room that had been his. Someone else took his place. He felt knotted by the anger and frustration of that imposture. It was his and no one else's. Custom and consent, spread over more than a quarter of a century so that it ought to be inalienable. How could property pass through a commercial transfer when it was the cornerstone of personality? He was overcome with the savage jealousy of his dispossession, loss of his dues which implied loss of some part of himself. Well, he would ascend. Nail and claw, he would rise by his own agency and damn them all.

He turned blackly on his heel, and then remembered the Geddes family. Was it too late to make a call? For a stranger, yes; himself, no. Besides, he had an invitation and a question that made the errand legitimate, coming to the councillor for advice like any other householder in the ward. He went across the gravel to the front door and, ignoring the conventions of the hour, rang the bell.

"Why, Fergus," a woman exclaimed as she opened up the porch door. "How good to see you."

The caller was enveloped by Irene Geddes' chief quality, her politeness which resided in her consideration of others first and herself second. A hundred women would have implied, What kind of hour is this to ring? But she was able to move on to the altruistic plane of assuming there was sufficient cause.

For her part, she did falter in her welcome, not that it was partial, but because an embrace would have been more freely given at one time. The new reserve between them measured a two-year distance, widened by his access to full manhood. He left promising and returned having accomplished it, so she was shy with his adult body although he was as known to her as her own son.

"I wonder if I could have a word with the professor? Is he home?" He conceded something to her hesitancy. "I realise it's late."

"Oh you know we're night birds, but he's busy marking papers for the University examinations." She wavered, wondering which claim was stronger, his to an audience or her husband's to uninterrupted privacy. She noticed that Fergus' hair was damp from walking in the night air and glistened as if wet. Why does one warm to him, she asked herself. Why does one care?

"I'll just go and tell him you've come. He said he'd seen you recently."

Fergus waited in the vestibule, hearing their voices in subdued consultation until he was admitted. Marriage, behind closed doors, secluded and intimate the way it ought to be. The professor sat in his panelled dining room with papers strewn over the floor and table. "Good evening to you, Fergus. Do tread carefully," he admonished, not attempting to get up. "And take a seat. I'll have that bundle, thank you."

Irene bent to stoke the fire which had died down and sparks flew loose, igniting for a second the flakes of soot accumulated on the grate.

63

"I believe we have to congratulate you, Fergus," she said, turning round.

Fergus was baffled. How could the woman know he was to be married when he only decided it himself two hours before?

"The lectureship," Professor Geddes amplified. "I heard about it through the Senate, before the official announcement." He didn't add that he had guided a hand, swayed a panel in the decision, being a quiet benefactor.

"Yes, it makes a difference having that settled," Fergus could say but, like Irene, was too new with his own advance in status to define why.

"What can we do for you?" the man urged, anxious about his schedule with the scripts. So many a day. So many an hour.

"I'm not sure you can do anything." Saying this, Fergus realised the pointlessness of coming. He glanced towards Irene who sat encouraging him visibly, glad to see him without reason. Why had he come? Belief that their security was unimpeachable and that, encountering them, he might encounter it. Casting his eye about the room, he landed on a copy of the *Scotsman*, turned inside out with intensive readings. "You saw the verdict?"

"Yes," said Irene quickly. "I was distraught for you both."

This 'both' distressed Fergus too, excluding three who might have been involved. Even the proportions of family alliance were weighted against Michael.

"I don't know how closely you followed the case—"

"Closely."

"Then do you think there's any point in lodging an appeal?"

The professor put down the papers on his lap and removed his glasses to focus on his interlocutor. They were soft and pliable glasses and he was able to unpeel them from behind his ears.

"Why?"

"Because the judgment is wrong."

"Wrong," said the legalist, "wrong."

Fergus found himself perennially daunted by this man. Even his head was out of the run of the other heads that he knew. Whatever was irrelevant to intellect was excised from the professor's concern and he carried as little spare human cargo as he could. He didn't suffer fools, gladly or otherwise, and terrorised his council meetings and his tutorials with implacable logic.

"Wrong is two words," the man went on. "In your sense it is moral. You are morally outraged by what you see as a miscarriage of justice. But that is not the view of the judiciary. The correct processes have been enacted, and a judgment has been arrived at with the assistance of a judge and jury who – you will admit – have been free of bribery or duress. A free trial, and that is not easily overturned."

"It wasn't unanimous."

"So I see. Eight to seven. A verdict so close it's almost worthless. But that is the law as it stands."

"One more person could have made that difference? Well, the system is absurd."

"It's the human factor, Fergus. If you look for pinpoint accuracy in the law, to the fifth decimal place, you are mistaken. I am a perfectionist too, and I tell you perfection is not to be found, not in our legal system and not in anybody's. Justice is perfect, as a concept, but the law is a very variable interpreter of it."

Irene made a movement, an adjustment in her chair, which registered her impatience with the abstract.

On his own example, Fergus was more pragmatic. If he had been able to influence that one juror who made the difference between yea and nay, not bribed or threatened, but persuaded, he would have done it by any means, wooed him by the powerful argument that the small share of hesitancy he might feel, added to the committed doubters, made the sum of negation which the law allowed. Eight-fifteenths as against seven was enough to tip the scales. Find that missing factor and a man's life was altered.

"There has to be a line drawn somewhere, Fergus, and on either side of it the plus or minus is indeed fractional. You wouldn't be any more satisfied if the verdict were unanimous, or 'Not proven' had been given. You don't agree with the outcome, and that is all there is to it."

Irene watched the young man cogitate, oblivious to the externals of the room. It was a handsome head, the sort of head the Romans could depict in wax, or a mosaic; curled, neat, with passive eyes. It had Byzantine overtones, not unlike the faces that looked out from the wall of a basilica. This passivity was not inactive. It was a screen pulled down for private thought, behind which both his intellect and his religion made their observance.

"No," he said at last, "that's only the starting point, dissatisfaction for my personal cause. It leads me on to a general principle which is that the fallibility of the legal system is too great. Yes, as you say, there's an in-built corrector but it may not be a wide enough margin for error. How many of those fifteen actually understood the evidence of the case as it was laid before them? It was complex. I knew the facts and I found it confusing."

"For fraud you may need experts?"

Fergus nodded. "And maybe fifteen is too many. The larger the number on a panel, the more difficult it is to decide in a way that satisfies all of them. You know that from your council meetings. What is a bare majority on important matters? And who would dare to hold the casting vote?"

"But Fergus," the professor leaned forward, excited by the instantaneous fusion of his two selves, the legal and municipal adviser, "you are indicting democracy. What you are saying, that only those versed in a subject should decide either on points of law or on the administration of public funds, is a denial of the democratic principle. You are suggesting a form of oligarchy in the legal system. Trial by jury is democracy, done and seen to be done. The people will decide."

"The people are ignorant."

"True. So change that instead." The professor thought he resolved the argument with a sophistry, the impossible conundrum, but Fergus was either younger in experience or more positive by nature. He believed that it was possible. Knowledge was wisdom.

There was a long and battling silence, during which the fire roared up the chimney, gulping air.

"Have you seen your mother, Fergus?" Irene ventured.

"No. Why should I?"

She had the advantage over Leonie in confronting this question, a combination of maturity and long association with the family of Petries, as well as her own fearlessness. "Because she is your mother."

"Biology," said Fergus slowly. "Biology can fail." Sometimes the looks he gave chilled her, hinting at the implacable. She came up against the graphite in his temperament, hard and grey as flint.

"You should go," she urged mildly.

"She doesn't come to see us," said Fergus, "but sends directives in brown envelopes. No," he held up his hand to stem the plea that she might make, "understand that if it weren't for the separation, he wouldn't be bankrupt, or in jail tonight."

"That's a surmise," chided the professor.

"I beg your pardon. It is fact. You can see it every day on the Stock Exchange. A rumour gets about and confidence falters. Prices go down and then the company goes into liquidation. Ten million pounds wiped off the value of a company in one day, because of some pernicious rumour that may not even be true. That's what she achieved single-handed. She drew out her own assets from Petrie Incorporated and the whole financial structure collapsed because, in that business, it's only credibility you trade on and good faith."

The couple sat willing themselves to make a conciliatory remark but his expression was an impediment to facile hopes, as well as the memory they retained of the woman who had been their neighbour for so long and had disturbed their peace of tenure with every form of transgression they might imagine. She was a woman who was capable of argument over the height of a communal hedge, the lighting of her gardener's bonfire, the parking of cars to restrict their access – every goddam thing she could argue about – and they never breathed with more genuine relief than when she moved away. So the subject lapsed, not because they had nothing to say but because there was too much.

"Is Matthew not at home?" the visitor asked of his long-standing friend, trying to re-assert civility.

"Why, Matthew's gone back to Oxford. He's taking his finals next month," supplied the mother, amazed at the growth of her own son.

"He's reading . . ."

"PPE. He phoned the other day and mentioned he'd seen Leonie in Shakespeare at the Playhouse. What was it? I've forgotten."

But Fergus couldn't remember either; neither the play nor the part. Perhaps to cover this omission, he volunteered at last the second source of congratulation. "Leonie and I are engaged. In fact, you're the first people I've told."

Irene expanded, "Ah, that's . . ." Good, right, timely? She couldn't find a word that was truthful to her feelings and so she said the paltry, "nice".

As he rose, Fergus stepped over the papers, marked and unmarked on the floor. "Any good?" he asked.

James Geddes made a face peculiar to himself which consisted of a dimpling of one cheek. It looked impudent in the context of his solemn features, greyed with authority. "A fine inventive way with spelling, but that's the major talent. Otherwise it's misquoted acts and conclusions quite unrelated to the hypotheses. I wouldn't place too much reliance on a jury made of these. I wonder how such fools find their way into my lectures. Perhaps I made them fools and they are a symptom of my dotage, though I cannot easily believe it since I have never been as frankly stupid as they. Not in my cradle." He re-sealed the spectacles from ear to ear. "You may laugh. This will come to you in time."

As she bade him goodnight at the door, Irene Geddes said, "And come back soon. You've been away too long." The night was warm, and he was comforted by it in the embrace of words.

When he arrived back at the flat in Canaan Lane, the euphoria of contact with their solidity and their old fondness for him was quickly dispelled. As he put the light on in the bedroom ready for undressing, he found the curtains closed, a relic of love-making if almost the only one, and on the floor where Leonie had left it was the full spread of the *Scotsman*. Its pertinent headline still accused. His instinct was to fold it up like shame, hide it, burn it, do away with the last evidence in his consciousness.

Then he remembered that the Geddes had their own version of scandal delivered, and others too. He thought of the endless duplication, the hundreds and hundreds of copies of that edition run off by the printing presses and dispersed to homes throughout the city, throughout the rest of Scotland for all that he knew, as far as the Western Isles. He saw the five-word headline arriving at so many breakfast tables, read with interest or dismissed. Thousands of people saying, Fancy that.

Fergus perceived that as long as there were no reporting restrictions, everything that happened in the Court of Session was public property. His father's trial was not a confession of sins, mortal or venial, whispered in private. It was a trial, a test of strength, a battle of forces both defending and prosecuting over one man's transgressions. Even if the judge in his summing-up had found him innocent, with the words, 'I can find no fault in this man' and recommended his release, still the press could crucify him with publicity.

Irene put out the bedside light and lay for some time in the dark. "He's become something of a Puritan, don't you think? A shame, when he was so open as a young man."

"Puritanical? Not altogether. A purist maybe."

She would have liked to pursue her husband on why he made such a fine distinction, but the abstruse frightened her and she held to the concrete. "Michael in prison. What an appalling thought."

"I'll go to see him." Her husband admitted the resolution made hours before.

"Ah, that is what I hoped for," she said. "But who goes to see Fergus?"

"Yes," he agreed to the unspoken parallel, reading her mind more accurately than she did his. "Imprisonment really is a farce when the family is going to be incarcerated by the effects of a scandal as much as the guilty member. Oscar Wilde was right. Society is infinitely more brutalised by the consistent application of justice than it is by the occasional indulgence of petty crime."

The words lay inertly in the dark, like lettering made with phosphates on a sheet of paper, invisible to the naked eye. She knew them but like most of her knowledge, it was encoded until he released it. The words began to make sense, lit by his utterance, and uncurled in a trail of thought so that they glowed insistently in the dark, a firebrand or smoke signal whose method of transmission made it sinister.

MENE MENE TEKEL UPHARSIN

burned in tablets looked like the hand of God.

Fergus sat up half that night, drawing signs with pen and paper. He didn't waste his time on doodles or cartoons or lines of ill-made poetry or sketches of the things that lay about the room; the outline of the conventional imagination didn't interest him. He drew

69

symbols, concrete symbols, hard fact. He drew numbers down the page and connected them with signs, making up mathematical knots for his computer to unravel.

Who said that it was an arid study? He didn't find it dry. It was exciting and profound. It was the essence of the Ancients, a conversation that took place with Archimedes and Pythagoras without having to go through the intervening medium of classical grammar. The lexis was simple, dramatic, universal. It was the language of abstract thought.

The linguistic signs were minimal: $\therefore$ $<$ $>$. Therefore, smaller than, greater than, but more succinct than wordy words. They embodied their own meaning, being properly representational and were legible at a glance while the geometric triangle, whether isosceles, equilateral or right-angled, contained for him the major conceptual drama. It was a mystery he had never tired of testing, that its angles added up to $180°$. And if he drew other symbols on the page

$$= \qquad \text{and} \qquad \simeq$$

they defined their difference visually. Two strokes for equality. Two strokes with a break for approximation. Such syllabic precision. Comprehensive meaning in two lines. That was realistic poetry.

But like poetry, it had to be more than a mental puzzle. This was a rudimentary alphabet he used, a method of expression which his mind had always sped through without mistakes. But where did it tend? What was the purpose? He saw the science as an intermediary to others. Mathematics was a tool, the implement of physics or statistics, proving theories and examples inarguably. It was indispensable to the counting of stars, or the molecules in an atom. Pure mathematicians could evolve a philosophy of absolutism; he had even heard of someone who proved the existence of a deity by numbers.

Truth then. It searched for truth. The power of it was that it contained no lie. Angles did not fluctuate, ellipses didn't curve away from their prescribed course. The science posed a problem to which there was always an answer even if it went to the tenth decimal place or the thousandth part of a fraction: there was a provable and true outcome.

He fell under the influence of that truth, that absolutism, and wanted to explore it for himself. When he read the biographies of the great mathematicians of the past, Descartes, Everiste Gaulois, Napier, Einstein, he heard an echo of himself. Dedication from an early age, a prodigal understanding of these sophisticated numerical languages, but identifying the goal and the ability of other men didn't help him to define his own. They had absorbed all the space there was; logarithms, the quantum theory, relativity and the fourth dimension. What had they left for him in the way of fame? Whatever new was there to postulate in the field of mathematics? He despaired of finding his own niche.

Then, when he was still a schoolboy, someone showed him a computer installed in the civil service department at St Andrew's House, the first generation of working computers after the sequential digital decoders of the second world war. They told him there was a man whose genius for numbers was such that he was brought in once a year to check the computer's accuracy, but that he couldn't work for very long because mechanical computation was so tiring. The two facts fused. The man was better than the machine in conceptual analysis, but the machine superseded its operator in reliability. The huge semantic network of computing opened up to Fergus and he perceived where it was that his work lay. Machine language seized him with its perfectible lucidity, superior to human speech which ended at guesses and approximation.

8

_____

Past midnight, half a mile away at Greenbank, Muriel put down the newspaper which they had all read during the course of that day, Petrie, Moncrieffe, Barr and Geddes scattered over the city, relaying its information to parties interested and disinterested. So it was done. She sighed with relief that the trial had been concluded without her name being mentioned, or her evidence being exacted by the court. She had succeeded in maintaining her neutrality in the eyes of the law and she read this success as the best justification of her actions, ends and means being inseparable to her. Michael's conviction for fraud was a demonstrable proof of her innocence.

At the same time she felt wafts of pity for a man in a prison cell which were disconnected from any of the factors that had put him there. So she could mutter 'What a shame' with a genuine feeling which would never be translated into genuine action. Within the space of half an hour, Muriel would weep tears for the harshness of the conviction, rail against the fact that they were all Petries by name and contaminated by the outcome Michael had wished on them, and bristle with self-righteous determination that she was fully justified in what she'd done. It was her business as well. She had kept it ticking over for years. In many ways, Fergus was right in saying the business collapsed when she withdrew her backing. She *was* the business, but felt that like any partner, married or not, she was entitled to say, 'I've had enough. I'm selling out.' Her reasoning was that, if she didn't, they all faced ruin and it was better to survive on fifty per cent of assets than risk their entire capital.

Besides, she was fighting her own legal battle. She was locked in combat with a solicitor whom she was trying to sue for professional negligence. He had omitted to point out a clause in the purchase agreement of her present house and she deemed herself to have suffered financially as a result of his failure to advise. She was determined to force reparation from this firm of solicitors. They weren't, in the normal sense, family solicitors. She and Michael had had separate representation for a long time and at various stages of their disagreements had held meetings with all four parties, to try and work out the fine details of a marriage confused by business interests to define who paid for what. At times the two lawyers were bemused at being treated as marriage guidance counsellors, called to decree on matters that were, in normal households, settled by tact or common sense, the unwritten law of matrimonial contract. The woman's lawyer found her favoured invocation was to 'slap a court order' on the husband's bank account until he did as he was told.

Muriel was finding out how difficult it was to sue professionals who were wary enough of the litigious public to cover themselves with indemnifying clauses. She had resorted to two further legal practices who refused to handle a matter that dealt with their colleagues, and was forced to go lower and lower down the professional register, reaching the levels of the incompetent and the unprincipled who were ready to give out any old advice as long as it made them money. Fifty pounds a letter. Why quibble over the contents? Muriel was their ideal client, determined to wrest the answer she wanted from the law, even if it meant changing it. She would have been loath to fund a full court hearing, if it came to that, or a decision that went against her, but she seldom thought through to consequences, carried along by the rages of personal injustice. She had no notion of giving up her suit against the unwary evaluator and, in the abeyance of specific legal progress, was restricted to a private campaign of harrying. She wrote a letter of complaint to the Scottish Law Society, reporting the misconduct and requesting mediation. The body couldn't actually tell her to get lost and stop bothering them, but most emphatically thought so. Letters came and went and she sharpened her legalistic phrasing with much use of ergo, prima facie and restitution of rights. Muriel was strong on rights, shaky on duties, especially her own. 'Request' changed imperceptibly into 'demand'.

She sat alone in her living room waiting for something to materialise. She looked to her children for entertainment or company rather than making her own, and was disgruntled when they found it elsewhere, frequently complaining when they didn't ask

73

her along on an evening jaunt. Harris would roll his eyes in disbelief at the suggestion. Taking his mother to the pub or tennis club? His friends would think he'd gone potty. So she spent another evening between the fire and the newspaper in a room that was composed of calamitous and strident tastes, demonstrating the principle that nothing was effective unless it was loud. Gold was a favourite theme, or its gaudy imitants, brass, gilt and the spray paint with which she tricked her picture frames. It was a place without respite, even visual.

It was almost one o'clock before she heard someone come in. Harris stood in the doorway, tall and fair and lax-limbed, closer to her physically than her other children, a similarity she often mistook for emotional identity. "Where have you been?" was the habitual question he dodged.

"Out." Muriel looked at her watch, implying that the pubs had closed long ago and, reading the gesture, Harris obstructed with, "Here and there. Is Alison not back?"

"No." She deviated along the route he laid for her. "Do you know where she is?"

"Not now. I saw her early on in the evening."

"Who was she with?"

Harris resented this spying, both as agent or as its subject. Muriel had never realised that her children kept an ancient pact of loyalty and didn't tell her anything repeatable or usable about the others. Acting daft was instinctive when it meant preserving their own identity in the face of her skewering inquiry. "Some students. I didn't know them."

Mother and son sat on opposite sides of the fireplace which burned artificial coals supplying the dominant sound now that the television had finished the evening's transmission. Harris drummed his fingers unconsciously on the armrest of the chair where the cloth, as taut as hide, gave back a booming resonance.

"You could have given her a lift home. Nobody else seems to get much use out of that car I bought you."

He stopped drumming. "Alison has her own friends. She doesn't want to hang about with me." He was as secretive with Alison's affairs as if they were his own.

Muriel was frustrated at having to abandon this line of cross-questioning and let it lapse for only a moment before picking up

74

another. "You forgot to leave me your house-keeping money this morning."

On the first Friday of the month his lodging fees fell due, twelve times a year, and he had as many excuses for not paying it on the nail. "I didn't manage to get to the bank today."

"Funny. You work next door to one."

"We've been busy with Stock Exchange fluctuations when the pound's been so dicey." The government shook and trading confidence with it.

"A cheque then."

"Ah yes. A cheque." He flourished out his cheque book and found his pen before he spread the cover. "Oh damn," he said. "I'm right out. I forgot I used the last one yesterday for petrol. Too bad."

She compressed her lips, saving the major invective for later. She noted the printing on the cheque book cover. "I thought you banked with Clydesdale."

"I did. I changed to the Royal Bank of Scotland a few weeks ago."

"Why?"

"Something to do with business. My own."

Silence grew again, a cornered silence in which the two of them tussled for supremacy, rehearsing and cancelling many options before Muriel, leaning up to the mantelpiece, finally said, "Your business isn't looking too healthy. I opened this by mistake this morning."

Harris seized the envelope and read the note it contained, angry at it and the fact that she had got to it before him. By mistake my foot. Her mistakes were too regular to be an accident. Mis-taking was built into her nature. In the envelope was a bill accompanied by a solicitor's letter threatening action if it were not settled forthwith. Timeously was the word used. A timeous settlement of the outstanding debt. The bill came from a men's outfitter's where he charged his clothes, a bespoke suit which he felt was imperative when he started work in his accounting firm, the sports jacket he was wearing and other casual clothes. All necessary. Nothing over the top. He hadn't paid the bill but that paled beside the fact that he needed these items to continue in his lifestyle. They *were* his, or indispensable to his ego.

"I gave you the money for that suit as part of your Christmas present," his mother pointed out.

"I used it for something else at the time."

"What else?"

"Oh, this and that. Anyway, I sent them a cheque last week. They obviously haven't had it yet."

She was placated momentarily by the lie while Harris moved on to wonder how he would settle the bill in reality. Write a cheque against the Royal Bank, or the Clydesdale? They were likely to be as ineffective as one another. Return the suit? Pity it was worn. Paying back the money became an immediate issue, but parallel to the problem ran a sudden eagerness to escape from his mother's questions, at once and for good. Not to have the debt thrust in front of his attention was one way of solving it. He measured his alternatives. He could stay on at Greenbank and submit to having his letters opened and his affairs pried into, or move out – to his own flat? He couldn't afford real independence. A landlady might be just as speiring as Muriel, and have worse grub. She wasn't actually going to turf him out as long as he was either inventive or consistent with his excuses for defaulting. Hang on for a bit longer. A bed. A meal. At two a.m. freedom was less pressing than the creature comforts.

"I can see you're running yourself into debt," Muriel went on.

"Oh don't exaggerate. It's only one bill. An oversight."

"It's a bad start."

"You don't know what you're talking about. And anyway, it's got nothing to do with you."

She humped. "One thief in the family is enough. And don't think I'll bail you out if you get into real trouble. You're on your own."

Harris didn't esteem his mother's charity any more highly than Fergus did, but he avoided the crucial issues more assiduously than his older brother, content to live in the short term so that the eternities were of scant relevance. He was a hedonist without debauchery and lived on the crest of the minute where pleasure and displeasure came equally easily to him. His main aim was to side-step confrontation. He'd lived on the principle of daily survival for so long that the consequences for tomorrow, a sleep or a meal or a day's work away, were remote. 'Get through today' was a touchstone to brusque, dismissive answers.

"I don't appreciate being called a thief without substance. Or can you back it up?"

"That's the way you're going."

"You watch what you say," he warned and stood over her chair to reinforce the threat. Harris was the largest of her menfolk, tall and heavily built and irascible, a combination she ducked. She often goaded him into a burst of feeling and then stood by while he paced like a captive, backwards and forwards in frustration. His financial and emotional dependence on her blocked him in.

Muriel wasn't blind to her younger son's weaknesses. She noticed the small faults of organisation but, because she wanted to shed her own responsibility for them, attached blame rather than understanding. She genuinely wanted to prevent the repetition of past mistakes. She cared but couldn't convert that into warmth or concern or even an open-mindedness which would make discussion possible. Compression of others entailed a corresponding expansion of herself and she squeezed continually in economic and emotive terms, when this measured her own power to do so.

The main door opened and they heard Alison come in and lock it again. The cold air in her clothes wafted other rooms and other people towards them, stuck stuffily beside their home fire, while her face was full of light and elation carried over from the free interchange of Ellice Barr's salon.

"Where have you been?" asked Muriel, dimming the enthusiasm.

Over her head, her children exchanged glances. 'I will back you up whatever you say,' was implicit in Harris's.

"Here and there," answered Alison lightly. "I saw Harris in the pub and then we split up and I went on to a party." She avoided mention of Ellice and Leonie because they impinged on the out-of-favour Fergus, but Alison wasn't a good liar and consciousness that she should have been able to announce her brother's engagement blithely made her falter. Lies and evasion became the mechanism of self-defence, although Alison was scrupulous enough to regret it.

"Have you seen your brother?" Muriel demanded to know.

"No," she said, relieved that truthfulness was not breached. "I haven't seen Fergus."

77

"Goodness knows what people must be thinking when he lives on his own like that." Alison and Harris, moving about the room in search of a newspaper or an ashtray, tensed themselves for the standard diatribe on Fergus who, by putting himself outside her control, incurred the inverse of Muriel's maternalism. They both liked Fergus and looked back on the days of childhood under his guiding seniority as the only peaceable ones they could remember. He was in many ways their parent, adviser and pattern setter and so the break in their family wasn't clean but compound, hurting deeply and maybe beyond mending. They hated meeting their brother only accidentally, Harris at the tennis club or as an occasional visitor to Canaan Lane, Alison bumping into him in the streets near the University where she was a student in Economics. And then the woman made one of her characteristic turn-abouts. She lapsed into the semi-maudlin. "When I'm sitting here by myself, I can't help thinking about Fergus doing the same. Just sitting on his own, night after night. When all's said and done, he's the most like me out of all of you. It's such a pity we can't be under one roof again."

Harris was taken in by this sentiment or gave it more than a transitory importance. He felt the surge of wishfulness, a yearning that blotted out the contra-indications of the past. Yes. Fergus back home, creating a small haven of peace. Alison was more objective. She thought it was transparently unrealistic, only a ploy to enlist sympathy for Muriel's solitary evenings. Nice idea. Impossible to enforce. Embarrassment made her head for the door.

"Before you go, Alison," her mother said quickly, "the house-keeping was due this morning."

"Oh yes," mumbled the girl. "I was in a hurry when I left." Alison was meek about this payment. As a student receiving a state grant, she relied on her mother to boost the allowance up to the statutory level. This difference was not forthcoming, however, though Muriel still exacted the same monthly sum as Harris paid for his keep, so that Alison had virtually nothing left over for clothes, stationery or books and had to plan her bus routes carefully to economise. The inequities did not strike the mother, or not to the point where she resolved them. Alison stumped up and the notes were then deposited in the black leather handbag that never left Muriel's side.

78

"And incidentally," said their mother, "I'm just warning you I may have to put it up. What I'm getting from you isn't enough to go round any more." They remembered the interminable wrangling over the payment of bills and house-keeping expenses at the Hermitage, and were silently daunted by the recurrences of attitude.

They dispersed separately.

9

"You stood me up," said Charles Moncrieffe of Torrisaig, coming down to breakfast on Sunday morning and finding his nephew ensconced over a plate of such hearty victuals that he was daunted by the sight, and walked past the sideboard where they were on offer, making for the pot of coffee. "A girl?"

"A girl," Watson conceded. "But not just any girl. Anyway, it was a waste of time. She turned out to be spoken for."

"Lost causes always were your favourite."

"Don't bait me, Charlie. I'm feeling raw about it."

"Oh? Piqued?"

"No, rather less philanthropic. More murderous."

"What you need," said Charlie, straddling a chair as though it were a mount, "is a wife. Marriage, not a love affair."

"You make it sound like castor oil. A good emetic."

"There are some reasonable women about. For heaven's sake find one and start breeding." Sometimes, like kings, they did address themselves to the problem of the succession. Watson forebore to say that if his uncle had done exactly that and provided himself with his own heirs, he wouldn't be in the predicament of looking to his brother's son to carry on the line. All he had perpetuated were his problems.

"What you forget," said Watson, "is that I tried that once."

Charlie found his coffee unsweet and leaned over the expanse of patinated table to the covered sugar bowl, adding another spoonful thoughtfully. He had come to look on Watson as his adoptive son as well as the heir apparent. The nephew had been primed to inherit Torrisaig and its string of attendant titles through long sojourns on the estate which developed him insidiously towards his uncle's tastes rather than his father's. Watson's father had been an Edinburgh lawyer of some standing, tipped for the judiciary and elevation to his own entitlement to 'Lordship' if he'd been called to the bench. But he had died of a liver complaint shortly after Watson's marriage. Watson's mother remarried, an American, a business man and her junior, aberrations so large as to be thought unforgivable by blood Moncrieffes.

Edward had been an Edinburgh man through and through, urban rather than urbane, impatient with the pace at Wester Ross but equally restive in London where he found no niche. Watson and Charlie enlarged to wider extremes than his and found the itinerant rôle, which joined the rural and ancestral place to the cosmopolitan one, a pleasing proportion. They weren't sure if the work at Westminster justified Torrisaig or vice versa, but didn't hurry to tamper with a golden mean, long proven. The whole range of their experience as politicians, Scotsmen in an English Parliament, kin and countrymen in every sense, meant that there was no bar to where they went conversationally. They were at home in each other's thoughts. Except women. It was possibly the single differentiation between natural and adoptive parenthood, or was concomitant with Charlie's own problems with the sex. He didn't know the specific causes of Watson's divorce and did not ask, turning his face stonily from gossip.

"Well, get back up and try again," was an answer that did neither of them justice.

"The trouble is," said Watson, looking out over the lawn to greater pleasures than this memory, "I broke every bone of my body in the fall."

Torrisaig was at the inland extremity of a long sea loch, maybe ten miles long, which ran from the Minch deep inside a range of hills. Normally there was a marked drop in temperature beside sea lochs but the situation of the original castle had been chosen by some Celtic ancestor not least because of its benign weather. It had a climate all of its own. The mountains between the estate and the open sea acted as a watershed so the spot was both warm and dry, a beneficiary of the Gulf Stream that brought a touch of the tropics to Inverewe.

The most typical and functionary castles of the western Highlands were like Dunvegan and Eilean Donan, at one time inaccessible by land. Causeways might be added making the fortress into a peninsula but the sense of dislocation remained. Torrisaig was different. It was a mainland castle and fronted the enemy, relying on architecture rather than geography for defence. A thousand years had proved it was impregnable. The clan might suffer a reversal but its stronghold hadn't fallen. Torrisaig had been able to evolve over ten centuries of uninterrupted habitation from fort to domicile which showed up like strata on a knoll of rock, keep, dungeon, a chapel, solar swelling up with the social ambition and affluence of the family until the last Regency additions called a halt. It was its own history book of Scottish baronial architecture and students in the summer months came to draw its ground plan with as much solemnity as if they took brass rubbings, a pound a time.

The gardens of Torrisaig were not Inverewe but, as he walked out in the keen sunshine of a May morning, Watson did not think they were deficient. Formality erupted here and there in rectilinear walks and regular planting, but for the most part the garden roved and let the eye do likewise. The early flowering bulbs planted in a carpet of meadow were on the wane, but the spikes of the harebell, the Scottish bluebell, had started to replace them making a haze on top of the grasses, a nub of potential. The place was one grassed meadow, rich from the alluvial silt of the denuded mountains, and this was a reversion that broke through in patches where more stringent forms of horticulture were difficult; reeds prevailed by the loch, cowslip and buttercup dominated the swathes under the fruit trees, but the delta of land that supported the house was still a unit. Banks of flowering shrubs overshot their original allocation, higher and wider than they should have grown, in theory, because the soil was fertile and pruning only stimulated growth. There was a waterfall that fell from a shelf of the mountains, and its ledges housed a water garden, happy in the lime-free spring. The backing hills were covered in coniferous forest but the Regency aficionado had planted some of the ornamental trees from Japan so that the dun green of the native hillside was enlightened by the decorative foliage of the japonicas, an oriental note that might have jarred on the purist. The incipient colour of the cultivated rhododendron started to show through, and here and there a curl of azalea mollis.

Watson knew that he lived in black and white in London and in Edinburgh; only at Torrisaig did he start to live fully and in colour. Even the clothes kept in his dressing room felt more real, a Norfolk jacket and breeches made from thorn-proof tweed, and the impregnable waxed cotton waterproof. Many were as old as his manhood and some were Charlie's hand-me-downs from a slimmer youth, clothes in a form of continuity with the landscape which they deferred to and were a product of. Hunting pink or Savile Row were a joke of fashionable smartness in this context and there was no surer way of distinguishing a newcomer than by new clothes. He felt comfortable with himself at Torrisaig, slack and unpretentious.

He looked at his walking shoes and up at the waterfall that connected the loch to the mountain, and wondered if one could tackle the other. The new season brought out the trampling urge and his mind threaded its way up the gully to the higher spurs where the forest ended, and the moors were broken only by the compelling stream. But he was detained.

"Good day to you, sir." The factor approached from his Range Rover. "We were not expecting you today."

"No. I wasn't expecting myself. A change of heart," he explained and wished he'd found a different phrase.

"Going walking?"

The habit was effete. The countryside was for work, not walking in. "I shouldn't be so self-indulgent." Watson turned in Donald Macleod's direction, people the perennial magnet. "I've reading to do."

"Anything of interest to us?"

"This fisheries bill. It was a rowdy meeting last night in Portree and I don't know how you balance livelihood now as against livelihood in the future if there's over-fishing. But I can see why the islanders feel hard done by. I said I'd look at the final drafting for my uncle before it goes to the Lords' Third Reading. And there's a private member's bill on the table next week which I've taken an interest in." He diverted, realising his own work, though compelling to him, was not a communicable pleasure. "How are things with you?"

Donald Macleod found himself, like most of the workers at Torrisaig, torn in his loyalties between the present and the future Lord, who were referred to behind their back as the Old and Young Pretender. This glib analogy was more accurate than it seemed; Charlie was the incumbent but his nephew brought such swing and glamour with him that it was hard to remember he was only lord-in-waiting. He might be an outsider, a visitor whose sporadic appearances were worth comment, but he was the one who had a more realistic understanding of the problems of the estate and was therefore more skilful in minimising them. So the factor was silent, wishing he could discuss the urgent matters with this man but knowing the old king had inherent rights.

They headed towards the greenhouses where Charlie would be spending the two hours before lunch. Lord Moncrieffe had a specialised claim to fame: he had a rose named after him, two in fact. 'Torrisaig,' which was a yellow hybrid tea with distinctive coral flashes, a more colourful bloom than 'Peace' but just as vigorous, and 'Charlie's Darling', a fine rambler with the open, rather fragile flower of the dog rose in a deep shade of hips and haws, a long-established favourite with the cottage gardener. He had set his heart, however, on developing the elusive black rose, which was his own lost cause.

The greenhouse was meticulously kept. John Innes compound in varying strengths was stored in plastic bins, scrubbed pots were piled up in among balls of twine and sticks for labelling. Charlie maintained it as scrupulously as a laboratory, and jotted down the progressive stages of his experiments in a methodical record book. Sometimes he worked from briar stock and grafted the new bud into the wood with a pruning knife which he wielded like a scalpel to make a clean cut, then bound the joint to a reinforcing splint in mimic surgery. Or alternatively used two developed plants, cross-pollinating delicately until he had ripe hips from which he sowed the achenes, keeping careful watch until they germinated. He had evolved hundreds of these strains and there was a patch given over to the experimental bushes beside the greenhouse, trench dug in alternating seasons. But they fell prey to disease, or the stock rejected the implant, or the flower was mis-shapen or poorly coloured in regressive reds, and he felt all the frustration of a Mendel knowing that the answer was simple – once he discovered it.

He dusted off his hands when Watson and Macleod came into view. His peace was over for the day. Business and papers were anathema to Charlie, and so he included his nephew willingly in the discussion. All three men went to the estate office, the first room inside the covered entry at the rear of the castle.

Macleod was responsible for signing fishing permits for the

reaches of the River Torrisaig owned by the estate, the tributary stream where the Atlantic salmon spawned, a good if unspectacular source of income, then the deer-stalking parties were given final clearance. Charlie liked to vet his paying guests, although they only paid to use his sporting rights and domiciled themselves in the hotel at the far end of the loch, because he might well encounter them himself on the moors and wanted to make sure that they were civil folk who knew something of upland etiquette.

This leasing of rights and the venison sold to market was the major income of the estate, together with letting of the one-time tied cottages to holiday tenants, and timber from about four thousand acres of forest. There was a herd of black-faced sheep that grazed the stubborn upland pasture, but it was a revenue that was far from secure. At times Lord Moncrieffe was at his wits' end wondering how to balance incomings against outgoings, prayed for a television company to need a castle as a set, held more fairs and fêtes in the grounds than he could honestly endure, but so far had resisted the temptation to sell parcels of poor land in order to maintain the more profitable, saying, What I have inherited I will pass on intact.

So when Donald Macleod said reluctantly at the end of the meeting, "Bad tidings now. The younger shepherd means to leave after the lambing and we'll be hard put to it to find another," it was a small disaster.

"He seemed so keen."

"He got married at the back end of the year and his wife has not settled. They'll go to Inverness." He said this as of one who departed willingly for Sodom and Gomorrah.

"What about the cottage?"

"Aye, we spent a wheen doing it up. Another for letting."

Watson did some hasty arithmetic. That left twelve. Only twelve workers on the estate. It fell too low, a draining reservoir of human energy. In its heyday, even between the wars, the estate employed over a hundred workers, either in the house or on the land. But the fish stocks fell, the number of deer remained static according to what the land could yield in grazing and the men who made their living from the produce left in consequence. Nothing was plentiful. The lines came to him,

Ill fares the land, to hast'ning ills a prey
Where wealth accumulates, and men decay.

then thought he was too much with Quercus and was in danger of falling into his erudite habit of mind. If only wealth did accumulate! Men and money drifted away together and were irreplaceable. Deserted villages sprang up all over the highlands as they had done since the Jacobite uprising through the Clearances to twentieth-century voluntary emigration. Though the villages didn't stay empty for long. Tourists came, sightseers or temporary residents from England and elsewhere, putting in cash but not human effort so that the houses were no more than façades, second homes or time-share properties. The indigenous waned: the parvenu flourished.

"It's the television," said Macleod by way of evidence.

"Television?" Watson imagined that the portrayal of urban mores might be a draw but couldn't imagine why.

"The picture we get over the hills is so poor it's not worth watching. All fuzz. It's the only entertainment the young ones care for."

"Well I'll be damned."

"What we need," said the factor slyly, "is our own transmitter. They've installed one at Achnaferran."

"Too expensive," said Lord Moncrieffe crisply. "Or not cost-effective. And don't forget, you still have to pay your licence fee to the BBC whether you can see the picture from their mast or not."

The hired man was silenced on economics.

A day at Torrisaig followed the natural curve, sunrise to sunset. It was unhurried. The newspapers arrived, like television signals, tardily and were the accompaniment not of breakfast but of lunch. As Watson spread the broadsheets, London and Edinburgh came surging back, querulous with debate. He had his own system of reading the papers, headlines first to get the shorthand of the day, the leader for analysis of what was significant, then the main stories covered by the leader. He read only the top half of each article, knowing the second half was padding or repetition, the inverse of good dialectic writing which built to a climax, then spent another half an hour on favourite columnists, often lobby

86

correspondents who relied on him for the feel of what was going on as much as he on them. When he had done this for three quality newspapers and two tabloids, he felt he was reasonably well informed.

Today, an arts editor in *The Sunday Times* interviewed a young Scottish actress who was making a name for herself in the classical repertoire, and England was beginning to discover what Scotland already knew. Watson looked at the photograph and read the article sceptically, as one who has inside information. It was out of date. There had been two advances in her career since this record was made of it. Six weeks in Shaw and an engagement to boot. Would she use Leonie Petrie as a stage name? Surely not. It was a jingle that grated on him, unaesthetic and unacceptable.

The face held him and he carried it through to the smoking room among the leather and the mahogany, knowing that he would revert to the page two or three times during the afternoon, that he would put that section in the Daimler meaning to read some other article when he had time, knew that he would never throw the bit of paper away, whilst not admitting it.

"Time for some moves?" asked Charlie breezing through with his own supplements tucked under his arm.

Their last chess game lay waiting for a conclusion. All round the room on boards of diverse origin were a dozen different chess games in the throes of completion. They waited like interrupted conversations, maybe for months, until the opponent came back to Torrisaig to finish his end game.

Watson got up and went to the side table where their contest hung a month between moves. Yes, he remembered it now. He was black. He didn't favour black when white had the advantage of the opening and after only a dozen moves it looked as if Charlie had positional superiority. He followed through the tangled middle game to its likely outcome and the prospect of probable loss didn't tempt him to struggle for the draw.

"I think I concede."

"How sensible of you," said Charlie, childish when it came to winning.

"We'll begin again this evening."

"Oh, will you stay?"

"Yes, I'll make a dawn start."

"What a bonus. Shall you work now?"

"Yes, I must. Just for an hour or two."

Watson took his newspaper carefully upstairs and went along the gallery to his own rooms. He began to dawdle before he got there. The sunlight spilled across the landing, discovering bright striations in the oak and making the rugs, which normally faded into nonentity, suddenly vivid with men and horses woven into a motif he hadn't noticed for years. He slowed down, arriving at a moment of physical and mental cessation. He wanted the day and the sun and the paper under his arm to go on indefinitely, not to become tomorrow and discoloured with disappointment. He was – not happy – but content.

The landing where he stood was a long gallery, where ladies would have taken exercise over the winter. The walls were covered with portraits of his forebears, handsome men and women indifferently rendered for the most part, though one ancestral grandmother was painted by Raeburn, another by Wilkie and they hung beautiful and ethereal in gauze above the panelling. His own portrait, painted at his majority, was the most recent addition. He had refused the formality of kilt and sporran and sat defiantly in shirt sleeves, bringing a breath of fresh air along the stuffy gallery.

He turned and passed a line of antique fighting instruments which were hung up on the plaster with inscriptions to instruct the castle's paying visitors. There were targes with bossing and leather armatures and broadswords and claymores wielded by his ancestors. The claymore had a praeternatural significance, for it was orb and sceptre to the chieftain, a symbol of the natural power by which he ruled his clann or children but it was also his mace, laid ceremonially on the judge's table at the court sessions where he would preside. Sometimes, putting his hand inside the guard, Watson would marvel at the size of such men. His own fist didn't fill it. He thought of not just lifting the sword but of wielding it in battle. Those muscles in his clan had atrophied, reminding him that his was merely paper power.

And even his family tree, illuminated on parchment as painstakingly as a mediaeval book of hours, with heraldic crests painted in the corners, lion rampant, gules, azure and argent, made up an intimidating document. His line stretched back to the beginning of history and entered legend. One ancestor had fought with

Kenneth MacAlpin, so it was claimed, another was mentioned at the battle of Maldon, a third came over with William in the Norman Conquest and a more recent landed with Mary of Guise, the unhappy mother of the Scottish Mary. His family could trace its lineage back as far as the origins of the nation and had acted in all its important moments. Pedigree. They had pedigree. They were prime human stock, a race almost sufficient to themselves.

Except that the shape of the chart on the wall visually suggested a termination. It was an inverted triangle, smaller at the base than at the top. They were dying out, these Moncrieffes of Torrisaig, becoming extinct. Watson followed the generations down the page like a thread through a maze, or a waterfall reduced through hazard to a trickle. Three male members in the Great War, a branch of cousins exterminated in the second world war, his grandfather killed in action in North Africa, his own father less illustriously dead so that Watson Abercrombie Moncrieffe was the last male member, the last of his line. His own name was the final addition to the genealogy. No, not quite the last. Beside his name was the small letter m and a full stop, which was married, followed by the name of his erstwhile wife, Elizabeth Scott-Kirkpatrick. A lady's name, worth linking to his own, proved even to the fifth generation. It was an arranged marriage which he had disarranged, so that his line of issue was defunct. He wanted to cry like Henry, Dei Gratia Rex, Defensor Fidei – I need a son! But sons were not to be had without mothers and he sank into a massive disappointment with himself that the basic human comforts eluded him.

His depression at this chart was not unique. He couldn't know it, but Leonie Barr felt an equal desperation when she saw its replica on a wall at Inveresk. He was disappointed at the termination of the marriage, she at its enforcement. For he flattered himself in thinking all the facts about his life were common knowledge. She hadn't heard that bit of society scandal and when they met and in the car and during the evening at her mother's house, she thought he was still married and so doubly an adventurer.

10

Fergus came back to the flat after a day spent inconsequently. With his thesis behind him, the viva a success confirming that the research prize was his, he felt he could afford a day off on his hobby, although it was a hobby not so far removed from work proper. He'd spent the day at a chess tournament in the Assembly Rooms. Six games, an hour apiece. Not a strenuous day but somehow a stressful one.

He came away with a score of four. Three wins, two draws, one loss. There were only three possible results and the outcome never reflected how close the contest was or how little it was lost by. There were no consolation prizes in chess. So this lost game annoyed him unreasonably and as soon as he got in he set up his board with pieces and followed through the sequence of the defeat which he'd written down move by move. He'd kept a score of every game he'd ever played since being awarded a grade by the British Chess Federation. He could see, even without consulting his reference books, where he'd gone wrong. Left a file weak in his race for a promotion. Attack undermined defence. It was an oversight that wouldn't have occurred with more time. He wasn't talented at speed chess. His natural game, which was a build-up of systematic duress, tended to disintegrate at speed and the fact that most tournaments were necessarily these quick-fire rallies meant his methodology counted for less.

He was a percentage player, as in tennis. Long chances, boundary decisions, going for the line. He hated the lost game, and would instinctively settle for the draw and equal points rather than go for the win and risk losing. This median approach had its drawbacks. Relying on safety margins or your opponent's errors wasn't enough in the echelons of excellence. There was one word that bedevilled Fergus, be it in chess or tennis or his career, and that was flair. He deeply mistrusted this word flair because he couldn't define it and neither could anybody else. Knack, skill, je ne sais quoi, all nebulous terms without the hard edge of substantive accuracy. It implied a missing factor, or that effort and equipment weren't adequate provision for success and this element of vagarious chance did rile him, mostly because it provided a too easy opt-out clause for being second rate when he firmly believed that greater effort infallibly brought greater reward. Failures hadn't tried.

The game wasn't all loss. He learned from it constructively. For some time he'd been working on his own computer chess programmes, guided by Botvinnik's *Chess, Computers and Long-Range Planning*, the major text on the problems of computer analysis. It foresaw a future which still hadn't been realised, machines playing as analytically as men, not in the 'explosive' technique that followed every possibility, but pursuing only those 'most likely to succeed'. Machines as good as Grandmasters? It was a long way off. Fergus had spent years digesting the formulation of the classic openings and their variants and fed these into his own programmes, but still the machine played like an idiot on occasion, allowing its queen and king to be forked by an errant knight, developing blind spots on the back rank or misjudging the moves to a promotion.

Fergus admitted that he was a keen rather than a brilliant player. He began too late for genius, at the age of twelve. He thought enviously of the Institutes in Russian cities where young chess players could meet and learn from Masters, but the British were more haphazard with their talent. He would gladly have sacrificed his career as a mathematician to be an International Grandmaster, while recognising a forlorn ambition. He played postal games with two British champions, and often keyed their moves into the console as possible variations, but he didn't beat these experts. Part practice, part disposition – he lacked the human aggressiveness that top players had in their temperament, wanted to play the game, not the people, or he was more interested in broad analysis of theory than in the pursuit of a single line of reasoning and found his mind tangential in a crisis.

His defeat had been on black, beginning disadvantaged. Not such a disgrace to lose on black. Black won on average only forty games to white's sixty. Fergus found this a striking disparity in success rates, quite disproportionate to the premium of having the opening move. That single move resulted in a 3:2 ratio of wins. Then he remembered that even a coin tossed a hundred times wasn't likely to land in egalitarian fifty-fifty, heads to tails. On pure mathematical grounds he couldn't explain the disparities between theory and practice. Chance was a factor he couldn't gauge on the laws of probability.

Fergus keyed in the moves to the point of his mistake and then played it as a normal game, himself against the computer. He was patient with the machine, more patient than he would have been with a human opponent, because the thing mirrored his own limitations, being the inverse image of his brain. He noted its faults meticulously to correct them, knowing that he wasn't improving his own level of play but the machine's, so that ultimately it might prove an equal or even a superior opponent.

He heard a bell ring in the distance, down the hallway of the Canaan Lane flat. It was such an unusual sound, the unexpected caller, that he ignored it and it was only when it rang again twice and was unanswered by the occupants of the other flats in the block that Fergus realised it was his own front door bell and rose to satisfy it.

Not even the imperiousness of the ring had prepared him for the advent of his brother, who stood with his finger pressing the button in continuous summons.

"Stop that, Harris," the older brother instructed. "You'll have everybody out." And he did desist.

"Come and see my new machine," the visitor invited and Fergus unwillingly complied, thinking it would be a moped propped against the kerb. He braced himself to feel a base envy, base in its cause and debasing in effect.

It wasn't a motorcycle, however, but a car that was parked alongside the pavement and Fergus was privy to a larger share of jealousy than he would have admitted.

"Nifty, isn't it?" Harris went through its catalogue of merits, its fuel capacity and top speed, its fashionable metallic paintwork and chrome trim. "My birthday present. It only took me a couple of minutes to buzz down here."

Fergus nodded. He would not learn to drive a car because he found the machine an offence against ecology. The responsible citizen walked or took public transport, but all the same it did grieve him that his junior was motorised when he was privileged to go on foot. Harris would one day aspire to be a man of property but his elder took some solace from the fact that already property entailed its burdens. A complex anti-theft device was fitted which locked the steering wheel. Harris' instinct to jump in and execute manoeuvres to dizzy his brother was therefore temporarily thwarted.

"Come back inside. I'm just going to have something to eat."

"Nothing for me, thank you. I've had dinner."

"I wasn't going to make anything for you. It's me who's hungry."

Harris strolled indoors, picking up things here and there, and watching the preparations, finding it hard to imagine himself fiddling about like this with slices of bacon in a pan. Woman's work. "What a dump," he said by way of commiseration. "I mean this really is a dump." Soot had fallen down the chimney over the beige tiles and hadn't been swept for weeks. The small stains it made in the hearthrug were a pitting which it distressed Harris to observe, because it was so unnecessarily squalid. 'Can't you get a woman in?' was a question that flitted across his mind, and was quickly dismissed. Even dailies didn't come that cheap.

Fergus sat down by the empty fire grate and ate his supper, then shared a pot of tea with his visitor who was fastidious about tea leaves, removing them singly from his lip onto the edge of his saucer. There was nothing in particular to say and so Harris picked up the text book from the table, asking, "What's this you're reading?" and lost his place.

"Fuzzy sets, Probability and the Nature of Uncertainty."

"Oh God, you do let yourself in for some ghastly things."

Fergus hesitated to express in what regard computing was unghastly but the pleasure was more elusive than the pleasure to be had from a new car, or winning at tennis, so he deflected the subject from the effacing self onto his more flamboyant sibling. "I heard you won the other month at Mortonhall."

"Yes." Harris suppressed a grin. "Easy. Matthew Geddes isn't as good as he makes out." Harris often derided the opposition in this way. He liked a vast margin of victory, whereas Fergus preferred to defeat a close rival, and in a match would often let points slip to equalise the talents and make it, for a time anyway, approximate to a draw. In fact, Harris would have gained more satisfaction from a walkover and was fond of the phrase 'No contest' as if rivals had backed off from his reputation. There was another minor irritant. Professor Geddes' only son fell between the Petrie brothers in age and tastes. The firmer friendship had been between Fergus and Matthew, and the fact that he was so readily replaced was a small hurt, as if his sibling ousted him in every regard. Especially when Harris disparaged their mutual friend behind his back, further slighting the thing Fergus had valued. "It was a silver trophy. Engraving's being done. Tinny bit of stuff really. Only plate, hardly worth showing off. But I think I'm the youngest person to have won it."

"No," corrected Fergus, punctilious over numerals. "I was younger than you when I won it for the first time."

Harris could see they were drifting close to their habitual state of bickering and yet he hadn't come to pick a quarrel with his senior. He stopped himself and fell silent while Fergus, peeved at having been drawn into overt competitiveness when he would rather have been sophisticated and aloof, picked up the book on fuzzy logic and found the correct page again.

Harris wandered restively round the room and coming to the dresser, started to pull out the folders in which Fergus kept his stamp collection. "Hey, do you still save these?"

"I hang on to them, but I don't work at it now." An expensive hobby. It had had its origins in the playground at George Heriot's over fifteen years before when it was the vogue to trade stamps at break time. Fergus did well at it simply because he was more methodical than his classmates. He saved sets; runs and series fascinated him and he would spend days hunting for the missing items, doing the round of dealers from Leith Walk to Tollcross. He mounted his finds on slips of card, like file indexes, and annotated them with details lifted from the Stanley Gibbons catalogue. There was something so professional about his presentation that his school fellows were ready traders, impressed by his insistence on tweezers and a certain make of hinge. In time, he came by some good items, Victorian envelopes franked over a penny red and a whole unperforated sheet which was said to be valuable. Jingling Geordie would have approved the profiteering industry.

Harris whistled. "These must be worth a bit."

Loose items fell to the ground and Harris lifted them with his fingers. "Don't," said Fergus. "Don't touch those things."

"Okay, okay," Harris dropped them back into the loose leaf binder and returned it to the shelf, but out of sequence.

It was growing dark and Harris was anxious to leave. A thousand alternative distractions came up with the street lights. He sat down again opposite Fergus and plunging in said, "Bad luck about the old man, wasn't it?"

Fergus raised his eyes from the formulae which made consummate sense to him, more compact than conversation. "Luck? I don't think luck had much to do with the case."

"Well," Harris shifted, wanting to steer clear of accusations, "it's a bit tough on you. I'm sure you didn't expect this."

"I'm all right." He returned to his infallible codes.

"What are you going to do?" Harris insisted.

"What do you mean? I'm going to do the same as I always intended."

"No, how are you going to live?"

"Here, on my own earnings, until Michael comes out." Fergus deleted the fact of his marriage to Leonie, sensing the strangeness of her absence.

"For two years?"

So he'd been reading his newspapers as well. Good of him to show such interest. "Remission for good behaviour. Could be half." The glib tone mimicked his brother's but Harris overlooked the jibe, determined to be amicable and even generous.

"You could come back, you know."

"Come back?"

"To the house."

Fergus could see that an invitation of sorts was being extended but it filtered down to him by such devious methods that he wondered who the originator was. They avoided mention of their mother, so that Fergus found himself affixing the offer, reconciliation or whatever it was, to a vacuum. He hadn't seen his mother's new house at Greenbank in the two years of the separation, and hadn't seen her either.

"Is she going ahead with the divorce?"

"You know as well as I do, there's no point in hanging on."

They were agreed on that, as each remembered the scourging of their childhood with parental disagreements. Fergus, seeing ahead with more accuracy than the messenger, anticipated how, if he had been willing to return to the maternal home, he could become a useful substitute for his father in these outbursts, a foil, a target to hurl words at, or household objects. A glazier came almost by contract to the house at Hermitage to replace the windows which had been smashed in a temper. Perhaps his mother missed having someone to argue with and asked him back to fill the void. He foresaw how she would have demeaned him into some sort of servility to his brother and sister, who had remained staunch throughout the run-up to the trial. His primogeniture would be whittled away by mean acts: the smallest bedroom would be his, his birthday overlooked instead of crowned with expensive toys, he would continually have the words 'please' and 'thank you' stuffed into his mouth. Obeisance? Never. Beggary was better.

"I'll be here when Michael comes out," was his reply.

"For goodness' sake!" Harris was genuinely exasperated. "At least come while he's inside. What's the point of driving yourself like this, trying to study and live off a research grant when you could be comfortable? I just don't get it."

"Sometimes, neither do I, but that's the way it is."

"I don't know which of you is the more stubborn."

"Me or him?" asked Fergus, almost pleased that he had a share of his father's moral tenacity.

"You or her."

Moral tenacity became mere selfishness.

"I tell you what," Harris suggested, fishing in his jacket pocket. "Take the key. Come any time you want. I mean that. Just come whenever you want." He put the Yale key down on the table, beside a pile of print-out paper.

"How's Alison?" asked Fergus of the one incentive to a visit.

"Oh, in love again apparently. Quite pretty these days," he added, with a touch of amazement that the girl he had tormented in her pigtailed schooldays had the trace elements of femininity somewhere in her make-up. "I think she misses you."

Fergus wondered who his sister was in love with now. Or rather, who was in love with her. She attracted an astonishing number of admirers, though they followed the same pattern of initial idealism which was disappointed when it came to serious knowing. "Ah well." She was a sacrifice he made to the absolutism of his position, but whether this absolute was good or bad, whether it derived from his father or his mother in its quality, he wasn't sure now that Harris had suggested it might be either.

Left alone, Fergus looked back at the print-out and saw the computer had responded to his latest move. It forced an exchange of queens, a move which he favoured because the piece was, in the balance of each game, too powerful. He removed both pieces from his board, black queen and white. The playing characters of chess were the only ones which had imaginative substance for him. Strong queen, vulnerable king, the bishop firm but limited on its diagonal, the side-stepping knight and the walled fortress which backed them all, castle or rook or tower. Chess had the distinction over lesser games of each piece being honed to its part, like numbers, so that the interplay was both an exposition of mathematical choices, and a characterisation of them in a drama. Playing was not in moves but people.

11

Leaving the Oxford Playhouse by the stage door on a Friday evening after the performance, Leonie collided with a young woman who was rushing headlong down the outside passageway.

"There you are. I've been looking for you everywhere."

The voice was vexed but Leonie was too tired to feel guilty at not having been where she was sought. It was Alison, breathless, rushed and tired herself having travelled by coach from Edinburgh without forewarning.

"I was on stage. Where else would I be?"

"Well, I seem to have missed you all round. Did you get my letter?"

"I did."

Leonie headed towards her rooms which were a ten-minute walk through the thick of the colleges, and Alison tagged behind.

"You didn't mind?" The younger woman slowed and Leonie turned back to look at her. Alison's eyes filled with remorse at having been a bother, which only increased the exasperation she aroused.

"What was there to mind about?"

"Well, it was such a . . . personal letter."

Personal to you, thought Leonie, but not personal to me. Not that she'd dismissed its contents as irrelevant to self. It had taken up more than time. It had occupied a large share of her thinking since she received it a week before – and here was Alison herself as postscript.

"I'm tired out, Alison. The audience was like lead tonight. Or maybe I was. I want a cup of something hot and to go to sleep. I've got two performances tomorrow. If you're going in this direction, shall we walk together?"

Alison acceded with her presence. As they passed the colleges along St Giles and Broad Street, they had glimpses inside the grassed quadrangles where, towards midnight, lamps were still burning in study or in revelry.

"Isn't it romantic!" Alison breathed.

Porters locked up lodges for the night. Those without pass keys were homeless.

"No. It isn't romantic. It's just old and wealthy."

"Oh, you're so prosaic, Leonie. This is just utterly beautiful and perfect."

Leonie looked round her at colleges endowed with charter or benefice, or chapels where in the early evening, as she went to the theatre, she could hear the organist practising a recital of church anthems, in Missa Solemnis or Te Deum. Mediaeval music and mediaeval architecture, denoting something so rare that Alison's words of eulogy were inadequate, glossing the momentous experience into something trite. Leonie had spent a month feeling her way along the stones and found an instant judgment unacceptable.

"Where are you staying, Alison?"

"Well, I . . . I did wonder if I could stay with you tonight. Just one night," she hurried on.

"There's only one bed," was the practical objection.

"It doesn't matter. Anywhere. The floor."

Alison sounded so bemused herself that Leonie couldn't refuse. Petrie trouble. She knew the feel of Petrie trouble by now. A quarrel. A shouting match leading to a decampment, but why should it be to her doorstep? Did you have to marry a man's relatives as well? Apparently, and fight in all their internecine wars.

Leonie was lucky in her lodgings. She had two rooms, a bedroom and a sitting room, which were let 'en suite' during the season. Visitors were thin on the ground in May, however, and especially those wanting a billet for a month, so the landlady took her at half rate. They had a lumpish solidity, something not easily defaced, and so when a bed was made up on the floor and a taper put to the gas fire, purring, it felt secure.

Alison hugged the warmth while Leonie made hot chocolate straight from the kettle, hot milk being beyond her resources, but she'd lived so long in rooms that she'd developed a fine knack with dried powdered milk and the drink was creamy as well as hot.

"You *are* going back?" Leonie wanted to assure herself before she retired.

"Oh yes. I haven't run away – exactly."

Above all, Leonie wanted to avoid an all-night confessional and so she left at once, saying, "I sleep till midday quite often. If you want to go out, try to creep."

When she was in bed herself, Leonie picked up a book to unwind and found she'd used Alison's letter as a marker. Frowning, she read it again.

My dear Leonie,

I know it seems odd to have been with you last week and not have found an opportunity to talk. I called at the flat again on Sunday, but neither you nor Ellice was at home. There's so much I wanted to say to you that I don't quite know where to begin and hope you'll bear with me for a while.

I think you'll be thunderstruck to learn that Alec and I have decided to stop going out together. I know our relationship had started to look like one of the fixtures of the calendar but I suspect this was due to a superficial affinity – seeing each other every day, researching the same projects, our work experience was even in the same company – rather than the sort of bond which a long-term arrangement called for. This division, of liking someone very much but not being in love with him, caused me much puzzlement and not a little pain. At what point do you say, This has ceased to be rewarding? It was a very rewarding friendship and a hopeless love affair but you can see how the attributes of one often spread into the other. Witty, companionable and charmingly persistent, he was the man of my dreams except that I didn't dream about him!

You know how difficult it is to abandon a relationship that has evolved into mere custom, because that can be very comforting and the hardship of making a clean break made it seem almost wilful, causing pain for no good cause. Alec's view was more median than mine: he didn't feel the conflict between friendship and love as sharply as I did and was very happy to drift into the rôle of loving escort. I wanted something deeper and couldn't disguise from myself that spending time with Alec, however pleasantly, wasn't going to further my progress towards a significant involvement elsewhere. Whenever the situation became emotional with the assessment of these conflicts, the happy tenor of our meetings was disrupted. The outcome was as you know already.

In the event, a decision which I might never have arrived at by my

100

own volition was forced on me. When I was away at Easter taking part in the march to Aldermaston, Alec joined me for a day and he reintroduced me to someone I've known for so many years, I'd actually forgotten the acquaintance. Matthew Geddes, our old neighbour. He's in his final year at Oxford and I haven't seen him for quite a while. The meeting was an experience I'm not likely to forget. A showery day, sun breaking through, cheering us a little when we stopped for hot drinks, that wonderful sense of communion with your fellows, and then suddenly Alec was introducing me to someone I knew so well, as if he were a stranger. The words, I blush to admit them, which came into my mind were 'Ecce homo.' Maybe it was the mood, the place, the mission, but I was carried away. Alec left for Edinburgh and Matthew and I were thrown together more and more during the last, culminating days of the march. In the course of two days' shared living, I got to know him better than I will ever know Alec. By the end of the week, I knew that I was in love. It seems a well-worn and almost meaningless phrase to express such a profound and wonderful emotion, but never in my life before have I felt the inadequacy of words to the same extent as in the past few weeks. Just to be near him is a sort of glory which makes everything else, past or present, fade into insignificance. I know that I will never love anyone else like this as long as I live. If it were possible, I should gladly marry him tomorrow. In a matter of hours my whole life has been given new meaning by this one man. Incredible as it sounds, I feel I have always loved him – this is what I have been waiting for and at last it has come.

Forgive the lyrical outburst, my dear Leonie. Perhaps it doesn't seem very 'me'! I assure you, however, that I meant every word. Maybe you are wondering just what sort of person he can be who has become so important to me in such a short time. I shall only give you a very brief picture here, because I still find it difficult to describe him with any proper degree of justice. Well, he's very tall, slimly built, with dark brown hair; he mightn't be everyone's idea of handsome, but he does have lovely eyes (a sort of mixture of colours but predominantly grey-blue) and the most attractive curly eyelashes! He's twenty-four years old and quite a man of the world. He won his place at Keble on an Exhibition in seventh term and spent the remainder of that year travelling the world, just to convince himself he was an academic and not a lay-about! He has a fund of marvellous experiences culled from that year, sheep-farming in Australia, a spell in Hong Kong living on his wits, a kibbutz. He grew up quickly. He has very interesting ideas and is a thorough-going individualist. Well-read, fond of music, plays the saxophone and writes the most wonderful letters. In short I adore him!

101

But I feel this letter has taken up quite enough of your time already, and so I shall bring it to a close now. I hope you will give me a ring when you get back from Oxford. We could perhaps meet for coffee and a chat.

This letter caused Leonie anguish, and for many reasons. She had met Alec Ramsey and was relieved to see him cast off, an unsuitable and rather brash accountancy student. But Morningside had its own cliques and she also knew Professor Geddes' son from long ago, even before she met Fergus, and was surprised that the blinkered Alison hadn't connected with the fact. How many endless hours had she played ball boy and umpire in Fergus versus Matthew tournaments! Alas, she didn't think him much of a replacement, partly because she knew more than Alison seemed to. There was a long-standing affair with a girl at Oxford and Leonie was anxious that her shadow was cast more strongly over this letter for being erased. Though Alison had a bad effect on young men, she reflected, because she listened to them and their problems so sympathetically that they fell in love with her. Leonie tended to dismiss her admirers curtly, refusing to indulge their fantasies about themselves or about her which led to these pangs of mutual self-deception called love.

Alison's letter conveyed her in person, the rather nervous voice and mannerisms. She had a voice not unlike Fergus, light and pleasant but under stress it turned into a monotone without resonance or depth, fluting too shrilly. It was Leonie's expertise, and so she listened to voices and catalogued them carefully.

She thought the letter strained and maybe affected, with a marked contrast between maturity of intellect and immaturity of judgment when applied to individuals. That it should be committed to paper at all – and sent to her – was a fact that astonished her. Why her? She didn't want to be the surrogate mother to a grown woman. The sentiment was both naïve and pedantic, or was that only because she didn't share it? Other people's love affairs were fatuous. Romantic was coupled with comedy in Leonie's repertoire. All that saved the victims from being caricatures was self-mockery, which Alison lacked. She could imagine the tears that welled in her eyes at the analysis of her own emotions while the speciousness of 'Ecce homo' applied to so mortal an individual

102

as Matthew Geddes affronted her all the more because she was without religious adherence. It was like 'crusade', an uncomfortable misapplication. Other Alisonisms came to mind, that love between the sexes should have a spiritual basis, that every kiss was sacred, that she, in short, adored him!

Leonie thought of the afternoons in Canaan Lane and didn't find a great deal spiritual in the energy and inventiveness which she and Fergus expended behind the cretonne curtains. Platonic? Well, even the Hermitage of Braid in the infancy of their courtship was not platonic. Open air love; his coat spread, her blouse open, his head buried. Their bodies were permanently hungry for warmth and consolation and found it in each other. Leonie ran back over the words of the Christian marriage service and thought them practical rather than spiritual, union as sanctioned by the Church being realistic. Better to marry than to burn. But maybe Alison didn't burn. She found the sentence again, 'Whenever the situation became emotional . . .' Emotional? Leonie had come across the pair at student parties and thought sexual might be more exact. The male wanting, the female not. The sacred kiss was a principle which an unscrupulous young man might postulate in order to obtain the carnal one.

Alison used to laugh about the sexual education handed down by her mother. A clinical schedule, it involves this and this and this: but you must not on any account do it. That was the Scottish version. Or rather, you must not on any account be discovered doing it, otherwise termed hypocrisy. A strange woman, Muriel Petrie. Leonie remembered a typical conversation with her which ended, of course, in a heated argument. She had been reading *Sons and Lovers* and carried it with her one day when she was visiting the house at the Hermitage, before the separation.

"Not D. H. Lawrence!" exclaimed the woman.

"Why not?"

"Isn't it filth?"

"I haven't noticed. Have you read it?"

"Of course not. I wouldn't have it in the house."

"I think it's on the University Literature syllabus at the moment."

"Then," pronounced the matron in triumphant logic, "the Senate of the University is wrong."

103

Leonie was commanded to remove the offending book, and accompanied it, never to return.

This was Alison's account of love, was it, a watered down religious ecstasy? If so, it was a passion Leonie didn't share. But did Fergus? She recalled the word Ellice used repeatedly of Fergus when she disparaged him, pious. The echoes of voice carried over into attitude disquietingly. Leonie didn't care for some of the material brother and sister had inherited in common. Theory first, practice later. She thought the deepest rift was between those who discussed life and those who lived it. Leonie had lacked occasion for self-analysis, seldom being herself, but re-shaped weekly, daily, into different parts. She thought all relationships were exploratory or interpretative and the pat phrases of the letter alarmed her, as if there were a text book on the human situation she should have read providing the catechism of questions and ready answers. Her own attitude was formed by the economics of the theatre. What will work? What will run? A practical philosophy.

It struck her on a second reading that Alison didn't discuss Michael or Fergus or even Viola, but was much fascinated by herself, without just cause.

So it turned out to be an all-night session after all, not spent with Alison but with herself.

It was midday before Leonie woke up and, although her bed and holdall stayed on the floor, Alison had gone. Probably to Keble, and Leonie wondered if Matthew Geddes was any better pleased at the visitation than she was.

She filled some hours scanning her copy of Shaw. She would go back to Edinburgh on Sunday and be ready for casting with Stuart at the Lyceum the following day. Her schedules were as relentless as Moncrieffe's and her work hours every bit as unsocial. It called for a lop-sided nature to tackle evening sessions in the House or in the Playhouse, or a fluid one which was happy outside the régimes of convention.

Alison came back after five when Leonie had finished the afternoon performance. She'd searched for Matthew and missed him too, doing another round of frustration, but left a message with the porter that she would go back to the college at eight, having no intention of seeing Leonie act at the Playhouse that evening, or of going home to Edinburgh. One night on the floor turned without asking into two, the arithmetic of egotism.

They made toast and tea and Leonie braced herself to being told the ineluctable all.

"What happened," said Alison, "is that Muriel found a letter of Matthew's and read it. Well, she was utterly shocked. There wasn't anything very outré, I can assure you, but it was enough to set her off."

So Matthew was as indiscreet with his letters as she was with hers. "Why enough?"

"Oh just . . ." Alison grew warm with embarrassment, "wishing we could be together, today, forever, lovers. Very moderate stuff. She went off the deep end, of course. Really quite out of proportion. Threatening to phone Matthew and warn him off, or going to see Professor and Mrs Geddes and showing them the letter. What it had to do with them, I can't imagine, but you know what Muriel's like when she gets carried away."

"So you thought it was better to clear out from Greenbank for a while?"

"And let the temperature drop. Coming to see Matthew himself felt like the sensible thing to do."

"But you didn't let him know beforehand?"

"No."

"And you can't find him?"

"No."

Leonie compared this hasty evacuation with her own to be with Fergus a fortnight earlier, in the opposite direction. Maybe she wasn't as immune to the excesses of irrational behaviour as she thought. There was little difference in the two flights of love, except that in one sense she had been summoned and the man was where he should be, where she placed him mentally. Matthew was missing and the shape of that vacuum was filled, for Leonie, by his former girlfriend. Should she say anything? Forewarned is forearmed. The trite was comforting. Theatrical tenet or example was Leonie's mainstay, but the dogma of the classical canon was in itself divisive. Lear's lack of self-knowledge was all important, So she was obliged to say, 'Alison, be careful. I think Matthew has a roving eye. I know for sure he was living with a girl for two years before he met you.' But before she could speak it, Ibsen interrupted and said in the example of *The Wild Duck*, that the saving lie was necessary. People needed self-deception to survive. These two motives cancelled each other out, and she was silent, in hesitation rather than in ready acquiescence to the second code. She never had decided about Gregers, soothsayer or charlatan.

The best she could do was to be kind and let eventuality tell the truth. "Well, it's a busy time. His finals fall soon. I'm sure you'll sort it out later when he gets your message." But she thought that Alison ought to absorb her own tensions, not heap them on her or on the unsuspecting Matthew who had enough to think about in the run-up to exams apart from decamping and marginally neurotic females, however lovely on the eye.

She poured more tea and Alison suddenly noticed the hand in movement. "Why Leonie, you're wearing a ring."

"Yes. Fergus and I were married on Monday. We decided the weekend I saw you. Now don't, for God's sake, say it was romantic. It wasn't. It was the civil contract we opted to abide by. No frills."

And Alison, in whose eyes candles were continually lit, extinguished them in acknowledgement of the grey of everyday.

Leonie had in her possession another letter, arriving that morning which she considered to be properly personal. She'd re-read it so many times already that the corners were a little furred.

Dear Leonie,
Much news but nothing of note. We're in for an election in the autumn and I'm busy laying the groundplan for our campaign. Archibald, our PPC, is so limp on political organisation. I think I might make a better fist of being the candidate myself, except that I couldn't abide living south if I had the mischance to be elected. As I go about, people ask me, 'What is the mood of the country?' to which I reply, 'The mood of the country is divisive.' I still find it a shock, after almost sixty years of politicking, that the human race hasn't come up with a standardised form of government. The simplistic notion of a whacking majority so that the country can get on with a legislative programme – and dictatorship *is* the most effective form of rule – is the converse of the theoretical truth behind 'one man, one vote' which my mind defers to. And if I cannot resolve the anomalies of different interests within

myself, how can the nation? But I know I'm tired of being this exclusive minority, Scot, woman and nationalist. I must think big.

I spoke to our Independent councillor, James Geddes, last week. He delivered a fine peroration to the City Chambers about their finance programme, especially their proposed spending on transport. Traffic will choke Edinburgh in time and he can see no adequate long-term projection to cope. He doesn't like the present Conservative council but consoles himself that he would like a Labour one less. He is a remarkable speaker, favouring the selective method of saying little to good effect. I note the council follows his directive – how else can one describe so imperious an opinion – nine times out of ten in the vote. That is power; discretion. He balances on feasibility, doesn't give a damn for his own prestige and in the end that is the most impressive testament.

I wish I could say the same for our other Independent, Watson Moncrieffe, a reputation builder if ever I saw one. He takes after his grandmother now styled the Dowager Lady Frances, whom I once knew very well. Before she married into the peerage, you understand. Her father was Lord Advocate and hers and mine were couthie with each other. A formidable woman, the dynastic matriarch. She kills with comparisons. No wonder other women depart the family in droves. Watson's mother and wife both took off within a couple of years of each other, and are happily remarried I understand.

James Geddes said he was going to see Michael Petrie, and I decided to go too since we are now, it appears, related. I did find it dispiriting, even after all those years of prison visiting. There's an odd atmosphere, compound of torpor and frenzy, in men's prisons where the male energy is pent up to the level of demonic. I hate zoos and especially I hate human zoos with bystanders like me coming to poke between the bars, like ignorami. I thought he looked less fraught than in the last two years. Indecision has gone and a vacuum has supervened which is more restful. But he wanders, in his mind. Living in books, in fiction, in fantasy. Something he said triggered off a thought and I went to look up the essay by Wilde: *De Profundis*. A worthwhile document, a pleasing antidote to the silly, quip-happy side of Wilde, the comic dramatist. I can see why he wanted to be taken seriously as a tragic writer; *De Profundis* confirms the potential for the grand theme in the way that *Salomé* doesn't. He says that among working people, imprisonment is no stigma, is in fact seen as a form of shared experience. It is called 'going inside', euphemistically. But the middle classes suffer more because of the loss of respectability which they see themselves as upholding, and undergo a multiple punishment to reputation which is largely self-imposed.

107

I note what you say about your marriage to Fergus, which took place it seems yesterday. I am surprised at the haste, even if I was prepared by your engagement and, not least, surprised at hearing of the event in a letter as though you expected a rebuke if you had ventured to tell me in person. Yes, I do rebuke you for the form and content of that envoy. I find it hard to separate the particular from the general. I am not pro-matrimony as a state. It seems to me to succeed in two rare conditions, a fragile orchidaceous growth that is quickly blighted except in conditions of complete equality or complete inequality. The former is so miraculous as to verge on the impossible; the latter requires the woman (in general) to subserve to the male, sexually, financially, in social status, adopting even his name, and above all, in parity of employment. No, I don't understand the theatre as a version of work but I can perceive that it doesn't cross-fertilise with any other vocation. In my view you are not adapted to wear the yoke of conformity. Coupling, pairing, jointure – no, not for the free-spirited or the achieving woman.

Fergus, well. Why did we quarrel all those years ago? I've forgotten because it was so imbued in personality. These violent disagreements are interesting in showing up the fault lines of the human landscape, the whole and hidden truth. He and I are utterly at odds. If I try to define what I mistrust about Fergus Petrie I come up with things I ought to admire, an industry so rigorous it is humbling, the adherence to a single point of view ad infinitum, the subordination of the minor to the major on all personal issues. These are his faults and they are praiseworthy. But I wonder how such a man can warm to passion, or even humour. I fear his endless capacity for dogma and for flawless justice that can turn into revenge. I wouldn't like to fall foul of such a man but, having said that, I think he is an outstanding individual. He is spoken of as a genius by men who distrust the hyperbolic word, a prophet in his field, though prophets must make such uncomfortable friends. The final indictment is maybe against the Petrie clan. They are users of other people, invisibly parasitic. Wean out Petrie and he may be a fully evolved person. But who am I to advise? I never bent my will to anything I didn't want to do in seventy-five years, so I advise you with the voice of failure rather than the voice of authority. I never needed a bedfellow, political or human and I don't know what it is to compromise the privacy of self.

A curse or benediction? Hard to tell.

II

12

Quercus couldn't find the member for Ross, Cromarty and Skye in any of his Westminster haunts. Though it wasn't surprising that he proved elusive. The House was in an uproar after the tellers returned from the division. Everyone who could come had been present, whipped in to vote, apart from two members who were ill and an all-party group on an official visit to an Eastern bloc country. Six hundred and thirty in a space designed for two hundred fewer. For six hours, the MPs had argued in an earnest, bitter debate on the credibility of the government over national security. The MPs stood up to try and catch the Speaker's eye and sat down again disappointed, fifteen at a time. Member followed member on the floor until midnight when a division was forced on the government. No wonder he'd lost sight of Moncrieffe in the corridors.

He found him eventually in the library which had abandoned reading, silence and seclusion for the time being and was in hubbub.

"How did you vote?" asked Watson, catching his senior by the elbow. "I didn't see you in the Lobby."

"I abstained," Quercus admitted shamefacedly.

"That was more benign than you felt."

"No, but I couldn't go against my conscience." Quercus was often his party's most vociferous critic, no bad thing, and exercised the back-bencher's pleasure in voting against it, when the issue was not so crucial as to be fatal.

The noise from a group of members drowned their voices out again and Watson, whose flat nearby was being commandeered as the most convenient venue to continue the drama of the night, was approached by men who wanted an invitation to one of the livelier exchanges of opinion. "Will you come?" The question was conveyed over intervening heads by mouthing and Quercus nodded. He had his own key for emergencies and half a dozen MPs followed him out, among them the two men he had wanted to ask to Oxford on May Day, John Laidlaw, a Border Liberal and Simon Dunns, the penultimate SNP member, from Fife. They were jokingly called 'The Four Apostles' mostly because they spread the gospel of electoral reform from different platforms. The Scottish Nationalists shared the Liberal problem of coming repeatedly second in a winner-takes-all system, whereas Quercus and Moncrieffe were more ideological in their support of PR – or eccentric. It wasn't likely to do them any personal good.

Big Ben showed one thirty, etched in the sky like one of the phases of the moon. It was a chill night. A little mist came up from the river and hung on the green spaces of the Embankment and Parliament Square. It surprised Watson that the Houses and the Abbey and the offices across the Thames were floodlit at this time of night. It made it feel like a celebration, as if a fountain had started to play or music flowed from a bandstand, marking the end of an epoch. It was an epoch. He'd spent almost a decade at Westminster. The policeman came round the corner on his beat, intoning like a sergeant-at-arms, "Who goes home?" and when he saw Moncrieffe, added "Goodnight, sir."

Quercus made it to the flat ahead of him and the entourage had already dug into his whisky and his chairs by the time he arrived.

"Did you ever?" queried John Laidlaw.

"No, I never did."

Fifteen men looked back on an astonishing week. Crisis had been in the air all spring, with the Tory government relying on a three-line whip so often it became its own danger signal. When it came to the real crisis, the ranks came as near to mutiny as they dared. The dénouement began over a trifle. The budget hadn't been popular. It only squeaked home. A spy scandal brought the government's handling of security into question and in a queasy atmosphere all it needed was a leaked communiqué about . . . did anyone remember what it was about? The opposition tabled a motion of no confidence and the government, with its performance put to the vote, won by so small a victory that it entered the phase of Pyrrhic. The Liberals, thirty strong, went with Labour. The Nationalists and a band of rebels headed by Quercus abstained. Backbenchers had started to misbehave or become stroppy about the party line. They seized their own freedoms, a

112

dangerous practice in the rigid demarcations of British democracy. The government sneaked in with a majority of seven. By such slim margins Parliament and juries reached a verdict.

Moncrieffe's flat, close enough to the Commons to fall inside the division bell area, was an elegant place, a tonal exercise in black and white which was an indulgence of masculinity. Sometimes he thought it looked too much like a set from a Noël Coward drawing room comedy, a baby grand piano for the musical numbers, a balcony for romantic scenes of which there were precious few, a spiral staircase for hasty exits and entrances. Colour looked extraneous when he tried to introduce it, so he stuck with monochrome and the arch sophistication of what was too highly selective.

His guests sprawled and he joined them, delegating the tasks of host to others so that he instigated moves towards coffee or ashtrays by remote control and managed to appear a visitor in his own home, relaxed and unforced. Someone tried to tune in to a World Service radio broadcast, to hear news of themselves. They had almost brought the government down and paused to count the cost. Cool-headed and a little anxious, they looked ahead.

"They can't, in all decency, go on cliff-hanging like this. Cadogan must call an election before it's forced on him," said Laidlaw.

"This is a pack of temporisers," said the Nationalist Dunns with disgust, as if all honour were Caledonian.

"Let's hope we see out the summer. Imagine a mid-summer election with everyone on holiday."

Each man in turn thought how a July election might affect his own constituency, Labour or Tory held, children educated at the state or private schools north and south of the border, trades holiday or the Bahamas, and of the potential bearing this had on the majority he had to defend.

"Perhaps not. Perhaps they'll hang on till October. But not much later. I'll put money on October." Quercus' opinion was deferred to as the senior statesman, a man who was only two or three places away from being deemed 'the father of the House' which, if he achieved it, would be his highest distinction, although Watson noticed he spoke as if he were outside his own party, as much an onlooker as himself to government decisions.

"The Home Secretary muffed his speech on the government's

handling of security, you know," Laidlaw accused. "He's a has-been. You want to give him the sack."

"His constituency may do that for us," answered Quercus drily. He won't be free-wheeling this summer."

He and Watson drifted away from the main discussion for the sudden threat to the status quo affected them differently from the other members present. The size of their majority gave them a wider scope of decision so Moncrieffe's question, "Should I stand again?" was interpreted not as electoral nervousness, shying away from the hustings, but a more serious pause for personal redirection.

"Would you dare to stand down?" was Quercus' reply. "Uncle Charlie would never forgive you. Anyway, what would you do instead?"

"Write. I've spent eight years fiddling about with that biography of Horace Walpole. I'm so goddam sick of Strawberry Hill and the letters to his chum in Naples."

"You've done other things in between," the older reassured, smiling. He had a monograph on Cicero that had the same effect on him. There was no surer way of killing an enthusiasm than to write about it.

"Just one monumental book, you know. The definitive text. Or I could climb mountains and write about that instead. I'll never make the Himalayas at this rate."

Quercus drew aside the curtain which was an abstract bought from Heal's, and looked out at the Thames, inking its way between embankments. Sometimes he was grief-stricken for Moncrieffe, recognising the shortfall between ambition and its attainment, a gap which was identical to his own. Able men, the ablest, but cursed by something that precluded a complete success. He had spent a very long time defining this omission, no easy task, scribing an empty space, and he still hadn't decided if failure were internal or external in origin. The corridors of Westminster had seen more of their type than most vocations. A first-class combination of second-class abilities was the requisite formula for success. The aphorism wore away at him. He thought perhaps that they failed in Parliament because they transmuted this norm, being a second-class combination of first-class qualities. In vanity, he said they were too honest, too philosophical or simply too diverse. Like

114

Watson, if he dropped out he could fill his days three times over by translating Martial and Horace and Juvenal, the silver age of Roman literature, and take up the study of archaeology which had so far eluded him. He could sustain an alternative existence in antiquity, a retroactive incarnation he found more engrossing than the present one. Maybe their failure was in being dissatisfied with what they'd done because they were multiple, or simply luck that fell repeatedly for rouge instead of noir, in defiance of numerical predictions.

So he let the curtain fall, fearing that Abu Simbel and Everest might be beyond them, trapped in the current of the belittling present.

The others had begun their favourite pastime, played as heartily as Moncrieffe and Quercus played it on the way to Oxford, but now given point by its imminence. They told fortunes. They found a piece of paper and a pen and charted the future. A block of seats to the right was the present government, a block to the left Labour and in the middle were the amorphous and floating groups who cast their votes to either extreme, yea or nay, when subtleties of vote were outside the British system. The whole made up a group of disparate islands analogous to the geographic map of Britain, not really a unit except through the accidents of history.

The men present were themselves eclectic, drawn from every party in the House. Whisky and emergency loosened their tongues into shades of indiscretion, admitting seats their party considered vulnerable to swings of opinion, which were in any case the target seats of their opponents.

"Tom says they hate that by-pass. He expects to lose next time."

"Or have the deuce of a fight."

"I think the shires will come through," said Quercus. He smoked very small cigars which over the years had stained his moustache as well as his fingers, but took more pleasure in contemplating these mid-air than smoking them. "They'll stay Tory." When the shires went to Liberal, the end was come.

So they shifted blocks around like children, blocks of primary colour, red and blue without subtlety, aligning themselves in patterns they didn't question because these were adopted at birth along with male and female, rich and poor, a genetic pattern they inherited from right-wing or left-wing parents which they didn't fundamentally alter in their re-arrangement. Quercus totalled by one method, in subtraction, and Laidlaw by the percentage swing of the latest opinion poll, but either way they came to the same conclusion. The election, when it came, was going to be one of the closest of the century, and therefore the most interesting.

"The next one could be your Parliament, Watson," joked the Border Scot. "You could have the casting vote."

They laughed, excepting two. Quercus, looking round the room, thought it ironical that each man present disregarded the political significance of Moncrieffe, seeing him as a lone runner, a quirky and interesting phenomenon who might merit a one-line footnote in a history book with his dates of tenure like a puppet king.

But powerless. A political makeweight, a man outside the pairing system, not subject to whips whether two- or three-line, a man who sacrificed office or preferment for the sake of a principle – an idle theorist. They overlooked the fact that they were gathered in this room because of him. His flat was a forum where members of variegated opinion gathered without arousing the comment of the Lobby journalists, so that he managed to break unobtrusively into the cabals of party. They categorised him as an anachronism, the man of the past, but Quercus, wise in political philosophy, thought he might be the man of the future too. He personally regretted the loss of Independents in the House and the dashing freedoms they had brought to the debating chamber. He didn't think proportional representation quite the panacea Moncrieffe imagined it, and certainly the party list system would oust Independents for good, but he had lived long enough to enjoy rather than fear exceptions, which were by definition a minority. A House of Independents, no, that was unworkable. A handful certainly.

Watson left them and went up the spiral staircase to the roof. His was the one flat in the block that had access to the roof, which he found a rare privilege in sultry London summers when he could come into the thin, fine air of altitude and feel a mile away from pavements and the crowds they carried on a conveyor belt of tourism.

He had tried to make a garden. He was no Charlie but he was

116

attentive to things that were already rooted and didn't let his plants become pot bound or dry out. It was a completely private garden on the top of the building. No windows overlooked him. No washing flapped offensively in view. In the middle of the metropolis, he was alone and he was refreshed by growing vegetation. The paradox never failed to stimulate him.

He had come away because the talk below was facile. His colleagues concerned themselves with their own share of the future and seemed to him to omit the central issue, the nature of re-alignment. They talked persistently of sides, drew up lines of battle, left and right, because the images of adversity were implicit in their political thinking. The piece of paper with their projections was about as perceptive as a child's cartoon. Even the Liberal, John Laidlaw, considered his seat was safeish on a three thousand majority and, inured to being out of office, let the bigger parties fight over control, content to be peripheral.

When he was a political novice, a school debater rather than a Parliamentary one, Watson had believed that the apportioning of discussion time in the House was fair, at least in ratio to the elected members, by a wise and headmasterly intervention. Not so. He was almost amused at the naïvety of that idea now. There were a mere twenty-nine out of the hundred and sixty sitting days each year when the opposition had the right to choose the subject for debate. In general, the Speaker who controlled proceedings and the introduction of members to that debate, belonged to the governing party – about as unbiased as choosing the judge from prosecuting or defending counsel. A member could rise a dozen times to his feet and fail, somehow, to catch the Speaker's eye. Disfavour would ensure his anonymity and eternal silence.

The debate itself was neither here nor there. The division was the thing and as long as an overall majority prevailed, the government could vote in any measure it pleased, and it became law. These men downstairs, balancing by whatever pounds and ounces they were in preponderance over their rivals, overlooked the avoirdupois that went unrepresented, the great mass of the disenfranchised, Labour south, Conservative north and Liberals overall. The sheer force of law entering the statute book, when it was supported by a party that might represent no more than forty per cent of the population, sickened him of the word democracy. The rule of the people was undercut by the simplistic notion that a majority of one prevailed in rigid absolutism, ignoring the multiple anomalies of constituency variation.

So the talk below of majorities enraged him and highlighted his own powerlessness. Yes, without party backing he was a political eunuch, functional but unproductive. He could have no political heirs. Not that he had the slightest inclination to join with any of the three main parties, or the Nationalists, in order to beget one. If he carried on, he would do it under the flag of Independence. A third term. A third campaign to fight. His first was a sheer thrill, at twenty-six, newly married and playing roulette with his future. Five years under Labour sobered him. He worked hard and earnestly for his constituents and learned a modesty from men who'd come up by a harder route than himself. Men who lived off their MP's salary while he lost his in tax. And he had scored an exceptional success in the Commons. He had actually guided a measure through the narrow straits of a private member's bill in his first term. A small matter of family law, but he was hailed as the latest of a new breed of private members who achieved small justices.

The second election consolidated his constituency gains. He had increased his share of the vote by a thousand. A third term? A third would make him a Commons fixture. It demanded a permanent commitment, something for which he didn't have an aptitude. He would have to fight it alone. Liz, for all her faults, had been a first-rate canvasser. He didn't know if he had the heart to tackle it again, twenty thousand people looking over his shoulder and saying, 'Where's your wife?' He had no party machinery to fall back on and had to rely on a few dozen helpers who gave their time voluntarily out of respect for the Moncrieffes. But it was a long and lonely battle, for less money in a year than he would earn seeing off Horace Walpole at last.

The hands moved together on Big Ben. Four twenty-two. Perhaps it was a night that was too historic to go to bed. He walked up and down the boarding which made a pathway between the containers, testing the moisture levels in the more vulnerable of them. Really a ridiculous and unnatural occupation, lugging clay pots and bags of sphagnum peat and hosepipes for water, all for the sake of making a personal oasis in a rooftop desert. It defied

118

gravity. It defied horticulture. It defied common sense. Couldn't he just forget it, let it wither away and die instead of this precocious insistence on upheaval, putting soil into the sky which was mere contradiction.

Among the many anxieties of the evening, the largest was occasioned by Quercus' excuse for his abstention. Imagine, a man like Quercus – whom they called the Senator for his air of tribune as well as the Latin translation – abstaining from such a critical issue. His exculpation was 'I could not vote against my conscience.' The fallacy of Parliamentary logic had trapped even such a mind. His conscience in this case was tantamount to party, and he dishonoured one rather than topple the other. His mind was not free to decide when party allegiance held sway. Party favour was a bribe, the promise of ministerial office a coercion that debased principle in the duress of the lobby. Few men's opinions were their own but they let themselves be herded into right or left, like cattle.

He leaned over the parapet of the building at the southern edge. London lay at his feet like a map of the mind, alien, divided, full of contradiction – but mighty. Day began to break towards Greenwich in bands of aquamarine that widened, absorbing the taller buildings, skyscrapers, offices, churches, tower block flats like a separate river of light. It swelled up towards his vantage point until a filament of sunlight struck the retaining wall of the cornice, warming the rooftop garden with colour and with heat. Geranium Fleuriste, Chérie and Sprinter, begonia semperflorens and pelargonia with zoned leaves responded vividly, putting new heart into him. It was worth it, if only for the satisfaction of saying – I did it. I kept going. I didn't let it die.

What an appalling host, he thought, as he went down the spiral stairs to join the party below. Could he breakfast fifteen? Perhaps to scrambled eggs. Or should they invade the café on the corner that kept Parisian hours, relying on routiers for dawn customers. The drivers were used to MPs falling out of the House after all-night sessions, and tolerated them because they'd worked that shift themselves, sharing their exhaustion if not their love of talk and sat bemused over mugs and wedges watching the antics of their representatives.

13

Edinburgh's prison was built on a dull plateau of land to the west of the city, in the middle of a treeless landscape. It was a long, low building of rectilinear symmetry broken by pointless baronial ornaments, a clock on a turret and sandstone corners. Who was to admire or tell the time, apart from those on the outside? It had the look of a Victorian Hydro or a schoolhouse, institutional correction of one kind or another.

Michael Petrie's cell was ten foot by twelve and north facing into one of the courtyards of the prison. He thought that was better on the whole, for the weather and outlook to be restricted to the bleak. He was alone, in solitary confinement that was accidental. Pressure of space wasn't acute during the term of his sentence. At times his internment had the feel of the timeless leisure of a hospital, wards, restricted exercise, brief spells of communal interaction, long, long hours alone in bed healing an undiagnosed sickness.

He had a mind that was well attuned to solitude, like his elder son, and he occupied himself with books and chess, looking up the problem in the prison newspaper every morning and trying to solve it before the solution was printed the next day. He was determined to make some use of his detention, so that his thinking was diverse in ratio to the narrowness of his living.

Still, it wasn't good. The worst moment of the protracted experience was when he stood in the dock and correctly foresaw infinity. A terrifying concept, infinity when it was split into daily units. He could see no end, but not because the horizon was ample and limitless; the prospect was as terminal as his outlook from the window. One day made no significant diminution in the total.

When he was a child and went to the dentist, the drilling was done on a foot drill, a slow burning away at the dentine towards the pulp. To distract his mind from the discomfort and the nauseating calcinated smell, he used to add up the bricks in the wall opposite the surgery, as men were said to count sheep waiting for sleep. Why sheep, he never knew. These bricks became a tally, like worry beads, counted over and over again, a rosary for the eye diminishing time and diminishing pain. So the wall opposite his cell was told in singles. There was a change in mortar colour under one of the windows, like prison Sundays, a minute differentiation in the blank tedium of a wall but one which created a focus of excitement. Why was it different? Was it the first hint of the decay of damp rot, or a mistake by the builder in mixing the aggregates of his cement, or a subsequent alteration? The new mortar was weaker than the rest and crumbled. A single seed had lodged in the crack, and germinated in this unlikely spot without the benefit of soil or irrigation, apart from rain, and even flourished. He couldn't tell what it was at this distance, just a bright splash of green with leaves of dentelle. A weed, one of the prosperous weeds like thrift or speedwell, a visual parable in the context of the prison cell.

This word 'cell' was, like much of the English language, a puzzle to Mihail Petrovitch. He found that English words had several meanings and sometimes they were contradictory. Homophones and homonyms bemused him and, because he had a mind that dwelt on tiny particulars rather than the broad view, he became bogged down by the double meanings indigenous to this language. 'Cell' defined isolation, but it also had organic inference, one cell of the body retaining the pattern of the corporate identity. He looked along the corridor at fellow prisoners, men with different backgrounds, different crimes, violent, pathetic, irresponsible; some men who missed brilliance by a hair's breadth and were driven to commit an offence almost in good faith, because successful crime would have made them millionaires. They made up a remaindered job lot of humanity, in which he was by definition one cell, holding in common with the rest the tissue damage of failure.

He was not a bad man. He didn't think that he was bad. The problem lay in language, codes of expression which made him dyslexic or aphasic, failing on a test that was extraneous to either morality or motive. He didn't want to cheat the law or his creditors or his own family of the security which underpinned them, but found that willy-nilly he had been guilty of public and private transgressions.

James Geddes came to the visitors' room and sat on a green metal and canvas stacking chair. The professor wasn't much concerned with visuals but noticed that the walls and the square tiles of the floor were scrupulously clean, clean to the point of baldness, scrubbed bare of lustre. He measured the hours expended in perfecting that cleanliness. There was an odour of disinfectant, and of institution. He too picked up the hints of infirmary and felt like a hospital visitor, carrying evidence of health and freedom that was almost rude.

"I brought you a book. Irene was short with me and said you must have read it before, so I apologise if you have. But this is a new translation, said to be very good." He passed over a paperback edition of *Anna Karenina*.

"Yes, I have read it before. Of course. But in Russian, twice in Russian. I am glad to make Anna's acquaintance in English. She will be good for me."

"How dull of me not to anticipate. I am so sorry."

"No. Not dull. Inspired. Other people's choices are so much more interesting than your own."

The professor accepted this but thought its fatalism was the flaw in the other's character, a deferential trait which made him easily put upon. For himself, he would have registered a pointed disapproval, perhaps even sent it back.

"You have heard the news of Fergus?" Michael asked.

"Engaged. He came to see us."

"No, married."

"Sudden."

"Marry in haste, repent at leisure." Like many foreigners, Michael placed much faith in axioms which native speakers had worn threadbare.

"Not hasty," corrected the professor. "Expeditious."

"I think Fergus knows his own mind. I am not certain he knows Leonie's."

James Geddes was more disposed towards Leonie than his wife, seeing an unusual face that was also pleasing, but he didn't accord the face a mind of any more significance than Irene's; to know or not to know its contents was immaterial. And anyway he wished his own son would prove as unswerving with the girlfriend in Oxford. "Have you seen Fergus recently?"

"A week ago. I don't let him come oftener. Too . . ."

James didn't let the sentence fall quite to the ground before he caught it up again. "Then you haven't heard about his windfall?" Michael shook his head, covering a moment's confusion about the idiom which sounded the harbinger of something evil. "It transpires one of the chess players he corresponds with has links with an American computer company. As a consultant. They contacted Fergus about the chess programmes he's been writing and it seems likely they will make him an offer for the copyright. The machine which he has evolved is capable of play to an international rating of a hundred and fifty, whatever that is. I am not terribly up on chess or computers. But they say it's unusual for an amateur to have developed such a sophisticated level of analysis. Machine Intelligence may have something after all. I met him in the Old Quad yesterday. Astonishing piece of luck."

"Luck. Fergus will always have luck with money. He will earn it, and Harris will spend it."

The professor became embarrassed. The fact not the psychology of the case was his brief. He rather liked Fergus and his wife and thought it odd of his old neighbour to voice a prophecy that was malevolent, when it went against the rewards of diligence or talent. Then he dismissed it, thinking he had misread a nuance.

"Have you thought what you will do after your release?"

Michael smiled. He liked the blunt approach. Other people used the euphemisms, 'afterwards', 'when you come out', like medical discharges which assured the illness wasn't terminal. "My release may be unforeseeable."

"Come now. It's June already. Another year at most. You must prepare." He chided pessimism.

"There are a lot of days in a year." Michael had thought very hard about his professional prospects. "An undischarged bankrupt *has* no future. His treatment by the law is worse than a murderer. I may not have a bank account or write cheques. I may not enter into a hire purchase agreement. I may not run a business, so I cannot be self-employed. My expertise is void, so I am not likely to be employed by someone else except as an unskilled labourer. A bankrupt, that I can live with, hope to pay back some day, but a fraud – that's so dishonourable. I am done for, make no mistake."

123

James listened to the list of exclusions and thought they were severe. Life-long penalties. They brought back something of the Victorian debtors' prison where a man might rot in Winchelsea waiting to discharge his creditors, which was impossible when he couldn't work. The circuits of the law were strange. He thought this the sharp end of jurisprudence, where theory broke down. The man had no skill or aptitude apart from his work. By depriving him of labour, the law penalised him ad infinitum. "I'll come back in a month's time," he said, "and we'll put our minds to this."

No point, thought Michael. This is not something you recover from. You only start to die more slowly.

Michael opened the book nervously, his hands trembling with emotion. Anna. Anna re-appearing after so many years like a lover he had lost sight of and met again by accident, with renewed passion.

Eight hundred and fifty pages. He measured the likely term of his incarceration as four hundred days and thought he would restrict himself to reading two pages a day. Anna Karenina, said the frontispiece and below, as if they were an introduction, the words were printed

VENGEANCE IS MINE, AND I WILL REPAY.

He folded back the pages one at a time, preciously, and arrived at the opening sentence which was one of the remarkable few quoted in translation. 'All happy families are alike but an unhappy family is unhappy after its own fashion.' He experienced the frisson of recognition. Anna might have changed in the interval of absence, as he had, but it was because she was written out of his life and mirrored it in every stage. They had grown old in synchronisation, even if they were apart.

He had read the book for the first time when he was twenty, and it made an impression unaffected by the glamorising of Garbo. He was repeatedly shocked by it, expecting a love story and, instead, found it harrowingly anti-romantic, a book larger than its reputation. Tolstoy used the story of Anna and Vronsky as a moral warning against the self-indulgence of romantic and adulterous notions, which amounted to profanity in his eyes, and as a foil to the 'sacred' marriage of Kitty and Levin. Vronsky was an adventurer, a man of talent who was destroyed by the power of his obsessions and was destructive to others. He broke the back of his horse when he had almost won the race, as Anna would fall in time under adultery. When he was twenty, Kitty and Levin had been solid and appealing, a domestic ideal he might aspire to. He accepted the author's version.

The second reading was more troubled, some score of years on. His loyalties swung again. He detested the boorish and self-righteous Levin, too transparently Tolstoy himself and begrudging praise to every other individual in the book. Scornful of his brother-in-law's philandering when he was a worse reprobate in real life. By this age, Michael was himself sickened of love, and fixed more avidly on the description of the social network, agriculture, politics, the shooting party, the small characters who had no moral purpose but filled space like the essential mortar in the fabric of the tale, its strength.

Now, at the last reading, it was death.

The fear of death welled up at him from every page and almost every sentence, sometimes measured in actual mortality, sometimes futility. Unhappiness was so pervasive, it swamped the effort to combat it. At the same time, the book uplifted because it was not real life, which was intolerable, but writing. He fell in love with Anna all over again and longed on each page, each day, to catch a glimpse of her, to know her better, for some forgotten aspect of their love affair to be revealed.

The book did not know of revolution, but it scented it. When the peasants took up their pitchforks, anarchy was in the air and Levin controlled them only by being an enlightened despot. Tolstoy anticipated the failure of the patrician system of land ownership and led on to the collective, a different failure but a progressive one. The book rocked on the precipice of history, its own fulcrum reform. It cried out for a change in the divorce laws to free its victims, for the storming of the Winter Palace which encapsulated so many effete lives, for the end of Empire and the arrival of egalitarian régimes. Every line imprecated revolution.

In translation, it gave him more than a little difficulty. The resonances were lost. Tolstoy avoided euphonic language, image, epithet but in Russian the effect was hard and masculine; in English it could feel rough and unfinished. The names clattered discordantly. Peculiar that sounds which were rhythmic in one language should be ugly in another. So with his own name. He reflected on the difficulties of Petrovitch to Scots' tongues, rounded down to Petrie. Petersburg to Leningrad by a different vowel shift. He felt the tremors of revolution, even so far away in time and place, disturbing people. Names should not change. They were all that was left sometimes to tell you who you were.

14

Fergus stood outside his mother's house at Greenbank with some reluctance. Harris pestered him with visits, urging him to come, and Irene Geddes thought he should try again. He started to think that his attitude had been too severe and judgmental and that now the trial was over there was no point in prolonging a disagreement in which he was marginal. A new start. The improvement in his own prospects made it easier to be generous with forgiveness and, humanly, he wanted to boast about his progress.

The house was the last in a crescent on the top of an escarpment, before the ground fell away towards Craiglockhart. It sat on the top of a promontory with an embattled skyline unsoftened by trees or hills, which would have been reminiscent of a scale more impressive than the suburban. Not as pretty a property as the Hermitage, he thought with a touch of spite. She had come down a fraction in the world as well. No one was at home. Four thirty; he'd hoped to catch Alison after classes and speak to her alone before Harris got in. But Alison, though he did not know it, was in Oxford and Harris made one of his many detours before calling at home. Fergus was deterred, then turning to leave remembered the Yale key which he'd added to his own key ring. He could let himself in and wait.

But it felt like a forced entry, seeing the old belongings in a new setting, the converse of his sensation as he stood outside the house at the Hermitage. The ground plan of this house was easy to read, with the rooms laid out symmetrically from a central corridor and he drifted towards the kitchen on his right. He wasn't happy at wandering about on his own like this and hesitated to sit down uninvited. He decided that he would leave after all, but when he was out in the hall again he heard a noise upstairs and realised the house wasn't empty. It was a noise made by a human and though he hadn't heard it before, Leonie didn't make it, he recognised it on instinct. Like the death rattle, or the birth cry, it was unmistakable.

The phrase 'in flagrante delicto' sprang to mind. Caught in the very act. It was, as the words implied, a coarse sound, the noise of the byre, deep and animalistic, man and woman on the verge of sexual climax.

Harris, entertaining, he thought. It was cunning of him to hide his car somewhere out of sight. Fergus made up his mind to discomfit his younger brother and went back into the kitchen, deliberately making as much clatter as possible to advertise his intrusion, and refusing to be put out himself.

The lowing overhead stopped when his presence below became obvious. There was an interval of some minutes and then voices came carrying down the stairs in forced normality, a male and female making conversation. The door of the kitchen was pushed open and a woman did appear, followed by a man who had dressed hastily and wore his coat and hat, in an attempt to emphasise that he had not been undressed in the first place. It wasn't Harris with one of his casual girlfriends, but his mother Muriel Petrie who stood in the doorway.

Her face as she saw her estranged son was a masterpiece of contradiction and control. She had composed herself for Harris, or Alison running back as inexplicably as she'd run away, but found her first-born instead. She had an excuse already formulated, "Mr Anderson has been estimating for the decoration," and spoke it before the pointlessness of a cover story struck her. Fergus was the last person she needed to impress.

Mr Anderson walked away pretending to take measurements. Muriel turned on her heels and followed him, keeping up an immaculate flow of artifice. Fergus was shocked in spite of his earlier resolution to be brazen. He hadn't imagined Muriel would be faithful to his father in this more than in any other regard, but the audible and physical evidence was shockingly real. Who was this man with his preposterous hat and coat? He didn't look like a gentleman. A salesman or a dealer on the antiques ring, a fence man, a spiv. Her sort perhaps. After some time, the pair bade each other a professional farewell and when the front door had closed the woman came back, having dispensed with the unctuous, frozen with sneer.

"What do you think you are doing snooping round here?"

"I'm not snooping. Harris asked me to come and gave me a key."

"He'd no business doing that."

"I thought you'd told him to do it."

Her silence instructed him that indirectly she had, and for once remembered what she'd said. She made tea from the kettle he had boiled and put two cups on the table so that he assumed he was to join her. Her movements were like the furnishings, remembered with less than fondness. She was a striking woman with a figure that was still, in her fifties, elegant. Flesh hadn't had time to settle on her when she was dauntingly energetic, or managed to give that impression. She ran her new business from home, and designated one room as an office on her tax returns. She called herself an antiques collector, but Fergus considered her a high-class scavenger and in their less friendly moments had said so. She bought house-loads of furniture usually from people who were emigrating, or old folk moving into homes or the dead who had dispensed with the necessaries. She scanned the small ads in the *Edinburgh Evening News* for notices of house sales, and phoned or drove systematically round them, ignoring the caveat of 'No dealers'. She had a good line in alibi, said she was setting her son up in a flat which made her sound philanthropic, and was careful not to dress too flashily and to appear ignorant about the better pieces that might be adrift in a sea of ordinariness. She had a contact who worked in one of the societies for indigent gentlefolk and when someone moved into a sheltered home she was quick to land on the pickings. Her most profitable seam was in the obituary columns. Where addresses were given, she arrived with the undertaker and, among condolences, made offers for the contents. Lock, stock and barrel.

Fergus thought it a carrion industry, not even a large and magnificent killing but the crow come to pick clean the remains. Most of the stuff was nondescript and filtered down through the strata of the second hand, auction rooms and boot sales until the rubbish was palmed on the Salvation Army. But once in a while there was a gem, a little gleaming brilliant which she panned carefully from a ton of silt. Fergus would have respected the effort if she'd kept the lyre-back or the bergère for herself, but they went to London salerooms with a carrier or, to avoid paying the auctioneer's fee, were sold privately in the paper under the heading of 'Antiques', goods endlessly re-cycled.

The energy which she expended was massive and Fergus linked her mentally with Ellice Barr for stamina, although their cause and personality were polarised extremes. He had often imagined a confrontation between these two and wondered which would annihilate the other first, cleverness versus cunning.

She poured tea and opened the milk bottle by puncturing the foil top with her nail. A little cream, which had not been dispersed by shaking, clung to the jagged edges. As always in her presence, Fergus found that his reactions became divergent. He wanted to leave, quite avidly, to flee the place. But at the same time he was hypnotised by the force of her personality, which he measured himself against. Sometimes it felt a dangerous contest, a mental free-fall which he executed while praying that gravity and his wits would save him from smashing to the ground, or rupturing a vital organ.

"So you think you're coming back?" She gloated for a moment, thinking he had come to grovel, couldn't make it on his own, needed the security she had managed to salvage from the wreck of bankruptcy.

"No. I'm not coming back. I only came to say . . . that Leonie and I are married."

Perhaps he hesitated in the wrong place. Her withering scorn of him made it difficult to be forceful.

"Why tell me if it's a fait accompli? I wasn't invited so you won't be expecting a wedding present. And even if you had asked me," she raised her voice dogmatically to drown out his objection that he wanted nothing material or maternal from her, now or ever, "I wouldn't have come."

Trained in systematic logic, Fergus found that following his mother's version of it was a tortuous experience. He assumed most people tried to be consistent in their attitudes, when continuous non-sequiturs were designated madness. If she had been invited, the couple would have been rewarded with tangible gratitude, but even if she had been asked, she wouldn't have come. This unravelling took him so long he was often silent in her company trying to reduce these imperfect statements to sense.

"It was by registrar's licence," he went on explaining patiently.

"Why? Why the haste? Did you manage to get her pregnant? Well, don't come and ask me for help."

"No," said Fergus. "We just got married."

She gave a snort. "Another sexless marriage. You certainly are your father's son."

"Rather that than my mother's."

She gathered herself up. "It's sheer proximity with you and Leonie. You've nothing in common. I give you two years at the most. That's all it'll last."

"I would have thought even you could count to more than two. Leonie and I have known each other for almost seven years." He held up both his hands with the fingers extended in illiterate symbolism.

They paused, winded with blows, and assessed an insurmountable dislike of each other. It went back very far; to her own unwanted pregnancy which propelled her into an unsuitable marriage with a man she scorned as pedantic rather than forceful. Fergus was a ready scapegoat on whom she vented her loss of freedom, her boredom with matrimony and one man, and the end of youth. He exacerbated this by being scrupulous, even as a child. He sliced open the fruit of her thinking time after time and showed her its worm. He found her embarrassing at both extremes of her character, the contemptuous alternating with the sentimental, which she thought of as deep feeling. She would gush about his achievements, his tennis, his chess, his school prizes in front of his friends in a way that made his toes curl because he knew the converse of her opinion. She boycotted the prizegivings, leaving him alone among the laureates unsupported. She mocked his stammer when they were alone with the words, Get on with it. He couldn't reconcile the two halves of her thinking, public praise, private opprobrium. She believed passionately in each sentence that she uttered, for the duration of the utterance. Spoken, it was erased from memory.

Once, more enduringly, he came across a piece of paper with the words,

Harris and Alison are the best children

written over and over again in her handwriting. It was a valid opinion, but they were 'best' only because they were more docile, or more easily cowed. The words had cut at the time, because he wondered why favouritism couldn't operate for him. No, that wasn't true. He didn't want to be anyone's favourite. He wanted fairness, that was all. But the words 'It's not fair' conveyed such a huge emotional weight for him, the admission of being discriminated against, that he couldn't speak them. Pride wouldn't let him object, and so he went on being treated unfairly. Harris would have picked the paper up and shown her, and others to circulate her views. Fergus was more reticent or sensitive. The murderous atmosphere which Muriel engendered in their house, setting one against the other or picking needless quarrels, made it inevitable that Fergus sided with his father in the split. Perhaps that was his final condemnation, that his mother hadn't put her own disappointments to one side and made a home for her emotionally battered children. Self was paramount and was uncontrolled. They lived in daily hell.

Muriel saw it differently. Fergus was awkward, spiteful, sanctimonious. He followed his father into the Roman Catholic Church only to be intractable. Mathematicians couldn't be believers in an unknown and insubstantial god. Fish Fridays and Sunday Mass were observances she tried to eradicate by ignoring or mocking them or making them difficult. No Popery was her slogan for a while. Or, Go hungry then if it doesn't suit you. She thought it unwise to adhere to a minority religion and one that had so evil a history of persecution of its opponents, which justified her in persecuting them. In practical terms, Fergus didn't know the difficulty of living on the strength of a business which was perennially in flux. Was she to stand by and watch the entire fabric of their lives swallowed by negligence? Michael had once made a man redundant and almost pauperised himself with generous payments. She had salvaged what she could and kept a roof over her dependants' heads.

So they drew on long draughts of bitterness, acid with affiliation. Where everything was known, there was no refuge. He didn't want to talk about Harris or Alison or Michael which would fuel their disagreements, as mention of Leonie had. She wouldn't ask the polite questions about his thesis and his future prospects and so they parted without a formal farewell, damning silently.

At the front door, he remembered the key by which he had made his entrance, and stopped to slip it from the ring. It was hard to free it from the other keys and she came into the hall when she didn't hear him go straight out, and stood watching him prise the Yale up and round the loop of metal. He looked at her and put it wordlessly on the hallstand.

"Jangle your jailer's keys," she said.

Fergus told himself that he had been a fool to try. In a family as riven as theirs, a mediator mustn't be one of the protagonists. It was beyond repair. Once, after a diabolical night which had ended with the police being called to terminate the squalid, domestic brawl – yes, in elevated Hermitage, with Muriel threatening to jump from an upper window, and crockery fractured all over the kitchen – Fergus swore that nothing would ever touch him again. His stringency with his emotions was self-protection in case the world was full of mothers. The normality of attitude that he wanted to wring from her was missing and he went on repudiating her actions and her opinions as a proof of the healthiness of his own. Black and white. Two sides that were irreconcilable. Leave it at that.

He came back to Canaan Lane determined to work himself to a standstill. He tried to think positively ahead to his lecture schedule for the autumn, and one or two refinements he wanted to make to the chess programmes. He had played a standard Benko opening the day before and discovered a flaw in the computer's response. He sank himself with relief into the abstract and perfectible.

He needed a book from the dresser and put his hand on it. His eye fell on the albums which held the stamp collection on a lower shelf, and he noticed that one of them was out of order. He thought of the evenings Harris came and made himself at home while Fergus went about his own business, ignoring him as much as possible. He took the irregular album out and went to replace it in the correct position. And then, on an apprehension, he thumbed through the pages, sifting unconsciously. He came to the end and started again. But a second perusal didn't uncover the valuable sheet of stamps without perforations. It was easy to mislay a single sheet, he told himself. He went through a third time and then thought it might be caught up in one of the other folders. But it was so distinctive, that one page, that it would declare itself at a glance. It had gone, and he realised that Harris had taken it.

Fergus was stunned. Which of the two acts he'd experienced that day, adultery or theft, was the more offensive, he couldn't gauge. Crimes against the person, crimes against property. It ought to be the former, but the missing sheet was such a personal abstraction that it outweighed the first. He imagined Harris selling the page to one of the philatelic specialists, a page that was hard won, the product of effort rather than cash investment. His own dividend was always work and to have his brother thieve from him, and convert the proceeds into something as vapid as an evening's drinking, or a flutter on a horse at Musselburgh or Ayr races, was a denial of his own worth. He had striven for nothing.

Pale, sick, trembling, he gathered up the albums and went out of the back entrance of the flat to an alleyway where rubbish bins were kept under cover, one to a house. There was a row of metal dustbins, with the number of each flat painted on the lid. They'd been emptied that morning and Fergus tore apart the cardboard cover of one of the binders, dropping it into the bin and added a lighted match. It flared immediately. He dropped the sheets of stamps in afterwards, one at a time and watched the different incendiary rates of mount and exhibit. The dustbin made an excellent brazier, fireproof, contained. For half an hour, he stood implacably tearing and burning the sheets which, carefully gathered in his childhood, were its last memento. His face, lit by the flames, was immutable. The cast of his features was ferocious through it all, iron-hard. No one would steal his belongings again. No hand but his own would touch the thing he valued.

15

On top of everything else, the male lead went sick mid-run at the Edinburgh Lyceum. Stuart had managed to hold on to one week in his own theatre out of the Festival's three, but that was the least of his worries.

Leonie, when Stuart broke the news that Kenneth Frew had laryngitis and it probably meant a lengthy lay-off, was unperturbed. "Roddy will manage, and so will I." They both knew a change of lead would put a strain on her as much as the understudy for the part.

Stuart wasn't so sure. Roddy was Ricky-Ticky-Tavy to the core and no match for the larger than life size Kenneth Frew who played Shaw's *Man and Superman*. Ken was the only member of the company with an international reputation, made by television's bigger budget. His illness would mean a drop in the standard of production as well as a loss of audience pulling power. Stuart was proud of his casting. Frew and Leonie sparred well on stage. Leonie had a way with Shaw's women, from virgin St Joan through to the much married Candida. She knew them inside out and acted them as women who were driven by intellect and not by passion, the way the playwright had wished the sex could be reconstructed to suit himself.

Stuart left her backstage to finish her make-up and went to his office one floor up, inscribed on the door 'Artistic Director'. He would like to have been one of the species of hybrids: the actor-manager, time honoured in the theatre from Burbage through Keene to Granville Barker, or the cinema's actor-director or even actor-writer. As it was, he fulfilled a dual purpose when commerce and art were inseparable. His years doing a circuit of Edinburgh theatres, with one after another closing behind him, not through his incompetence, pointed to the fact that you couldn't mount a play in a financial vacuum nowadays. On one side of his desk there was a pile of bills, left by the manager for his perusal, and on the other a pile of posters. There were reviews cut from Festival programmes and souvenirs and newspapers, a hundred letters covering everything from complaints about the temperature of the coffee served at the interval to one from the Festival Director pointing out a small infringement of copyright, together with a typescript of a play by an unknown he thought he might try out in the February doldrums; these were the parameters of a job specification which on rational days he felt no sane being would undertake.

Mid-run was a bad time, see-sawing between different kinds of uncertainty. Or maybe the doubts attached themselves to the midpoint of a career. Moncrieffe would have called them mid-term blues.

He wandered back down the left side corridor to the coffee shop where the attendant was already boiling water and laying out the cups to stem the interval rush. He bought a bar of a sweetmeat he was addicted to, Swiss Milk tablet, then changed his mind and bought two. These were the mainstay of his diet and he broke off corners in his jacket pocket all evening and let the sugary cubes dissolve slowly on his tongue.

He tended to leave economics to this slot of the day, the half hour before the curtain went up when he was so jittery anyway he was numb to the imbalances of pounds and pence. He wrote down the figures for the Shaw season, made up of funding from the Scottish Arts Council, sponsorship through advertising, the grant from Edinburgh City Council and box office receipts. Then added them up. Two thousand pounds short so far. Wonderful. Good reviews, Kenneth Frew and Leonie outstanding. Maybe, if anybody had the wit to notice it, one of the definitive performances, at least in London somebody would have picked up the quality, but they were only Scottish actors relegated to the provincial and the half column notice. Packed houses, good value given, but they still fell short of break-even point.

He doodled a little, making despondent marks like questions end to end. He was running the theatre into debt. He would pull back a little in the run-up to Christmas and the New Year with some solid family entertainment, a Hogmanay knees-up, lowish budget; there was a dance company booked for two weeks in January who were pretty well guaranteed income. But if he went

136

ahead with this new play which he considered artistic, literate, dramatically exciting, he would be heading off in the direction of deficit again.

There were three types of theatre, commercial, experimental and subsidised. In the halcyon days of youth, he imagined it was possible to combine them, if not in a single production, then in a single company, to provide a balanced menu and he laboured as hard as anyone to give variety. Try as he might, it was just notoriously hard to get bottoms on seats. He touted all the usual offers, discount on four bookings, season tickets, supporters' outings to Glasgow theatres, anything to prise people away from their fireside on wet evenings. Out of Edinburgh's half million inhabitants, one per cent were theatre-goers and those five thousand represented the whole spectrum of taste. Half of them hated Shaw on principle, because he was a damned socialist, or family entertainment, or dance companies. Who would set about pleasing the majority?

He went backstage, meandering in and out of dressing rooms. Greasepaint had the whiff of excitement, like ballet dancers' rosin making a small squeal against the leather pumps, or the tuning-up of the orchestra, practical moments but suspenseful when they entailed an imminent performance. The call bells started to ring. "All right?" he asked the anxious understudy who wanted to be professional and play without the book but carried a copy in his pocket just in case.

"All right," Roddy gave back, knowing that his own understudy, upgraded in the shuffle, was more nervous still.

The foyer and the bar emptied. The auditorium filled. Progressive layers of silence fell. Stuart was eternally amused at the way a Scottish audience clung to their coats, either because they wouldn't pay the cloakroom fee or because they were susceptible to draughts. He tended to agree with them. The natural air-conditioning was chillingly efficient.

A nervousness communicated itself invisibly, which he added to by explaining in his preamble from the stage that the star was voiceless. They thought they got short commons by the exchange and really, they weren't far wrong. Roddy wasn't imposing enough in physique or diction. Leonie would swamp him.

Stuart hung around the wings listening apprehensively to the silence of response behind the dialogue in the opening scene, while Leonie stood opposite waiting for her cue. She thought it was rough too. A cold canvass or worse, a hostile debate, coming in as seconder when your proposer has already created the wrong climate. How to redeem it and make the points bite. How? You couldn't tell them to stop squirming and listen, the way you could with hecklers. It brought out beads of sweat along her nose. All she thought of in these crises was the lesson she'd been given at primary school for reading aloud; stand up, book up, speak up. It was the best anyone could do.

And she was on. When she was playing opposite Kenneth, their voices were so well matched that they made a duet. The metre of his speech supplied hers and, if she pitched it right, they made a counterpoint in the staccato wit of the text. It was as though they linked hands in a chain and made an unbreakable knot.

Roddy was a change to minor key, marking an uncomfortable shift when there was no time for a rehearsal. Stuart, waiting as impatiently as she did for her lead-in, heard her hit a different note when her turn came. Or the same note an octave down. Less colour. Less brilliance, but true to the character of Ann Whitefield and Leonie's own interpretation of it. She was able to create the same mood with quite a different partner so that the proportions of the play remained intact. And that, as far as he was concerned, was the basic element of theatrical workmanship. It was the facility which some composers had of scoring a work for any instrument in the orchestra, or the virtuosity of writing a hundred variations from the same melodic theme. It wasn't creativity itself, but was often a good indicator of it.

Roddy relaxed, feeling the female lead had things in hand. He took her pace and they began the vocal flirtation of the drama. It was going to be fine. Stuart left, assured that nobody was going to ask for his money back.

Professor Geddes and his son Matthew were among the audience and left well satisfied with the performance.

They weren't quite so satisfied with each other, having drawn into opposing factions of youth versus experience over Matthew's dallying. His father called it dalliance. They had suspended the interchange during the play, but resumed it when they reached the car which the professor parked in a side street off Castle Terrace. It was a handsome, rolling car with a walnut fascia and blue leather upholstery, an old fashioned vehicle that had been preserved for so long that it had acquired its own majesty and was a landmark, as much a novelty as Jack Tanner's on the stage, if for converse reasons.

"You tell me you love two young women and I tell you it isn't possible."

"Well, I feel I do."

"And equally?"

"Equally."

His father snorted. They had arrived at the roundabout of Tollcross where a new traffic flow was being implemented, to the accompaniment of several sets of traffic lights. The system, which had won the sanction of the City Chambers without the benefit of his vote, was so unaesthetic that the professor never saw it without registering disgust and disbelief. Town planning went awry.

"You have committed a solecism which proves to me that you don't know what you think. To love is to perceive and esteem the distinguishing quality. It is therefore possible to love God or the law or Princes Street, but not to love them equally because all things are unequal. You must redefine your terms. You lust after them equally. That I allow."

The shops in Tollcross were lit and the pavements carried a carnival of Festival visitors in a procession towards the North British or the Caledonian at either end of Princes Street, hotels and railway stations the concomitants of tourism. Matthew was, like Fergus Petrie, daunted by the professor's dismissive analysis of human motive.

"If you proceed to the next stage and say you do not know which you should espouse, that also I allow and make bold to advise you on. Marry a woman who will not become an infernal bore. Marry a talent or a sense of humour or, if you are really hard put to it, even an intellect. But do not marry a pretty face in isolation because after ten years it will start to look astonishingly plain as prettier faces supervene. Prettiness wanes. Talents increase."

Silently, James Geddes compared the two young women under review who were now rather hazy in his memory. Ann Whitefield

139

was much sharper. He wouldn't forget the sharp-witted delineaments of Jack Tanner's Ann in a hurry. The girl from his son's Oxford phase, Jennifer Davis, had passed through one Easter holiday and Alison Petrie was also at one remove. He found himself formulating a wedding announcement for the latter, with a divorce pending in the family, and her father an ex-convict. The royal family might allow divorcees in the box at Ascot. Edinburgh did not. The nuptials didn't have the makings of a ceremony in St Giles Cathedral. Not really a connection to boast of. Regretfully, he thought the Petries were not the best his son could do. There was a vast gulf between prison visiting and inter-marriage.

"Above all," he went on as the lights changed at Bruntsfield Place, "confirm that the woman you choose will be more than functional in bed. Empty sexual vessels are excruciatingly little fun."

And the car rolled in its impressive cavalcade towards Morningside.

Leonie hurried to catch the last bus to Canaan Lane and was rather cavalier with the removal of her make-up. Stuart came to congratulate her in person for bearing up so well but said nothing, thinking his person was enough. He watched her carefully dispense with the cotton wool and the top of the bottle of astringent. Her dressing table was laid out in formation, an unvarying ritual not because it was important but because it was simpler that way.

"I've had an offer, Leonie. I had a phone call from my agent this morning."

"Oh?" She finished on her face and changed out of Edwardiana while he, disinterested in this professional nudity which only looked like another costume going on, turned his back.

"I've been offered a three-month opening at the Haymarket. An Ibsen play. Hedda Gabler's my first choice."

"But that's wonderful. Aren't you cock-a-hoop?"

"Well. You know."

She read the hesitation correctly. "You can forget a Scottish National Theatre, Stuart. I mean, how long have they been arguing about the Opera House? Procrastination has become a civic pastime. And even if you could actively bring it closer, going to London and earning yourself a bit of national prestige is about as

140

good as anything."

"Yes, I'd probably get twice the funding if I had some London success behind me. But you know, it's not how we set out to do it. We always meant to be indigenous."

Leonie shrugged. "Abandon the theory and go for it."

"You won't think I've run out?"

"No. Not at all."

He swung back and found her not greatly altered. She wore divided skirts that belonged on a penny farthing.

"How about you?" he asked.

"Oh, nothing much in the pipeline."

"Would you come?"

"To the Haymarket? For three months? Well." Oxford was good. Edinburgh was better. She heard a distant roar: a London accolade, louder because it was larger. "Are you serious?"

"Never more so. I know it sounds like a takeover bid but Ken is free. He hopes you would come too."

The light bulbs round her mirror framed a dubious face. "There's just one problem, Stuart. I'm pregnant."

And she wasn't joking either. "Oh Leonie, what an amateurish bit of timing. That's not like you. Some pipeline." He puffed his cheeks out. There was no room for the tender response. "You'd better sign yourself up for some radio then. You won't be any Puss in Boots this Christmas." He got up from his stool and paced about the room, breaking off lumps of tablet to dissolve. He might have added a corollary to James Geddes' advice to his son. Marriage was the swiftest detraction from both prettiness and talent in women. He was wholly exasperated that the professional skills of the best young actress he had worked with were to be renounced for predictable maternity. Then catching sight of her face, he stopped himself and said, "Well, congratulations or something. When?"

"March."

"Can't you dump the baby and come anyway? It won't open till June."

"I'd have to miss out on the pre-run around the provinces. And who would I dump the baby with? Fergus does have his own work. I don't suppose babies are the best audio-visual aid for a lecture in Applied Mathematics."

"Oh I don't know."

"Or Ellice? I really can't see Ellice fitting a newly born baby into the council chambers. And she's just too old. She was too old to be a mother, never mind a grandmother."

"Three months old. It won't be new. It'll be quite aged by then. That's standard maternity leave," he said, suddenly wise.

"Oh Stuart, really."

"Would Fergus let you go?"

It occurred to both of them that this was taken for granted and indeed, she was surprised he asked it. "*Let* me go? Of course, if I wanted it."

"Well then."

And she nodded, knowing it was a verbal contract and that marriage need not be terminal to development.

16

Quercus was right. The government spent a summer of postponement and the general election was called for Thursday 23rd October.

In Ross, Cromarty and Skye, the three weeks of official campaigning was a peculiar affair when it was the most idiosyncratic
constituency in the British Isles. Door-to-door canvassing was non-
productive in such a scattered community, simply because the
doors were too far apart. Moncrieffe had developed a three-
pronged attack of radio broadcasts, local press coverage which was
generally well disposed towards him, and large well-advertised
public meetings in the key areas of the constituency. The Conservatives put up a paper candidate, knowing the incumbent drew
largely from their traditional support, but Labour had a strong
contender in the shape of Andrew Neil who was a mining engineer
and geologist as well as a local man from Inverness, and had a
technocratic skill in giving just enough detail to sound convincing
about the future of North Sea oil and its spin-off for the economy of
the region, to niggle at Moncrieffe's support. And although he was
outside them, the Independent was squeezed by party politics.
The national mood went left and, so often associated with Conservative by default, he felt the pinch.

Not that he was particularly frightened. It would take a landslide
and a half to shift him but being a third-term runner did have its
repercussions. He wanted to do himself justice and increase his
share of the vote, like building profits in a sound company, not go
backwards. It was the main evidence of how he'd performed in the
eyes of the electorate in the preceding five years, and was an
accolade he honestly thought he deserved. On the other hand, he
acquired the tedious fixity of permanence, or had changed from
the dashing young freelancer to the restless oddball, and divorced
to boot. He had to work harder to go on making an impression,
running to stand still.

His agent was another Macleod, Alistair, who was, in the clan of Ross Macleods, a distant cousin of the factor at Torrisaig. He lived in Dingwall and was the deputy headmaster of a school on the Black Isle, so an October election falling over a mid-term suited him well enough. They drove to a meeting in a village hall near Achnasheen, anticipating maybe fifty in the audience. Thin pickings in the country. It was all country, Watson reflected as they drove across the lonely uplands of Strath Bran with only the railway line and the stream for company along the road, a three-way network practically void of traffic. Moorland, sheep, the treeless landscape. Occasionally, he had to draw the Daimler in to one of the passing places along the single track, but not often in October. Campaigning was easy in the extremes of east or west where townships were larger. It was the empty middle that was impossible to canvass, reflecting a national pattern of ideological vacuity. How did you target vast open spaces?

In the back of the car was a reporter from the *Ross-shire Journal* who tagged devotedly after Moncrieffe. It was one way of ensuring coverage.

"What will they want to know in Achnasheen?" Watson asked his agent.

In Skye it was the unending battle between those who registered as crofters and paid half rates on their property and the men who said they worked too hard at road-building or fishing or running their business to pretend that they were farmers with a sheep or two on a pocket handkerchief of land. In Invergordon, he tried to soothe the conservationists who feared the scars that would be left on the inlet, one of the messier by-products of oil; elsewhere, he pacified the natives who were sick to death of conservationists telling them what they should or shouldn't grow or kill or breed. Overall, it was a compromise between a thin and exhausted seam of land and the men who tried to live from it in the gradations between prosperity and tradition. He was, whether he liked it or not, the agent of government explaining the disbursement of subsidies like a fertiliser on the land but a fertiliser which some said killed the soil, replacing natural sediments with the synthetic junk crop of the south.

"I could not say for sure what it will be in Achnasheen," said Alistair Macleod.

Moncrieffe was certain he wouldn't be able to supply it, whatever it was they wanted from him, proofs or reassurance. Where did he stand on devolution? What was his line on unilateral nuclear disarmament? Did he agree Scotland was becoming a nuclear dumping ground for England? Plant nuclear reactors instead of forests. What was to happen to the Flow Country? How did he suggest a man survive when fish harvests were controlled to below realistic market levels? And the rates . . . again and again and again. In vain, he tried to explain the demarcation between regional and constituency matters, but the blurring of bureaucracy remained. He didn't know the answers a lot of the time and was tired of being God's fall-guy when it all went wrong. Where did he stand on anything, that was the question. The honest answer was, I am a pragmatist. I judge each situation on its merits according to my experience and common sense. And every other politician is the same, even if none of us dare say so in case we are castigated for displaying an unseemly lack of principle. It was convenient for opposing factions to group under the strident banners of capitalism or socialism, the heraldic lion or the heraldic unicorn, emblems so clear they were recognisable at a distance. He found that brash, unsubtle, untruthful. He would not trust a man who did not trust his own judgment in a crisis but had to rely on the tags of party to tell him what to do. Though, at election time, he admitted a handful of party mottoes would have been a respite from incessantly thinking on his feet.

Leonie rested, which wasn't a euphemism for being unemployed. She took a rest as well as Stuart's advice, having been in continuous stage productions for the three years since she left Edinburgh. She had appeared in rep at Bristol, had a summer at Pitlochry, a season at the Crucible, the Festival Fringe for so many years she had lost count, Oxford Playhouse, Edinburgh Lyceum, and now the Haymarket if she wanted it. She didn't broach Stuart's offer to Fergus but kept it a warm potential, like maternity itself, something she hugged and was afraid of in alternation. Her career began to look serious, a curriculum vitae instead of a pastime. She took on several radio engagements over the autumn and winter and grew lax with time, or more normal. Normality was a rest in itself.

During the day she would go to her mother's flat and help the election volunteers who used it as a base. The official headquarters was a rented slice of a shop in Comiston Road, blazing with posters and stickers and rosettes, but the day usually opened and closed at Ellice Barr's.

It was a different campaign from Moncrieffe's. The urban constituency was comparatively tight, one of the close-knit kind possible in the city complex. Personal contact counted, so that teams were brought in from other constituencies which had no SNP candidate of their own. Archibald was the resident incumbent who was re-adopted and, after the initial canvass, he used his time wisely, knocking only on those doors that sheltered the floating voters, a definite yes or no being outside persuasion.

Leonie and Ellice joined the team that swept ahead of him. Ellice Barr had a talent for doorstep politics. She'd perfected her opening technique into a single sentence which was always different and was matched to the householder who came to the door, so that it sounded intuitively close to his interests. 'Do you care that there are forty children in some city classrooms?' 'Does it worry you that there aren't enough hospital beds for the elderly?' 'Are you dissatisfied with the way the government is spending Scotland's oil revenue?' She asked the bottomless question. There had to be a yes. No decent, self-respecting person said, No, I don't care. It led to more questions and more yesses. It was her foot in the door and after that it was virtually impossible to send her away.

If Ellice met with out-and-out opposition, there was nothing she could do about it, but if her interlocutor was misinformed or out of date or simply indifferent, she swept into a dramatic monologue like the busker who had the knack of playing to the mood of the hour or the crowd, and charmed pennies out of pockets in the process.

Her message was maybe unoriginal, fact plus sentiment, but it was unbeatable for that reason. She knew the gross national spending on Scottish investments under successive governments for the last fifty years and was crisp on detail. But round this rather drab solidity, she spun the enticements of national independence, emotive and unanalytical.

Ah! Freedom is a noble thing!
Freedom makes man to have liking;
Freedom all solace to man gives;
He lives at ease that freely lives!

The watchwords of separatism weren't stated. They didn't need to be. They were built into the national subconscious and every Scot who'd read a history book was ten per cent for devolution, in theory. She had the gift of extracting that tithe.

It was her delivery that was original. She looked so extraordinary, an Angel Gabriel coming like a clarion to the doorstep, and in Morningside too, re-incarnated in the hermaphrodite dress of kilt and jacket. An angel in tartan? Well, maybe not. Every now and then, with people who were inclined to be argumentative about her offer of salvation, usually men who had strong voices which they could employ to cut off the end of her sentence, she had an unanswerable reply. She soared her voice above theirs in a long crescendo, as if she were in a stage musical and in the middle of a humdrum speech, suddenly burst into song. She sang at them. They looked on dumbfounded, which was a good enough silencing.

You had to listen to her, hate or love, you listened. In the main, she got her donation, if that was what she was after, and sometimes a subscription. She reckoned she could palm a hundred leaflets in a session, or get a hundred signatories to a petition. No envelope stuffer; she always knocked. Above all, she left them with a laugh or a good impression, the sense that they'd been entertained because they didn't really want to be hectored on the doorstep. Humour was the best persuader. They went away feeling they'd been amused rather than berated, a euphoria that might last an hour, a week, or with luck until polling day.

Leonie, who should have been good at doorstep persuasion, was actually diffident about its long-term effectiveness. She followed the banner 'Party' with the rest: only fainthearts stayed at home, but the images of militarism were not inept. Target areas. Campaign. Divisional headquarters. Attack was built in. It did seem too frontal, accosting people in their own homes, walking up their drives to push something through their letter box they didn't want and wouldn't read. She read her brief, covered her area, gave her spiel, but the performance lacked absolute conviction and was a delivery by rote. Something lacked.

Watson visited the community north-west of Achnasheen, taking the boat that plied the inlet twice a day, weather permitting. There was no road because, although the Highland Regional Council was prepared to build and maintain one at public expense, the inhabitants of Carse said they'd gone there to get away from civilisation and didn't want it transported to their doorstep. So sheep and flour and tools, and even a piano for the school, went by rowboat under tarpaulins.

It was a personal rather than a professional visit. There were forty adults in the village but the election meant as little to them as the road. They were self-governing. He went to see an Edinburgh and Oxford friend, Sandy Govan, who'd dropped out of the hierarchies of success and built boats. Good boats they were too. He caulked the planks of an upended hull outside the workshop which he ran beside the shore. His brother shared a bench when he was at home. More often he was out on site, being the odd job man in Carse, and he had developed a simple wind vane that supplied each household with enough power for rudimentary lighting, so he was much in demand installing and repairing these.

"You'll not ask me to go fifteen miles by boat to put a cross on a bit of paper?" asked Sandy. On the western edge of Britain, the poll was a stranger custom than a counsel of elders. Parliament gave way to the witenagemot.

"No obligation."

"Ah, I can relax then. Except I see you've brought your press photographer."

"I can't seem to shake him off."

"I suppose you must cull your votes somehow." The cynicism with all systems had not diminished in half a dozen years at Carse. "If I smile and shake your hand for the camera, will the journey be worthwhile? We could find a baby for you to hold."

The photographer had never been to Carse and after a shot or two of the Independent, he staggered off to snap the cottagers instead. It was likely a Pictish settlement, a fertile spur, deep fishing, and the black houses didn't contradict the impression of prehistory. The families who re-inhabited abandoned homesteads on the peninsula were seldom Scots. There was one Shetland woman who couldn't abide to watch the oil rigs spawn in the open sea, and helicopters droning back and forth all day long, but the rest were English, Dutch, Hungarian, a Swede, opting out of the commercial affray. They followed strange trades alongside crofting. There was a rush mat weaver and a man who made the traditional Orkney chair and a lapidarist, who mined and polished his own gems and made them up in the Celtic shapes, the serpent and the cross, stylised temptation and salvation side by side.

Carse made the visitor uneasy. Visually, it was a mess. Tumble-down cottages, the turf-roofed but and ben, ruins made water-tight, disused byres and outhouses pressed into service as living quarters; quite sophisticated people living in the discomfort of slums for the sake of a principle. Even the buildings were anarchic. You could tell from the other side of the loch that Carse was a cell of industry. Smoke, the bright green of silage, a schoolhouse with newly pointed walls as primitive as a child's version of brickwork, but it had sealed itself off from reality, a cul-de-sac, a closed road. He couldn't decide which had failed, the men who shunned the city-state, or the state itself which hadn't supplied their needs.

He and Sandy walked along the bay where the seagrass grew high. The air was benign, a million miles from the fume and smut of London. He measured the temptations of the natural life. "How are things?"

"We do quite well. There's been a number of newcomers since you were here last. One couple from Derbyshire. He's a good farmer and his wife's taken over the school, which is why it's so spick and span. I hope their enthusiasm doesn't wear off. The others." He shook his head. "She keeps getting pregnant and the horse died, so they've fallen below subsistence. I don't think they'll make it."

"Do you get used to that? People coming and going?"

"Oh yes. There's no room for sentiment. This is the roughest life of all. There isn't any margin for error. One wet season and you've had it. By God, you understand the potato famine when you've been here a year or two."

Sandy didn't look hard pressed himself; he had a full order book and set his own price on his work, in demand all over the British Isles. "Yes," he said, reading the glance, "I'm flush. But I'm not raising a family."

"No wife appeared yet?"

The boat builder looked amused. "Out here? What chance. And anyway," he went carefully, knowing the sore point, "you and I need women who'll marry a way of life. Not everybody would take to this. I hear Liz has re-married."

"Yes. And children."

The wind freshened and in a moment the sea, which had been blue and sparkling set with islands in the western archipelago from Skye across to the Hebrides, turned dark, threatening a squall. Moncrieffe noticed that the prevailing wind had blown the trees into a point.

"Don't hang about," said the expert, "or you'll have a rough crossing."

They came back through the settlement avoiding the rough ground of boulders. "You know," said Sandy, "every man Jack of us *ought* to turn out to vote. We live off the government. Every household relies on a grant or a subsidy of some kind. Maternity payment, child benefit, so much per head of sheep. We're only kidding ourselves we're living self-sufficiently." He looked over the lean fingers of land stretching into the sea. His face had the wry look of the disappointed idealist. "We're trying to turn the clock back at Carse and think we've bucked the system, but if we didn't have the Giro cheques and the helicopter for emergencies, we'd be dead within a year."

"Does it matter? That it's subsidised?"

"We're rather a forlorn bunch, don't you think, if we can't pay our way. Misfits. It's St Kilda all over again, just clinging on. You can't fight large-scale economic trends."

"You're a long way from St Kilda. It's not as hard as collecting fulmar and puffin down a cliff face, surely?"

Sandy laughed and remembered how much he had enjoyed Moncrieffe's company at Oxford, and how he missed a sharp mind. "Do you know, on St Kilda an adult male had to have woven his own length of horsehair rope before he was allowed to marry. Because he couldn't scale the cliffs otherwise and would have been a burden on the rest of the community."

"A not inappropriate noose."

They shook hands by the water's edge once Watson had rounded up the agent and the photographer whose supply of film

150

hadn't matched his enthusiasm. "Come for longer next time. Steal a day or two. I can put you up all right."

Govan raised his hand as the boat pulled away from the shore and bobbed in the choppy waters towards mechanisation and the mainland.

Moncrieffe thought he would write to the returning officer and say it was high time Carse school was an official polling station. He could have done with the forty votes.

Leonie watched her mother and half a dozen other women spread a copy of the Register of Electors for the constituency and write the names and addresses which were listed in it onto brown envelopes. They wrote the names according to the particular canon of the party, all persons with the same address and the same surname onto one envelope, but initialled separately. Someone else would put an election manifesto into each envelope, and then take them to the GPO who delivered them with the mail. And all this canvassing and addressing was only part of the pre-election activity. Public meetings, posters, notices in the newspaper, telling and checking rolls on the day – these women's lives were filled with the small detail of politics, helping to run the machinery of party with voluntary service. Leonie watched the ferment of industry that went on behind the scenes, invisible to the people who took no part in local or national politics. And in houses up and down the country, Labour and Liberal and Tory women did the same. Women. The men took the platform, the women got them there by such minute addenda to success as writing names on envelopes.

What did they achieve by it? The Nationalists knew they hadn't a hope of winning Edinburgh Pentlands, but when the results were read out by the returning officer they would congratulate themselves on the statistics. Leonie remembered past jubilations that accompanied failure and was baffled. A seventy-two per cent turnout, making it a good poll, a ten per cent share of the vote for SNP, a swing of six per cent. They juggled the figures and came up with a victory of sorts. Of course, if every Edinburgh supporter of devolution lived inside the boundary of Pentlands they would return their candidate, but in the meantime they contented themselves with a better failure than before.

Leonie asked herself the salutary question, Why? What did the people do with the leaflets and the election address? Put them in the rubbish bin. Screwed them in a ball and threw them away. What happened to the petition Ellice Barr spent two months on, collecting ten thousand signatures? A remarkable achievement, everybody said. No one else had done as much to resist the demolition of a local landmark, which was demolished anyway. It lay about the office in Charlotte Square for months or maybe years before it too was destroyed, but more neatly than the pamphlets, by incineration. What did the party do with the money she collected? Bought more leaflets. Why? she asked herself. Why she could not answer. The political machine was drowning in bits of paper. Leonie couldn't bring herself to believe in such diffuseness, a confetti of information. She hankered after something more direct than pavement pounding or collecting and distributing sheets with printed words on them, potential litter. Active intervention, active participation, not all this paperwork. She admired the conscientious attention which the party gave to detail, thought it was necessary, but knew it missed its mark, a voice too small for the auditorium it should have filled.

Moncrieffe spent the last night before the election at Torrisaig. He was exhausted. The campaign was a protracted royal tour, ten engagements to be undertaken every day, always in the public eye, always talking, meeting people, shaking a thousand hands and smiling, oh God, smiling while he did it. That was the bugbear. Being nice. Saying the conventional thing because he didn't dare offend. No respite, even in therapeutic rudeness.

Macleod went back to Dingwall alone and the MP drove to the estate in the Daimler. He passed over the cattle grid and drew level with the lodge, slowing down so that he didn't wake the factor though the factor heard him pass at one a.m. The car headlights picked out the rowans that proliferated in the grounds, which were thickly berried. Didn't the country folk say that meant a winter of hard frost? He must ask.

Charlie was sensibly in bed and Watson went to his own rooms where a fire had been lit and he put on another log to catch the embers before they died completely. He remembered he'd got his feet wet somewhere that day. Where was it? Somewhere on Skye, in the morning, but it did seem several days ago. He sat in front of the blaze and pulled his boots off. Even his feet felt ancient tonight. He noticed that a Thermos flask had been left on a sidetable and he felt grateful for the multiple welcomes of the place. He looked over at the bed with its coverlet ready turned back, and postponed its loneliness. Whatever the cook had put in the flask was good and slowly he unwound.

The bed reminded him that it was three years since he had had a woman. Had a woman? Liz would have objected to the phrase as contravening feminist principles. Okay, Liz. Made love, then. She probably would have found something to pick at in that as well. There were a lot of empty nights in three years, but surprisingly he found that making love was something of an acquired habit. He'd tried to regain it. He took women to social events, kissed one or two, even got as far as taking his clothes off on one occasion, then changed his mind. He had become dispassionate about the act. Reversion to celibacy wasn't as hard as he'd imagined and he could see how men with low sexual motivation, or sworn celibates in the priesthood or other professional bachelors, could live without women. The shocks of his divorce, brutish, nasty but not short, had reduced his libido for some time, and he began to feel intercourse was an addiction you could break yourself of if you tried.

Until the first of May. Since then, he'd had five and a half months of fairly continuous torment. Was it the woman, he asked himself, or the time of life? He put Leonie Barr out of his mind, said she was married, he had come too late. Forget it. But he couldn't put her out of his physical consciousness, why he didn't know. She wasn't like any other woman he had been attracted to. Maybe that was the cause, distinctiveness. He didn't normally like the colour of her hair and he didn't care for tall women as a rule. He told himself that over and over again, and didn't listen. She kept coming back in spite of his denials. Her voice in a radio play startled him that same evening in the car. He didn't know it was being broadcast and, switching on, was transfixed by the particular catch of her phrasing. The car was filled with her again from Portree to Lochalsh, a mauve gown and a piece of lace visionary beside him.

I am not in love, he said. I refuse to be in love with a woman who is wholly indifferent to my existence.

He went to bed when the log had burned itself out, but didn't sleep better than fitfully. He got up at daybreak and looked out of the window, glad that he had come out of his way after all. The mountains of Wester Ross went on fisting themselves upwards, camouflaged in heather, fern and scree, hard, challenging, a masculine conquest. Love and mountain climbing, the extremes of female and male in his personality came back at him, tempting him to try them again. The lower slopes were clothed in trees, and from this distance he could almost feel the forest transpiring, warming the air. Some trees hung on impossible ledges, their roots deeply embedded in the rock face so that it was hard to tell if the tree were fracturing the stone, or holding it together. He took in the smell of the morning with a mist lifting in a harbinger of a fine day. These were places without vulgarity. They might electrify a fence, widen a road but the land prevailed.

He went down to the church before breakfast, realising he hadn't been inside it for at least a year. When the estate was in full manpower, of course, it had had its resident minister and the pews weren't adequate on Sundays. Now, a preacher came by rote one week out of three. Watson noticed that the churchyard, like all the graveyards in the Highlands, was well tended. He wondered who put the work into keeping the dead so close and dear; his ancestors and their dependants laid to rest and loved still, by somebody. Nothing ornate, no urns or statues. The headstones were granite or marble with sharp lettering, as precise as memory. His grandfather and his cousins fallen in the line. Charlie would be laid to rest here, and himself in time. But his father was buried in the churchyard of St Michael's at Inveresk, and his grandmother would choose that resting place instead of the bleak shores of Torrisaig. Even the cemetery waned.

The door to the church was open. A decent, quiet place and maybe right for him to come to at this juncture, the knight praying before battle, Let me defeat my enemies and in a just cause. That was a foolish notion. It was won or lost already, and was all too secular. Today was only the reckoning, although the sense of dedication remained. If I do prevail, let me use my power wisely.

17

Leonie found it hard to break herself of the schedules of the theatre, and still went to bed and slept late even when she wasn't working. She thought it was unwifely, however, to let Fergus leave in the morning without seeing her and so she struggled out of the comatose sleep of night people to sit with him over breakfast which he'd set and made himself.

He peeled an orange for her and fed her a segment at a time, interested because his own child was the ultimate beneficiary. She didn't enjoy the orange as much as the giving fingers.

Fergus had been up for some time, and had been out to collect a newspaper which lay partly read on the table beside the mail. He didn't buy a paper every day but knew Leonie would want to read an account of the election and those results which had been declared in time for the morning edition. Today, he had an interest of his own he followed up.

"What's this?" asked Leonie, picking up an air mail envelope with an American stamp.

"Good news. Amazing news in fact." He passed her the letter and a cheque which came with it, but because the cheque was made payable in dollars and cents, it didn't mean much to her. Fergus was shrewd about money. He was indebted to his father for his facility with numbers, but to his mother for the knack of making them total to good effect. When Paragon Electronics bought the copyright for his chess programme, he didn't take the cash. He converted it into shares in the company, tantamount to taking a wager on his own chances of doing well, because he knew the small electronics industry was booming in the States, with TV and hi-fi systems available to the home-owner, and the first inexpensive computers in demand for the domestic market. He'd had the great good fortune to catch a peak. The quarterly dividend from investment in this first wave of computerised technology brought a lump sum which was staggering, in his terms, half of his annual salary as a University lecturer, all in one go.

"What's the exchange rate?" She tried to carry out the conversion in her head. "Have you been looking that up?"

"It's a lot of money, Leonie. Enough to put down a deposit on a house."

She noticed that the *Scotsman* wasn't turned to the business section with its list of currencies, but to the property guide. "Which house?" She knew how his mind would run. Not a day lost in investing his capital.

He showed her on the page of newsprint. "The house at the Hermitage is for sale again. I saw it advertised at the beginning of the week and went round to see it yesterday, just for old times' sake really. I thought it would be impossible for us to buy it, but this money brings it within reach."

"Fergus. That house. You don't really want to live there again?"

"There's nothing I'd like better."

She didn't know. It was an example of Scottish Baronial architecture with crow-stepped gables, turrets, keystone windows and a stone archway for a porch, all cut down to fit suburbia. Not so much stockbroker Tudor as stockbroker Gothic. It struck Leonie as a piece of fantasy, unreal escape into the days of yore. It was certainly a handsome, commodious house and in a prime location but the thought of living in the shadow of Muriel and Michael cancelled out the material benefit. Was it obsessive and unhealthy for Fergus to want that repetition, or a natural desire to return to the place that he was fond of? They lived on in Canaan Lane with its tawdry fittings, but if economics had squeezed hard enough they would have moved in beside her mother. Was that any different? What did it matter where they lived? In condemning the house, which was neutral and innocent, she thought she might be falling prey to the curses of property, ascribing status and character and omens to what were only walls.

"And what have you done about it?" Maybe made a verbal contract like her own with Stuart, in pursuit of the differing ideologies of self which weren't always to be married in a partner. She was sharp in the question.

"Nothing. There was nothing I could do without the cash. But when I went yesterday, I was hoping against hope that something would happen. I saw Irene Geddes. She would give anything, of

156

course, for us to be back there."

That was understandable. Leonie was a shade put out, all the same, that Irene Geddes was addressed on the subject before she was, and that Fergus used this generic title 'we' in relation to their return, which wasn't one as far as concerned her, but a new arrival. She didn't spend time in niggly quarrelling, however, but converted the terms he used into the strength of his volition; to be seen to do so well, so young.

"Are the present owners the people you sold to?" She became casual herself about pronouns.

"Yes. The husband's moving down south again with his company. They remembered me. I think they might be disposed to accept my offer, just for . . . neatness."

"So what do you want to do next?"

"I'll have to arrange a mortgage for the rest of the purchase price but that shouldn't be any problem with my salary guaranteed and your earnings too."

"I would have to be a party to this mortgage?"

"Yes of course. The house would be half yours."

She counted, at least in earning capacity. "The baby will mean there won't be much coming in next year."

On the edge of the *Scotsman*, Fergus jotted down his salary and then, working on the current interest rates, the monthly repayment on the differential he would have to borrow to meet the upset price. A helping hand from Leonie would have been useful.

She drew breath to put out the suggestion that had been shaping for two months. "Stuart Ainslie's going to direct a production at the London Haymarket, for three months initially. Kenneth Frew will go with him and they want me, starting next June. The baby would be three months old."

"What have you done about it?"

"Stuart knows I'd like to go, professionally, but that it's virtually impossible with a youngster."

"Well paid?"

"London rates and star billing. It's what it would lead to that's important, becoming established in a West End theatre. Ken's a good launching platform, too. I like working with him and his reputation is absolutely secure. I can't see it going wrong."

"I'd rather you didn't, altogether, with the baby."

157

"I told Stuart it was impractical."

Fergus drew the argument in files. They needed the money all right, but he wasn't as convinced as Leonie that this opportunity was uniquely good for the career. The patterns of a theatrical career were so diffuse that they were lost on him. He knew where he was going in rigid, measured steps and paced himself chronologically against his peers. Leonie made up her own pattern as she went along. And it wasn't a serious career, not bread-winning, mortgage-paying serious. Seeing Irene again reminded him of the norms of housewifeliness, a good woman making a good home, and he didn't think that decamping to London to live in digs was the best way to start a crèche. The two factors were plus and minus, bringing him to zero again. He was strict in logic. He remembered as accurately as Leonie the terms he had offered in the marriage contract. Freedom of movement and freedom of association. Not easy to reconcile with the eccentric and particularised demands of theatre. He wondered suddenly if he'd given away too much in those conditions, but he couldn't withdraw them now, or not completely, without incurring the charge he made against lesser intellects, of being self-contradictory. He didn't want to, but felt he was compelled to maintain that original open-handedness, although it was a split vote.

Leonie watched his conclusion formulate itself, by analysis. She proceeded differently, by gut reaction. She didn't know exactly why she'd been quiet about the Haymarket offer but now that she had produced it, it looked a cunning trade-off. My career for your house. She was in no doubt that it was his house, just as it was his marriage and his baby. But where did she come in? She hacked a little corner for herself and said it was a career, but maybe it was defiance at the enclosure of free space, hoisting the flag of independence over one hectare of her life.

"You know," he said with some excitement at having arrived at a sound deductive settlement, "it could come right. If we lived at the Hermitage, Irene Geddes would mind the baby for some hours of the day while I was at work. Not for ever but for a while. And Ellice could take a turn. Even Ellice can push a pram doing her leafletting."

"Just like old times," said Leonie. The senior woman couldn't manage full-time nursery care, but she could manage part.

Fergus couldn't remember seeing Leonie in the pram, but believed it might be true. It was Irene herself who could recall Ellice Barr and the flask of warm milk which she would decant into a bottle on the pavement and feed the baby by remote control, the bottle being propped against a pillow. She had described it once to the adult Leonie. Scandalised by it. No way to bring a child up, she had thought, and there was the child grown up the same way to prove it. Irene, the instinctive mother. Yes, she would not only raise Fergus' child but do it better than Leonie, with half an eye on her script and frantic to be working, burning with the same fervour as her mother which viewed the personal as self-indulgent and the public dutiful. Irene provided the grounds of compromise, unasked, but both Leonie and Fergus acquiesced to the other's demands of marriage, knowing the woman's surrogacy was assured. They noted in passing that they wouldn't trust their child for one second to Muriel's untender mercies.

"Should I go ahead, then?" The answer was yes to both.

When Fergus had left for the University, Leonie turned back to the newspaper to read the result of the night's count. It looked bad for the Conservative government. They'd lost a couple of the Home Counties after all, one to Liberal, one to Labour. Dissatisfaction bit closer to home than they had expected. The results were printed in long columns split geographically into England, Wales, Northern Ireland, Scotland and then alphabetically by constituency. She ran speedily down these lists, bypassing Edinburgh Pentlands and arrived breathless at Ross, Cromarty and Skye. It was laid out like a bill.

Watson Moncrieffe (Ind)	13,302
Andrew Neil (Lab)	8,838
John Sanderson (Cons)	2,976

A sixty-nine per cent turnout, a majority of 4,464 over his nearest rival though, to the electoral reformer, this would look a waste of some two thousand votes when all he needed was a win by one. He had an increase of 1,027 over his last result. He was home and dry, and with honour.

She poured another cup of coffee from the pot Fergus left and drank it thoughtfully, not noticing it was tepid. She scanned the other results. These lines of figures made more sense to her than rates of exchange or chess moves, d2×d4, numbers in isolation from people. She could read the totals of the election as if they were the outline plot of a play, made up of protagonists who were vivid and real to her. She knew very many of them, if not in person, then by reputation. She knew Andrew Neil had stood before, somewhere in Aberdeenshire, and ought to win next time if his party did the decent thing and gave him a winnable seat at a by-election. Names came up at her like old friends she had rumours of, devoutly interested in how they were getting along. It was better than a gossip column, the print-out of these results, because they were true and they were factual, and she charted the new developments across the graph of her memory, fascinated by the statistical pattern they made. 'So he has gone.' 'I wonder why he didn't stand last time.' 'He ought to give up now. Four tries without a hit. Pack it in.'

Archibald had lost but saved his deposit. That was the disgrace, being booed off stage. You could come back another time, but only if you were a fool. If you hadn't convinced even a ten per cent minority that you had something valuable to say, then the chances were that you didn't.

Running her eye down the list of names, Leonie registered the lack of women in the political arena, the two public stages being parallel in this. There weren't many significant rôles for women, an occasional star part against an all-male sky, but politics and the theatre asked too much from their female aspirants, and resulted in the classic inequalities of the cast list. Where were the eponymous heroines of the English stage? The Duchess of Malfi at best, put to death for an illicit love, but even Shakespeare didn't attempt to draw an Elizabeth as heroine, queen, decision-maker, skilful economist because the portrait was too exceptional. As well as being quite difficult to play in Tudor drag. Dreary Lears staggered on incompetently instead.

And yet French drama had its great women, and Greek; majestic, compassionate women written over the full range of feeling. Medea. Phèdre. Antigone. Iphigenia. Maria Stuart was only a heroine in German. Was there a valid connection between the placement of women in drama and their social standing? If so, British women were a very secondary breed. The stage was male

160

ground apart from whores, harridans and tearful Ophelias. The English were unreasonably proud of their theatrical history – in continuous production for four centuries (bar the Commonwealth) – just as they were proud of their version of democracy which they regarded as the universal model, a product of the island mind which clung to precious fallacies rather than import an idea from abroad. Not so much perfidious as injudicious Albion.

Leonie and Fergus had a singular conversation after they were married. They agreed that her stage name was a personal trade mark which it was stupid to change, but there was something illogical about being Barr professionally and Petrie in private. And the fact that Fergus was Petrie by assimilation compounded this unease. Why should she take his name when it wasn't really his anyway? They discussed whether she should renounce Petrie altogether but the Inland Revenue and banks and registrars made almost insuperable obstacles to the practice of married women retaining their maiden name. So they compromised. They changed both their names by deed poll to Barr-Petrie, having held lengthy discussions on which half should go first, but settled at last on euphonic as well as alphabetical priorities, and were as well pleased as if they'd established a new dynastic title. In practice she went on being Leonie Barr and he Fergus Petrie just the same.

So with the disposition of the day. Fergus was absent during the whole of the working day. He didn't have many lectures to give, twelve a week, three tutorial groups, quite hefty marking which he kept in his room in the department, but he worked overtime at his own research on the computer, seeing with something like vision-ary insight what the applications of ready numeracy might be once the hardware was cheap enough to be accessible to everyone. Leonie's day was the reverse. She waited for nightfall to begin living. The season at the Lyceum had been a valuable transition period, leaving for work at six, home before midnight so that the two places weren't too far removed in time or spirit. These emphatic work schedules gave way to the cyclic waiting of maternity. She missed the live theatre. The radio recordings she made in bleak daylight weren't the same. The sound-proofed studio was dead; unresponsive microphones, edits and cuts and

161

re-runs until the producer was satisfied with clipped little cassettes of sound. She couldn't listen to the finished broadcasts, hearing their artifice a mile away. Give it live, faults and all, because that way it was spontaneous.

At nightfall she put her coat on and went out, somewhere, anywhere, but out. The election had been a stop-gap, filling space with people, and now that its activity was over she wondered what she would do with evenings. So she drifted, looking for the meeting place, drifted unconsciously towards her mother's flat where the rooms, full of familiar chat and faces, were a substitute for theatre. She was welcomed, applauded, listened to, made much of. This was her milieu, not solitary domesticity.

That evening, mad festivities were taking place at Ellice Barr's, like a wake in the middle of post mortem. Archibald was there and a group of the city's Nationalists who clustered round their oldest campaigner to celebrate their three new victories overall in Scotland, in Ayrshire, one in Glasgow and in Aberdeen, which brought their representation at Westminster up to five, including Simon Dunns and the great man of the SNP, their elder statesman from Shetland who'd hung on to his seat for almost thirty years.

Archibald was a self-educated man, and impatient with the abstruse or effete elements in Ellice's entourage, so that when Alison arrived late in the evening to congratulate him on improving on his result and say how thrilled she was for the party nationally, he wasn't disposed to be charmed.

"Thrilled?" he queried sourly. "Surprised as much as anything, I would think, considering how little we've seen of you at campaign headquarters over the last three weeks."

"Ah," said Alison. "Well, you know . . . it's my last year." If she'd done a round of leafletting for him, he'd have forgiven her much.

Her real distraction from things political accompanied her.

"There's no need to introduce us," Matthew Geddes said when they came by the thronged detours of the room towards Leonie, who clung to a window space for fresh air.

"Why, you sly thing, Leonie. You never said you'd met."

Alison had a way of standing by the elbow of the person she was talking to, an inch too close for comfort as though in a while she would whisper a childish secret, all girls together. Leonie moved aside.

162

"And you never paused to ask. Three years, isn't it, Matthew?"

"At least. I saw you quite recently, although you didn't know it. I came to see your Viola at Oxford. It was mandatory viewing in my College. You were out of the conversation if you hadn't seen the mauve gown. One of my friends came six times."

"Did he indeed?"

"How's Fergus doing? I hear he's on the staff now and producing research a mile a minute." At twenty, Matthew had been one of the gilded youth of the city, like Fergus himself, of whom imminent greatness was expected. But whereas Fergus drove on and on and on with relentless single-mindedness, Matthew dallied. He took a year out before going up to Oxford, instructive and expansive perhaps, but not a notch up on a career ladder. Then he changed subjects, adding another year to studentship. Almost Fergus' contemporary, he started to lag behind, perhaps too multi-talented to be a devotee of any one thing. Jazz concerts and practices for his own band were frequent diversions. He posed a little with his talents, more concerned to display than to develop them. His dress was dandyish, yellow string gloves and a boater in the summer not unreasonable in Oxford but drifting into posture at the Hermitage. Nor had he made his expected first, but scored a near miss which disappointed him less than his father, who didn't omit to upbraid him for the female distractions. Matthew began to wear the air of grievance, as if someone had cheated him. The gilding wore off.

"Oh yes, Fergus knows how to be busy."

"And you, what are you doing spending all this time in the provinces?"

So she told them, half-reluctantly, about her plans.

"The Haymarket, London?" queried Alison sharply. "Oh I couldn't do that. Once I was married, I would have to be with my husband all the time. I mean really throw myself into our joint lives and make a go of it. It would be all or nothing with me."

Perhaps the major irritant in this response was that it bypassed Fergus, simply an excuse for preaching and, like most of Alison's hypothesising, done in a vacuum of experience. Leonie couldn't contain a curt reply. "Why, Alison, what happened to the feminist cause, women forging ahead and using their abilities, not being bogged down by traditional rôle-playing. Or was that last month's theory?"

163

Matthew laughed, which made Alison flush and protest, "That wasn't what I said."

A large silence fell. Leonie didn't feel inclined to add her pregnancy to the material for censoriousness, or the house at Hermitage. None of Alison's business, she thought, but she sensed that if she'd been allowed to talk to Matthew alone, she might have spoken more fully. Indeed, by a flicker of his eye, she imagined he was informed on both counts via his mother and also held his tongue.

They were engulfed by the dominant conversation of the evening. "The problem is," said Archibald, "that we've got to Westminster, but what do we do now? What can five SNP members do to make themselves into some sort of force? Give themselves real weight."

"They can throw themselves behind full devolution, of course," said another of the city's candidates who'd come closer than Archibald to getting there, and felt entitled to cap his statements. "Refuse to co-operate with the government until Westminster stops dragging its feet over a Scottish Parliament. It's about all a minority can do, be obstructive."

The Nationalists found themselves in a cleft stick over the continuous postponement of devolution. Scotland's political map, made up of minorities, was complex. Many seats were fought four-way, with more marked contrasts from one election to the next than in England, so that Scotland's result was not necessarily reflected in the disunited kingdom as a whole. Politics were a more unstable and combustible mix than south but at the same time, resignation – rather than apathy – towards a system that looked unshakeable was widespread.

"And who's going to notice? A power base of five is nil."

The room itself partitioned, for and against devolution, a stronger say at Westminster or full blown separatism, and in its corners the same points were made in different levels of shrillness and accuracy, until Ellice Barr, frustrated by the chatter, called them to order by the exercise of her seniority.

"The worst thing that ever happened to the Nationalists," she said, "was when the leadership decided in 1948 that members with dual loyalties would have to state their preference. SNP or nothing. Labour, Liberal, Tory were out. I think that was unequivocally wrong. I remember a time when the colour of your blood group didn't matter, red or blue, and we were all the better for being less partisan. Nationalism ought to be a point of view, not a party. I can see why it happened. We were becoming a debating club instead of a political force, but it's a small man who doesn't hold two opinions concurrently. And any opinion which subverts all other opinions is suspect. So I am a Nationalist and a socialist, not equally, but harmoniously. Parties are a spectrum, are they not?

"So if the SNP withdraws into a little clique of five members and refuses to take part in the broader debate, it'll cut off its nose to spite its face again. It's stupid from the stance of ideology and it's stupid for practical politics. These five can be our bargaining power. The way the results look tonight, everybody will be after our five votes and we ought to make sure they're bought at a price."

Murmurs of bribery were heard.

"Yes, bribery. Legal, honourable, but bribery."

"Ellice, how can you?" Alison grew vexed.

"Because the voice of my experience tells me so. Change from within is the only kind that works. If we want to change Parliament and the shape of Scottish affairs, we'll have to do it from the inside. These men that we've worked so hard to put into their places must capitalise on the significance of their vote, win privileges, ask for debating time. A trade-off is required. Alas, but it is so."

She didn't silence them for long. They came back clamorously.

"Yes, Ellice," said Archibald, the only man in the room who could say yes and mean no, "but that's ignoring the principle of a political base. Are we right or left? How do we vote? Who are our running partners? It looks tonight as though we've got a socialist government but you know our five members at Westminster aren't all Labour men. In fact, they're just about everything you could think of. So getting them to pull as a team is hard enough. Getting them to be a force at Westminster is asking for divine intervention."

"David slew Goliath."

"The trouble is, we need more sophisticated weaponry than sling or stones."

There was uproar. The smoke added to the heat and heaviness of the room. Leonie had the overwhelming impression of home, not a

165

place but a person: Fergus, who found these argumentative evenings quite pointless and sat, wherever he was, doing, doing something, with his hands or with his brain. Whisky and smoke and talk were indulgences he didn't have to forgive in himself.

Fergus was disappointed to find that Leonie had gone out that evening. It foreshadowed longer separations. He'd fitted in several business appointments during the course of the day, a building society, a surveyor, given instructions to a solicitor to make an offer for the property. He had wanted to talk it over with Leonie, but ate what she left and set to work again afterwards. Paragon Electronics considered that there was a place for a computer manual on the standard chess openings, a compilation which would appeal across the whole range of international chess play and, with that in mind, put him in touch with a New York publishing house. He was a quarter way there already with his systematic notation of classic games and variations, while his access to a computer bank made the documentation of them easy. He added some hours to his daily schedule on this vast work of collation and updating.

But Leonie came in earlier than he had expected, like a whirlwind.

She sat on his knee and kissed him fiercely, supplanting the papers that he worked from. He knew her in this febrile mood and indulged her, smoothing away their mutual frustrations with the outside world, political or personal, and they rocked together in exclusivity.

18

Moncrieffe spent a day in Dingwall thanking his supporters, renewing his pledges for the coming session and resting. It was a short rest, however, before the machinery started to roll again, like presses, churning out his daily effort. He stopped over for a day in Edinburgh on his way to Westminster and picked up the pieces there. Charlie, delayed because he had a tour of duty as Justice of the Peace at Fort William, was to join him later so that they could drive to London together for the start of the new Parliamentary session.

The mail filled a drawer in the desk of the morning room where his grandmother stored it. Frances Moncrieffe brought a tray of coffee and sat with him while he sorted his way through the bundles.

Saturday morning at Inveresk was a particular form of limbo. Watson made the house a staging post between the two more vital locations, his constituency and his place of work which were fixed by abode, the habitats he'd shaped himself or which had shaped him. For all that he had grown up at Inveresk, he felt that he was passing through. It was phasic rather than generic. This house was preserved, not functional, in its statement of antiquity, whereas Torrisaig which was an architectural scrapbook had a rumbustious kindness that shone through its inconsistencies. Sometimes he was afraid to tread too heavily here in case he damaged the irreplaceable. At Inveresk, he entered a time capsule of childhood as much as Regency.

Frances compounded this. Whenever Watson saw his grandmother, he was reminded of the Victorian injunction against ladies letting their back come into contact with the chair. She had a spine like a ramrod. Etiquette and the correctness of procedure were a brace holding her in position and reinforcing two powerful distinctions from the common run, her seniority and class. She was as proud of being eighty as of being Lady Moncrieffe, for she had proved empirically that you could survive democratising change intact. At the same time, she avoided the niggles of old age and didn't complain about the rising cost of living or recall when a pan loaf cost a penny ha'penny. She accepted inflationary spirals as evidence of the expanding middle class and kept as close a watch on her bills as on her deportment, holding both in line.

"I went to Carse a week ago," Watson said as he tore open his envelopes, the typed first, the handwritten second, A4 before A5. One of his chief pleasures was the game of guessing who his correspondent was before he opened the letter: usually a greater pleasure than the contents.

"Oh did you? And how is Sandy Govan?" Frances asked after an old favourite. He had to be impressed by her exact location of one name out of the vast calendar of his associates. His grandmother was still a shrewd observer.

"He's thriving, but it was quite thought-provoking to see how things have shaped. They think they've dropped out of the system, but all they've done is reconstruct a replica of it at Carse. They've got the prototype village there, a historical model of a pre-Clearance, pre-industrial village, with all the standard hierarchies and Sandy, even if he doesn't know it, is the head man. Literally. He's got the best brain. I find that quite remarkable. People ditch one form of government and replace it with something so damn close you wouldn't know the difference. They think they're making their own decisions but they're not. The decisions are being imposed on them by the weather and hard economics. The natural laws. And they're more inflexible than any man-made ones."

His grandmother nodded. "Are they actually destitute?"

"No, it's a different kind of poverty. Poverty of resources, I would say. A life without stimulus, like an unrelieved diet of oats and herring, wholesome but dull. Though that's the view of the city-dweller." He was distracted by the pouring of coffee, and drank a little before he resumed. "And Carse is a microcosm of the Highlands. Intelligent, dedicated, hard-working people not managing to make a go of it. I find that depressing. I don't know. I'm inspired by the fact that they go on trying, that anybody goes on trying to make his own way. Why should people be so dedicated to doing the difficult thing? But I can't bring myself to believe finally in anything unless it's successful. Unless it bears fruit.

Otherwise it seems theoretical, hot air and that's what's dispiriting, thinking so many worthy people have wasted their time."

Himself included. Himself most of all.

Frances grew impatient with her grandson's reflectiveness. "Free choice," she said crisply. "They were in command of their decisions at the time."

"Is anybody ever that?" he wondered.

Their dialogues habitually followed this pattern, he ample, she curt, and missed being conversation by almost half a century of attitude. Frances liked her men to be archetypally decisive and loathed the open-ended question. Her grandson was the most difficult of the Moncrieffe men, husband and two sons, and she put this down to the wayward influence of his mother who was not greatly concerned with a growing boy, and the consequence that Charlie had been let loose with him scallywagging. She was proud of Watson; they had many distinguished men along the line but no other democratically elected member of the House. But she was equally infuriated by his ambivalence. All questions had solutions in her day. Quod erat demonstrandum was his business.

The two were often at odds. Watson's upbringing had been irregular, partially adopted by uncle and grandmother while his parents spread themselves into the advocate life of Edinburgh, ticketed receptions to patronise the arts, sherry luncheons and claret-tasting sessions before the vintage port, a full social programme to imbibe. The grandmother had had more handling of the boy than the mother. She worried that she had inculcated too high a sense of destiny whereby the normal or the everyday failed to stimulate. She knew she made invidious comparisons; said he was like his grandfather, or the Lord Advocate, more often than he could endure especially when his memory of one was hazy and the other nil. It took him all his time to be himself, far less exceed his male forebears.

Watson resisted the matriarch in her. She didn't have the raw material for power which was people. The dwindling family meant a corresponding limit to her status although he knew others ascribed the two remarriages to her iron rule. In fact, both his mother and his wife had liked Frances Moncrieffe but modernity had amplified their rôles beyond either the domestic or the dynastic prototypes she happened to exemplify. She did not indulge, was neither fond nor fondling towards other people, having in general a higher regard for their ability than for their character. Attitudes were inflexible and she could seldom be persuaded on any subject.

Charlie arrived, having taken four hours cross-country from Fort William, and damned the road network that followed the contours of loch and mountain instead of going direct. On the car radio, he'd heard the latest results from the more scattered constituencies. "It's marvellous about your majority. And very deserved." He took the coffee that his mother passed him. "But how do you think it's going to fall out? It's looking very tight for the Conservatives."

"I just don't know. Cadogan is out, that's for sure. But is Fleming in?"

"What's left to come? Northern Ireland. That'll make no material difference to the outcome. So Labour's the largest party?"

"But with an overall majority of only six."

"Can Fleming form a government on that?"

"He can try. But honestly, it makes me smile when advocates of the first-past-the-post system decry PR by saying it leads to a hung Parliament. What will this be but a hung Parliament, and with years of scrabbling around making pacts and wooing minorities."

"Including Independents?"

"Heaven help the country that has to come down to one vote, even if it is mine."

"Whose rather than yours?"

"Nobody's. No one individual has the right to decide on issues of national importance. What's a law worth that's voted in by one? You know you've seen legislation rail-roaded through Parliament that turns out to be unworkable in the courts." He waited for reluctant agreement from the JP and demanded the answer when it didn't come. "Haven't you?"

"Well, yes," agreed his lordship, who'd seen some appalling bills pass into acts. "Not criminal law. That changes surprisingly little. But certainly trade union law is unenforceable in some cases."

"The law's becoming the scapegoat of our unbalanced political system. A party with a majority can put measures on the statute book that encourage its own access to power because they please its adherents. Now I think that's the end, when the law is brought into disrepute by being nothing better than the tool of one faction against the other. Bad law is worse than any other form of badness, because it encourages defiance of all legislative procedure."

Charlie Moncrieffe was a practical man, skilful and hard-headed. He didn't philosophise but worked with the tools someone else put in his hand. He found conversation on political theory with his nephew unsettling, like a miner at the work face who talks to an engineer in nuclear fuel in terms of megatons. The scale staggered him and made continuation on the small and the manual almost impossible. Neither the message his nephew postulated, nor his eccentric means of transmission – the voice crying in the wilderness – fell within the scope of his normality and he was troubled by the obsessional. "A free election, anyway, and that's not easily overturned."

Watson went on opening the envelopes which came to hand. There was a backlog of material forwarded from Westminster by his secretary. Some of it had been chasing him up and down the country for weeks, frightful dull stuff too. Requests for him to speak at dinners, seed catalogues, in among personal notes from Edinburgh friends warm on his renewal of contract and a letter from a lady admirer who enclosed a photograph of herself for his approval. It might have met with greater success if she had left her clothes on.

He worked his way down the stack, systematically throwing the envelope and the wastage in the basket and forming a pile of those that required an answer. It was a daily chore, swollen by three weeks' absence from it. And then he almost fell out of his chair in surprise. In his hand was a sheet with the words, 'My Congratulations. Leonie' on it.

So she wasn't wholly indifferent to his existence after all. She had taken note of his progress and he was flushed with gratitude at this personal commendation of his efforts. He *had* won. He had triumphed after all.

When the surprise faded, he peered at the sheet of paper and recognised it consciously, while realising that one part of his initial shock had lain in someone writing to him on his own notepaper. The Inveresk notepaper returned home. Looking more closely at it, he could read its age. There was a change in the printing of the

171

telephone code for the area since this batch came from the stationer's. It was a ten-year anachronism and enabled him to reconstruct her offence. So that was all she'd taken from his room. One sheet of paper. It kept its original creases, slightly off the square as if she'd folded it in a hurry to avoid the eye of the steward in the room. How had she hidden it? Where did girls of fifteen hide a thing like that? A billet doux. In the bodice of her dress possibly, an intimate seclusion.

And he had actually been angry with her when she confessed the theft, thinking she'd lifted one of the miniatures his grandmother prized. What had Leonie said to him? 'I will return it with interest.' This interest was a bonus then, a compound sum accreted over many years. Every stroke of her pen was a matter of intrigue. The lack of a date, the omission of her own address superimposed on Inveresk which read as hers by adoption. Where did she live now that she was married? Why only Leonie? It denied surnames of any kind and was familiar in the signature of friend. The document fascinated him. He would have scratched the surface of the paper if it could have told him more.

Then, when he'd drained the page of its invisible messages, he remembered the envelope and picked it back out of the basket. Well, that reverted to formality. The Hon Watson Moncrieffe MP. Not many people called themselves 'The Honourable' these days and he could hear her voice in its characteristic banter, teasing him with titles which might be due but not deserved.

His grandmother came past the window, carrying a sprig of herbs rescued before the frost. He noticed something about her that was so distinctive, he wondered how he'd never seen it before. She dressed to match the season, not tweed versus voile, but in colour harmonies. She wore the same kind of clothes all year round, a fine wool in which she was neither hot nor cold, a teagown long out of fashion but perpetuated in a style that became her own. Always with a base of cream, pastels in the spring, a plummy autumn, she came and went like perennials that picked their way between the brash and the drab. A lady. Ladylike was her predominant tone.

He longed for woman, for the gracious to descend in his own life. He underestimated the dowager, or didn't love her according to her deserts. He would compliment the dress and be less boorish over lunch, noticing the herbs she added to the sauce.

19

Now that she was cast in the rôle of mother, Leonie looked round for some hints on how she ought to play the part. She knew her own upbringing was abnormal and thought it wise not to take that as a model. But whose was the perfect performance? Certainly not the Petrie version of child raising. It would be hard to imagine five blood relations who had less in common, physically or temperamentally, apart from a common height and handsomeness. Like the five fragmented states of the British Isles, they were similar only where they were contiguous, but were at their most bitter along precisely those borders, scoring deep dividing lines of territory. On the other hand, was the peaceable Irene Geddes so very successful with her son? Harmony reigned because there was absolute deference to the household god, the professor. Matthew didn't look an entirely happy man in competition.

Leonie thought there might be some advantage after all in being an amoeba. She often felt she had divided from the cells of her mother, or was the product of encephalogenesis, the brain child as much as the body child. The genetic system of fission did at least preclude argument. No one individual had to defer to any other and the offspring was at once the equal of the parent. Uncommonly, Ellice had the requisite balance of male and female in her own personality to be an ideal parent, singular. Discipline and indulgence, the father and mother of character formation, were matched in equal proportions. Leonie hadn't missed out on either. Or she was the offspring of community, people coming and going in an unstoppable variety. That could provide its own social patterning.

In Leonie's case all the rules of good parenthood had been broken. The domestic system was breached daily in favour of a higher regimen. Food, sleep and even cleanliness gave way to elections, by-elections, public meetings and rallies which Leonie attended almost from infancy. In a world of serious-minded adults, she didn't dare to over-demonstrate the child and quickly learned silence and invisibility, entertaining herself through long periods of boredom by developing the habit of internal monologue and its source material, observation.

One of the strongest caveats of her childhood, however, had been against 'telling stories'. It was twenty years on before she realised that the Scots idiom fused two meanings which were distinct in English. To tell a story was to lie. A story-teller in Scotland was a liar and was castigated as much as the hated bearer of tales, the clipe, the northern equivalent of the nosey parker, the type Orwell rightly pinpointed as the one nobody would admit to being. Ellice dismissed the entire canon of literature with the words, 'Whoever would want to *make up* stories, or to listen to them? Give me a good history book every time.' That was the other taboo. Make up was a falsification and anathema to the exact chronologist.

In Leonie's childhood, there was history in plenty. History came leafletting too. Round the uneventful streets of Morningside, Ellice recounted the terrible and dramatic history of Scotland, fighting off invasion by the Roman legions, by the Vikings who were confined to the islands, by the more persistent English, though in the end the noble and freedom-loving country was subjugated to its neighbour through the stupidity of a woman who couldn't marry the right man and so safeguard her own or her nation's independence in crown or Parliament. Ellice Barr had as little good to say of Mary Queen of Scotland as John Knox did. History was stacked against the Scots in Ellice's version. Weak rulers and their unemancipated consorts. One king after another was a pernicious fool and either fell over a cliff like Alexander III or lost a strategic battle like James V or handed over power to his unruly knights, putting his ranks in disarray so that England only had to capture the skittish queen to prevail. Sovereignty was gone.

The didactic was so strong in these lessons it drove out the colouring of the frivolous, or the fictitious. History was morality or religion, and was not to be tampered with. Ellice Barr condemned the popular Scottish writers, Stevenson and Scott, for meddling with the facts in their historical romances. She endorsed only some non-amorous poetry by the Ettrick shepherd and the sober Burns of 'The Cotter's Saturday Night'. The nearest Ellice came to

174

imaginative speculation was, 'What would have happened to British politics if Beatrice Potter had married Joseph Chamberlain instead of Sidney Webb?' This was her variant on an inch on Cleopatra's nose, and as inconclusive except that it proved nineteenth-century politicians were as foolish as Roman generals when it came to judging the quality of women.

Leonie had to reconstruct the imaginative or creative aspect of language for herself and started on the self-indoctrination as soon as she could read. Ellice found a much-worn copy of Arthur Mee's *Children's Encyclopaedia* and put it in her hands, assuming the girl would absorb some of the facts, however outdated or over-simplified, which it contained. Covertly, the child turned to *Aesop's Fables* and the stories of Alice or the water babies, the outlines of Bunyan, Shakespeare or Harriet Beecher Stowe, history only incidentally. They might be bald in précis, but characters came tumbling out of them providing companions who were better than contemporaries. Leonie expanded the thin narrative of the text with playlets in which the major flaw was the necessity of speaking all the parts herself.

Harris, who was attached to his sister-in-law, often came to see her and, after the election, brought Matthew Geddes over the lunch hour when they escaped from the office building of the Mercantile Company where they both worked, at different levels of responsibility. Matthew, after his degree in Economics at Oxford, was being groomed for an area he termed 'middle management'. Harris, who had no patience with examinations, was restricted to the clerical but they renewed their old affinity of defiance. Over- or under-qualified, they were both impatient with bonds, equities, unit trusts, dividends, pension plans, endowment mortgages and the whole caboodle of investment financing, mainly because they were denied a share of its profits. They lived for lunch hours and escape.

They descended on Canaan Lane in hilarity one day about noon with Alison in the back of Harris' car. "We're meant to be doing a job, Leonie. A dull old audit but we said we're going out on site. Which we are. But not the site they think. It's the last race meeting at Musselburgh. Will you come?"

"You're a bad influence, Harris."

175

"I know. Come and keep us good."

The sun came out. The flat was void; Fergus wouldn't be home till six. The enticement was too much. She sat in the front with Harris while the lovers held hands, doe-eyed in the back. How long was it, thought Leonie. Easter they met. Surely by October they were beyond holding hands in public. Harris drove through the village settlements of Midlothian, past the miners' rows and fishermen's cottages which made up the economic landscape until they touched the sea line at Musselburgh and turned east across the market square.

Harris knew his way round the race course and parked under a tree where the car would stay cool throughout the afternoon. He had an excess of nervous energy, Harris, and kept as long and eccentric hours as Leonie but seemed driven without purpose. The excitement of the race meeting focused him. He bought programmes for them which outlined the pedigree of the horses entered for the six races of the afternoon and then fell into a trance with his own copy, marking cryptic codes down the margin. He checked his watch against the clock beside the grandstand for the time when starting prices would firm. He brought his party closer to the paddock rails so that he could get his own impression of the condition of the horses, but once he'd settled them in one spot, he wandered off alone through the crowd without an explanation, but clearly visible even from a distance.

Leonie looked at the layout of her programme mystified.

"That's the name of the race, if it applies," Matthew explained, running his finger down the details. "Then the age of the horses. Two-year-olds in the first race. That's the length it's run over, seven, eight furlongs, whatever. Then the prize money, for the owner that is. The three o'clock is the wealthiest race which is why it's attracted the biggest field."

"How very organised."

"It has to be. This is a full-time occupation for some people, Harris included. Haven't you been to a race course before?"

"Goodness no. What would Ellice think of this? Not a good spot for pamphletting round here. All I know about horse racing is that Emily Davison was killed by the king's horse at the Derby."

Matthew looked about him at the spectators who were a strange cross-section. It wasn't Epsom or Newmarket but there were

176

people who in England would be called the county set, people who knew about horses, owned, trained or rode them to a meet. The leisurely aristocrats. Women in brogues, men with shooting sticks who came prepared to make a serious study of the business of horse flesh. At the other extreme was a motley selection of people who'd been worn down to the rims, usually men, usually middle-aged. They were the addictive gamblers, strained, living between the minutes of the clock, cautious with their energy as they went from the bookmakers to the tote, with minds like mathematicians when it came to calculating the odds, the chances of return on accumulator totals which they hardly ever reached. They were people who survived on marginal results, compelled to think the next race would be release from the losing averages weighted against them. And these were the more sanguine of the compulsive gamblers. The frayed ends didn't come in person but hung around the bookies' shops or phoned their bets in and watched the television screen for the result at home. Hooked, inescapably hooked. But in between was a swell of jolly folk out for the day, as jauntily as if it were the shows six miles along the road at Longniddry, or the Tattoo, or the dogs at Powderhall. Somewhere to go for a bit of fun, a bit of the action.

Harris came back breezily. He'd discovered Stuart Ainslie in the crowd and brought him along to join them. The director greeted them with nonchalance. "Throwing Fergus' money away, Leonie?"

"I've none to throw."

"The property market's more lucrative?"

Strange, thought Leonie. One turn of luck made them enviable.

"You will bet, though? It's a dull afternoon watching other people's horses win," said her brother-in-law.

"Haz has come back with some hot tips from the jockeys' changing rooms you can use," said Stuart Ainslie.

"A friend of mine lets me in on what's happening," said Harris modestly and they each fell to marking out their favourites.

"What's all this about 'Haz'?" asked Leonie in private.

"Snappy, isn't it? An improvement."

"I don't think there's much wrong with 'Harris' actually."

He pulled a long face. "A bit trad. Like tweed."

"But it suits the climate."

177

The prices were on the move, jostling ahead of the starter's orders for prime place. The ticker men signalled from the stands down to the bookmakers' stall in the enclosure, in the indecipherable codes of fingers, elbows, tapping rhythm.

"What do they mean by the tote?" Leonie asked.

"The totaliser. It's an official betting office run by the course. Their prices tend not to be as keen as some of the freelance bookies."

"And the first three earn a dividend?"

"A proportionate win for second and third place."

Better than elections.

"And what's an accumulator total?"

"A roll-up." Harris knew all the percentages. "You go for first place on every race and if all six win you're into a grand."

"A grand what?"

"Good God, Leonie. You may be a dab hand at Shakespeare but how about giving the twentieth century a try? A thousand pounds."

"I thought you meant a grand draw of some kind. I fancy a thousand pounds."

"Tell me who doesn't. The chances are minute. Several thousand to one against. But go for it if you want. In at the deep end."

They chose their horses according to their different systems of decision. Harris relied on his inside information, which he confirmed by the fitness of each horse when it paraded in the paddock. Stuart backed hunches, and often theatrical ones. "Pygmalion. We'll have that," irrespective of whether the horse was three parts lame or not. Matthew was a man for form and studied the pedigree details which were printed on the programme beside the record of wins over the season, and paid meticulous attention to blinkers, the number drawn, jockey and trainer. He had theories for all these incidences which he didn't disclose, being superstitious about luck and wishes. Alison used the pin method after an excruciating debate with herself and anyone else who would listen. Leonie stuck with her accumulator and put five pounds on six horses which were selected not quite at random, but through an intuitive maze that derived an element from all the other systems.

"It's not your sort of thing, surely, all this lottery," Stuart

178

challenged Alison. "It's a far cry from Aldermaston. Or are you slumming deliberately to pick up some humanitarian tips? You want to be careful, Allie, it'll be soup kitchens next."

"Don't call me Allie," she replied with hauteur, but couldn't establish in principle why she'd missed a day at classes, or was shy of saying it was simply to be with Matthew.

"Lend me your binoculars, will you, Stuart?" said Leonie, drawing his fire.

"You can't see even through binoculars, can you?" Stuart was often amused at Leonie's groping across the stage in the vague direction of a door or chair.

"True, but the colour's better."

Through the lenses, the jockeys wore a quite distinctive emblazonment that owed something to the ancient shapes of heraldry; lozenge and stripe and parti-colour patterns were sharp against the field. The horses were restive at the starting line. Horses? That was too mundane. More like steeds, man and mount were chevaliers or realigned in a new biological form like the fabulous centaur. Leonie hadn't seen horses close up and understood how the mistake could have come about. The intelligence of the man and the physique of the animal were such an exact complement that they appeared inseparable. Leonie agreed with Harris that you should look for evidence of partnership before you backed the combination, and regretted her hasty, uninformed selection.

Stuart enjoyed this spectacle but had no overwhelming desire to participate in it. He came when theatreless afternoons were empty. He was pleased to latch on to the young people because they added character to the background of the running, giving him problems to solve. Why did the beautiful Alison attach herself to such anaemic young men? Following the siring of horses so solemnly like a court genealogist! A nit-picker if ever he saw one. Why did brother and sister go on seeing Leonie when they didn't fraternise publicly with the third sibling? And what, above all, what would the absent Fergus say about this expedition? A fiver on a horse? He would blanch as much as Ellice Barr at the wastrel and the prodigal elements in spendthrift. These were mysteries of the living text he tried to elucidate as he went along, not thinking to resolve them but to make more dramatic clashes in production.

179

Leonie and Harris won the first race, black on red. Matthew came second. Leonie didn't collect but carried forward more than thirty pounds to the next race, while Harris' sum went undisclosed but was enough to make him withdrawn, juggling how much he could afford to put on his second horse. "I'll go for a place," he judged eventually.

"Well," said Stuart, looking glumly at his programme. "Our systems don't seem to be so patent, Alison. Should we pool our resources? Matthew here is the academic, so maybe you and I should take a leaf out of his book. Show me how you work out the pedigree again."

Matthew launched into sire and mare and stud, the copulatory conventions allowable in horses, while Stuart po-faced, interposed, "You don't say," from time to time.

Alison took it as gospel.

"So what will your colours be this time, Alison? Capricious? Sporting colours white and gold. Argent and or. Fair enough when it's going to cost us a packet. I'll follow your lead. Let me escort you to the bookmaker," he said chivalrously and drew her arm through his.

"Why does he fool about like that?" asked Harris as they disappeared and Matthew went along by the other arm.

"He fancies her," said Leonie.

"Fancies Alison? Does he really?"

"I reckon so. He's always twice the idiot with her. Same thing."

"Come a bit late to the starting gate, hasn't he?"

Leonie turned to equestrian races.

Stuart didn't win throughout the afternoon but became more and more impetuous in his losses, not caring if the money in his pocket were frittered away when it brought out a laugh or Alison's solicitude. She put her hand on his arm to advise against more desperate hazard and gave him worse palpitations. Matthew found that pedigree was a poor index of performance. Repeatedly, he came second and often gained less on short odds than his stake, which wasn't excessive. Alison came nowhere. But Leonie and Harris entered a secondary concourse of which of them would win more. By the last race Leonie, with beginners' luck, had won each time and almost four hundred pounds stood on a horse which she'd chosen blind, a three-year-old chestnut called Castle Rock, quoted favourite at two to one. The win of eight hundred pounds plus her stake was a sum so astronomical in her reckoning that rolling dice with it was a fickleness she'd not been able to indulge in before. She wasn't a gambler, however, and would as soon have had the five pound note back in her pocket than risk it all again. But she was in for it now. The parable of the talents came to mind, demonstrating that the Biblical talent was a coin to be invested somehow and made to yield a profit. She wanted that money. She wanted the win, not for the cash only but because losing was so paltry. Its scale added frenzy to the outing. Success would make it a famous afternoon. Harris had been more moderate. He'd won something on every race, hedging, laying off, and by the last race was fifty pounds up on the day. He liked a palomino called Cheyenne, a flamboyant name to go with frisky looks that caught his eye. It was a horse with a nervous temperament, easily distracted and a handful for his jockey, but ridden hard had the constitution of a champion. Harris decided to put fifty pounds on it for a win. Five to one, not spectacular odds, but it had been a lucky afternoon.

The field of ten started to mass towards the line. Stuart and Alison went for Elsinore, Matthew thought Castle Rock was reliable stock, but settled for a place. The field bunched at the beginning and from where the five of them stood it was imposs-ible, with the distance and foreshortening, to pick out the leader. The colours merged. It lowered the tension when the field passed round the far side of the course beside the shore and they didn't have to try and pick between them. At the final bend it was still neck and neck. Their three horses were straining every muscle towards the finishing line, running in close formation. But on the rails a fourth horse made vast strides so that it was all decided in the last furlong. In one sense they wanted any of themselves to win so long as it squeezed the outsider who came up so rapidly from nowhere, cutting in.

The leaders passed under their eyes. They were larger than other horses because more was staked on them. They thundered on the ground as they went by, and the harness, bit, rein, saddle, stirrup were one continuous noise of creaking leather, striking metal mixed with a heavy snorting through the enlarged nostrils of the beasts. And a rush of air like contusion, leaving the onlookers stunned. Killing animals close up, dangerous metal hooves, teeth in a snarl. The charger and the carthorse were implicit behind the raceground thoroughbred, pounding the earth.

"Are you all right, Leonie?" Stuart asked. "You're very white."

"It's too much money really."

"It's only money," he said, "and you haven't had to work for it."

"It feels harder than work."

The finishing post was a hundred yards ahead of their position and the buzz which was let loose at other finishes, as the signal of victory, was stemmed by an inconclusive outcome. The also-rans straggled home indifferently. Over the tannoy system, the marshal relayed that there was a photo finish. Only a hair in it. The judges' decision would be announced shortly. Then a few moments later another broadcast explained to the impatient crowd, who were anxious to pick up their winnings and be off, that a stewards' inquiry had been called on whether there had been deliberate barging, but the horse accused of this offence was unnamed, so each of the five wondered if their potential win was to be frustrated after all by a technical infringement.

Leonie did feel sick during this wait for the result and swore she would never gamble again. Faintness, a sense of draining into the hands and feet, nausea at having been caught in the traps of chance; she could see why people became addicted to the pumping adrenalin of lotteries, a self-induced narcosis.

The result came through at last. Elsinore who had been first past the post was disqualified. Stuart and Alison were denied their one win, but the director found this a triumphant failure. "It was a brilliant win, Alison, make no mistake. And we were cheated. Yes, we were cheated in the end."

The outsider came first by default, and Castle Rock was second so that Leonie had failed to achieve her accumulated total by one place. Harris came third on Cheyenne but having gone for the win, forfeited his fifty pounds. The only winner was Matthew who was cautiously placed on Castle Rock, a fully covered insurer. So he came out on top overall, in spite of the predictors.

Harris tore up his betting slip disconsolately. "I should have been more chary," he said. "And you should have gone for a three-way accumulator. Ah well. Live and learn and all that tiresome

182

stuff." He walked from the enclosure beside his sister-in-law, compressed by the crowds who were massing towards the car park. "Can you lend me a fiver, Leonie?"

"A fiver? What for?"

"I'm broke."

"Well, so am I. I've just lost one fiver and I don't want to throw another one away."

"I'll pay you back," he assured.

"Yes but when?" she wanted to know. "And how?" They were both demonstrating an inability to hold on to five pounds for more than a corresponding number of minutes.

More oddly perhaps, Alison said secretively to her as they dropped her off at Canaan Lane, "You won't tell, will you?"

"No," Leonie assured. "I won't tell."

These two questions rolled around in her head, attracting different answers from the ones she'd actually given. What was Harris doing putting on bets of fifty pounds when he could barely pay for the petrol home? How could five pounds be of such urgency when fifty didn't matter? And who was it that Leonie was not to tell about the afternoon escapade? Muriel? Fergus? Professor and Mrs Geddes? Or was it Matthew's presence that was the prohibition? You may say where I went but not who I was with. Any or all of the putative answers were possible. Strange people, to be so inhibited about their legitimate business.

20

Telling became unavoidable. As luck would have it, Fergus had come back early that afternoon meaning to keep Leonie company. With his full membership of the department established, he had his own terminal linked up to the IBM mainframe in George Square and could work directly from the computer at home. He was sitting at this keyboard and studying the print-out record of his work when Leonie came back towards seven.

She put her arms round him with pleasure; his the face she knew and trusted most.

"Where have you been?"

It was the easiest thing to say she'd been with her mother, or to a studio recording, when he wouldn't be inquisitive enough to ask the follow-up. But she told the truth. "Harris came by at lunch time in the car with Alison and Matthew Geddes. They were going to the Musselburgh races and I went with them. We met Stuart later on."

Fergus thought for a moment. "Stuart Ainslie, was that? Well, I thought Matthew Geddes would have had more sense."

This remark, which excluded her and her professional friend from rationality, triggered the unease which she felt about many aspects of the expedition. "A harmless enough pursuit, Fergus. We just put in an afternoon."

He sat back in his armchair and turned his head to her with great deliberateness. "You're quite mistaken, you know. Lottery is a very harmful pursuit and I'm scandalised that you can go to something like that and then say blandly it's only entertainment. Do stop and think what you're doing, Leonie. I distrust the money that isn't honestly earned. And I distrust the belief gamblers have that winning money will solve the problems that drove them to gambling in the first place. I'm afraid of it. Speculation. It's all speculation."

These speeches terrified her, prophetic and Biblical in delivery, like the rod of Moses which turned into a snake and back again. His words writhed and were still, demonstrating the power of faith. She felt scourged by his indictment of human fallibility. "Yes I know. I understand. I'm not condoning gambling on the large scale, or on any scale but I meant it's possible to go there without meaning harm. It *is* an experience, Fergus. Surely a taste of any experience is valuable."

She walked round the table where he worked, his lecture notes strictly segregated from the personal files, the chess programmes which he went on improving step by step in line with the manual he was preparing. Foreseeing that he would have less time in the future if he had care of the child, he adjusted his output to meet his publication deadlines.

"That's a fallacy. You don't need to experience a horse race to realise how harmful it is. Your mind ought to tell you that much. People's lives have been destroyed by as little as that, the fall of the dice or the turn of a card. It's not a game, Leonie. It's mental and spiritual erosion."

Remembering the finger-bitten men who hung around the bookies' stands, Leonie utterly agreed with him, but his premises were like her mother's, so incontrovertible that she looked for the loophole almost for the sake of variety, so that the world was not monotone. It seemed that all her life she had been testing the immaculate hypotheses they handed down to her, like tabernacles from the mount. She repeatedly found the weakness in the application of these tablets, though they were both so trenchant in their attitudes that they implied it wasn't the law, whether moral or spiritual or natural, that was endangered by her transgression of it. Its inviolability remained intact. All she had proved was that she could not perform to its expectations. Her failure was a measure of its strength, and so the exception went on proving the rule. She tried to live up to their absolute and exclusive standards and continually fell short. Her marriage did not meet her mother's requirements. Her politics were reviled by her husband. They both despised the trivialising play, laughs and stories without a moral aim. Woe betide the Cavalier caught between two sermonising Roundheads. It was a form of civil war.

"I knew that before I went, Fergus, and I know it better now."

He took this as admission of guilt, or penitence, and accepted.

"You didn't bet?"

"Well, yes I did." She decided to be scrupulous. "I lost five pounds."

"This is irresponsible," he judged. He put his hand to his back pocket and pulled out a wallet which he had had as a schoolboy to show his bus pass. Many hands had mended its leather sections, his own included. He took out another five pound note and put it on the desk near where she stood. "Here. You need money to spend."

She didn't know whether the gesture was magnanimous or humiliating. Forgiveness or blame, both implied his was the higher authority, so she didn't pick the bill up but looked at it for a very long time. "I have my own money," she said. "I don't need you to pay my debts."

"As you please." He too left the note in the open.

"Have you eaten?" she asked.

"Yes. I waited until six."

Their timing missed by fractions. She went to the kitchenette and made a snack of bread and cheese which she ate from her lap as he watched.

"You should be eating more, you know."

In the atmosphere of disapproval, his solicitude went astray. Leonie was convinced he cared not so much about the woman as about the carrier of his child.

"I know, but I don't feel like eating." The fine distinction between concentrated knowledge and expansive feeling was one only a skilled speaker could make. Her voice descended scathingly on knowledge.

"More protein, nutrients."

"For heaven's sake, Fergus, don't henpeck me."

"You look tired, that's all."

"No, I'm not tired. I'm frayed. I miss work," she admitted. "Work is the escape. I can't wait to get back to it. It's easier for you, Fergus. You take your occupation with you wherever you go, but mine is on location. I should have been the man. I really should." The moment she said it, she realised how such a proposition would infuriate him. Unworkable. Delete. She *was* a woman, or at best was one in the majority. Hoping to avoid a reproof for this idle remark, she said, "Harris and Alison seem well. Though Harris has started to describe himself in abbreviation. Haz Petrie. I ask you."

"Do you see them often?"

"Alison less so now that Matthew's on the scene, but we meet fairly frequently at Ellice's. Harris comes here maybe once a week."

"But always when I'm absent."

"That's coincidence. He comes over the lunch hour."

Fergus moved and switched off the terminal, then carefully bent down and unplugged it from the electricity supply. Yes, he thought, his stamp collection went to fund a spree at horse racing. "I'd rather you didn't see them if you can avoid it. If you meet them accidentally, that's fine, but don't go out of your way to encourage them."

Leonie listened in astonishment. She went on seeing his brother and sister partly to reinstate normality in their dealings, but mostly because she liked them and counted them genuinely among her friends. Maddening at times. Imperious with their own interests, but who wasn't? And they were his relations she tried to cultivate, a duty surely among these so-called families. "You speak for yourself when it comes to that, Fergus, but you will never speak for me."

"I realise I was asking as a favour, not a right."

His seriousness took her breath away. He actually meant it. Leonie felt an anger which was beyond reason, an anger based on instinct. Who was denied at her mother's door? If Cadogan or Fleming had pitched up at Morningside, she'd have given them a whisky and a chair like anybody else. No better, but no worse. She did not insult with exclusions which were petty. If there was to be an argument on dialectic, it would be an open one, a grand, glorious scrap – not this hateful and hating secrecy.

"You make yourself into too much of a recluse, Fergus. You're becoming disconnected from reality. You don't speak to your mother and you refuse to see mine. The causes are past," she held up her hand to warn against the circuitous discussion of why he was impeccably in the right. "And now you want to go on with a vendetta against Harris and Alison. Where's the sense? And who will we see if you carry on like this? I can assure you that when I live at the Hermitage, I won't be holding coffee mornings with Irene

187

Geddes or anyone else you deem to be a suitable or safe companion. You won't make my friends for me, Fergus, or unmake them."

Fergus heard the rising note of passion in her voice and, behind it, implied criticism of his stance. He didn't feel comfortable with the strong feelings inherent in her choice of words, recluse, vendetta, which brought with them overtones of his mother and a constriction in his own emotion if not in his thinking. "These histrionics are uncalled for."

Leonie was indignant. She knew how to give vent all right. She could be spectacularly violent if she chose, a Cleopatra tearing her hair, her clothes, her opponents into shreds, but he had unwittingly defused the theatricality of such an outburst with his comment. For the first time in seven years she had the specific urge to walk away from him, to walk out. The problem was, where did she go? She was worn out after a day standing on her feet at the races. She wasn't going to walk round the streets of Morningside for the fun of it. The only person she might confide in, her mother, would solace her with nothing more comforting than 'I told you so' and dismiss these disagreements as inevitable once you let yourself in for marriage. So she sat on in her chair and stifled an emotive scream.

"Let's not trade insults, Fergus. There's no point."

"My experience isn't yours," he replied. "You can't know how I feel about the trial and the sentence and everything that went on before it. How can I see any of them, Leonie, when no one ever goes to see Michael in prison? Think of what it would mean to him if somebody made the effort. I really can't excuse that. You go. I go. What's the matter with his other children? Their treatment of Michael is so callous. Whatever the power is that Muriel manages to exert over them and I think it's moral, or amoral, as much as monetary, it's basically stupid not to decide the issue for themselves." He hesitated, calm and controlled among the ill-arranged feelings. He wasn't inclined to calumniate needlessly, but thought that to explain and justify his own position he must produce the theft of the sheet of stamps. So he explained how Harris, meeting some urgent need, had stooped to pilfering from his own brother.

Leonie, who wasn't normally perceptive about material objects, looked up from her easy chair and saw the space the stamp albums used to occupy. "What happened to the rest of the collection?"

"I burned it."

"You burned it? All?"

"Yes. I was so disgusted that he would steal from me. It was a rash act."

"I'll say it was." She was half-admiring. "But Fergus, it was so valuable."

"Not really. Only sentimental value."

That was enough. Her eye caught the five pound note. And he had the effrontery to upbraid her for waste! "Have you talked to Harris about it?" She reconstructed the incident with ease, and his omissions in the narrative.

"No. I said nothing."

"Then you don't know for sure he did it. That's judging without evidence."

"The sheet had gone. That was conclusive. And I know he's guilty. He hasn't come to see me since."

"Circumstantial."

He shook his head, not to be gainsaid.

"Well, I am surprised at you, Fergus. You should have challenged him as soon as you noticed it was missing but you went and destroyed your own proof by burning the books. You should have nailed him. Made him pay you back if that's what you wanted. But the incident's entirely hypothetical. You've no evidence and he would deny it now. But to go on punishing him, or yourself, on the grounds of such feeble suspicion, is ridiculous. You criticise Harris and Alison for taking someone else's word instead of trusting to their own judgment, but you've done exactly the same. Prejudice. That's all."

This was Leonie's hold over him. She was remorseless in her way and her skill in placing him in the focus of her own logic was chastising. That she brought a quality of imaginative colour to deductive thinking wasn't lost on him. He saw his own faults very clearly when she brought them to light. "Yes, that was incompetent. I over-reacted."

At the same time, she couldn't escape the memory of her identical theft, even if she had made a recent reparation. She rounded it down, of course, to the lesser offence of misappropriation, a borrowing only. Fergus's reaction resurrected Moncrieffe.

189

He'd been equally angry at being the victim of theft, but less extreme. She couldn't imagine the politician putting a match to anything, because he was secure. Whatever he was deprived of in success or goods or affection, he had the vast infrastructure of position and class to bolster him. This wasn't simply a buffer but a source of example. What he did was right because that was what his people did. To Fergus who made his own way, singular and unaided, each check was a huge reversal. He elevated himself mentally, but was quite simplistic in many of his social attitudes because he was his own pattern-setter and had no stronger influence than self to fall back on.

Although she understood his reasons, it was impossible for her to confess the theft of the sheet of writing paper. Realising that, she had an insight into how much she didn't tell him. Not about Alison's curious debunking to Oxford, or her initial fears about Matthew Geddes. That Harris had unsettling elements in his character, not least immaturity, wasn't an easy subject to broach, too close to home. A large segment of interaction was shut off between them.

He appeared to follow this contour by his reply. "I can't change, Leonie. It goes too deep. But you must do as you think fit. Whoever you choose to see is your affair. I think, on the whole, I don't want to know about it."

She nodded, relieved that they had reached a compromise without an open quarrel.

When she had gone to bed, Fergus sat for a while mulling over her advice. He found an old account book, ruled in columns, and headed a page with 'Harris Petrie'. With the assistance of his diary, he entered two dates and added 'Last visit by H' against one and 'Sheet of stamps missing. Destroyed the remainder' by the other. He started on a register of his fraternal dealings.

21

Fleming caught up with Moncrieffe as they left the chamber and they walked along the inner corridor side by side. "Have you got a minute?" asked the older man. "Right. We'll go to my room."

Moncrieffe didn't resist the oblique invitation to an audience. Fleming was the third Prime Minister during his tenure at Westminster, and the most able. His background was surprisingly like Moncrieffe's own, which was common énough in Parliament where Oxford and the law and some political affiliation in the family were the standard entrée. Fleming's family was an ancient one and his great-grandfather had been a distinguished Liberal cabinet minister, a fact he didn't over-advertise. Although they lost their title at the end of the nineteenth century, they had hung on to their estate. Fleming himself counted it good fortune to be born into a family of younger sons, out of the line of succession, so that he wasn't compelled to forfeit a title on either ideological or practical grounds, to further his career in the Labour party. He was an Anglo-Scot, with an emphasis on the prefix and he looked on Scotland more distantly than Moncrieffe as 'the old country'. His sympathies were grounded in history rather than the present and he was a summer visitor only.

He had replaced his predecessor almost three years earlier, half way through Cadogan's Tory administration, a wise move by the party managers since he'd brought the Labour party into government and avoided two successive electoral defeats. He had sloughed the aura of failure, but sustaining a daily Parliamentary majority was proving harder than winning a one-off election. Cadogan, a baying Conservative if ever there was one, who sported his county tie of Warwickshire with bears and bear-baiting in unintentional self-parody, had been an indifferent Prime Minister. His man-management was poor. He had no social ease, no oratorical power and no charisma, the indefinable attraction to self which boosted a man once he'd worked his way into a position of authority, so although he got to power it was impossible to stay there. In opposition, Cadogan was proving to be another man altogether, or his assets counted for more, wily, shrewd with Commons tactics, an excellent harrier and blocker. He was fighting for his own political credibility. After one session, Fleming was exhausted by the snapping at his heels and found himself a Gulliver, continually brought down by littleness. He didn't have an adequate working majority, that was the trouble, which was tantamount to running a business that was under-capitalised. Without reverses, he eked by. One major set-back and he was finished.

There had been plenty of reverses, even in the short life of this Parliament. The Liberals came his way, but only with daily persuasion. The splits within the thirty-strong group were deeper in spite of being narrower. He was inclined to offer the Liberal leader a ministerial position to seal his loyalty, but the grass roots were against such an open affiliation. At best, Fleming rocked on a fulcrum of half a dozen votes, and the internal balance of his own party was far from secure. His back-benchers were a frisky bunch, left or left-haters on the outer flanks. He was often reliant on the backing of the five Scottish Nationalists and their votes were only to be had if he promised Parliamentary time for the discussion of the devolution issue. With an extensive socialist programme promised in his manifesto, he had little time left for this, apart from disinclination. He felt himself beleaguered like Agricola by the pestilential Scots. Yes, they bit like midges, not a disabling but an intolerable irritant.

The room which the Prime Minister kept as an ancillary to the rooms at Downing Street, a Westminster post box and not much bigger, was snug out of a draughty January day. A one-bar fire, a tray of tea, gave it the air of headmaster's study and Moncrieffe like the head boy waiting for a private word. Inevitably, there were messages and a bundle of constituency letters from the midday delivery which his PPS left for attention before rounding everything up at the end of each working day and transporting it to number 10 for sifting there. Fleming shuffled these missives like cards to see if there were any aces, then turned his attention to Moncrieffe.

"How's life at Torrisaig?" the Prime Minister asked with intentional cosiness.

"Slipping a notch or two. We can't get the manpower."

Fleming nodded. His father and elder brother complained of the same but, in the Borders, neither the labour shortage nor the adversity of the climate was so acute as in Wester Ross. His own visits to Torrisaig were restricted to half a dozen stalks when he was a young man, just after the war, but he retained a strong sentimental attachment to the place if only because he'd met his wife on one of them, a beautiful if troublesome woman. He recalled Watson as a small boy, uncaged, given the run of the estate, wild and lonely as the terrain. "I think that may change, you know. We're committed to increase the investment aid for crofting to try and sustain viable communities on the ground. And I suspect, however hard we try to avoid it, that unemployment's going to soar. That, ironically, may help to keep the Highlands and Islands together. Off the record," he added, although Moncrieffe had assumed that embargo the moment the door was shut behind them.

The Independent didn't think the Prime Minister of the day took him to one side to express solicitude about the emptying rural communities, but was silent and apprehensive, wondering exactly what was the purpose of the interview and how it would be broached.

"It's been bad news for us about the Solicitor-General," said Fleming as an aside.

"He was an able man."

"Except that he never learned to say no. I do deplore yes men."

Just as the new administration was finding its feet, there had been a scandal before Christmas involving a decision by the Solicitor-General for Scotland. It ought to have been a matter dealt with by the Secretary of State for Scotland and the Scottish Office between them, but timing was against discretion. It was the season of Saturnalia; men were absent from their posts, and the press took over in the vacuum of serious political news, blowing the episode into a nine-day wonder. The law man began to look a vacillating fool and, to protect himself, Fleming had to hint at resignation which was offered after the recess, when the lawyer returned to the back benches after an inglorious three months. The position was still vacant.

Moncrieffe felt his way cautiously. "If relations were better with the Liberals, it would have been an ideal post for Laidlaw."

Fleming flashed him a look in which gratitude was prevalent. Intelligence did so cut down on wasteful documentation. They moved on to confidentiality. "I thought so too. It's a pity about the Liberal groundswell. I would have seen it, quite impartially, as a prime opportunity for them to gain experience in government, but there we are. We work with realities, don't we, not ideals." The warning was given and heeded. No theories were to be expected from him. He was talking tactics. "What it did demonstrate to me is the comparative weakness of the Scottish executive at the moment. When I look round for somebody suitable there seems to be a dearth of Scottish lawyers. I can't think of such a shortage for the last thirty years."

Moncrieffe held his breath. He was being primed for the offer of a position in the Scottish administration. He had never been solicited before, because nobody had needed him that badly. One vote put an added premium on his talents but he felt he could hardly say to the Prime Minister, 'Exactly what are your terms?' and so he kept his peace.

"How far have you come?" asked Fleming with less ceremony than his guest. "In ten years what have you achieved?"

Watson was caught off guard by this direct approach and floundered a little.

The older man supplied his own answer. "You've won three elections in a notoriously difficult constituency and you've increased your majority on each re-run. You're probably unbeatable now. You have life tenancy at Ross, Cromarty and Skye if you want it. And I appreciate it's not been easy alone." He snapped a ginger biscuit in half as he drank tea, to test the accuracy of its trade description. "You know you've made yourself into an expert on the wording of legislation. I was at the Home Office when we helped your family custody bill through, wasn't I? You must have had a hand in more private member's bills than anybody currently in the House. You have achieved a very rare thing for a back-bencher and someone who's never held office. You have actually established an identity, in the constituency, in the Commons and I would say nationally." A copy of *The Times* lay on the work table and the Prime Minister flipped its margins rather dismissively. "I can tell you, there are six hundred and thirty MPs who wouldn't mind being quoted as a political oracle as often as you are. Yes, I know it has its irritating side but that's publicity for you."

Moncrieffe was quiet, mesmerised by the accuracy of this review.

"What I am giving you is a picture of power, or the elements of power. These three things are necessary if a politician is to make headway. Now you have these three qualities and yet, if you will forgive my boldness, you have made no headway and never will if you persist in the wholly admirable ambition of being a one-man band."

Fleming allowed some moments to elapse. He thought being an outlaw to established political systems was nothing short of lunacy, like those ill-advised egotists before the bench who decreed that they would conduct their own defence without benefit of counsel. You could not do it competently, even if the law did extend you the privilege of making an ass of yourself. He had come to detest a vogue phrase and the sentiment it expressed: 'going it alone'. It implied some Herculean feat, walking to both Poles, circumnavigating the world single-handed, which he felt attracted a false aura in an age when men walked on the moon. If machines or co-operation could get you there faster, what was the point of doing it alone? The Independent status, implicit in divorce and climbing mountains, was a delineation of solitude the Prime Minister didn't fear, but despised. They were wasteful and anti-social pursuits in the broadest sense, putting the ego before the corporate identity.

"But the one-man band is a music to which I have an aversion. You cannot play all the instruments yourself, Watson, or not without being a bloody freak. A party of one? No. Every political instinct in me rebels at that. Politics is the congregation of people into groups, a merging in the common identity. What you represent is very interesting, historically. This is an age of loners and dissidents, but dissidence is a fringe activity, mere negation, and it grieves me to see a man of your ability continually on the periphery in spite of hard work and high esteem." He paused. He was the master of dramatic pauses. "This is not flattery but fact. Will you think about joining us?"

"For the Solicitor-Generalship?"

Fleming allowed himself a smile. "Oh well, neither of us would

195

want to incur the charge of bribery. It might be seen as rather too expeditious. The vacancy simply drew my attention to a lack of trained legislators. But I do promise you a position in one of the major ministries, within the current session. And looking ahead, we have so few Labour Lords."

"And what about electoral reform?"

"Oh PR! That's a bit of a fad, isn't it? I don't think you get very stable government with a hung Parliament."

Watson's expression lost its respect, a nuance which Fleming picked up, and the Prime Minister adjusted his response to a more thoughtful one, drawing the correct conclusion.

"I am surely living proof of what I say. Parliament needs a majority."

"That's because we balance on a majority of one. With PR hopefully we might achieve the radical change and operate on consensus over the party boundaries."

In fact, long before Moncrieffe could recall, Fleming had been an advocate of some form of constitutional change but was dissuaded in the face of the difficult How? not the simple Why? Some of this interest was reflected in his reply. "We boast," he said, "about the great unwritten constitution of British politics. A lex non scripta. But it does share with ius publica, common law, the marked resistance – imperviousness even – to change. It evolves and sometimes over centuries. Certainly so slowly that it may be felt to be at odds with a contemporary trend. I think this is no bad thing. It obviates over-hasty change. And at any rate reformers might reflect that change from within is easier and more beneficial. Change from without is revolution, and that's mercifully unlikely."

The correspondence pressed. The mailbag waited for his signature. "I will be very interested to hear what you decide." He rose and came to the door of the office, stopping to shake hands before he opened it. "Whatever."

The handshake was not a pact, which would have been condescending, but an acknowledgement that in essence they had the equal status of men who made solitary decisions.

January was not a good month for revolution. Political revolution took place traditionally at Easter or in October, the equinox providing the best campaigning season. Popular uprisings were in July, the month for barricades and street riots, passions boiling over with the temperature. January ought to be immobile, quiet, reflective. Every wise general after Napoleon knew it was a bad time for the assault.

Moncrieffe left the Palace of Westminster and went across Parliament Square towards his flat. Office workers and bank employees dashed for a bus or a tube or a train, in a hasty exodus from the barren core of London. There was a smir of snow in the air which hurried them on. He lagged, a day-round city dweller with nowhere to go tonight except the circuitous detour of his thoughts.

He passed one of the south entrances to St James's Park and thought he would meander along its paths rather than go indoors again. It was empty at nightfall, and the lamps threw little illumination into the cold shrubbery. It was a bitter winter. For a fortnight past, the daytime temperature in London had hardly risen above zero, and at night plunged to ten below. The trees in St James's Park were frosted, bark and bough white along their entire length so that they looked artificial in the twilight, silver filigree against the dun brownness of the enclosing city. The contrasts were so sharp they looked unnatural. Petrified trees, warm stone. Winter was an inversion, making thought or movement or emotional upheaval a painful paradox.

He was flattered. Of course he was flattered. One part of him said, 'Recognition at last', as if he were an ordinary politician in an ordinary career. Setting vanity aside, he could appreciate Fleming's point that if proportional representation were to be introduced into the British electoral system, it might be achieved more swiftly through the internal machinery of a party. But that had been said for a hundred years. Yes, a century ago, John Stuart Mill and John Lubbock, Albert Grey and C.P. Scott led the way in electoral reform, all-party, all-class but Parliament clung to ancient forms. A century was a longish interval even by Fleming's standards of political evolution. The two main parties had their cells of enlightened reformists but as long as the first-past-the-post system ensured at least an alternating spell in office, neither Labour nor Tory party was going to unseat itself willingly. The odds for a two-horse were safer than for a three-horse race. God rot minorities. A win and not a place on every bet.

So Watson had no illusions about altruism. Fleming might well admire his capabilities, but he wanted his vote in the Lobbies and needed it for his own survival. The offer, urbane, unquotably diffuse, was still in translation a cry for help, but to give it was to endorse the adversarial politics he condemned.

He gave a cry too, a long groan of indecision along the frozen verges of the ornamental lake. He wanted desperately to externalise the factors of his dilemma, a personal for and against, professional for and against, the four quadrants of any decision-making problem. He simply did not know which was best. Position versus material. Which strategy in the long term would prevail?

It was easy enough to predict the reaction of half a dozen confidantes if he put the hypothetical 'Should I?' to them. His political agent would be overjoyed. Success. Definable progress in promotion, since he supported Moncrieffe irrespective of why. It was reward for his own labours too. But Charlie would say, 'Over my dead body.' Lord Moncrieffe was askance that Cadogan was a grammar school, scholarship boy, come up through the ranks and good luck to him but not the thing at all for a Tory Prime Minister, just as he was about Fleming's mixed pedigree with a Liberal title dropped along the way. He liked the political map to be definitive in boundary and kept to his cross-benches in part because neutrality was the sole position that could not shift. Charlie distrusted the political turncoat, the man who crossed the floor of the house to the other side, no matter how distinguished. Sandy Govan would shake his head. Political chicanery in any shape or form was odium to the anarchist and, if pressed, he would argue that Moncrieffe was better employed at the sheep dip than in wheeling and dealing at Westminster, paddling in the waters of ethical corruption. Quercus would avoid a conclusion and the crisis of conscience with an apt quotation. 'Quot homines tot sententiae.' True but not consolatory.

There was no index of what he should do because nobody stood in his shoes. Nobody ever had. Uniqueness was a miserable state. The difficulty of the decision was a temptation in itself to capitulate, to abandon the rôle of being a one-off, eternally the outsider and unpartnered. He tasted the joys of party conviviality; the meetings in committee rooms, the annual conference at a seaside watering place, the social chat among the whips relaying gossip, the pairing which excused attendance at the duller debates. There were no dull debates for Moncrieffe. Every one was an establishment of the isolationist principle and he was obliged to vote at all those he could attend to underscore his existence. The sheer weight of the reading material required to make a balanced judgment, instead of following where his party led, was crushing. He wouldn't flip a coin and say I'll go heads today, lads, tails tomorrow. He thought each issue through but knew the free vote was the most harrowing. He was tired of the intolerable tensions of maintaining a median approach, without counsellor or friend.

He thought inevitably of the actress, non-partisan like himself. He did notice that his mental advisers were all men and regretted the inability he seemed to have to make friendships or relationships with women. Boarding school, an all-male college and the Law, followed by the sexist House of Commons. Perhaps he had shouted women down too often in his life. What, if he gave her ample space, would Leonie Barr think of his dilemma? She would give it time and her full consideration. Mindful, chary, aware of all the contingencies running through the sequence of his life. What would she say?

As he walked, he noticed that at the edge of the semi-frozen lake half a dozen boys had gathered and were making a slide along the margin of the ice. Watson looked on apprehensively. The repeated passage of their feet made a long glissando. It was such a slippery route that the challenge was to stay upright along the whole length of the course. The boys waved their arms like tightrope walkers to keep their balance and spent the time when they weren't on the slide discussing their footwear in the ideal compromise between adhesion and slipperiness. Watson was anxious about them, in the grip of vicarious parenthood. He didn't think the ice was thick enough to take their weight but was disinclined to cast himself as killjoy when it was harmless fun. Equally, he couldn't walk away and leave them to their own resources if there should be an accident. So he hovered, cold, concerned and wishing secretly that he could have a go himself.

After almost an hour, the boys grew hungry and filtered home. When they'd gone, Watson found a large stone and threw it into the mass of ice about five feet from the edge. Sure enough, it broke and from the hole a maze of cracks appeared, ruining the icy playground. No one would go down in the black waters of St James's Park if he could help it.

The flat was a haven, warm, clean, private and he came gratefully to its insularities even if conversely it did remind him how much larger was the bleak outside.

He wanted to belong, to be an insider in the political game. But a socialist? He didn't think he could swallow the socialist canon, which aspired to an anti-capitalist, anti-nuclear, state-owned society. It was a shining and unworkable Utopia. If, when Leonie Barr purloined that something from his property, he'd been able to respond, 'Yes, go ahead, take. I own in excess and only the unfairness of our undemocratic system prevents you from sharing my estate,' then he might have the makings of a socialist. But sentiment would not marry with the facts. He couldn't live with that ideological naïvety, or wouldn't expose himself to its continuous disappointment. So he got out a sheet of paper and wrote on it,

> I have grown accustomed to being the No man at Westminster, and regretfully decline the invitation to join the Yesses.
>
> W.

22

Alison and Matthew came to the bridge that connected the paths of Blackford to the Hermitage of Braid and Craigmillar Park, in a three-way intersection. It was a wooden bridge where some of the planks were missing and, remembering how hard it was to step across these gaps, they came to a halt and re-directed themselves through the valley of the Hermitage instead. A January day gave no protection. The sky towards sunset was an icy blue. The trees were leafless and a sharp wind blew through them. They were disconsolate and didn't walk hand in hand like lovers, denying themselves the warmth of the physique. Alison turned up the brown velvet collar on camelhair, a picture.

"And you say you called in simply by accident?" Alison tried to assure herself that they would still be happy but for chance.

"Yes." Matthew had spent a few days before Christmas and the New Year with a friend in Oxford and, before he drove north, stopped off near Woodstock to see his former girlfriend, Jennifer Davis. "A social call. Just for a cup of tea."

The narrative which they had run through half a dozen times didn't become more probable with repetition. "And how long was it since you saw her?"

"Eight months. The last time I saw her was the week before we met at Aldermaston."

Alison checked back for herself. The end of April to the end of December. Right enough. "Why did she never tell you, or try to get in touch?"

"I don't know. Jenny always was pretty self-sufficient."

At this moment, Alison envied the entity of self-containment. She felt fractured. Her lover had had another lover, hinted at rather than confessed, but here was irrefutable proof of the liaison. "And what was she going to tell everyone?"

This 'everyone' was familiar to Matthew Geddes, because the name was so frequently invoked. It was a uniquely Scottish personage, an amalgam of neighbour, gossip, telltale, sneak, but during the four years of his studentship he'd managed to forget about the power of this ubiquitous critic who was Calvinistic and unfriendly. It was the inverse of the laissez-faire spirit which prevailed at Oxford. Alison, the closest, was the easiest to tell about the failures of intimacy but, at her use of the word, he remembered the others who would sit in judgment on him, Jenny's parents as well as his own and, heaven help him, Muriel. Gratuitously, they would feel obliged to have their say, no offence and with all due respect, but offensive and disrespectful none the less. Previewing the massive censoriousness that lay in store for him, he was infused by defiance against their provincialism. What say they? Let them say! This was hard to live up to in Edinburgh.

He leaned against the guard rail of Braid Burn. "I don't know what she intended, but it took some courage, didn't it?"

Eight months pregnant and not a word to anyone, least of all the father who, in an outburst of cumulative quarrelling, walked out of the relationship and fell in love elsewhere. Discovering he was so imminently a father was an unlooked-for means of reconciliation with the mother.

Matthew was divided between the two women of his choice as much as he had ever been. The route back to the first would have been straightforward had it not been for the second but he actually found, then and now, that it was the pairing that was fascinating. Singleness was dull besides duality. The ménage à trois, albeit a mental one, was a concept that appealed strongly to him. He didn't think it was immoral, when so many religions and societies conceded its value, or even impractical. It was a matter of finding two women who were, in every sense, complementary. A sensible wife for the homely amenities plus a cultural companion, to provide the escape route from domesticity. Where was the harm? Dante did it. Simple monogamy was too linear to be fundamentally interesting. He liked the binary complexities, and although this wasn't the method of arriving at the ideal which he would have chosen, enforcement had its own attractions. Even in the last stages of pregnancy Jennifer was warm and sensuous. She made any room a seductive venue, and welcomed him back without recrimination or too much talk. At one time, they had made love in all the rooms at Woodstock, even the smallest. He remembered the

202

frankness of their two-year intimacy with a rush. Heady, strong, the pulse of youth was undeniable. It was hard to imagine Alison in those abandoned embraces. He had never brought her close. Alison deliberated well, drawing out a touch with unendurable finesse but kept him waiting beyond satiety. The temperamental virgin and the frank eroticist were irreconcilable, except in his appetite for both. Oxford, composed of freedom and self-indulgence, or Edinburgh with its restraints of chastening work, prudery and high intellect. Body and mind, characteristic of the women he associated with either place. If only the women were transposed, mixed or re-assembled! Soberly, he faced the difficulty that they might not be as enthusiastic about each other as he was for the combination.

Alison couldn't make this escape into sophistication. She saw her own precious ideal of a spiritual love affair dwindle beneath the realities. It was a dream. The great platonic union, the marriage of true minds, collapsed when it was obvious that the male partner needed physical gratification elsewhere. She was an extra, not the lead. A mental bit on the side. The division in Matthew's thinking underlined her own, but while he was capable of proceeding on both fronts, she tracked more single-mindedly along her private prejudice. This unwanted and unwelcome child *proved* the error of carnality from which she continued in her determination to remain aloof.

"So what will you do?" She asked the question as if he knew the answer.

"What you think is best."

They walked on through the enclosure of the Hermitage and, at a turn in the path, Alison looked up to her right and found the gate which led into their old house. The lights that burned through the trees were Fergus and Leonie's. Married. Waiting for their own child, successfully ensconced in that private universe while she walked outside, cold and lonely. They did well after all or better than she did. She saw, later than Matthew, how this event of theirs would be reported among their relatives. Muriel declaring she had had her worst fears confirmed – Exactly what I would have expected! – which justified retroactively all the rows she had had with the Geddes neighbours and the mental slights she had wreaked on them since. Matthew's reputation would be aired disparagingly to every passing stranger, given his character in twenty words, while Alison winced at her own indictment for poor judgment. She couldn't face that daily harangue and wavered for a moment about being discreet. Saying nothing, and hanging on to him. If that was what she thought was best, and he seemed to concede the decision to her, why not let Jenny have the child while she kept the man, body and mind divisible after all. Then she saw that such a choice was unworkable in the face of wholesale publicity. Besides, a chill little thought entered her head. She was no longer sure she wanted him when he had wanted someone else so primitively.

"I think," she said after a protracted pause, "that the rights of the innocent are strongest. Your child should have your allegiance."

He took her hand at dusk and kissed it, pressing the palm against his cheek.

But she had already moved on and formed the phrase, as if posthumously, It was a self-sacrifice but too many people stood between us, and foresaw Leonie as the most likely recipient of this résumé.

They underestimated the ensuing furore. So Muriel termed it, in amongst to-do, rumpus, ruction and show-down, which she did her best to make it.

"Madam," Professor Geddes was reported to have said when she descended on the bewildered parents, demanding reparation, "I would gladly make such amends, if I knew what they consisted of. You feel cheated, and yet you were equally displeased when Matthew and Alison first walked out. Perhaps it would suit you better if my son had impregnated your daughter instead. No? Well then, what do you suggest? That we change the custom of the country and institute the arranged marriage? A higher incidence of success, I hear. But I would not be so foolhardy as to prompt my son's choice and neither, I imagine, would you. It is impossible to restrict the freedom of young men and women in this generation but I give you leave to do your best with your offspring and I shall continue to do my best with mine. It may be wiser to accept at the outset that neither of us is likely to succeed and they will go on making their own mistakes as we did, impervious to advice."

204

So Matthew told Leonie when he came on one of his daytime visits. It did seem reversionary to visit the neighbouring house again with Fergus in residence and a different, more welcoming mistress. Leonie spent the dull part of her own pregnancy painting the walls of Hermitage Drive into acceptable neutrals.

"She actually tried to bribe me, you know. Mrs Petrie."

"Muriel? How?"

"Said she was thinking of buying a flat and Alison and I could have it."

"How odd."

"A volte-face at any rate. Not long ago she was trying to buy me off."

"So what did you say?"

"The other side had bid twice as much for me to marry their daughter."

This flippancy was maybe called for when Muriel quickly established the lowest and most common denominator among her fellow beings, but it indicated a want of seriousness in his emotions. Alison, for all her vaporising, deserved better than the philanderer. Matthew was disinclined to examine his own motives, possibly because they had already had such a thorough going-over by the professor who played the heavy parent to excess. Buying or bullying; Matthew evaded both stresses by prevarication. He didn't regret his own impartiality and Leonie failed to make him come down on one side or the other.

"You don't seriously imagine you could live with two women in one house? Not in Morningside."

"No," he consented. "More likely in the purlieus of London. But one to one is limiting wherever you are. Confess now, Leonie. It is dull, however good the view." He looked out of the lounge window into the tree tops of the Hermitage which were only thirty feet away, a blue haze that blotted out mundane suburbia. "Have you never hankered after someone else?"

Leonie came down from the step ladder and removed the rubber glove which protected her right hand. In spite of her best efforts to control the emulsion, a spatter of flecks landed on her face. "Am I blotchy?" she asked in response to his gaze.

"Not hideously so."

"Hankered?" She wrapped a plastic bag round the head of the

205

brush to keep it supple for the afternoon session. "Will you stay for lunch?"

"If you answer me honestly. Thank you."

The kitchen to which they removed was vast by Leonie's standards, after her mother's flat and Canaan Lane and bedsit kitchenettes, but all the same she rummaged for rather longer than was needful to find bread and cheese and pickles. She kept her back deliberately to her guest, masking her feelings with diffidence, as he did.

"Well?" he insisted on his answer.

"Hankered physically, do you mean? I'm not sure. Sex is only hunger. Does it matter what you eat to satisfy it?"

"How unfastidious of you."

"Yes, but yours may be sexual greed, the gourmand rather than the gourmet. Insisting on more."

He cut and tasted. "But you see, you buy such good cheese in the first place."

"Delicatessen," she replied, taking up the tease.

"I'll look with more interest next time I pass." They ate for a while before he pressed, "You haven't answered truthfully."

"Do I notice other men? Incessantly. How else could I act? You're on the look-out for partners all the time. But only stage partners. Just someone to externalise what you are, or make a dialogue with. It doesn't mean very much."

"And that's enough of a release?"

"That's enough."

He thought he had his answer but Leonie knew it was not an entirely honest one.

He left reluctantly to go back to his desk and spend another afternoon balancing figures, but no sooner had he gone out of the rear door from the kitchen than there was a ring at the front one. Leonie went to open it and found her husband's mother, much furred. Muriel didn't readily part with words of greeting and so instead of Hello or How are you or Good-day, she said, "Ay, ay," which fell between assurance and a question so that Leonie found no reply which was adequate.

"Perhaps I could have a word," the visitant said. "In private."

Leonie didn't want to ask the other Mrs Petrie indoors but recalled how she had chastised Fergus for falling out with the members of his family. She had nothing to hide and so held wide the door to let her pass.

Admitted, Muriel stood in the open hallway where a staircase rose in some majesty above her head with an oak balustrade, and sniffed. "Painting?" she asked.

"The lounge."

The woman followed the smell of paint through the doorway and stood examining Leonie's handiwork with a critical eye. She picked up a corner of its dust sheet from an easy chair a little scornfully, whether because the sheet was indeed just that, demoted from its original use, or the chair was unpretentious and not really worth such elaborate protection, Leonie didn't know. "Spatters," she said. "Where *can* we sit?"

"The kitchen."

Muriel knew the way well enough but didn't go directly there. She made a detour via the dining room and then the room downstairs which Fergus used as a study, filled with bookshelves and the computer terminal which fed out sheets of paper that his mother lifted and looked at without understanding. "Chess," she said and sniffed again.

Leonie didn't hurry her on, sensing how disturbing it must be to revisit in this guise a house which she had occupied herself and which had passed without natural inheritance to her son. The young woman waited for signs of recognition, a strip of wallpaper evoking memories of when and how, but none was forthcoming. Leonie didn't know it but every scrap of the moveable had been torn out. The last tack was prised from the carpet, the light bulbs from their sockets, even the hooks out of the curtain rails. The initial M in Muriel's alphabet was for mine. There was nothing left of attachment which she might recognise. No, it was a different reconnaissance which the woman carried out. She performed a rapid inventory of their goods, a running total that she carried in her head of how much they were worth before she came up with the total. "I reckon it must have taken you all your time to buy this place. Not much left for trimmings."

"True," said Leonie, unperturbed.

"I wasn't much older than you when I moved into this house and I had all my furnishings made to measure from Jenners. The place looked very well then."

Even associations were competitive. "And I wish you joy of it. Furnishings are such a consolation."

The older Mrs Petrie looked at the younger and remembered she did not care for her. Too independent for her liking. One of the modern women who didn't know the meaning of establishment and seniority. "A quotation, I presume, from some play."

The actress didn't disagree but led the way into the kitchen, finding the two sets of dishes where she and Matthew had left them carelessly. Muriel's eye was quick. "Does Fergus have time to come home for lunch?" knowing full well that the journey by bus would be too protracted for a lunch hour. Leonie wouldn't cover up but let the accusatory plates lie as they were.

Muriel sat down at the kitchen table and moved the setting aside disdainfully. She said, summoning the purpose of the visit, "I want you to know that I hold you responsible for this."

Leonie quickly ran through the things she might have held against her. The bankruptcy, divorce, Fergus' disaffection, or simply the dishes which stridently proclaimed the presence of the vilified Matthew. She gave up guessing. "For what?"

"Pardon me if I am mistaken, but it is my understanding that you had prior knowledge of Matthew Geddes' affairs."

Some dawning of intelligence came through these words. Muriel had a remarkable way with a sentence. She was able to pick out the highlights of an event or attitude and string these together in a semblance of logic, while missing out the salient ordinariness of the conjunctions. So the word affairs was loaded with plurality. Why should Leonie deny that she once met Jennifer Davis, and yet to admit it was to incur some unspecified blame. She was drawn reluctantly along the warped camber of the allegations.

"I am correct in my assumptions, am I not?" Muriel pressed for answers, a multiple impertinence.

Leonie saw that if Matthew or Alison had made the acquaintance obvious, there was no point in falsifying. "Yes, I did meet Jenny once."

"Then," said Muriel, triumphantly right, "I consider that you have failed in your duty."

"Oh? And what duty was that?"

"To inform me of the undesirable background of that young man."

208

"I didn't think it was undesirable."

"Well," the woman retorted, "I cannot tell how low you have sunk in your standards."

"To emulate Alison's, you mean? She didn't seem to find him so undesirable."

"To deceive. I consider this a disgraceful turn of events. My daughter . . ."

"Come on, Muriel. Make some allowances for human nature. There's no point in playing the outraged matron. You yourself were married with less than the statutory nine months to spare. I wouldn't disparage Matthew, or Jenny, too readily if I were you."

Muriel ground to a halt. She had a blind spot in the area of self and having her own past cast up to her by someone who was both in a position to know about it and to be unaffected by consequent slander was a novel experience. She couldn't find the lever for emotional extortion with Leonie, which normally had its root in fear of the truth. Most people, thwarted in this way, would give up or say moderately, Fair enough. There's a point in that, and so concede something to the opposition. Not Muriel. She rose and consumed opposition in a tidal wave of unreason, flattening the landscape of normality as she went.

"Don't throw Fergus' pedigree back at me. At least he has a father which is greater, I believe, than your endowment."

And Leonie did the unforgivable thing. She laughed. "It's a waste of time trying to threaten me, Muriel. I'm unthreatenable because I simply don't care. No. My mother has had less use for men than you, that's true enough. Honest or dishonest, she made her own way."

The woman was blocked again but this time didn't dare to proceed, remembering in a glimmer the man Fergus had encountered at Greenbank. She assumed all talk was as scurrilous as hers and that Leonie sat smug on information.

"Well, I'm very disappointed that you condone behaviour which is harmful to someone who is your friend and also your sister-in-law. I think you have abetted it. If you had come clean we might never have found ourselves in this humiliating position. Alison is devastated."

"I'm sorry if that's so. But she's the victim of circumstance, not ill-will on anybody's part. She'll find someone else."

"I wish I could feel as self-satisfied about the outcome as you do. When your turn comes, you may know what it feels like to be disappointed in your children."

"As they will in their parents, like as not."

"I only hope you never have as much reason to call on our loyalty as we have had to call on yours." And Muriel rose to her feet and went, with neither word nor look of valediction. For a long time afterwards the rooms throbbed with the minatory tensions she set up, waves of hostility for no known cause. In an abstracted state, Leonie cleared the surfaces in the kitchen, thinking it odd that Fergus' mother hadn't once called her by name, or made a direct reference to the baby, or a single propitiatory remark. It was all negation.

Passing through the hall, she remembered the paintwork waiting for her and, peeling off the plastic coating round the brush, set to work again. As she brushed, however, she noticed that hard specks had entered the emulsion, ruining the surface. She peered at the bristles. The paint had caked and flecks of it hardened on the wall and mixed with the majority in the tin. Sift it? Wash it all off and start again? It would take hours of futile effort to put it right. She was incensed that her handiwork, a labour of need and not of love, should be spoiled by these people with their unsolicited interruptions.

Sitting on the bare floorboards of the lounge, Leonie saw herself in focus. Downstage. A domestic drama full of vulgar brawling. Smocks and flat shoes. Unglamorous. The play had run six months and it was time to close, or move on to something more rewarding. She was suddenly tired of this tour of the provinces and had a strong impression of the metropolitan appeal, gowns cut to the body, a ripple of sophisticated wit. She was hungry for audience and watched herself as she went to exit left.

III

23

Monday 25th May, London

I arrive on schedule but hit an unexpected vacuum. I ought to be city hardened by now. Who's pounded as many pavements or walked more urban miles? Trains, taxis, tubes, dodging the bag-and body-snatchers, I should know my way round the city complex. London's the place I always meant to come to, capital, but either it's different from other cities or the transition is in me.

I find I'm apprehensive. There's no welcome. I know nobody. Stuart has sorted out an address for me in King's Cross where the landlady has left a salad, and gone out. London rolls on oblivious to my arrival. At one time, a suitcase and a script would have been remedy against the traveller's sickness but I feel vulnerable and unprepared.

I notice how ugly these digs are. Badly hung wallpaper and the soiled bedspread remind me of the place I've left, pristine, efficient and maybe beautiful, called home. Why do I do it? I don't know. Why would anybody up sticks and do what I'm doing if they weren't crazy or egotistical, catapulting down here to meet impossible deadlines, and for what? They couldn't believe in the hospital that I asked for my book before I asked for my baby. But I can't wallow in maternity. I've done that job to the best of my ability and have to move on to the next one. I've always fought sentimental self-indulgence, can't say 'My child is the most important thing in the world because it's mine.' Am happier unconsciously with the removed concept of child rather than baby. Look on the intimate or subjective with suspicion – but this is to define a guilt, or an inadequacy. I am no paragon.

I go out in the afternoon and mix with the Bank Holiday crowds who mill around Hyde Park. The buildings are taller in London; you feel dwarfed walking under them and the traffic goes faster until it melts into a polychromic blur with hansom cabs periodically

213

black to punctuate a rush hour. The crowds are overwhelming, immeasurable because I can't break them into individuals yet. Someone stands on Speaker's Corner and harangues them about pollution or abortion or meat-free diets while they go on throwing wrappers on the ground and kissing as if it didn't lead to consequences, ya-booing silently. It's a long way from the bottom of the Mound on Sunday mornings where a brave soul takes the soap box to a polite and reasonable assembly of ten. Here the crowd is witty and bantering, 'Wrap it up mate,' says one while another caps the remark, 'And I'll post it back to you,' in unanswerable scorn. Policemen keep a watchful presence and the amplifier spreads the message as far as a competing band from which it is indistinguishable.

Soon, I'll have to get up in front of all these people and convince them on my own behalf. Not easy. They're blasé. They down the likes of me and go ramping on for more. Only the extremes excite them, the very loud, the very famous. They'll pelt me with indifference.

In the evening, I settle down to practise on my face in front of a water-marked mirror that adds pobbles. Stuart has told me I've got a good enough face, professionally speaking, and it's all the better for not being pretty. Well and good. Doll features are no good for anything but playing dolls. He points out that my features are more asymmetrical than most, one side happy, the other sad. Like palms, he says, the left etched with potential, the right with achievement. He reassures me that this lop-sidedness has its advantages; I can be comic or tragic according to which side I turn towards the audience. But I think it's a grim forecast. His throw-away words eat their way into the subconscious, like a horoscope you dismiss rationally, but remember, and I look at my face as fragments instead of a unit.

I've spent years practising on this face to make it better, more supple, stronger. Other people think of their face as something very personal; I think of mine as neutral, fluid, raw material, mere ectoplasm. I won't prink or pretty it. My features are a set of slack muscles I put through their paces every day to keep them fit, all inelegant exercises in the way of callisthenics, pull, stretch, bend, relax. My face is a bit of elastic or chewing gum, stretched to the limit and then twanged back into position again. I've put this flesh of mine through hours of torture because, like a ballerina, I'll feel much worse if I don't. But I look as silly as she does warming up in her swaddling socks when I go through my own girning routine, a toothless, boneless, shapeless grandad.

This is the unglamorous side, the bit nobody sees, you sitting alone in a dreary back room, pummelling yourself into vocal shape. It's so specialised and abnormal that you sometimes doubt your sanity, as you listen to yourself saying the same words over and over again and suddenly notice they don't make a bit of sense. Or you breathe to a pattern, like a pianist working out the fingering in a difficult passage. We all breathe, but the actor learns to breathe in a rarefied way, measuring his lines so that he doesn't run out of sound power, has something left to reach the upper notes.

That's my entire equipment, breath and body, and it looks so fragile in this mood as I overhaul it. I don't produce anything but sound and shapes. I haven't even got a good voice. I don't know which is more unexceptional, my face or my voice. Pleasant to listen to, useful, but verging on monotony. I have to work harder than other actors to get myself up and down the ranges, singing scales that push me to the limits. Other people hear the music, but you know how the notes are made, ground out of a resisting anatomy. And I've never heard of anyone taking out an insurance policy against the common cold.

This is by way of anxiety. I've got an attack of stage nerves, only London's the stage and today's the play and I'm shy of going on. Maybe I expected fanfares and realise I've got to earn them.

Something else is inhibiting me. A fresh part is hard enough but in the middle of the ongoing stress I'm trying to relocate a new me, or the old one with new developments. I'm exhuming an aptitude I've let slip and the exercise hurts after sluggish intervening motherhood. But motherhood lurks in the cell, deny it how I may. As night falls, I wonder what's happening north, which is a sub-location of the conscious place I'm in. Is the child asleep, my child, and if not, who is with him? Is he warm, well, happy? The questions crowd out concentration. They say there's a sickness youngsters suffer from in the Third World, a form of malnutrition which sets in when the mother suckles the second infant. I'm adjusting to that painful reality – the physical limit of my own

215

resources. I can't nurture two at once. I've taken on a new life and must deliver myself of that obligation in time. I fell again too suddenly.

Thursday 28th May
I join the cast at the Haymarket. They've had four weeks already, moving from Bristol to Bath to Guildford and could go straight into the London run. Normally would. But I'm given a week's extra grace by our director to rehearse my way into the part. After all, this would happen mid-run with a change of lead, so I can't complain. Want the work? Accept the conditions. But I have to be on top of the part even before I set foot on the stage. The others enjoy the time to polish and to re-acquaint themselves with nuance.

We started on Tuesday, quite democratically, with Stuart pretending he was only the chairman and officiating. Seven of us sat round on the stage and read our parts lazily from the script. I like working from dead authors. You don't have to cope with them in person. When I was in rep in Bristol and the playwright kept
    a) changing his mind
    b) changing his characters
    c) telling us we weren't acting it as he'd imagined anyway,
I nearly went insane. Death does set your parameters. Dead authors in translation are the best. With the English classics, there's always some buff who knows it off by heart and writes in to say you fluffed a line or didn't pronounce pollacks properly to allow for all the various interpretations. Though I remember hearing Compton Mackenzie, who went on the stage as a very young man like his sister Fay Compton, say he'd replaced 'million' in one play by 'thousand'. The onomatopoeia, if not the sense, was more appropriate to immensity and the author who happened to be in the audience didn't object. So Ibsen suits me perfectly, dead enough to improve. Stuart takes me to one side afterwards and says, 'I know your trick. You'll improvise on what you think ought to be there. Okay for you, but think of the other actor looking for his cue.' I know this rebuke is justified but I find it difficult to be word perfect. Approximating lets me feel it more, as if I'd just made it up. Not an idea to float to your director, however.

We chat pleasantly, agreeing on the space we allow for others.

216

Ken promises not to boom me out. I promise not to crowd him on the stage by swishing my long skirt in front of his position. We have long rambling discussions, very like an impromptu student seminar, about what the play means and what Ibsen took from Chekhov and Shaw took from Ibsen. Dialectic. We feel pepped up afterwards, overflowing with intellect – which isn't theatre. We spend the evening in a pub round the corner which has tubs full of roasted peanuts in the shell. Stuart eats mountains of them and ends up with a fine matting of straw threads down the front of his jacket. He's a shambles, both mad and professorial.

Today we're less hot on theory. The set is hung, transported bit by bit from one theatre to another. The steep rake of this stage is something new to me and I feel as if I'm leaning backwards, or on board ship. Exits and entrances are focused. So many paces on this line. So many yards to cover between the end of that delivery and reaching the French window. How to fill the silence actively. How to be tense for just those seconds, as if I didn't know that Jörgen would come back with his learned publications and the play unfold along its set course. It comes down to precision timing. I often think of Fergus and discipline on stage – moves over the surface of the board, strategy, position, knowledge of the ultimate goal. I suppose any play or piece of writing is founded on the principles of chess, good and evil, protagonists working their way to a solution which is the neatest ending. It helps to think that when it all feels messy and pointless, to recall the underlying structure of what we mean. It also prevents over-emphasis of one part. As Fergus tells me over and over again, it's combination in play that matters.

Friday 29th May

Stuart becomes less democratic. Each decision we make cuts down the ensuing decisions. The setting and the costumes are contemporary with the play, 1890. He is particular about the fashion of ladies' hats and whether the bustle has come or gone. What would Hedda's underwear be if she is pregnant – *because* she is pregnant. Her undisclosed pregnancy runs like a dye through her character. We spend an hour discussing corsetry, whalebones and somehow end up on Moby Dick and the endangered baleen. And though all this seems affably discursive, Stuart is guiding not participating. I am sensible that he is allowing us to digress in the assumption that we are making a contribution, holding a forum. In reality, he made the important decisions long ago, when he accepted the contract, chose his cast, his play, his period. He is a despot, albeit of the most enlightened variety.

Stuart says to me, perhaps jocularly, 'You can play this one from life, Leonie.' And it's true. Re-reading the play last night ready for rehearsal, I was impaled by something that's happened to me only two or three times before. Recognition. The feeling – and it's almost horrific – of identification. I am, or could be, Hedda. Her husband isn't Fergus, precisely, but I know him well enough. His doctorate, his yearning for a professorship, the honeymoon spent at work arranging and collecting material for a book by a man for whom rummaging in libraries is the most entrancing occupation, "and learned men are not entertaining travelling companions" – this is first-hand familiar. So I read Hedda Gabler with a growing fear, the house fortuitously for sale, the husband eager for a child and an imbalance sets in whereby similarities between her situation and mine become disproportionate. Up till now, it's been the audience that superimposes the part on me the player, while I am conscious of the disparities and how I am supplementing the rôle artificially – or by art. Now Hedda threatens to engulf me. I am deliberately *not* being Ms Gabler (but why, like me, does she not use her married name?) and this is bad stage practice. If I go on this way, I'll be in danger of muffing up not only my performance but everybody else's, through emotional withdrawal from her which creates a vacuum of sympathy. Yes, I abhor Hedda for her boredom and her coldness and her lack of intellectual curiosity. I am not Hedda but have to believe I could be this way if the stifling atmosphere of nineteenth-century Norway had done its worst. Northernness may be a catching malady, like narrow-mindedness, environment bred.

I think about Hedda late into the night. She comes between me and myself, splitting the real and the imagined or theatrical life into atomic particles. She makes me think about myself and that is always painful when I am most happy to be plastic, squeezed between rôle-playing, which prevents my being anyone in particular.

That visiting lecturer in Anthropology who was my father, all I know about him is that he was a Norseman, a twentieth-century Viking who came to sow but not to settle in the Lowlands. Has he passed on a taste for Ibsen that's stronger than rationality? Do I know these characters through and through because the complex molecular structure of identification is inbred? Or is it simply the cast of mind that inquires, and rejects conformity in whatever century or place? Maybe so. But I am unaccountably, through Hedda's agency, less comfortable with myself and look in the mirror at skeletal emotions.

Sunday 31st May

We are into costume and set. The echo has been taken off the stage. The dressing rooms are inhabited by our belongings which give a comfortable padding. We actors are fetishists about the dressing table, laying out make-up and clothes for the performance with almost religious fervour. Pathetic really, to have to rely on such little boosters to get going. Thinking that making the sign of the cross will make it come right. My room at the Haymarket is a delight, right at the top of the building, light and airy, painted cream with the dressing table between two high windows. A fireplace, an easy chair, a wardrobe big enough to walk in and a bed with chintzy covers. A beautiful desk at which generations of actors have sat penning notes to friends, or reading them. I could set up house here and am loath to leave each evening for some of the shabbier enclaves of N1.

It is a home, this theatre. Ken has appeared here twice before in his career and knows the technicians and staff by name. They chat like old friends and he picks up news of other actors by the way. The building is squeaking clean, steps scrubbed every day and polished brass knobs and name plates on the principal doors, while round every corner is a little fireplace or a lovely architrave over a door that was lifted straight from a Sheridan set and put there to last. Long panelled corridors are hung with old placards and mementoes, going back nearly two and a half centuries. The names of long-dead actors fascinate. Who on earth were they, perpetuated only in a programme signature? Hedda suits the physical shape of this theatre, darkly marbled and I notice co-incidentally that the carpet is monogrammed with the initial H. She belongs here and I follow in her footsteps.

We work well together, cast and crew, and make rapid progress.

In the page-burning scene, and I react to the ritual sacrifice of paper with personal vividness, Stuart watches me without moving. He says almost nothing in these final stages, letting you flow naturally along the terrain he has already prescribed, but I know perfectly well he's in a crisis of attention. Timing, pace, the physical distribution on the stage, the colour balance of the set and costumes, the subtlety of the lighting – he's modulating it all, and with a pencil makes editor's signs in the margin of the text which will be interpreted later into changes of minute significance, minute to everyone but him. It's such a comprehensive form of intelligence that we, limited to our single on-stage view, can hardly encompass it. I thought I was as near as dammit perfect and he said, 'Put the sheets in with the left hand, will you.'

Stuart is very patient with detail but not with explanation, so I don't ask for one. Why on earth should it matter which hand I use? Is Hedda to be a left-handed woman, gauche throughout? Then when I do it, I find I tremble and create a different physical tension to control it. She looks more vulnerable in spite of her huge crime.

Ken is a good Judge Brack, slicing his way between suave and menacing, at once a lady's man and a man's man. Fifty, bearded, tidily large with that threat of being gross, physically and mentally, if he let himself go. "I assure you that sort of – shall I call it triangular relationship? – is actually a very pleasant thing for everybody concerned." That sends shivers down my spine. I marvel at the way Ibsen, within the moral conventions of his day, manages to imply all the nuances of adultery and sexual practice. His restraint is his intensity. Say it all, show it all, and it's banal. Twentieth-century exposé. Of course, I would translate the word as 'pleasing' instead of 'pleasant' and try to work on Stuart and Ken to alter it, to no avail. Pleasant is limp. Pleasing is rippled with the erotic; pleasurable strokes the auditory senses.

Ken is most amusing to rehearse with. By the time he knows his words, he can't be bothered to say them. So he does a running mutter and a hum to fill the space. Tra-la-la he goes, reminding me of Pooh bear. He's a generous actor. He's every reason to feel peeved that I've been given so large a share of stardom, but is professional enough to be content with playing his own part to perfection and knows that for this he needs me. On the stage there's no point in being selfish or sexist. Men need women, women men. The performing arts are the most egalitarian.

We have a wonderful surprise at six when Alan Mills comes over from the Old Vic and sits watching us through Act Three. Alan says he admires Stuart's work but complains he has no ear and I have to deplore the nit-pick jealousy. Then we all go to the pub afterwards and have a good chinwag about Oxford and old times. Thirteen months since Viola. She seems an infant compared with the me I am now.

Monday 1st June
Hedda wears away at me and becomes merged with her close relatives, Emma Bovary and Anna Karenina. They are her forerunners, coming out in 1857 and 1877 respectively, whereas Hedda only emerged in 1890, in a slow northern drift of the malaise of the bourgeois woman. They're all three the same woman in effect, recast according to the nature of her partner, the man who knew and wrote about her, but they're also linked by similarities of type which are more powerful than coincidence. They're connected by their adultery, different adulteries admittedly and in Protestant Norway the woman rebels, but maybe not so much at sex as at the servitude it will bring. They're each alienated from their husbands and their children, with only passing interest in motherhood. They die uniformly by suicide, though again this is modulated by circumstance, arsenic, the train or pistols being symbolic of some image in the piece or in themselves, the husband's profession or modernity or romantic escapism which triggers the destructive elements of their collective character.

I am uneasy in this feminist atmosphere. The writings are a cry by pre-suffrage women for work or for some engagement with life other than men and children. But a hundred years on, after the vote, the bomb, the pill, have Heddas become impossible? No, there are thousands of them in Edinburgh and Birmingham and Bath dying of ennui and I too, in spite of being post-suffrage and *making* myself employment in this bizarre and probably self-centred way, cast myself privately as one who bears the stigma of these bored, vain women, seeming not to care about family and home.

221

Fergus opened these sheets of ruled file paper once a week when they arrived on Monday morning, posted Saturday. He smoothed them out and sorted them systematically to make sure Leonie had put them in chronological order and then he punched holes in the left hand margin, and filed them in the series of folders he'd bought specially for the purpose. They were her letters home.

He filed them in the spirit in which they were sent, as archival material which she would draw on at some time in the future when she wrote her autobiography. When she was eighty and beyond Hamlet even with the aid of a wooden leg, she would write her stage memoirs. That was a thought. An eighty-year-old theatrical Dame, alongside Flora Robson, Anna Neagle, Sybil Thorndike and Edith Evans. Dame of the British Empire. What a frumpy title, not like the sleek salutation of Sir. 'Dame', with its overtones of drag or slag, was an odd choice for the highest female honour of the realm.

So Fergus stored these missives, diary, letter, notebook, but he didn't read them.

24

Leonie did edit her letters home. Some incidents were unconsciously left out.

One evening, a couple of days before she opened in *Hedda Gabler*, she left the Haymarket Theatre alone and took the back route behind Trafalgar Square. After seven o'clock, London started to muster itself for a switch of mood. Entertainment and performance rounded off the working day and the city-dwellers didn't bother to go home between times. The queues were already starting to form outside the cinemas in Leicester Square, queues longer than the ones which the theatre round the corner was capable of drawing and Leonie dawdled among the crowds enviously, looking at the posters and billboards. Not far from the National Portrait Gallery, she passed a church hall that carried its own announcement outside in large lettering but she hardly bothered to glance at it, presuming it would proclaim either salvation or the nighness of the end of the world, equally remote at seven on Tuesday. But a name caught her eye as she passed and she went back again and re-read the wording of the poster carefully letter by letter. It was a political and not a religious benediction that was being offered in the church hall that evening. Watson Moncrieffe was due to give a lecture at eight p.m. on the theme – Proportional Representation at Westminster: the reality.

A small congregation had arrived by the time Leonie joined them, mostly old and mostly men but the women who came along were recognisable as derivatives of her mother, even so far afield from Edinburgh Pentlands. The audience was stern and informed, combative as only politicos and religious diehards could be. Leonie settled herself among them towards the back of the hall on pew benches which were drilled in a pattern of holes and embossed with metal studs, neither of which was conducive to a state of complacency about the lecture they were going to hear. It was a warm evening and musty inside the hall. A man beside her went to open one of the high windows using a cord on a ratchet but the air that came in was hotter still, activated by traffic and crowds. She thought she was mad to sit there in the fug, in among fifty people breathing the same air, re-cycling the same opinions, used and secondhand, but an exodus before the speaker had so much as opened was more dismissive than walking out of the theatre in the interval. Wait until half way at any rate.

Moncrieffe arrived with only a minute or two to spare and Leonie was glad she'd sat to one side, out of his line of vision, and edged a little closer to an obscuring pillar to be inconspicuous. He looked tired, a long way from the playboy of his public image. He'd come straight from the House where mischief was brewing over the second reading of a transport bill the government had pledged itself to in its election manifesto and was still struggling to carry against the wishes of its minority supporters. Watson balanced his views with as much autonomy as ever, following his own lead. The subject, less controversial than a hundred others, touched everyone personally and had aroused fiercer battles than he could remember in the House. Labour, who had always favoured the railway network for heavy goods transportation and avoided direct acknowledgment of the EEC when it could, far less co-operate with it, now found they had to modify both stances. Legislation on a standardisation of the size and weight of Community juggernauts was a small clause that had merited hours of discussion in a packed chamber. The single issue enlarged to incorporate unwieldy principles.

It was with difficulty that he dragged his mind back to the lecture which his audience had come to hear. He looked down at the notes on electoral reform which he rejigged every time he spoke, but which were substantially ten years old and unoriginal, as the exhaustion of endless repetition overcame him. Why hadn't these good people gone round the corner to the picture house, bought a paper from the news vendor on the pavement outside or read a book instead? What was the point of spreading the gospel to this multitude of fifty? Some important decisions were in the making at Westminster and here he was, going over the same old ground for no return.

This lasted for a moment or two, and was a form of stage fright.

Then the compulsion of meeting the expectations of his audience revitalised him. They had come to listen to his argument. That was enough.

Why reform and why proportional representation? He began as usual, retrospectively, with a look at the Reform Bill of 1832, its advance on rotten boroughs and bribery as well as its residual flaws. He talked of the men who recognised these omissions and how close PR had come to being introduced in 1919. Throughout this historical preamble, he began to settle and get the feel of the audience by the small signals of interaction between them, where they laughed or fell silent. They weren't a restive audience but the evening was too hot for total concentration. Alternative sounds to his own voice impinged distractingly through the open window.

"I'm often asked," he said, "why I don't join one of the two larger parties and the answer is that I can't subscribe to a system which I feel is inequitable. Any statistician will tell you that, to obtain a true count, you must subtract a weighting of the negatives as against the positives. There's no mathematical justice in the British electoral system when a quarter of the vote can gain a tenth of the seats, or a party with a reduced majority can increase its representation in the House. There's a basic flaw in the principles of addition we're using. It's like playing a game with loaded dice, or saying in football that team A's goals are worth less than team B's – simply put."

He searched round, as all platform speakers did, for the attentive face he could relate to, the head that would nod, the eye that would follow. He found it, to his massive surprise, towards the back of the hall and reticent behind a pillar. He sharpened his delivery to convince.

"There are many arguments put forward for retaining the first-past-the-post method at elections, the most facile being that PR is too difficult for the electorate to understand. But anyone here who's a member of a union is likely to have used the single transferable vote which only needs the capacity to add up to five or so. The X marking of the ballot paper, which took account of mass illiteracy, hasn't moved on from the colour coding that's used for Third World country candidates and surely we can achieve a higher level of sophistication in identifying issues than that. If Europe on the whole can understand the mechanics of PR, why not

Britain? Anyone who can grasp the principle of the water wheel is on his way to understanding proportional representation. In fact it's much the same theory, maximum efficiency with minimum wastage. Instead of having a huge overspill, each MP is voted in by just the majority required in that constituency and other votes cast for him are re-allocated to the second choice recorded. Every vote like every drop of water counts for something in a multi-member constituency.

"It's said that our present system ensures strong government, though that's a notion put about by would-be governments. For strong read monopolistic. Successive administrations in Britain are veering to such wild extremes, nationalise, de-nationalise, reduce taxation, increase taxation, with an inbuilt refusal to co-operate with the opposition which I think is the most damaging aspect of adversarial politics. It rubs off on the nation. Sometimes the opposition *does* have good ideas. Why not use them? The public are tired of the extremists, the sectarianism of the left where there's no common unity and the totalitarianism of the right where there's no dissent. Most voters recognise the blatant self-interest of British political parties."

He drank from the water jug on the table, tasting its dust and room temperature tepidity more than its quenching. "But what is the real point? We're saddled with a primitive method of bungling – and honest men on both sides of the House admit to that – but aren't all methods and administrations bungling at bottom? I trained as a lawyer and my first concern at Westminster is the law-making process. The passing of legislation with less than fifty per cent backing in the country is the most flagrant example of the break-down of democracy. What force can the law have when it's repealed by the next administration? Factional law is always bad, because it represents the power of might over reason. If this is democracy, give me a dictatorship. At least a dictatorship can fall to a revolution, but this quasi-democracy can keep itself in power indefinitely by saying it's the will of the people. Every election in Britain is subject to rigging by the flaws of mathematical computation to the highest score."

He felt very tired, reliving as he spoke the failures of his career and his ideals. It wasn't the right evening for dialectic. They came so hopefully, wanting a simple commandment to go away and cherish, something that would apply to every situation but all he could say was, It is complex. It needs a programme of re-education that nobody will fund. And these were the ones who cared.

"Let's have an example," he said. "Give me a show of hands. That's as good a vote as any. How many of you this evening came by public transport?" He counted quickly. "Now here we have a situation that's like any opinion poll. It happens that those taking the bus or tube are in the majority. Imagine that these people have power over directing funds into transport services. They'll follow their own interests. The rest of you, if a vote goes with a simple majority, don't have a chance to put your point of view effectively. You'll always be outvoted. It's the most obvious form of injustice, this half of the room having the power of veto over the other half. It's a trivial example, but you assume a consensus of interests in a democracy and that the majority won't penalise the minority because it's lacking a vote or two."

They laughed, taking the slight point, which they knew was being multiplied by hundreds in the Commons debate that evening.

Leonie took it more personally. She found the message troubling and at first ascribed it to the quality of his voice which was distinctive in public. It had elements of her own voice recast, like the wax sleeve on an old phonograph which sent up a scratchy and imperfect version of an otherwise familiar tune. His speech fell into the same cadence as hers. She recognised the plosive quality of the consonants and a mellowness in the middle of certain words, which was a Scots rise and fall breaking through the strictures of English enunciation, the voice forming a duet by itself. Its roughness intrigued her when it released a vibration in the air so that a sensate experience preceded the mental reception of what he actually said. A trick: or instinct? Either way, it was the oratorical power to keep the audience listening and she was sufficiently impressed by his skill in delivery to be objective and, behind analysis, moved.

His physique too changed on the public platform. He was rather ponderous in private life but a different phase of mobility came over him in performance, facial and gestural. He worked at it but not with the tricks of the demagogue, air sawing, table thumping. The delivery matched the message, often so deeply felt that the

227

effect was painful as both the voice and the manner surged from a well of conviction.

"Minority. Majority," he went on. "That's what it always comes back to. How do you make an effective compromise between powerful and less powerful factions? The problem in Britain may be related to our attitude to that word 'compromise'. It ought to convey simple mediation, a practical solution to the day-to-day problems of government and every politician knows he has to modify his best laid plans. But then it has these undesirable overtones of compromising one's principles, adulterating some ideal by absorbing an alternative, and that's almost impossible to eradicate from our subconscious thinking. Coalition is a dirty word except in time of war. I don't know why. Other countries are less partisan." He thought aloud. Leonie caught the tide of mood as it changed from exposition to reflection, provable to unprovable, and was carried along by her own difficulties with compromise. She knew that 'I' could not always supervene in a decision. Res publica was never singular, but was splintered into plural interests.

"What's wrong with the British Parliamentary system," he specified, "is that it doesn't properly protect the interests of minorities. It does allow them to come into existence and imagines that's the full scope of democracy. But the mother of Parliaments ought to be like the best of mothers, and protect its minors as though they might one day attain seniority, not stifle them with a repressive hand. Minors, minorities, there's no difference. Suppress Nationalists, or individualists or people who lobby on a single issue, and eventually you build up a core of resentment. Or apathy. I'm discouraged by the fact that the great mass of people in this country have become cynical about politics and think there's no way they can influence Westminster decisions. They're tired of hysterics. They're tired of fluctuation. They end up diffident, thinking of Parliament as a talking shop, when they ought to have more active involvement."

Leonie hardly listened to the ensuing questions, caught up in his reasoning which was the final deduction from the materials of dissent she had been gathering for years. Scot, woman, Nationalist, Ellice Barr had specified the confines of her own minority position. Leonie could add a few more. Height and vocation and temperament singled her out further from the statutory norms for women. Minority within minority down to uniqueness, the lonely state of one.

Moncrieffe drew the parallel between people and political units which she had overlooked. This parenting of nascent ideologies was all-important. Minors and minorities. The link in language and theory explored the nucleus of social conflict, political, theatrical, familial, wherever groups evolved which were unlikely to be monocracies. His message was utterly obvious, while being as obscure as cliché. No single point of view was compulsory. Proportional opinion added up to the whole spectrum of free thought in which everyone did have the right of choice even when external compression threatened it. There was no distinction between political and personal bullying. She was not obliged to be the same as the next person because disagreement was neither mischievous nor perverse but a right, the basic freedom. She had confused the yoke of conformity, as her mother called it, with obedience. She grew heady from the thought that she did not actually have to do as she was told ever again.

Leonie noticed that in spite of the incubating heat of the day, Moncrieffe carried a raincoat, rolled up on his chair. It symbolised pessimism. It was a dark raincoat, not the beige, glamorised macintosh of secret agents. This was a guarantee against soiling, often rolled into the overhead rack of train or aeroplane. It was a true gaberdine, with a percentage of woollen fibre like the one she'd worn herself at one time, navy and belted, the unisex garment. She found it a human evocation of his susceptibility to rain and was troubled over and over again by the delineation of her own experience in his.

He finished speaking and the chairman for the evening wound up. The room emptied. Leonie stood hesitating by a door, ready to filter out incognito but Moncrieffe was too perceptive to let her slip away. He came quickly across from the side door he could have used and caught her by the arm saying, "Not so fast," and together they joined the stream heading towards the entrance, a mass that buoyed and resisted passage. They walked across the hallway unsure of the words they spoke to each other which were made thrilling by their inconsequence. Have you been waiting long? Where have you come from today? So you walked, did you? They knew they begged the central question because they avoided the imminent, Where to? Where now?

The floor of the church hall was chequered in black and white marble squares making up a grid pattern. Leonie watched her step, careful to place her foot, as children did, firmly within a square and avoided standing on the cracks which brought bad luck. Her foot was encased alternately in black or white. She accepted this measurement until they gained the outer door and the free flow of the open air.

They took a taxi back to Moncrieffe's flat on the Embankment a little south of Westminster where, as he anticipated, Quercus had let himself in with half a dozen other MPs to prolong the divisions of the house.

"Why here comes Viola!" Quercus turned round from their discussion and shook the new arrival by the hand.

"Oh, were you at the Playhouse too? It's been a long year since."

"You'll find they shorten reassuringly as you get older. But I shouldn't harp on your past successes. You're opening in *Hedda*, I believe. There's quite a stir. I couldn't come by tickets for the opening night."

Leonie hadn't expected this instantaneous exposure to Moncrieffe's milieu and was taken aback by so much attention from a man her mother had taught her to admire. Quercus' political books sat on the shelves at Morningside, unusually bought, unusually re-read. Ellice thought he was a better prose writer than Churchill, more pure and more distinctive if less witty. Meeting a prophet in person would have been disconcerting if Leonie hadn't passed her childhood in the company of learned men and knew they wanted an opinion less than an audience.

"Don't think of coming to the first night," she said. "Give me a week at least to tune in to the part."

"Come now, you're not nervous, are you?"

"A London début? Of course I am. And the others have had a month at it. I'm on cold."

"Well," he reassured, "maiden speeches are soon over and seldom held against you. Look at Disraeli."

Moncrieffe circulated. Women weren't entirely a novelty at these ante-chamber gatherings and so he made no exceptions for her. Leonie, after the first shock of initiation, wondered if her established reputation was the passport to this circle or if Moncrieffe brought home so many strays that they were unremarkable. Was she herself here, or his current companion?

"How did the vote go?" asked the absentee.

"Closer than you thought. A scrape home by two," said John Laidlaw. "Fleming's having a horribly rocky time, not a year into office. You've got to feel quite sorry for him. A majority of half a dozen may make for exciting evenings, but it's not good government." Laidlaw was a true Liberal, being free from dogma. He was the Presbyterian of politics with onus on individual responsibility, but often thought it would be much easier to belong to one of the collective religions like Roman Catholicism than be a daily decision taker.

"Do you know what they're talking about?" Quercus asked Leonie attentively as they stood by the open window on the balcony and the narrowness of the country's security caught up with them like cool draughts from the river.

"Of course. The government's trying to push through a transport bill that'll give developers more power and speed up their road building programme. But now the Tories, who were always pro-motorway, turn round and say it's in undemocratic haste."

"Frightfully banal, isn't it?" the senior statesman confided. "Like the plot of *Hamlet* in fifty words. But it's the incident that's so engrossing, and the style. Parliamentary style is much more interesting than you'd think. Or I've lived long enough to read the nuances. This is one of the better pieces of Westminster drama. My party had almost identical legislation planned but can't deny themselves the fun of being spoilers. Labour really want the electoral backing of big industry who are crying out for an improved road network and distribution but even Labour's own supporters in the Commons are playing hard to get. A motorway may be good for the country but it's bad for the constituency. I value my seat more than my principles is an important maxim for back-benchers to memorise."

Leonie gave him a long look, measuring this cynicism which came as an unexpected contrast to Moncrieffe's reflective delivery an hour before. She preferred earnest wrong-headedness.

Quercus read the look correctly and was a little abashed. "I know. It corrodes the ideals after a while. Is this an indecent glee

231

we derive? Maybe it's forced on us by being perennial bystanders. The country doesn't make enough use of its able men."

"You wouldn't be an advocate of a cross-party government?" she asked, thinking all Conservatives must be small c as well.

"Well, why not?"

"It does make you wonder why not when the Americans appoint advisers as ministers from outside Congress. It has its attractions, but you can't think it's workable here. We're too entrenched."

Quercus wasn't often surprised, and certainly not by women from whom he maintained an objective detachment based on the failure to charm. The swift and pertinent reply shook him a little as he allowed her more insidious attractions than face and talent. "Yes, the nearest we come to that is calling down cabinet ministers from the Lords. Hardly the wilderness."

"But coalition is a dirty word."

"Ah," said the man, "Moncrieffe has been baptising."

The host watched these two guests together a little anxiously, in case they showed signs of not liking one another. He caught the ripple of surprise as Quercus reappraised her with more seriousness. A formal gallantry stole over him that amused the younger man. Was Leonie actually flirting with his mentor? No, he thought it was something more subversive than flirtation. It wasn't a physical or even an emotional chord she struck with men. She manipulated the mind of the person she was in conversation with, entering the brain cell. She teased not in the sexual sense but as unravelling. And he remembered Stuart Ainslie telling him she was a director's dream and could adapt her voice to make a harmonic duo with each one of her stage partners. Find a note, strike a chord; the vocal metaphors were apt.

A twinge of jealousy afflicted Watson at this, the old soreness of wounded pride, wanting the woman to stay, be attentive, be his. Here he was stealing moments of her time and flattering himself that they were precious and unique. Well, they were, if he was sensible about it. They might be all he had. He shouldn't waste them in predictable responses.

Leonie unbent. It was a room in which nothing was strange, either in the setting or people. John Laidlaw, who was a fine musician, played a version of 'the Red Flag forever' on the piano, merging its chords into other political anthems and finally the national one. Dunns, the Scottish Nationalist, was the Celtic prototype; his hair was sand-coloured and crinkly, he was laconic until he passed the half way mark on a bottle of whisky, when he became unstoppable and he was pugnaciously adamant about what was effective in politics. He found that it was his turn to pour the drinks and he and Leonie exchanged reminiscences beside the ice bucket, having unknowingly attended several party conferences together. "Is your mother fighting fit?" he asked. It was only the flat at Morningside made larger and more regular, giving her the distance from provincialism. She entered the arena of their concerns not as a complete outsider but an initiate, informed and argumentative, on their terms as a means to knowing.

While she spoke to this one and that, Leonie watched Moncrieffe out of the corner of her eye, as he circulated without joining. She was acutely aware of him in the room, sitting, standing, making those blunt-ended gestures as he spoke. But he spoke less than he listened and by choice would have eavesdropped on all the conversations, hoisting antennae to catch the quiet rumours.

They counteracted brandy and Quercus' addictive port with coffee, mellowing into a stimulated weariness.

"D'you know," said Dunns, "I wilted this evening when our Right Honourable friend got to his feet and reeled off those smug statistics about Labour's splendid building programme. So many hospitals, so many houses in the public sector, so many miles of roads. And going back to the post-war administration! How can he be such a chump? It's so unsophisticated. And it'll be in all tomorrow's papers. They don't seem to realise the public switch off when they're being brow-beaten with figures."

"Yes," agreed Moncrieffe, thinking uneasily of his lecture that evening. How to improve? How to convince? How to reduce the irreducible complexities? "In politics we're always applying the lessons of yesterday to today. We don't seem to notice that times have moved on and the old standards don't apply."

The voice of Quercus came through the darkness that crept slowly from the window across the room. "Tempora mutant et nos mutamur in illis. We *ought* to be changed by them is the correct translation."

"We keep on using an inflexible formula to altered circumstances

233

and are surprised when the problem doesn't come out," opined the Nationalist.

This was a familiar idiom to Leonie and roused her out of a slumberous corner. "What we need to do is teach politicians how to use calculus instead of algebra."

The company paused, then laughed at a remark which was apt, if also accidental. Only two men present realised the full import of what she'd said, and they were silent. Moncrieffe was struck by the spectre of her husband which she'd raised; Quercus at the intellectual apparition. He was deterred at the thought of convincing most politicians, who couldn't even fill in their tax returns correctly, of the subtlety of that calculation, never mind explaining the difference between fixed and shifting values to the electorate. So they were both quiet in the middle of hilarity, one sunk in personal and the other in universal gloom.

They left towards midnight. Leonie stayed on, expanded by the congenial company to the point where hurrying back to one room was masochistic.

"I haven't congratulated you," Watson said from the far side of a Chesterfield. "You have a son."

"How did you know about that?"

"I read my *Scotsman* too. The sixteenth of March, wasn't it?"

"Yes, the sixteenth." A wary silence fell through which Leonie sensed his criticism. "I think you blame me for leaving my son behind and tearing off to London to do my own thing like this. Maybe I blame myself. I'd already contracted with Stuart and the Haymarket to do this play and I told myself last summer that it was only for a month or two. But Andrew hadn't been born last summer and it was much harder to come away than I thought it would be. I probably should have broken my agreement but chances like this are so hard to get."

She had changed over that year. Unlike most women who acquired a rounded self-satisfaction, she seemed physically and mentally more sculptured, as if maternity removed the last excess of youth. He remembered the impetuous responses of the first of May, and thought she would be different now, cooler, wiser, maybe more guarded. She wouldn't come his way.

"What's your son like?" Moncrieffe asked, not without envy.

234

"Andrew – he's like Fergus. He's a most sagacious child. He doesn't play with toys. He studies them. Though he did laugh just before I left and that was delightful. It was Fergus who made him laugh, not me. He was knocking a ball against a wall before we painted it and suddenly the baby chuckled."

"Rapid movement. Always engaging."

She smiled, sad. "I keep thinking of these phases that I'm missing out on and how they won't come again. It's very damaging, really, when I'm not doing either of the jobs well."

"Of mothering?" He mused among the few mothers that he knew. "What does mothering consist of? You're not essential to his physical well-being at the moment. You would be frustrated if you thought you'd settled for . . ." he searched for a word that wasn't derisory, "the easy route. At least now you know."

"When you spoke this evening about mothers having a duty to protect the interests of minorities, I couldn't help thinking that for me that doesn't mean being with my child all the time. His interests may be best served by someone else. That's not a facile attempt to rationalise. It's not easy admitting you're dispensable to anyone's happiness." She was consoled a little none the less.

Moncrieffe, on the other hand, found that their conversations were disturbing because they went awry. As on their car journey, they started well along the line suggested by his prompting until she gave an answer that veered away from the predicted one. The average woman, legitimately following her own career would have said, I miss my child agonisingly but the nurse copes so well, putting an end to speculation. Her picture of missed laughter, a child already wise at birth, the vignette of Fergus doing something as unacademic as hitting a tennis ball pelota-fashion against an indoor wall – these were sharp and unpretentious truths that troubled him. The images he built up of her as a womanly force, for she did still vibrate for him like a source of heat, focal and compulsive in any room, or as a mental one slipping in and out of his perceptions without reserve, became more complex with the shading of her personality. The lived woman was a translucent medium; no mystery, no secrets. The thought woman was a spectrum of rotating pattern that shifted just as he felt he'd caught it. Juxtaposed, the two parts of her character set up a paradox that

235

was as enigmatic as a riddle. She was out of kilter with the norm. Out of kilter? Yes, that too. She evoked the Scottish idiom in his thinking which he instinctively trusted more than the acquired English one. Above all, he found himself little bored.

"Must you go?" he asked, leaning forward to convince. "You can stay here."

Leonie had folded herself comfortably into the cushions of his furniture but at the suggestion of permanency, she uncurled again and put her feet firmly on the ground. Well, he was a man after all though he wasn't to be blamed if she had misled him. "No, I'll take a taxi, thank you, if you could call me one."

The prim thank you made him smile. "Where would the taxi take you?"

"An Edwardian terraced street behind King's Cross."

"Is it grim?"

"I've lived in shoddier houses. But there's something so dismal about red brick."

"I really mean it. You can stay here until the end of your run. You need somewhere more restful to live than King's Cross. I have it. I'm not often here so you can come and go as you please. I'd appreciate that."

Oh God, it sounded suave. She had never been more deftly propositioned. She faced the idea squarely. "Perhaps your career survives that kind of scandal. Mine wouldn't."

"Scandal? That's an Edinburgh term. Behaviour can be redefined in London. Nobody knows and even if they did, nobody cares." He became a fraction haughty. "This is a four-room apartment. A kitchen, a drawing room and two bedrooms. You are most welcome to one of them. Many people use this as a resting place, passing through. Men and women. Be my guest. The after-dinner conversation can be stimulating."

She did feel gauche and provincial in the face of such liberal generosity. It was only what Alison had done, bunking down in a bedsit in Oxford when there was nowhere else to go. It seemed as though she could be neither a gracious guest nor host. Moncrieffe got to his feet while she watched herself hesitating over a simple change of address, redirecting poste restante as she'd done so often in her travels, theatre to digs. He came back and put a key in her hand which she acknowledged as the symbol of her nightly privacy.

She did not lock her door and he did not test the fermature.

25

Alison took her final examinations and by the middle of June was ready for her release from the dull and chrysalis state of studentship. On the verge of a decision about her future and her career, she had located something elusive in her personality, or possibly indeterminate, which other people had been mocking gently all her life. They said she was idealistic without being practical. It was true, she found it easier to react than to act. She had a marked response in the negative, as a neutraliser to wrongs and conditions she disliked, though she told herself this was quite genuinely motivated. Given freedom from constraints, however, she didn't know what to do with herself and drifted.

Conditions round about her changed. Muriel had eventually done what she'd proposed to do for years and bought a separate flat in Grange Loan where she installed Harris as caretaker. It was meant to be a money-making speculation, Harris living on a reduced rental provided that he monitor the comings and goings of three other paying tenants. He agreed to the principle, but defaulted on the payment. They became his mates. He didn't care to exact their rent as punctiliously as his mother would. They all colluded in defrauding the safeguards of the meter system and then found they couldn't pay the quarterly bills. They laughed at debt, knowing that Muriel could afford to stretch their credit by a month or two and were only motivated to cancel it when her temper ran short, a measure which they calculated to perfection. Muriel found that instead of one prodigal son, she had created four and although she threatened to evict them, sue them or make an official complaint to their employers, they remained incorrigible.

The pipe dream Alison had entertained of setting up a liberal, come as you please household with her brother melted away. Harris had no assets as a living partner apart from good humour and even that was dispensed sporadically. She longed for something more sustained and permanent. The separation of her parents, the trial, the falling-out with Fergus meant that one family member after another had peeled off, all the supportive menfolk, until she and her mother were left bruisingly alone in the gaunt house at Greenbank, deprived of buffers. Sometimes, she was moved to go and see Fergus and her nephew. Michael's sentence had been completed, a total of fifteen months with remission, and he lived with his son and grandson in the house at the Hermitage. A full reinstatement between them was the most natural move, but Alison recognised that, having turned her back on them in adversity, she was excluded from sharing their respite. Besides, that street was haunted. Old happinesses hung on there and an old love affair.

Work provided no alternative allure. Her training for it was mechanical and had stretched neither her abilities, which were as acute as Fergus's if less directed, nor her imagination. Fergus lived for the symbolic truth of mathematics, an assertive core of faith, but Alison found economics less absolute because it started to tip over into areas of profit and loss, about which she was uneasy. No, she had no inclination to become an economist, macro or micro, and thought her apprenticeship was wasted.

What did she want to do, positively? She didn't know. She looked out of an office window into St Andrew's Square, summed by the headquarters of the Royal Bank of Scotland, and loathed the rectilinear nine to five. One friend was setting up his own advertising agency and she daydreamed for a while about the independence of the self-employed, hard work for high returns. She searched among her own skills for the profit-making capacity and failed to locate it. Her facility with words was less than with numbers. She could neither organise other people nor stimulate herself to the exceptional effort, obeying a schedule only when it was imposed. She was a follower, not a leader. She faced an unpleasant possibility; she had a taste for the eccentric but no talent. Devoid of creativity, she was compelled into secondary forms of employment, a wage earner rather than freelance.

A means of escape from both restrictions, work and home, had presented itself of late. She'd had an invitation to an opening night in London. *Hedda Gabler* at the Haymarket. Should she accept? It meant a day or two in London, stretching to a week and the hope that something would turn up to delay her return. She might see

Leonie. The attractions mounted, though she misgave at moments on the conditions implicit on her acceptance. How would she tell Muriel that she was absconding yet again? Then the two thoughts fused, Leonie and London. How easy to imply she was going purposely to see the actress, as she had for her trip to Oxford, instead of admitting that she went at the invitation of the director.

Stuart Ainslie had a run of luck with his London opening. The theatre critic of *The Guardian* postponed his holiday by a day, came to the preview and gave them a rave notice which was printed to coincide with the official first night. There was an air of gala at the Haymarket Theatre. Evening dress proliferated in the stalls and made sporadic outbursts along the balcony. The audience suspended its critical judgment, glad to have a known play performed to standards of excellence by familiar voices. Someone breathed that the production was unadventurous, and so it was. It was safe, non-experimental but professional. The director's eye, which was so negligent about everyday appearances, was meticulous in matching the colour of a gown to a detail of wallpaper on set and in this recessionary socialist-drab season the audience gawped at opulence. They took four curtain calls that turned into a standing ovation. A rumour ran that the production was to be televised. They were a hit.

Backstage, Leonie and Kenneth Frew were swamped by well-wishers and champagne, spilling over from the royal retiring room to the passageways behind the stage and into the manager's office. It was almost midnight before the real celebration party of the cast headed towards the restaurant in Covent Garden where supper was booked.

There were a good many extras. Moncrieffe standing in her dressing room doorway shouldn't have unsettled Leonie but he did. She had been in his flat for two days, though it was such a hectic time for both of them, all-night sittings at the House and Stuart's perfectionist rehearsals, that they met only in passing. He hadn't said that he would go to the performance and she didn't anticipate that he would bribe and corrupt to have a front seat in the stalls. Or possibly he had bought his ticket long ago, intending to turn up at her dressing room the way he'd done in Oxford. He was a man for the flamboyant gesture. At any rate, his appearance

240

put the clock back.

"I am so very pleased to see you," she said, unconsciously repeating herself.

"I thought that you could probably do with some support."

The other members of the cast gathered on the pavement waiting for taxis while the two of them went ahead in the Daimler, weaving their way across Trafalgar Square through the traffic that was still dense at midnight. Support, he said. The phrase succeeded in demoralising her. She realised that neither her mother nor Fergus had ever seen a performance of hers, amateur or professional, and the notion that someone might show a technical interest in her career revealed not self-aggrandisement but the fact that, in modesty, she hadn't expected anyone to back her. Watson's response was simpler, couched in friendship and human curiosity. At the same time, she could appreciate that he might feel his own solitary career went unsupported by his family so that they shared the bond of outcasts and loners. Recognition of this was access to compatibility.

"No criticism?" she was trusting enough to ask while they waited for lights to change at the bottom of the Strand.

"I thought that you found Brack more attractive than sinister, so the suicide was perhaps fickle instead of being properly . . . moral. Hedda needs to be moral if she's going to be tragic."

"That's true. I did. He played the part as an entertaining man and was oddly solicitous. Their relationship is the only honest one in the play, or at least it's not founded on deception. You sound as if you dislike Hedda very much."

"Dislike? Yes, maybe I do. You tend to dislike someone you know so very intimately. Nothing's hidden and that's shocking. We're very fond of deceiving ourselves about how fine and high-principled we are and rebel at being shown that we aren't, as a race. That's the real catharsis of play-going. It's a horrible self-exposure, if we're watching with our minds. At the same time, I'd vouch for disliking every character on the stage of *King Lear* and it doesn't affect the momentum of the drama for me. Like or dislike is immaterial. It is."

They arrived at the restaurant and were shown to an upper room ahead of the main party who came noisily behind. Leonie was absorbed arranging for Moncrieffe's extra place but, hearing

241

Stuart's voice, turned to forestall his comment. The rest of the cast came up the stairway in a surge, carried on the high of their success and disrupting the conversation of other after-theatre diners who looked round.

A single face emerged as individual and half smiled up at Leonie. It was Alison's face distinctively featured in the crowd. Alison again. Leonie didn't smile down in reply but stood astonished and rather put out as her sister-in-law approached up the staircase towards her.

Alison's smile was less of a greeting than an appeasement. No theatre-goer, she knew she'd seen something remarkable at the Haymarket that evening and it elevated the actress from the familiar in her scale to the exceptional, an uncomfortable transition in the close domestic circle. That she'd never had the measure of Leonie's ability embarrassed her and put a screen of self-consciousness between them. She couldn't find a single generous or congratulatory thing to say. And then there was Leonie's appearance. The actress wore a black dress which Alison recognised as a Fortuny gown. Pre-war or new, she didn't know. Leonie was quite likely to have bought it on a second hand stall in the King's Road. Her sources were often discreditable. It was a garment singularly suited to her height and figure, with its crushed pleats falling heavily like the folds of Grecian drapery turned into stone. She wore her hair loose in a sheaf and its crimp rippled like the dress. Leonie, who was an oddity in Edinburgh, London made statuesque and even regal.

This was no more restful a transition than her acquiring fame.

"You should have told me you were coming," said Leonie, aware how removed this was from her welcome to Moncrieffe half an hour earlier in the theatre. Consciousness of him pulsed at the back of her brain, signal of a guilt that she hadn't made her change of lodging known, to Fergus, to Stuart, in fact to anyone. Forewarning was what she begged so that she could fabricate a story.

"There was no time." Alison reached the same level while Moncrieffe, recognising the ardent girl, withdrew into the background.

"You *do* have somewhere to stay?" The question was kindly meant, if disingenuous, with Leonie praying she wouldn't want a bed from her at the old King's Cross address.

Alison looked defensive and told the truth since she suspected it was already known. "I'm staying in Stuart's flat while I'm down here."

Leonie's progress towards their dinner table was arrested, the two of them blocking the way to other guests for a while. "Stuart Ainslie?"

"Yes, he asked me down for the first night."

Leonie controlled herself and the imperative questions. Does Muriel know what you are doing? In what sense are you staying with Stuart? She didn't want to know the answers which might bear too direct a relevance to herself. Her director and her sister-in-law became suspect if they were sharing a flat, man and woman, an opprobrium from which of course she and Moncrieffe were exempt. What had he said – We're always deceiving ourselves about how fine and high-principled we are – and here was the proof, in the form of her suspicions and her own guardedness, that she wasn't so noble at all. So the two women moved tentatively along the table, glad of sideways interruptions.

There was a photo call during supper, more champagne, toasts and laudatory speeches. There were twenty people at their table but the four who had met for the first time in Ellice Barr's flat and were reassembled here in a different shape as two co-habiting couples, according to appearances, were sharply self-aware among the mass of celebrants. Moncrieffe's presence at the party was as livening an event to the director as Alison's was to his leading lady. Four quadrants, they touched but dared not mix.

"Are you pleased?" Stuart asked Leonie. "Was it worth it, worth a minor domestic inconvenience?" Moncrieffe came distantly into his line of vision and he added, "Or maybe a major one."

For once, Stuart's jibes misfired or found a sensitive spot. Leonie, raw and out of sorts, couldn't restrain herself from answering waspishly, "It may be major indeed. Does Alison know that you are married?"

The director halted and his teasing smile went through several gradations towards the wry. "Fancy you remembering that." The midnight confession five years before, whisky-induced, was fuzzy in Stuart's memory but sharp in hers. His wife was a nurse, Helen, based in Perth, who classically misunderstood or wasn't sympathetic to his vocation. This excused many sexual excursions.

243

Leonie had been irritated at the time principally because he'd treated her to such an unoriginal narrative. This suppressed partner was the missing emphasis in Stuart's private life, which looked on the surface free or floating but was also obscure. He often returned to Perth for a wash and brush-up by a woman of regular and unpretentious habits who tolerated him well.

"I remember all the important lines, precisely. Be very careful, Stuart."

"For me, or for Alison?"

True. Why should it matter? "For all of us." The imbroglio of family life loomed, with Muriel rushing to restore damaged reputations and family honour as they each moved into the orbit of Petrie. Yes, that was the first reaction as she saw Alison mount the stairs of the restaurant, annoyance that she conveyed the waft of Petrie like a bad conscience to spoil her celebratory evening. Another fact she wished she didn't know. Another sadness that Alison chose so badly from among menfolk.

They drew apart and after a little while, Watson passed her a glass of champagne and asked, "Are you all right?"

The observative concern hurt. "Fine."

"We'll go as soon as you say you've had enough. It's been a long day for you."

"Very well, we'll wait for the first editions. We have to hear what the papers say." She was brusque, covering the shameful impulse he produced in her to self-indulgence or reliance on the nearest arm. His attentiveness highlighted other neglects. There was no card or telegram from Fergus; only his own needs were phrased in the imperative.

In the small hours they left as they arrived, together, a fact that went not entirely unobserved.

26

Fergus rose towards happiness. He came home every day about five o'clock and walked all the way up the hill from Morningside, a journey which was so well established in his life that it had taken on the veneration of a pilgrimage. The stones were shrines he deferred to as he passed. It was a warm season. The streets baked, sunk under the particular stupor of a northern sun, low and penetrating in the sky. It made him expansive, adding to the sense he carried these days of being in total possession.

He had marked his last batch of examination papers for the year and submitted them to the moderator. His first academic season had been a success. There was no problem over his renewal of contract, in fact there was talk already of a promotion to 'reader' status which meant he'd have less student contact time. Not that he objected to his teaching schedule as such. Bred on the pernick-etiness of chess notation, he was well used to breaking down a complex formula into its smallest components and applied this to his teaching method. He knew he didn't have remarkable powers of delivery, erring on the side of a correct, unemotional monotone, but the sheer perfectionism of his methodology kept a lecture theatre full of students straining in their seats in case they missed one essential word from the logical cohesion of the argument. Tautology was not his problem. No one skipped with Dr. Petrie. He was illustrious in his way. The serious mathematicians wanted to emulate him; the non-serious admired his overpowering competence. He had worked himself into a position of power and authority and was recognised as a significant addition to his department, a man who would one day be a national and maybe an international figure.

The irritant was personal. He had spent seven years as a student who was talented enough to follow his own disciplines. Serving others came hard. Just at the moment when an idea became interesting, he had to stop and decode it for lesser minds. Research was his forte. Anybody could do this degree cycling. So in the middle of completeness there was a wistful note that the task was not ultimately of his choosing.

Irene Geddes worked in the garden throughout the afternoon which had grown in intensity rather than fading. The wind had dropped and in sheltered corners the concentration of warmth and moisture from overnight rain made for a midsummer lushness in which the vegetation could be seen or felt to grow. She pulled the dead heads from the roses which were already past their best, using gloves which were leather on the backs and palms, with cotton gussets. It was through this less protected gore that a thorn pricked her. She pulled the glove off and pulled out the thorn which had broken. A point of blood appeared, and she smeared it impatiently before carrying on with the job until the whole rosebed was tidy. The soil work she left to the gardener and so she brought a lounging chair out of the sunhouse, brushing off its dust, and lay back in it for a while, comfortable in its padded insulation. The sun flickered and the leaves rippled transparently overhead. Her eyelids dropped towards repose.

Happiness? Yes, she was happy too and the mood wasn't unconnected with Fergus Petrie's. She knew she placed her chair where she would see him as he passed in front of the gates to her gravel drive. The return of the Petries, even in part, had given her life added dimension. The mornings when she looked after the baby were full and purposeful. She was needed. Child care brought her incidentally closer to her daughter-in-law who lived in Balerno, a house in the outlying villages being all that the newly married couple could afford, but near enough at that. Matthew and Jennifer also had a son whom they called Adam. Irene shed years as she drove her own charge out to Balerno, organised shopping trips, systematised her erratic days to fit the regulations of infancy and stepped back into rejuvenating motherhood. The chores weren't burdensome. She never complained, even mentally, and in fact dreaded Leonie's homecoming which would remove the new pivot of her existence.

Why? Did one child matter so very much? No, not the morning but the evening she waited for, when Fergus came to see her for a moment or two before taking over from Ellice Barr's shift. She coaxed him to talk a little and he continued the habit of confiding in her. He found her an exemplary confidante, patient, silent, sympathetic and utterly discreet, a repository of secrets which were never divulged, unbreakable alphameric codes.

And here he came. She stood up languidly to meet his footsteps, as if they weren't counted out like heartbeats.

"All done now," he said, waiting only a moment before they headed back down the Geddes drive together to his own.

She could interpret his most cryptic phrases. "You can concentrate on the book now. You'll meet that September deadline after all."

"It looks like it." Publication next May, an alternative success and one that would do his prime career no harm.

This manual had revived Irene's own interest in chess, for she was a passable player, of Fergus' standard if not better. She'd taken on herself the work of checking the computer print-out of each game, ensuring with a three-dimensional board and pieces that the moves were at least legal. This was important because a clean type-ready script brought Fergus an enhanced fee. She added one or two minor suggestions for clarity of layout which he appreciated, aware that she represented the average, non-specialist reader. Occasionally in the evening she brought the proof-read sheets to his study and they would consult over them, losing their personalities in the abstract perfection of the symbols. He didn't talk down to her. He didn't need to. She understood with an acute, formed intelligence just what he was driving at.

"How's Michael been?"

"So-so. He stayed at home this morning but we had lunch together."

He did feel guilty about this imposition. She baby-sat Michael as well, more helpless and dependent than the child. The man was in an acutely depressive state because there was nothing he could do. There was no business or form of employment he could return to and so work his way back to respectability, or even self-respect. Fergus, who filled every minute to excess, was frustrated by his father's passivity. He recognised the legal restraints but goddammit, the man could do something with himself instead of stagnating between the morning and the evening delivery of the newspapers.

247

"I don't know what to suggest," he said.

"Give him time."

He nodded, taking the placebo which would be unacceptably weak from anyone else, and noticed the bloodstain on her finger. "You should cover that," he admonished. "For tetanus. Do you have plasters in the house?"

"Of course. It's nothing."

The driveway ended and, without a formal goodbye, which would have been as redundant as between members of the same household, they parted.

His garden wasn't as kempt as Irene's, he thought, passing between its borders. He couldn't afford a handyman as yet, or the time to learn about planting schedules which he reserved as future potential. He'd had a major overhaul of the site in the spring, but was more a pruner than a grower. His only talent so far was compost, being determined to have a chemical-free garden that didn't offend against ecological standards.

As he went into the hallway through the stone arch, Fergus overheard a strange one-sided conversation. It was Ellice speaking to her three-month grandson, a dialogue of unanswered questions and comments which amused the father. The running commentary covered her planned itinerary for the evening, snippets from the day's newspaper or observations about the people she'd met in the course of their afternoon walk. Irene drove the child; Ellice pushed him about in a pram worthy of the title baby carriage. The hood was firmly folded down so that he could observe the passing world. Perhaps the most comic element of the monologue was that it made no concessions to baby talk. It was a fully adult, polysyllabic speech to which the child listened attentively, as compelled by the music of her voice as everyone else she met.

The woman straightened up when Fergus entered and her indulgent expression changed to formal politeness, as she turned from son to father. They mellowed towards each other in behaviour, but not in principle. They could share a room in the physical sense but moods were disparate.

"How are you?" was the phrase he had evolved as striking the right balance between the concerned and intimate.

"Quite well. We've been to Duddingston today." She employed

248

this 'we' about the inexpressive child and he found it had a taking innocence.

"A longish way. You must be tired."

"We can step out." She was dismissive, but knew he expressed solicitude in his way.

Compared with Michael's inertia, her briskness was engaging. In truth, Fergus liked the eclectic household he had gathered round him. In spite of being a private man, the idea of the commune, even an intellectual commune, appealed to one side of his character. He was one of the academics who believed that knowledge should be shared, grew impatient with researchers' secrecy and espionage when it meant two faculties in Bonn and California might be working on identical material at the same time. Wasteful if nothing else. Sharing and equality were deeply ingrained in his attitudes. Each to his specialism was a refinement on this. That Irene cared for his child physically and Ellice mentally, while Michael could be trusted as guardian for the sleeping hours, struck him as a perfect blend of talents. The odd assorted household represented an ideal philosophy of the harmonic whole, each member different, each contributory.

It was his own job to put his son to bed; patient and deft-handed, he found the routine agreeable. The boy, a robust, dark-skinned child with vigorous limbs, seemed to understand the need for changing from one set of clothes into another and didn't flail. Handling him, Fergus was reminded of something he'd been told about paintings of the Madonna and child. The infant Christ was never represented by Old Masters as asleep or lolling. The eyes were open, the face alert even at birth.

His own son did sleep but as soon as he awoke Fergus felt he was in the presence of an alternative intelligence, watchful, receptive, maybe at times analytical. He didn't so much play with his son as experiment with his perceptions, carrying out the tests of the child psychologist. He looked up the work of Piaget and Anastasi and evolved his own battery of tests to measure his son's ability, manual and perceptual. Strong grip. Strong eye. The child had an immediate response to changes of facial expression and tended to watch his mouth as he spoke, relating sound to lip shape. Fergus knew this was in advance of most infant development and read analyses of the gifted child to prove his point, discovering that a

249

child prodigy was frequently the first born of a professional father with exceptional physical as well as mental prowess. Fergus grew excited by the arc of this potential which led into infinity. He began to spend some part of the evening talking to his son, not like Ellice over his head but slowly, deliberately in the same phrases with the aid of tangible objects. He modified a simple string of coloured beads to make a rudimentary abacus and counted from right to left, one to ten laboriously.

And the child watched and absorbed it all. His attention did not waver. Fergus grew frustrated, certain that the intellect was ready to learn but was impeded by physical immaturity. He exercised the boy's limbs in sequential patterning, hurrying him on over the slow exploratory stages of growth and sharpening his reactions with contrasts of hot and cold, sweet and sour, bright and dim. It was a passionate, all-encompassing interest and when the boy was finally put to bed Fergus was both worn out and exhilarated by the shaping mind.

His study waited quietly for him each evening, a shadowy over-hung spot looking into the Hermitage trees. No one disturbed it except Irene putting the mail on his desk to be opened at leisure when the bulk of the day's work was done.

He dealt swiftly with the bills, writing out cheques at once in payment, wrote a quick note in answer to an American correspondent who hoped to visit Edinburgh in the summer, inviting him to stay, and so worked his way down to the less definable missives. One, with a typed address, was from the moderator for the First Ordinary mathematics course. It queried one of his fails. Fergus had deliberated long and hard about the fate of this particular student, a bright but indolent lad who happened to be one of Fergus' tutees, whom he knew to be hopelessly erratic about handing in work to schedule. The area of doubt was two deductive questions on a paper of four where the answers were far adrift of the right one. Nothing unusual in that. Perfectly correct answers were in a minority but a student could still pass by showing sound mechanics and a knowledge of method. Fergus felt this student could neither calculate nor reason adequately. He applied the wrong formula and made a slapdash error in computation, so that Fergus gave him no credit for the little he had got right which resulted in the fail. The moderator disagreed by half a dozen marks and wished to refer the paper to the professor.

It was the first disagreement of the day, of the entire academic year and Fergus was angered by it. He didn't like the student, found something familiarly loose-willed or misdirected about him, while the letter troubled his conscience about apparent prejudice. The student was the son of a wealthy family, educated at an English public school, and Fergus couldn't control the physical shrinking from his arrogant airs. Over-exercise of his authority was his compensation. So he wrote a reply that was cursory. 'It will do Master Williamson no harm at all to spend the summer with his text books as remedy for a winter spent on the rugby field.'

This referral clinched a decision. He'd been attracted a year before to the department of Machine Intelligence which was entirely research-orientated and the offer of a lectureship without student responsibilities had been repeated recently. He'd spend no more time with layabouts. His work was worth more than these petty queries. There were half a dozen projects in AI that drew him, voice imitants, a mathematical problem with robotics called 'singularity', a term which denied its multiple facets. He would be engrossed.

The last item was an envelope with a London postmark which contained no letter but a photograph, a newspaper clipping in fact, without any covering note. He unfolded it warily and found a picture of his wife taken at a party after the first night of her new play. The caption printed underneath told him that much. He wasn't sure if he would have recognised her otherwise. He'd not seen her with that loose hair style before, a contradiction of the clinging gown. The image shocked him a little because of its sophistication and its portrayal of a life beyond these walls or his involvement. It asserted independence more than Leonie's real absence because it highlighted for the first time what she actually did in that removed existence. She had become demonstrably beautiful whereas he had been the only person to think so at one time, and achieving. These two aspects, refining each other, propelled her into a different orbit from his exclusive one. He didn't feel regret, for he was proud of what she did and that his belief in her ability was justified, but sadness that he couldn't supply the full scope for her talents.

He noticed that the sender had added a single arrow to the cutting and terminated it with an exclamation mark. Tracing the line back to its source, through the dot matrices of newsprint, he found it related to the figure of a man in evening dress who stood immediately behind his wife as if she'd broken off a conversation with him to face the camera. He knew this unnamed man, knew he was Moncrieffe, the only son of Edward Moncrieffe QC, a Member of Parliament, a potential Lord – the upper cases mounted enhancing his entitlement. Lady Moncrieffe had given ample testimony at the Court of Session of her business transactions with Michael Petrie. A strong pursuant of claims. Was her grandson an associate of Leonie's, and a closet one? Why hadn't she mentioned him openly and honestly to her husband? Because he was an enemy of Fergus Petrie's interests, and a dishonest friend.

He put the clipping down and carried on a long train of association. Leonie had come back once during her month's absence, towards the end of rehearsal time when she could be spared for a day or two. She'd flown up, which in itself marked a new phase in their lives. Time was in shorter supply than money nowadays. It wasn't a successful trip. Leonie was reassured to find the household running on wheels in her absence, but excluded by its efficiency. She spoke about London and the play as of a country which he hadn't visited and couldn't understand. They had an emotional block compounded of distance and shyness. Michael had been in the house for the first time and he unwittingly imposed a physical restraint on them. The house had ears. They heard him walk the floor hour after hour, night after night, creating a silent inhibition. In fact, Fergus recounted ruefully, their marriage hadn't been reconsummated after Andrew's birth. A long recovery plus a professional absence prolonged their separation to the point where they became self-conscious about ending it.

So the face of the man in evening dress filled an emotional vacuum in him after a long period of puzzlement about Leonie's behaviour, to which he thought his own standards of methodical progression applied. He didn't understand the circumstantial. The fact that this photograph existed and was sent made it look like evidence and, uncharacteristically, Fergus drew conclusions without concrete proof. Assumptions, misapplied premises, errors in calculation flawed his logic. Who was so malicious as to send this poison-pen photograph with anonymous intent? He couldn't think of anyone who had such intimate knowledge of their lives and, failing to pinpoint an individual, he ascribed the envoy to general knowledge. Perhaps this man explained Leonie's devious insistence on pursuing her London career in the first place. Perhaps . . . many things.

His instinct was to throw the cutting away, as with the newspaper coverage of the trial, or burn it, but he had learned unpleasantness was inescapable. Print was proof. The photograph ultimately confirmed his own shunning of publicity. Success to Leonie was overt, not discreet while his natural reticence was repelled by such obvious reportage. These banner headlines were the antithesis of his protective privacy. Thank goodness, after all, she didn't use the name of Petrie. There was a noise in the room, an expulsion of air as if someone had difficulty with his breathing which ended in a cough, or sob. He stopped himself in time. No, none of that. Hadn't he promised that nothing would ever hurt him again?

He looked down at her face which was happy and even radiant in a way he seldom remembered it. This other life was a release for her, although he measured in minus quantity how that happiness was achieved at his expense.

27

Moncrieffe didn't imagine he was a great mountaineer, but he thought he was a good one. In the spring, John Laidlaw had come to stay at Torrisaig and when another friend of theirs, Roger Prior, passed through Wester Ross on his way to the Cuillins of Skye, they decided to make a trip to one of the mountains between Torrisaig and the Kyle of Lochalsh.

It was an ancient mountain said by geologists to be over seven billion years old. That day it did feel monumental and the three men, approaching the more challenging west face, felt minimal, foolhardy even tackling the ascent. The snow line had receded with the spring which had the effect of stretching the mountain higher than its three and a half thousand feet. The heather of the lower slopes was slippery with a thin ice glaze and they had to stop themselves from sliding backwards by using the axe as an anchor.

John Laidlaw was an experienced climber. He'd climbed in the Alps since adolescence and had been, to Moncrieffe's envy, a member of an international expedition to Annapurna, ill-fated as it happened because of atrocious weather which confined half the party to base camp. Prior was a rock climber more than anything and this was his first climb on ice and snow. In experienced hands, he was able to relax, chattering euphorically about the pure air, the view over the valley as the perspective opened up, the unexpected warmth of the sun reflected from the snow – wasting precious energy, thought Moncrieffe, who wouldn't answer.

On the summit ridge there was a slight rise in temperature which caused lumps of snow and ice to break away. The spindrift started to cascade down at an alarming rate. Laidlaw was in the lead, Prior next. As they approached the ridge, they found that an overhanging cornice was blocking the direct route to the top and the anxiety of this frustration transmitted itself along the rope like a telegraph wire. Laidlaw hacked away the loose snow to drive in a spike, but this incidentally removed the surface for the next man to clamp himself to. They belayed slowly across this overhang, with the rope an insurance against the serious or fatal fall. The bowline tied round the waist was comforting, but ultimately it was an impediment like walking in harness. Moncrieffe admired the steady hand above. Laidlaw was a neat climber, with a physique both slim and strong so that his footwork was a species of juggling, or a tricky beam exercise as he edged forwards, creating footholds and handholds in the ice with no spare movement. Moncrieffe himself was too top-heavy for real athleticism; ratio of weight to muscle was wrong although sustained fitness meant his breathing was evenly controlled. He grew impatient with the flustered scrambling of the novice ahead of him who puffed and panted.

At last the three men cleared the ridge and stood on the summit. There wasn't a movement in the air. The sun poured down with fluid brilliance colouring the drifts in the ravines a piercing blue. It was a wild exhilarating moment. There was no hurry. Midday and all the time in the world to make the descent before the sun started to move off the mountain.

Moncrieffe slipped his karabiner from the line and said, "I'm going over to that crevasse. I'll be half an hour or so. Roger can get his breath back."

Laidlaw looked along the ridge where the broken crust of the rocks showed through the snow covering as the sun melted it. "For the descent we'll take the straight line down." It was a simple gully, easy for downhill work.

Moncrieffe walked away, relieved that the party split and he had some time alone. He raised his hand after two hundred yards and seeing the two men proceed along the ridge, called, "Don't walk about roped together without one of you being belayed."

The crevasse on the far side of the ridge, which was quite a famous landmark, was menacing. Heavy falls of snow had narrowed it into a vertical chimney; passing inside its shadow, Moncrieffe was chilled by the intolerable contrast between sun and shade. Comparisons of temperature or skin reaction were trivial. His lungs compressed in the squeeze of the thin dry air. His face puckered in pain. Yes, it made you gasp with fear. Why did you do it, walk into the valley of the shadow of death? To test something internal, lungs or endurance. Mountaineers had the stuff of martyrs or hermits in them, the sustained alone. He wasn't entirely happy above the snow line, feeling it marked a transition from sanity, the recoverable position, to insanity. Climbing was a curious obsession when, after so much planning and so much effort, even success had nothing to show for itself. There was no win, no certificate of excellence, not a single proof to people down below that you had actually done what you said you'd done. It was a pursuit where you were bound by honour. Challenging the unspecified forced its own truth. You couldn't lie about the outcome because whatever mountain you climbed, winter, summer, in good or bad conditions, it was a scaled face of the self.

So the adventure made him strong by forcing recognition of his limits. He wasn't superhuman. He wasn't immortal. Testing it, however, was a proof of stamina along which he edged himself precipitously. His mountain boots approached their own coming of age. Bought for an expedition in the Cairngorms, they were unrecognisable from student outings. The eyelets were grooved by the pressure of the laces, his sweat stained them dark and the leather turned to bruises. But they still carried him forwards. He felt a different man when he put them on, braced, adhered.

He turned, sending a shiver of loose snow down the mountainside that coned outwards. He reached the ridge effortlessly and saw that Laidlaw and Prior had walked ahead to the point of descent, a broad escarpment of snow. He thought they underestimated the precarious edge, and was annoyed to see the novice and the expert were still harnessed together by the rope, without being anchored. A warning signal in himself made him hurry forward.

But almost as if his movement started a catastrophe, a footfall to an avalanche, the men fell. They fell softly and plungingly over the rim of the snow which the creeping sun had melted. Moncrieffe watched them bowl helplessly down the chute. He knew that they were dead, grotesquely bound by the nylon line at either end of which they lurched in unison. He knew there was no point in running towards them. A hopeless feat running in snow like rowing against a high tide. Then the motion stopped as suddenly as it had begun, the two forms dangling at each end of a noose which had caught on a spur of sandstone three inches wide that protruded through the snow. Relying on his axe to give a handhold, Moncrieffe quickly worked his way down towards the bodies, not so much aghast as numb.

They weren't dead. Both men were breathing and Moncrieffe knew he was charged with the responsibility for keeping them alive. Prior lay in the open while Laidlaw had come to rest on a narrow shelf, but they were both unconscious. The onus on the third man was virtually self-defeating. There were so many alternatives, he didn't know which to choose. The mountainside was resoundingly empty and unhelpful, the sun remorselessly descending until they were cast in shadow.

His first objective was to separate the men from the rope that was strangulating them. He made sure that Laidlaw wasn't likely to slip from the ledge and worked his way back up to the critical point of the spur. He couldn't simply cut the line and let Prior fall into the chasm. A belay point was provided by the axe and using this, he tied the spare rope he carried to Prior and then for a moment or two, while he transferred Laidlaw's line to an ice screw, had to support the combined weight of both men.

Inch by inch he lowered Prior on the second line towards Laidlaw's more sheltered position, avoiding a jagged outcrop of rocks. His own body alternately sweated with exertion or froze in a chill of fear. He thought that Prior had several broken bones. He grated audibly. All Moncrieffe could do was leave them and go for help. A three-hour descent. Nightfall. A rescue party in the dark with no helicopters possible. The agonising slowness of it deterred him. He had a spare windcheater in his pack and, undoing it, was faced with the choice of which man needed it more. Prior did. His colour was bad, breath rasping. But it struck Moncrieffe that Laidlaw was the further from death, by degrees. He fastened the jacket on him and began the long descent.

Not easy. The surface was patchy, deep drifts through which he plunged and rolled himself, hardly upright and then a frozen crust he had to labour over. The snow was more straightforward than the approach slopes of intractable heather. By now his own exhaustion was advanced. The continual pumping of adrenalin as he went through manoeuvres he knew contravened basic safety rules, like climbing down an ice gully unroped, drained his reserve of strength. He buckled. Sometimes he fell. Diminishing will-power made him sluggish and putting his head down on the turf, he thought, I must sleep for a while and get back some energy. He saw a raven circle overhead, symbol of death, and he fought the impulse to end his own life-saving momentum.

Seven miles. A last ditch was insuperable and all it was was a trickle of a burn. He couldn't climb up the rock sides to the cottages he knew were a hundred yards away and lay half in the stream, licking the salts of the water, mouth to earth. The sub-vertebrate lapping reminded him of something. In his pocket was a bar of chocolate, half melted and then frozen like himself. He crammed it in his mouth and the food exploded through his system like a heat shock. Revived, he struggled to his feet and carried on.

The woman in the first cottage phoned to the rescue base at Fort William. Hours passed in which Moncrieffe knew he had to conserve his strength so that he could climb back up the mountain again and show the team the exact spot. He ate, dried himself, rested in a state of semi-hallucination, wishing there were some way he could transfer his knowledge onto somebody else, or shirk its enactment.

But he could not. He was with the final party which took Prior off the mountainside, dead from exposure and internal injuries, while John Laidlaw spent three months recuperating from a broken foot and ribs, but he did live.

The episode didn't take place that spring, or the previous one but seven years earlier. It didn't take place once, but dozens of times, over and over again in nightmare. It was a good month when Moncrieffe was so tired that he didn't relive the three acute moments of the descent; the instant of the fall, the decision about the windcheater and the despair of his own ebbing strength. They were the crises of elemental drama. Knowing the end didn't alleviate the stress of its unfolding action.

He woke up this time to find that Leonie was standing at the door of his room with a light shining behind her from the corridor.

"I'll make you tea, shall I?"

The woman in the cottage had said the same and he nodded impassively.

Rude, he thought, and embarrassing, as he got up to put on a dressing gown and follow her into the kitchen. This was a stark and stylish place, white cup on black saucer, spotlit and it glared at him jaggedly in the middle of a broken night. The street outside was silent, so that he could plot the time between revellers going home and milk carts starting on their rounds. The woman blurred these hard edges, providing heat, colour and a little comfort.

"Was I making a lot of noise?"

"Enough to wake me up. I thought it was a burglar."

Charlie told him he shouted in these dreams and Liz used to move into another room when the bouts were on. He'd forgotten the impact of the nightmare on other people. "I don't seem to be able to shake this one off."

"Is it a recurring dream then?"

"Yes. Other people dream about the dentist, or being chased by trains. I dream about a climbing accident I had in Wester Ross." And he told her, scene by scene, of the calamity.

Leonie watched him closely as she listened. She'd become used to the facets of his ugliness. He was ugly, in the way of men, with a combination of features to which the euphemism of rugged or strong was applied. The only good line in his face was his jaw, like an emphatic underscoring to finish off the business. The mouth she found intriguing with its changing roll through linear to full which marked a shift in emphasis, as comma to full stop. She studied him with a professional eye, coldly, a cold outer casing to harden her against too much sympathy. She did feel for him because the lonely despairing moment of the fall and its midnight revival embodied much of what she'd learned about the man in the space of six weeks. His arrogance had its source in scruple. He couldn't prevaricate or shirk the consequences but spoke his mind forthrightly, and she recognised that isolation was the price he paid for independence.

"I wonder why you can't put the memory to rest. What is it that bothers you most about the accident?"

He hadn't thought of it as cause and effect, but lay down helplessly under the suffering. He searched back through the dream for clues to the reality. "That I anticipated it. The thing that's unbearable is that I actually warned them. I wish I hadn't seen them, or hadn't called out. To know what's going to happen and be overruled, that does seem fatalistic. Or if I'd not said anything at all, it mightn't have come about."

"Why, that's Aeschylean. Tragedy fulfilling the prophecy of the oracle. Do you think you're oracular?"

259

The night wore thin the edges of discretion and self-containment. "Maybe. I feel I know everything, but lack the ability to direct events." His political life impinged in living parallel to his nightmare. "I'd rather have a better balance of talents, know less, achieve more."

This couldn't be gainsaid, and Leonie sat mulling on the enervating effect of too much scruple. Not to care, not to be haunted by one's actions or suffer from retrospective analysis invested a human being with such power. Unreflecting action. Wonderful! "But then you might implement a wrong decision, bull-headed."

"I'm not convinced my decisions are right however much thought I put in. Perhaps I should have given that jacket to Prior. When I think about it, I deferred in extremis to a principle I don't admire, the survival of the fittest. If I'd done something different, they might both have lived."

"Or both died."

"That's so. But I'm disappointed that the most significant decision I've ever taken without advice reverted to something so primitive. That's not the way I want to function. I wanted to think something more impartial, more profound."

"But heavens, Watson, you're tormenting yourself because a man died, in impossible circumstances. In your shoes, I'd be saying, I saved a man's life. Or even more basically, I saved my own. There's nothing angers me as much as the parable of the good shepherd. That he should endanger the ninety-nine for the sake of one is culpable negligence. I wouldn't trust a religion based on that premise."

"You think religion should run on more secure averages of salvation?" He was amused, out of the blackness of the night redeeming laughter.

"The greatest good of the greatest number. Yes."

He was impressed not by the quotation but her unwavering pronouncement of it, feeling the stamp of her personality which contained a battlingness, a lack of nonsense he hadn't established before. "But you, you must have had doubts about your own decisions now and then."

"Women are more pragmatic." She thought of her marriage which deferred to Fergus, her career a contra-indication. "It may come down to selfishness with us, balancing what we owe to others against what we owe to ourselves. And you can't reach a perfect compromise every time. Men beleaguer themselves with the abstract. We just struggle through the day-to-day, quite resigned to botches."

She spoke in earnest and he was struck by the careful neutrality of her opinions which abrogated self, as well as the introspection that had gone into forming this conclusion, in spite of her practical severeness. He felt she hadn't been encouraged to indulge her whims and imagined Ellice Barr saying, Pooh, get on with it, to any hesitation. His house guest made a marked impression on him. Her elbows came out of her robe, exposing graceful forearms. Her face at that hour was atypical. He realised that for the most part he saw her before or after a performance, with a lacquer of make-up that looked not exactly artificial but highly coloured. The night refined her. Underneath the rôles was a face of extreme simplicity, adaptable, almost blank. He admired the elongation of features in which there was nothing spare or fleshy. Minimalism of speech, body, possessions – habits he didn't share – were attractive by opposites.

They came to the end of confidentiality and the pot of tea. Light softened the window. He hurried, over-impatient, to define the mood before it disappeared.

"I must say this, in case I can't again. You know I wish that you were coming back to bed with me. No, I'm not asking you but it is foolish not to admit it. I am in love with you, as far as I know what it is I feel. I've only been in love once before," he went on, empowered by her receptive silence, "and that didn't last for very long, so I don't trust the feeling. Maybe I over-rationalise what I feel about you. When you're hungry everything promises to sustain. I don't put much faith in so-called attraction or sex appeal. I am attracted, in some measure, to every woman I meet though that's only defining one area of my response. But I think I'm genuine about this. You're completely different from me and completely the same. I haven't been able to come to terms with that yet. Sometimes when I'm in a room with you, all the time in fact, I know what it is you're feeling. I'm not guessing – or identifying. I can feel you in the other corner. I don't know what you're thinking, maybe I'll never know the shape of the words that are going through your head, but there's a physical pulse I'm picking up that

261

I can't ignore. I try to dissociate myself from it but I can't. You leap out at me from every page. Things are only real in as much as they relate to you. In spite of everything I've done to put this off, I am in love with you."

Leonie said nothing, side-stepping the dangerous moment. Perhaps she should have interrupted the flow more promptly, but the flattery of the speech and its delivery carried her along fascinated and unresisting. He took this as encouragement.

"I think I should have behaved differently on the first of May last year. I meant to. I had such a positive reaction when we met that I intended to be assertive. But it didn't come about and you eluded me, through misapprehensions really. What I can't forgive is my inability to close. To see, to know and not to compel events. That's my flaw, time and time again."

He grew wary of her silence as it continued over minutes and formed itself into a hostile rather than benign mood. He had a strong temptation to snatch, to seize a physical closeness with her. These weeks had given him many opportunities for seduction, brushing his hand upwards against a breast to find the irresistible area of response. He knew how to do it but kept himself in check. "Perhaps you find these feelings a burden. I hope that you won't go away. I don't want to pressurise you like that. I won't speak of this again."

To say anything was to adulterate. She rose, determined not to agree, condemn, qualify, or even hear since a response of any kind compounded what he said. She went back to her room, chilled by the enormous absence in her bed. She lay down and, turning to the wall, stared at the solitary anguish of the barren and unresponsive mountainside.

28

Kenneth Frew met his director for lunch at a wine bar in the City. Both of the venues were Alison's choice. The men weren't at home with either. It was a frenzied, chrome and cuisine place that couldn't decide if it were a restaurant or bar, didn't serve the blissful beer, and was full of City gents whose points of conversation reached them now and then, as sharp and glittering as the fitments. Alison had registered with an employment agency who sent her temping as a book-keeper, and she would come by later.

Stuart had called in at the theatre on his way to pick up the mail, a daily compulsion not unlike checking an Ansafone, not for the relayed messages themselves but because it assured him that he was needed. A pile of reviews from monthly periodicals was waiting for him and he brought these on for Ken to read and Alison to keep. For himself, Stuart had gone beyond the making of scrapbooks though Alison started to paste up cuttings for him in a ledger.

"Good on the whole?" Frew asked of their reviews. He tried not to pay excess attention to his transitory reputation. A week in the theatre was a shorter time than in politics.

"Oh yes." Stuart pushed the more obscure coverage towards the actor. "Maybe too good."

"Surely there's no such thing."

"Too successful then. I think the management may suggest extending to a longer run than we'd envisaged."

The equivocal tone of this cheered the actor. He'd come to ask for quittance as soon as their prescribed three months were up. "I'm out for one. I've been offered Macbeth at the Old Vic. Rehearsals start in September, opening the end of the month."

"You'll have to lose a bit of weight," jibed Ainslie looking over the table. "And how's your swordsmanship these days? Rusty, I would think."

Frew knew better than to look for congratulations. "I was

worried about breaking up our happy band and wanted to let you know before you heard it elsewhere."

Stuart would have liked to make him apologise for the defection, wringing him with how a long run would have established them for years, changes in cast being so unsettling to the faithful etcetera; but his mockery dwindled. He was tired of the fortnight-old production himself. He slaved during rehearsal, spent tortured nights debating the infinitesimal and once it had opened, lost interest. Time to move on to something new. He was a craftsman who was involved in the making, not in permanence. "We've done well though, haven't we?" was as close as he could come to flattery, even self-flattery.

"Earned more than we ever did at home."

"That's a bit sporranish, isn't it? Or are you saving up for your retirement?" Stuart was penniless on principle when the rich were axiomatically idle.

Seeing there was no alternative, Frew rubbed Judge Brack's beard which was going to give double service to Macbeth, and joined the mawkish lament for wealth and reputation. "Yes, I've booked myself into the retired actors' home in Brighton." They often talked of their imaginary pension plans.

"And they've got a vacancy sorted out for you already?"

"Two singles. Don't say I never think about you. You can come along next week."

They cuffed each other with words and sat back lightly winded in good humour, although the precariousness of their real fortunes often impinged.

"Do you think Leonie will be disappointed if she has the chance to carry on with Hedda?"

"Ah, Leonie. Who knows?"

"Has she got anything else lined up?"

The director stifled a risible comment. "I don't know if Leonie's private life would stand a protracted spell in London." Stuart edged them nearer an exchange of confidence, balanced on innuendo. Had Frew noticed the MP at their inaugural party? Did he know something more substantial about the affair worth sharing? The theatre, which was a tight circuit, thrived on gossip and Stuart was engaged in circulating it, not venomously but because it was the stuff of interchange. A new liaison was seized on in the profession with the same avid interest as a sex scandal in the House. He did think this demonstrated a wilful naïvety on the part of the British masses, still surprised that men and women went to bed tògether in public as in private life. Yes, the press could have a silly season with more Moncrieffe revelations.

Kenneth Frew had known Leonie almost as long as their director, conspicuous in the small world of Edinburgh theatre. He could recall her student performance as St Joan on which he'd based the recommendation that led to her Bristol season. He didn't deceive himself that he had made her – she made herself – but he was paternalistic about her talents. He felt not the slightest envy at the size of the letters billposted in her name, because he knew how hard it was for women to rise to stardom in the theatre. A flush season of prettiness, a comic Shakespeare, some precision Priestley then a dwindle into Tennessee Williams, followed by obscurity. A tiny proportion of the juvenile leads made it to the larger classical rôles. He'd seen generations of fine actresses disappear into wedlock and knew that Leonie was at a point of transition which he was determined to help her over, more altruistically than her younger friend. Stuart Ainslie wanted her to do well in his productions; Frew wanted her to do well.

Yes, he'd heard the two names coupled and observed more than Ainslie did, that Leonie left the theatre by a different route each evening, west instead of north. He didn't come to any conclusion about the relationship but waited for developments, though he admitted London was a better venue for a stage career than Edinburgh, and her supporting men might well be cast accordingly.

"Actually, it's Alan Mills who'll do *Macbeth* and he wondered if it was worthwhile approaching Leonie."

"For Lady M? Well." They were all going to have fun and Stuart felt some pique, as if it were a party he hadn't been invited to. "Not inappropriate," he conceded. "She's young but she might pull it off."

"Do you think she'd consider it?"

"I would think she has a soft spot for the Scottish play. And it's a wise move." Stuart thought she did have overtones of Ellen Terry in her deportment, Lady Macbeth crowning herself in his illustrated Shakespeare. Her majesty, if not the polyphonic voice. It was so maddening that you didn't have an authentic record of those early voices. Irving as Hamlet. What he'd give to hear that! Or Sarah Bernhardt. It drove him wild that her contemporaries described her voice as golden and he'd never get a chance to test the purity of its tone for himself. Perhaps it was as well. There were fashions in voices as much as faces. On neither count could he take John Barrymore or Valentino very seriously. The stage was kindlier than the cinema in letting vogue performances die, embalming them in fondness. "You'd better watch out. Leonie'll upstage you," he added savagely.

"Minor must defer to major talent. Who ever adequately part-nered Garbo? Playing opposite her was the best that men could do."

The experienced actor spoke the truth, in a waft of generosity which had the effect of a rebuke. Stuart picked up the reviews again and wondered if he was right, if Leonie was headed for the canonisation of the stage. Garbo, Bernhardt, Ellen Terry – the great names of legend had a resonance which was built up from a combination of their voice and talent but the vital ingredient was a physical lyricism which had impressed their generation. The craft liked its heroines to be not necessarily beautiful, but distinctive. He often puzzled about the element in acting that made its adherents androgynous. You turned yourself on day after day; it *was* the auto-erotic art. Not everybody cared for this male-female quality. Among the reviews he held, Stuart noticed a repeated harping on Leonie's physique. A new shape and a new interpretation chal-lenged the preconceived. He regretted that women had to leap this hurdle of physical acceptability before their acting talents were esteemed. Looking the part came first. Men were more easily evaluated on what they did. It was discrimination in its most subtle form, when both sexes were guilty of expecting decorativeness as well as talent from women. The plain actress was a very fine actress indeed.

That his protégée might go from the Old Vic to the Aldwych to the Royal Shakespeare Company – and on to Broadway – seemed a likely outcome. He followed the arc of her achievement like a rainbow, elusive, haunting, obscure in source and destiny.

Alison arrived, trim and shining. A captivating girl, thought Frew, and accompanied it with the regret that she didn't act. She wore a dress that reminded the older man of the forties, something called

266

Art Silk which swished and clung erotically to his imagination. Maybe not the cloth but the times, women devoted, men heroic, when flesh yielded to pressure, willow waisted. Bygone passions wafted over him.

"How was this morning?"

Alison was sent ad hoc to various merchant banks and stock-broking companies where she felt she might get a taster of something permanent; but she found she was instrumental, allowed not much more responsibility than expression through the telephone or typewriter. "Dull. I keep thinking the next job they give me will be the exciting one, but it isn't. And you?"

"Let's order first."

This was a protracted business, deciding on the merits of prosciutto versus prawns but after sending the waiter away twice, they finally chose. Kenneth passed Alison the reviews which she read before the arrival of their meal, but this turned out not to be a good aperitif.

"There are only two here that even mention the director," she exclaimed. " 'A faithfully detailed production' and 'Ainslie has extracted the maximum from his exciting cast'. And reams about the actors. It's just not fair. Everybody gets the credit except you. Scriptwriters, technicians, costume department, never you."

Why should she make scrapbooks about other people? She was angry to the point of trembling. A man at the adjacent table, catching the intensity in her voice, looked round thinking it was a quarrel. Stuart became alarmed when she went off at a tangent like this. Mocking her, the way he'd done for years, wasn't an adequate reaction when they were intimate. "Let's not forget, I'd be nothing without the actors." He exonerated the profession in front of Frew who sat back pondering.

"It's not them I blame. It's the public who're so ignorant and even the press. 'Smash hit' doesn't concede that the director engineered it."

Stuart realised, forking a dish of antipasta, that he seldom understood what Alison was driving at. She felt so powerfully about the things he took for granted. It confused him to have to go back to basics, explaining every one of his terms of reference, and frequently felt she was criticising him when she let off steam like this, as if there were something he should be actively changing. He tried hard to be reasonable. "No," he said. "It's more complex than that. I don't engineer anything. I'm just a co-ordinator of other people's talents. In some experimental companies, one of the actors can take over as director perfectly well. Ken's done that before now." The man nodded in agreement, silent and judicious. "A hit's an accident anyway, or success succeeding. Good reviews are pot luck. There's not one critic in a dozen knows what he's really watching so you have to hope the other eleven are well disposed, or follow the one who does. The situation's not as bad as in New York, anyway, where one critic can close a show."

Alison had already grown frustrated by the shapelessness of theatre. Amorphous people floating in and out of each other's lives, no core, no general consensus and, worst of all, the ephemeral nature of the production. Yesterday different from today and both forgotten tomorrow. She wanted to resolve its anomalies – film rich, stage poor – with a theory she could rely on. Genius goes unrecognised was the best that she could do. She still believed vaguely in the standards of a qualification for the job, and hype was a word she couldn't bring herself to say, far less perpetuate by indulging in its vapid standards. She thought Stuart should push himself more, but against what or with what, she didn't know.

"It is, regrettably, a chancy business," said Ken. "And we're the fortunate ones. Maybe one per cent of triers make it to the London West End. If we knew at the outset what it meant, we'd probably stay at home and go into the bank. No, maybe not. I can't see Leonie as a telling clerk, can you?"

Stuart winced as he got to the name. He'd prayed Ken wouldn't mention her, wouldn't stray onto the *Macbeth* offer, anticipating Alison's response.

"Of course it could be seen as a cop-out from responsibilities, and I really can't approve of that," Alison answered in just the prudish and self-satisfied way that exasperated. He knew this defensiveness came from insecurity; she was not remarkable and had the misfortune to be thrown against more striking talents, but found her precisions hard to forgive. "It must be very easy to use the creative process as an excuse to avoid duty."

Stuart noticed her modulation. She tended to emphasise every syllable, Scots fashion, so that 'verray' had Chaucerian overtones, pedantic or charming according to mood. It was the Edinburgh voice, lacking pace and humour.

Ken, half way through a pizza, remembered his fencing agility and wasn't hungry. "I remember someone telling me the tiresome thing about saints was that they'd never been tempted. It confirmed me on the side of honest sinners."

"If sin is the price of fame, let's settle for failure."

Ken stared at her and for Stuart's sake desisted. "Actually, I mustn't be long. I've an appointment for three. It was so nice to have had a chance to speak to you," he saluted Alison blandly and left.

To correct her was to invite argument, and so Stuart asked, "Have you written to Muriel?" to change if not to lighten the conversation.

He asked this every day, and every day the answer was the same, "Not yet." Alison knew she dealt with difficulties by ignoring them. As long as she didn't write the letter spelling out the new conditions of her life, a flat and work, albeit temporary, she didn't have to address mentally the connective and permanent factor of her relationship with the director. Her mother would not approve. This word 'approve' shaped itself often in Alison's mind and became mixed with the tangible proofs of why not. She knew her mother's potential objections to the man, too old for her, too unconventional, a battered leather jacket not at all easy among the suits and polished toecaps of Edinburgh predictables. She knew her mother yearned for acquired status, and looked to Alison to make a good and respectable match, not for Alison's sake but for Muriel's. Stuart and the theatre and the former wife were disqualifiers from this elevation. The term which so captivated her – artistic director – would have less influence on her mother when it wasn't subsidised by the largeness of impresario, resident consultant or OBE. As long as she kept the two sides separate, she needn't square their disparities, which lay in the irreconcilable nature of what her mother termed her duty versus her own inclination. That she had run away as much as Leonie was blurred.

"Let's go back to the flat," said Stuart, finding that the proximity of breast and thigh through summer undress had started to form outlines on his attention.

An impression of drawn blinds flickered across Alison's eyes, he naked and moving in her arms, an image so new and so appealing she hadn't grown accustomed to its shock. She had surprised herself by basic liking and by the patience he put into instruction, slow on breast, slow on thigh, the fascinating inevitability of the act. Her body grew turgid at the thoughts.

"But work?" she wondered as of conscience.

"Blow work. It's only four hours' piece rate." He lifted the longest curl from her shoulder and bent it back into place. "And I pay overtime."

Alison was sexually besotted. They lay joined at the hip for hours throughout the afternoon as she went on testing her ability to retain him. She had discovered a dozen internal muscles like a new and unexpected range of notes in her voice and rejoiced in exercising them. The complexities of her body became simple when he applied himself to them, the breast shaped this way for an entirely logical reason, the legs parting to a purpose. Man. And Stuart was purposeful, producing one effect after another, a little in awe himself at the delight of response as he shifted through finger and lip to tongue. She was like a child in water, idiotic, frenzied, craving sensation. They curled and uncurled together like different tensile substances, distant along their similarity.

Alison private was a delight; Alison public was captious. Her rudeness to the actor was typical of bêtises he'd thought he would eradicate, and hadn't. What was the matter with her? Was she just daft or was it more deep-seated? He remembered when he gave her a play to read and the following day found her sitting with a commentary about it, reading avidly, which impressed him with its dedication. 'Finished the play already?' he asked. 'No,' she said, 'I thought I'd read an analysis first. I don't know what to make of a book until I've had someone else's opinion.' This floored him, reliant on his own judgment. It implied a mindlessness, or subservience to the strongest viewpoint. And yet, when he thought that he might programme her into common sense, he failed. He wanted the serious love affair, couldn't believe his good luck in securing her and yet, and yet . . .

'When we are married' began to be a discernible possibility. Leonie's rejoinder about his existing marriage had jarred Stuart's conscience troublingly about the deception. Like faith, marriage

270

was something he had tended to let lapse. He'd said to Alison that he *had* been married, but didn't effect the transition to the present which defined its aoristic tense. He rather liked his wife, saw no pressing reason to divorce her and in fact they made love whenever they met, once or twice a year, as old friends going out to dinner. Immoral? Well, blow me down. They were married, weren't they? 'You're an awful man,' was Helen's worst censure of him and very probably he was.

Alison angling for permanence on the basis of 'What would my mother think of this?' wasn't an inspiring alternative. He turned his better side towards her but only he knew what was cast in shadow. A divorce wouldn't be to her liking and so he elided the facts into an acceptable version simply to suit.

He had some reservations. Alison he was extremely fond of . . . but the Petrie clan en masse? Bailing Harris out of gambling debts, the fearsome Muriel, and Fergus delivering a lecture on the Mount? Did he really want to be Leonie's brother-in-law? He fought shy of dynastic stage families, indeed of families together. Alison had elements of Helen, good background, poor foreground material. Free-wheeling. That was his style, So he toyed, looking on his own life as a bit part, some soap opera on radio where he made a guest appearance to stay solvent, but his real life passed more grandiloquently in the theatre, written large and colourful and in better prose.

29

The last meeting of the Scottish Grand Committee for that session was held in one of the larger rooms on the Committee Corridor at Westminster on a Wednesday morning in July. It was very hot so that the leaded windows which overlooked the Embankment and the Thames were open. Like the chamber of the Commons, the architecture borrowed something from the layout of a church, with wooden pews arranged in two banks. The original chapel of St Stephen's had influenced more than the seating arrangements. The confrontation of right and left, rather than the gradations of an amphitheatre which was typical of most democratic assemblies, had shaped the attitude of the British Parliament. Opposition was mental as well as physical and Watson regretted the lack of politics in the round because in that spectrum he might have found an established place off centre.

The minority Conservatives sat with their backs to the river. Labour MPs faced it while the Liberals, Nationalists and Mon- crieffe made a front row break in these extreme divisions. There was almost a full complement of members that day and in fact attendance throughout the session when votes were so finely balanced had been high. But the attitude of Scottish MPs to their nominal assembly was equivocal. The few who were English by birth or education felt ill at ease among the broader accents and humour of the Grand Committee, and were never fully integrated in it. Equally, the two or three Scots-born ministers of the crown felt they'd graduated to higher things and didn't often condescend to appear.

This pointed to the comparative weakness of the Scottish mem- bership. They were evidence of a higher level of representation per capita than in England and Wales but they were still, cross-party, a minority group. All went well when the balance of opinion in the Grand Committee matched that in the Commons as a whole. This session the seventy-one Scots felt an enhanced sense of purpose when Labour was in a healthier preponderance in the smaller than in the larger domain. They felt they showed the way. They emerged from the political limbo of Cadogan's Conservative administration when, by a gentleman's agreement, the Grand Committee hadn't taken a formal vote on its debates because it would be uniformly and discreditably overruled downstairs. They were happy now to pull in harness with the majority.

Today they were holiday happy.

Heat got to them. Unused to temperatures in the eighties, they abandoned themselves to the ferial mood of London sweltering in July. It was the weather for char-à-bancs and seaside outings. As the Labour Scottish whip said afterwards, If you'd given them paper hats and streamers, they'd have used them.

Watson liked the sessions of the Grand Committee and never missed them, in Westminster or Edinburgh. Yes, they were a headstrong bunch. They'd been in politics long enough to know each other intimately and, in the way of Scots, spoke out. They catcalled with greater pertinency than the English who booed and rubbished with a sad lack of inventiveness. "Sit down man. You're havering. You've not read your brief. You don't even start to think until you've got up on your feet," silenced an Edinburgh lawyer-turned-politician with the truth.

The same convention as in the House of Lords prevailed with the current speaker breaking off his speech as soon as he was challenged from the floor, and this allowed for good-mannered and discursive interruption. A well-made speech was appreciated and applauded irrespective of its political bias. Ellice Barr wouldn't have been out of place, thought Moncrieffe, looking round but he noted that women were in even shorter supply than in the Commons overall. The warlike Picts weren't likely to defer to distaff. Women doctors, dentists, lawyers were perennially suspect in the north.

At the same time, the quips and repartee were of a higher calibre than in the sour, dour, earnest chambers below. There were many educated men and classicists who delighted in the apophthegm, like Quercus. The small assembly indulged them without the tiresome heckling of the Commons which cut across wit. So in the middle of a discussion on tourism in Scotland which tended towards criticism of poor signposting and road marking, the

273

Honourable Member for Strathclyde got to his feet and said, 'The Scottish Tourist Board might indeed see its way to clarifying the signwriting. Most confusing it is for the visitor arriving at Strome-ferry to find a placard on which are inscribed the words: This is not the Ballachulish ferry.'

Watson had laughed with the rest, but sensed the game they played was as negative as the signpost. The real place was somewhere else. Their comments and recommendations were laboriously recorded by the scribe, read by a minor civil servant in the department of the Secretary of State for Scotland, and shelved among mile-long corridors of other documents. The debate was pointless, even if it was a genial pointlessness.

Today the agenda had more gravamen. They addressed themselves to the last legislative item from the spring budget which affected the aid central government was prepared to give to problem areas, which were euphemistically redefined as development regions. Fleming's long-term prophecy about the young inclining to stay in the depopulated regions of Scotland was far from being fulfilled. Speaker after speaker commented on the drain of youth and talent from his particular constituency, where the combination of falling school rolls and thin opportunity emptied the straths and smaller, non-industrial townships. The oil rigs at Aberdeen employed some but the drift south was unending, woven into the emigrant subconscious of the nation. The MPs fell into a lament for Scotland and the Clearances, a mood in which they all wore the white cockade of Jacobite.

After the opening speeches by spokesmen from the main parties, Watson got to his feet and said, "I always felt that the Scottish Development Agency was a valuable piece of short-term legislation. The agency has demonstrated its usefulness in sustaining traditional industry and launching new ones. The sum we are debating today and will vote on tomorrow is not unreasonable. But the principle of subsidy in this form begs the central issue of how to keep the workforce stable. Putting a small proportion back once it has gone isn't remedial, because it doesn't ensure that it will stay. These grants will provide training, but not long-term work." Putting a patient on a life-long intravenous drip, he thought.

"One of the major and unrecognised problems in the north of Scotland is the comparatively high cost of living. Aberdeen is normally quoted as emulating London prices in housing, but a report published two months ago by the Rural Scotland Price Survey establishes that the cost of living is substantially higher in the Highlands, with wide regional variations. Housing, basic foods and transport-related costs are inflated in comparison with Aberdeen and the UK as a whole. Taking the Aberdeen index as 100, the cost of living in the Highlands and Islands is on average 109.4. That's almost ten per cent over and above the admittedly expensive Granite City.

"Workers in London receive the 'London Weighting Allowance', with inner and outer scales adjusted to location. And yet salaries are already boosted by the buoyant economy of the south, while the people who are living and working in the north of Scotland enjoy only the basic salary scale, and incur increased expenditure which amounts to an unwarranted differential. What is needed isn't a cosmetic facelift but a comprehensive review of actual incentives to live in the north. A method of subsidy that benefits the whole community rather than this emphasis on the unemployed or the young would be of greater long-term value." And good television reception over the mountains would help.

Laidlaw thought that the 'Highlands and Islands Weighting' might be scenery and pollution-free air. The member for Caithness and Sutherland reminded him of the fact of nuclear reactors and the offshore oil refineries, as they headed into their favourite cul-de-sac.

At last the toughest Labour man got to his feet, silencing periphrasis. "This development fund we are voting on is insufficient in size and concept. It is to be patchily administered and discriminatory in tendency. What are these redeployment centres to be set up in rural areas? This is mere tinkering, occupational therapy for the long-term unemployed. What we need is jobs to regenerate the Scottish economy and this may indeed be a small-scale, cottage economy rather than a fully mechanised industrial one. But my objection to the Development Agency is that its components are, per se, contradictory. Build a factory *and* preserve the scenery? How? The proposals overlook the claims of small towns which have been badly hit by the decline in traditional industry, fishing, building as well as agriculture. We don't want a spawn of craft shops and tourist tea rooms across the north. We work for our living and wholly reject the government's proposal to relegate the Scottish workforce into secondary, non-regenerative employment. This is a badly-planned, badly-worded piece of legislation and in the Third Reading I, for one, will vote against it."

Laidlaw, Dunns, Moncrieffe looked round from their bench in astonishment. A hubbub was let loose at the man's intention of voting against his own side. He was an awkward cuss. This was the man who had ruffled the Edinburgh lawyer, anti-royalist, anti-feminist, son of a Fife miner, the outspoken stereotype Scot who feared no one. He was reputed to have given his agent a hard time in the October general election when he was defending a slender three hundred majority. Walking down the High Street of a small mid-Fife town a week before polling day, they were approached by the stalwart figure of Miss McCormack, leader of the local SNP. 'Get on her right side,' breathed the agent. 'You need her couple of hundred votes.' So the Labour man accosted her with the words, 'Good morning, Miss McCormack. What's all this I hear about voting for the fucking Nationalists?' He scraped in with fifty, on the third recount.

The Conservatives would have made him a life peer for services to something or other and got shot of him. As it was, he hung on to harry successive administrations, right- and left-handed like the true wielder of the claymore. He'd made it manifest to Fleming that he thought he deserved a post and didn't get it, so he kicked back with obstructionism in his own way. He was going to give the Secretary of State for Scotland a rough ride at that afternoon's Scottish question time and maybe lead a damaging revolt in Thursday's division on the bill.

Miraculously, as other members rose one after the other and echoed his sentiments, word leaked out of the room and the number of journalists doubled. Three to six, six to twelve in minutes. The big Scottish dailies sent their political correspondents scurrying from other parts of the building to cover this phenomenon – the Grand Committee apparently about to come out in unison against a piece of legislation deemed to benefit the north and a respected Labour politician intent on toppling his own administration.

There was only one MP who kept his head in the mood of jamboree, or two including Moncrieffe who noted that a fragment

276

of every man present was nationalist, not separatist, but indelibly defiant to English mores and English laws. The clansman was anarchic and like the feral species could never be entirely trusted in domestic habitat. The schisms and septs proliferated with northern Labour and Conservative men by no means whole-hearted about their London leaders. They often liked each other more as fellow Scots than they liked their southern partisans.

But Moncrieffe had nothing to lose by objectivism. His vote was academic. The Labour Scottish whip, answerable to his Prime Minister, did. He asked the chairman for a brief adjournment while he tried to rein in the stampede.

In the corridor, the Labour Scots made a huddle. "Look, work it out for yourselves. What's going to happen if you lose your heads and vote against the motion on Thursday?"

"An election?"

"I'm not going to say any more."

"The PM's resignation?"

"I'm not committing myself. You're big lads. You can work it out for yourselves. But," he said, turning to the rabble rouser, "I wouldn't like to be you in August going round defending the constituency on your majority."

The intending rebels foresaw the Prime Minister cancelling Friday's business for a vote of confidence on the government's performance and every man jack of them would have to trot out and vote the other way. They anticipated their absurdity in the lobbies, in the press, in their constituency and desisted from too much foolishness.

They went back into the Committee, toned down their objections and abided by the party rules.

"So what did you make of it?" asked Quercus, hearing the rigmarole late that night at Moncrieffe's flat. With the last flurry of business in the House before the long recess, the MPs and Leonie often arrived back together from their respective performances.

"It certainly would have been one of the more adroit own goals of modern politics."

"Do you think he really would have done it?"

"No, he just wanted to be bolshie," said Moncrieffe.

"And how will you vote on the Third Reading?" he asked.

"For, I think. I don't like this piffling fund but it may be all we get. At the same time, I feel it's attempting to reverse the irreversible. It won't solve the problem, and so it's a waste of resources."

"Did you ever get through *The Wealth of Nations*? Laissez-faire economics are so attractively simplistic in theory and so ineffective in practice. Supply and demand of employment doesn't seem to operate in the technological era. Or results in the poverty of weaker nations. What is the answer? Tourism?"

"Heaven forbid. I can see why that makes our Fife friend bilious. Not man's work, is it?"

Leonie searched back through effect to cause. "You know, the southern drift is part of a conditioning that's so subversive we don't even realise it's happening. The regional accents aren't fashionable. Every one of the 'provinces' feels that there's some magic or sophistication attached to the south. Partly wealth, I suppose. The pavements of London are still figuratively gold. But it's more than earning power. Look at us. We've both had to follow our careers to London. We couldn't do what we're doing in Scotland. London houses a quite disproportionate number of the amenities of the United Kingdom. As well as being the centre of government, it has the Stock Exchange. All the entertainments are here, the majority of orchestras and ballet and opera not to mention art galleries. Journalism, publishing houses. It goes on and on. The income from all of that is simply massive. And maybe more persuasively, radio and television are here. The BBC projects its view of Britain in standard English and that must become the norm most people aspire to. A bit of vernacular radio doesn't go far to balancing the accounts.

"I remember," she said, "when I was a very young aspirant to the stage, Kenneth Frew warned me that I'd never be a classical actress with a Scottish accent. I couldn't play Shakespeare without changing my natural intonation, even though his sixteenth-century English was probably much closer to Scots than the accent we call received pronunciation. We all have to conform, one way or another."

"And you resent that?"

"No. It's a fact of life. But you can't counteract the pull of London with the odd subsidy to the regional development boards. London weighting is a subtle metaphor for its magnetic field, its pull power."

278

The men admired this phrase.

"Yes," said Moncrieffe, "there's a sad validity in the remark that if you stand in Piccadilly long enough, you'll meet everybody you ever knew. Sad if you're a Scot at any rate."

"Come now," rejoined Quercus, "the whole world passes along Princes Street at least once in its life."

They drank chilled white wine at midnight and went onto the roof obeying the topsy-turvy conventions of this capital when in the northern one people would be sensibly in bed. The buildings along the Embankment were floodlit as far as the eye could see and the streets below were busy with restaurants still open for business and parties in full swing. It was warm and the three of them walked about among the container-grown flowers which, in the sultry inversions of the night life, seemed not inappropriate. A pleasure barge went down the Thames leaving a wistful trail of music as people danced on deck.

"Alan Mills came backstage this evening," said Leonie. "Do you remember, he directed the *Twelfth Night* you saw in Oxford. He's at the Old Vic now and thought I might try Lady Macbeth."

"That's marvellous," said Moncrieffe who understood these discernible advances and knew they were hard won.

"Yes, it would be a breakthrough. But *Macbeth*'s not a popular play."

"You will accept?" Quercus asked, breathing Havana scents into the air.

Leonie didn't answer, standing apart from them beside the balustrade. She found it interesting that these men, whose achievement ran along the same path, encouraged hers. London, the irresistible, pulled them together. She couldn't entirely rationalise its draw by her list of the capital's attractions. It was something more than an amalgam of tourist spots, perhaps because the people who chose to collect near the pulse in turn became energised by it. It was the centre, that was all. Elsewhere was irrelevant. So she didn't reply to whether she would or would not succumb to the gravitational force of the city, buoyed temporarily on the high of being asked.

30

Michael's days were void. He sifted through the newspapers methodically, ringing the potential jobs with a red pen. Qualified accountants were in demand, and he wrote dozens of letters of application, mentally. A little part-time job. He prepared himself to go for interviews, steering carefully between elation now and disappointment later. A pressed suit, a white shirt would give him the respectable appearance but in the board room, round the rosewood committee table, he knew that something would go amiss. He knew that he would falter under a barrage of questioning. The blank spaces of his curriculum vitae waited to be filled and he could neither lie nor bluff. And they would say afterwards, 'We'll be in touch' with the forlorn ring of a prognosis never likely to be fulfilled. He would have done the same as an employer. The theoretical code for employing ex-cons was something you didn't test on frauds. However James Geddes might put his mind to the problem, there was no solution to the circuits of undischarged bankruptcy. Credibility, credential, credit were closer than semantic cousins. In the business world they were inseparable.

Loneliness. Such loneliness. The world went about its occupation while he had none. Redundancy or disability he would have preferred when he could have blamed external factors, not least bad luck, but when the cause was his own judgment, there was no relief from self-accusation.

Matthew Geddes breezed into his parents' house one Saturday forenoon and joined them over coffee in the garden. He didn't often find them alone these days. The Petries, one or several, would swell the household and even Ellice Barr was pulled into the orbit of the Hermitage.

Having their private ear, Matthew confided, "I've had a huge bill for repairing the car."

"You should have changed it in the spring when I advised," was the professor's consolation, turning over the pages of the weekend review.

"It was running soundly then. Such bad luck the gear box going."

"You drive it too hard. I've had the same car for twenty years without a change of gear box."

"You only potter about town. I was going up and down to Oxford three times a year in mine."

"Well, there you are. And this is your first expenditure. Cheap motoring."

Matthew waited for his irritability to subside. "I don't suppose you could see your way to lending me five hundred pounds to tide me over?"

"I don't suppose I could. I live within my salary and my investments I don't touch. A sound policy."

The professor's life insurance and bonds happened to be held with Matthew's company and he'd managed to sneak a look at them. Forbidden but never mind. He knew to the decimal point how much his father's annuities were worth. He'd even thought of borrowing on the strength of his eventual inheritance from the family estate, knowing there were brokers who would stoop to handling such post mortem benefits. Matthew needed the money now, not in twenty years' time. He thought his parents could have been more generous when he got married since his mother was an only child and had a substantial private income of her own. They had no concept of how difficult it was to start with mortgage, marriage and a child to pay for out of one salary. At the same time, his father was the first to comment on a lapse from the sartorial standards becoming to a professional gentleman and pointedly gave him clothes as presents or a voucher to be used at Gieves in George Street. Matthew wondered how shocked they'd be if he admitted to having sold a set of quite useless Edwardian dress studs inherited from his grandfather. 'Down to the pawnbroker next,' his father would probably say, 'with the family silver.' He grieved a little himself at the loss of a sentimental keepsake, but the facts of life pressed harder.

"Are you actually . . . destitute?" Irene asked.

In the setting, such a possibility sounded ludicrous. The professor had security of tenure with the University until he retired, or for life if he wanted it. He lived under a red tiled roof, down a red gravel drive, which were the adjuncts of security. Matthew foresaw twenty years without change or upheaval, a human eternity. He found his parents were insulated from the realities by a double barrier of wealth and ignorance. "Not destitute. That's into receivership. I'm only broke, a temporary embarrassment. In business it's what they call a cash flow problem."

"And in private life, mismanagement. Cutting one's coat according to an exact yardage is a useful skill. Acquire it."

Matthew got up and walked about the garden on his own, sullen and resentful. There wasn't much right about the way the world arranged itself. So much superfluity here and such a slog at home. Even the annuals his mother put into the flowering beds cost more than their monthly grocery bill. Carnation and delphinium and drifts of nepeta went on thriving at his expense, using up his soil. Grievances flooded in on him. They could have settled an endowment on his son like any reasonable grandparents of their income bracket. Or a covenant for school fees. They couldn't read his problems sympathetically, to the point where they might alleviate them.

He came to the boundary wall between their garden and the Petries' behind which lay the tennis court he and Fergus had played on as boys. It was a wanton parallel at this moment, Fergus his contemporary escalating and himself descending. Buying his old house! He turned and looked back at the Geddes' establishment, and knew it was a dozen years beyond his expectations. The differential between himself and Fergus grew at compound rate. 'How well Fergus is doing for himself' was a phrase not spoken but implied and with it the innuendo that the neighbour would have been closer to their ideal son. He remembered all the ways in which his father belittled him until he started to think of himself as a failed first. Wrong parents. Wrong children. A woeful mismatch as bad as marriage partners. The sheer lottery of being happy in the company of one's kinfolk struck him with its lengthy odds.

Irene waited until her husband went indoors before she joined her son. Crossing the lawn, she reflected on the partisan divisions of their home. Conversation was with one or other of them. A tripartite discussion was too angular. The men didn't talk as much as jab at each other and she began to hate the role of go-between, blamed by both sides for wilful misinterpretation of the other, or bias. She had become the fulcrum of a see-saw and its stress point.

"My dividends are payable shortly," she said, breaking off an idle stem in the border. "I can let you have five hundred pounds, for a while."

"Are you sure?"

"It is my dress allowance for the year. So if you can make sure I have it back by, say, the end of October. That's three months. Can you manage that?"

"I would think so." He tried to sound enthusiastic, finding direct thanks inaccessible when he felt the offer should have been spontaneous and couched as an outright gift and not a loan. Her dress allowance! And he could barely meet his daily expenses.

Michael went out on the hills behind the house two or three times a week. He had evolved several alternative routes, walking down Midmar Drive and entering the park area alongside Blackford Pond, or going by the back gate from the house directly into the Hermitage, or walking much further up towards Mortonhall golf club and tackling the hills from Buckstone Snab so that it was never a dull outing, with paths snaking and converging unexpectedly. It was a large complex of hills, Braid connected to Blackford geographically although they were severed by the through road to Liberton, the natural by-ways conforming to the practical in a way that pleased no one.

It struck him that he had always been a city dweller testing the uneasy compromise between places and people, first Leningrad and then Edinburgh – capitals which were not wholly dissimilar, neo-classical, grand, a little grey, although in the city of his childhood it was the greyness of water that dominated and in his maturity, hills. This lesser Hermitage was a transmutation of the other, the Winter Palace of St Petersburg, a scaled-down version like his own existence from the otiose and indulged phases of boyhood, an echo muted over the intervening distance of civil war and flight. The Hermitage was a public art gallery now. He supposed that was as good as anything. This minor Palladian mansion had been turned into a study centre: he'd seen boy scouts and youth groups out collecting specimens of wild life. Not in private ownership any longer but municipal. Even buildings lost their original function and their gloss. Why Hermitage? The word recurred in several European cities. A retreat, a place of contemplation for the spirit to gather itself, a sanctuary. They were aptly places' of retreat, cells of contemplation for him as well as the Romanoffs, figuring as the tail end of a personal dynasty.

His two lives connected occasionally along the same latitude, names and words. How few English words he had known before he left Russia, and how few Russian ones stayed within his lexical range. It was a forgotten form of self-expression. He had made the transference long ago to thinking in English. The generous language had adopted a few substantives, the ethnic words, balalaika, samovar, babushka, troika. Nothing profound. But the one Russian word he used again and again mentally was 'pravda' in all regards superior to English 'truth', which implied a test against the straight flight of an arrow or the quality of steel in a simple metaphor for true. Pravda was related to prava, the word for law and also the right hand, the agent with which he'd sworn to tell the truth on the holy Bible. This complex verbal network puzzled him, lines tied with less definition than the huge empty spaces they left blank. Had he told the truth? And if he had, was the law able to recognise it? He sifted his own evidence and came back repeatedly to the conclusion that if words themselves weren't false, his sentence was just and all his consequent suffering deserved. But maybe it was words that were the cheats and liars.

Later that afternoon, Irene opened her door in welcome to her neighbour, feeling he filled the space her son left and diverted her from a sense of guilt at having gone, as it were, behind her husband's back since the loan to Matthew contradicted the spirit of his decree.

"Have you been out walking?"

"Yes, I took a breather."

Irene noticed that fresh air didn't invigorate the man. He came back from his walks looking pale and morose and so she bustled cheerfully about the spick blue and white kitchen where they generally sat, making him tea. She was glad that her husband was out on a call, for he became restive at the constant annexation of her time, as if it were in some way his and not free for her to give. It didn't escape her how often their house was used as a consultancy, his professional, hers personal. "At least," the professor would admit, "I am paid for my advice. You don't need to be so liberal."

But she smiled and listened.

"What can I do with my time, Madam Geddes? It hangs heavy."

"There's no need to do anything, Michael. You've worked enough. You're over seventy. Most men have retired by then. Just be."

"Women can afford to be. Men must work."

"We're not entirely idle," Irene protested by words and doing.

"Oh no. It was a qualitative statement."

Irene had a pair of kitchen scales on her work top, functional but pretty with Slavic flowers in enamel work. Brass pans and a pyramid of weights completed the balance. Michael found himself mentally separating the weights which ran from a quarter of an ounce to two pounds, as he tried to equate them. He knew beforehand that he couldn't. Whatever piles he made, he couldn't get the two halves precisely balanced. Of course they were designed that way but it did irritate a pedantic neatness in him that so small a measure, no more than a handful of grains, impaired a visual perfection.

The housewife didn't smile or soften her irksomeness, and so to cajole her a little he said, "You are a completely good woman, Irene. Perhaps the only one I ever met. I know nothing bad of you."

"That's not so."

"Tell me something bad then."

"Well," she did smile, "something Blake says – Nurse unacted desires."

"You do surprise me. What unacted desires do you nurse?"

"No," she said, shy of so much self-analysis, "I only meant we can't know everything about each other or ourselves. I'm not particularly good. I'm just simple. Your daughter," she went on, "and your daughter-in-law are much more complex and more interesting women than I. I've no special talent."

He thought of Alison and Leonie, unusual women yes, if not comfortable. "Talent may be a curse as much as money. And the desire for a talent you don't have may be the worst of all. Alison admires excessively because she has no strong motivation of her own. It clouds her judgment. A kink in perception. I don't think

285

these are good women, or at any rate I pity the men who marry them."

"That's too severe," she chided, "they have many merits."

"Irene," he said in the Russian pronunciation. "Peace-maker."

She thought that he would banish the lingering aura of her son but instead Irene found the two personalities futile and depressive. Looking along the curve of Matthew's career, Irene could see the parabola bend in the shape of Michael's. An enforced marriage, the first-born son and a drift into accounting work for which he had no aptitude. They both had the etiolated looks of handsome men whose lifestyle didn't suit them. A strain showed. Above all, the word Matthew used that morning, 'receivership', set up troubling reverberations. It was glibly said but the prophetic was often overlooked at the time. No, it couldn't be that her son was condemned by a chance word. She turned away from fearful destiny.

Anna died for the third time, and it was an irreversible death. He would never read that book again, it or any book, good or bad. It was the end of imaginative escape. Like Vronsky, he couldn't believe that Anna would have left him like that to be assailed by doubts and self-recrimination for the rest of his days. Yes, a quick heroic suicide in battle was better than lingering. He couldn't believe that Anna would have defaced her beauty by such an unseemly death, trapped by the engines of destruction. There was no consolation in the living: Kitty and Levin with their son in the domestic entourage, such banal people, not even knowing they were living in shadow when the light had gone out of the sky.

31

By the end of July, the House had exhausted its stamina for debate and was impatiently calling for the Prime Minister to dissolve Parliament for that session. The closest mood to this was the impending announcement of a general election, a frenzy of attending to last-minute details and a winding down at the same time which created the bi-valve into a different mental condition. The MPs wanted to be away with their school-age children, paddling or sailing at the coast, wanted to reacquaint themselves for more than a weekend at a time with the women they called their wives. London emptied round about them as systematically as Paris in August, a ghost city apart from visitors.

The final Friday came. It was also the last week for Leonie and the production at the Haymarket, their finale. *Hedda* followed the pattern of most successful stagings. Critics had applauded at the opening, the box office was steadily appreciative and then, as soon as the closing date was announced, they were mobbed. Standing room only for the last two weeks. Tickets changed hands between tout and queue for three times the face value and those agencies which had had the foresight to make block bookings of fifty early on mopped up.

All the same, it was a trying time. These packed houses weren't necessarily the most attentive. There was a percentage of tourists struggling with the English text, sixth-formers who'd been taken out for an end-of-year treat but rustling, rustling distractingly in the circle and slow on the sophisticated response. On Monday, always a bad night, Kenneth Frew had very nearly lost his temper, slammed a book down on Hedda's desk to focus the wandering attention of the audience and waited for silence before he carried on, an embarrassed silence which fell with pendulous slowness.

Leonie and Watson were wary and avoided each other after their broken night, unless Quercus or Laidlaw or one of the others were present. They circumvented the future and how that might be related to whatever Leonie decided about Lady Macbeth, so he sat back and let the allure of the rôle work for him. They had agreed to drive to Edinburgh together during Sunday and let eventuality take its course.

After Friday's performance, Leonie went back to her dressing room and found a deputation waiting for her. The MPs had been celebrating their release from the schedules of Westminster and, making an impromptu party, Quercus and Laidlaw and Moncrieffe had come to collect her before going on to a nightclub.

"Come as you are," urged Quercus for speed of exit.

"That depends on where you're going." Whatever the bachelor might think, Hedda's sombre afternoon gown wasn't in party style.

"We should have dinner," said Laidlaw wistfully on an empty stomach.

"Why don't we do both?" resolved Watson. "If we go to the Park Lane Club you can still have your dinner and the rest of us can have slightly more riotous fun."

"Park Lane Club?" asked Leonie, looking for clues on dress.

"A casino," admitted Quercus, setting down the word gingerly as if he were nervous of its Italianate, seedy connotations. "But the restaurant does happen to have a first-rate supply of oysters."

"And Scotch beef," capped Laidlaw.

"Park Lane then. Why don't you ask Stuart and some of the others. We're all suffering from overwork."

So they left in search of more escapees while Leonie changed into the pleated Fortuny gown. The face which in the dressing table mirror had looked tired at the end of Act Three revitalised again as she tilted the brass lamp for a different angle. The hair combed out from Hedda's severe chignon was released into new anticipation. Under the make-up was herself, headed for some hard-won irresponsibility.

It was a group of seven that gathered in the foyer, among them Stuart and Kenneth Frew and the actress who played Thea Elvsted, a golden-haired girl called Amy Ross. They squeezed into two taxis which set them down on Park Lane, two hundred yards below Marble Arch. It was the affluent location where property had started to escalate out of the hands of individuals into corporate businesses or Arab sheiks heading oil conglomerates. Nothing ostentatious showed. The stucco was immaculate, the bow windows were polished so that they reflected the beech and oak leaves on the other side of Hyde Park with precision on a dark night. Not that nights in London were strict according to the word; they were alternative days with people emerging from the torpor of daylight to extend the small hours into largeness. The substratum came up to the surface or a lid lifted showing the citizens of an underworld who were engaged in hidden pursuits. The city didn't sleep but dozed in phases.

The casino was busy long before they came. The gaming rooms where they looked in before going up the circular staircase to the restaurant – a staircase drawn in the political cartoons of Rowland-son, baroque or arabesque curls with caricatures of people going up and down – hummed with a quiet studiousness that was more reminiscent of the library. It was a handsome building, late Regency, constructed with the classical balance of vast scale and particular detail. A wall that ran sheer up sixty feet had on its panels egg and cup moulding no bigger than an inch.

Beef followed oysters, liqueurs coffee. They were replete and a little foolhardy from the satiety of work and nourishment, output and input in a momentary equilibrium.

"So what's your next engagement?" Watson asked Stuart who was always reluctant to admit the future in case he became its slave. He stayed mentally evasive even when in practice he had committed himself.

"This and that. Some experimental things at the Edinburgh Festival. A University group who are very promising. More daring really than the professional stage. Not so much hangs on it. I'm sick of squaring the books. Then I'm freelancing. My cast are going to overtake me. They're moving on to much more illustrious things." He disguised the fact that he'd wanted a London theatre for a year's stint as artistic director and wasn't going to get it. In such moments, Stuart resented that his career was a precarious tightrope between overwork and unemployment.

"Macbeth!" pondered Quercus to his neighbour, Kenneth Frew. "That is a challenge. Do you know what strikes me now when I read Shakespeare? The statecraft, or kingship since there were no party politics in his day. The plays are studies in authority. The major heroes were all rulers of some kind, king, general, whatever,

289

and have a public image to maintain while all this turbulence goes on in their private lives."

"Their emotional breakdown is a symbol for the administrative one?"

"Yes, Shakespeare was terrified of civic disorder. Maybe that's part of the plays' impressiveness. Men speak for nations, France, Albany and so forth. It enlarges. Kings have gone out of fashion as heroes. Imagine 'Prime Minister Fleming' as a viable title."

"Do the speeches stand politically nowadays?" wondered the actor, always ready to call on others' expertise.

"Oh there are some good floor of the House speeches. Mark Anthony in *Caesar* knew the manipulative tricks of the professional politician. But it's too simplistic and authoritarian a view of government. Personalities not issues, the feudal hierarchy. That's changed out of recognition. We're all Polonius nowadays, dry old windbags, not really making decisions but putting on the air that we do."

"Who would you be if you had to choose one part?" This was Frew's parlour game, a typecasting that could reveal interesting delusions.

"Among the whole Shakespearian canon? Kent," he said emphatically. "He talked some sense, which is the privilege of the peripheral. You have that in your face which I would fain call master, that's my shot at being a politician, only unfortunately I'm still looking for the face." Quercus finished an after-dinner cheroot then marshalled the diners towards the gaming tables below. "What do they play here? Chemin de fer or baccarat? Not that it matters, I forget the rules between visits and lose every time."

"Do you have money?" Watson asked Leonie going down the coil of staircase again.

"As much as I'm prepared to risk."

"And how much is that?" He wanted to know, amused at what he felt was her instinctive parsimony, desiring not so much to have money as to discount it.

"Ten pounds or so."

"Let me take it to the cashier for you."

"Shouldn't ladies go to banks then?"

"Not in evening dress."

The chips he put back in her hand amounted to fifty rather than ten pounds' worth.

There were three rooms with gaming tables, rooms in which there was no distinguishing feature apart from décor. Silver and gold and Chinese suites ran into one another through double doors, each one of which was lit in subdued points by a chandelier or lantern which gave off the glow of opulence and glamour. The high rooms tapered into a cupola and gilt mirrors with candle sconces supplied a visual echo, furnishings doubled up from wall to wall. The carpets were inch deep. They padded out the harshness of extraneous sound. Each table could accommodate sixteen players under its weighted lampshades, but easy chairs were arranged near the occasional tables and the bar which ran along the corridor of the three chambers sent up a distant but connective chink, so that the pressure to gamble was subtly disguised.

"Decadent," said Leonie.

"Come now. Not so censorious. Look on it as a tenner at the theatre. It may or may not be an elevating experience but what you make of it is yours."

They settled themselves in groups, Quercus and Frew taking themselves off to the Chinese room, for which they professed an aesthetic fondness.

Watson was a judicious player. He played the red numbers of column three in rotation and hedged this by simultaneously backing black which at least protected his stake. Not much but steady, though twenty-one was lucky twice, confirming its superstitious power.

"Dear oh dear," complained Stuart, "I never thought you were such a cautious player. It's all or nothing with me." He hazarded the former and ended up with the latter, emptying his pockets one after another in the search for more coins in buffoonery.

Amy Ross was entertained by his antics and played up to them, passing him her own chips to play with.

Leonie watched the run of the roulette ball for a long time before staking anything, making the calculations of chance. The gamblers were a different breed from the race course at Musselburgh or rather the same cross-section in a higher stratum. The luxury of the private club debarred the down-and-outs who'd hovered round the fringes of the paddock; members and members' guests were an exclusive fraternity, filtering narrowly through pricey entrance

fees and recommendations of good credit. But there were the same
desperate men around, black-eyed with worry, throwing money
away that would have bought them a suit or peace of mind if they
were capable of settling for either form of humdrum. Something
else enticed. The mirrors picked it up and deluded with a false and
glamorised image, multiplied into infinity. A million or more. The
chips weren't real money and this wasn't real time, but the
vacuous space between going to bed and rising which didn't count
or was wasted by doing the conventional. Excitement and glitter
had hypnotised them.

In the Chinese room, Quercus wandered away from the play
which was only a diversionary centrepiece, an excuse for revelry in
which he had no compelling involvement, and said to his new
acquaintance in whom he recognised the delineaments of friend,
"I am very concerned, you know. Perhaps it's old womanish of
me. I've noticed old men do have this alarming capacity to become
neuters but I never thought the condition would befall me." He
ruminated, wondering how indiscreet he should allow himself to
be. "Leonie is married?"

"And has a son," said Frew, turning on his heel with more
interest in the conversation than the betting percentages.

"So I had heard. That is cause for concern. A young son."

They walked beside a fretwork screen, perforated in a hundred
lattices which were both transparent and obscuring.

"Why? If they are consenting adults."

Quercus didn't care for this modish phrase which implied both
deviance and a trivialising acceptance of it. A social man rather
than an individual one, he couldn't ignore the corporate entity. A
weighty sense of responsibility for his actions had hindered progress in his own emotional life. "Mess," he specified. "Watson has
already acquired an ethos which isn't wholly justified, or helpful."

"Yes. His divorce was a blood-letting event."

"Oh, you remember that? Rather a silly girl, his wife, out to
make an issue. That vulgar publicising. So many strident wrongs
to be aired in the name of the injured women, and overlooking
injuries inflicted. Fine, he had committed a peccadillo but what
successful politician hasn't? If she'd had a grain of sense, she'd
have scolded him and then taken him back. Lonely times, you

know, away from home and family."

"My calling has the same defect," said the actor. "My wife is long-suffering."

They raised an eyebrow at each other and walked on.

"He's one of those unfortunate men who's attractive to women, but fastidious. They tend to throw themselves at him. Some extraordinary compulsion women have about men in public life. They treat politicians like film stars. If I thought Leonie would come and go, I might be less uneasy."

Frew thought this an accurate résumé of what he might say of the actress. Fancies passed; but the serious involvement was a fixture because it was necessary to their temperament, both escapist and self-compensating.

"Imagine if this became public. I think in Wester Ross, a second scandal would finish even the nephew of Lord Moncrieffe."

Kenneth revolved what might be expected of him in the way of counsel. He thought the actress's career more singular than any politician's. "I've no sway with Leonie. I suspect nobody has. Or you can be sure by saying something, you'd drive her the other way."

"Thrawn," supplied the Anglo-Saxon from the older tongue.

"Thrawn indeed. No, not deliberately but determinedly."

"Dear," said Quercus. "To be out of it all oneself but forced to watch others making the same grievous mistakes. I thought old age would be light-hearted, but it isn't. A shift from major to minor, but no change in tone."

"I can tell you this. Leonie's husband isn't inclined to scold and take back any more than Elizabeth Moncrieffe. He is intractable and maybe moralistic."

"Ah. That is the one thing I hoped not to hear you say."

Leonie had the repeated misfortune to win. She didn't place a bet on every turn of the wheel but the times that she did the ball came to rest on her colour. The quandary of unsubstantiated success came her way.

"Good God, Leonie, you've got uncanny luck," said Stuart, more admiring of chance than skill. He remembered how at Musselburgh she'd come close to winning the legendary grand. A level eye. A steady hand.

"I wish you could take it from me. I don't like being this lucky."

"One more turn," urged Watson, not caring if his small investment of forty pounds ended up with the croupier. He was diverted to see the cool-headed Leonie so baffled by the unexpected rewards.

"I've had enough I think."

"One more throw. Why don't you put the whole lot on a single number. Thirty-five to one. What the hell." He pushed her out, underwritten by a bank balance which would stand thousands of such debits. "Live dangerously. What's it worth if you don't risk everything?"

"You didn't."

"Then I will." He gathered up his piles of counters and made to put them on nine.

"No," she deterred him. "That's come up twice earlier this evening. It won't come again. I'll put on another stake but don't rush me."

"Faites vos jeux, Mesdames, Messieurs. Faites vos jeux," came like a warning bell to curtain.

She waited while the wheel revolved for other players, committed to colour or number. She thought she must have five hundred pounds in front of her, ten times her original holding. That she could multiply it by so much on one toss had a pure conceptual appeal. It wasn't actual money, only counterfeit tokens, and it wasn't even hers. If she had the facility of good luck, it was a denial of power not to use it and increase the investment. But against this, there was the memory of Fergus inveighing against lottery and the speculative bent. Money dishonestly come by was a continuing corruption. Between the two contrary motives, actually deciding on a throw was hard.

Stuart could read her hesitation better than Moncrieffe. Women's faces didn't wear a formal front as often as men's but reflected their feelings through a translucent medium of skin, inner to outer. Doubt and cupidity, not for the win but for the event of winning, battled across her features like the simple personification in a mediaeval morality play. Knight slays Dragon. Good triumphs over evil and suchlike trumpery. No wonder they were such tedious dramas when, in an equal contest, the good and knightly were also fatally wounded. He personally found Greed

294

and Sloth and Lust rather more intriguing characters than Friendship or Wise Counsel. He always wanted Noah to go down in the Flude, the three kings not to make it to Bethlehem because of a sandstorm, adding a bit of a twist, or other edifying disasters to subvert the course of the one-dimensional parable with its happy ending.

"Don't tempt me, Stuart."

"I never said a thing."

"Well, stop thinking. I'm trying to concentrate."

"In for a penny, in for a pound."

"Those economics made you a pauper."

Amy had a flutter, leaning across her director's arm to place it. A long gold hair clung to his sleeve afterwards like an iridescent thread caught up in its fibre by accident. She lost her stake, without regrets.

The colours alternated symbolistically, the numbers ran like a series whose logic would be manifest at the end of the night's dealings. Their sequential patterning seemed random at this moment, so many disconnected digits, but there was surely a unifying theme that wound through the incidence of chance. To find it, to believe in it, to make it work. It was only the strength of mind which, focusing on one point, brought character to bear on hazard. It wasn't the croupier who spun the wheel, or those long-sheared Fates but the self-selecting process behind choice. Be certain and you will succeed was an attractively accessible touchstone to reward.

Colour and number pulled her in opposite directions until she succumbed to the negative force of indecision. Half of her chips went on Première, the numbers one to twelve, the other half on black. Even as she placed the stakes, she realised there were a dozen possible outcomes that would bring her no return. A high red would take her back to zero status, wiping out the evening in dissipating failure.

The man rotated the wheel and it was the only thing in the room that moved. There was a glitter from the gold quadruple knob of the roulette wheel that looked in its speed as if it were counter-rotating while the ivory ball made a continuous whirr against the higher planes of the circuit as velocity threw it out, then a clatter as it fell down against the sections that partitioned one number from another.

Irresponsibility, thought Leonie, it's hard-won indeed. She didn't care now which way it fell out, only to be done with suspense.

The ball came to rest. Black eleven it was and the croupier returned her stake with a covering number of chips, two to one in number. The grand and more came her way after all and the table applauded a win they shared by involvement.

"You pick it up," she said to Moncrieffe. "It's yours."

"No. No. You must cash it in."

"Must I really?"

"Your win."

They turned to go. It was three in the morning. The rooms hadn't thinned since they arrived, but relaxed from the earlier state of intensity. The fortunes of the night were told as men resigned themselves to running out winners or losers for that day. Stuart went to round up the rest of their dispersed party, with Amy tagging along. Going through the central gold room to the entrance hall, Leonie was arrested by the sight of a figure sitting at its table, so familiar it was distinctive even when least expected.

"Harris," she said, walking up to him without reflection while Watson followed her. "What are you doing here?"

"The same as you it seems." He stood up and grinned, thinking it an uncommonly long time since he'd seen his sister-in-law but not otherwise put out.

"This is Watson Moncrieffe," she introduced the figure who hovered disconcertingly close to her shoulder.

"Haz Petrie," the younger man advanced.

Fergus' brother, he deduced. But the trio stood incomplete in Watson's eyes and he strained to gauge between the appearance of the brother and sister he had already met, how the last sibling might look.

"What are you doing here?" she asked again. "Where are you staying?" The apparition was as unlooked for as Alison coming up the stairs of the restaurant at her first night party and when Stuart was the unspoken effector then, she looked for a similar justification now. For all she knew, Fergus might have followed the others – one two three – down south and be sitting in the next room watching her moves. Annoyance mixed hastily with confusion.

296

"I'm not staying anywhere. I caught the late flight down from Edinburgh last night and I'll take the first flight back in the morning. I'm running a syndicate."

"A what?"

"A syndicate. With Matthew Geddes. We've got a good system going."

"There aren't any good systems." She looked down severely at his chips which profusely contradicted her assertion.

"We're doing okay."

"I wouldn't have thought you or Matthew Geddes could afford to risk as much as the air fare."

"Don't you go to The Lantern in Edinburgh?" asked Moncrieffe, dipping into the jargon of experienced gamblers.

"Oh yes," said Harris, relieved to find a man after his own inclination, "but you know they have a thousand pound limit."

Leonie was horrified. The money which she had won after so much angst that evening was Harris' starting point. A thousand pounds limit on the turn of a wheel wasn't enough. "Would you mind going to the cashier for me after all, Watson? I haven't seen Harris for some time." The actress with her mouth and eyes in that determined set was not to be thwarted. Moncrieffe left them, scalded with curiosity as to what it was all about.

"You're flying back up?" Leonie confirmed from her brother-in-law.

"At seven from Heathrow."

"Is it really Matthew Geddes' money you're gambling with?"

"Some of it's my own."

"You've never got two pennies to rub together."

"Well," he admitted reluctantly, "Fergus did lend me five hundred pounds."

She drew breath from her inquisition. So Fergus lent him money, contrary to his first impulse and contrary to his instincts about what Harris was likely to do with the buckshee. The brothers had made up in her absence, but why? She sensed some ulterior motive in Fergus' mind when he was not the man to overlook a slight. Revenge loomed, revenge and power. Five hundred pounds! The sum she had ventured herself took on an altered valuation when it was Fergus who dispensed it out of earnings, and from her earnings as like as not. A fortnight's performances for

Fergus to disburse, indeed.

"How have you done tonight?"

"Up about six thousand overall."

The scale and ease of the admission staggered her. Fretting for him and the nervous tension that drove him to these straits, she could find nothing to say that wasn't hypocritical. Go home and work hard at being good – the tenets of socialism were scant comfort when, lifted over the impasse of immediate need, he and Matthew and hundreds of impatient ambitious young men might prosper by conventional capitalism. All things will come to those who wait was a miserly aphorism when you were twenty-five.

"I don't like this, Harris. I don't like to see you here. These nocturnal comings and goings, they're not natural."

"Oh relax, Leonie. I'm all right."

Tall, blond, not readily suspicious, he was a larger moving target than he realised. She put her hand on his arm. "Don't do it. Don't be beholden to Fergus. Go back and pay him what you owe him and don't ever borrow from him again."

"As you say."

"You're not carrying all that money about with you?"

"Of course," he said. "In a briefcase."

"What if somebody mugs you going out of here?"

"Oh I always get the doorman to order me a taxi first."

Always! How repetitiously it sounded.

"A cheque would be safer," she pointed out.

"Cheques," he laughed, "have to go through banks. And banks, contrary to rumour, are very dodgy places to deposit money. It looks as if you're off now," he said as Moncrieffe appeared again in the main doorway, shadowing her. "Cheers. And you'll keep mum about this?"

They smiled wryly at the Petrie caveat and parted.

"Who was that?" Watson wanted confirmation in their separate taxi home.

"My brother-in-law."

"An older brother?"

"No. A younger. Younger than me."

"You wouldn't think it."

The compliment grated. It pointed to a hastened ageing process in the man, not youthful any more but bowed under cares of his own making.

When Stuart got back to his flat in Little Venice, he groped his way tentatively round the hall remembering that Alison was likely to be asleep. But she wasn't. After a few seconds she put on the light and came through to the lounge bleary-eyed.

"Why, where have you been until this hour, Stuart? I've been worried sick." Even to Alison, this had striking overtones of Muriel, the woman left out of celebration because her company wasn't a vital ingredient to enjoyment.

Stuart hadn't thought about her until the moment he put his key in the latch and was smitten with a temporary remorse. He really should have called and a more expeditious liar would have said he had but the lines were blocked etcetera. Stuart was inclined to be more direct since having enjoyed free range for so long, he fretted at the restrictive curbs women imposed, which included the labour of inventing alibis. He felt it was important to stake out his future liberties. "It was a hurried get-together sort of outing. I didn't know where we were going till we went and I'm not sure you'd have fitted in."

This defined exactly how Alison felt he allocated her, as a pleasant diversion but not an intrinsic part of his life in the theatre. The theatre people talked a coded language, a quick shorthand of reference from which she was excluded, not intentionally but because she was a foreigner. Their jokes and quips seemed fascinating while she didn't understand them and trivial when she did. "I might have liked to decide that for myself."

That was the dignified reply he couldn't ignore. "Is there any coffee?" he asked, to stall.

"I expect there is. And if you ask me to make you some, I will."

"Thank you. If you would."

He flopped, suddenly exhausted by her steely opposition which he hadn't looked for. He hadn't known that Alison had an incorrigible will, right or wrong.

"Who was there?" she asked from the kitchen.

"Leonie and Ken."

"Moncrieffe?"

"Yes. He came. His idea. And his cronies."

"And Amy Ross?"

He did some hasty calculation on how likely Alison was to find that out from someone else, balancing a quiet time now against a reckoning later. "Amy? Yes, they asked her too."

"And where was it you went?"

"The Park Lane Club."

"Who was the member who signed you in?"

"Moncrieffe, I think."

"I didn't know he was a gambler. I expect you lost."

"A bit. I tell you who *was* there. Harris. We had a long chat."

Alison evinced no surprise, not greatly interested in what her brother did with his time, his money or anyone else's for that matter, as long as it wasn't hers. "I think you should bring your friends back here, don't you? That's right and proper. Then I can be included," she said decidedly.

He was pleased by this solution and impressed. It marked a willingness to try. Helen, meeting his friends, designated them 'gey queer folk' which in terms of district nurse they no doubt were. Mostly he was relieved that Alison wasn't weepy. The one woman he detested was the tearful mop, the woman who clung without being close and every time her man went over the doorstep and threatened to enjoy himself, made her own and his life a misery. Perhaps Alison meant to manage him wisely after all.

At the Westminster flat, the lights had been left burning for security. Leonie went about dimming them and closed the curtains so that she and Watson drew inside a seclusion that felt restful, kicking off shoes, removing a necktie in the aftermath of an evening out.

"In vacant or in pensive mood?" he asked.

"Oh, vacant. I'm past it for pensiveness."

He assessed the deflecting remark. Her reaction was always a put-off, always a shield. To say she was thoughtful prompted an inquiry which she shied away from, but for once he risked offending her privateness and probed behind the defence. "You hadn't expected to see your brother-in-law this evening."

"No."

"And he upset you?"

"In a way," she conceded.

300

"Is he a compulsive gambler?"

"I suppose he is. In some form or another since . . . well, since he was below the legal age. Ten years maybe."

"A serious addict. Has he tried Gamblers' Anonymous?"

"He would have to get to the point of admitting there's a problem first. I've no idea how much money he gets through but he had six thousand pounds in a briefcase this evening. And he's pulling in someone else who's even more vulnerable." Her face twisted into grief as she thought of Matthew's debilitating taste for luxury, boaters, gloves, expensive cars which a trainee's salary didn't accommodate.

"Your husband?"

"Fergus? Goodness no. Fergus is no libertine. You possibly know who it is. Professor Geddes' son."

"Of Jurisprudence? Yes, I know. James Geddes was a friend of my father's. I seem to remember they were old sparring partners at the Law Society debates. An amicable enmity." Edinburgh's ambit drew tighter than any other city's where the same school or the same profession made interlocking cliques. "Look, Leonie, these are grown men whose worries you're shouldering. Get out of the syndrome of the confessional. It's egotism really. And you're starting to talk like a politician, going about righting the world's endemic wrongs. I sometimes think if I ever give up politics I'll switch over to the priesthood. I've no doubt you think you shouldn't have been gambling in the first place and certainly shouldn't have won. Much more virtuous to lose. Fun is such an unScottish term and invariably has its source in vice. Occasionally, it might be therapeutic to waste time and to waste money. Not as general habits but to test economy."

Her gown splayed out like a fan of plumes over the slubbed linen of his chairs, an exotic creature, or an odd one who kept him talking into the small hours, when with any other woman he'd have moved by now into the routines of flattery and seduction. He didn't even dare to pay her a compliment but hung back from the personal, tongue-tied with inhibitions. He was losing his grip.

Leonie found that the way his life was integrated along the planes of hers was a mixed blessing. It did away with circuitous explanations. It reassured. His opinions were comforting partly because they were semi-familiar, patterns thrown up from the silhouette of the known, but intensified by his sharper illumination. These had been her own arguments to Fergus' objections. Life – not abstinence or abstention. It also troubled. She knew her husband better than she knew this man but only because of the bonds of marriage. The calibre of his mind was lost on her. Mathematics might be Fergus' version of Esperanto but it was still a foreign language to her, theoretical and not people-based. Communication between them was through the physical or the accidental; they were deep strangers, however sympathetic.

Her thinking drooped and Moncrieffe put out a hand to support her, a hand which she didn't brush aside. Self-reliance was so very tiring. Sometimes unburdening was easeful. He went on touching her without embracing and she let him release the tension knots around her neck. She looked at the man who had done everything that was humanly possible to sustain her during these months, while adding immeasurably to her problems. They called him difficult; he was, difficult to place, to contradict, to ignore.

"I wonder if I am being very unfair to you?" she asked. "I think I'm abusing your feelings. I give nothing in return, not a thing."

"I'm not the man to make you do anything you don't want."

She removed the hand from its massaging and held it open studiously. "I don't know who we're kidding. I've been in love with you for ten years, on and off."

"Me or a house?"

"An impression that wasn't wrong, at any rate."

His other hand ruffled the random creases of the dress where they fell into a satin cuff. He had promised not to force, but it was hard to keep his word when he felt volition was equal on her side and that they were separated only by the thing they had just defined, a cowardly negativeness towards being alive.

Her eye and then her hand moved down the face that was known for so long it had become the prototype of male. Ferocious brows, a misformed nose and the mouth shifting from precise to sensuous. She kissed it in a tardy acknowledgement of the latter. Why was it particular? Out of the kisses which were exchanged in the course of a lifetime, patient, bored, dutiful, ceremonious, why should one contain the elements of union? The roll of his lip inside hers, narrow to broad, was surprising and intense over an anterior stretch of feeling while his eye in retreat challenged. He wouldn't let her off lightly on anything.

"I'm too tired to make love, Watson," she said honestly. "But I don't mean to cheat. And anyway, people hurry over this too much. I want to wait a little. Just this pause has its appeal. We can go to bed and sleep together, if you want."

He wouldn't disagree at having her turn into his arms. It was the end of mental celibacy and maybe the promise was better than simple or singular possession. They didn't sleep in the end but talked out the night. It reminded him of birthdays when he was young, staying awake with fever but then when he was faced with the reality in the morning, he couldn't undo the parcels all at once, and they laughed at him for the delay. One at a time, and over days.

The light came up by degrees with the tide. She was right. These hours were not to be hurried. Tomorrow would be logical or prosaic, attached to the parameters of cause and effect. He abandoned the notion of sleep that night. Sleep was for dotards.

She got up about five o'clock and opened the long windows onto the river. Bargees taking advantage of the rise might have observed her. Immodest, was she? Then London mornings had seen a good few of these women leaning out of balconies. The Dark Lady of the sonnets, though people now said that it was Shakespeare's patron and a man, not their shared mistress at all, but Watson liked his own version and would go on believing what he wanted in the face of advanced scholarship. And Nell Gwyn and Emma Hamilton and Lily Langtry defying the restriction of their different centuries and carrying off kings, lords and princes who were more entertained by the actress parvenu than by the courtly ladies. Tiresome, ill-bred women? That was the judgment of the tired and over-bred, and envious.

32

"I'll come to the theatre for you tonight," Watson said. "Can I stand in the wings and watch?"

"Aren't you tired of seeing that play?"

He lifted the hair which she was trying to bind and kissed her until it all fell down again. "The play, yes. You in it, no."

"Don't idolise me, Watson. Remember I am completely mortal."

He sat behind her on the dressing stool, impeding the movement of her arms as she went to fasten up the sprigs of hair, frankly bothering her because he was in the hapless, tumbled state of infatuation and went in and out of her clothes to convince himself of underlying substance.

"I want to make love now," he said.

"I know." They pulled away from the embrace that shaped itself unmistakably as sexual, a drawing to centre. "It seems perverse to go on like this but if I can, I'd rather be open with Fergus. I don't want to deceive him."

Watson accepted the conditional because the long term which her words proposed was a permanence, the thing he'd feared to ask. So the ensuing kisses were a contradiction, yes and no.

She abandoned the tidiness of her hair and trying to avoid him. His physical passion began to overpower her in its repetition and intensity, because she saw it wasn't self-motivated like most men's need, seeking the most convenient object, but was actually sprung by her. She wasn't instrumental but pivotal. She was his obsession. Yes, he was a man given to the single obsession, not irrational but selective, which he would pursue doggedly against a run of difficulties, hostile opposition, even the natural rewards of labour, on and on and on until the bitter end.

"Let me go now, Watson."

"I can't."

He came for the last act, having spent the day packing and tidying out the flat ready for a long summer in the constituency. It wasn't going to be a vacation as such. Alistair Macleod had arranged a hefty schedule of events, political among the social so that one day he was briefed to see two farmers about grants for drainage and land reclamation, the next opening a country fair at Evanton. These were pleasures in store, out and doing, putting on his boots and tramping across fields and moor, unable to predict what the day would bring in the way of sun or rain storms, so he was either hot or wet and often both. He packed for Leonie as well, a small compensation for having held her back all day, and this was a distinctive joy, folding her clothes inside a suitcase as if their journey north again were a continuum, not finite. He tried to do what he so seldom could, suspend the future and circumscribe his vision to the next hour, or two, a blinkered happiness.

He stood in the wings, in evening dress, since he had thought he would take Leonie to supper afterwards. Listening to her delivery, he registered misgivings about holding any sort of celebration. It was the flattest performance he'd heard her give and aroused considerable guilt in him that the sleepless night together, loving without love-making, had made her so exhausted, and for the last performance too which should have been memorable for something better than an anti-climax. He fretted, finding he couldn't watch her doing less than her best because he shared in the acute disappointment. Failed speeches; he knew how those dwindled away into air. It was too hurriedly done, brusque on the emotional interaction with the other characters where normally she excelled. Her mind was elsewhere and she'd reached the point of cut-off from the audience because all she wanted was to finish. Rather on the closing than the opening night was the best consolation he could wring.

When he went upstairs to the dressing room afterwards, she was sitting with her head in her hands in front of the illuminated mirror, rubbing her temples.

"Not that bad," he cheered. "Six curtain calls."

Her face was grey and pained. "I was abominable," she said. "But they were in the mood to applaud anything."

"That *is* success."

She pulled out the pins of the chignon and the hair fell down, but differently from in the morning. The same act in a changed mood shed the erotic and was merely tired or dispirited as if the extra weight of grips and hair on top of her head was intolerable. He wished he could find something to alleviate such fatigue.

"What can I get you?"

"Not a thing." She moved her hand towards her brush and came across the telegram which was waiting for her when she arrived at the theatre that evening and passed it over for him to read.

MICHAEL DIED. FERGUS

"I've told Stuart to let Alison know. He'll drive her up tomorrow." The fact that the man's death compelled public acknowledgement from the members of his family, when in life he was so easy to overlook, was evident to both the director and the actress.

Goddam Fergus and his telegrams, thought Moncrieffe. Goddam all Petries with their troublesome, invasive existence, turning up whenever they were least wanted, demanding and imperious. This put them back weeks, months in terms of progress. The selfish dominated.

"What do you think it was? Was he ill?"

"I don't know. I am afraid in case it wasn't . . . natural causes."

"Suicide?"

"The man was terminally depressed, had been for years."

"Were you fond of him?"

"Yes. But he'd no real interest in me. He thought women should be either domestic or decorative. And I wasn't a Roman Catholic."

"And he was? Then it's not likely to be suicide. The religion forbids it."

"That's why I'm so afraid. For Fergus. He'll feel such a burden of failure if it was."

"Today's date. If he died today, the funeral will be on Tuesday at the latest. What do you want to do? Go now?" He was at his best in crisis, swift and clear-sighted on the options.

She looked out of her high window into the dark night, punctuated discordantly by brakes and car engines accelerating at the traffic lights down Haymarket and the passage of feet which troubled stillness. "We wouldn't sleep, would we? Do you think we should go at once?"

A twelve-hour advance on their plans. "If we're in the car, that will be two nights without rest. Can you manage?"

"Oh I can manage. But you'll be doing the driving again."

"A small spurt of madness won't do me any harm. The cases are ready. I'll go round to the flat and put them in the car and be back here in a quarter of an hour."

He drove to Park Lane and then north round Marble Arch, places which already were past history.

"Do you know what day it is?" he asked as they drove through the monotonous urban clearway until they found the access to the M1, heading towards Northampton and the M6 turn-off.

"Saturday."

"The date?"

"I should have noticed on the telegram. I don't know."

"The first of August."

"Ah, the first again."

"Fifteen firsts since Oxford."

"So there are."

"Have you lived a long time since then?"

It wasn't possible and yet, checking back on his chronology, she affirmed that one year and a quarter contained so much, marriage, motherhood, two stage rôles, a house bought and decorated, Michael's imprisonment and death, a love affair begun then and on the verge of fulfilment now, all crammed in between other people's lives. "Longer than real time and longer than you, I think."

"That'll always be the case. You'll live three to our one."

She wondered how true that was. She looked out into a contemplative dark which should have soothed the tired brain, but its quiet recesses behind the car window gave back a picture of herself in giddy motion, hurtling from place to place, and denied the time for adequate reflection. Why was she compelled towards this bizarre form of achievement, burning herself up for something that was by nature evanescent and maybe worthless beyond its superficial entertainment value? Hedda, who had cost her so much effort and self-searching, was already dead the moment she walked off the stage and into a waiting Daimler. Fame? Money? There were easier ways to come by either. The answer lay in her feelings as she headed north, involuntarily, to the ancestral city. Her life in

Edinburgh, or her life denuded of acting, was narrow and mundane. What was waiting for her at the Hermitage? A set of human problems which she knew couldn't be resolved by hers or anybody's intervention – judge, jury, Prime Minister, no-one – and that invalidated the attempt. To struggle all one's life to solve the insoluble was insane, Fergus writing down rules by which the perfect game of chess was playable, although the perfect game was an illusion. Mathematical truths did not apply to life which remained an awkward polygon conforming to no known standard of measurement. Life was always drawn freehand. The northern life was boxed in and claustrophobic whereas London spelled the multitudinous, peopled, varied existence. How many people had she met in the last three months? Hundreds of people and she could name them all, faces and occupations and conversations recorded in detail in a memory bank which was more complex and more accurate than any computer. Total recall was a human and not a mechanical capacity. The solitary, domestic life denied access to that resource which sustained her. The single pursuit, as against the layered strata of other characters and other parts, ironically made too many demands. She was unable to settle for day-to-day reality any more than gamblers, chasing their high. The thrill of chance and risk made going straight impossible.

"You're too far away," he said. He lifted his left hand from the wheel and put it behind her head, rubbing the distant cheek with the back of his hand. "A good argument for automatic cars."

"You are a practised philanderer, Mr Moncrieffe."

"And you are an accomplished sexualist."

"More honest, sir."

"More honest."

They reached the junction with the other motorway and drove west, traversing the country in a swathe away from true north which the body followed with its own compass as instinctive as circadian rhythm.

"I'm hungry," she said. "When did we last eat?"

"Days ago, wasn't it? Friday night in Park Lane and it's Sunday morning now. Shall we stop at the next motorway café."

"What a pair. You in a dinner suit and me in Hedda's best. Why can't we go about looking like normal people?"

"Mostly because we aren't."

They ate a breakfast of some dimension, advertised as 'Full American'.

"Why American?"

"I don't know. Waffles. Or maybe the way they fry the eggs. In America eggs are either easy over or sunny side up. Isn't that a happy connotation? A sunny egg. They always look like suns to me now."

"You've been to America?"

"Several times to visit my mother in Illinois, about as far distant from Torrisaig as you could go. It's funny to see how she's changed. She even wears quite different clothes, younger maybe, or socially elusive. I think she always was a Republican."

Leonie wondered about this woman who leaped so precipitately into the unknown, and was predisposed to like her.

"I tend to go with Quercus because he has American cousins and that keeps us on the move. We see our publishers in New York and put it down to business expenses." She felt his life spiral outwards. He could pick up the telephone and dial a hundred numbers, world-wide, to people who would extend hospitality, so that he could travel for a year between old colleagues like the state visits of dignitaries. The House *was* a club and if you valued your membership and obeyed the rules, it guaranteed friendship for life. "Quercus brought out a biography of Truman a few years ago that made him famous, at least on Government Hill. Though he's much more at home with Martial's epigrams. The slackness of modern prosody has consistently been too much for him. He's going to translate Catullus when he retires."

"I had a Catullus phase at one time. 'Glubit magnanimi Remi nepotes.'"

"Construe please."

"I can't. It's untranslatable. A sexual pun. Glubit is rub the ears of corn to extract the kernel, or masturbate. Rubbing up is maybe the nearest. How exciting if he could make it topical. Sons of Thames instead of Sons of Tiber."

"Well. I didn't know there were incidental attractions to the task. Horace Walpole isn't nearly so engrossing."

"I know. The twentieth century goes on behaving as if it had invented sex but the Romans were rather more cleverly licentious. Nobody wrote filth as artistically as Ovid and Catullus."

309

"Ars erotica."

"Ars amoris," she corrected.

She thought when they came back to the car that he must be feeling drowsy. A heavy meal on top of sleeplessness wasn't conducive to steady driving but the road was clear, the moon high and to keep his attention sharp she went on talking to him to prod him awake.

"That evening," she began, "after you'd had the nightmare, you said a strange thing. I haven't been able to forget it."

"Oh? I'm not usually so wise. What was it?"

"You said you felt you knew everything."

"Middle of the night egotism. I do apologise."

"But that you weren't able to enact what you knew."

"That's a bit more realistic. Why did it make an impression on you?"

"It was one of the things you said, you say them all the time, that I've been thinking for years and never vocalise. At least you get to the stage of fitting words to what you feel. I seldom get that far."

He was quiet, steering steadily north past the intersections of Birmingham, best viewed at night when the urban street lights made a pleasing sideral pattern which daylight dispelled. In fact, he recalled very precisely saying that he never knew what it was she thought, and sensed that after fifteen months of not knowing her at all, except through parts, exits, borrowings, that she was gravitating to the point of self-analysis, self-exposition for his benefit. "Does that matter to you? Most people are so wordy about themselves to no effect."

"I've begun to suspect it means the self is not so very interesting. Or rather that I am no one in particular but am capable of being everyone."

He remembered the note which he'd sent to Fleming after the offer of preferment. 'I have grown accustomed to being the No man at Westminster.' He had meant it as the opposite of Yes man, but saw in the light of her comment that it had ripples of the Homeric Nemo, the self-styling decoy of Ulysses who sees with two eyes to avoid the rage of the uni-visioned Cyclops he must blind. The no-man's-land he had described was spiritual, an arid, embattled place, scorched with many contrary motives.

"Have you ever noticed," he asked, "that of your own choice,

310

you always wear neutrals? I thought it was very astute of Ainslie to pick that up. He dressed you in white for the opening act of *Hedda* and black at the end."

"Bride and then bereaved? No, I hadn't thought about why Stuart decided to do that. Do you think I really am neutral then?"

"You make it sound insipid. Neutrality is interesting. It can be a quite conscious as well as a passive state. The contradictions of black and white are strong and very dramatic. They do provoke thought."

"You may have something there, you know. I can't remember having a single opinion. I mean a singular one. I always had two quite opposite feelings at the same time, about everything. Yes and no together. Is that what's wrong with me?"

"What's right with you. Imagine how dull people are who're convinced of their own infallible correctness. I am petrified by the man who has no doubts."

"But you think you are right."

"Politically, you mean? No, I don't think I'm always right. I simply say there are more obvious and harmful forms of wrong-headedness than mine."

The road started to be recognisable north of Birmingham, where they had joined it in the drive from Oxford. The parallels between that night and this made comparisons forcible, a telegram as summons, a stage costume carried over into reality, a man appearing to propel her towards an episode in which he had no part. So much the two journeys had in common but the differences were larger.

"Are you harbouring regrets?" he asked, following the path of her thoughts. "I don't regret these fifteen months. I'm happy, consciously happy, not in the deluded state and I thank you for that. But it's simpler for me."

"No, I don't find it simple. This is adultery, Watson. Make no mistake about it. You can't wrap it up with glosses about love and happiness. I hate the adulterous tendency of our times more than I can tell you and here I am caught up in it all the same."

"Would you rather not have known me?" He asked only because she would have to refute the hypothetical and he was new enough to the emotion to seek affirmatives.

"No. You are the final dimension."

"Can we talk about what will happen ahead?"

"There's no point. It's all conjecture from now on."

"It can at least be an informed guess. I've no idea how things will be for you when you get back and of course I worry."

"Try not to think about me for the next month."

"Don't be absurd—"

"All right. Think as little about me as you can."

"Will you answer me one rather personal question, to set my mind at rest."

"If I can."

"Is your husband . . . kind?"

"Benevolent? No, he's not a kindly man as you would term it. He's fair, like the rod of justice."

"Or correction."

"And he is very possessive."

She had meant perhaps to say protective of his own, but the stronger motive expressed itself, releasing a suspicion that Fergus cared a great deal more for things than people. Or people were possessions over whom he exercised the rights of ownership, incontrovertibly, legally his, or not his. He stressed belonging and was rooted in one place. Leonie realised she obeyed a different system of attachment. Movement or momentum, social interchange gave her a security that was at best precarious and volatile, but was more valuable than an inventory of goods, degrees, publications in one's name which added to the accretions of self. Her habits were diffuse, his contracted.

The word possessive triggered a subsidiary line of thinking in Moncrieffe, disturbing a conscience he'd imagined was long buried. "Where do you think my income comes from, Leonie?"

"I don't know. Your salary as an MP?"

"That's about a tenth of it. And my salary doesn't cover election expenses. I have to pay my own. I haven't got party coffers to dip into, no big business or trade unions backing me. So I need to have an alternative income."

"Family assets? I never really thought about it."

He smiled at the inbuilt assumption that landed and titled families were wealthy. "Torrisaig and Inveresk are hanging by a thread. Charlie says he'll go bust every year. There is no family money. We have plenty of things, objects, houses but they're a

312

drain on upkeep. When I was twenty-one and actually looked at our accounts and holdings, I realised it was all up with the Moncrieffes unless I made myself an independent income. I finished my Law degree at Oxford and then, to everybody's disgust, went into the Stock Exchange. Didn't you know that?"

"No, I didn't. I suppose there are three or four years unaccounted for."

"I was with a good company in the City, highly respected and I was given a lot of responsibility. There's a manoeuvre that's frowned on in stock market dealings, but isn't illegal as such. Buying shares and not declaring in whose name they're bought until you see how they're moving. I handled maybe twenty large portfolios. When the market went down, I entered the shares in their name and they made the loss. When it went up, I profited. It was a very subtle form of borrowing."

"And you were never found out?"

"No. I left after three years with an impeccable reference. And I had built up an investment fund of my own that'll put me out of need for the rest of my life."

"Did you do this thing often?"

"Only half a dozen times. It was enough to get me started and I operated legitimately after that. I made my firm and my clients a great deal of money in the long run, but I wasn't going to be cut out myself."

"How rich are you?"

He prevaricated. "Americans would call me a millionaire. But I hide it very carefully. It doesn't do to flout it."

"Why are you telling me?"

"I'm not sure. So you've got something you can use against me. I've never told anyone else, with some foresight. My wife would have sued me to the ends of the earth if she'd known."

"You trust me that much?"

"Yes, I think I do. And I was so very comdemnatory when you said you took something from Inveresk. You know, pompous."

"So you were."

"A sheet of paper too."

Paper. So much paper bearing the imprint of money, words and numbers. Watson's gambling system wasn't much at variance with Harris's, except that his character controlled excess. Cheating the bank's advantage was their prime ambition. Leonie had seen the printed diagrams of probability curves for gaming as well as electoral returns that pinned down statistical certainties to formula. She too had begun to ascribe to eleven the power of magic, a prime number, symmetrical, the sign for parallel, heaping on significance to make it lucky again because it was lucky once. In actuality, the curves did not converge unless by a fluke. She distanced herself from their profiteering, whatever the motive, in case they were all filchers.

33

_____

When Leonie arrived at the Hermitage in the small hours, Fergus didn't ask, 'How did you get here?' He hadn't asked it on the previous occasion, because it didn't occur to him. It was presentiment of the answer that debarred him now, and this silence throbbed between them like an unnatural vacuum waiting to be filled.

The house too pulsed with strange reverberations. Leonie went at once to look at her son, his arms and legs splayed out in a trustful sleep. Was this exquisite child really hers? She bent down beside the bars of his cot to look more closely into the features which had already lost the babyish imprecision and were marked in their mature proportions. Dark hair replaced the nondescript fuzz of birth. A person in the making, growing even while he slept. He opened his eyes and looked at her steadily in the dark. She smiled and he gave back the reflex smile which made her breath catch, as if he recognised her on a subconscious plane, knew her in spite of absence. But immediately he shut his eyes again and closed her off.

Fergus came upstairs onto the first floor landing as she stood outside the nursery door, tall, drawn, utterly correct. She always forgot what a fine individual he was as if, too perfect physically, he became confused with a mental ideal it was hard to think of as an embodiment. "Do you want to see him?" he asked.

"I've just looked in," she said. "He's asleep."

"No. Michael I meant."

"Michael?" she recoiled. "You mean he's still in the house?"

"Upstairs in the room where he died. Of course he's here. He's only dead. The dead don't turn into different people from when they were alive. Where else should he be? Death doesn't have to be so clinical, shovelled into nursing homes and hospital bays the way we do with the old and sick. They're our responsibility. This was his home. I want him to be buried from this house."

This was said in the tones of quiet reason, and Leonie in logic couldn't fault it. Repressing a squeamishness about the morbid which was in character as much as flesh, she said, "I'll come with you if you want me to."

He took her hand and they went up the final flight of stairs to the landing of the attic flat. Michael's was a room with a turret and long slits of window that were uncurtained summer and winter. The undertaker had come during the course of the day to dress the body which lay on the bed in a repose that was still formal. No one could make the mistake of thinking that the man was asleep.

They didn't put the light on, as a mark of inner respect and, when standing onlookers felt voyeuristic, they knelt, Leonie resting on her calves because the attitudes of prayer were unseemly to her mind if she didn't have faith. The emotions of the encounter with the man's recumbent body couldn't be transmitted through religion or consoled by it. He looked tired. In cessation, he was an older man than she had noticed in movement. A lined face and hands that lay creased and folded, were evocative of half a century of work that hadn't come to fruition. Disappointment that his life had aroused so little charity overcame her, and the resources of a stoical endurance with which he'd met neglect. He wasn't an assertive man but neither was he a complainer. She remembered how a very long time ago he had said to her, 'When I die, grieve only for one day. It will come as a release for me.' The phrase had passed unnoticed at the time, and was the cause of the largest regret. In spite of being so close in kinship they hadn't known each other intimately but glanced past. The times hadn't been right for friendliness or trust. Deprived of the traditional condolences, spiritual or denominational, she could only murmur to herself the words of a popular song. 'All my trials, Lord, soon be over.'

The funeral service was held in St Peter's Roman Catholic Church in Falcon Avenue. Michael had walked over there many times from the Hermitage, and from Canaan Lane, and in an earlier era driven to the door in style. He was one of the best known members of the congregation, having been a regular communicant for almost forty years. It was a church of no architectural or positional grandeur, oddly sited, somehow Castilian in design, but had been his haven all the same.

Fergus and Leonie arrived early with the cortège and sat to the right side of the church stalls. The whole of the Geddes family followed in support, including Jenny, and Ellice Barr came too, glad to pay her last respects because she couldn't avoid remembering the small spitefulness when she had bypassed Michael during the days of his trial. A word of comfort at that time might have meant more than prison visits or walks along the Hermitage or funeral attendance, hindsighted. The woman sat grieving, rocklike with judgment on herself for petty-mindedness. Too late to make amends.

There was a very large gathering of mourners. Edinburgh had its quota of Russian expatriates, Red as well as White, Ukrainian, Georgian, Siberian – refugees driven ahead of the Bolsheviks and stranded in the desolation of civil war, homeless, exiled, deprived of their livelihood because of the shifting freak of battle grounds. They'd come to settle in the compatible zone not so far across the North Sea. There were men from the more recent exodus of the second world war who still had sons and wives in the Soviets or the satellite countries, on the other side of a political divide, men for whom a family celebration meant wrapping up parcels, not certain if they would arrive since those sent in return were always intercepted. One ex-soldier who was illiterate brought his letters from home for Michael to read to him, and tears would spurt out of his eyes at the simple messages of love and hope they contained. My good greetings to you, Father. May we meet soon. All these men turned out for one of their own, quiet, shuffling, blackbanded.

There were members of the business community who said to themselves, There but for the grace of God go I. Bankruptcy and premature death were curses they came to expiate vicariously. Michael Petrie hadn't been so long removed from the current of their activity that they'd forgotten him. But they hadn't shown that they'd remembered. They came in force, bankers, financiers, insurance and building society managers to show they weren't thoughtless or bad men, only busy.

The priest in surplice came from the vestry to begin the incantational prayers.

In the middle of this settled fraternity, head down in contemplation as the organ played the last mourners in, there was a sound of disturbance. The other Petries had arrived. The alienate Muriel came in and bore down the aisle with the air of a woman determined not to be omitted. She wore a full set of weeds, black from head to toe and was not unimpressive. Harris and Alison came in her train as well as Stuart Ainslie who, having been the means of transport, was reluctantly included. The three family members came the full length of the church to sit in the front row on the left, level with Fergus and Leonie. A schism emerged. Stuart realised too late that he would have to jump one way or the other, or retreat in full view of the congregation. Should he back his girlfriend or his inclinations? Muriel looked round and seeing him vacillate, called, "There's just enough room for you at the end of our row."

Fergus was multiply offended. Muriel and Michael were not finally divorced since the decree waited at one of the lock gates of the law for passage. She was still technically his wife and technically entitled to appear. But after all that happened! After infidelity, revilement, every form of injurious action, to turn up in the suit of widow. The woman was adept at ruining occasions. A fight before an anniversary, a birthday spoiled by quarrels, a fit of the vapours over Christmas; she had perfected the art of mischief.

Fergus grew pale with suppressed fury when he wanted to be calm, to pray and think constructively about the man departed. His mother knew that he wouldn't insult the consecrated place by making a commotion. Her skill was in manipulating that aura of sanctity against him. Yes, she came into the hallowed house after all the taunts she'd levelled at their Church. A minority religion she called the great Church of Rome. The flagellators, sign-makers and idol worshippers she taunted them. Her presence was an affront on many counts, chief among them inconsistency. The two opposite sides of the chapel vibrated in ill-feeling, confirming the effective apartheid of family.

"Ignore her," said Leonie, moving closer to Fergus' side. "Just keep your head up and forget about her."

She was not to be blotted out, however, but invaded his senses and his memories with insult. The two women, mother and wife, to left and right of him, etched deeply over his mind like acid and neutraliser, the latter unable to remove the pits, but sealing them indelibly when he remembered that Leonie too was absent from her husband in times of need, was not a co-religionist and behaved obscurely out of his sight. What heresies did she also harbour under the overt sympathies of wife? So the devilment ate its way into his brain, confusing shades and gradations until everything ahead of him looked black and evil.

Muriel considered that she had every right to come. More than twenty-five years of living together were not invalidated by demise. The arithmetic of time was in her favour. She had outlived him so that the final phase, the final word was hers. This was deemed to be the place of forgiveness, and so she came forgiving.

The mourners were confused. The Petries suffered from the egotism of thinking their doings were of universal interest, but in fact the great majority of those gathered together had no notion of the family circumstances and hadn't observed the segregation in the front pews. Her non-appearance during the trial had been to that extent effective. When Muriel, pushing her way to the head of the mourners, said to each, "You will come back to my house at Greenbank for a glass of something?" they accepted, innocent of wrongdoing. Wife into widow. Subtleties were none of their concern.

James Geddes refused his invitation. "Thank you, madam, no. This day has been too long already for the friends of Michael Petrie." His frock coat flapped, superfluous to August but not to mood.

Muriel cast an eye over the remainder of his party. His dithery wife Irene who couldn't say yes or no for herself and wasn't worth asking, the reprobate Matthew and his newish wife. She lumped them all as Geddes minuses. At length she approached her own son, as one who has not been included in the first choice of a side but asked along to carry bags. "Will you come, Fergus?"

"No. I go home to my own house. You hounded me from yours when I came before. I'll not step inside it again."

She stood her ground among so many onlookers and held out her hand in a formality of reconciliation. "Will you not shake hands now, forgive and forget?"

He looked at it and saw only the glove, looked at her and saw only the hat. Who she was in reality was unknown to him, a set of features beyond recognition because they were masked in life-long antipathy. "No. I won't."

319

"I did ask you. Remember that." She raised her voice to be audible.

"I think your offer was conditional on my refusal. Go away now. You've stayed too long where you're not wanted."

The larger party left in cars and the Geddes family too departed until only Leonie and Fergus stood on the dusty pavement outside the church gates, a little wind stirring debris in the gutter. Leonie felt powerless in the face of factionalism. Harris, Alison and worst of all Stuart, ranged in the other camp and she, by nature noncombatant, was forced to participate. Such odd alignments too. Harris and Matthew were constrained against speaking to each other under Muriel's eye and yet it transpired they ran a syndicate together in London casinos! Alison must turn her back on an old lover and an old friend. The divisions went on being perpetuated.

"Did you notice?" asked Fergus. "She even had the biggest, showiest wreath."

Fergus shut the front door behind them after they'd walked home, saying cryptically, "Our life begins now."

Leonie flung open all the windows to let the sun in and ventilate the stuffy interior, stripped Michael's room of its moveables and fed them systematically into the washing machine. The ordinariness of doing was a relief. The northern dusk fell through the house, finely pollinated and with the smell of resin from the trees in the Hermitage. It cleansed. They slowly re-established the pleasures of being alone together and with their child who, used to many hands, accepted his own mother uncomplainingly. He was a child who didn't cry but watched the world steadfastly out of black eyes. Fergus had bought him a walker like a hammock on wheels and, supported by this, he could actually rotate himself about the living room and keep his interest on the move. Strong and purposeful, he marched the contraption into corners, shouting with rage when he got himself firmly wedged. He laughed when tickled, slept when fed and was in all regards content.

Rapprochement with Fergus was more complex. They had let intimacy lapse, a celibacy which was older now than their son. The evening drew towards bedtime when something should be reinstated in the course of normality. She wanted to come close to him again and offer him the warmth and oblivion of the physical to combat other coldnesses. A man wasn't so different from a child

320

in that, take him in her lap, comfort him at her breast. Sex without love? Not much stranger than love without sex. She waited for a signal of consent as they went about the last chores of the evening.

He fidgeted. He came and went, kitchen to study, switching on and switching off, burning up excess energy to no end.

"Do settle, Fergus. You're unnerving me."

He left her to carry on with the ironing but came back in a minute or two with a piece of paper in his hand. It was the certificate of death, correctly signed by their family doctor, confirming that the cause of Michael's death was natural.

"Of course," said Fergus, "the GP wasn't the doctor who'd been prescribing these." In his other hand was an empty plastic bottle. "I think they're sleeping pills. He must have had them for a long time, or been saving them up. I think he was allowed one a day in prison for insomnia."

Leonie took the container from him, revolving the chemical formula. Valium, the common sedative. "And you didn't tell the GP that he'd been taking these? That's maybe wise. You didn't want an inquest, did you?"

He did appreciate the deductive speed that led to his motives without condemning them. He relied on a strong, impartial mind. "No, although an inquest would have prevented this afternoon's fiasco. In the witness box, I could have laid the blame where it belongs."

"Don't agitate about that. Revenge will destroy you if you let it."

Fergus managed in a stationary pose to give off energy, like convected heat rising from him in a vapour. His face was so concentrated it became inanimate and hard, the thinking terminals deactivating the emotional ones. Whenever his feelings were powerful, or unignorable, he became confused or simply negative and inarticulate, the child in man form.

"What is it that you're trying to say to me? Do you regret not telling the doctor about the Valium? But you didn't do it at the time, so you must have had good reason."

"You know we think self-killing is a mortal sin so my first reaction was to deny it. There *were* tablets left in that bottle and I threw them away. But now it strikes me they could have been anything – even codeine for his migraine. I should have let a chemist analyse them for a coroner's inquest and the actual truth

321

be known. Then I wouldn't have been in this state of doubt myself about whether he did or didn't commit suicide."

She followed the course of his actions along an old and familiar route. "You jumped to conclusions again, Fergus. And you destroyed your own evidence. You can't go back and change your story at this stage without risking the doctor's integrity, or throwing suspicion on your own. If the doctor had been chary about the circumstances of death, he wouldn't have signed the certificate in the first place, so what you think might not be true. Or if Michael did take his own life and you covered it up, you'll have to live with that responsibility."

Her words resolved something in his confusions. Responsibility. The onus of giving true answers to oneself. He came closer to where she stood, moving over the patterned tiles of the floor into adjacent blocks. "It's not the cover-up," he said in misery, "it's the fact. I couldn't prevent it or instil in my own father the will to live."

Sadly, she put her arm round him and he leaned into her shoulder.

"I think back to the times I was short with him, or angry because I didn't understand what he was up against. I would never go out walking with him because I had other things to do. Books, I ask you. I left him for hours on his own. He used to take the bus into town, and it was so hard for him to have to speak to people, when I could have paid for taxis. Small comforts I denied him because I didn't even think about it. I included him out. I could have saved him if he'd been able to rely on me." He wept, the hoarse weeping without tears while Leonie, rubbing the nervous spine, recalled the other grief for a man on a mountainside. Perhaps when someone died there was always an instinct for self-blame in the survivor which acted as the valve for sorrow. Or were these men who turned to her with the same anxieties, weighed down by too much scruple?

She told Fergus what Michael had said, anticipating death, and if it didn't solace the son, it diverted him with its self-abnegation or acceptance that seemed to devolve on mourners. Just for one day he would grieve.

"It's time to sleep," she said. The lights had gone out long ago in the Geddes household. The Hermitage, as they passed the landing windows, was covered in a lacquer of darkness, patinated under the influence of a moon which was on the wane from the height of its brilliance the night she drove north with Moncrieffe. Three nights ago she was on the stage in London.

Fergus didn't undress to join her in bed but walked up and down in front of the window looking out at the spectral gardens. "There's something I must say, Leonie, that's been worrying me and I ought to make my position clear before we go any further."

A guilt rose and choked her.

"I want very much to bring Andrew up in the faith. I never discussed this with you before he was born but I would want your agreement before I went ahead."

Better than raising a doubter, she thought. You could always renounce your faith but it was damned hard to acquire it without an early training. "I wouldn't object to that."

"And something else. If he and I are in the Church, why not you? I begin to feel that marriage in a registry office isn't good enough, isn't valid. It would mean so much to me if we could take the sacrament. As it is, I feel our marriage isn't . . . . blessed."

Piety came chill and even the mood to embrace him couldn't warm it. "Fergus," she said firmly, "you offered me one form of marriage and I accepted that. Freedom of movement and freedom of association. By my reckoning, that includes religious freedom unless you want to start persecuting me for non-observance. You keep changing the conditions of our contract and I don't think that's fair of you. Andrew I agree to, but I couldn't promise to even think of a conversion. I wouldn't be easily committed to a single point of view."

The arguments for faithlessness were not new to him. His mother had aired them many times. "I won't argue. It just seemed more harmonious."

The instant formed in crystalline precision. Now. Say it. Be honest with him. It was only one more infidelity which, with religious if not human compassion, he might understand. At the compelling moment, she didn't have the heart to say it and heap more troubles on him. His absolute uprightness shamed her into silence.

Although they kissed, it was conciliatory not passionate and the lines came back from a student production in which she'd played the ill-fated Duchess of Malfi.

> your kiss is colder
> Than that I have seen an holy anchorite
> Give to a dead man's skull.

IV

34

Stuart was homeless in his native city. After they retired, his parents had followed his emigrant sister and brother to Australia. He'd never had a place of his own in Edinburgh, bought or rented, sensing he was passing through although it was a transit that had lasted a decade, but was happy enough to doss down on a floor or in somebody's box-room, which was the Scots upgrading for a cupboard. He grew intimate with these four encroaching walls of box-room; they opened off another room, were windowless or at best had a fan or a skylight and in these plusher, walk-in days were often converted into hanging wardrobes so that if he wasn't careful, he woke up in the morning smothered in coats. They weren't originally for storing trunks at all but accommodated the odd guest, grown-up sons or daughters in service who came home one weekend out of four. A mattress, a box or truckle bed, an extended chair or cushions, Stuart could sleep on anything. If he was pushed, he'd make a night of it in his car.

He made no long-term plans; he knew he had three weeks' work during the Edinburgh Festival and a fortnight's run-up to it, but the problem of where to stay didn't impress itself on him until he arrived expeditiously with Alison. He didn't entirely see why he couldn't go to Greenbank although, having met Muriel once, he decided that was probably enough.

He wandered along to Morningside and asked Ellice for a bed. She was the superior type of landlady; she gave him a hearty breakfast, a latch key and let him shift for the rest. The amenities plus the decencies. What more did he want? So it was Leonie's room he woke up in, furnished with the spartan chest and iron bed and wicker chair that Ellice had probably bought from the Salvation Army depot for the price of a loaf of bread. And Leonie was upping it with titles. The bizarre affinities made him smile.

The evening after the funeral, Stuart came back from Greenbank and found his hostess unusually alone, rocking with one foot as she read.

"I've had the weirdest day of my life, Ellice."

"Did your cast walk out of rehearsal?"

"The rehearsal was the easy bit, even if it was in Leith Town Hall. Actors aren't anything like as awkward as ordinary people. No, this morning I went round to see Alison. Even you must admit, Ellice, it's a bit of an anomaly when we've been living together for months in London and yet, three hundred miles north, we have to pretend we've never set eyes on each other except in the street."

"Muriel didn't find you inamorato?"

"No, Muriel had gone off on her rounds first thing. Alison and I were in the kitchen having the most innocuous cup of coffee when the front door bell rang and Alison leaped a foot in the air and said, I forgot. It's window-cleaning day. He's a notorious chinwag. You'd better not let him see you here or it'll be all over the South Side. So I belt upstairs thinking, blow, I'll have to go and sit inside another wardrobe, when I hear footsteps coming along the hall-way behind me. What Alison hasn't told me is that this window cleaner does the insides as well as the outsides. I make a bolt for Alison's room and think the best thing I can do to preserve my incognito is to lock the door and keep him out." Stuart, no mean mimic, stood up signalling the turn of the key and his ensuing relief, arms folded. "Only there isn't any key in the lock and the man who's apparently going to blow my cover and Alison's good name for life is coming up the stairs two at a time. I think about getting under the bed, but it's a divan. The wardrobe is match-wood and will fall over if I get inside it. So the only thing I can do is hang on to the door knob for dear life. Up he comes and tries it while I'm straining fit to burst to keep the thing from opening. After a few rattles, he goes on to the next room along the landing. What a let-off! But then I turn round and there's his mate on top of a long ladder doing the outside window. He's about two feet away from me and gazing in disbelief at this pantomime, wiping with his chamois to get a better view."

"Stuart," she laughed, "you thrive on it."

"Alison was very annoyed that I hadn't made a swifter exit."

"You've survived worse scrapes than that one."

"Well. I don't think I *have* come out of today wholly unscathed."

328

In these haphazard rooms, an amalgam of ugliness that managed to be interestingly eclectic, quips and cut-outs from three foregoing centuries, five continents and tolerant of all of them, the strict contemporary attitudes were irrelevant or mean, an era of bad taste that the next would blur.

"I went back again to Greenbank after the rehearsal and walked into the most extraordinary scene it's been my misfortune to be a party to. Muriel was succeeding in having two momentous quarrels at once. Alison had taken leave of her senses and told her mother spontaneously that we were living together in the flat in London. I felt guilty, she said to me, so I had to tell her."

"Alison doesn't have the sense she was born with," the woman tutted.

"You're right. I think she had more nous ten years ago. I suppose I did kick up this morning, hiding from the window cleaner, I ask you. At my time of life, it doesn't do much for a sense of dignity. I think I told her to sort her mother out."

"Not easily sorted, that one."

"So I discover. We had the ranting plus the raving. How that woman can go on! What had I done? I'd seduced her unblemished daughter. I'd taken advantage of her hospitality – she'd been generous to a fault, though its material effects have managed to pass me by – I'd all but killed her husband for whom she seems to have developed a sudden affection now he's dead. It's so cockeyed you don't know where to begin to apply sense to it. I was frankly lost for words."

"And Alison meanwhile?"

"Oh, Alison doesn't keep her head in a crisis. Shout at her long enough, and she'll jump the way she's told. The upshot was Muriel demanding I marry her daughter."

"You'll not manage that in a hurry," said Ellice, who'd long ago wised up on Stuart's singularity.

"That's what I said. I was quite blasé by this time. I said I was already supplied with a wife."

"And all hell was let loose."

"Right. The unthinkable. An Affair with a Married Man." He illustrated it with caps, a neon light, a screaming headline.

"You're a fool, Stuart Ainslie, getting yourself mixed up with the bourgeoisie. They've such a dampening effect on high spirits. So you've promised to get a divorce pronto and put everything to rights. But you're the most unmarrying man I've ever met and now you've saddled yourself with two wives instead of one. What a piece of stupidity. And what will you do with Alison once you've married her? Put her in a house that you'll try not to go back to six nights of the week. You exasperate me, you and Leonie, boxing yourself into corners."

"Here, Ellice, won't you be an indirect mother-in-law of mine?"

"I do feel sorry for Alison. A routine enough girl with these emotional blockages. She doesn't seem to be able to find a man who hasn't got a past. All d'occasion. Second hand. You should have behaved better."

Stuart got up and found his token whisky bottle on the blue enamel trolley and poured them both a dram. "You haven't heard the best of it. Harris had come in about six, a social visit because Alison was there – he doesn't call normally – and in amongst brow-beating us, Muriel started to nag him about not paying his rent. It's months overdue for the flat at Grange Loan, it seems, and she just can't nail him on it. She finally threw him the mortgage payment book and told him he could be responsible for it in future. Have you ever noticed, Muriel Petrie can make a phrase like 'in future' feel like a pistol to your head? I wish I could get her on the stage."

"Melodrama has gone out of fashion."

"Oh, she'd manage to make it pay, or else . . . "

"Did Harris agree?"

"Well, Harris is slow to rile but when he blows, he blows. The four of us are sitting in the living room – what does she call it, sitting room, one up for the middle class – and she's going on about me being a fornicator and Harris being a liar and suddenly he lunges at her. Now he's no lightweight. He's six foot four and fourteen stone if he's a pound and he's throttling her in her chair. He actually has his hands round her neck and she's going that very distinctive de-oxygenated colour."

"Don't tell me you felt morally obliged to intervene?"

"I thought it wouldn't be very nice for Alison if her brother was done for matricide."

In spite of her intention to be serious, Ellice hooted. "So you came to the aid?"

"I did my damndest. Harris is a big bloke. And he was intent on

asphyxia, I can tell you. All the time I'm fending him off, unpluck-
ing one of his fingers at a time from round her throat, I'm thinking,
What am I doing this for? I ought to be helping him to choke her."

"I wouldn't have put the Petries down as violent," she said,
wondering what strains her daughter might incur.

"I don't think they are. He just hit a blind spot. I bit into my
tongue while I was struggling with him, bloody painful. But the
old girl was bruised and badly shaken. It doesn't take much to kill
someone. I've learned that. Really, she should have gone to
hospital but what do you write down as the cause of accident? My
son tried to strangle me, with some justification. Then you're into,
Do you want to press charges and Harris is in the cells for the
night."

Ellice Barr was quiet but not as shocked as Stuart was, in spite of
his displays of comic bravura. You didn't go prison visiting twice a
month without learning the inside story of some odd families.
Drug abuse, incest, murder and not confined to Edinburgh's
council estates either. The fine folk did some funny things at home.
Weren't seventy per cent of murder cases within the family circle?
Crime passionel needn't turn on sexual passion either, as Lizzie
Borden testified.

"How long ago was that?"

"A couple of hours. I tried to calm everyone down. Alison got
Muriel to bed. She was pretty nearly hysterical herself. I drove
Harris back to the Grange in his car. He was a bag of nerves and not
to be trusted behind the wheel. And then I walked up here."

"What now?"

"I'd like to get Alison out of that madhouse." He hummed and
hawed, taking draughts of whisky. "You don't think you could
have her here? I know it's an imposition."

Ellice looked up to the ceiling where she noticed that an endemic
crack she had filled in, papered over and painted the camouflaging
brown had begun to show through all the layers of disguise. "I'd
like to, Stuart, but I'll have Muriel hammering on my door accusing
me of connivance or some quasi-legalistic charge. My own I take in,
yes, but I don't want to have any more to do with that woman than
I can help."

"Understood."

"Why can't Alison go back to London for the next month?"

"Yes, it may come to that, but she's not keen."

The woman watched the permutations roll. Alison would be uneasy about too many of Stuart's evenings unaccounted for out of her presence. She wasn't confident about any of her assets, except virtue and high principle, and those she'd already degraded. She was afraid of the roving male in men. For Stuart, there was the suspicion that Alison wouldn't be an acceptable house guest to his more unconventional friends. She'd be dousing somebody else's kitchen and bathroom with bleach to make sure they conformed to health and safety regulations, nor restrain herself from quoting these if she were challenged. Alisonisms stuck in the gullet of a free flow conversation. The woman, who could stretch to friendship with both, couldn't volunteer to be the compromise solution between two such extremes of human style.

"I don't honestly know," said Stuart, heading towards bed, "if today was tragedy or farce."

" 'Stuart Embroiled.' A light-hearted sexual comedy I think."

"I must ask Helen to the opening. She always knew I had it in me."

When Stuart had retired for the night, Ellice Barr sat for a long time watching shadows thicken. She was filled with an insidious sadness at the politics of people. This was her own patch, these young men and women the best of their generation, Stuart, Alison, Fergus, Leonie, interesting each one of them, full of potential, but unable to strike their personal bargain with happiness. Adversarial families made them deficient in the ingredients of good sense or wise choice. She traced a fault back to the Petrie household, and her own. God knows she wasn't smug. That she wasn't confidential with her daughter was manifest. She had been wrong to oppose the stage career, wrong to oppose Fergus. Whatever it was that lined Leonie's forehead, and put the hesitancy in her step, the mother couldn't alleviate now. In a relationship devoid of intimacy or even concurrence, they talked of every subject except themselves.

Only once had they approached the personal. She asked Leonie when the girl was twenty, Are you sleeping with your young man?

The answer came back true enough, although it hesitated on rebuke. Yes, I am.

And do you enjoy it? the mother asked.

Yes, I do.

That's good, because when you don't, you must stop and find someone you do enjoy it with.

She didn't know at this remove what she'd been advocating, certainly not promiscuity or random sexual experiment. What could she sensibly advise on sex with a man? Strange, the human race passed on every kind of wisdom except that one. She could remember only two occasions, neither of them glorious. Had she been warning against Fergus, first love, or the endangered freedoms? Or did the edict borrow the enhancement of all prophecies, true because they have come true? Man trouble, woman trouble. Was there any other kind?

Leonie had said a sobering thing, deflecting her advice. Enjoyment's easy enough. It's the responsibility that's hard. If I ever become pregnant, I'll keep the child. That inhibits too much philandering.

Ellice wondered for a long time about this as a standard for morality and how far it derived from herself, looking on love between the sexes as procreative rather than creative. She couldn't fathom these sexual tensions, or what it was about men and women that drove each other to such extremes. All for some groping in the dark, some seed spilled, adding up to a baffling pleasure. What was so compelling about desire? She was well off without it. She remembered Muriel Petrie saying she had never come across a man who was stronger than she was. Odd statement. Ellice *thought* so but was wise enough to know where male strengths lay and how they could be harnessed not necessarily by descending to feminine wiles and wheedling. Fair play was a standard most men could be ruled by, home or away. But a sexual war of attrition, drawn ranks, sworn enemies, non-co-operation between sides, what was the point? She didn't hate men any more than she hated anyone. There were degrees of avoidance, preferences stated by omission, but no one finally barred. Perhaps that was the root of tolerance, neutrality. She needed no one and loathed no one; need and loathing fed each other.

She rocked quietly by the window, balancing a hypothesis on runners. Her thoughts sped repeatedly to the woman who lived half a mile away in suburban Greenbank and who, if she weren't careful, she might become. She knew a great deal about Muriel Petrie, knew how she feared loneliness, as who did not? The empty house, the empty life reverberating as she walked from room to room accompanied by the friendless, pointless self. As Muriel grew old, she feared to die alone, feared her own death because it marked such a small transition in the enormity of space. Muriel made her own loneliness and her own living death. The example served. Ellice considered she had failed with her daughter, so much loved and wanted but now the fierceness and the independence had gone their own way. She determined not to fail again. She gave thanks for the grandson she and Muriel shared, who grew up in her sight, not out of it. Stuart Ainslie called of his own free will. Her son-in-law didn't turn her from his door, whatever their past differences. She clung to the littleness of life when the grand gesture was stark and bare.

35

Dear Leonie,

I know I shouldn't do this but whether I send it or not, I must write something. It's been a week without any news of you and I'm straining every nerve trying to catch a rumour of how you are, but we're in a rift valley here and nothing reaches us over the hills.

Torrisaig in August is all bustle and rather surprised by its own access of energy. Charlie's in his element with the shooting season opening on the twelfth, polishing his guns and putting dubbin on his shoes and loving the influx of red setters. We have no grouse to speak of in the west but he goes on tour in August, swapping our deer and salmon for other people's moors. We'll have a dozen people staying in the house till mid-September and it has its appeal, a hurly-burly of animals and visitors and the gun room smelling of oil, bristling with cartridges. The factor locks up the gun racks every evening with ceremonial precision. Even his lordship isn't allowed a gun after hours when there are 'strangers about'. I go out for one or two days on the hills, to prove that London hasn't made me into a milksop, but I find deer stalking and fishing counter-productive of conversation, quantity as well as quality, and make constituency excuses. A wonderful exeat, by the by, much like you saying, I'm going to learn my lines. The occupation without definition, or disproof and entirely legitimate.

I brought my grandmother up a week ago by car from Inveresk. She gave me a thorough drubbing on the way. She manages to catch me in moments when I can't escape or proffer the above excuse. She had cut out a photograph from one of the nationals in June, the opening night of *Hedda*, where you are prominent and I hover ignominiously in the background. She asks questions. I damn the press pointing out to her the accuracy of my visual positioning. But the old devise such cunning. She knows the set of my shoulders, the parting of my hair and is impossible to deceive. She cannot forgive me for failing to be the ideal, clean-cut, torch-bearing Moncrieffe. I find myself forced into defensive and self-explanatory attitudes when she's around, Alas that I am me which I think is offensively pusillanimous, because more aggressive statements like Mind your own business are disrespectful to the atavistic gene.

She focuses my wavering attention on the main point. What am I doing with myself? Where am I going? I can't give her answers beyond admitting I have made a mess of things again, though I go on pulling out the shape of this entanglement all week.

I know what's off limits between us, Leonie Barr, don't look at me that way. I can see you looking lengthwise across the page, with your mouth shaped in surmise and disapproval. Do you suppose I haven't studied those looks in detail, on and off the stage? Why, I've even read the plays you've appeared in. How's that for devotion? If I'm not a better man than I was a year ago, I am at least better read.

It's my misfortune to come too late to the thing that matters. I know what this is – I don't deceive myself – this is the direction I want to go. You are the woman, the, definite article. Not one of a series but the full stop. Declarations usually pre-condition a response. I am fully cognisant that you can't give one or won't. So don't say anything if you don't want to. I am resigned to being on the periphery.

Dear Watson,

No, you shouldn't have sent such an injudicious letter, even to my mother's house. Its typed address came through arousing as little comment as its plain brown envelope. A fan letter, I say, that's been misdirected and wonder if this is a veritas in vino. The half-truth smacks of the callow deceits of common adultery and, equally deceitfully, I reply, your correspondent.

I think it's strange that you enjoy a houseful of people – maybe because you live alone most of the year, or have always got somewhere else to retire to. I abhor people under my feet. At the Hermitage we're in a state of invasion. Stuart and Alison are our unwelcome guests, Muriel having threatened him with extermination if he doesn't 'do the decent thing'. Those months in London were damaging for me. They confirmed impatience with hypocrisy which I see is not a universal malaise, but a provincial one. Fergus sucks in his cheeks and could tell a tale or two, but won't. He doesn't even point out to his sister the slights of the past but takes her in when no one else will. I like Stuart and I like my sister-in-law, separately, but the juxtaposition is unendurable. What she has done to the insouciant man I can't imagine. They spent half an hour yesterday arguing about whether they ate pizza or pasta in an Italian restaurant within the City walls. The story had some other purpose which was lost in the burden of supplementaries, with Stuart determined to be amusing at the expense of accuracy and Alison pedantic over detail, busily contradicting each other in spirit as well as fact. What do you do? Grin and bear it? You're so right. I rise and say, I must go and learn my lines, off into the ever ready exit.

I really don't object to people as such. Quite the reverse. I object to living with people. I suffer from a particular disease which hasn't been clinically diagnosed as yet; perhaps it could be named after me. Leonie Agoraphile. I crave the meeting place, symposium, conference, assembly hall, concourse, public gathering or even a sports stadium if the worst really comes to the worst, anywhere that two or three are gathered together is the most interesting place on earth.

Oddly, when I'm not smitten by individuals, I do adore the public. I'm a sucker for that good old political bait, dangled by both sides indiscriminately, *our* people, and fall for it every time. SPQR strikes me as the best banner or battle cry ever devised – the senate AND the people of Rome. It's the slogan to end all slogans, simple, unitary, convincing. The people rule me linguistically through their derivatives, vox populi, common consent, the man in the street. I am particularly besotted with that man in the street; he is the finest critic, the astute perceiver of pretension, the rounder-down, subtle mickey-taker who doesn't submit to being fooled much, if any, of the time. Give me the common man.

So the masses don't alarm me. Crowds are fascinating. I don't see groups but individuals, hundreds of separate incidents gathered in one location. Or maybe I'm the worst kind of dema-gogue, I know how I can manipulate them for my own ends, jerk a tear, get a round of applause. Claptrap? Just so. We all need to be clapped.

Individuals are another species altogether. You can observe

everything impartially but want to live with very little of it. It occurs to me, and this does step out of bounds, that you're the public side of my make-up, demonstrative and attention-seeking, or possibly that the need for performance is the mutual territory where we meet. Fergus is the private. I can't deny that he exercises a mental tranquillity over me because he's consistently in touch with a subject he believes in and will master. I don't admire the end product but I do admire the relentless process. I find myself bedevilled by questions. Fergus *does*, day and daily. His is a solitary, retiring occupation and its self-sufficiency astonishes me. I can do nothing by myself. A one-woman show with no technicians, backing, audience? It won't even open. But give Fergus a piece of paper and a pen and he can not only entertain himself for fifteen hours but he can make money at it and add something to knowledge. Brain power. I don't have it. His integrity is complete and I mean that mathematically.

I recognise that the private life is one I have no talent for at the moment. The gregarious instinct gets the better of me every time. I can't bypass a room with people in it or turn down an invitation. Talk draws me. Even if I don't contribute, I must hear what's being said in the world at large. But when I'm fifty, I may develop this rare capacity for being still, or being myself whoever I am. Marriage, sealed and protected, is a bet I've laid on futurity. I do have a craving to be normal. Most people imagine they are approximately normal, but I know that I'm not. I enjoy the remote prospect that someday I'll be like everybody else, content with a man and a house and grandchildren. Like my neighbour, Irene Geddes, the home-maker, satisfied with equanimity and managing to make other people's lives the most important work of women.

Dear Leonie,
I've read your letter fifty times. My eyes are strained reading between its lines. I thought I'd got over the simpleton stage of mumbling sentences by rote. I read it on the hills, belly down in wet heather while the stalker crawls towards the deer. 'You'll no get there by reading maps, Your Honour.' Very true. I read it in the car, I read it rain or shine. Like you its author, it changes with the venue and is always elusive. It transmits in a dozen different voices which may be nothing more than an echo of my own mood,

338

alternating between despair and a spurious elation.

I find myself quite irate with you for aspiring to be ordinary when the world is very well equipped with ordinariness as it is. The romance of that common man has got to you and made you seize up with an attack of the democratic, levelling conscience which tries to convince us we're deeply wicked if we aren't socialist, by birth or inclination. Don't fall for the persuasive jargon of mediocrity, giving all your goods to feed the poor. John 12 verse 8 is pretty emphatic about those priorities. Leonie – normal? Goddammit woman, acknowledge your ability for what it is. Admire each man for the thing he can do by all means but make the distinction between hierarchies of talent. I hate a deferential reticence or false modesty. I've never understood why people are shy of being clever or beautiful or successful and feel obligated to apologise for being more than averagely good at anything. Equality has got us by the tail in this country. The English dictionary must be the only one in the world where 'intellectual' is located under obscenities. I am an unashamed meritocrat. What should we invest in if not the exceptional?

One sentence slips out and makes me sing. You get up to learn your lines. Are you, in spite of the declared fondness for house-keeping duties, really learning to be that devastating termagant, Lady Macbeth? And does this mean London in September for rehearsals? Yes would make me a happy man.

I am busy, busy every day from dawn to dusk. I had a man come to see me yesterday at a surgery in Dingwall. I could see the justice of his case. Water pressure in his area – he farms at the top of a hill – isn't sufficient for irrigation and livestock needs and he wants to know if the local authority isn't obliged to provide a water supply. This is correctly speaking out of my jurisdiction, but constituents turn to me hoping I'll endorse every sort of complaint they have against the Inland Revenue or the School Board for sending their child out of the district. More often than not I am powerless or sit in the seat of counsellor. Lawyers and doctors must feel the same, giving advice that isn't curative of ills. I am doing no more than interpreting regulations for people who live on the wrong side of a boundary, are too old or too young, have ceased to qualify for benefits because of missing contributions, while the logic of democracy makes no exceptions. They think that I am God, or an omniscient and comprehensive social worker, patient, strong and tactful, the modern god or ombudsman. This is tiresome in the extreme, my equivalent of housework I suppose, both exhausting and repetitive. Like you, I admit to liking the people I meet and wish I could do more for them. I am endlessly touched by their belief in me as a righter of endemic wrongs. At the same time, I think an enlightened laird or factor was probably a better friend than the modern MP bound by his rule book.

Write soon. I miss you. Being busy doesn't obviate the persistent loneliness. I am empty when most full.

Dear Watson,
I think that this must be the last. What am I to do with these letters of yours once I've read them? Throw them away or hide them? Either offends against somebody.

And the same with yes. Yes makes you happy, Fergus unhappy. In fact, I had committed myself to Lady Macbeth at once but didn't broadcast it until I had a chance to talk to Fergus alone. No easy feat with these two house guests and a troupe of hangers-on we hadn't bargained for. I send them over to Ellice most evenings, and then follow later.

The more I pursue my career, the more my marriage disintegrates. We can't build up any continuity. There are several complicating factors – Fergus is not deeply interested in the arts, London is distant from Edinburgh, I have become involved with a man who is
a) available
b) sympathetic to what I do.
Is this crudely put? That is how outsiders would put it. There are other things which are more emotive. I have a son who's changing every day. I adore this child, objectively, without cosseting. I adore him not because he's mine but because he's a dynamic and resourceful individual. 'Mother love' which excuses all faults is a form of self-doting I can't indulge in. The objectivity I suffer from is very cruel. I love and I can't give way to love in any form.

Fergus has undergone a worrying character disturbance. He's in a state of withdrawal from life and from me. This has become a relationship without relations and my absconding again couldn't come at a worse time for either of them because these two people

340

do actually need me. I curse the indiscriminateness of this talent you extol. Why couldn't I be something more manageable or adaptable to circumstances like a painter or a writer or a musician, any of the arts which I could exercise alone. I'd cheerfully settle for the Scottish National Orchestra, even percussion section, to be more conveniently placed than at the Old Vic.

So I say yes to the stage and Fergus looks at me with a justifiable aversion. I signed a contract for both agreements, so which one do I renege on? I am in two minds. That phrase becomes an incantation by the women who try to achieve on both fronts, and who love twice. It is one of the most banal lines of situational drama and I discover I am called on to deliver it with conviction. Life is so mean. You learn, you practise, you rehearse and it can still go wilfully wrong in spite of your applied efforts. I am tired of reconciliation, not between other people but different parts of myself.

There's something else that's unsettling me. We spoke about my father-in-law when we came north and whether his death was natural. Michael had very few belongings, as you will understand, but he did manage to keep one or two books and Fergus handed me a copy of *Anna Karenina*, which he had inscribed For Leonie very definitely on the frontispiece under the words,

VENGEANCE IS MINE, AND I WILL REPAY

as if he intended me to have it. So I re-read the book. I've been taking Andrew out for walks in the pram and read along the way to alleviate the boredom. Isn't it so like Ellice to upgrade the motor activity by doing something else alongside, but I've skipped on the leafletting for now.

Anna has got a hold of me and no mistake, and of Michael too who annotated his three phases of reaction to the book very carefully. They begin to obsess me jointly, she and he, and I can't separate them. It's hard to read the book through his laborious notes like a screen in front of the text obscuring it. Conversely, he was so enamoured of Anna that I get insights into him as a man which I find disturbing, private, maybe even shameful, like reading a diary that's intrusive when the writer's dead. He had perfect calligraphy, baroque sloping letters and what he says is very perceptive. Sensitive, literate, even academic – how did I miss knowing this man while he was alive? More than that, how did he miss out on first-hand contact himself? What flaw made him, in spite of being a loving man, so unloved? Accurate on the page, he foundered on direct application, a Fergus in the making.

His notes are negative towards the end and I feel he certainly thought of taking his own life. You can see the mind spiral downwards into despair until, when Anna died, he gave up altogether. This is privileged information I don't want to have. I resent the burden of responsibility placed on me by the inscription.

Estrangement is a word I sift meaning by meaning for a core clue on how to avoid the state. Moving inside other people like this fragments the identity; Anna, Michael, Lady Macbeth occupy small corners of my mind and every so often old parts, dead and gone, come back at me, nuances which these present people throw on the past so I am permanently in a state of occupation, or siege. At times I feel I'm hosting a malignancy that will destroy the central me. Acting makes lying generic because it paralyses reality. Living nine-tenths in a state of deception means in the end I can't say what I think. I am aware of being on the outward edge of a centrifugal force I can't control, spun but not by my own hand. Or am I becoming unbalanced too?

Dear Leonie,

This is the very last letter, I promise. Sensible and business-like. Relax. You've given yourself a punishing schedule, taking on two major rôles without a break and I'll wring Stuart Ainslie's neck for being a nuisance. Calm down and be pleased to be nobody for a while. Let go, of something.

That pain, yes I know that pain inside the skull; it's the self-inflicted torment of the perfectionist and I wouldn't be so dismissive as to pretend I think it'll ever go away. What pain-killers do I take for mine? Repeat after me, I wouldn't want to do anything else in life and what I do is valuable. These are the palliatives of public service – your mother must have passed the powders on to you – and I swallow the words three times a day with water. Acting *is* valuable. Its dissimulation is the two-way valve to the most intense reality but I'm sure those who do it to standards of excellence must feel sacrificial. It matters. Go on.

What troubles me is the question of whether I am helping or hindering you. I can apply the same diviners to the personal. I don't want any other woman and I believe this relationship is valuable. Can you say as much? I promise to bow out if you can't. I feel, presupposing your reply, that we suffer from being mixed with work and its related tensions. I would like to see you after hours and would give a great deal to have you come to Wester Ross. We have a party or a ball in mid-September, excuse for shindig. Think about it.

I seem to have trespassed after all. As for London and rehearsals, you have your own key to the flat so do whatever you want about using it if you are down before me. I am scheduled for a couple of meetings in London before Parliament re-opens. Till then or sooner.

Yours.

36

The kitchens at Torrisaig were sited next to the other public offices and had evolved from some of the oldest parts of the building, functional and unpretentious. The open fire had a chain-winched spit which, although in good working order, was kept for show and, like the brass pans and fish kettles, impressed the visitor because they were venerable but also because they were part of the momentum of continuity. The most humble object, from fire dogs to basting ladle, was monogrammed and stamped with the shield of Moncrieffe.

It was hard to believe on an August morning that these chambers were a section of an oubliette in the lawless days of clan warfare, and that a belligerent chieftain had imprisoned his enemies here until they wasted and were forgotten in a subterranean Bastille. The wars were small but ruthless and fighting men had disappeared into lengthy captivity until they were reprieved by an exchange of prisoners or became too old to lead an army.

This morning, with the sun shining through two transomed windows, its feel was the antithesis of enmity. Men came backwards and forwards from the gun room looking for their lunches and their flasks. Watson didn't know from one day to the next who'd come down to breakfast because the stalk was open season too for hospitality. Anyone was free to drop in while, in the evening, reciprocal parties from the neighbouring estates made a gathering of twenty or twenty-five a regular event.

The Moncrieffes, uncle and nephew, weren't headed for the hills. Charlie and John Laidlaw, who took two days out of Border politics to visit them, had reserved a stretch of the river to get in some fishing, leaving the management of guns that day to Donald Macleod. While two guests with their stalker drove east onto the rough ground where the deer roamed, and the main party made an expedition to grouse moors in Sutherland, starting at five, the three dissidents went north to the river which fed Loch Torrisaig

344

from above, draining out of inland fresh water lochs.

The terrain here was still high, but densely forested so that the river which cut along a natural rocky culvert was sheltered, with no outlook except along the single track road that brought them in and another road going west towards a plantation leased by the Forestry Commission. It was warm. The sun could beat down with surprising heat in these coombs although the running water as Charlie tested it was still glacial, reminiscent of its source high up in the meltwaters of the mountains which might be free of snow for less than half of the year.

Watson went to open up the Daimler and unpack the fishing tackle. As the boot flew up, however, there was an ominous crack and Charlie, hearing it, came up hurriedly from the river bank to inspect. Their three rods were tied for easy transport across the boot and should have been untied before it was lifted. The opening motion broke one of the rods unusably.

"That was mighty careless of you," complained Lord Moncrieffe, nursing the fracture. "I reckon that lets you out for today."

His nephew was no better pleased. It was not a valuable but a favourite rod.

"Can't be helped," said Laidlaw, "I don't mind standing down. Or we could rotate morning and afternoon." He made the best offer he could.

Three-quarters of an hour drive back to the house for a replacement rod? No, it wasn't worth it. "Not at all. You've come here to fish and fish you shall. My fault entirely. I'll busy myself making up some flies. It serves me right," said Watson.

But he was angry at the avoidable mishap all the same and spending a morning sitting on the bank, cut out of his share of the sport, was scant comfort. Charlie was above him on the same bank of the river, Laidlaw below, facing into the sun. Conditions were right; the water warming slowly through the morning and several salmon showing. Charlie had perfect timing of the back cast and was able to use the current to take the fly past the fish temptingly. He knew every pool and underhang of the river. But though he changed his fly from light to dark as the sun came and went, there wasn't as much as passing interest from a fish.

Watson resigned himself to enforced passivity and settled back to enjoy a spell of mindlessness instead. He opened the fly boxes which looked like tobacco tins and were selected from dozens stored in the gun room at the house. They held different sizes of hook and the coloured feathers that went to making up the various flies. Watson had spent hours examining the combinations of artificial fly in a book when he was a boy, more flies than he had ever seen in the sky. He thought it was astonishing that salmon and trout had a preference for one or the other and that their tastes changed according to sunny or overcast conditions. Stoat's Tail and Hairy Mary and Garry Dog were the patented favourites but Charlie had one or two invented novelties of his own and to palliate for the broken rod Watson made up a couple of these, twisting with small pliers kept alongside the feathers.

It was frustrating, this sitting still, but he did so little of it that he was interested to see how it nevertheless exercised the ingenuity of the body. He watched his limbs move. His physique changed after a day or two at Torrisaig. Years of climbing made his skin respond to exposure so he was brown and, never wholly unfit, soon looked healthy with the outdoor life. Even his hands felt different after one washing in the native, lime-free water. The snags and sores he brought with him from London rubbed away and he uncovered a new skin in himself. He began to ripple, to ease into the natural spring of life in Wester Ross.

Around twelve, John Laidlaw had a bite and Charlie up above looked on enviously as the fish struggled and the man controlled it, reel and line, playing it towards him slowly. Plucky, it played too, threshing in the light so that the twenty-yard stretch was glistening with beads of water in the air, cold and clean itself. At last John had it close enough to land and finished it off with the gaff. An eight-pounder, not glorious but good and Charlie was almost as well pleased at his guest having the haul as if he'd landed it himself. It went some way to redeem the disappointment of the snapped rod.

They broke for lunch, a large basketed affair that spread out on the verges of the river. They ate and addressed themselves to the philosophies of cast fishermen; did the fish take more readily at specific temperatures – on Speyside the locals wouldn't even turn out until the water reached a certain degree; did the difference in fly really contribute anything to the sport; and why, when they didn't feed in fresh water, did the fish take the bait in the first place? They joyfully revolved the unanswerable question.

"Macleod thinks we'll be badly hit by poachers before the end of this season," said Charlie.

"They don't account for much, surely?" thought the incomer.

"The traditional poacher doesn't. The odd snatch in the night is a cull we've got to resign ourselves to, five per cent for pilferage against profits, like any business. But these fellows come out in organised gangs. They net the fish in a single stretch and can clean out all the best holding pools in a night. The real rogues net the loch at the river entrance as the salmon wait for the sea water level to rise."

"Rather unsportsmanlike."

"Not the game at all. But the worst of it is, apart from ruining our sport, they deplete the breeding stocks. A few seasons of that and you've got no working capital, so to speak. And London restaurants don't ask to see the licence salmon were caught under. Cheap at the price."

As he talked and ate, Charlie went on sorting his own fly with silk, thinking he'd indulge himself in a touch of his faddish orange fleck and disdaining Watson's attempts. Charlie was nimble-fingered with these mounts, as particular to detail as he was with the splints and labels of his roses. It seemed a physical impossibility for such a big man, who could cast a fourteen-foot rod without difficulty, to work in millimetres.

"Penalties aren't stiff enough to be a deterrent," Charlie complained. "Not that I want another mass of laws to deal with it. The three of us spend our time putting more and more legislation on the statute book when what we want is less. As it is, we probably break the law twice a day without knowing it. A better common-sense approach by the courts is needed, upgrading the offence from poaching to theft. We don't seem to think rustling is serious, but livestock is wealth round here, just as much as money in City institutions."

Their minds turned on a change of wind direction towards Westminster.

"Tell me," said Laidlaw, "what Cadogan buttonholed you about on the last day of the session. I never had a chance to ask you."

Watson damned the gossip of the House, which played a game like Chinese Whispers, repetition plus distortion. "Touting for allies. Could he count on my support next session?"

347

"At a price?"

"At a price."

"Well, what was he offering? Lean pickings to tempt anybody with, I would have thought. Or was he going to play Moses and bring you all out of the wilderness?" Laidlaw was scathing, afraid that the neutral man had joined forces with the Tories after a decade of forswearing allegiance. If he joined anyone, it ought to be the Liberals.

"A place in the shadow cabinet the year after next."

"And shadowing for the foreseeable future if he's party leader."

"Did you accept?" asked Charlie, tying his threads as deftly as the Brussels lace maker, bobbin to spool.

Watson swithered, tormenting them. "Well, what do you think I should have done? That's much more interesting."

Laidlaw was a Liberal and a Scot, a common enough combination when the Liberals had their best representation, apart from in the West Country, north of the border. A dislike of extremes, the reliance on the intellectual precepts of honest men and a sophisticated land-owning heritage, something in the landscape of their minds, had adhered generations of Scots to Liberalism. Liberality was another matter. For instance, John Laidlaw distrusted his friend's new companion, partly because she was married, was another Scot and ought to know better but mainly because she was an actress, an occupation to which he attached the scorn of Covenanters. He actually loathed conservatism and socialism as philosophies, while admiring many followers of either doctrine for their human or practical qualities. He was, too, proprietorial about Moncrieffe. He knew he owed him his life, never forgot it day to day. The man had bust his gut to rescue him as well as Prior, and he recognised he himself didn't have the strength to hold the saving winch with one hand, or walk the seven miles to the cottages and back again. That obligation made him sensitive to everything the Independent did, a primitive bonding, but he would almost have considered his enormous debt cancelled if Moncrieffe had perpetrated so gross a betrayal of principle. "I hope to God you didn't accept," was not an idle blasphemy.

"Well," said Charlie, camouflaged in tweed against green and brown, only his moving fingers distinguishing him from the background rocks, "I've changed my tune on this one. I think it's

348

time that you did belong. I can't tell you who you should join, but I think you should join somebody. In time," this phrase was a gentleman's euphemism for when he died and Watson succeeded to the title, designed to spare unseemly shows of feeling, "you'll go to the Lords. Now I'm not a good member of the Upper House, as you well know. I haven't got the patience with the bits of paper and I'll only turn up when it's pertinent to me and mine. But I do like the organisation. I think the Lords is a very useful corrective to some of the wilder fantasies of the Commons men and Watson is an expert law-maker. Mustn't let that go to waste."

The recipient of this laudation was amused that it wouldn't have been spoken one to one. Always with an intermediary present and in the third person. You was too intimate a pronoun.

"Being a cross-bencher suits me well enough. You can throw in some quite effective spanners from that position, without endangering anyone else. But you would have proper, systematic work to do and you've a much better chance of being listened to and getting on committees if you belong. The Liberal peers would be my first choice but anyone rather than no one. You should join up now to get the full benefit of your membership."

Watson thought the argument was reasonable enough. It had just one flaw, the unthinkable premise that he might relinquish his title which, since he had no issue, would accelerate the end of the line by the mere thirty or forty years of the remainder of his lifetime. It would leave him free to continue in the Commons as he was, given the blessing of the electorate. To Charlie, that would be a heinous possibility. The lands, the title must have an heir and the idea that Watson might resign his trusteeship voluntarily was an affront to their joint inheritance.

"That's political philandering," said Laidlaw. "You can't trust men who make bedfellows of anyone who happens to be available."

Watson shot him a dangerous look.

"I'm recommending one," said Charlie. "Just one."

Laidlaw bit his tongue about the suitability of choice depending on trying them all out first.

"You can set your mind at rest. It won't be Cadogan. He was offensive, actually, for a man who was asking favours." He thought back to Fleming's like-minded approach in the winter

when things were going badly for him. Fleming was a wheedler, a
skilful manipulator who praised and commended only to create
the predisposition to his own point of view. The Conservative
leader had no such refinement. "I've heard the speech-maker too
often in Cadogan. He didn't even have the courtesy to take me to a
private room but turned round and addressed me in the corridor
with other people listening. He booms like a street barker. Set 'em
up and knock 'em down, with as little subtlety as the coconut shy.
He said to me, In the long term the butter's thicker on this side,
Moncrieffe."

"So what did you say? I've become a vegan?"

"He wouldn't have known what that meant. The man's an
ignoramus." This was a variant on the phrase 'the man's got no
breeding' commonly said of Cadogan, as if the Conservative party
were a club that had let standards of entry slide during his
stewardship.

"Sun's going," said Charlie. "Easier fishing," and the two
dedicated anglers got to their feet.

Watson left them to the fickle sport and took the Forestry Commission path towards the mountains on the west. At intervals along
the way there were metal signposts warning against fire and a pair
of brooms tied to each post to help with fire-beating. He passed
round the edge of an enclosure surrounded by a stone dyke which
was used for experimentation, out of the prevailing wind. He'd
met a man up here the previous summer who'd spent fifteen years
accumulating data on sequoia which unbelievably turned out to do
better in Scotland than their native Sierra Nevada. So far north,
they had an extra four hours a day of sunshine during the growing
summer months. The Highland region was comparatively storm-
free so the major danger to tall trees of being struck by lightning
was minimal. The climate was mild, warm and humid but not
susceptible to the scorching dry winds of the south and it looked as
though the Great Caledonian Forest, cut down for the shipbuilding
of James IV, might be replaced in time with more exotic species
growing to phenomenal heights, two hundred feet or more.

It was fine open country, spanned by nothing but a road and
telegraph poles. The road was the artery of the community and
roadmenders and stonebreakers were in continuous occupation

when floods and frost could strip a tarmac surface in a winter. He passed a car and automatically raised his hand in greeting as though it must contain a friend. He climbed steadily upwards, traversing the forest of Douglas fir and Norway spruce until he came to the top of a pass and could see west over the inlet of the Minch to Skye and the Outer Hebrides, no more definite than clouds on the horizon, and south towards the Kyle of Lochalsh. Inland, there was Torrisaig surrounded by its delta of cultivation, the hotel further down the loch dispensing wood smoke and in the distance, not a village, but an assortment of houses set at all angles to each other, like their occupants, men of independent thought who deferred only to the lie of the land. The houses were rolled down like the boulders they were made of, stark and surprising out of the ground. Whitewashed or natural stone, they were nodules and outcrops of the hills, unadorned by gardens. In this part of the world, any man who planted a flower with his own hand was a Jessie.

All familiar territory. A six-hour walk in any direction from Torrisaig was inside Moncrieffe lands. Though this might have contained the solace of ownership, Watson found that wherever he went, he was dogged by the question his grandmother framed, Where am I going? What am I doing with myself? Like most men, he inclined to temporise about his motives, stalling the long term with attention to the urgent. But every so often the scenery parted and the long view made its impact on the mind.

He would inherit Torrisaig and the responsibility for its preservation. There was no denying that the eccentric, asymmetrical outline of the house, seen in an unusual perspective from this vantage point, brought tears to his eyes. He wasn't ashamed of sentiment but recognised it confused hard-headed economics. He had several options. He could go on running the estate the way Charlie did, hand to mouth, year to year, in habitual crisis, not admitting it was impossible to keep up the broad style of the Edwardian gentry without its manpower. He could try to specialise, become a gentleman farmer striving to increase his yield and profitability. Deer farming for commercial venison was the thing these days, or trout and salmon tanks and ensure the catch was all legitimately sent to market. Or he could stock the woods with the majestic, high-growing sequoia. Afforestation drew substantial

351

grants. He smiled to think how deftly he could employ the systems of central and regional government, the way those in the know would live off their insurance policies.

Or would the castle make a successful country house hotel, four star, AA and RAC approved, offering A Taste of Scotland on its menus. It could come to that, its antique amenities formulated into the jargon of holiday brochures and himself the modern landlord, pulling pints. It might go the way of other great family houses, from private into public ownership. Art galleries, municipal parks, hotels. Going public might be a democratic impulse, but it terminated an ancient bond that was no doubt feudal and outdated but, for that reason, historic. The rocky garrison of Torrisaig was more embattled than ever in the twentieth century.

Facile solutions were seldom operative. These hills were full of cranks searching for an Eldorado, not inherent in wealth as much as in fable or romance. There were the men of Carse, aspiring to a Utopian commune, and rich drop-outs setting up fish-canning factories or woollen mills, liable to defeat by a small error of miscalculation which was perhaps nothing more than their poor resistance to hardship. The fate of the country was bound up in its lack of give. The hills defied, the sea defied, the weather defied the most earnest labours of man and he was an Ozyɪ andian fool if he thought that he could harness them.

In the heart of this mood was a personal anguish. Where did he fit in to the sequences of landscape and heritage? The talk at lunch time unsettled him when he could identify himself as the vagabond poacher, no overheads, no responsibility but grabbing what he could without replenishing. What was he giving back to this place? Or for that matter to Westminster? He suspected he dodged commitment, avoided the final belonging because, as for Leonie, the alternatives kept up a state of vacillation or of freedom that was very dear. Laziness? Inadequacy? He couldn't name his fault but didn't honestly think it attributable to an omission as much as an excess. Plump for one was the most difficult instruction to obey. And even when he did, as with Leonie, the circumstances of choice seemed deliberately to confound a settled outcome. But plump he must as time ran out for him, for Torrisaig and maybe for Scotland, dependencies all.

37

Alison was summoned by her mother to an interview at the Grange Loan flat and went, powerless to utter the emphatic 'No'.

She walked all the way from Fergus' house at the Hermitage, and was an eye-catching sight along the tree-lined boulevards that ran between Blackford and Marchmont. It was lunchtime. Blinds were down, doors were locked for the hour, one to two p.m. precisely. Commerce mattered less than the conventions. Workmen eating their lunch out of doors turned round or watched the girl out of the corner of their eye. A chestnut beauty, high and prancing, too thoroughbred for whistling at.

The calm was outer. Inside, Alison was agitated, didn't notice whether the shops were open or closed, or that the men who mended the road and the roof followed her progress. She wished for calm, but calm was like a shadow. Step on it and it moved.

Her life was in fragments. Bits split off. Her father had gone, confirming their long estrangement. She tried to think when it was she'd last spoken to him, and couldn't. She remembered with shame one occasion when she could have intervened on his behalf with Muriel, an impression corrected, a fact put right, but she hadn't put it right so the quarrel between them which the mistake mounted went on raging. Too weak? Parental savagery made them craven. Except Fergus latterly, and Fergus was turning, turned, gone off somewhere on his own where nobody could reach him. His solitary stances hadn't helped the rest of them.

The physical confrontation between Harris and Muriel a week before had a special significance in Alison's eyes because it was carried out in front of a third party, bad move that, publicity, but it wasn't the first of murderous family brawls by any means. Alison tried not to dwell for too long on these ugly battles, sealing them away in a submerged portion of the mind like dreams, but this latest one had broken them out of the subconscious again to haunt. When she was seventeen, Michael had come into her room to show her a gash on his hand and said, She did this to me. He bled visibly, audibly onto the book that she was reading. Underneath her churning reaction to the triangular wound was the dismayed suspicion that it was self-inflicted, and that she was being shown it because at some time she would be called upon to say so. Or on different occasions Muriel, who became hysterical with the rage of not having what she wanted now, at once, pushing lighted newspaper under the door of a room where Michael had barricaded himself, making a noise between sob and scream, as singeing smoke rose from the carpet, burn the house down to make a point, why not; or lying in front of a gas fire she'd switched on, trying to die; or threatening to jump from an upper window: mock suicides that foreshadowed the real one. Their deaths were many. The children were repeatedly called on to testify against one or other of their parents and the simple loyalties were perjured by the need for their self-preservation.

Stuart: what did he understand about these traumas, burbling along in his own make believe? She had fallen into the trap of escape that he offered. A love affair had looked better than the alternatives but bent deviously back into the familiar ground, dishonesty and infidelity of which she had a loathing. Here came another person for whom she must make perjury of standards. He laughed about the Petries because he didn't live with them or in them. He gave her no support. He had no final gravity. Oh why was it not easy? She looked round her with envy at the people who lived innocuous lives, the postman who could whistle on his rounds, Irene taking letters from his hand not fearing what they might contain. Emergencies could be dealt with when there was solidarity between man and woman, but she suspected she had built on sand with Stuart.

Alison approached the flat in Grange Loan with some foreboding. She didn't like to snoop. Looking round Harris' flat when he wasn't there was an offensive act, as if she were aiding his eviction. She climbed the three flights of stairs in a heavy anticipation, only to find that the door to the apartment was locked and she had to ring for entry, ring and wait but no one came. Yes, that was in the run of her mother's character, she thought, to make her walk all this way and not be there to meet her at the appointed hour. The sun falling across the common landing suddenly exhausted her

354

and she turned back downstairs to go home, weary-footed.

About a quarter of a mile from the flat, in sight of Blackford Pond, Alison saw her mother's car come up the hill towards her. A forgiveness flooded her. Maybe it was she who had mistaken the time. She waited for the car to draw alongside and pick her up but instead, as she came level with her daughter, Muriel put her foot down on the accelerator and zoomed past, while Alison stood on the kerb dumbfounded. Had her mother seen her? The spurt suggested it. The girl had no idea what to do, walk tediously back up to the flat or go on to the Hermitage as if she hadn't noticed the deliberate snub, but then she would have to repeat the whole performance another day. The thought of incurring extra time penalties deterred her. She trudged back up the hill again.

Muriel waited indoors for her daughter to retrace her steps, feeling high indignation. It was a recurring mood, though she was wary of it ever since Fergus had told her it was only a prefix away from being undignified. She walked about the rooms of her flat, adjusting curtains and straightening a rug. The sun full on the windows made her irritable, as well as queues in the shops and the broken petrol pump that had made her late. This temper accentuated many faults. The rooms looked shoddy in its light. A small mark on a chair cover undermined perfection. She recalled precisely which of her tenants had spilled the wine and how scrubbing hadn't shifted it. She was dissatisfied with everything she owned, couldn't somehow make the furnished rooms here or at Greenbank gel into an aesthetic presence or a home and was tormented by having sold a better settee or desk by way of trade. The exigencies of the makeshift grated on her eye, reminding her of what might have been.

'Why do the bad things in life always happen to me?' was a corollary to this mood. She had tried, hadn't she, worked harder than other women and was repaid with a spendthrift husband, one ungrateful and one wastrel son and now a profligate daughter. Disappointments were as vivid as stains. They marred her enjoyment. The eye, travelling over the interiors of her life, observed only omissions. That a quality might reside in attitude occasionally struck her, as when she sold a table to a friend only to find, maddeningly, that it looked better in her house, more lovely because it was more loved. That objects and people borrowed a lustre from their environment was evident but the elusive, charismatic quality of that concept depressed her because of something resident in self which she could neither purchase nor control so she went on admiring other people's houses and lives more than her own, which was afflicted with the shabbiness of second best.

When Alison arrived, no reference was made to the incident with the car, the mother lofty, the daughter meek. They spoke in the kitchen and refreshments were not offered. Alison's eye took in the untidy room with tea chests at one end, in process of being packed.

"Well, I can't say I've not been let down badly by what you've done but I suppose we'll have to put a good face on it and redeem what we can. I had hoped for better things from you."

This was what her menfolk wouldn't stand for, the slow torture of emotional bullying. In the end they would get up and strangle her with muscle, trying inarticulately to say that obligations were owing as well as owed. Alison wasn't so beefy. She listened out of gentility, finding the one element of truth among ninety-nine falsehoods. Yes, it was disappointing. Yes, Muriel had no other daughter and wasn't likely to have another one now. She too would have liked a grand white spotless wedding. Such occasions could be fun. Fergus had married without as much as informing anyone and now Alison had done the next worst thing. These were errors not of fact but of interpretation, and harder to correct.

"Tell me," said the mother, "did you *know* that Stuart was married?"

The test of Solomon! No, I didn't know and I was deceived by him or yes I did know and I colluded in deception. The two extremes ignored the vast middle ground of knowing without admitting it to herself. Three options struggled towards a compromise in the young woman; keeping faith with the director, retaining at least the rudiments of communication with her mother or telling them both to get lost and walking out, the female equivalent of throttling. But Alison had seen too many people disappear into ostracism so she clung on, making the best of it. She was a positive, simple thinker and lacked guile. The fact that she was in love with Stuart and aspired to marry him conditioned her responses.

"Yes, I knew that he was married." The form of words could occlude the truth.

"And has he done anything about a divorce, or is all this pretence?"

"His wife doesn't object. The marriage has been nominal for a long time."

"A divorce shouldn't take too long at any rate, on the grounds of your adultery."

Alison winced, too wounded to make comparisons.

"If you are quite sure it is marriage that you want. Men like that can't be relied on. You needn't think this will be a one-off for him. Others before you and others after. Though you may not mind his past amours. You don't appear to have put up much resistance to his approaches."

"It wasn't like that," said Alison, beaten back, less and less sure of her ground.

"What, did you beg him then?"

The afternoons in London shuttered; old film jarring on the spool. Flicker, flicker and then stop. Alison recalled the pleasure of turning in his arms, holding him on and on, pictures spoiled with the acid drops spilled from sordid.

"It wasn't like that," the girl murmured.

"Oh *love* – was it – I'd forgotten about *love*. We all fall for that one, once."

Alison was silent while Muriel twitched a curtain into place.

"In the meantime, it strikes me you ought to have somewhere permanent to live. I don't think you would want to come back to Greenbank, though goodness knows, there's enough room. I needn't have bought such a big house if I'd known you'd all take off like this." She was ample with her arm. "But I want to cut down on my expenses. In the circumstances, I'd be prepared to let you have this flat for a reasonable price."

Alison knew this sentence off by heart, not its particulars but its grammatical construction. 'Prepared' and 'let' and 'have' formed the shape of a concession and her mother's concomitant generosity. But it was not an outright gift. There would be some hold or leverage to weight the bargain. They hadn't discussed price and wouldn't till the principle was established, by which Muriel would dangle her on a verbal commitment.

"And Harris? Where will he go?"

"It's out of my hands. I thought I was doing my son a favour by putting a roof over his head but it's misfired. He's running up huge debts and I can't be responsible for them any more. You don't happen to know what it is he's up to?"

The suddenness of the question, pistol after bludgeon, surprised Alison. "Stuart did meet him at a London gambling casino last month. He seems to know his way about the Park Lane tables."

Muriel was silenced, but as little surprised as Alison had been at the emergence of a wife, skeletally cupboarded. Secrets made their own vacuous space. "Then we might be doing him a service by making him move back home to Greenbank where I can keep an eye on him."

The therapy of extraneous control sounded reasonable. As she thought about it, Alison found the idea of having their own flat in Edinburgh more attractive. It put an end to Stuart's straying. Engagements in Scotland became easier. They could entertain friends at home instead of being boarded out to the Hermitage or Ellice Barr's. A place of their own, symbol of the serious relationship. Status. Security. The Petrie standards of success compelled.

They got up to look round the apartment, Muriel disdainfully closing doors and drawers of the tenants on whom she had served notice to quit. They waived their tenants' rights as long as they didn't have to settle their arrears. Glad to see the back of them, she consented.

In the middle of this property inspection, the main door opened and Harris came in without warning. Three in the afternoon, wordlessly. He nodded to Alison but strode past his mother.

"Not at work?" Muriel demanded.

"TOIL," he explained. "Time off in lieu. I worked yesterday evening on a shares flotation."

"Not off to the London casinos?" she taunted.

Harris had reached the windows where the crates were stacked, erupting sports equipment, records and a jumble of clothes. He looked back at his sister and her eyes dropped. He didn't blame her because the most innocent piece of information could be turned by Muriel into an offensive weapon. He had a sudden image of the night at Park Lane when he met Stuart and Leonie, and knew that of the two witnesses, it was the former who had been suborned.

Leonie would not have split on him like this. The ancient pact of sibling loyalty had been broken and he felt daunted and friendless.

He lifted his belongings from the floor and dropped them in the boxes without the slightest interest in them. "Are you actually thinking of taking this place on when I go, Alison? Well, I wish you joy of your landlady. I'm warning you, she lets herself in when you're not here and rummages through your belongings. I've tested it, forensically. She even reads your letters. If there's food in your cupboards, she'll eat it. She meets her gentlemen friends here when it's not convenient to take them to Greenbank where the neighbours have got sharper eyes. You can ask for the key back and she'll give it, but she's made another copy without telling you. You're welcome to it all."

He was quietly spoken, embarrassed by his uncontrolled outburst of the previous week when Muriel's goading had got the better of him and, in this steely mood, sounded like Michael, scathing but under-motivated to open hostility. He looked down at the ground, shoes among sweaters. He noticed in the glare of the sun that his jacket had a spot on the lapel and he scratched at it. Then saw one lower on his trousers. Dry cleaners, he remembered. He had other suits at the cleaners, somewhere. He wondered what had happened to the tickets. He was so tired. Tired of this bickering, of nine to five with the insurance prudential forms, of haring up and down on Fridays to London to pay off one bank or another before it prosecuted him for debt. What did he spend the money on? How did he get into this mess? It was a nightmare of exhaustion in which he felt physically sick or debilitated when it came to making decisions. He could no longer decide adequately. His life had become a juggling act, more and more items in the air, a magnificent feat of showmanship except that he knew his credibility consisted of never stopping. He could not ever stop the compulsive rotation of figures and accounts.

"Where will you stay, Harris?" His sister's voice was kindly, masking intent.

He shook his head. He could take up Stuart's role as genial itinerant, bunking down on odd settees in city bed-sits but he knew his taste for the bohemian wasn't marked. Or Fergus. He felt a rush of gratitude knowing he could trade places in both directions with his sister, a straight exchange. Fergus would take him

359

in. His brother, who had borne no ill-will against him, and the glorious child. He recognised that the alternative residence at the Hermitage sheltered the outlaws from Muriel's banishment; Michael, Alison and then himself were in turn accommodated without demur. He tested his brother's generosity and didn't find it stinted. They undervalued Fergus, silent, staunch. It would be a going home in every sense.

He looked up at the women, selfish he thought and hard. He'd made a mistake long ago throwing in his lot with them. His own kind were more reliable, so when he said softly under his breath, God damn you all, it was general against the betraying sex.

Muriel dropped Alison back at the Hermitage, more pally than before.

"You won't have to grovel to your sister-in-law for much longer."

"Leonie? Oh Leonie's too busy to be objectionable. She's going back to London, you know, for Lady Macbeth."

"Is she indeed. And I bet Fergus isn't too pleased when she asserts her independence."

Alison under-weighed her words. Vulnerability put her beyond guardedness. She had moved back firmly into Muriel's camp, a renewed alliance, a contract rephrased. She resented that she had incurred so much blame for her relationship with the director when the actress managed to avoid it, actually by being secretive which she thought was more reprehensible, when she had come clean. Honesty didn't look much like the best policy. She had noticed Leonie's aloofness with them around the house, and that she was not surprised at revelations. It was infuriating that her sister-in-law, drawing on a wider range of contacts, knew about Geddes and Ainslie doings before she did. Pique at excess discretion made her answer airily, "But Watson Moncrieffe is pleased."

"The MP?" Muriel followed the personalities if not the politics of Westminster.

"Yes."

No more was said but the name gave off a lasting resonance as Muriel went on to think, Why couldn't you have got your hands on him instead?

38

Leonie came away promptly from the final rehearsal for Act Four and caught a taxi to Heathrow for the last flight of the day to Inverness. The tightness of her schedule compressed like the flow of traffic out to the airport at six p.m. on Friday, a build-up of anxiety which became increasingly urgent but self-defeating. What if she missed the plane? These two days had been so difficult to negotiate out of rehearsals, persuading Alan Mills to keep to a chronological plan so that she would finish in time for the ball at Torrisaig, and then pay off her conscience with a week at the Hermitage when she must finally square up with Fergus. A separation, a divorce, a something to be broached so that she wasn't compelled to go on being the middle ground between two conflicting hypotheses.

In the event, she caught the flight with ten minutes to spare and, already used to routine domestic flights, started to get out her papers to work on. Yes, Moncrieffe would do this too, do exactly this every Friday evening while the House was in session. Heathrow to Inverness, one hour thirty-five minutes, with the Daimler ready waiting at the other end for the drive to Torrisaig. She'd used the Westminster flat for five weeks while Watson was in the constituency but to be in his place, whether it was his plane seat or his flat, without his presence defined the limited insights of an impersonation. To accompany was more than to substitute. London was not the same without him and neither was life.

As well as her stage copy of the text, Leonie had a second folder made up of separate sheets of the script interleaved with plain paper where she'd filled in Alan Mills' comments and the other actors' ideas as they went along which, over the weeks of rehearsal, grew into a massive compendium of diverse thoughts about *Macbeth*, setting, period, the layout of the stage and how she should move between the lines. She drew diagrams of stage positions like dancers' feet. In the margins were stray academic notes about mediaeval architecture, notions of kingship divine or otherwise and the history of the stone of Scone. Hours of work she'd put into building up this part, quite scholarly, quite disciplined – although none of it had brought her any closer to the woman she was trying to portray.

It was a complex role. Hedda had been all of a piece when she was the main character and almost always on the stage. Lady Macbeth had two areas of contradiction that made playing her more demanding. She was only an ancillary to her husband and mustn't overstep that limited supporting role. But there were times when, self-evidently, she was Macbeth's courage, motivator, moral fibre whether that was good or bad and at those moments she dominated the drama as well as him. How to be strong without making him look too enervated to be a believable monarch or undermining his tragic status at the close; that balance was hard to find. As she moved deeper into the personality, Leonie saw that the cause of this ambivalence in the woman was something very familiar. Lady Macbeth was obsessed with masculinity and harped on it throughout the play so that when Macbeth said she should bring forth men children only, it bit like a known truth. She was a woman who had no patience with women. At the same time, she was a fully sexed being. Her hold over her husband was physical because unless there was a consuming sexual love between them, there was no credibility in their relationship. That was the point when she challenged him with lack of virility; it was his sexual potency she scorned as much as half-realised ambition.

These were difficult paradoxes to resolve when they had to be achieved by technical means. Leonie turned back to two sets of charts she'd made out which she transferred into the folio for each new part she undertook. They were charts of the consonants and vowels laid out in their phonetic symbols and according to where they were articulated in the mouth. These were the basic tools of acting, the component elements of sound, the consonants masculine – accurate and precise – and the feminine vowels which contributed the quality to language. Leonie spent a long time juggling with the harmonies of sound for each character she acted, finding the right vocal field. Hedda had looked appealing in her long flowing gowns but the actress had given her a hard, edged voice, emphasising the way she'd felt about the brittle and egotistical woman. Lady Macbeth might be interesting to play in reverse, with manly gestures, frontal, dark clothed but very attractive in sound, full of the warm and sinking vowels.

Moods, phrases, variations up and down the scale of notes a thousand times, practising on the way to perfection. It was a passion. Nobody would do it otherwise. It called for limitless self-discipline or self-examination when the dedicated actor had to watch himself being recast time and again, dismembered and reformed with an almost ghoulish objectivity.

Whatever else, Leonie was grateful for the ample rehearsal time she could give to this role. Alan Mills was a perfectionist in a different way from Stuart who excelled at the visual effects and was arguably best suited to just those playwrights he'd directed Leonie in, Shaw and Ibsen, where the physical interaction on the stage, people colliding in space, was more marked than the verbal. Dialogue was subordinate in nineteenth-century plays to theme, or hadn't had time to attract the exegesis of the poetic dramas. Alan was a scholar and impeccable on the speaking of a Shakespearian text. He carried out a full edit even before they started, deciding between the alternative readings according to his own interpretation, and never forgot about linguistic finesse. Stuart tended to work in three-dimensional metaphor, Mills in editing the soundtrack.

It did strike her that the Old Vic might not be the best auditorium for these delicate sensations. It was a vast hall, wide where the Haymarket was narrow, and high. It was an insight into the richness of London's stage history that these two dissimilar theatres could be built within half a dozen years of each other, but the Old Vic with its original four thousand capacity had been intended for the big scenario, variety or spectacular and could engulf straight playing if it were too quiet. The origins of the place were hard to conceal, showy and nearly vulgar. It had briefly descended into notoriety as a drinking den and assignation place before being rescued by the remarkable Lilian Baylis who took over from her aunt at the turn of the century. She mounted ballet and opera and all the Shakespearian plays of the First Folio on alternating schedules. What a woman, the plain spoken and exacting institutrice. Her compelling discomfiture lingered on backstage like a challenge to weak wills. The intimate warmth of the

Haymarket came back nostalgically, small, gemmed, personal. The Old Vic threatened with its size and with its unwieldy reputation. The giants had walked here. They said all theatres were haunted and, if so, it was the recent great who stalked these corridors in spirit, Olivier and Richardson and most of all, Gielgud whose company in the fifties had changed the direction of Shakespearian playing. Everyone trod these boards with respect. The Old Vic was cosmic, not domestic, and both play and performer had to match the grandiose setting or be lost. Leonie knew her Lady Macbeth had to meet eternal standards.

The plane hurtled motionlessly north, spurring this mood of dangerous achievement. The velocity of its movement matched her own. The ground twenty thousand feet below was infinitesimal, reduced in scale to a mottle of green and brown and was anywhere or any time. They said that from outer space no human mark was discernible apart from the Great Wall of China. Lakes, chains of mountains, rift valleys showed up in minute detail but transient man left virtually no impression on the planet. It was hard to credit that, when you were surrounded by a hundred other men and women who checked their watches, mindful of who was meeting them, who they'd left, how they fitted into the connective schedules of there and here. They were important but only momentarily. To the thoughtful such enormity of scale was humbling, but in the ambitious it prompted notions of greatness. The sun settled over the westerly seas in empyrean splendour, not real, not representative, exaggerated as the moment was by the superstructure of clouds which blurred an exact horizon, but the event did stimulate the desire to blaze, not so much in emulation of that splash of colour as defiance of the encroaching darkness and annihilation.

It was true that Leonie couldn't shake off the play that had started to occupy a portion of every waking day, another life carried on parallel to her own. It was impossible not to see things through the requirements of the part. Driving away from Inverness, she looked round for Macbeth's castle, crenellated on a hilltop, though Watson said if it was anywhere it would be a ruin by now. He told her Macbeth had suffered from the same slanders as Richard III, was in fact a just and equitable king with a better claim to the throne than

Duncan but the heirs of Malcolm who slew him promoted, like the Tudors, the theory of their own priority and his evil, a victim of history rewritten.

In the absence of the authentic, Torrisaig would serve as a model backdrop for *Macbeth*. It was a crag of a castle which had repelled the attempts of later centuries at domestication. Leonie could put the clock back nearly a thousand years when she found stones in the foundation walls that had been hand-cut from a mountain quarry and shifted since only as graves shift, under the weight of their own past. These Highland castles were built of men and war, a human rustication. She looked for the places which were mentioned in the play, the porter's lodge, the lady's bower and battlements from which messengers were spied riding at a distance. She came into contact with the brutality of Torrisaig, overawed when it personified fastness.

Watson and Leonie went by the long back stairs to the sectioned suite of rooms that was his private apartment, known as the tower house. A fire had been lit by someone, as it had on the night of the election, a fire lit every evening from September to May when he was in residence and some supper left ready.

"What is this room?"

"Mine. I was born here."

A gloomy enough place to start life in. The walls had been rendered but that was the one concession to modernity. A high oak bed, stone fireplace and wall hangings that some pre-Union Mistress Moncrieffe had spent forty winters labouring over in embroidery with her tiring women, a Scottish Bayeux with badly drawn horses and red-clad warlords with armour like fish scales, not because they were red but because the blue and yellow dyes had faded. Presses on either side of the fireplace were fitted with glass fronts like show cases to house old books and family memorabilia that weren't worth putting on public display. To Leonie, who could pack her personal items on tour in ten minutes flat, the accumulation of objects was daunting. The sheer responsibility for keeping the dust on the move! A lifetime's servitude to one's forebears was an appalling thought.

The fireglow threw additional shadows into the recesses, Watson moving among them at home but not at rest. His guest disturbed. Sitting in the damask fireside chair, she occupied the central position while he was forced to walk or to lie or to stand by contrast, rotating from her pivot. Leonie bent down to rearrange the fire, pulling the outer coals towards the middle, and was lit from the ring of flames, lit internally as she leaned over them. When he came nearer to take the benefit, she put up her hand and brought him to kneel alongside.

Leonie fitted her face against his, probing with her features the format of his own, eye against mouth, nose along the chin. It was a strange experience, this nuzzling, she used to one shape, he grown accustomed to none over the years. It built up into a pattern of the familiarly forgotten, revisiting a landscape that has passed into memory but finding it still vital in current as well as former knowledge. The kisses that followed were exploratory. They took up the nearer references of their last night in London and pushed out to the unknown or denied, the shape of shoulders below a sweater, the arms under shirt sleeves until the whole was revealed out of sexual synecdoche.

She embraced him whole. Lying side by side, it was still hard for Watson to separate the compass of her acceptance from preceding refusals. Physical encouragement after a long abstinence or emotional rejection wasn't actually joyous – food after fast. Interruptus was not the best prelude to coitus. It shocked the system without quickening because his mind was intent on watching his body function without being involved, in abeyance of real willpower.

Feeling this, Leonie slowed. Her legs were as long as his so that by winding she could twist them together, and then she leaned away from him with her hands lifted behind her head, coupled and uncoupled together.

"You seem so misgiving," she said.

"No, I don't misgive." He smiled at her precision. "I hesitate."

"Why?"

Why indeed? The most distinctive woman of his acquaintance, loved, wanted, wooed systematically over eighteen months was in his apartment and in his arms, if not ultimately in his power. Perhaps that was the last bastion of arrogance to fall; notional mastery. Watson had precious concepts of masculine behaviour which a decade of mistakes began to modify. 'I'm not the man to make you do anything you don't want to' was not an ideal he'd started out with. Equalising tendencies were hard won and harder

366

to apply. In allowing her freedom of choice, he incurred the wait, the unendurable wait for choice to land on him. He had learned that men forced the issue inadvisedly even though the rôle reversal of traditional passivity and activity didn't suit him. He was a doer. Leonie stretched round him like his own potential, wanting only fulfilment. Typically, at the critical moment, his mind vaporised as a dozen failures came back to taunt him in the form of a failed marriage and an imperfect career, each indicative of his inability to join. Nemo, the no man rose in vacuity to frustrate.

"Such doubts, why such doubts," said Leonie and took his head between her hands, combing it. Her face was on a level with his. She kissed him again in recapitulation and continued the caress. Her voice bathed. A change in tempo, a catch in phrasing compelled his interest. What was the act? Not what he had once thought, a taking. It was an allocation or a share. A committal. Or going further, a pledge that the future might not be bereft of mutuality.

There were a hundred guests who'd come to Torrisaig with an invitation to take supper which was served out of the kitchens in the Great Hall, turned banqueting hall once a year. Refectory tables were arranged to make the letter E, in three side tables and a top table at which Leonie found herself fifth from the centre and next to Watson. She hadn't expected so much formality, or publicity. Charlie presided, paying her no particular attention when he was busy with more familiar guests. Leonie's notion of banquets was Elizabethan, culled from her background reading and had evolved from impressions of culinary centrepieces like statues carved in butter or ice according to the climate, the regal roast swan and sturgeon or a boar's head agape on a pomeroy. Charlie was much more sensible than that: edibility was his prime criterion. They ate simply but they ate well of what was to hand on the estate. The Savoy cabbage and the curly kale weren't despised because they were native, any more than trout or salmon or venison, and the Torrisaig cook had worked overtime on a batch of apple tartlet which in London might have been called tarte or torte but locally was plain and good, glazed with a pressed fruit syrup.

¹n the gallery overhead a quartet played madrigals and the music rose up into the oak beams of the roof where Leonie followed it

until it fell down again in a shower of sound, notes evaporating followed by condensation.

"What are you looking at?" asked Watson.

"I'm listening. The acoustics are spot on. How did builders know what the sound waves would do before they had scientific audiometers?"

"What's wrong with the ear?"

"True enough. They say Epidauros is the perfect amphitheatre, still. You can hear every word without amplifiers or microphones."

"Shall we go there?" A Greek holiday surfaced in the shared imagination. Island hopping with sun, wine and making love; a multiple intoxicant.

"And see Irene Papas in *Aeschylus*?"

"We could."

"Yes, we could," she agreed but the intention shifted from future to hypothetical.

The party became diffuse after supper, breaking up into cliques that scattered over the hall and grounds. A marquee had been erected on the sheltered side of the house, not the garden party variety, but borrowing something from its setting. It became the movable tent of war, its canopy turreted and embattled, its tables campaigning, with men and uniforms in the majority as regimental and clan insignia came out of retirement.

At ten o'clock as many people again had come in from the surrounding countryside, to dance if not to eat or, if not to dance, to say they'd been there and seen the sights. The quartet kept up the serenade indoors with the measured steps of a minuet or quadrille, while in the marquee a band gave out the heartier notes of the ballroom classics which, as the evening progressed, slipped gradually into a medley of folk and pop, the quickstep and the strathspey and the jive rolled into one glorious phantasmagoria of improvised sound, impure but fun.

Watson's responsibilities as co-host were pressing. In public, he was never off duty but obliged to be civil when he might have wanted to be private. A gathering of two hundred people on home territory was the best means there was of temperature testing. Not much in the year since the general election had found favour with the electorate in Ross, Cromarty or Skye. They objected to the fish quotas imposed by the previous government, distrusted the transport bill of the present one and were sceptical of redevelopment grants – patching a boot with cardboard as one farmer called it.

Leonie caught sight of him over shoulders, talking with his forehead on the move trying to explain or palliate, working at the business of conviction. She understood. She didn't expect him to be the gallant escort and found her chief regret lay in not being able to join openly in the conversation. She kept a low profile. She knew why it was compellingly interesting to him, this talking out. Other people would find so much speechifying wearisome but for both of them, the mechanism of voicing was fascinating stuff, watching how your interlocutors slowly turned round and were convinced by your point of view or the projection of your personality. Turning listeners into believers; it was a form of egotism at base, and calling it art or politics didn't reduce the megalomaniac tendency in their character, where the self was transmuted endlessly into causes. Putting on a show? Yes, but the show was extroversion. Watson gave an impressive display, neither bored nor rude nor indulgent. Sheer force of numbers meant he couldn't spare more than half a dozen sentences to each and when someone threatened to become tendentious, he could move on with a nod of egalitarian charm.

Leonie smiled, recognising his self-sufficiency and left him to his profession. She passed through the double embrasure of the Great Hall to the covered walkway that led to the marquee where the musical medley attracted the largest crowds.

The quality of the night stopped her progress. It was a beautiful night, something you could almost feel with your fingers, fine, silky, so transparent it was a revelation, like having a film removed from the retina to sharpen experience. There was a full array of stars which appeared to hang low, larger and weightier than London constellations. The particular colour of this sky was enchanting, the living aphorism of midnight blue, a phrase she'd thought infelicitous till then. Ahead of her, the band rocked on but its noise was contained. It didn't shatter the impenetrable silence of the place; in fact it was the sound of a piping flute, the hautboy, that carried the furthest being lighter than the rest, like a sparrow more buoyant in the fragile night than swooping birds. The purpose of music was to make silence throb. Torrisaig rose above

369

temporalities, stern, rebuking and also tolerant of the passing hour. It made her catch her breath.

Charlie, who was kilted in dress tartan for the occasion and wore the ceremonial silver buttoned jacket, came by and commandeered her. "We're being appallingly rude, Watson and I."

"No, I don't mind." They moved together down the canvas-covered passage, met by a funnel of warm air from the marquee that was pulsing with a hundred bodies.

"Have you danced yet?" Charlie asked. "Then let's take the floor. This is something which I was taught to do as part of my social repertoire, a Military Two-step. It's very bizarre to think of dancing classes in our curriculum. Watson's much more heavy-footed because they don't bother now with social graces."

She thought of who Charlie's partners were likely to be in a boys' own school.

"Oh, they shipped girls in from a ladies' college nearby. Once a week in the sixth. All very formal. I rather liked Miss Baxter but Miss Baxter didn't like me. Perhaps I birled her too fast on the turns."

In fact, Charlie was a nimble dancer, as with everything else he did. Massively dainty, in thirty seconds he had outlined what the Military Two-step ought to be and made her succumb to its phrasing. She grew warm changing hands and directions. "Something to do with swordsmanship, I'm sure, and the passage of arms."

"I wouldn't like to be doing this in full kit."

"No, indeed." A progressive dance formed while they cooled and Charlie assumed she would join it and, having joined the circle of the dance, she was caught up in the succeeding one so that the best part of two hours was spent on the floor. Hereabouts, a woman who had shown her inclination to dance wasn't allowed to sit down again until her feet gave out. She spoke to twenty men, pressed hands and passed on. Farmers, lordlings, fishermen, newcomers, in the broad mix of Moncrieffe and Highland where hospitality meant that no man who wanted to come was excluded.

After midnight, she found herself back with Charlie, who was not in the slightest puffed. "Have you enjoyed yourself then? But it's sweltering in here with so much swat and reeking. Shall we take a breath of fresh air or will you get chill?"

Leonie thought her velvet would protect and nodded. They took a gravel path until they reached the top of the bank and went down a flight of steps towards the rose garden. It was a longish walk, bordered by a clipped yew hedge which in the way of yew had started to grow unruly and spread outwards. Charlie tutted a little, thinking how it would need to be sawn into shape again and what a straggly couple of intervening seasons that would mean. Besides, who could be spared from the estate for such decorative pruning? He explained, as he went along, about the hybridisation of his roses and the testing process at the National Rose Garden at Wisley and registering the flower once he had developed it with the Plants Variety Rights Office, talking and listening but each aware of the hiatus of more urgent concerns.

"Past their best, of course," he said, handling the blooms as if they were fragile, "but at the end of the season, the bud stays a better shape than when it's very hot. And is well perfumed. Quite a bonus when proliferation has passed."

Autumns pressed. So many autumns and still the thing not done. The man saddened personally and they turned back along the path, weighted with silence. Charlie cast his eye over the house which was lit from all its portals, a dozen different types of window shining out over the centuries, mullioned, oriel and sash. Celebration at Torrisaig was always nostalgic. Impelled by future unease, he asked "Are you serious about my nephew?"

The woman reflected for a long time, wondering what it was he wanted to hear. "Oh yes. This is a serious accident."

Charlie stopped at an intersection of paths and directed them along a slight detour to prolong the moment, past a stone bench and a piece of classical statuary, some goddess breezily disported. The Regency fan had put her there. Not quite appropriate but accepted because it was done. He shouldn't have asked the question, and didn't know how to handle her reply, so he said obliquely, "We Moncrieffes have such terrible trouble with our women. I was in love for ten years with a woman who was quite unsuitable. Not disreputable, you understand, but not headed for Debrett's."

Leonie met the insidious notions of genealogy and was at the point of disclaiming any interest in pedigree when he went on.

"But then, I'm talking of a pre-war standard. Fellows seem to

371

marry Americans now as well as commoners and divorcees. You'll laugh at me, but the abdication was the beginning of the end for the British peerage. All three in one."

She didn't know what to say, shock or disappoint him. If I got out of one marriage, I'd be chary of stepping inside another. And what's so pure about the peerage or royalty for that matter, with their spawn of bastards, that I'm not good enough to join them? The double rejection of the norm read as contradictory. Abstraction might be safest. "Briar stock, Lord Moncrieffe, is the strength of genus. You don't revitalise by so much inbreeding."

"You're quite right," he answered, pleased. "And nowadays, I'd marry Jean and hang the lot of them."

"Why don't you still?"

"Oh. Too late. She married, in her own class. No," he summed, as a waft of heat and music caught them down a garden channel, "I'm deceiving myself. She'd have hated this. Found it oppressive. We make scapegoats of our failures, but in essence they have got the better of us."

Watson came suddenly into view at the end of an avenue and bore down on them, aggressive and bristling, suspecting that his uncle was giving Leonie a wigging. Charlie knew him in this mood and ducked out good-humouredly towards the house on the excuse of guests waiting to leave.

"Was he talking out of turn?"

"Oh no. Every inch the gentleman."

They bent back towards the water, out of the confines of the ordered garden, where the rushes made a stiff fringe. He drew his arm through hers, velvet and lace warmer than barathea. "I'm nervous," he said, "when I can't see you."

"Then that must be for the most part."

Charlie reached the top of the bank again and looked back before he joined his guests. The man and the woman were silhouetted against the loch, dark on dark. Only the white shirt of his nephew moved as a point of brilliance showing their route. An intriguing enough woman to defy the standards for inclusion in Debrett's. She left an impression that was hard to analyse, in her foliar dress separated petal by petal by petal. The black rose came to Torrisaig, albeit non-organic.

39

Sandy Govan watched the rowing boat pull away from the far bank and draw slowly towards the landing cove before he went out to meet it. The politician came at last, and accompanied. Rumour reached even this outpost of the western shores and the host and head man was fully prepared. Just this morning, a man who had dined at Torrisaig had spoken to a man who brought the weekly mail by this same boat, gossip preceding the event.

"I feel I ought to break into a series of All hails," said Watson, disembarking. "It's Leonie's fault. The play's got into my blood-stream. Do stop me if I begin talking in iambics. I'm taking you up on your invitation a year late, Sandy. Is it still open?"

"Always open house. You've chosen a good night to visit us. We're having a ceilidh this evening. Maybe," the host suggested, turning to Leonie, "you could speak for us. Most of us haven't seen the inside of a theatre for years."

Watson was relieved at patent knowledge which excused explanations. At the same time, he began to realise how naïve he'd been to say to Leonie that behaviour could be redefined in London: all information was ultimately relayed to source. They went along the shore towards Sandy's boathouse where a hull with planks missing was upended.

"The owner stoved this in doing some Cape Wrath race and I've got it back to repair." Sandy picked out splinters disap-provingly.

"Good for business."

"I'd rather make than mend."

Leonie lifted up his mallet from the ground, an oversized gavel, and went inside the boathouse to put it back on the work bench. Sandy measured the distance of fifteen feet she put between herself and them, in respect for an established friendship and he moved up to close it again in case she felt ill at ease or unwelcome. "I'll pack up for today. That's why we like visitors so much in

Carse. It means a holiday. We'll walk around, shall we, and bother everyone for cups of tea."

"So what's been happening?" asked Moncrieffe. "A good year or a bad? The schoolmistress stayed, I hope. And did the fecund couple make it through the winter?"

Sandy grudgingly acknowledged the politician's adhesion to facts which he put down to an inherent one-up-manship. The voters did so like to be remembered. He'd discounted this facility ever since he'd read of one American President's wife who kept a file box with names of their party workers, listing wife, children, interests, all on index cards beside the telephone ready to impress. 'Hi, Gerry. How's Tina? Dropped the golf handicap yet?' He loathed this ballyhoo on-the-make philosophy and half suspected Moncrieffe of storing these cue cards himself to prompt his interest before he did his rounds, until he considered that there was no political mileage in people who eschewed their own enfranchisement and didn't mark their ballot paper with an X for him or anybody.

"No. The couple left. But the school is going strong. We'll drop in there later. Our big problem has come about since you were here last." The boat-builder looked over the potholed escarpment which spread out between them and the sea, with broken dykes and rough pasture or unsquare fields, towards a wall on the northern boundary of the land spur, which was neatly built. "A newcomer. He's started some sort of school of meditation."

"Fair enough."

"Well," said Govan, "I'm all right on meditation when it's private. This is organised. They practise doing some weird things."

"Such as?" Moncrieffe skirted a patch of beans that rose up elegant trusses in somebody's back yard. The homesteaders couldn't freeze or can them so they must either salt them over the winter, or pack them into water jars. What a thought! Was there any nourishment left after the processing or were the vegetables reduced to the taste and texture of cattle fodder?

"They go in for fasting till they hallucinate. And something called hyperventilating."

"What's that?"

374

"Expanding the lungs and contracting again in quick succession."

"In the long term, it's meant to aid physical and cerebral control," said Leonie, who'd been introduced to the theory by a psychedelic actor in Bristol, strobe-lit on and off the stage.

"No harm in that," considered the politician.

"I'm not so sure. They can become comatose. And they play strange music—"

"Stranger than the bagpipes?"

"I know," said Govan thoughtfully, "it has all the makings of prejudice when we'd forsworn the standards of ordinary society. Live and let live. But it's not so easy to be tolerant when people are making inroads into your chosen and secluded way of life." He snorted, listening to himself. "The mot juste. They're campaigning to open up the highway so we can have droves of meditators in."

"Oh, they can't affect you all that badly, surely?"

"It's a very subtle form of antipathy. They're rich, some offshoot of an American-funded organisation, and we're poor. We work. They don't. That becomes damned annoying after a while."

Watson suppressed his comment that opposition in miniature had come to disrupt a socialist Utopia. The alternative use of communal space presented the same problem as the village green. Grazing geese and playing cricket on it weren't compatible pursuits. "So who will arbitrate?"

"We don't have any mechanism for that. It's developing into confrontation. A radio mast is broken, a wall gets pushed down in the night."

"Don't mediate; retaliate."

"There are two school-age children who're a blithering nuisance. Same thing. You can't actually discipline or debar them."

Co-operation was a rotten form of self-government without penalties. Watson found the continuing proof of mighty right was demoralising. Even anarchy couldn't contain an out and out rebel.

Leonie struck out on her own, poking her head into cottages where there was smoke rising, or going up to the women who were working outdoors, asking frank questions of the gem cutter and his wife and the rush mat weavers. What did they eat? Where were the children schooled after the age of eleven? Did they listen to the BBC news? She found the starkness of the community penal as well as reformative, stone-breaking, clod-splitting. The voluntary reversion to a bygone way of life was baffling and, like Moncrieffe, she wondered if they deluded themselves, a bunch of misfits, hideaway, castaway, runaway failures, romanticising on days of yore and the good life; or if western civilisation really had broken down to the point where it couldn't absorb loners. The lessons for self were compelling. Integration mattered more than isolation.

The schoolmistress was pleased to show off her children's progress to their distinguished visitors, a sampler of cross-stitch embroidery, a new hymn sung to the accompaniment of a ship's piano, the one brought over on the boat, little but stirring, a frieze of highly coloured seasons running along a wall. It had a settlement simplicity which Leonie found arresting because it was in earnest, a strict Protestant interior as depicted by the Dutch school, or her mother's flat swept clean of clutter, where plainness was attendant on function. Children in hand-knit Aran sweaters, faces scoured by wind and water, had a raw purpose showing through their scholastic interests when they already knew what was productive learning, vocational not academic. She would have been completely convinced by it at the turn of the century but found herself disturbed by its anachronistic conceit. Access to civilisation, like faith, was surely a birthright. She felt these parents misdirected when they made retreats from reality into hardship, a canon their children could not be expected to follow. Or was it really the ark of hope, forty brave souls and their livestock preserving the last goodness from the flood of a corrupt world?

Moncrieffe wandered off mentally as Sandy used the occasion to catch up on village concerns, the hardiness of the black-faced sheep, the fate of a consignment of sweaters with patterns like runes which the Shetland woman turned out for fancy Edinburgh shops to sell at ten times her profit, or a baby who'd come down with suspected measles. Where had the infection come from? How would it be contained? They would need to fetch the doctor over from the mainland, a four-hour round trip.

Watson listened in but his eye roved. The disarray of Carse upset him. He liked wild wilderness but neat dwellings. He had an essentially tidy mind, despaired of waste and especially wasted effort. He thought everybody liked to live four-square and shanty towns of corrugated roofs and cardboard walls, or the unkempt plot, weed-attractive, signalled defeat to him. Black squatter townships on the outskirts of Johannesburg, the no-go areas of Calcutta, unpoliceable, the squalid urban slums of South America, he'd seen them all and knew the fear of the contagion of irrational disorder. Perhaps he had a prettifying strain in him. He remembered seeing country folk, when he was very young, put conch shells on either side of their whitewashed doorstep, whether purely decoratively or as the universal symbol of fertility, he didn't know and probably neither did they. But he did believe that when people were happy, when there was excess, they turned their hand to ornamentation. It was a basic instinct. A life so denuded of aesthetics struck him as centrally barren and a visual symbol of misery.

Or was this maturity come creeping on him with its greyness of attitude, precursor of old age? He noticed raggedness compulsively, as if it were his duty to mend it. The woodsmen didn't seem to cut and stack the logs as tidily as they once did. The purple flowering vetch was more beautiful in his youth, long plumes of foxglove simulars; now he knew it was a weed and endemically invasive. He fell himself into the traps of bygonism, which was a measure of his responsibility for the present.

"What are those?" asked Leonie, coming up to him beside the tidy wall of the infiltrators. An opening between the houses gave them a view north to a longer spur of land jutting out into the Minch, with three stone roundhouses on it.

"Brochs," he answered.

"What are brochs?"

"No one's sure but probably pre-Pictish fortified dwellings. When the enemy came, you barricaded yourself inside."

"That's why they've got no windows?"

"They're hollow. With galleries. The windows are on the inside, onto round courtyards, a bit like huge stone doocots."

"I'd like to have seen those."

"Another time," he said, considering the long drive round these fiord-like inlets. But the future hour chimed oddly.

Watson and Leonie walked instead, while Sandy took the boat and then borrowed the Daimler parked on the mainland to call the nearest doctor.

377

They walked up to an isolated spot Watson had known long before the commune re-inhabited the village houses on the shore. The place wasn't a beauty spot but he took her there because it was quiet and more typical than the grand scenic views which made the postcards, or more attuned to his own taste when it was rugged and unimproved. It was high up on the moor above the tree line so that on rougher days than this it bore a likeness to the blasted heath as Leonie had imagined it; browns and a purply pink, nothing more penetrating to the eye than the natural colours of rock, with a scree on the exposed side of the hills and water gulleys like scar tissue so old and pit-marked that they would never mend. The burn which had its source nearby purled slowly across the upland landscape, which in a rainy season could turn into a sodden peat bog. This bog was a spongy organic mass like a water meadow, maybe a hundred feet deep and built up of layers of flowers and grass that had died but didn't decompose because of the natural minerals in the spring water, and so formed the subsoil for next year's growth. The flowers were the tundra variety, with heads so small you'd have to put them under a microscope to see the colour, bells, clover and miniature orchids mottling the heather. They made a thick and buoyant carpet under them. Crushed, they sent up the aroma of the herbalist.

They lay in the lee of a shieling which had been built by shepherds for the lambing, while the sun made a sporadic appearance between clouds to warm them in starts. The two figures closed and separated again, embracing without hurry. Hand moved over limbs, reconstructing forms. Her person began to contain the universe for Moncrieffe, providing all things, pleasure, interest, challenge, mirth, a sum which he hadn't expected to find in one embodiment.

"Shall we swim?" she asked, rolling away.

"What in?" Watson was particular about bathing apparel.

She considered the options; a bikini made of underwear that would have to be worn sopping wet afterwards or simple nudity which in the open air was less prudish. "The river will do."

It was easy bathing with no rocks underfoot and the water, which could have been chill, had spread out benignly over the expanse of moorland and absorbed some of its insulated heat.

She paddled, stationary in the shallow stream. "This is like a jacuzzi."

"No, it isn't. It's a perishing Scottish burn and we're mad to do this in September."

"Oh you've lived a soft life. It's bliss. The water's full of bubbles. Very energising."

True enough. When he pressed down with his foot, a pocket of gas was released as if a shoal of fish had gone swimming underneath him. The effect was curiously sensuous with explosions of air against the skin. "The plants I suppose. Or air trapped in the bog."

"It does," she said, spouting the water which was blue and clear, "oxygenate the blood."

And his as she went gliding past, legs threshing in the sun. The water dazzled, elementally different from other water, a lime- and salt- and fluoride-free liquid, spared the harsh additives of civilisation. He tried to trap her as she swam and their voices were magnified into shouting by the echo of the flat ox-bow stream and the reverberating emptiness of the hills. Her hair floated out behind her like a clump of moss and flora which had become dislodged from the river edge and her body hair, as she kept herself level with the surface by rippling her feet and hands, a minor plantain. After the first shock of immersion, his body warmed up and he started to desire her cool and slippery embrace all over again. But making love in water was notoriously hard and all they did was add to the effervescence of the stream as they threshed about, trampling its bed. They rolled over and over like rocks brought downstream by a current.

When she got out, breathless with avoiding him, she pulled handfuls of the grass to rub herself down.

"You don't seem to mind being naked," he said, admiring the fact that her body didn't glare or look indecent in the open.

"No. I would be a natural nudist. You soon lose whatever prudery you had in a communal dressing room. Three minutes for a costume change doesn't leave you much time for being shy and retiring."

He rubbed her hair with his hands, drying by friction until it stood out on end, sun shone.

Watson tested her on her lines as she gabbled through them, lying on her back, face into the sun. He took up the rhythm of murderous Macbeth, and they entered the duet of man and wife.

She experimented with the various voices she had worked out for his ear, a dedicated enthusiasm which astonished him. "Do you live yourself?" he wondered. "Or always vicariously?"

"Oh I live. I'm enjoying this. Being in the sun for once. I've not done too much sun-bathing in my life. I could become a glutton for it. This is the first time I've been in what you would call the country. Not a single house in sight." They perched on a high plateau, the nearest habitation five miles below.

"Impossible."

"It's true. I've always lived in cities. There's no call for a theatre in the middle of the countryside, is there? I went to Pitlochry one season but our lodgings were in the High Street and I didn't see much green."

A bird circled overhead and he turned on his back to get a better sighting.

"An eagle?" she asked hopefully.

"No, too small. But a bird of prey."

"Raptors," she said. "*Macbeth* is full of raptors and bird images. The gentle martlet and the wren and chicks all fall prey to the carrion birds."

"I think it's a small hawk. Which raptors does he mention?"

"The raven," she said, checking back from memory, "and crow and rook and falcon and owl. And choughs, they have red legs don't they, and the maggot-pies, as Shakespeare calls them."

"Yes, you might see all of those. How do you know the names of birds," he wondered, "if you've never lived in the country?"

"A bit of luck, like my plant recognition. But it's hazy. Don't risk me out on the moors or I'll be shooting larks."

"A great Tudor delicacy," he laughed, "like blackbird pie." He grew quiet, thinking she had touched on an idea he hadn't dared examine too directly. What was she doing here in the game season? He had put up the decoy that she was tired and needed a break, but gallivanting cross-country was no rest. The London to Inverness flight plus a journey as long by car across Strath Bran, all for three days purloined from rehearsal while the rest of the cast finished Act Five. Not restful at all. The excuse would not serve. He asked her to see how well she fitted in, if she could be a country as well as a city dweller.

She looked right. Just as new clothes made men conspicuous on the hills, bright ones did women. That was the advantage of her preferred neutrality. She was as unremarkable at Torrisaig as the doe, the blend of tones she thought was dull but was in fact lastingly vivid, the grey and cream harmony of which the eye didn't tire. She wore a garment he'd often seen her in, a pair of things like gaucho leggings or the divided skirt of cowgirls and Edwardian cyclists, pedalling to suffrage, the original unisex clothing of trousers in disguise. Above all, she didn't commit the blunder of city slickers, come perched on heels or showing too much midge-susceptible flesh. She did.

He knew that their association in London was limited. A few hours after both houses had shut down, seldom alone but mixed with people who weren't intimate, but professional friends. Three-quarters of the human repertoire was outside their range, the eating, walking, waking mundanity. He asked her here to know her better, to know her well. Then he took himself in hand. No fantasising. No romancing. This was not a try-out for the part of Lady Moncrieffe. Even if he were to be emphatic about the formulative plan, she would look in the other direction and answer with those blandly tutored vowels. She should have been a diplomat, giving nothing in negotiation, especially offence. Decisions were not to be wrung out of this woman so that he was forced to admire, even when it worked against him, the operation of independent thought.

"Back to work," he ordered, and they spent the afternoon perfecting caesura, elision and enjambment in and out of context.

The ceilidh that evening was held at Sandy's house. The nearest thing Leonie had seen to this was T.E. Lawrence's spartan cottage at Clouds Hill, rough-hewn rooms and unfussy masculine furniture, with yards of cloth or hide tacked onto old upholstery shapes. Their bed which sat in the middle of the main room was at least six foot square and, laid on the floor, wasn't far different from a makeshift platform which Sandy confirmed by throwing a rug over the bedclothes for the evening. A stage or generous seating; either purpose justified its size. Sheepskin proliferated on floor and wall and chair. It made a snug lining to an easy chair and the visitors went about all evening with long tufts of wool hanging from their clothes, in semi-moult.

381

They lit hurricane lamps outdoors to show the way and laid a table with tapestry weave ready for offerings. You brought your own food to these communal gatherings and over the course of the evening a plenitude of dishes appeared, the inestimable black bun outweighing its pastry case and potted hough, closer to banquet fare than Torrisaig. And they drank! Home fermented ale and wine that didn't disclose too readily its source of nettle or berry, which was a gentle brew the men avoided in favour of unblended malt though Moncrieffe, forewarned, diluted his glass with burn water while children kept to the real lemonade not commercial carbonated syrup, but made from pressed lemon and citric acid, or ginger beer out of stone bottles.

The wind vane turning on the roof gave out a haphazard flicker of light, supplemented by a wood fire that settled lower in a hand-forged basket, the depth of the stone hearth necessary to guard against its spatters. Crusie lamps of oil stood where they wouldn't be a fire risk, sending out a guttering light together with heat and smell as the floating wicks smoked rather than burned. The adult faces in this penumbra had the look of the children in the school-room, simply older children who were marked by time instead of stress. They weathered well, these outdoor people, like oak or stone or wool. Age was irrelevant compared with strength or sex or the character written broadly in their features, like the men and women in the ballads who performed the function of types in a world where nuances were effete. They endured and had that stamped.

The violin maker gave them songs, better at producing the instrument than its music, but they joined in to blur his more erratic notes. The schoolmistress had had six men carry the piano over and the two of them gave a recital, the Moonlight Sonata and Für Elise among the Scottish melodies. Nobody hogged the show. A child told a joke he'd seen printed in the *Sunday Post*, and everyone laughed although they'd read it too. The Shetland woman put down her pins to sing them a song about the oil rigs. It was in Gaelic and nobody understood but the plangent notes of lament for a passing way of life were recognisable through the plainsong of her unaccompanied chanting. Times were changing. Times were hard.

Leonie got to her feet in the centre of the improvised stage and

382

recited for them. Neither visitor could muster better in the way of
entertainment so she had to speak for both of them.

> I will arise and go now, and go to Innisfree,
> And a small cabin build there, of clay and wattles made;
> Nine bean rows will I have there, a hive for the honey bee,
>   And live alone in the bee-loud glade.
>
> And I shall have some peace there, for peace comes dropping slow,
> Dropping from the veils of the morning to where the cricket sings;
> There midnight's all a-glimmer, and noon a purple glow,
>   And evening full of the linnet's wings.
>
> I will arise and go now, for always night and day
> I hear loch water lapping with low sounds by the shore;
> While I stand on the roadway, or on the pavements gray,
>   I hear it in the deep heart's core.

She said it simply, consonant hard without a hint of that intrusive
tremor of poetry, relying on logic not sentiment to convince them.
It might seem inappropriate, a Yeatsian turn-of-the-century Ireland but with some typical substitution, she put in loch where lake
should be. It was the epitaph for Carse, for the Celtic cultural
minorities, the yearning of the fringe people of the British Isles for
their own place. Moncrieffe thought the lines an inspired choice,
to the point where they felt written for the occasion. As they rose
out of the anthologies of childhood to fill the room with wistful-
ness and reminiscence, he found himself unaccountably moved.
Her voice had for him the instant access to emotion. Technique as
well as feeling held him. That she could deliver to a group of
strangers an ode that surged spontaneously out of the tenor of
their own lives, the row of beans, the connective roadway they
fought against, and did it without books to hand, from the
repertoire of her own mind, surprised him. He would not tire of
this woman or her range. He had that capacity after all, undying-
ness.

To stop himself from actually shedding tears he had to yawn, a
protective device he'd hit on long before. The movement simulated
tedium but also mechanically cleared the throat of its constriction.
She caught his eye during the applause and understood.

The night spent in the firelight wouldn't burn out but stayed wakeful like embers. As she turned, she said, "This is the sin. Being so happy."

"Isn't happiness a right?"

"No. It's earned. And you don't know how this will count in our debentures."

40

Lying became unavoidable.

The internal flight from Inverness arrived an hour later than the shuttle from Heathrow, a schedule which Fergus knew off pat, and so in answer to his question, "Why are you so late? Was the departure delayed?" Leonie had to fabricate. He might be moved to check the fact, systematically, and so she replied, "No. They'd mislaid my bag. And the taxi seemed to take for ever in the traffic from Turnhouse." The tissue of deceit thickened.

"Odd. On Monday."

The afternoon was heavy-set, solidifying Edinburgh at the end of September. There was a haze which hung about between heat and mist, gathering vapours. A cloud sat at the end of the garden at the Hermitage, blurring the rhododendron bushes, and pockets of it had filtered indoors making the landing spectral, the rooms fitfully coloured like a film taken at the wrong exposure.

The house vacillated too between precision and vagueness, work and holiday. It was Fergus' last week before the new term started and the days ran out like the lees of indolence, intoxicating with an aftertaste of bitterness because there was to be no more. He was a little shiftless, going to his study for a book then outside to catch a burst of late sun intense under a stone wall. Harris came back after four. He was, strangely enough, the most amenable member of the Petrie family who had taken refuge in the house, good-humoured and busy where Michael and Alison had been idle, because he was determined not to be a burden. Leonie left the brothers playing tennis, making the best of the erratic light while she wheeled the baby round in his high-sided perambulator to see her mother and stopped off at the shops at Comiston along the way to buy meat for supper, fulfilling the shape of the everyday. Plain walking was exhilarating after cars and aeroplanes. Speed slowed in suburbia.

Ellice was pleased to see her, but better pleased to see her charge who'd been rarely consigned to her over the summer while Fergus was at home, and grew fascinatingly between meetings. Andrew spoke some words now and was fond of 'No.' Old and young played together, or thwarted each other's diverse ambitions while Leonie watched, amused at the incipient gagadom of her mother.

"Have you seen Stuart and Alison of late?"

"Hm. Setting up in unmarried life together seems just as hard as the married style. I went round to Grange Loan last week. Stuart moithered because there's no work although his Festival production with the students was a sell-out rave. And Muriel makes their flat her calling-off point almost every evening and sits like a sore head in the corner. What a favour I did selling you this flat. What would you have done without me? So on and so forth."

"But how are they?"

"Ah well," the woman drew her wits together. "I found Alison making a cake which is a performance of epic proportions. A measure of this and a measure of that, all exact you understand to the grain, no happy guesses with Alison, backwards and forwards to the cookery book, slaistering on with egg white in a bowl until the kitchen was in upheaval. Attention to detail can be injurious to scale. And Stuart adding hints, who's not so much as stirred a pan of porridge in his life. I was never so exhausted trying to make a conversation."

Leonie laughed. Her mother had a gleeful accuracy for type. "And did it taste good?"

"No. It tasted awful although, to be fair, we did eat it hot out of the tin. Alison's cakes will always fall flat because she beats at them too much."

"She's a trier."

"There's a wisdom in trying what you can accomplish. I'll stick to shop cakes or none at all thank you," said the prudent shopper. "Alison has a love of potted plants and in time will adopt a cat."

"I must go and see them sometime." But not too soon.

The vignette stayed with Leonie, curling round the edges of her mouth at its pertinence. She was careful to add a dash of the carefree to her own cooking that evening, the ultimate salt. She and Fergus and Harris ate in the kitchen, a Petrie-spirited meal if ever there was one, neither of them sitting still but wandering

386

away from the table for different errands between forkfuls, discussing computer programmes with each other.

"Fergus is teaching me how to use the computer," explained Harris.

"You and computers?" Leonie was disbelieving.

"I'm not all that dim."

"I never said you were. I just can't see you having the patience with machine technology, that's all."

"They have one in the office now. Not that I'm allowed to use it. Matthew Geddes is the boffin. He keeps disappearing on courses with titles like 'Administering Retrieval Systems'."

"The coming age," said Fergus. "I'm going to be doing some new work myself this year on language programming." He worked at home on his first project for the department of Artificial Intelligence, having made the transference from teaching to research as he intended. At this point he strayed away from the table and came back with a sheet of phonemes Leonie recognised from the phonetic transcription which she'd had to learn for speaking her lines in a foreign language. The theory he was propounding, close to her own interests, caught her attention. "It's easy to get a computer to think numerically, because that operates on the basis of correct or incorrect, or a provable right and wrong. It's much harder to programme in language where deduction and logic come into play."

"Can't a computer obey instructions written in words, then?" she asked.

"Well it can, in Algol or Basic or one of the other computer languages, but when words are ambiguous, say a verb and noun are homophones, it can't resolve shades of meaning as readily as the human mind. Experts are trying to work out a code language that a machine can comprehend, or use to check its own conclusions. Why do I think what I think is something a machine can't answer yet. So it may arrive at the wrong deduction because it doesn't understand its own mental processes, if you like. Has no self-regulating device."

Leonie looked at the sheet of phonemes. "How do these fit in?"

"One of the units in the Artificial Intelligence department has been working for a number of years on a project to convert the English language into sounds a machine will obey."

387

"Voice synthesisers?"

"Well, very approximately speaking."

"What's the point of a talking machine?" She was edgy when her own expertise was threatened.

"A lot of point. Imagine being able to speak into a typewriter that had the computer facility to convert all these phonemes into alphabetic symbols. What a breakthrough for the blind. Or the physically disabled could give oral instructions to the machines they rely on, say a wheelchair. Even in the office, you could simplify the majority of secretarial work instead of going through shorthand or the dictaphone, by speaking into them directly. Pilots controlling flight by voice alone. The applications are endless." His enthusiasm was convincing.

"So what's the problem?" Leonie wondered.

"The human voice box and the human ear are so subtle. Human beings can make and distinguish thousands of different sounds which we have to try to convert into electronic sound waves using only a very rough Morse code of bleeps like a radar detection device. So far, it isn't precise enough. A 'd' for example is different, light or dark, according to whether it's the initial or the middle letter and if it's followed by a vowel or a consonant. 'D' is in fact one of four different sounds which are difficult to reproduce or interpret accurately."

She'd heard one of his talking chess computers imported from America intone in its sexless flattened drawl. "For all that, the machines still sound execrable."

"That doesn't matter at all," Fergus said severely. "Euphonics don't come into it. As long as it works. The function far outweighs mere rhythmics."

"So much for you and all that actressy stuff," observed Harris, rising to leave for his nightspot. He said it with glee, landing on the favoured Scottish diminutive for her profession.

"So much for me indeed."

She got up to clear the plates, annoyed at her brother-in-law's facile intervention. The snub was adequate – and deserved – without his amelioration. Standing at this spot on the traverses of the kitchen floor, she remembered that it was precisely here that Matthew Geddes had spoken to her eighteen months before, about the supposed attractions of the ménage à trois. The phrase had its

388

own ambiguities. For the best part of this year, she and Fergus hadn't had this household to themselves. There was always a third party to accommodate, a medium through which husband and wife made interchange that ended up as an imperfect translation of their thoughts and wishes. The course of this conversation might have been quite different if they'd been alone, accompanied by gesture banned in front of others or a visual closeness that was withdrawn.

Or would it? The other ménage presented itself more forcibly. Matthew had considered a threesome the sophisticated ideal, unworkable she'd thought in Edinburgh Pentlands. She had a moment's illusion of herself and Fergus and Watson in a similar three-way compromise, living under one roof together. But which roof? Westminster, Torrisaig or the Hermitage? She tried to imagine Moncrieffe settling down in these rooms to read constituency documents, House papers green or white, and it wouldn't work. He was too extreme even in a physical sense, zooming from far north to far south, to settle on the median of Edinburgh. The polarities came home to her. Even if Fergus could tolerate Moncrieffe as the politician seemed to tolerate him, perforce, the practical arrangement ruled it out. She remembered her mother saying marriage only worked where there was total equality or total inequality of interests. More difficult with three parties than with two.

And heirs. That Moncrieffe urgency had impressed itself on her at Torrisaig, as Maldon and Guise and MacAlpin cried out to be perpetuated. She'd already had one son. In time, Lord Moncrieffe might demand another. Woman as breeder was not a thought to inspire, and yet the curve of the relationship tended to that outcome. He'd given her a photograph of himself as a schoolboy, one that stood on his desk when she'd taken the notepaper. A squint cap, a tie undone and the face too making a tilt at the conventions, wryly dismissive of itself. She kept it close, folded in her wallet, but it faded rapidly with so much creasing. The eyes that looked out of it started to seem ancient, haggard with denial, not Moncrieffe's eyes at all but his son's, waiting for his time to come.

"You're looking very well," said Fergus watching her from the kitchen table. "I suppose you must get some fresh air in London."

She nodded, silently perjured. The sun stain deepened the other falsehood, layer on layer.

"And so do all of you. I haven't seen Harris look so relaxed for a long time."

"No. He has the knack of making everyone else take the pressure."

Leonie heard the sharp inflexion behind this. "Does he pay anything towards his keep?" she asked, thinking finance was the most likely cause of disagreement between Petries.

"In theory. I put it on the slate."

"You'd need a long slate with Harris. I never knew anyone with so many sudden holes in his pocket."

"I keep tabs on him."

The phrase was awesome; a tabulation made up of columns, totals, debits. She recalled how she'd advised her husband to make a proper record of dealings with his brother and wondered, chillingly, if this had been carried into scrupulous deed.

Harris, who had been humming through the house, suddenly put his head round the door and said, "I'm off then, folks. I'll see you sometime," and disappeared. They heard his car pull down the gravel drive, making a sharp ping of acceleration against the stones and Fergus anticipated how he would have to sweep the chippings laboriously back into place in the morning.

"It's funny. He always manages to avoid lifting a dish. Does it very well."

Leonie realised for all his hospitality, in spite of the tennis matches and the hours of instruction on the computer terminal, Fergus quietly resented his guest and was unforgiving of past wrongs. She was fixated by the many duplicities of the moment, Harris disguising wherever it was he went, Fergus' passive surface and her own, an overlay to deep and anxious feelings they wouldn't admit, liars all.

"Where's he gone?"

Fergus shrugged. "I'm not his keeper."

He did kiss her. It was a kiss that delivered many shocks. It declared, like the observation about her tan, an interest in the restitution of rights. In the context of his crushing indifference about her rehearsals or the stress of her rôle – she doubted if her husband would be able to name the theatre where she'd be appearing – the gesture didn't woo as much as it offended. He'd lost sight of who she was, because her personality had always been obscure. As she developed and expanded, his incomprehension grew in ratio. It wasn't intellectual stupidity but personal, relating to personalities. Fergus stopped short at people's function without moving on to explore their motives while character was an indecipherable mystery.

His body lying down the length of hers between the marital sheets was the most familiar object and the most alien. Carnal knowledge didn't assist any other kind. She was still grieved on the point he'd made after the funeral about their marriage being unsanctified. So what was this then? A lesser adultery, contravening emotional or spiritual ties but not the civil ones? After the funeral, she'd wanted to be kind, to comfort him but in the intervening month the major change had taken place, from being involved with Moncrieffe to being in love with him and being his lover.

To put Fergus off or to resist was to admit this central shift in loyalty. She lay reliving the dream of Tolstoy's Anna when she'd imagined she was married to Vronsky as well as Karenin, the men bigamously her husbands who made love to her in turn. Anna had found this triangular bedding a means of quietus with her own conscience; it made Leonie's flesh crawl. That Monday morning she'd lain with the other man in the smoke-filled living room at Carse, not eighteen hours ago. Here came the same proposition again in different form, unsolicited, positively unwanted but unavoidable. She shrank from the unendurable mechanics of it when the act was carried out without mental foreplay. Man into woman, robotic. Her stiffness wasn't tumescence but a lack of pliability to his will. Or guilt, knocking at the seat of the affections. Take guilt away and there was no plot. That thought was prevalent. An easy conscience made for such an uncluttered life.

Fergus could make her but not make her. The frightful moments lunged on endlessly. It wasn't pain as much as the indignity, which every woman must have experienced at some time, of not wanting in return. This can't go on, she thought, as the moon rose sequential on the sun. The moment of release would be just that, the escape from detention not an escape into pleasure. But without

391

reaching consummation, her husband rolled away from her and Leonie saw how he might subversively despise her as much as he despised his brother.

"It's impossible," he said, "with a bad conscience."

"Why bad?" she asked although she knew her internal reason.

"What I said after Michael died. It feels wrong when we haven't taken the marriage sacrament. I can't give and neither can you."

The opinion stunned. His shoulder blade wedging open the night patterned so many nights in bed. Eight years of making love non-sacramentally and not a word of objection to the act. She thought of all the times she'd gone against her own inclination to suit his, undressed in the afternoon behind curtains without demur. Corrupted him, had she? Less than the hypocrite or unworkable religion.

"And the Church comes out against contraception. I suppose that's another sin," she couldn't stop herself from goading.

"Procreation is the—"

"I know," she intercepted. "I've read your pamphlets too."

Leonie didn't dwell on anger for relief was itself an antidote. Perhaps the dictum of the Church of Rome was Fergus' saving lie, an unconscious escape from the clinches of a marriage that started to bruise them both, but she felt sore for a long time afterwards.

Harris came back in the middle of the night. He didn't make a sound but he did leave a door ajar somewhere in the house. It banged irritatingly, went on banging against the jamb while Leonie lay awake and listened, too lazy or too tired to get up and close it. The hammering went on and on like the knocking at the gate, knocking and hammering as if someone demanded entry which startled the disquiet mind.

At seven o'clock, she heard the baby move and got up to make his breakfast, returning with it to his room. By six months, Andrew was as developed as most children twice his age. He thrived on continuous adult attention and, handling him, Leonie was aware of a formative brain. It was Fergus' work, she conceded, keying in responses to the point where the primitive intellect started to think for itself, question, analyse.

He wasn't a precocious child but managed to be physically taking, with the curl of her hair and the colour of Fergus', brown-skinned, grey-eyed, the amalgam of physique and, for all she knew, tendency. When he was fed and washed he crawled about the room, picking up his toys from the plastic boxes where they were stored and bringing them over to her one by one, a three-legged animal when he crawled because one hand was incapacitated by the toy. Half a dozen objects he brought her to approve and she did it respectfully, assuming these were favourites, turned them over and put them to one side. She hadn't seen these before and was a little hurt that he hadn't brought the new duck she'd bought from Harrods, a carved wooden toy on wheels that sounded like a klaxon as it was pulled along.

And then her heart rate leaped. She hadn't seen these six toys before and he knew it. He hadn't brought her own gift in the pile because it was superfluous. He showed her his new possessions as his résumé on what had happened in her absence, already connecting people and objects in time. No, it wasn't possible. A child of that age couldn't make the intellectual assumptions of her foreknowledge. It was a mere accident of selection.

He moved over to the window bench where she was sitting and hauled himself upright against her knees. Wordless thoughts passed between them and then he did what she had never seen him do with anyone else, Irene or Fergus or Ellice, he put his head down sideways on her lap evoking the long forgotten phrase, matris in gremio. She stroked his head comfortingly, noticing tufts. Abandon him? How?

She had spent a week convalescing from the birth in the Simpson Memorial Maternity ward overlooking the Meadows. A tiny precinct contained their vital activities, George Square to the Mound. Fergus had come every day after his lectures and all she had wanted to do was get up and go to London. She shunned the maternalistic dialogues of other women, functional and maybe crude, with so much talk of fluids, when Hedda was there to be read and imagined, in a transubstantiation of herself.

The child grew without her further help and embodied the lessons she had learned at Carse. What was for the best? Did she have the right to prejudice her child's upbringing? Half hers, he might produce talents equivalent to her own and in her absence who would foster them? Natural, human, evocative, he deserved wholeness.

393

She heard Fergus get up and listened as he went downstairs. He would look for her, missing in bed and board, but the minutes passed and he didn't come. Extraordinary, such self-reliance or lack of sociability. He was a man who might wait all day before opening a letter, so incurious about its contents. Moncrieffe? He would have got up at the same time as her, shared the breakfast ritual with the child and talked about the fistful of presents Andrew brought to show his mother. The idealised image broke again into its components. It was not so.

Leonie remembered how, when buying the house was first broached, she had feared to walk in the shadow of the elder Petries. Something leaked out of these walls, or the echoes reverberated more powerfully than elsewhere, built up from association. She was, at bottom, what Muriel was, a faithless wife thinking of asking a wholly innocent husband for a divorce, injurious to those around her and contravening motherhood. She was no better than the worst.

"Isn't it disgraceful about the miners?"

Leonie met her sister-in-law sooner than she'd intended. She bumped into her at the bottom of the Mound, each shopping and they headed towards the sedateness of Jenners' tea room.

Leonie was so withdrawn from Alison's mental ambit that she foolishly thought the question related to minors and wondered what law relating to under-age drinking or work hours was coming up for review. "What about minors?"

"The Scottish Secretary announcing the closure of three more pits."

"Ah."

"I mean . . . "

They circulated slowly round the self-service counter. Tuesday at three wasn't deserted. The room was full of women, indeed Edinburgh was full of women in the afternoon, women who didn't work and didn't need to, the beneficiaries of professionalism. So many women of a certain age! Widows on protected pensions, mothers of children at the fee-paying schools, grandmothers of distinction who contrived amongst themselves to keep the hat in fashion – surely a greater array of bonnetry than anywhere else in Britain. Velvet mob cap, raffish velour, tartan toorie all subscribed

394

to warmth. They were so silent. Fifty women humming quietly together like tops. 'No, I don't think I will dear. I'll just have the scone,' like an incantation of assent over the tea cups. The English were shrill with their concerns, assuming every train passenger or diner in the restaurant wanted to overhear their business. In this parlour, Alison's voice was the most audible, cutting through blandness like the lemon in Madeira cake.

"This is supposed to be a socialist government and they're wilfully depriving workers of their livelihood."

"Yes, Alison, but—"

"Do you know in the USSR they have an employment register which is computed by usefulness to society? We have one in Britain but of course the Whitehall version is a snob's charter, a professional index of A grade workers made up of doctors, lawyers and top civil servants, and so on down to the blue-collar Cs."

"The theatre must be round about E minus."

"Of course, you can't categorise artists or the intelligentsia. But in Russia, the most socially useful people are ranked as being first the miners because nothing runs without fuel and then the teachers. They've got it right. This is a national disgrace. I mean national. Scotland's being victimised again. More closures last year than in the whole of England and Wales put together."

Leonie did find pause to wonder what a deep-face miner would make of Alison. See her as not very far removed from the behatted ladies sipping tea. Moncrieffe's perennial question had rubbed off on her. 'What can I do?' The is man, not the ought. He detested speechifying without action and Alison's vapidity began to irritate more than it had done before. Much was forgivable in the girl that wasn't in the woman. What did Alison do about anything apart from theorise? "Take it up with your MP."

"Oh that's no earthly good."

"Perhaps somebody's organising a march."

"Yes, we need to raise public consciousness and attract media attention."

"Or you could go over to solid fuel as a token gesture."

Alison was finally silenced drinking, perhaps ideologically, Russian tea. "When do you open?" she asked.

"I'm taking the early flight tomorrow. And it's into dress rehearsal. Critics' night is Thursday."

"Stuart's following something up in London. He may be flying down at the same time as you, though really taking the coach would be more sensible."

"Has he had an offer?"

"I'm not sure. He doesn't like to build up my hopes."

"What will you do with the flat at Grange Loan if he takes up work in London?"

Alison sighed at the disparities of place. "I don't know. We were so stupid to take the flat on. Stuart's – former wife has been so slick. She's got hold of a much more unscrupulous lawyer than ours and of course Stuart has admitted everything about us, so she's suing to retain the house in Perth on the grounds of desertion. He may end up having to pay the mortgage on that too. His finances are in pretty bad shape."

"Have you bought the flat, signed contracts?"

"No, but it's a gentleman's agreement."

"Well, I'd face Muriel's wrath and back out. She'll hardly sue you for not proceeding."

"You never know."

"Muriel can't expect you to raise much of a mortgage surely?"

"My earnings plus Stuart's very erratic income just about cover it. She's wanting a lot, even for a prime-site flat." Prime-site! That was a neat euphemism for attic, adding a thousand to the upset price. "It does seem so unfair. You couldn't lend us something to get started could you, Leonie?"

"Me?" The Petries were an astonishing clan. She didn't know if they were spongers or truly unlucky, never able to pay their way. "I'm trying to run my own show, Alison, and my earnings only just cover the expenses."

Alisons eyes dipped. "Stuart said you won over a thousand pounds last month."

"So I did. And I invested it."

"Oh to have a private bank."

The phrase jarred. 'A private bank account' would have gone unremarked but this was tantamount to banker, the unlicensed source of revenue via Moncrieffe. In fact, he didn't pay for anything, her flight to Inverness and her clothes were out of her own purse, but she did live free at Westminster. There was a hint of menace in the truncation, or was she being unduly sensitive?

"In joint names," Leonie asseverated.

"But which joint names?"

The allegation came close, a fist of threat. Leonie looked up over the rim of her tea-cup, deliberating on what was meant. "Blackmail doesn't become you, Alison."

"Blackmail? What would I have to blackmail you with?"

Leonie looked down the long course of her friendship with this woman, outgrown girl, observing signposts that were landmarks rather than directional. They didn't go together. Travelling over the same terrain, they happened to catch a glimpse of each other now and then but they were never companions except in need. The actress sighed for wasted time in pretending it was otherwise. She wouldn't confide problems to Alison and resented being made confidante to hers. Accidents of place and family threw them together in a simulacrum of compatibility, a mini-marriage that had developed rifts under stress. No need whatsoever to continue with it if it failed to please so, anticipating the ultimate divergence of their interests, Leonie got up and walked away.

41

Black Rod had struck the barred doors to the House three times and gained admittance. Behind him, as he went stockinged up the aisle, came the line of MPs. It was almost a full attendance. The galleries of the chamber of the Upper House were ringed with visitors, the two sides packed from one tier of benches to the next, commoners, Lords in scarlet and ermine with the Law Lords taking precedence in the body of the floor, Charlie corpulent amongst the rest. At the end of October, the lights hung low over the assembly which was an amalgam of politics, ceremony, religious dedication and pure theatricality. It was a darkroom clipping from a forgotten history film, sumptuous in detail, perfectly managed but one whose interest was mainly archival.

The dais was prepared with the attendants of regalia, and Her Majesty, dressed in the robes of state, flanked by consort, other members of the royal household and her ladies-in-waiting, began to read the speech from the throne. The ritual might have become stultifying or unreal, done for effect. The cameras did roll, microphones discreetly dangling overhead picked up the script, the audience in the chamber and the country waited for the delivery. It was saved from the accusation of sham by two forms of realism. It had evolved. Each of the conditions of ceremonial, like orb and sceptre and anointing ampulla, had a special significance in the compromise between monarch and people, sovereignty and individuality so that Moncrieffe felt himself to be privileged to witness the event. History made could be as compelling as history in the making.

The queen's speech was not Her Majesty's. That was one of the more intriguing constitutional devices. They were the words of the Cabinet Office officials that filtered out into the chamber, outlining the government's programme for the coming year. The repeated 'Let us' and 'Let us not' of Parliamentary debating style took on the tone of Biblical peroration, as if Moses had temporarily descended with a new fistful of tabernacles from the Mount, invoking the saving dispensations of socialism, DV. Deo volente, though Parliament willing was a stricter authorisation still. The packed chamber strained to catch the drift. Fleming had suffered yet another reversal in the long recess. A Yorkshire member had resigned for reasons of ill-health, reducing his majority to five. The Prime Minister's freedom to manoeuvre became more and more restricted. The by-election in November was no foregone conclusion. Two Labour candidates appeared representing moderate and extreme left-wing tendencies so even the selection process was an election in miniature. Against such pressure, Fleming had shown a wise expediency in an agenda that was socialist but not outrageously so. Neither his critics nor his advocates could reasonably berate him, though they probably would do so all the same.

As he listened, Moncrieffe's eye wandered off into the roof beams of the building, while he assimilated the political theorem indirectly. The outline of the schedule and this moment in chapel-like surroundings reminded him of the start of a new academic year, at school or Oxford. A curriculum had been planned by someone else which it was his task to follow through in practice. He broke it down mentally into units. Half a dozen major pieces of legislation including improved social benefits and an altered structure of maternity payments. He decoded the phrases into bills, reports, committees and he could anticipate, even before the first drafting, where the problems would lie and how they ought to be resolved. Law was a foolproof form of words and it gave him pleasure to cogitate on how to bind language fast from loopholes. He admired the legislative process and how all the pressure groups and factions and vested interests contributed to that final dictum 'La reine le veult', and were in turn controlled by it. It was a feat of logic, addition, subtraction, emendation until the act emerged as a perfect equation of sides, the will of the people and of the government in balance.

Charlie had told no more than the truth. He was a skilled legislator. He'd never practised law but his father's trade devolved on him as a ready rule of thumb. He knew how it would work, how one test case could find the flaw in the wording, conclusion not fit premise. At the same time, he wasn't a perfectionist like some legalistic MPs, squeezing the life out of a bill until it was defunct or ran out of Parliamentary time, guillotined to death. The thing was, and it was perhaps shocking to think it, profane even in this setting, he didn't greatly care what the law contained as long as it was good law.

Was that a heresy? Maybe, but one that could only be thought with impunity in the Palace of Westminster while the words of Her Majesty's cabinet went on being intoned against the eternal backdrop, like organ notes. Monarchs came and went, outlasting most political careers, but here, the best part of a thousand years on, the unwritten constitution prevailed. Whatever was categorised in law could be taken off the statute book this year, or next, but some essence remained undefined. The law and government and Parliament were an ongoing hybridisation. In each mutation, something of the best was retained. That no administration was likely to be entirely corrupt was manifest and a source of consolation for someone who sought to improve. That was his credo; the instinct to improve, not implying that all precedent or outdated statutes were wrong. Simply that they could be better.

In spite of that open attitude or absence of dogma, his own freedom to manoeuvre was as inhibited as Fleming's. He was mindful of Charlie's advice. Time to join. Time to belong. There were periods when his wilful abstention from a decision could be read as irresponsible, like being a conscientious objector in time of war or when national security was threatened. There was a constitutional crisis in Britain, silent and unadmitted, the crisis of default when the present state of things was unsatisfactory to the electorate. During the lifetime of this Parliament, maybe during the current session, he ought to come off that excruciatingly uncomfortable fence. He listened, testing not only the feasibility of this programme but his desire to back it whole-heartedly. Difficult when, to the rational mind, all verbal statements were half-truths. It was an acknowledgement of the alternative point of view that made them whole.

The year ahead was mapped out professionally but, like a rock cave suddenly enlarging into a chute, it illuminated the path by which he'd travelled in the dark. It was one year to the day since the general election. For a moment, he recreated the elation of that victory, empty because it wasn't shared. That was the largest change. This evening he would go back to the flat and Leonie would come in by midnight, prolonging the day's event. To some extent, he lived experience in double for her benefit, recording as he went along so that he could tell her how the Lord Chancellor nodded off, his wig askew, that Cadogan looked more ursine every year, growling at being brought down by a meagre six pups, and what the queen's dress was made of, cloth of gold. She sharpened in absentia his responses.

The talk in Annie's Bar afterwards wasn't confined to Westminster.

"So," said the government chief whip to Moncrieffe as he threaded his way across the crowded lounge, "the Irish have done what you've always wanted."

"Eire's got a marginally closer result than yours last year, I will admit."

The whips on both sides detested the Independent as one who lay outside their power, reducing it. "Proportional representation isn't proving to be much of a solution over the water. They've got another stalemate in Dublin." Fine Gael was three short of overall majority over Fianna Fáil. "It'll mean the leader buying up votes with some seedy bribe or other and weakening his economic package. God knows, Eire needs a firm hand."

Watson smiled. The chief whip imagined himself omniscient in the corridors, but his Prime Minister was rather more knowing. The offer of a post to the Independent to join ranks was obviously closet and Moncrieffe had the fleeting desire to say so and breach the unofficial secrets act. It was having nothing to do with touts and totters like this man that kept him out of party politics.

"You shouldn't be so holier than thou. You've got a hung Parliament now, as near as dammit, under the first-past-the-post system. And you needn't tell me Fleming isn't doing a bit of insider dealing with the Liberals and Nationalists. He wouldn't have survived a year without it, not with your unruly back-benchers. The difference is, the Irish will do their trading in the open."

"No insider dealing," protested the Labour man.

"Ignorance is bliss in your case, but not good management policy."

The whip faltered. Fleming had a sneak strain. He was a man who thrived on cabals and it was true, his most devout followers didn't know how he was manipulating them.

Laidlaw and Quercus rescued him, concerned not so much with Dublin or Westminster as with their own constituency imbalances. They stood talking to John Prosser, the chief political correspondent on one of the quality Scottish dailies.

"An election before the year's out," was his forecast.

"Cadogan back again?" groaned the Liberal.

"No. Fleming will increase his majority."

"The polls don't favour that result."

"The polls," sneered the newspaperman. "The polls were nearly ten per cent wrong in Ireland. When the situation's volatile they can't predict any more accurately than straws."

They liked Prosser, hard-headed in spite of being hard-drinking, and trusted him which was better still and were inclined to believe his soundings. It was a two-way interchange. He relayed opinion in return for usable facts on the tacit assumption that neither would be ascribed to source. More than once Moncrieffe had turned to Prosser and asked, 'What's the feeling about this down the line?' and acted on his advice. Like himself, the newspaperman had no political allegiance beyond a desire for fair play, or a good story to fill his bi-weekly article. His main problem was parochial; the MPs of the city where he was based wanted to see themselves represented glowingly in his columns. Why didn't you report my speech? was a complaint he frequently had to field. Because it was a boring speech, Prosser would reply, and I don't have a licence to bore my readers. The MPs' version was different. Prosser had turned Tory since he went to live in the south and couldn't understand the views of a Scottish Labour stronghold any more. Power corrupted.

"I was reading about a new system of armchair voting," said Laidlaw, who lived in hope of enforcing turnout to the ballot box, endorsed by a fine. "You press buttons on your television set like a cashpoint card that validate your polling number and then register your preference."

"It'll be the end of my claim to fame if it comes," said Prosser the cynic. "I was going to set up a party of my own. The spoiled ballot paper party. The last count I was at the returning officer spent an hour deciphering which box the cross fell closest to, with a ruler! There were more spoils than votes for one candidate. I thought, hey, there's glory in this."

"I once saw a local election where there was a dead tie, decided on the toss of a coin."

"Fair dos," considered Prosser. "Good as anything."

"The television remote control would be a good pollster," said Quercus. "Accurate. Though I am frankly sick of polls. I could hold twenty today and come up with a different message every time."

"Swingometer and clapometer in one," said Moncrieffe. "Why not? The television set has taken over in elections. It's the medium for informing and wooing the voters, so it might as well count them too."

The men often played political tomfoolery.

"Did you have a good summer?" the Conservative asked Moncrieffe. "You've a good tan anyway. Often the same thing."

"They tell me," said Prosser, interrupting, "that sea water is better than loch water for promoting one."

The remark meant nothing to the other politicians but Moncrieffe was dumbfounded. Was it a good guess or based on some second hand knowledge? A leak, a leak, his instinct cried. Had someone really seen him in the burn above Carse, for that swim with Leonie was the only dip he'd taken in the summer. How the hell . . . He was as shocked as if the man had whipped a sneak photograph out of his notebook, taken through telescopic lens, and confronted him with the court-acceptable evidence.

"But so much more unpleasant to drink," was his thin defence.

Prosser was well intentioned. He didn't mean to pry and the words were intended as a warning. The politician felt the hair rise along the back of his neck, the stag's response to the clink of a gun or a scent carried down wind. Danger. The pack was onto him.

Moncrieffe left the bar early. He had a meeting to go to that evening at the Electoral Reform Society and took a taxi south of the river to its headquarters. Twenty men met in the first floor library, all known to him because they lectured on electoral reform and kept up a network of association with each other. They were much more commanding experts on the subject than he was – men who could tell you without notes which returning system was used in each of the world's democracies. Some could even give you verbatim the results of the latest general election throughout Europe, party by party, a felicity with numbers Moncrieffe found verged on the prodigious.

Their business that evening was to select a panel to go as observers to East Africa. A former British protectorate was holding its first democratic election and invited international inspectors to ensure correct procedures were applied. Moncrieffe had been a member of one such party to the Far East, when ballot boxes went mysteriously missing, voters in the villages they had just left were bribed or threatened, and the corrupt government was returned with a whacking majority. They still called themselves a democracy and one bout of cynicism was enough for Moncrieffe. He wouldn't go to Africa.

They sat round the vast committee table where the counting of votes was carried out for the trade and professional unions who engaged the society to oversee elections and count their referenda. The room pleased him, like a reliquary to an ideal. The walls were lined with bookshelves, a word which didn't give an accurate impression because it implied uniformity or system. Here there were roughly carpentered shelves in amongst cabinet made cases, different heights, different woods, but every inch was loaded with documentation. Some of it was a hundred years old, historical papers on the foundation of the society and its pattern of development, more successful abroad than at home. It had spawned a dozen daughter societies world-wide. Rickety, priceless, archetypal institution.

His eye roved along the uneven shelves, box files and large brown paper envelopes mixed in with leather-bound volumes. What a mess. He donated five hundred pounds anonymously each year to the society's funds but it didn't go far. At the foot of the stairs was a box of incoming mail, again box a misnomer. Metal crates, six by six, stacked with unopened envelopes. A thousand packages waiting their own documentation through the meticulous but undermanned filtration systems of the society. It reminded him of one of those arithmetical problems – if a tank of water empties at such and such a rate and is simultaneously filled from above at a differing one, how long before it runs dry? Or floods? It made him itch to help speed the process. He'd spent some time rooting among these archives for material to use in his own lectures and came across interesting snippets, not least the men who'd believed PR was preferable to other forms of computation. George Bernard Shaw and H.G. Wells and most astonishingly Lewis Carroll who, in his other life as Charles Dodgson, wrote an erudite and reasoned pamphlet on the mathematical validity of PR in 1884.

The inequities of the first-past-the-post system had been obvious a century before.

> *The injustice of this method may be illustrated from two points of view.*
> *Suppose a bare majority of Electors to be of one party and the rest of the opposite party; eg let 6-11ths be 'red' and 5-11ths be 'blue'. Then as a matter of abstract justice, about 6-11ths of the House ought to be 'red' and 5-11ths 'blue'. But practically this would have no chance of occurring: if the 'reds' and 'blues' were evenly distributed throughout the Kingdom, a 'red' would be returned in every District and the whole House would be of one party! Yet this distribution is, by the Laws of Probability, more likely than any other one distribution, and, the nearer the distribution to the most probable one, the nearer we come to this monstrous injustice.*

The man spoke of the nineteenth-century two-party system, Liberal versus Tory. The inequalities were even greater with three.

Prompted by this find, Moncrieffe had gone away and re-read *Alice in Wonderland* and was convinced it was an allegorical account of the newcomer's arrival at Westminster where Red and White Queens battled with ill-disguised savagery and the menagerie of mad animal and human composites was familiar in type. He knew several Mad Hatters in the House, and not a few dormice. 'Off with his head' was the traditional Parliamentary answer to opposition, elided into 'heads will roll' as threatened therapy. Had anyone analysed *Alice* as a contemporary social satire, much like *Gulliver's Travels*, purveyed to children but cryptically adult in intent? He sensed an essay in the making and docketed it under 'Future projects'. The academic life made its appeal against the brutish conflicts of the House. A donnish seclusion, steeped in papers, the most dramatic event of the day the arrival of the morning post. He fitted himself against the silhouette of scholar and found they didn't match. He was more of a White Rabbit, rushing never to arrive.

The day that had begun passively in the past tense turned with nightfall into the aggressive, turmoil-ridden present. His encounter with the Labour whip and the lobby correspondent read as a bad prognosis for the current session. No star-gazer, his profession nevertheless trained him to give due weight to mood and signs. The polls for the career of Moncrieffe took a downward turn. The political squeeze was on him. Each time he went into the division lobby, six hundred pairs of eyes wondered why he chose that door. Prosser confirmed the personal pressure. His activities had been noted and would be used against him by his enemies.

He moved and seconded but his mind was a mile from the agenda on the table.

42

The new term inaugurated a different mood at the Hermitage as decisively as it did at Westminster. Irene's first session as minder to her neighbour's house and child was carried on in the early summer, and had been as light-hearted as the weather and exploratory of a new and burgeoning self. Autumn sealed that growth. Hope and change hardened into permanence, like established wood.

The woman shed one part of herself when she walked out of her marital home; took up another in the adjacent house, more demanding, varied, urgent and maybe personal. One relationship was set, wife and mother, requiring no further adjustments. Fergus didn't make her feel so matronly. Mutual need pulled them into a proximity that was practical as much as intellectual but gradually spread into her emotional life so that she couldn't imagine a return to the cloistered, undiverting world of home.

She tended Fergus' house with care, admiring its stern bleakness. Her own house was padded with much materialism and flowered like the garden, in riots of chintz and Wilton colour that weren't always harmonious. Fergus carried the solemnity of his own garden indoors, non-floral, emphasising structure and texture before more obvious attractions. It was ascetic in the extreme, with wooden furniture preferred before upholstery and a deal of grey, the perfect interior of Scottish and baronial. Fergus put it together not by selection but by accident although everything that passed through the process of his choice was minimal and quiet, so that the effect of the house was a display of dried grasses picked from the hills, bleached, subdued but repeatedly fascinating and restful because preserved life was a final inversion of the green and seasonal one.

Being often in one place carried its responsibilities. About eleven o'clock one weekday morning, Irene answered the doorbell at Fergus' house, rummaging in her head for who it might be at this hour as she went.

"Mrs Petrie?" asked a man who'd parked his car, an electric-blue sports model, across the entrance to the drive effectively blocking it. She bridled at the rudeness which implied she might have tried to make a hasty exodus, and was a mental vulgarism.

"No. Mrs Petrie doesn't live here any more," she said, thinking he must mean Muriel when she instinctively omitted Leonie. She had intended to point to the enamelled sign on the gates that read 'No hawkers, no circulars', because he looked that type, a travelling salesman for polish or maybe more up-market, for encyclopaedias, but his use of the family name stopped her. For all she knew, his business might be prearranged.

"Who are *you* then?"

"Not Mrs Petrie, at any rate." Automatically, she closed the door a fraction, then remembered that Andrew was asleep in his pram a yard or two from the porch. She couldn't be completely dismissive with the man because his manner was harshly brusque and intimidating. He was heavy-jowled, shaved but rough around the eyes as if he hadn't seen the inside of his bed last night. She didn't trust him, kidnapper, housebreaker, anything.

"Does Haz Petrie live here?"

"Harris Petrie." The alteration gave it away and Irene could have bitten her tongue. She'd never get rid of him now. Her brain started to race in self-justification. A browse through the telephone directory would confirm this was a Petrie household or he could have consulted other neighbours or shopkeepers for directions. Why should she lie anyway to cover up? The stranger's errand mixed with his pushy manner, making him unacceptable. Her eye dropped on reflex to the ground to see if he'd wedged his foot in the doorway. What if she had to phone the police to get rid of him? How to snatch the baby and come indoors again without letting the caller in? Maybe she should leave the house open and run round to her own. People safe before property. Let him take what he wanted as long as he didn't harm that child. Mad solutions pounded.

"Yes. Harris Petrie."

"No. This isn't his house."

"This is the address he gives."

"That may be." A decade of awkward bell-ringers for the local councillor should have taught her to give nothing away.

"Well, you know him, don't you?" said the man heavily, tired of argy-bargy. "Do you know where I can get hold of him?"

"Not at this moment."

"Look, lady, he owes us money and we've come to get it. This is where he lives. He knows who we are and he knows how much he owes us. Tell him we're coming back to call on him every day until he stumps up. Every day we'll be here. Tell him that. Tell him his number's up."

The repeated words of he and we sounded confrontational, a linguistic battle in which the woman was caught up involuntarily.

Once or twice in her life Irene had been physically threatened. Walking home from school when she was a girl, fifteen or so, a lout had come towards her down an empty street, clanking in hobnailed boots. He looked dangerous. On an impulse, she started to cross over the road before they passed when, two feet away from her and for no good reason, he suddenly kicked out at her with unbelievable venom. Seven o'clock on a Tuesday evening coming home from the Literary and Debating Society. The blow on her shin would have broken it, if it had landed. She walked on, steeling herself to calmness.

Her heart seized now in the same way, with inarticulate fear.

"No offence, but you tell him we're on his tail."

The accent lingered malevolently like bad breath. An impression of a ragged fingernail stabbing the outer door repeatedly to underscore his message.

When he went, Irene ran outside and lifted the child out of the pram, holding him too close until he fought her off, startled out of his sleep, and yelled. She wanted to pick him up and run before the coming storm.

Fergus listened attentively to her account.

"I'm sorry you've had that unpleasantness, Irene. I'll speak to Harris when I see him, though I haven't seen much of him recently." He pulled out a notepad and made jottings. Exact time, date, résumé of the conversation, man's appearance like the report of an incident in a police officer's notebook, eye witness valid. "And nothing to indicate who he was?"

"If I'd had my wits about me, I'd have taken the number of his car. But I didn't."

409

"You did well as it was."

The praise sufficed and calmed the palpitations that broke out whenever she thought of the episode as if she were the wrongdoer.

"We can't have this sort of thing, though, can we? Harris will have to go."

"Where can be go now?" Irene worried in case she was responsible for ousting him from his last shelter.

"Alison could have him now that Ainslie's domiciled down south."

"They don't really get on." The phrase, relating to the siblings, reverberated against the lovers.

"That's not our concern, is it?"

She admired the circumspect phrase, unwilling to partake in gossip, but thought he might also mean Harris' welfare wasn't their business. And there she differed. She was the habitual good shepherd, saviour of prodigal sons – did not remind Matthew that his own debt was due for repayment – and quiet pacifier.

"I would like to see Harris settled."

"So would I and settling his debts comes first."

She rose ahead of disagreements. The professor would be home. Her own allocations became complex in time and duty. "Till tomorrow," was promissory.

Fergus tore the top sheet off the notepad and opened a drawer of his desk to file the document. He picked up an account book that was lying there and flicked over several pages until he came to a sheet with a list of entries which he'd headed *Harris Petrie*. He had written down the five hundred pounds he'd lent his brother then a weekly sum for board and lodging, immaculately drawn up with dates, as well as other small lendings. These sums were ratified with the initials HP, perhaps ironically, and formed an effective register of debt. Maybe five thousand pounds in total and not a penny entered in the credit column. Nor was that all. The details of the missing stamp sheet were entered elsewhere, an illicit abstraction.

How was he going to recover the debt if other people had started to hound Harris too? This IOU probably wasn't worth the paper it was written on. How could he bring pressure to bear for payment of his debt first, a creditor anxious to move to the head of the queue in what looked like imminent insolvency. He could resort to threats, eviction, withdrawal of good will – Muriel tactics. If only he'd taken banking precautions and obtained a guarantor against the debt. Bad money – oh bad money.

Harris counted the steps beside the National Gallery as he went down them towards Princes Street. He'd been helping at an audit for one of the firm's clients and he decided to walk down from their office, thinking he wasn't getting enough exercise these days.

It was after sunset at the end of October, a chill, windswept season. The clocks had changed over to winter time and the nights drew in with a closeting suddenness, a squeeze on liberal and expansive summer. Princes Street was lit along the shopping side in a festoon of bulbs that neither drew nor jollied him, as they broke the flat glass frontages with the luminous allure of purchase. He couldn't remember when he'd last been inside a shop, couldn't think at this moment what he'd bought most recently. Money was for other things than spending on consumer durables.

He hurried on. A drink after work with Matthew Geddes in a Rose Street pub, back to the house hoping Fergus had made something to eat and a rest before going on to The Lantern. His priorities stacked themselves in a deck, dealt in order.

"It's your round," said Matthew. "I'm broke."

Harris played a game with his pockets, patting one after another until he found some small change and counted it out laboriously, to unimpress. It didn't do to go flashing rolls of notes around. "That'll just about stretch to a tot each and that's your lot." He was generous with Matthew.

"How was your audit?"

"Oh, the senior accountant did most of the donkey work. I made notes and the tea."

"Mine was heavy going. They're installing a computer and I had to run a check on their system. They buy the hardware without training the personnel properly. The chap who's handling the installation is machine-illiterate. I had to go back to first principles. It's a shame Fergus isn't into the commercial thing. He could make a fortune."

"And legitimately too."

The word struck an odd note. Matthew, finding the brandy he

had drunk warming, dug into the recesses of his wallet and found the last fiver, buying them two doubles. By rights, Jenny should have had it but that was tomorrow's problem. Passing back from the mirrored, Dickensian refurbished bar, Matthew noticed that his hair was thinning miserably. His father had such a vigorous head of hair too. By the same age, he'd be bald.

"I've had enough," he said when he came back to his seat, instantly maudlin on an empty stomach.

"I know," Harris agreed, "it's the slog."

"Companies that couldn't carry on without us, and are making millions in investments, pay us a pittance. Do you know what I took home last month?"

"More than me," specified Harris.

"Yes but you live for nix. I'm paying for a mortgage and wife and child."

"You had a thousand at the beginning of August from that trip I made to London."

"All gone." The glass emptied dismally.

"Here, have another," said Harris, suddenly relenting on austerity. The truth was, he hadn't given Matthew an equal cut of the winnings from Park Lane and suffered a momentary pang. He brought back two more single brandies.

"What I don't understand is how Fergus gets ahead. Two years ago he started out with nothing. He should have been grinding like us."

"Ah, he's had the breaks."

"We've never had the breaks."

"No. That's very true. We've had bad luck."

The mood of self-pitying indulgence lasted for an hour until Matthew recalled his family and a long drive out to Balerno and left, listing.

Harris drank alone, disappointed in alcohol and towards eight thought he'd become bored with the people in the bar who were unsmart, unwitty, unrich. He recollected that he'd left his car at the top of the Mound and cursed at the long uphill walk he'd let himself in for. Getting to his feet, he stubbed his foot on something hard and realised that Matthew had been witless enough to leave his briefcase on the pub floor. Matthew tended to treat the office documents as classified files and wouldn't leave them in his car

412

where they were vulnerable to theft. Harris saw he'd have to lug it all the way up the Mound steps, against the pull of gravity.

He'd forgotten the total he'd arrived at on the way down and started counting again as he climbed. His ambitions ran parallel. If he took a chance on everything he owned, he could double it in a night or even treble it and not only clear his backlog of outstanding repayments but have enough to set himself up somewhere, a house, a business of his own, go abroad or emigrate, start again with a clean slate escalating rapidly out of this suburban mediocrity.

The high proof of alcohol didn't elate as much as it clarified, reducing the peripheral clutter of immediate concerns. He didn't think his gambling was a problem, or immoral, or any of that Gamblers' Anonymous twaddle. It was a skill he possessed. He found it easy to remember sequential patterning and was able to take risks. That was all it was. And gambling was an instinct. Everybody did it sometime, buy a raffle ticket, invest in government bonds, take a share in the office sweepstake for the Grand National – it was all chance, the thrilling stuff of speculation. Why, you could get odds on everything from a world-class fight to the names of the next royal baby. Everybody had a flutter. It wasn't like backing the blood sports, cock-fighting or badger-baiting, watching animals gouge each other to death for fun. Not a vice. Rolling numbers was harmless stuff, nothing other than a short cut from the tedium of employment. Once he'd got a start, he'd work hard enough at his own business but working for the bosses was a bore. He just needed some capital to float him.

He got to twenty-six and realised he was short of breath.

So with his debts. It wasn't a crime to borrow. All the people who were stupid enough to lend him money could afford it. He only borrowed when there was something to spare, a temporary transfer from one account to another. It wasn't like stealing. He'd pay everyone back eventually. The trouble was, he was suffering from a financial embarrassment whereby the money he had in his pocket at that moment was all he had. Lost on a week's bad results and nothing to get ahead on. He'd run out of the usual creditors. The bank withdrew his cheque book. The credit and charge companies closed his accounts. There were no more lenders. What he needed was a windfall. He'd make good use of that.

413

The word windfall made him chill, a gust sweeping across the unprotected space of Princes Street Gardens. Spires and pinnacles and historic battlements ringed him round but afforded precious little shelter as the wind swept down from the Forth, salt and smarting in the eye. This city wasn't built to face the climate, too high, too open, streets funnelling the draught like flues.

He remembered that when he and Fergus played competition tennis at Mortonhall as teenagers, and they were an invincible doubles partnership, right- and left-handed, Fergus used to take the long route home by the pavement and in at the main gate. Perfectly correct. Harris knew a shorter path, through the fencing of the Hermitage and along the ridge of the bank until he reached the back gate to the garden. At a walking pace, and they'd taken the trouble to time it, he could be home two minutes earlier than his brother. Why wouldn't Fergus come his way? It involved two small infringements of by-law. The park was closed at sunset. To enter after hours – and dozens of children as well as lovers did it – you needed to squeeze through the metal railings. Harris wouldn't have bent the posts himself but he would take advantage of a loophole made by someone else. You had to go past the lodge where the gatekeeper lived, and he could come out and warn you off at any time. Harris enjoyed the dodge.

The briefcase made him pant. He reached forty-three but couldn't remember if it was really thirty-four. He gave up counting. What was in it anyway? Lead piping? He stopped for a respite and opened up the compartments, thinking Matthew would flip if he could see him rooting in the official papers. They seemed to be documents relating to the new computer system. He spun through figures. A list of codes it seemed to be, numerical codes and Harris immediately realised this was the windfall. Account numbers and computer data for the firm's files and customer deposits. Top security. He looked up to the mediaeval turrets of the stalwart castle and pressed on.

Fergus went to put the cash book back in the drawer and then suddenly remembered that he had entered another debit in the accounts and started to look for it. It was the photograph of Leonie and Moncrieffe which he kept clipped in the back for future settlement. He searched the book in vain. He searched the drawer.

Omission reinforced the certainty of his missing sheet of stamps. It had gone forever and someone had stolen it.

Well, well. He sat back, folded in meditation. Who had removed it? Of those who had access to his papers in the last few months, he immediately exonerated Ellice and Irene and Michael and Stuart. He separated likely from impossible with ease. They had no motive. That left him with Harris, Alison or Leonie herself. Which of these was likely to poke about his study in his absence? He sifted probabilities but found he came up against a serious blockage, the nature of their character which impinged on the hypothetical. What *might* they do unbeknown to him? He felt that its disappearance was in some way connected with its arrival and was equally ominous. Someone meant him no good but pinning this intent onto one out of the three was hard. Not Leonie surely, his own wife, although she had most reason for destroying the evidence against herself, which confirmed its status as just that. The strangeness of her recent behaviour should prepare him for anything, eighteen months married and six of them down south until she was wholly alienated. Even her body changed, not pliant but merely accommodating, and streaked with an unpremeditated colouring, borrowed from awayness and adopted parts. The house consolidated, his career and their child grew in stature, but Leonie was an outsider, not much different from the hostile caller at his door that morning, shattering composure.

Was he moved? Did it hurt? He looked down at himself sitting in the chair, regular, controlled, the person others called reliable or dependable and yet he knew he was more complex than those bland and faded epithets. He held out his right hand and saw it steady and untrembling. Good, but his heart rate had pumped up with the discovery of the theft, which threatened the security of his household. He was moved. It did hurt, but he wouldn't demonstrate. Would he be more effective if he behaved differently, smashed and shouted the way his parents had done, even his mild-mannered father driven to the unseemly by provocation. No, his brain and his willpower controlled the nervous system, halting the shaking that he felt. Mind mattered.

He put the book away and turned to a small practical detail that had arisen in regard to Leonie which he wanted to finalise. The annual Register of Electors had arrived and under the heading of

415

persons resident at this address and entitled to vote in the constituency he had entered his own name but hesitated over hers. Perhaps it would be wiser if she applied for a postal vote, as for one often absent on business. He checked the dates to make sure this delay in consulting her didn't endanger his own franchise and thought he'd pen her a note, 'Do you vote here or do you vote in London?' Then he realised he didn't know her address, whether home or theatre, and was debarred from making contact.

43

Stuart Ainslie switched on the reading lamp over his desk and wrote under a heading of that day's date:

Tonight I went to see Leonie in *Macbeth*. I didn't want to be impressed on rather peevish grounds, because I hadn't directed the play myself, and even objectively I found a dozen faults in Alan Mills' production. He went for naturalism or realism, lots of raw brown rocks and castle walls and trumpets and so on. Stage Scottish baronial, a cliché and phoney because you know perfectly well the ramparts are only hardboard thick. I see the play as a piece of hammered silver, a Celtic brooch of intertwined motifs with the serpent of ambition devouring itself and so would have envisaged it as a more metaphysical winding round of power and guilt. The man has no eye. I thought his production was leaden, but part of this is because we hate the shape of someone else's imagination. I make a pact with my vanity and say his was a worthy if pedestrian version, though I would have done it better.

Despite the hoo-ha Leonie raises, and she is an immensely watchable figure on the stage, flickering before your eyes, I've always had my reservations about her development into a major classical actress. She's got the technique off pat, a highly distinctive voice, an ability to respond to the rest of the cast and this odd, troubling physicality that is febrile and makes the air vibrate. A travelling eye and spindle thin. Nothing to do with her looks, but there's no doubt she generates a high level of tension on the stage, which is a direct impact with the set and the audience, the real and three-dimensional space. She manages to draw power to herself, like a nucleus to protons, dragging something out of the air. She sees little things as big and big things as a blur which disturbs our own visual perception. When she strikes across a stage, she gives the impression that she may end up in the wrong corner. This assists the frisson of reality in her gestures, as if she lands in that

417

spot by accident, impromptu with the move as well as the word, keeping the whole thing on a nervous boil.

But, she didn't seem to suffer enough, acted with her head and not her heart. Was still playing at playing. Held back from total involvement. And I half suspected that by the time she'd reached the right level emotionally, she'd be too mature physically. I've said this to her more than once. That's her attitude to the profession. You can tell her the truth, straight up and she pays heed to it. I know I'm excessively critical of her because she has the most potential and you don't let talent off easily, and neither does she.

So I rolled along to the Old Vic feeling denigratory, not wanting to see success. What impressed me? Leonie and Ken have grown together so that in spite of age discrepancies they made a couple on the stage, splendid yoked. The lines were spoken with clarity and swept down like sword strokes, clean and cleaving. Dazzling stuff, so that at times I wanted to switch off the interfering visuals and concentrate on the text. They created the ideal balance of a duet, operatic, musical, building up vocal tension. Their held moments had a shimmering, the way a musical note sustained for some seconds doesn't end precisely when the singer ends but goes on resonating in the auditorium, swelling not dying and the listener waits for the trail of the diminuendo, and strains more achingly after that than a triumphant crash. Delicate in the extreme. I'm not convinced that this is drama, when one excellence ousts all others . . . but I quibble.

I dislike the role of Lady Macbeth and had thought Leonie might be miscast in it. Nevertheless she seized the part with fearlessness. She established the odd duality of that woman, unnatural and absorbing at the same time, the compulsion behind Macbeth as well as his downfall – ambition incarnate – and played her with such controlled power that neither Macbeth nor I knew what we were doing, and panted and expired and obeyed at her command.

I was amazed at the sheer might of what this woman could accomplish saying words. We fail? But screw your courage to the sticking place and we'll not fail. It's sad the great lines become so banal as to be unsayable. Leonie managed to give these a new twist. Every word of that was loaded with married innuendo. I swear I never noticed it before. I and the audience gasped to a man. The gesture that accompanied the line was explicit on metaphoric courage, grabbing if you knew. If you didn't, it passed as emphasis. It was a blow to the solar plexus that was uncomfortable, rude and exhilarating together. If only she could have put armour on, she'd have gone out and won at Dunsinane, Birnam Wood or not, and I really did want to rewrite the plays of Shakespeare to give the heroines more room.

There were some unexpectedly poignant episodes. The banquet Leonie played not as a harridan, screaming at their lordships to go, but humanely and magisterially to protect her spouse from the imputation of insanity in front of his peers, not shrill but reasoned from the head of the table. I was moved by these unforeseen aspects. The sleep-walking was a painful sight, bare-staged, elemental, nightdress against armour, actually more piteous than Desdemona murdered or Cordelia cast off because the woman has stamina and stature of her own, not a cipher or a simple counter-balance. The two of them played it tenderly and it was one of the most passionate love scenes I've sat through, tipping passion towards its darker elements of death, a harrowing farewell through which they occasionally recognised each other of old and clasped. Her madness somehow seals his fate but also enhances him as a man. Excruciating emotions. I came away with an impression of warmth and closeness the play's never induced in me before.

Yes, I was sitting in the front stalls, horribly conspicuous and after about an hour, I realised that the tears were rolling down my face into my collar, embarrassing my neighbour as much as me. I had to wipe them up, murmuring, 'It's hot' as cover. Why did I weep? I wept for human endeavour because as Leonie gradually turned into the regent, striving upwards and infuriated by middlingness in the people round about her, I located a spot I hadn't recognised before, why she has this powerful drive to succeed, to be unordinary, and that end softened me to her unforgivable means. It is a plea for mediocrity not to be encompassing. The actress made the rôle more sympathetic to me not just because of what she did but because of who she was. I couldn't split them, part and player. She is unstoppable, except by self. I was impressed by the quality of tenacity in the woman I know will go mad with guilt and by self and violent hands, take off her life. I know exactly what will happen and that doesn't matter. It's the happening that counts. I wept for the excellence of the pursuit I admire most. Leonie changed my perceptions of the play, of herself, of what the theatre is and should be, of my own purpose in it. She gave, maybe just on this one evening when I happened to see her, one of the best performances there will be in my lifetime. It put her among the greats. Whatever I thought objectively about the play or her speeches in it, was unimportant because the actual performance elevated them beyond analysis. She took me apart. Whys were temporarily answered. Faith stated, conviction rewarded by a sign. Life was recast. It was one of the moments in which one lives at extremity.

I walk all night, lit with enthusiasm. I walk over the river and watch the boats coming up the Thames with the tide, taking the bridges like lock gates, a hurdle at a time. Not easy when the river's rising and the helmsman must steer under the apex of an arch. The buildings visible from the banks are illuminated, the Tower, St Paul's, the South Bank complex in a thousand-year spectrum of history. Somehow it lives. It lives continuously, pulsing away whereas Edinburgh goes somnolent at six with the populace turning furtive after dark. Work, not pleasure, is the business of the day in the north. I wonder if I have become otiose, besotted with the warm and lazy south. Maybe. But my business *is* pleasure or relaxation. The theatres are more successful than they are elsewhere in Britain. I remember the struggle to fill the Lyceum, the quotidian imbalance between resource and aspiration so huge it became crippling, a debt to art I couldn't cancel. Here, things roll. There's more surplus. I'll keep turning up at the Edinburgh Festival or take the odd group round the Scottish provincial theatres as a sop to heritage, and struggle through *The Warld's End* or *The Thrie Estaites* or *Wallace* dutifully. But I diagnose a retrograde ailment, love of the past, nostalgia for a self-indulgent Scots Wha Hae era that never existed. The kail-yard of the playhouse, narrow, insular, dialectic. It's the Loch Ness myth of popular folklore, endless effort poured into resurrecting a pre-Neolithic monster we wouldn't know what to do about if we found it. Independence, nationalism? There's a laugh. It's a relic that's better buried.

The sad fact is that the theatre becomes the home. I have the wanderlust for good plays. Sitting on a stage with a dozen people and moulding air and space and words into a tangible construction is the most involving activity I know. The normal grates, rough and random compared with the thing you can control and perfect. It's the only form of the body politic, or city living, which I understand. The other day I was walking along the Strand and I heard a familiar voice, an actor I've never directed but would dearly like to. I thought, That sounds like Tom. And Tom it was, blethering aloud on his way to rehearsal. So we stopped and talked for half an hour. I've never run across him in Edinburgh. We drift, disconnected, but I have kept a running check on his career since we last met and he on mine. Between stage people, nothing slips because progress is corporate.

I find myself by Westminster Bridge overlooking Parliament, Big Ben and the Abbey, a cloistered world of mock Gothic which rules us in its own anachronistic way. Leonie and Moncrieffe have gone home by now and standing chilled on the Embankment – it is, after all, four of an autumn morning – I'm full of envy that they're tucked up and tidy while I'm on the prowl. Envy for the ease of their unconvention. Ellice said Leonie and I were fools to get ourselves boxed in with the bourgeoisie but then she's a woman who doesn't need anyone, or any one person in particular. Life's easy without sex. Give her a meeting to attend in a town hall and she's satisfied with haranguing. She can ignore the bourgeoisie because she's eschewed commerce and is brilliantly impractical. What an excuse, eh, to proffer for non-involvement. I can't do it. I can't sew, I can't cook, I can't marry. Leonie and I are either more honest or more ordinary. We try and the blasted bourgeoisie are always there to be a party to negotiation, pulling purse strings, banning nudes, upholding the everlasting standards of the crass.

Dawn was coming up by the time Stuart finished this expurgation and, noticing it, he switched off the redundant lamp. He'd spent all night in his clothes and felt lousy. Was it true your beard grew faster awake than when you were asleep, he wondered, rubbing his chin and going thoughtfully in search of something reviving. The kitchen in this miniature flat in Golders Green was only a step from the drinks cabinet, so water and whisky soon met.

After it, he felt sufficiently fortified to re-read the letter from Alison which had arrived that morning. No, he corrected the time lag. The morning before. He read it very slowly, giving his bloodstream and the pepped-up euphoria of the sleepless night time to fall back to normal levels. A sobering document. It was a peremptory letter the terms of which were, Come back or else. Or else what? Or else she would cease to be what she wasn't anyway. Muriel, he thought ruefully, was better at threatening than her daughter because she attacked in one of two soft spots: pride or the pocket.

He had been in London for a month, chasing leads, and had neither pride nor money left when suddenly two opportunities popped up, not one but two and his problem incongruously was, how to accept them both. He escaped ecstatically into these offers which provided their own exit from pressing realities. Costings touched him only for theatrical budgets. He planned furiously and excitedly for the hypothetical.

Was he a charlatan, he asked himself as he put Alison's querulous letter and his page about *Macbeth* side by side. He'd very much like to fulfil the expectations of the first, which were implicit in a phrase he found awesome, family man, but the demands of the second ruled out simple monogamous happiness. For twenty years women had been offering him terminal relationships without realising he was the last man to be a signatory to convention. Well, he would sign. He would say yes and default again and again on fulfilment. He sighed for his misleading tendencies. The fault lay in the theatre. The only truth he could adhere to was the aesthetic one.

44

Alison and Stuart gave a party at Grange Loan. The reason was openly given as house-warming but Alison privately thought of it as an engagement party since Stuart's decree nisi was formalised and they waited only for a decree absolute to marry; Stuart did too, but his was the engagement to take up a new offer of work in London.

They had moved into the flat but Muriel hadn't entirely moved out. She allowed them the use of her furniture until such time as they could afford their own chairs and beds, to replace her strictly segregated singles. These reliquary job lots added to Stuart's sense of displacement at the Grange, another rented room, another borrowed background. People were his only addition. He brought in large and dramatic people, like screens to hide the walls; Tom who was passing through town, Ken who visited his long-suffering wife, as well as Leonie and Amy Ross for whom no excuse was tendered. But these were regulation dull among a man who wore his cloak indoors, the caber-tossing Cuthbertson who took up too much space, the comedian pair from the King's pantomime and half a dozen others who annotated some part of Stuart's oblique connection with the city. Ellice Barr sat like a Grande Dame of theatre herself, resplendent in silver moiré whereas the three sibling Petries found themselves awed but ill-at-ease among so many buskins. Alison had no friends to speak of.

Sunday evening. Wet. After a while the air became as thick as mulled wine, a four-part brew composed of heat from bodies as well as the log fire which Stuart stoked, the vapour distilled from glasses and furious talk, stirring the cocktail. They opened the windows which only added a fifth element of misty rain like dogmatic sobriety.

Stuart dug himself into a space near Leonie, who came wearing her enhanced reputation. This modified his approach, turning cajolery into deference. "How long is your run?" he asked.

"Eighteen weeks planned, up till the end of January."

"Will they extend?"

"No. Something else is booked to follow on."

"Pity. They could have held that down for a year if they'd had the nerve to go for it."

"*I* couldn't," she said, and in fact the strain of playing at full stretch showed. Fatigue filled spare moments. She aged in experience ahead of time.

"You need a change."

Fergus came past and nodded curtly to the director, circulating as he'd done all day round his wife, moving without speaking, bottled up.

"I wanted to talk to you," said Stuart, turning his back against the hubbub of the room, where voices exploded like firecrackers, to make a quiet corner, "about two offers I've had."

"I thought you'd been secretive in London. Anything exciting?"

"Something good for television, if that's not contradictory. And the chance of a season as co-director at Stratford, Ontario." He gave it out nonchalantly but Leonie couldn't suppress an outburst of joy for him at the prestigious move, international outside national. "Sh. Not so loud. I haven't negotiated final terms yet." The roll of his eye was baleful, encouraging a guess at why.

"You mean you haven't told Alison about it? Well, you're a mutt not to get that over with."

Stuart swivelled his glass, making the liquid come dangerously close to the brim. Behind them, a pocket of silence opened to accommodate Tom, the acknowledged grandee of this evening, who entertained the company to a story about one of his very first Edinburgh Festivals. He had been appearing in a Tyrone Guthrie production and the two men were in a restaurant in Princes Street when the waitress came up to them and asked for Tom's autograph; the stripling play actor just out of his teens, simply because he was a local boy, a nobody compared with the renowned director who was the real star of the Festival. Guthrie had looked away and smiled with the consummate arrogance of the slighted great. Tom gave the hooded profile to perfection.

They laughed, half a dozen of them thinking back over their own favourite encounters with the man when Alison piped up, "Who's Tyrone Guthrie?"

424

The laughter soured. Stuart was aghast. All right, she was the wrong generation and the wrong milieu but surely anyone reasonably informed about the twentieth century had heard of the director? Maybe not, but that aside, he thought her tactlessness in spoiling Tom's anecdote was unforgivable. If he said anything corrective, she would reply. Well, I really did want to know. Why shouldn't I have asked? She was naïve to the point of being offensive and all he could do about it was button his lip. Amy Ross, sidling past her hostess, whispered, "You little dolt," under her breath.

Stuart's eye met Leonie's in collusion. That was exactly why he couldn't confide in Alison. She could neither come with him to Ontario nor easily let him go. "Anyway," he put that problem to one side, "my other proposition could concern you more. It's a six-part serial for Independent Television. It'll have to be made in London later this winter for transmission next autumn. On a big budget. They expect to sell the series abroad. *Anna Karenina*, if you're interested."

The name struck home. "Anna?"

"Seems uncanny, doesn't it, your third suicide in a row."

Uncanny. That was true, the woman wouldn't go away like a shadow she tried repeatedly to slough. "I'm not a television actress."

"Who is? I know we tend to think it's second best, but it would mean a breakthrough for you. A much wider public. Not many people can afford to sneer at that."

She conceded so much. Film often supplemented stage in an ideal balance, carbohydrate to protein in the diet; too much made one puffy. "When do you have to know by?"

"A week at the outside. Tomorrow would be better. The money men wanted an established TV name, so I had to fight for you. There's a queue if you don't want it." He turned round, indicating its tailback.

Division loomed again and blocked out smaller enjoyments. Leonie looked into the throng of the room made up of so many shifting groups. What was her mother saying to the pantomime pair that made them all hoot so irreverently? Fergus, who hadn't wanted to come found himself cornered with Kenneth Frew, agreeably surprised at discourse on phonetics. Alison came and

425

went to the kitchen, uncertain if guests were helping themselves to drinks which was easier or if she was serving them which was more economical, and fussed. An impasse of people. An unmix.

Leonie charted the last year and a half and how similarly her career and Stuart's had evolved, each professional advance matched by a personal regression, and both of them quite incapable of learning from the other's mistakes. You're a mutt not to get that over with. Simplistic remedies for other people's lives were inoperable in one's own. This assembly did represent several advances. Fergus had been drawn into the company of his brother and sister and his mother-in-law as Leonie had always wanted. Surface relations improved. They were speaking to each other but transitorily, in words that didn't build into communication. Fergus' relationships were partial, based on need and even that was seldom mutual. He prowled the room now, disconnected, like a roving conscience and wherever he stood was a point of actual distress in Leonie's eye. She went on dissimulating. Every fortnight she came home, flying up on Sunday morning, back Monday afternoon to keep in touch with Andrew. Pretended to be married. Pretended. The phrase get it over with reverberated with subconscious meanings. She acted the go-between but whether the continuance was brave or craven she couldn't say.

The doorbell rang: before anyone had time to answer it, a knock followed and Stuart hurried along the corridor wondering, Who now? He had scattered invitations freely and was gratified by the response.

This new arrival had not been invited. Muriel stood on his threshold which she still regarded as nominally her own, investing her with right of entry. It didn't occur to her that Stuart might tell her to vamoose, or him either. "A party?" she asked, cocking her head towards the sound.

"Of sorts."

"What are we celebrating? Pay day?"

Her scoffing habitually got the better of the genial man because an adequate riposte demanded lower cunning than he would descend to. He inclined, as with Alison, to give in. He opened the door wider, admitting her. As she passed him, Muriel noticed a mark on the hall carpet, her carpet, and while she didn't want to bend down and exclaim over it in his presence, she brought the toe

426

of her shoe across it and established to her satisfaction that it was a loose piece of dirt and not ingrained. Stuart mentally deducted her levy for wear and tear.

The room, twenty by fifteen, was too preoccupied to notice her although she stood for a long time in the doorway, picking over its occupants one by one. She wore a tweed suit with tippets of mink about the neck in which she thought she was unignorable. The draught, lowering the temperature, alerted Alison to a newcomer but turning round to greet, she reddened and grew flustered. Muriel's head went up in challenge. Why was *I* not invited? was unanswerable. There was Ellice Barr as representative of the older generation not excluded. There were the brothers, also sons. Here were the flotsam from theatricals, preferred above the mother! Such ingratitude. Trumpets and cymbals sounded like a siren.

Stuart's solution was the stiffest drink that would pour into a glass. Passing it over, he drew the interloper towards Cuthbertson who might be able to do something with her and would laugh about it if he couldn't. The move was wise. Circumference impressed Muriel. She grew expansive under the influence of man and liquor.

"I didn't expect to see you here," said Harris glibly to his mother.

"Why not?"

"Ah, well. I came over to see you this morning but you were out." He lied expertly. He never called at Greenbank, but often pretended he had done so when she was out on errands, serving notice of filial duty in absentia. He imagined how she would drive round these streets by the Grange in a reconnoitre, as she did on every evening when she wasn't otherwise engaged, snooping on the visitors his sister had, watching lights and curtains, plotting movements. He remembered when he was quite young being driven along city roads in the dark and asked to spy; whose car is in the drive, what lights are on, lounge, bedroom, none? He hadn't understood at the time, an adult game whose point only became apparent latterly. She was obsessed by rivals, business, amorous, and often got the two entangled. She lived for intrigue.

Fergus on the other hand seethed at her unwarranted appearance when it reminded him of her intrusions at his house and at the funeral. He thought it was deliberate and that someone had tipped his mother off. A resentment began to boil that his peace of mind was continually shattered by these blood-related intruders. He didn't want them. He didn't enjoy their company. He was actually embarrassed by their inanities. He could have spent an evening at home doing something constructive, three hours on the problems of singularity instead of vapid socialising. He moved over the room towards Leonie thinking that by midnight they could decently leave.

Amy Ross was privy to the filming of *Anna Karenina* and unwisely congratulated Leonie in her husband's hearing.

"I haven't accepted it," excused Leonie hurriedly, safeguarding one day's peace.

"You haven't turned it down?" Amy was askance for contrary reasons. The opportunity she might wait a lifetime for, dismissed out of hand!

"No, not that. I simply haven't decided."

Amy was brusque. She'd worked in the shadow of three actresses, wrong place, wrong time, relegated to being their understudy. She prayed for Leonie to retire into provincial or marital obscurity, wished minor accidents or laryngitis on her. Had hoped that the Monday shuttle from Edinburgh to Heathrow would be fogbound so that she could have her chance as Hedda Gabler. Why did Leonie have all the luck while she was left with bit parts like other people's fag ends to pick up. Character actress! She hated the phrase that contradicted the heroine in her nature and soon she'd be too old for anybody's leading lady. "It wouldn't take me long to decide."

Stuart, fearing what might be said in front of Fergus that made positive responses difficult, moved in. "Come on," he said. "Help me get another round of drinks. Alison's not coping. She's spent the last ten minutes polishing that glass instead of putting something in it."

To reinforce the suggestion, the director put his hand into the small of Amy's back and almost without a pause she stepped forward at his touch, synchronised. It was nothing, merely happened and went unobserved except by Leonie who, expert in gesture as well as voice, gave it many interpretations. It was an intimate second, that forward propulsion and gave insights into where Stuart had been secreted during his weeks in London. Amy's bijou flat in Golders Green. It explained why he hesitated over informing Alison about his moves when Amy would be a more companionable asset in Stratford, Ontario and why the other actress had a bitterness in her voice that Leonie, the old friend, was still preferred for the choicest parts over the mistress. Cast on, cast off. The rounds repeated themselves.

Muriel slipped incautiously, skidding on gin.

"We hear a lot about you these days," she said to her daughter-in-law as she intercepted her exit. "Hear more than we see of you."

"I'm flattered that you take notice."

Muriel struggled boozily with what this angular phrasing might mean. She had always ascribed to Leonie the word 'superior' not because she was part of an élite, social, intellectual or even personal. Far from it. Her lowliness, up a stair at Morningside, was a clue to the interpretation of affected or condescending. "It takes us all our time to keep up with your cuttings."

A long file developed in Fergus' head from an incautious opening gambit in which he perceived the eventual dangers.

Leonie thought that anyone who read her clips didn't ostensibly harbour malice and stopped in the middle of saying her goodbyes to look more closely into the woman's intention.

"Quite a little bundle of goodies."

Muriel opened the vaulted black handbag over her arm and produced a newspaper photograph which she passed over to Leonie. It was the more bewildering to its subject in that she hadn't seen this one before, but that was less of a shock than the arrow ending in the exclamation mark in black ink and the words penned in red in a hand she knew as Fergus', 'Received anonymously 15th June'. Muriel managed magnificently to slight everyone concerned while looking, like Alison, quite guileless.

The actress handed it back to source. "A superfluity of captions."

Husband and wife walked back down the slope to Cluny and up again to the Hermitage, passing Blackford Pond. Fergus wouldn't wait for a taxi and so they strode out, their footsteps breaking a brittle post-midnight silence between the high reverberating walls of enclosed gardens. Silence raged between them as each accused the other and justified self. It looked to Leonie as if there had been a conspiracy along the way, Fergus and his mother less likely than

Muriel and Alison, to whom she attributed the original sending of the photograph, a sneak act on which she vented her own guilt. She could place the clip with accurate timing, remembering both that the relationship with Moncrieffe was innocuous at that stage and that Fergus had never mentioned its odd materialisation. Yes, he'd rather think ill of her than ask a direct question. Her husband was unendurably haughty and wouldn't condescend to explain himself.

They'd walked these streets for so long, seven, eight, nine years. The high toll confused. Such a long time since they'd headed back from student functions together. Dances? No, they hadn't danced like other couples. He'd spend an evening in the reading room while she was at rehearsal in Adam House or the Little Theatre or maybe a church hall, then walk her back to Morningside. But en route they had lopsided conversations, telling in turn rather than sharing.

"We should talk, Fergus," she said, dragging the present out of the past.

"There is nothing to talk about. You know your duty."

"We must talk about our marriage."

"There is nothing wrong with my marriage."

They had seldom quarrelled and didn't have the mechanism for airing grievances with each other. Besides, Fergus was impatient with all wordiness. Whenever he said, Oh don't talk about it, it was because he believed nothing was achieved by discussion. He had never changed his mind thanks to the hidden persuaders. Rights and wrongs didn't need justification; they were. So the curt phrase 'You know your duty' was explicit to someone who understood his mind. To acknowledge an idea such as adultery was to make it fact and so he moved away from needless argument, leaving it as a matter for individual conscience.

A car came towards them before they turned out of Cluny Drive and at five hundred yards it made them apprehensive, coming on too fast, too reckless, a souped-up fifties buggy with heavy rear tyres that gave it an unnatural nose dive. It wheeled towards them and as they turned round the corner just in time, there was a tremendous explosion at their feet followed by a shower of liquid. The car drove on. They were spattered up to their knees by something wet and cold. Stunned for the moment, they couldn't

430

work out what had happened but wiped themselves down distastefully. A burst balloon lay on the pavement. The jokesters filled them with tap water, at best, and threw them at the feet of pedestrians. It was a grotesque version of mugging.

The incident repelled but didn't draw its victims closer together. In that mood, wanton malevolence could be read as internal, a retribution she had called down on herself and him by adjunct.

They came up to the house in divergent extremes of mood; for Fergus the Hermitage confirmed arrival and security, its tight walls a retreat. It oppressed Leonie like a haunted house, emblematic of the undead as well as the unfulfilled aspirations that had been theirs at the outset. She went straight upstairs to wash off the nastiness of the evening while Fergus stayed below, talking to Irene. Leonie lay in the bath until it started to grow cold and in bed for longer but her husband didn't hurry to join her.

Alison came sharply into focus, highlighted by Stuart's disaffection, and Leonie recalled the letter sent to Oxford which, with hindsight, contained some of the most sensible things her sister-in-law had ever said. 'This division, of liking someone very much but not being in love with him, caused me much puzzlement and not a little pain. At what point do you say, this has ceased to be rewarding? It is difficult to abandon a relationship that has evolved into mere custom because that can be very comforting and the hardship of making a clean break of it made it seem almost wilful, causing pain for no good cause.' The phrases spanned aeons of development in which she admitted Alison might well be more advanced than herself, twice round the circuit since. It had come for both of them to the point of irretrievable breakdown for which nothing could prepare, not even precedent.

Leonie thought through several solutions, baby-snatching among them, but so many things hadn't been resolved that one cruel kidnapping didn't simplify. What would she do with Andrew in the Westminster flat, provided Watson agreed? Hire a nanny? What did they call these children, tug-of-love, pulled one way then another. Solomon's decree was wiser and prompted hers. She couldn't separate Fergus from his child and deprive him of father, wife and son in one year. Her caring for the child was greater than that, and for the man.

V

45

By nine months Andrew was walking sturdily, put words together in pairs or longer groups to which the definition of sentence couldn't actually be applied, and was capable of complex tasks of recognition by colour or shape. Fergus took him to the Child Development Unit at Moray House where diagnosticians said it was impossible to assess such a young infant but, in comparison with his peers, his intelligence quotient was outside the measurable scale. He was quite likely to be that phenomenal responsibility, the gifted child.

This didn't mean he was either dispassionate or, the curse of cleverness, precocious. He had a warm and loving nature. He kissed freely. Whenever a face was turned to him, father's or mother's, he put his head up and kissed back. They called him the kissing boy but tried not to spoil, him or themselves. Their games were instructional, involving long commands or difficult forms of hide and seek. "Aren't we in danger of making him into one of Pavlov's dogs?" worried Leonie, fascinated nevertheless at how quickly her son memorised a sequence of responses.

"No. It's more than a simple reflex. He's thinking as he goes along. When the circumstances change, his behaviour does too. He can recognise when the ball and the cup are in different positions."

"Do you think he really understands or is he just obeying the tone of our voice?"

They experimented wickedly with the baby's hatred of solitude. Close a door on him and he would yell indignantly, in part, they suspected, because he knew quite well how to open it if only he could reach. Andrew was compulsively human seeking and would spend up to an hour crawling and climbing laboriously round the house looking for them if they hid. They played dead then watched how he plucked at them to get a reaction and wouldn't leave them be until they opened an eye on life. Read a book when they were reading. Picked up a crayon and configurated too. It was a relationship in which they all became children, in sexless, ageless games.

It was the area of calm and so they spent as much time together as they could, which circumvented the awkward one-to-one. Threesomes had their comforts.

When she had gone again, Fergus withdrew into his hermit-like existence. Child devotion, work devotion. Now that he'd transferred to the department of Artificial Intelligence at Forrest Hill, work became more compulsive than ever. It wasn't scheduled like lectures. He had no students and no schemes of work to restrict him. Research was freedom but was also the ultimate commitment. The department offered him several advantages, not least its prestige. Established before the computer era, it had remained free of computing ideologies and snags. It was academic, uniquely among British Universities where the subject was often mixed with practical components. It was a protected department because of its importance to information technology and hadn't suffered the penalising government cuts of other subject areas. It attracted generous donors. Foreign companies gave machines for research while developers, as well as other students, came to visit so that the place was exciting to be in, a hum of activity going in and out. Robotics, photographic units developing recognition by an artificial 'eye', computer terminals with print-outs accumulating on a table, speech synthesisers – the tangibility of evidence pleased after so much mathematical abstraction. Industry and medicine and business organisation needed this cumulative expertise.

Jokingly, the departmental members called themselves the refugees. They took a form of intellectual refuge from related disciplines, mathematics, computing, psychology, philosophy – even the odd geographer came their way – working across the highly defined and dogmatic boundaries of academic study. It was an amalgam of ideas that engrossed him. Any hour of the day or night, there would be somebody at work in the building. Switch on the computer terminal and check who was working from it, never fewer than five simultaneously. Fergus found this twenty-four-hour watch inspirational, a metaphor for the brain that didn't sleep and its inquiry that wasn't satisfied with ready reckoned answers. But refugee camps had one drawback; they were easy to enter and impossible to leave. The men who congregated at Forrest Hill were the intellectual stateless. There was nowhere else to go. The stimulus of their individual projects and each other's company, casual, unsought, along corridors, was an acme of interaction they couldn't do without, a perpetual high all the more powerful to the bloodstream because it was self-administered and invisible, the adrenalin of thought.

Fergus sat at his bench forgetful of time. The department had been given a serial robot by Ferranti when they couldn't solve its technical problems by themselves. The French called this type of robot 'the left hand', adaptable for grasping while the parallel robot moved more like an arm through Cartesian space. This serial robot had a set of six calibrated rods, three pairs which in theory could move through 360 degrees of space unimpaired to perform any mechanical function. Unfortunately, they sometimes collided with each other in the process, one rod blocking the route of the others, or by misinterpreting a command all six moved above instead of below a given position. It was no good having a deft manipulator if it kept mangling itself in certain sequences. Fergus knew there was a solution, a mathematical formula to avoid practical error, if only he spent long enough on it. His predecessor had arrived at an equation with two hundred and fifty terms before he gave up in despair. Singularity indeed. Fergus abounded in patience and when the task felt too onerous, told himself it was no different from training a child. System. Regulation. Methodology paid off.

The room had windows that looked west into the grounds of George Heriot's school where he could watch the blue blazers as they threaded across the greenery. Only a few years till Andrew was enrolled, upholding a tradition. Just fifty yards spanned his own education and employment, back to back. Other people might have found that limiting, one cloister of academe running down the side of a quadrangle, but Fergus thought it was a proof of strength that those raised in a certain belief could be sustained by it. When the intellect was liberated, did it matter if the physical compass was circumscribed? So he didn't feel shackled by the known when his thesis waited like an unexplored universe, all-encompassing.

Relaxation was chess. Possibly the occupation should have warned him he was working too hard. Holiday? When had he had time off? Christmas approached, Andrew's first Christmas and so a special celebration but not a holiday as such. The department would nominally close over the administrative days but people with their own key would go in all the same. You couldn't wholly switch off from the cerebral.

He went home and played chess by himself on the machine to unwind. He hardly ever played against a person now. Errorless machine play made it hard to adapt to human opponents who didn't make the predicted or programmed response. Or they would make the correct moves in the wrong order and throw his defence off balance. He preferred perfection.

His play had changed as a result of his own computer training and the manual which they said was doing well, was into its third reprint. No one had reported a mistake at any rate. He was a better player, more competitive and more aggressive because he could completely discount the opposition as an emotional force. He actually enjoyed the slow throttle. The violence implicit in white pursuing black into a corner was exhilarating. He studied the swingeing attack with savagery. A long cunningly concealed diagonal. A pinned piece. He loved to outwit the machine, which was his own by-product, as one half of his brain tested the other half in the proof of excellence. The particular machine he used had no facility for capitulation. It couldn't offer 'I resign' as an option and so he always played to the end. Checkmate one way or the other. Shah maté. The king is dead.

That night he suffered the indignity, as he thought it, of losing to perpetual check. The same move made three times gave the machine its stalemate. Of the final options, Fergus loathed this so-called swindle, mostly because he felt he could have circumvented it. Too tired, that was his trouble, to avoid falling into the obvious trap. He beat his brains for their stupidity.

When he closed his eyes in the dark, he couldn't go to sleep. He started to semi-hallucinate from over-fatigue. The shadowy objects in the room were pieces, the chair a knight, the bed a rook, moving

438

across the floor in a lurid personification. The game wouldn't finish but went on possessing him in a mad mental whirl as doors and windows became displaced and went on hurtling in collision across the room. Stop, he wanted to shout to the activated terminals, but the machinery ignored him and went on smashing itself against the walls.

46

The Speaker held a reception in his private apartments at Westminster which was an unofficial part of the pre-Christmas festivities, drinks from six to seven. He was adept, this Speaker, at rising above political issues and so his guests included Cadogan as well as the Prime Minister and his wife. Otherwise, the men and women who met in the lift that delivered them inside the Speaker's house were a random mix. Moncrieffe had frequently been a guest at small formal dinners there, furbished with the state silver and some glittering company. His neutrality was a useful entrée to the social entertainments for visiting dignitaries who weren't political as such.

Leonie, arriving between Quercus and Charlie, was puzzled about her own invitation, separately sent, until she recognised a senior newscaster from the BBC as well as an interviewer, reputed to be more cranky than his subjects, whose interrogation was feared as much as Commons question time. Media people, the current names and faces, among whom she must number. It was the first time she had been inside the Palace of Westminster where the panelling and portraits, lit from above, and maze of connecting passages echoed a superior boarding school with the anonymity of institution. The real incumbents were the staff, retainers, flunkeys, footmen who put in fifteen years after early retirement from the armed forces, or civil servants who made a niche for themselves and knew the whole groundwork and mechanism of Parliament better than its successive residents.

No one made introductions. At a certain point it was assumed you weren't a nobody, could be recognised or at least were capable of explaining yourself. In half a dozen conversations, it was obvious to Leonie that this milieu kept itself informed. The talk ran high on these currencies; the topical play or film, exchange rates for sterling or who was controversial in the New Year's Honours list ahead of its announcement. Two people at different ends of the room said that Cadogan was about to face a challenge for the leadership of the Conservatives and ranked his likely successors. No wonder MPs left Westminster with reluctance and fought their seats to the point of acrimony, accepting three-line whips with token rebellion. To be out of the action, however lacking in the time to analyse it, was to fail.

"Can't you get me a couple of tickets for *Macbeth*?" the Prime Minister inquired of Leonie. "Even the agencies can't produce the miracle they're supposed to." His manner was flattering, hypnotic to the ego so that, instead of dismissing the request as she normally did, she gave it space.

In fact, Alan Mills kept back half a dozen director's tickets from each Friday and Saturday performance to trade as favours and Leonie wondered materially what she could negotiate against these. Another reception, or a dinner at Number Ten perhaps, leading into one of the season's highlights, Covent Garden Opera or a charity ball? What were two tickets worth by today's exchange rates? London corrupted giving standards. "I'll see what I can do. But we've been virtually sold out since the beginning. It's the tour operators. They make block bookings at the prestige theatres to put in with a holiday package. The Old Vic happens to be one of the London sights as far as most Americans are concerned."

"That can't be very gratifying for the cast if the audience comes to see the theatre, not the play."

She shrugged. "It's just like votes. Count the heads, don't weigh their opinion."

He laughed, becoming boyish. "I heard the production is transferring to the States," he said.

"That's still being negotiated, but it's not for me at any rate. I'm moving on. I start television filming at the end of January."

"Ah, none of us stands still for very long in public life. You'll be finished by the Easter recess? Why don't you," he suggested, lifting a flute of Kir Royale from a passing salver, "join us for a few days. We have a villa on Náxos and usually put together a house party. Watson's been before. It's paradise. Well, a mere sixth heaven compared to Wester Ross but the weather is more reliable than in that particular stratosphere. Good swimming and not bad sailing. We'd love to have you both if you can manage time out. You can fix it up with Helen."

441

Leonie nodded. That was what professional wives did, tie up the suggestions of their hard-pressed menfolk and make them workable, the secretaries of the bed. It appealed nonetheless. Their Greek vacation became feasible after all through the unlikely channel of the PM's house party with its official clearance. He must know, among all the knowledge that circulated that day, that she was Mrs Petrie – but chose to overlook the anomaly. Maybe she had started to acquire celebrity status which came with its unconventional rule book.

Charlie had accepted this invitation for old times' sake but complained about being fed cardboard canapés and retired early to his club in time for saddle of lamb. Quercus, hovering for a word with her, lifted an eyebrow to interrupt. "Charlie asked me to say goodbye for him. You were at the other side of the room when he left."

"Ah, has he gone?" Leonie looked down the length of the reception suite through double doors that required servitors to close them. She was sorry to have missed him.

The cocktail hour drew to a close. People moved on to dinner dates, working systematically down their diary of engagements so that at the end of the week they could claim to have lived to the full. Leonie made a dash for the theatre by taxi across London, close enough to deadline to give her director and the rest of the cast palpitations. Moncrieffe walked back to the flat alone, ready for an evening's work clearing his papers before the Christmas recess.

But he found the paperwork uncongenial this evening and pottered instead. The flat had changed over the six months or so of Leonie's co-habitation. She had asked him formally if she might change the second bedroom which she'd used at the beginning. He walked in there again, remembering how he'd expected her to order a new suite of furniture from Harrods and charge it to account, or have the decoration turned into something more outré than its grey silk walls. Murals? If that was what she wanted, so be it. In the event she only pushed the furniture about. The bed became a divan out of the way against a wall, hidden under bolsters. The dressing table doubled as a desk, paper one drawer, make-up the other. Inquisitively, he opened them and found small sticks of Leichner left over from the theatre which she used up at

442

home. No waste. It sometimes irritated him the way she drained bottles or counted out her change in coins before she broke into a note. The lessons of penury grated on him. He had once added up the small change in his dozen suits and accumulated fifty pounds which infuriated her, mostly because the weight ruined the lie of a pocket.

He touched the surface of the desk. Japanned. When had he gone in for lacquer ware? He couldn't recall buying it. He looked into the pattern for clues, flowers and birds preserved under layers of shellac. Must be a good piece because the inlay was mother of pearl, and probably old. Touching it confirmed an incidental fact. It was scrupulously clean. Leonie kept a duster in a drawer and wiped it down every day to remove her traces. In fact, a glance round showed no sign that the room was used; it was a guest room still. Her habits were not so much anonymous as unassuming. He wished she'd take more liberties.

He opened up the wardrobe that ran along one wall. A quarter full. Clothes hung in colour gradations, pale to dark. The Fortuny gown, the panne velvet, her divided skirt, garments that were locked into association for him and so charged with her personality that he couldn't imagine anyone else wearing them. They were her. Though only a portion was here. Others hung on a rail at the Old Vic and still more in the house at the Hermitage. Many locations she had and many parts. He sat down on the divan and looked into the wardrobe the way people study a picture in an art gallery. It was a composition of a sort, a gathering, a selection from infinity, designed and colour-controlled.

Perusal told him nothing more. It was not a painting but its frame. The real, the material was yet to come. She was not there and the room and clothes waited, as he did, for vitalisation. Yes, he liked gadabout women who satisfied their own deadlines and ambitions even if it did mean that he was put in the traditional female role of bystander and admirer while she took the platform. Perhaps that was the secret of this attraction. Himself mirrored in her and she in him.

What if she didn't come back this evening? He looked out of her dressing room across the lounge, encountering the ebony piano and the staircase to the roof garden, the starkly graphic curtain as far as the hallway and its unlatched door. What if she never came

443

through it again? Sometimes he dared to ask himself the question, Is this for real? For keeps? and the answer was no. A telegram could remove her at any time, franked with duty. He tried not to be resentful or make petty objections, having had wheedling lovers in the past, but the impermanence wore at him. All his life he had taken from relationships more than he had given, was master of his emotions and in control. This woman upturned such objectivity. She challenged male supremacies. Watson had no doubt that his was the larger dependency; without him Leonie's life would proceed with its own forward momentum, supported by its artistic energy and a batch of ready-made contacts. Without her – empty wardrobes, emptying rooms and days that drained him at the thought. He didn't want to love or to hurt so much, to be so needful of one person, but did all the same.

He stemmed a hatred of Fergus, rival and enemy, that might have become pathological. He didn't even want to know the answer to the question, Did husband and wife sleep together? A daily division; yes, it was exhausting. At the same time, he shunned the final solution of a divorce which meant making another man as unhappy as he had been. Turn and turn about. In both cases he was the wrongdoer, caught in adultery which did strike him as ironical when by most men's standards he was moderate. No one-night stands, no promiscuity, no false promises. Each relationship was a love affair in its way, in its time. He would find it hard to think of ten men in the House who'd led more blameless lives than he, but he attracted this opprobrium because everything he did was more newsworthy. He was depicted as the perennial spoiler of established systems. But third parties did exist, had feelings and even rights; anyone who pretended social demography could be split into two exclusive types, wife and husband, was a hypocrite.

She came. She unbuttoned her greatcoat, double-breasted, almost floor length, sparing in detail and put it on a bamboo hanger in the dressing room, switching on a favourite lamp as she went. She chafed at having to wait on for an extra hour every evening while Act Five played itself out before she could take her curtain call. She washed her face hurriedly afterwards and came back pale, leached from stage lights. In the mirror, she brushed a little extra colour

444

back into her face. "What are you doing sitting in here?" she asked, closing up the fronts of the wardrobe.

"Ruminating."

"How bovine of you."

She stood over him and folded his head against her body. Gone eleven o'clock and they found time for the first embrace of the day. What a life. She felt his tension, neck to spine, and looked into his face wondering at the cause. "I do," she said. "I do," refuting doubts. "Go on with you. Make us both a drink. It's too gloomy in here." She was brisk about the apartment. Lit a gas fire, spread a newspaper, made a huddle over them, six square feet a hurried re-setting.

"What did you think of our Prime Minister?" he asked, breaking into her arrangement from the settee.

"Hm. A very pleasant man. Not at all portentous. He asked us to his Greek villa in the Easter recess."

"Did he indeed. And did you accept for us?"

"I kept my options open by sending the tickets he asked for pronto."

"I didn't know you were such a schemer."

"I'm learning. His wife's more high and mighty than he is."

He pondered telling her about an incident that had taken place the first time he was their guest. Helen Fleming had been a notorious flirt and came close to finishing her husband's career. Ten years before, there had been rumour of a divorce and the Labour leader warned that a scandal wouldn't do him or the party any good. The couple patched it up. "She was off-hand in case you knew she'd propositioned me once."

"Did she indeed? How do women do that?"

"Straight up. We were dancing on somebody's lawn – there's rather an expatriate colony on Náxos – and she popped the question, four-letter frontal. Yes, the cabinet minister's wife as she was then, just so. Perhaps she used it as a term of endearment rather than biology, or to shock. I found it counter-productive. I thought I answered with considerable aplomb. Thank you very much but I've already eaten. She was tipsy. Maybe she didn't mean it. Some women like to collect dignitary scalps, an ambassador, a future lord, an admiral, like plastic cards to prove their credit rating even if they never use them. It's a common enough

445

trade, exploiting reputation and titles. Where would boards of directors be without it? Very possibly she told her friends I propositioned her and got her kicks that way."

"Do you suppose she remembers?"

"I think so." Odd, she wasn't jealous. Didn't even ask if he'd been tempted. Probably wouldn't be shocked if he had accepted, non-judgmental, only interested in why.

"Perhaps we'd better not go to Náxos after all."

"Well," he said, "don't rule it out for that. But I am very interested in why he put the invitation to you in the first place."

"Do you think he's still trying to rope you in?"

"He's desperate enough. The debate last night went to the Speaker's casting vote and because it was a Second Reading, he voted with the government. But at the Third Reading, if the returns are the same, he'll go against. He says it's not up to the Speaker to decide for the House on something as important as passing a law."

"You like the Speaker?"

"We share the politics of impartiality, and that's rare."

Leonie started to tell him about the people who'd been at her end of the room but after a few seconds of the performance couldn't resist getting up to show him how Cadogan had cut a group in half with rudeness and how Mr Speaker was left to salvage sensitive feelings.

She was unflinching, making a caricature of their voices and actions with devastating accuracy. People in public life had asked for it, and in fact the height of fame was to be recognised in a lampoon. She wouldn't have cringed at it herself. A pull of an eyelid, a slumping of the shoulder and she turned into someone else, heavy and male before his eyes. And she damned well remembered what they said. 'During my period of office' as a recitative in a dull man's monologue, the other eyes roaming away from him in boredom while he talked, knowing the phrase already consigned him to the mental zone of has-been. She observed it in the corner. It was the savage eye of the political cartoonists, Cruikshank through to Gerald Scarfe, where one twist of a line caught the expression better than the portrait truth. Mimicry and invention went together exposing the foolish or pretentious. She imitated the gesture of the interviewer, pushing his glasses back onto his nose with a wrinkle; Helen Fleming draping a hand on an arm too long until it turned from touch to feel. She observed from scraps, nothing more than looks and phrases, who the allies were and who the enemies, rating his circle by an alternative set of values that sometimes expanded his. So that was what had been happening all the time, he thought. It confirmed his own suspicions of would-be-ism. He laughed at her irreverence until he hurt about the eye and the windpipe and his face creased with exertion. No more, he said, no more.

She stopped and sat down again. "But maybe, you know, I'm the poseur. I go to these things to send them up. At least these people believe in them whereas I've become cynical from over-exposure. Soon I'll be saying, Oh they only served me white champagne, not pink."

"Do you hate the party-going?"

"No, I lap it up. As long as I don't start thinking it matters. I always suspected Henry James after I heard he'd attended a hundred and seven dinner parties in one London season. It was keeping the tally that was vainglorious. Yes, a score sheet like Helen Fleming. How many, not how much. What can you remember out of all that lot? Well, I suppose life would be pretty dull without any of it." Her thoughts flew back involuntarily to the Hermitage. When was Fergus likely to throw a party, dinner, house-warming, christening? He reproved her over the miles for gadding. "I'm as bad, really, selling my performance for an invitation. It may convey something, the big event, but I always feel slightly dissolute afterwards, as if I'm due for some floor-scrubbing as a penance."

"There speaks the indoctrinated Scot."

The room had expanded, warmer and more benign than two hours earlier. She sat on the floor with legs akimbo. The floor often did service as chair or bed. He'd seen her come in tired, switch the fire on and fall asleep on the hearth. Sleep in the day, wakeful after midnight, turning the hours inside out.

"I saw you speaking to Quercus. Did he tell you he means to stand down at Easter?"

"No," she said, surprised. "He didn't. A term's notice."

"The party managers have known for a while. He'll be seventy soon which is premature for political retirement but he feels it's time to go. The Conservatives need a transfusion of young blood.

447

Their average age is daunting. He thinks resigning now will safeguard the seat and give the new man time to build up his following before the next general election. It's the last act of a party loyalist, dying at the decent moment." He perceived the logic but was disappointed for his senior and for himself. Quercus bowed out after nearly forty years of distinguished but unrewarded service, providing a salient lesson for himself on talents misdirected. The others had constituency problems: Dunns uncovered a move to de-select him, moved by more radical Nationalists than himself and Laidlaw had sacked his agent among bitter and public recriminations. Oh God, the loneliness of the long-distance politician.

Leonie began to understand Watson's solitary wait in the dressing room, symptom of this mood of withdrawal. Charlie making an early exit to his club, Quercus going from the House for good, her own removal to the theatre when in the normal course of things they would all four have dined together or come back to the flat, forewarned of the larger separations that loomed. Watson would go to Inveresk for Christmas festivities and then on to Torrisaig for the New Year while she had to stay behind and take perfunctory breaks whenever she could. The holiday season was no relaxant in the theatre with the audience going to plays like panto or the Oxford Street lights, anything for a seasonal night out. Standards dipped depressingly. They wouldn't be together until Parliament re-opened and these absences started to define a vacuum which daunted the least unsocial or self-sufficient of men. The gloominess in the flat that evening was his own, deserted as he felt by inmates.

"Come," she said, lifting him.

He resisted the pull by gravity.

She left him there and went into the bedroom. She started to undress by the edge of the bed, just outside his line of vision although the unsheathing of a garment over her head was plain enough. He heard her pad barefoot about the room, setting an alarm, adjusting the blinds in ritual preparation for tomorrow with its departures. There were times when he found her acceptance of the inevitable maddening. She was rarely down. Found something to do. Never sat and brooded. Went into somebody else to diffuse the tensions of Leonie.

448

"Come *on*," she yelled with suppressed fury and at the dulcet command he went to stand in the doorway, amused at the sudden appearance of the termagant. Her position, arms folded fiercely over the bedclothes, was a parody of tidy sleep. "Don't languish, for pity's sake. You'd spoil today, out of spite that tomorrow might not be perfect. Get a hold. Stop thinking and live." Prehensile. Tougher-minded than he was, or able to control that exhaustive thinking. Give me the power to change what I can, the fortitude to endure what I cannot, and the wisdom to know the difference. Wisdom was hers.

He gave in gracefully.

The mouth was the orifice, the first O. She could kiss coitally, entering him with her tongue. She moved through the various positions, labial, labio-dental, alveolar until he was touched in every part, male into female, female into male, vowel or consonant incidental to the gender vocabulary of the whole. She rasped along the length. Maraichinage, effleurage in an oral caress. She stopped. Looked at him. Left him out of breath. A long wait of recovery while she tested the different surfaces that made up skin and sound, how fricative differed from plosive in practice. Virtuosity wasn't everything but it was much.

She circulated round his body like the bloodstream finding localised pulses, a distended vein in the neck, the flush of heightened temperature, swelling in the groin. He was taken by her, supply satisfying demand.

All along she said two words, repeating her earlier assertion. I do, I do. After a while, spoken fifty times, this could have meant anything. Action over inertia, a statement of faith still emphatic without its doing word or object, love or you, the finality of the marriage vows she hadn't taken. Or simply a breathing that escaped from the articulators of desire. She did, multiply.

Don't go.

I must.

They lay for a long time while the barges and motor boats went up and down the Thames, part of a continuous overnight traffic. Bridge lights caught the swell, flickered up against the windows and then rippled down the blinds like a spray, icy in mid-winter. In the distance, the gears of lorries rasped with the insistence of a chainsaw, cutting through the nervous system.

"A week to Christmas," she said. "Do you buy presents?"

"Yes, I buy presents."

"Well don't buy one for me. I won't."

"Not any sort of keepsake?"

She rolled over on her side. Her body was so spare, her flesh hardly moved in the shifting. "You only need mementoes for something past. Or are you about to pension me off?"

He lifted her jaw with his fist and rolled it along the knuckles watching the impertinence in her eyes not flinch from his. Cool grey confidence outstaring him. He would want to say she was the irreplaceable experience and if he did indulge himself in such a sentimental utterance she'd laugh at it, refusing données. Not protestations or gifts or replicate gestures but the essential thing.

"Shall we eat? We didn't have dinner this evening. When did we last have a meal?"

"About three days ago."

They raided the larder, coming up with exotic supplies which he'd laid down some time before by the converse of Ellice Barr's selection process from the grocery shelves; the most expensive packaging, the least nutritious contents. Bath Olivers and a tin of truffle pâté and something called drunken orange slices which in extremis served as relish to a camembert. They picnicked in bed, uncomfortable on crumbs.

Tomorrow had arrived and was irreversible. He resigned himself to it and relaxed. Leonie curled alongside him drowsily. She was a comfort creature. Food and heat and drink made her meek. When he kissed her again she scarcely moved but by drawing up against him indicated that she would, if made to.

Languidly passive, she forbore. No not so much pushing or striving could elicit a response, her eyes shut tight against the light. Submissiveness was another game she played, her mind performing a decoy of indifference while her body went on reacting subcutaneously, if only he could locate it. It was a challenge Watson couldn't ignore, turning this limpidity to passion. Stand, sit, kneel, lie she would encounter him. And then she turned about and looked up cunningly, the alibi abandoned, encircled him and was present in person.

Who was she, he didn't know. He had plunged into the wardrobe and came into contact with nothing, rifling vacant space. The deeper he plunged the less he found. The knowledge of return didn't reduce the emptying. Somewhere she eluded him and was, in spite of words or acts, unknowable. That was the core of interesting women; they gave less than they were given. Or alternating take and give, yes and no, kept up the momentum of inquiry. He couldn't fix a single value on to her, specific gravity or atomic weight, and be satisfied. She shifted and was many.

47

Fergus had difficulty with the twelve days of Christmas. He wasn't sure when they began. The commercial interest of shopkeepers in prolonging the annual spending spree had eroded correct traditions so that the festive period could be deemed to start from almost any point in the calendar, which became an arbitrary movable feast. He consulted several authorities and almanacs and discovered that the first day of Christmas was its Eve. That was the proper day to hoist your tree and decorate it.

They were in luck, he and Leonie. Christmas fell on Friday so she had a long weekend planned at the Hermitage, giving her understudy the break she wanted albeit on an ungrateful evening, so that she could fly up on Thursday.

Throughout Christmas Eve, Fergus prepared his tree. He'd been most select about its purchase. The greengrocers round Morningside and Comiston stacked some wilted evergreens on the pavement outside their frontages, trussed up with string. He'd no idea how long they'd been in transit or how soon they'd start to shed their needles. The shopkeepers ran out of good humour answering these questions. A quid a foot. What did he want for that? Someone said there was an alternative, two in fact. He could either go to a nurseryman who supplied trees with roots or track down one of the new species that was longlasting and guaranteed not to moult.

This prompted a long bus journey to a tree plantation on the outskirts of the city where they actually cut the fir or dug it out, roots and all, while you waited. He chose a prime specimen after protracted deliberation up and down the rows. An impasse evolved when Fergus asked for it to be delivered that day, still fresh, because the drivers' schedules were already arranged. At last, between exasperation and pity, the manager gave in, promising to bring it round in person.

It was a beauty and worth the effort, larger than most houses could accommodate and it stood in the hallway at the Hermitage where it could be seen from several vantage points. Fergus was proud of it and put more time into standing back and admiring the tree than in decorating it. He'd stored fir cones in the airing cupboard over the autumn and sprayed them when they opened out. Ivy too and holly berries, prolific in a hard winter, which he wound into bunches like a nosegay. A toyshop in the Canongate went out of business and he'dbought a box of wooden gadgets at a knockdown price, children on swings and seesaws, trains, boats, rocking horses that were satisfyingly well made and swung or rocked to order. There was an assortment of American decorations, odd bells and skating figures, with the wrong year printed on them, but what did such anachronisms matter? He wanted for the sake of visual harmony to burn real candles on the tree. He'd seen some Swedish holders that clipped onto the bough to hold the drips as well as making sure the candle didn't fall over and set the tree alight. He toyed with the idea for a day or two before common sense prevailed; he couldn't be certain that Andrew wouldn't upset the system, burning himself if not the tree. Fergus settled for conventional electricity.

Irene helped, enchanted. She spread, wrapped, tied obligingly among her own preparations, hurrying now against time with the professor coming home and Leonie's flight due in, compressing deadlines. By four they were done and Irene went home to cook the first celebration dinner of the holiday with Matthew, Jenny and her grandson coming as guests.

Harris breezed in to the Hermitage early on his way from one office party to another. "Very ethnic tree," he commented as he went through the hall. "Good Friends of the Earth stroke Greenpeace stuff. Though probably they don't approve of slaughtering wood stock in the first place. Blood on your hands, Fergus. Bit of a Druid ritual anyway. Ivy and holly and lights, opposite solstice from Midsummer. God knows what's Christian about it."

He picked up Andrew and, to tease, held his toy, the quacking roll-along duck Leonie had bought, at arm's length until the child kicked and struggled to reach it and then he laughed, setting them both down.

"You upset him, Harris."

"No. He's all right." His brother turned back, half way up the stairs. "Leonie's arriving soon, isn't she?"

"The flight's due in at seven. She should be here by half past, all being well."

"I'd like to have seen her."

The remark created a discord. "Well you will when she comes in."

"I've got to go straight out. I meant I'd like to have been here to greet her. But it can't be helped."

Harris clattered about upstairs, changing his clothes it seemed with much opening and closing of drawers, before he came into the kitchen where Fergus was clearing up. "I'll be seeing you then," said Harris.

In his way, Fergus was exasperated. He didn't have the heart to evict his brother, went on feeding, housing, basically supporting him without, as far as he could see, any return. Neither money nor convivial company came his way. Harris made a convenience of him and this suspicion of being used drew to a head. On Christmas Eve of all nights, with Leonie expected, surely he could stay in. Anger in Fergus diffused laterally into interrogative rather than the imperative.

"Are you sure you can't hang on?"

Harris paced across the floor to the window, staring into a glum and rainy evening. It didn't tempt but something whiplashed him to meet it. "No. I must go." He turned without warning on his heel and found Andrew who fell over at the brusqueness of the encounter, bumping his head. Harris set him on his feet again and rubbed the head. "Bye nipper," he said and left quickly, his coat tails flapping as he went.

Fergus noticed irritably that the outdoor shoe had left a scuff mark on a white square.

Shortly after six the doorbell went and Fergus opened up, thinking Leonie had caught an earlier flight, or had come by a different and unspecified method. But it was Professor Geddes on his doorstep, not bearing gifts or greetings.

"A word with you, Fergus, if I may."

They moved into the study which, strangely to the professor, had fewer books on the shelves than magazines and catalogues, and manuals whose spine was a coil of wire. There were several tables providing separate work areas and a computer terminal with a chess board wired to it that straggled leads across the room. Piles of paper caught the councillor's eye and, in spite of what was on his mind, he instinctively picked them up and sifted through the sheets of abstract. There were printed words, he discovered, but not words as he knew them. Phonemes, outline directional instructions, letters as initial codifiers, mathematical symbols; not meaningful. A model of the serial robot from the department of Artificial Intelligence sat on one desk, its knobs brightly coloured in primary red, yellow and blue for identification and to Professor Geddes it didn't look markedly different from the toy the toddler carried. A plaything merely, a simular that didn't amplify real life.

"A complication has arisen," started the professor. "May I sit?"

Fergus cleared the chairs of their paper load. He realised that he saw his neighbour very seldom, maybe twice over the last year compared with daily meetings with his wife. The thought produced an obscure guilt which, in the maze of feeling, he couldn't trace to source. The man had aged in the meantime. Or was the added greyness winter, draining the pallor? The head was higher, the features sharper as both hair and flesh receded. Against this, his acuity was heightened, or impatience.

"Have you seen Harris this evening?" the visitor demanded.

"Yes, he came and went an hour ago."

"Went where?"

"Who knows?"

James Geddes matched his fingers, left and right, but kept the thumbs unpaired. "A situation has evolved. A case. Details as follows. Matthew has been employed by his finance company for eighteen months. He is trusted as a trainee executive with prospects of becoming a director in time. He has responsibility for overseeing the installation of computers in the businesses they service and of necessity has access to their files. Really for instructional purposes." The professor paused, dry. He looked across at the computer terminal warily, compact as the human brain they said, analogous to its function in that it stored and remembered and sifted information, but not humane. It could not hurt. It could not tell the difference between an interpretative or moral right and wrong, and could not therefore divulge the truth. "What is it that

455

you do with this?" he waved to the watcher in the corner, its screen alive, alight.

"Oh, calculate. It does some of the complex mathematical work for me. There's a new piece of American software I'd like that would simplify my graphics." Fergus stopped himself from jargon. "But you were saying about Matthew . . ."

"Apparently they use these machines in banking and for storing records of accounts. By my understanding, which may well be flawed, it is possible for someone with knowledge of the correct serial codes to transfer money from one number, or bank account, to another. To go on moving money around until it's lost, or paid back."

"Computer fraud." The word didn't come easily to Fergus.

"You have it."

"It's so common companies are starting to introduce sophisticated fail-safe devices. But they have to write off five per cent for pilferage like any other business."

"So common?"

"A well known problem."

"Matthew has been accused of computer fraud."

Fergus was wholly unprepared for this statement. He braced himself for something, to being told that Matthew had been instrumental in uncovering such a fraud and that the professor's visit to this house was no accident. Fergus thought he came to warn. But his neighbour's son as the agent of deception? Never. Matthew was too simple in the best sense, and too adhesive to his respectability to commit an offence against it.

"This happened today?"

"A routine check carried out before the Bank Holidays threw it up. The first line of inquiry was to Matthew in case there had been a genuine error by the operator. He became more deeply implicated because the money, and very large sums of it, was cleared through other accounts his company handles. It was a job inside to his office and only he actually had all the information. Incriminating."

Fergus feared. He knew these traps. One by one the circumstantial details meant nothing but in accumulation condemned. Inarguable evidence!

"The computers unfortunately cannot tell who pressed the buttons, but the sequence of buttons appears to be the giveaway."

There was no signature to forge in this crime and no fingerprints. The professor found himself smack up against the modernity he knew he hadn't understood. Different values. Different methods for the criminologist to trace.

"So what has happened to date?"

"Matthew has been told he must answer questions to an internal tribunal next week or in the early New Year pending police investigation. He's suspended forthwith. He phoned me at my office. They're coming to dinner in a little while." He shook his head at the continuance of normality, food and festivities unreal. The narrative, which had been laid out with prudential competence, point by point, began to disintegrate. Random thoughts punctured the surface. "Have I been mean with my son that he should steal? His mother tells me disturbing things." The professor looked across at his young friend and dismissed a nervous reticence. Fergus was a graveyard of confidentiality. He could speak freely. "She lent him money in the summer, five hundred pounds, which was never returned. I didn't think Matthew was so seriously in need."

Five hundred, thought Fergus, doing his own sums. And a bit more.

"I don't know how such a thing as this can be hushed up. Even to be accused is to be indicted in a way."

Fergus' memory was more acute, long-term, than the other man's. Yes, he'd thought just that, and had lived through the consequences of intuition to see it justified. There was no recovery from a professional disgrace and just as Fergus carried the stigma, son of the bankrupt, so the professor would find himself with a new title, father of the fraudster. Their own good standing was distrained as asset.

"Why are you here?" asked Fergus pertinently. "Why are you telling me when this charge is no better than supposition?"

Age discrepancies faded. In practical wisdom the young man was the senior and the councillor came acknowledging the power of survival, as a touchstone to his own. "I wondered," he proceeded carefully, "if Harris could shed any light on this?"

"I think Harris could shed a great deal, if he were here." The brother was sorely tempted to make revelations, the comparable five hundred pounds he had lent in July, the endemic

457

gambling, the man who called at the Hermitage when Irene was at home and demanded with menaces, presumably paid off at least in part because he had not re-appeared. A sorry tale that added up to an implication in this criminal charge. Aiding and abetting? An accessory after the fact? A fence? Goodness knows.

"I never trusted Harris, even when he was young. Too slick. Slickness is not a thing I understand. We academics proceed differently from the known to the unknown in stages by an established heuristic principle. Harris cheats a little on both the question and the answer."

Fergus thought this résumé was its own judgment. There was no need for him to specify where Harris cheated. The professor on the other hand realised achingly that each word he spoke applied to his own son and what he had fundamentally disliked in the friend was that he had explicated these unreliable tendencies, companion in disrepute.

Fergus watched the other man fall into a trance. He knew that pain but could neither share nor alleviate it. It was the stare of Michael journeying back home from the Court of Session in a crowded bus which might as well have been empty, when he was unable to focus on the faces. It was the hysterical withdrawal he went into himself after his father's death, fearing suicide. The trance was still, a petit mal, but the brain went through nine gs, blacked out, exploded, fell to the ground, blazed meteorically in the space of seconds. The robot mangled itself to death as logic impelled it into impossible physical locations. Madness came close. The self suddenly collided with other dimensions, duty, morality, loyalty, the heraldic code words that didn't actually uphold or counsel when the fit was on but rather mocked, emblems of outdated honour. What, feeling round the professor's silence, could he comfort him with? All pain ceases. In the end we die.

"What time is it?" the professor asked, looking round the bare-walled room in confusion.

Time to move, thought Fergus, time to repay. "About seven."

"Then I must be off." He got up and propelled himself forwards to the hollow celebration. "This has upset my day more than somewhat." Fergus watched him disappear round the curve of the driveway, staggering.

Fergus picked up his boy and mounted the stairs. The lights from the Christmas tree shone upwards casting troubling shadows, like a face lit from below more cadaverous than human. Doors were foreshortened, banisters elongated weirdly. Small decorative details changed their shape like the circular knob on the handrail that turned into an ellipse.

The house was primordially tidy. Fergus had too few belongings to ruffle them and so his brother's haphazard way with objects was a source of friction. Harris' room became a no-go area. It was better not to see dishevelment than to scold about something that was native and incorrigible, a mental disorder, so Fergus stayed away.

One step inside this unfamiliar territory told him everything. The room returned to regularity because Harris had gone. Nothing out of place. No signs of ownership. The drawers were empty, the wardrobe bare. Not one thing was left except in the corner of the cupboard, a tennis racquet, the Lillywhite's steel frame left behind. Wherever Harris was going, he wasn't intending to play tennis.

Fergus set the boy down and thought. This timely evacuation proved an involvement with Matthew's problem. Was he implicit in that fraud and ran out, leaving an accomplice to face prosecution solo? Or was he in fact the perpetrator of the crime for which he framed his friend? Or was he wholly innocent but afraid of too many impinging questions? Or all coincidental? Fergus zoomed back and forth between the extreme degrees of blame and exoneration.

Andrew played meanwhile. He lifted up the tennis racquet, found that its netting fitted fingers, was transparent as a mesh, had a convenient handle and thereby established its strike power, swatting air. Fergus remembered the spongy ball he'd bought for Andrew's stocking in the morning, harmless indoors, and wondered about advancing the gift by a day but the child would need a lighter racquet than this one which he would put away for the future. Bye nipper. Left a present after all.

Fergus fell down shafts of thinking parallel to the professor's. Where had Harris gone? Had he crossed with Leonie on the way to and from Turnhouse? Was he now airborne to a distant destination? Had the ticket been pre-bought or was it the last thing he charged to his credit card? Perhaps he'd turned up at the airport and said, Where can you fly me to, and took pot luck. Who had he said goodbye to? Alison? Muriel? Nobody surely. He couldn't afford to forewarn of movements so necessarily hasty. Possibly he lifted the receiver at this moment and, pressing the button codes of a call box, dialled a farewell.

Harris had expunged himself from consequences and ran out on his debts. Who would pick them up? Matthew and the man who called and the firm and Fergus himself and any number of other creditors from banks to credit companies. Five thousand pounds outstanding to Fergus, fool that he was.

Well, not entirely a fool. He had elicited from Harris a document acknowledging the debt which had been underwritten by a guarantor. He sat on the edge of the bed, complacent at that thought. He'd get his money back all right, with interest – which would be the pleasure of extorting it. And then a horrific thought crossed his mind. Harris had sneaked his case out of the house without being seen. Could he have filched the guarantee as well?

Fergus picked up the child and sprang downstairs two at a time back to the study. He located his book of accounts in its drawer and found the piece of paper intact. Of course it wasn't worth lifting; what did it matter to Harris if Fergus collected the debt from someone else?

The beneficiary held it up to the light for ratification. A real signature was embossed on it. Ink dried in a pucker. It was Muriel Petrie who had guaranteed her younger son's commitment to her older and Fergus couldn't disguise from himself an avenging glee that events had so played to his advantage.

He heard a taxi roll down the drive and went out to meet Leonie.

48

Winter at Torrisaig was neither benign nor picturesque. Too inaccessible for ski-ing, too treacherous for climbing, the mountains reverted to being the habitat of the eagle in the dead months of the year. The peaks looked higher and more remote under snow because the white expanse obliterated actual distance. They rose in the perception which was immeasurable. How to track across that void of landscape and reach them baffled the eye, so the backdrop hung from the invisible gantry of space, not pinned to the real.

The estate and the gardens contracted under this immensity. Nobody went to the perimeter, even those who waited for arrival. The waterfall didn't freeze in an average year, but it did crystallise, frost bridging its way from rock to stream in solid granules. Ice pools formed out of the main current and grew or melted according to the temperature and time of day, a barometric clock. The trees were lopped, the yew hedge cut back, so that the space of paths had enlarged but there was nowhere to go along them. The sea loch came up and fell away again in tidal fluctuation, no event when the whole was grey, water, land, vegetation a slush. Movement against this monochrome was only a blurring. The snow dirtied.

Watson was no lover of snow, the pristine on the hills, the muddy underfoot. It got in the way of activity. Fresh falls made the drive across Strath Bran tedious. He carried a spade in the boot to dig himself out of drifts and arrived after a seven-hour journey from Edinburgh tired and dispirited. The cessation of momentum on the road was more than inconvenient. It reminded of frailty. If he didn't actively dig himself out of the drift, he could die of hypothermia in hours. As the wind whistled about his ears and threw ice points in his eyes, blinding his direction, that was a chastening thought. Forbidding the blockage of his own bloodstream was a primal motivator and so he dug his way mile by mile across the moor.

Even so, he lagged behind events. He came a week ahead of schedule, Christmas Eve instead of New Year's Eve and still arrived late.

The consultant who had made a journey of almost equivalent time if less distance was leaving the house as the Daimler drew up outside but he stopped to walk back along the length of the Great Hall to the smoking room which had been made ready for the younger Moncrieffe.

"What are the chances of a complete recovery from a stroke? Well, that's impossible to say. It's variable with the individual." The doctor was older by a decade than his patient and Watson remembered advice Quercus had once given him. Never consult an elderly professional: they've gone beyond caring. "People tend to recover from the first. But this is your uncle's second stroke."

"Is it? I didn't know that."

"As like as not, neither did he. But looking back on my notes, that's how I interpret the symptoms now."

"So what is a stroke?" Watson hurried him on. He was wet through from standing in snow up to the thighs and wanted quick-fire answers.

"It is a paralysis that originates in the brain or part of the brain."

"You mean he's paralysed?"

"Down one side."

"Which?" As if it mattered.

"The left. What they used to call apoplexy." The doctor, offered a post-consultative dram, didn't refuse it and took to a wing chair by the fire commodiously. Outside wasn't tempting. "It damages the nerve ends so motor control is lost temporarily and may be impaired for good thereafter."

Watson did not like this prognosis. "He will walk?"

"Oh, it's far too early to say. It only happened in the early hours of this morning. There may be a very long period of recuperation." The West Highland drawl was endless, placid but not comforting.

"He'll speak?"

"Oh yes. I think I can say that's likely."

"So sudden." Watson, in spite of the boorishness, took off his shoes and warmed his stocking soles at the logs.

"Yes, that's how it goes. And it's as well. What would we do if we had warning of calamity? Such apprehension would incapacitate us for good. I am eternally amazed at people reading the stars. Who wants to know the course of the future?"

Watson was in no mood for the rhetorical and emptied the glass quickly. The alcohol on an empty stomach vaporised immediately through his system making him feel befuddled without attendant relaxation. Enough of that, he thought, remembering how his father had died of the advocate's disease, too much drink. Edward and Charlie were both florid men and in the eighteenth century would have suffered from gout. He ought to try to resist the genetic strain that predisposed towards one infirmity or another. Ah, maybe that was the inhibition the medical man counselled against, restricting life for fear . . . for fear of death. Not so unwise after all, the old boy wasn't.

"Should he be hospitalised?"

"I can see no advantage in that whatever. He has a good nurse upstairs. Better there than in Fort William with strange ways. Not to mention the small problem of getting your uncle into town."

Watson nodded, pacified by the quiet. It was three in the afternoon. The day had already been eternal but would last another ten, which he could cope with if he paced himself. He slowed to local time.

Nothing that went before – not the alarmist phone call at seven in the morning, not the long hazardous drive north, not the medical definition of the case – could prepare Watson for the sight of Charlie Moncrieffe bed-ridden. It was too sudden a contradiction. The active man brought down by a minuscule failure of the brain, impossible. Watson had never seen his uncle in bed and couldn't think of more than three or four occasions when he'd visited his bedroom. They retired up different staircases at night. Theirs was the friendship of the field, the bench, the corridors of Westminster. It was its own agenda, composed of doing. They shared everything except intimacy, so the nephew was hesitant turning the door knob – it was absurd to knock – into the double strangeness of the personal and the debilitated state.

The room was shaded against the last of the light, muffling sounds as well as faces. A nurse came forward, a fresh-faced woman he half recognised. He'd seldom seen a nurse nearby and was disconcerted at uniform in a private setting, a cap and apron set just so.

463

"What is happening?"

"Lord Moncrieffe is asleep."

"Can I see him?"

She nodded and they went forward to the bed which was partially screened in a recess with hangings. The room, like his own, was vaguely shabby, decorated with cast-offs from the public rooms in a hasty choice. The curtains had real silver thread, now tarnished, and the Indian carpet was worn down to a drugget.

"I'll sit here for a while," he said, indicating her own vigilant place really to shake her off, and the nurse obligingly moved away.

Charlie had his eyes shut but Watson didn't think he was asleep at all. He flickered consciously. The face was ashen. In that attitude, resting, somnolent, nobody would have said it was Charles Moncrieffe, form without spirit, bulk without animation, like the wintry landscape round the house, withdrawn into a remoteness that was inert but chilling.

Charlie opened his eyes and looked at his nephew. "Damned nuisance," he said. Or seemed to say. The mouth turned awry and the words with it.

Watson smiled painfully. "It looks as though I'll have to unwrap your presents for you. Most inconsiderate timing."

Charlie smiled back. He tried to move but came up against the impediment; the right would, the left wouldn't and without propulsion from both sides, he was static. Push pull cancelled each other out. He struggled up and nothing happened. Tears of frustration and effort came into his eyes.

"Now go easy," said Watson, not sure if this exertion was damaging. "It'll take time to get things together so don't strain yourself."

Charlie turned a reproachful eye on him and Watson thought, My God, I'm already talking to him as though he were an imbecile. This is what it must be like when you're disabled, people talking down to you or talking over you – Is he allowed to sit up? – with the 'you' suddenly relegated to the third person and not directly in the conversation any more. It must exasperate. Watson wasn't clear about what he should do next. He didn't want to leave. He'd come all this way to see Charlie but equally he couldn't sit there in silence. He talked without hope of response.

"Frances is going out for dinner on Christmas Day. She sends her love and says you're not to worry. I thought it was better if she stayed behind in Edinburgh. Horrible journey up. Strath Bran was blocked in three different places." The euphemisms were transparent. Frances was so dithered by the news of a stroke, however much Watson played it down, that she would have been more of an encumbrance than help along the way, and so elderly the journey was a hazard she could do without. Friends had stepped into the gap and would distract her. He glossed.

Forced into a monologue, Watson told him about Westminster developments, Quercus' resignation and attendant anxieties, though he omitted the sudden death of a Labour back-bencher in a marginal seat bringing the majority down still further.

All the time that he was listening, nodding occasionally, Charlie flexed his hands against the bedclothes. Only the right one moved and Watson thought it must be horrific to see one half of your system not working although, as far as you knew, you were instructing both sides together. He remembered being told that it was the right side of the brain that controlled the left of the body, a stray fact that illuminated some of the schisms of the human frame and its symmetries which he'd taken for granted. Two of everything except the heart, the brain, the genitals and even these had left and right auricles and ventricles, hemispheres, testicles. Movement was necessary co-ordination.

The fragile equipoise of his own life, borne in on him that afternoon, was underlined again. It was so easy to stop. He didn't fear death, but dying. One entrance, many exits they said of life. How to die was the question he had touched on with the doctor, either suddenly as in falling down a mountainside and never regaining consciousness, or slowly, eyes open, aware of every cellular deterioration of mind and limb. That was no choice. Neither. He didn't want either of these options but to die an old man in his bed and in his sleep, or positively to some purpose. But above all, he wanted to live and clamorously. This proximity to feebleness stirred a basic determination. He would not die of accident, he would not fade away, he wouldn't sneak out of life like Michael Petrie, swallowing analgesics, all falling-offs, but would survive, himself and issue.

"That's enough," said the nurse. "Half an hour is long enough to start with."

Watson found a replacement pair of shoes in his cupboard and went back downstairs. Torrisaig was full of intemperate contrasts in the winter. It was centrally heated, but running the boilers at full capacity didn't combat the two main problems, old windows and high ceilings. Architecture and convenience met and parted again without co-operating. Some rooms, supplemented by fires, were so warm as to be soporific. Others froze, snow roll following sauna. Winter was a contraction indoors as well as out, confinement to the small or unwindowed like the smoking room and the library, a shutdown from the vast.

He caught sight of the factor down a corridor and changed direction towards him.

"Have you been in to see him, Donald?"

"Yes, I had a minute with his Lordship early on."

"You've done things quickly. I'm very grateful to you." The doctor, the nurse, the phone call summoning himself were Macleod's doing. Factotum, yes, the man who in a shrinking world did everything. "What do you think?"

"Ah well now." Donald Macleod was as cautious as the medical man, but bred on animal wisdom before human had a more objective view of the importance of one life. His honest opinion was that his Lordship would not rise from his bed again but he held back from voicing it from fear of hurting rather than fear of truth. "These things are slow to mend. My father was the same." Macleod senior had lived to ninety so Watson was reassured by omission.

"What is there to do? Perhaps there's some paperwork I ought to sign?"

Christmas Eve was not a work day by anybody's reckoning but the factor acknowledged business was a therapy in the middle of the passive. "I haven't looked into the office for a day or two. The wages were the last thing that we did."

The we shifted, henceforth more likely to be you and I instead of he and I. They found the keys to the office where Charlie kept up a rudimentary system of filing and book-keeping. Donald sorted through the various keys on the ring and they opened up the drawers in turn. Fish hooks mixed with paper, sisal twine with invoices. They felt like petty larcenists or worse, because the rifling exposed Charlie's incompetence and looked disrespectful while he

466

lay upstairs, unable to protest, as if they wilfully hastened his non-involvement with affairs. There was no room for squeamishness. It had to be done but they shrank from the insensitivity of their actions and avoided each other's eye.

Donald took him down the ledger of accounts, incoming, outgoing correctly tabulated but the dates of these entries troubled the perceptive reader. They came in blocks with ten or fifteen items written in during one single day which meant they'd hung around until Charlie found time. He wouldn't delegate the book-keeping to anyone else and didn't do it routinely himself. Absence and disinclination made a nonsense of efficiency. Watson came across a bill for several hundred pounds from a plumber in Fort William for servicing the entire estate, house, tied cottages, holiday homes, that attracted a five per cent discount if it was paid by a certain date. It wasn't.

Watson's heart sank as he catalogued more and more oversights. There was no need to buy in winter foodstuffs in this quantity if the men on the estate planted or harvested more systematically. Advertising the holiday cottages was costing too much. They ought to be put in the hands of an agent for a fee. Charlie was so miserly with fishing permits he choked his own profit. He should do a deal with the local hotel so that their guests had priority access instead of meeting with his veto. Mutual benefit wasn't Charlie's theme. Opportunities were missed, openings overlooked. Lordly attitudes were fine when things went well but the economic squeeze forced a reappraisal that Charlie was too unworldly or too haughty to accept.

The factor was silent except when spoken to. He cared about the entity more than the individuals, Torrisaig more than its servants. Lord Moncrieffe's stroke wasn't such a blight if it was the saving of the estate. He thought regretfully back over the last ten years of mismanagement when the Young Pretender could have imported more in the way of hard currency or entrepreneurial tactics than the Old.

Watson was dismayed by the task ahead of him. He came back to his original question. 'What are the chances of recovery from a stroke?' Charlie's prognosis and Torrisaig's were interdependent but in inverse ratio. The place was failing. If he recovered, it would fail. Year after year, as he flicked back over the ledger, it went into deeper deficit. Heartless or realistic, the see-saw image of survival impressed itself on him. How long had Donald's father lived? Till ninety! Imagine if Charlie went on like this for only another ten years, incapacitated, unable to wield authority but unwilling to resign it, what would that mean in real terms? At the moment, Watson could take on himself power of attorney but it was an emergency status without legality. He foresaw himself a cipher in both houses, domestic and political. Ten years of future shadowing on his part, signing without authorisation – or not signing. Nobody in charge. Piecemeal decisions, one countermanding the other. A full recovery? It looked a dismal prospect either way.

"We'll have to have a longer session together, Donald, when we know better how things stand."

It was almost dark by four o'clock in December. Watson walked outside to dispel the claustrophobia of rooms, made up of anxiety and sickness. He thought this was a cheating time of year, midwinter to spring. The shortest day had passed and the light was technically on the increase, but the bitter cold deceptively lay ahead. New Year was a misnomer, inaugurating the final wasting rather than a start. There was a two-month lag before the real beginning came.

The sun set, not spectacularly but a quiet folding away. He walked along the main path under the savaged yew hedge and down the steps towards the loch. The wind was keen off the sea and met him at the intersections. A contrary air poured down from the glacial mountains without a brake and made his eyes water. He thought of more sheltered avenues and looped along the paths until, losing himself a little in the maze, he drew near the greenhouse. It was warm inside, being heated automatically and as comfortable as a bivouac out of the wind. He didn't often come in here when it was Charlie's province and he didn't understand the finesse of hybridisation in the first place. There were plants in polythene bags, things germinating all year round. Signs of order pained. He thought of the nimble fingers, tying, trussing plant or fly and had an agonising sight of the same hands clumsy on the bedclothes. Charlie, always busy, always cheerful, reduced to a humiliating dependence, fed, washed, cleaned even by a woman from the village. It was not fair. It was not dignified.

468

Watson looked round the staging to see if there was something practical he could do. All it took was a day without water, a night without heat and everything in the greenhouse would be blighted. He'd been angry at Charlie's incompetence in the office but here he was the dullard, thought the capillary feed tank needed water and didn't even know where the nearest standpipe was. Did Charlie use rainwater from butts? Goodness knows. Did it matter if a hundred cuttings died from drought? Or should he turn his back on it and think, So what? Who wants a black rose anyway? He felt there was a moral obligation to sustain and so he poked about outside until he found a water butt that filled from the roof of the greenhouse itself in a cyclic neatness and topped up the tank. It earned a few days' grace, though what would happen when he went back to Edinburgh and London he couldn't guess.

The future fined like the quintessence of light over the Atlantic, most brilliant because it came to crisis. Soon to be extinguished, it pulled a black canopy of the past behind it. The moment reminded him precisely of the day of the election when he'd gone down to the churchyard and found the work of hands other than his own had gone into maintaining it. The greenhouse wasn't so very unlike the chapel, ribbed, vaulted, glazed, a little musty in the corners with disuse but green and vital still. Personal goals reduced in the presence of so many alternative forms of trying. They all died trying. Ancestry and endeavour sobered the ego. It might be time to retract on his own ambition and concentrate on Torrisaig. Perhaps this little acreage was all that he could save.

49

Leonie shed her greatcoat and walked past the Christmas tree without noticing it.

Fergus hung up the coat which he didn't recognise. Each time she came back there was something new. He didn't blame her for this indulgence, thinking she needed important clothes for important occasions, and didn't consider it wasteful as long as she was able to afford an extensive wardrobe but found the altered outline disconcerting when he habitually preferred the old and familiar. He noticed his own overcoat was tired by comparison, then remembered it was one of Michael's and possibly thirty years old. Leonie hadn't disdained such borrowing or patching at one time. Nowadays garments didn't last as far as signs of wear, never mind mending.

She swooped on Andrew who was developing a passive resistance to being adored by women and allowed himself to be cuddled for a minute or two before pandemic boredom set in.

"You're much later than I expected," said Fergus, waiting by for equivalent kindness.

"Yes." Leonie put her son down and watched his progress, space and time. "I just ran into Harris at the airport and we talked for half an hour."

"Ah. I wondered if you might cross."

Some foreknowledge on his part was a relief, if only because it abbreviated the repetition of her tale. "How much *do* you know?"

"James Geddes was here an hour past. He tells me that Matthew's facing charges of fraud against one of the companies he services. Computer fraud."

Following heat, Leonie had walked into the kitchen and sat down. Eight o'clock approached when, according to routine, a meal would have been cooked and eaten, the child put to bed. Today was exceptional in degree when she was very late and very tired, but in general her arrivals were disruptive. Billed as events, they often disappointed.

It was true. Fergus expected her to jump up and throw herself into the housewife with enthusiasm. She seemed to him idle, not because she did nothing but because she bypassed the things he felt were important.

"Why did James Geddes come here? It wasn't a thing to advertise."

Yes, he gave her that. She was astute when it came to human dealings. "He thought that Harris might shed some light on events."

Leonie turned over her conversation with Harris when, fraught with tension, he had probably said more than he should. She was divided. She wanted to help to clear Matthew since Harris wasn't willing, in spite of her best persuasion, to stay around to do it but wouldn't implicate her brother-in-law in the process. She didn't want to be the main witness for the defence on the grounds of 'Harris told me so'. Besides, she hadn't lived on the fringe of public life for so long without picking up a modicum of legal wisdom on what was quotable or not. Some of what she knew was hearsay. No point in repeating it when it wasn't material evidence.

"And Matthew protests his innocence?"

Fergus was thrown by the obvious. "I never established that. I presume he does. Matthew's with James and Irene now." He digressed into the non-sequential, overtaken by the fact that no, the professor had not specifically justified his son. Was that from a clinical impartiality, he wondered, or a suspicion that Matthew was tainted with the guilt of motive? Borrowing without repayment and gambling were almost equivalent sins, in the professor's scale, to fraud.

"Then I think I'll go over and see Matthew myself in a little while. There could be possibilities he's overlooked." Privy counsel might repair some of the breaches in his defence, a briefcase missing and subsequently returned.

"I'd rather you didn't do that," said Fergus, without reflecting on why.

Leonie's temper frayed. Every time she stepped off the plane at Turnhouse there was another Petrie furore to become embroiled in, none of her concern, none of her doing but imposing on her free mental space all the same. Her severance from Fergus and his circle was almost complete. Sadness at this failure matched the exhaustion of her London success. Both sapped. To be met by caveat and prohibition when the last thing she wanted was to be involved, was more than she could take.

"Any reason? Or simply a desire that I shouldn't act on my own account."

"No. I withdraw that," he said, mindful of preceding disagreements. "What you do is your affair."

Andrew sat himself down on the floor and scooted the duck round the squares, outlining them carefully. "Isn't he tired?" asked Leonie.

"No. I let him sleep later than usual this afternoon so that you could have more time with him now."

The implicit rôle reversal of this statement was sobering. Fergus was the mother of this child as well as father. She realised she took a minimal part in the spirit of the house at Hermitage and none in its organisation. Fergus hung her coat up, raised and decorated the tree which she observed at last through the hallway, planned every detail round about her as if she were the homecoming male. She responded as the worst of men, churlish, intransigent, egotistical, incomprehending of the domestic. Yes, she had absconded from her responsibilities as much as Harris, leaving others to pick up the tab. It was a choice of lucid simplicity: this child or her career. At least, it had been simple at the beginning. Latterly a dozen other factors impinged on it as the extremes widened to incorporate the results of that decision. They both expanded in interest, neither easy to relinquish. Her sympathies weren't so much separate as twinned.

"What did Harris say to you at Turnhouse? He took his things away with him, what there was of them. Did he tell you where he's going?"

"No. He said it was better if he didn't tell me that, so that I could give the straight answer. I've no idea. He said he was catching the last flight to Heathrow. Next stop the world." The phrase was wishful rather than glib. She turned into the traveller herself so the words were a prayer for safe arrival in whatever continent he chose to go to ground, though stopover was more likely than full stop.

Fergus got up to make a drink or food, whatever was needful, while she went on playing with Andrew, catching up on his new words and recent skills.

"Did he owe you very much money?" she wondered.

Fergus was perversely proud of the enormity. "Five thousand pounds."

She thought she had misheard and looked up from the game to verify. "Five thousand? Fergus, do you realise how much that is in relation to what I earn?"

He shrugged. "I'll get it back. I have an IOU."

"That's worthless when he's not here to honour it."

"But Muriel guaranteed it, with a solicitor's oath. A true affidavit."

She sat back on her heels and shaped a doubt. "All of them signed it in your presence?"

"Well, no. Harris produced it for me."

"And you intend to prise the cash from her?"

"My rights, I think. I have a perfect right."

She got up and lifted the child, warming her face against his hands. "This sounds wickedly like the pound of flesh to me, Fergus. What if she won't pay out, or can't?"

"I'll sue. A trial, imagine. Muriel in the witness box answering charges. I wouldn't shirk that." His manner as he said this wasn't gleeful as much as cold. Reversals satisfied by neatness. "Awarding costs."

Leonie paced up and down thinking, I don't believe this. I simply don't believe this family. They're all mad. First Michael, then Harris tangled in some money-getting scheme which may end in Matthew Geddes going to trial and now Fergus plots a contorted Machiavellian revenge against his mother. "I do not want you to proceed with this."

The kettle boiled and he filled the pot carefully. "Any reason?"

"For God's sake, Fergus, don't quibble. Humanity."

"That is not a virtue I have to spare."

"So I see." She looked at him directly. Nothing to spare. The months had made him fleshless but this didn't have the effect of enervating; quite the reverse. He was more compact and centred than before, tense with a force that was mental and heightened by celibacy or withdrawal so that she was reminded of the coiled spring, more powerful for being compressed. His movements round the room were precise. He was in all his aspects, body, gesture, speech, habit, mind, a denial of superfluity.

Leonie's scorn of the virtueless state made him re-examine his own categorical right and wrong. He did not know what he should have done differently. "Why? Why should I not exact?"

"Because this type of revenge is endless once you embark on it. Mafia-style attack and counter-attack. Who wins?" She rejected the other examples that came to mind along with Shylock and the Sicilian code, drama bound, in Montague and Capulet and the plays of Lorca, hot with Mediterranean passions that didn't transpose readily to Edinburgh on a winter's day. "You were a simpleton to lend your brother anything, given his record. How you bumped it up to five thousand pounds, I can't imagine."

"Some in lieu."

"I think you dangled him deliberately."

"No. I believed I was helping out."

If he didn't examine his motives too closely, it could look that way. "It is very bad for you to go ahead on this." She spoke with concentrated emphasis, bad for his character and bad in its social effect. The plain word 'bad', containing the pitch blend of immorality, struck him full on.

"Then what should I do? Waive the debt? I can't afford to. This is my money and yours and Andrew's. I won't waive it."

"If you could afford to part with it, you don't need it."

"I don't agree. I'll sacrifice the interest but not the capital."

Leonie heard his mother pinpoint her dues. Mine. What is mine is inalienable. In a sense, she admired Harris most out of the Petries because he was, for all his escapades, the least material. That was a radical test of priorities, if the individual could at any given moment pack a suitcase and go. If not, what was it that detained? Admittedly Harris did it under pressure and for non-ideological ends, but the removal from possessive ties had a strong attraction for her as the ultimate freedom. Passing through the eye of the needle baggageless.

"Does the money matter that much to you? Well then, what if I pay you back and cancel Harris' debts?"

The offer shocked him out of the cautious mode. "I didn't think you were so well endowed."

And neither did Leonie. Off the top of her head, the proposal delineated much that was unconscious. She didn't have that sum of money at her disposal but Moncrieffe did and she made the unfounded assumption that he would part with it for such an ignominious end. The scope of her own statement staggered her.

"Why would you do that?" he pressed. "Beggar yourself to absolve my brother?"

"Because pursuance of your claim is so harmful, Fergus. I think you should clear yourself of these feelings of malice. It's better to owe me than be owed by them."

He revolved this transfer of funds. "We always hate the person we borrow from because he's exposed our weakness."

"That wouldn't apply to me, surely?"

"But it might to your backer. Your fighting fund ought to be cleared first through your political agent."

Fergus was so seldom sardonic that the effect was doubled, a strike from the pacifist gaining by surprise. She hadn't thought he was so acute. The moment had come but not as Leonie would have wished it. Surfacing in the middle of an unrelated quarrel, it would take on that mood and the name would be spoken in anger.

"You mean Moncrieffe? He is not my agent or my backer."

Sure enough, the patronym brought out a shudder of antipathy. "How can you associate with such a person," he asked with trembling invective, "who was instrumental in my father's downfall?"

Well, thought Leonie, I have missed out on something in my upbringing. The clan gene that makes all wars tribal. The Petries found each other uncongenial but let them be attacked from outside and they closed in phalanx. Such an odd mentality, to take each other's quarrels on themselves and so multiply their native wrongs.

"It's unfortunate but hardly relevant," she interposed, "when he is no more responsible for Michael's lack of managerial acumen than I am."

"You are my wife," Fergus insisted. "You should—"

"Restrict my circle according to your diameter? Oh no, Fergus. This is old ground. Your trouble is, you say one thing and you mean quite another. You act the libertarian but you are very repressive underneath."

He was genuinely stupefied at this accusal. Who had more freedom than she did? When had he interfered with her wishes? He gave her the full scope of infinity, as he understood it.

"I know what you're thinking," she interrupted. "But you are not *interested*, Fergus. Not in me or what I do. Shall I tell you something? You haven't called me by my name today and not as long as I can remember. I am the person, the woman. You don't touch me spontaneously because you feel all impulses should be generated by me. The way you are with a quarrel, unforgiving, unapproachable. You think it's weakness to admit need. To depend. You've no real use for a wife. Marriage means a house to you and a son, your own image recast, but not a woman. You've no time for women."

Fergus took this point by point. He didn't believe it or think that she did. This was the way people behaved when they were impassioned. They exaggerated and distorted. Muriel laying her hand on every brickbat in a fight, ugly combat without rules or formal stylisation, the way the disaffected tore up roads to make a barricade. Who was to re-lay them? He could not precisely see how this hectoring had evolved from meeting Harris in a transit lounge and thought her merely overwrought. He would not similarly lose his head. And anyway, what was the point of using her name when there was no one else in the room?

"I mean it," she said. "I mean it. For once turn round and take cognisance of yourself."

"I don't need to. I have done no wrong."

She stood with the child girded round her body. Whether the increased heartbeat of the mother communicated itself to him or the raised voices dismayed, he burst into tears. He had never cried as such before, simply yelled in frustration, and so their shared response was 'Look what you have done.'

Leonie thought it was time he went to bed and there was a lull of argument in favour of activity. As she went about the house, Leonie noticed the quietness of Fergus' preparations, an oak refectory on the landing laid out with a display of cones and berries and miniature stockings, one for each of them, ready for hanging. She had done nothing except add Muriel's contribution of bad feeling to trouble an unexceptional Christmas Day. That was reprehensible. She tried to soothe the child and so herself.

She went downstairs and found Fergus fixing these stockings to the chimney piece. Perhaps he was excessively naïve, setting store by childish rituals or formalities, but there were times when it was

476

touching. Her methods broke continuance. She bowed her head against his back as he secured the toys.

"Can we be civilised?"

"I doubt it." But he half smiled. In light moods, he was a ravishing individual. First love, best love because it had no point of comparison.

"We've come so far this evening, I think the rest must be said." He didn't turn round so she was obliged to go on addressing his profile. "I love Moncrieffe and we have been lovers for some time. Not very long. Quite recently." As if minimising time reduced blame. "I am living with him in London."

"There's no need to tell me what I already know."

"Do you know? You indicate so little."

Fergus came to a halt, arms static in the air. "Well. Let me say this." He marshalled the diffuse strains. "You imply that I don't feel, as if feelings had to be expressed to be real. I think that's the fault of your calling, to superficialise. There are feelings that are quiet and strong but are never vented. I can't stop you following your career any more than I can stop you seeing this man, so I won't demean myself by trying. The woman isn't worth it who allows herself to be fought over."

Fine, if pontifical. Strange, all discussion with him slewed away from particularities and ended up in principle.

"What is it that you think I've done wrong?" he asked. "I'm ashamed of nothing that I've ever done. Nothing. Ever. If you can tell me of a single ignoble act, I'll apologise. But at the moment, I recant on nothing."

She had to be impressed by this authoritarian decree. I am the true Church. I am the way, the truth, the life. No, she wouldn't buy it as a philosophy beyond nodding to its monotheistic belief in its own righteousness as the sole path to salvation. There were more ways than one.

"No, you're not wrong, except in so far as you can't accommodate the rest of us who admit to being fallible."

Fergus was puzzled. Right and wrong ran like polarities of x and y across his thinking, the graph on which all acts were plotted, and could not be qualified. She argued as if fallibility or rule-breaking were an asset, mixing moralities and absolutes in a way he couldn't accept. She shifted ground, drawing parallels between one situation

477

and another that took him time to think out logically. His slowness of tongue didn't help. No sooner had he formulated one answer than she moved on to another plane.

"Tell me one thing," he said with a struggle. "How is he different from me?"

The question chastened. It was so shy. It had no concept of the cruelties she could inflict on him by wanton comparisons. "You're not different at all. You're the same men in a lot of ways. He's actually as unswerving in his beliefs as you are, or idealistic. I'm just a leveller. I don't have as many ideals as either of you. The only difference is, he's there and you're not. He's lived my rackety kind of life and you haven't. That's a bond. We racket on together."

It pained enough.

The stockings were filled. The night was set for Christmas. It was a frosty night in the valley of the Hermitage. The tops of the trees had caught a nip and were in turn silvered. A beautiful eve if one were so disposed to notice.

"Do you know what I'm going to do?" she asked. "I'm going to go to Midnight Mass at St Peter's. Do you mind staying in with Andrew?"

"No, I don't mind. Will you walk there?"

"Yes. I need to walk." He was pleased to have her go to Mass voluntarily, thinking it was a religious solace she stretched out towards, but it was simply the only meeting hall open at that time.

When she had left, Fergus went into the study and shut the door, wrapping himself in an assurance of the known. Here was the truth, unlying and unstinting. The events of that day were massive, a tree raised, much merriment with Irene, Harris passing through followed by the professor and Leonie's scourging follow-on. To come back to stillness described an interval of chaos so large as to be inconceivable.

The symbols on the page confirmed. He had been working on an equation and as he stared at them, twelve hours old, the numbers started to make sense again. Singularity. Yes, that was the place where he left off.

He moved the pair of screw-threaded rods with the blue knob and noted how the other two pairs immediately adjusted. He could see that, perceive the mathematical implications for the other two, knew it could be factorised – but do it! An equation with two hundred and fifty terms. It began to look as though he might fail on the same clumsiness of notation as his predecessor. Why had he chosen to take up that project out of dozens of easier alternatives? Out of a vanity that others had already failed. Not the combined brain power of Ferranti engineering had cracked the problem. The term itself lured and he cursed himself for falling into the word trap of singularity. It meant everything from exceptional to odd, embracing contradictory extremes of interpretation, high to low. Thinking this he suddenly remembered how his father had commented on this ability of English to mean two things at once. Such cheating words that made it possible to say the opposite of what you meant. When did π mean anything but itself? As he shifted the rods in turn, he was baffled by the misalliance between concept and expression, ideal and reality. The robotic brain would work if he could come up with a means of quantifying the pragmatic choice between position and material. Infinity to·formula. Ah, how?

By chance, the number that he wrote down on the next line of his calculations was 1, redolent of this singularity. A masculine shape. The straight line which was the shortest distance between two points and so the essence of logic. It was the prime number par excellence being a multiple of all others. He took it to himself, this 1 and noticed with a small but breathtaking insight that it was also the word for the first person.

$$1 = I$$

That equation was the neatest paradigm, although it did contain a mathematical solecism, that two sides should be so self-evidently equal. Left-hand side equals right-hand side was as close as he could come to simplifying the message.

Leonie's tirade had unsettled the objective capacity. As when his brain was overtired from chess, he began to confuse human and symbolic entities. This 1 was so pure, so absolute, so irreducible that it turned into the elemental mark. The jingle of a song 'One is one and all alone and evermore shall be so' appeared without forewarning on his thought screen, saved long ago. Singularity as in celibacy and temperamental aloneness might well be with him

479

for the rest of his days. The simplicity of the self equation he had arrived at, however trite, was also true.

He jotted down the three symbols again, one to one, and found another meaning in the process. Leonie had said they were the same men in many ways, he and Moncrieffe, the brace of male held together and separated by the equalising sign of the woman. I am just a leveller, she said. The trio of signs clung together with inevitable adhesion. The removal of one component required in logic the substitution of another. Then he rewrote it.

$$1 \simeq I$$

That was more revealing, however jokey. He and Moncrieffe were manifestly not equal, except perhaps in raw ability. They were not equal in status or in power or in her affections. She preferred the other man. Not equal. He thought Moncrieffe probably had flair, the elusive and unquantifiable asset. There was no such thing after all as equality. This thought revived the old aspiration during his father's trial in the Court of Session that man might be more equal before God than before the law, referral to the higher judgment, but this too in a black mood thinned as a creed to place reliance on. There was no parity that he could establish in the world around him. Man to man, man to woman, children in the affection of their parents, the human race in the sight of God – none. Dieu et mon Droit? Rubbish. A just deity would have served him better. He gave back word on God.

So scepticism devolved on robotics and his other credo, conceptual purity. If equals as a symbol was meaningless, contained a huge lie, what was the point of constructing these mathematical myths with it? It would crumble under pressure. There was no truth to be arrived at and no solution. Life was the quadratic equation made up of three undefined terms caught in an insoluble balance with each other and impervious to actual outcome.

50

Frances Moncrieffe drew back the door cautiously on Boxing Day and found a young woman of uncommon appearance, dressed in a long grey coat which she would normally have attributed to the costume department of the Victoria and Albert Museum, under Hussar or Cossack. She opened it cautiously because at four in the afternoon she expected no callers, having been recently delivered back from lunch with friends in Gilmerton, and had given her maid four days off in a row. Maid? Well, the anachronistic title served many functions, cook to cleaner and when not harassed she also answered the door.

Recognising the visitor, Lady Moncrieffe was less guarded and opened wide to admit. "Do go through," she said in tones that, for Leonie, walked out of political biographies. The London hostesses of the mid-war years had spoken that way, Nancy Cunard and Lady Mountbatten and Clemmy Churchill, and indeed Frances Moncrieffe had been a London debutante and socialite, pushed out by her father, the Lord Advocate, before settling for the remote orbit of a Scottish estate on the edge of Ultima Thule. Cast into outer darkness, she had said at one time, and lived only for the London season when her husband attended the House. But after his death she found there was a superfluity of widows on people's dinner lists and took up dowagerhood instead and the management of other people's lives.

"My grandson is not here," she said, joining Leonie in the blue room – rooms had colour connotations in this house, its Adam heritage preserved. "He is in Wester Ross but I am expecting him very shortly." The old lady consulted her watch, a gold lozenge where the face was distorted to suit the design more than accurate chronology. The minutes were exact but the hours mingled at the corners.

Knew who she was and that her business was with Watson but didn't throw her out. Perception and gentillesse offset each other.

481

"He telephoned at midday to say he was leaving Torrisaig but the roads have been so very bad. He hoped to be down by five." She thought the caller looked anxious and, because time hung heavily for her too until she heard the latest news of Charlie, she thought they might as well be frenetic together. "You are most welcome to wait. If it suits you. And an excellent excuse for tea."

Leonie removed the coat and waited. It was almost a dozen years since the steward had talked her round this room but the details had stayed more sharply than recent impressions. The walls were a powder blue, particular to the old fashioned distemper which was chalky and there was stucco work in oval panels picked out in white, garlands and bows made into ornamental trails. No, not white; it was off white into cream as atmosphere and time darkened its base tint. In stately homes this might be called the Wedgwood Room and have valuable pieces of jasperware in fireplace niches. But this house had lived as well as endured. The Wedgwood had been broken, or been re-allocated to another house, another room, not precious in the currency of function. The upholstery corners of an Empire day bed frayed. A water stain mottled the Cumberland table top but nobody hurried to renew or smarten.

Frances Moncrieffe came back with the silver service. Mere tea and wisps of biscuit but presented with a ritualistic show, the strainer, tongs on sugar cubes, a George III fluted cream jug. They tinkled, but didn't touch on the urgent questions. What had brought Leonie Barr to Inveresk on Boxing Day without forewarning and, on her side, why was Watson in Wester Ross and due back any time, when his visiting schedule had been planned in the reverse? Though Lady Moncrieffe passed the almond langues de chat and poured Melrose's tea, she offered not a shred of information, or asked it.

Aloof, gliding, but without the quality Leonie imagined was the prerogative of old ladies, spryness. The dowager was not an inch short of the actress's height and was far from fragile. Much of the face was familiar, Watson's features re-modelled on the female scale. The mouth had the same play about it so that Leonie watched intrigued while the identical shape and movement produced, from a feminine voice box, dissimilar sounds.

"My newspaper tells me that you will be appearing in a television series of *Anna Karenina*."

"Yes. We start quite soon."

"Odd woman, that Anna. Tolstoy was obsessed by her, don't you think, much more than the dreary little Kitty he tries to sell us – Kitty, Kitty what a name – but despises himself for it, or doesn't even know. Why did he call the book after Anna if we are meant to revile her? Very strange."

"Who do you like in the book then?"

"Like? My dear, I detest everybody in every book. Heroes and heroines are not my thing at all. Very naïve thinking. Their goodness doesn't deceive me for a minute. I always like the baddies. I admire survivors. Anna did not survive. No, the people I enjoyed most were the fallen women, the demi-mondaines of St Petersburg society, because they actually did what they wanted. Everyone else is so repressed by notions. Oh yes," she admitted, answering the astonished look Leonie gave her, "when you get very old you don't care about notionalism or even convention all that much. To live on is the issue. I'd be one of the fallen women before Kitty any day." She sighed, a dry and powdered sound, like flakes. "But that's because I was Kitty, a silly little gadabout who flirted all round, got hurt and then settled down and married a good man. A secure life in the country. Awfully dull. I even made jam with my husband's housekeeper and argued over recipes. Can you imagine? So I hate Kitty with good reason. But Tolstoy cheated us over Anna. She would have snapped her fingers at the men and said, To hell with all of you. Gone and set up a school for indigent gentlegirls like her little adopted friend. Though I suppose that isn't tragic enough. Tragedy is so very wearing on the nervous system. But as for trains and the engines of death, I ask you. I won't believe it, not even with seances and all thrown in."

Leonie saved this to relay to Stuart Ainslie. "Unfortunately, I have to act the version as it's written. I don't get to improvise on the ending of the classics."

"Well, I don't know. Garbo squashed that little Kitty out of existence. Edit it to suit you. I remember hearing Orson Welles say he didn't know for the life of him why he should film Kafka's version of Kafka. He was filming his. I go along with that. The classics aren't sacrosanct and if it suited Dr Bowdler to cut the naughty bits out of Shakespeare, I'm sure he had a good motive. It is simply interesting that the canon changes." She paused, thinking the almond fingers were as dry as dust and desisted from eating them. "Actually, that's it. We don't take the Bible seriously any more so we make literature into substitute 'good books' and treat them with undue reverence. Baloney. Give me bad books any day of the week. Sin is first rate for literature."

Minute and hour hand closed distinctively on twenty-five past five in the bottom quadrant. A pause while they noticed that in reality they waited. Snap their fingers? No, they still depended on male propulsion.

"I must say this," confided Frances Moncrieffe, dropping her discretion, "you are so very like your mother. She could have had her pick of the men but she went for the political instead of the domestic sciences. Yes, quite a different batch of recipes."

The Daimler arrived with a solid braking on the stone driveway. Watson hurried in, strained after the blinding headlights at the end of a journey which wasn't made any shorter by familiarity. Oh for a straight road, Fort William up. The impact of the two women sitting unexpectedly together hit him as he forestalled their unasked questions. One at a time, he thought, is all that I can take.

"Is the tea very ancient? I'll have one cup as it is but another pot would be appreciated, in half an hour."

And his grandmother rose, perceiving her cue to leave. Old women, she reflected, had as few breaks as old actresses. Needed for the matriarch from time to time, the brewer of tea, or the grotesque, a whiskered Judy for Punch to berate. Whereas men, ah! So many fun characters to choose from. Boardroom bullies, presidents in decline, gun-runners, blockade-busters, alcoholic artists and philanderers at every age – dirty old man, what luck! – any one would do, any one but Kitty Kitty the domestic cat.

"Has she been civil?" Watson asked.

"Most. I've been highly entertained."

"Yes. She can talk for half an hour on any given subject. A mine of misinformation."

"You're too hard. She was delightful. I learned a thing or two."

This interval of ten days since the party at the Speaker's House was the longest apart since September. Separations suited her better; she carried a strong mental image against which the present

484

was measured, noticed that he was very tired with a pulse ticking on the left temple, but was convinced of continuity. He wasn't. Alone, he was able to maintain his own equilibrium but emotional dependence unsettled. He'd forgotten this raw wanting, churning his guts like sickness. Time apart demoralised him. Each meeting was a new beginning when positions had to be restated, confidence established. In a testy mood there was no time and this added to irritability.

Leonie recognised herself of two days before and made allowances. "I'm sorry to have burst in on you unannounced. Maybe it should wait. You've got something else on your mind."

He tried to put the problems of Torrisaig to one side and pay attention to hers, although bridging the two locations in a matter of hours forced a different perspective on Inveresk and he couldn't see the frayed edge or the stain without taking on an added responsibility for them. And the tea was what they called wersh in Ross, bitter as outlook.

They had sat decorously apart under his grandmother's eye but moved together again, comfort touching. His body had an accommodating appeal, a corner to crawl into, shabby, rather worn but nonetheless congenial.

"What's up?"

"The stramash to end all."

He listened to her story, checking off the details in turn, the practised problem solver. "If he has any sense, your brother-in-law will have gone somewhere that doesn't have an extradition treaty with the UK. Israel for one. Matthew Geddes? It may not be the end for him but it'll be the end of the professor. What a blow for him. The University and the council chambers won't be lenient when he's been such a stickler in the past. Houses in order and so forth. Matthew will need a good barrister to represent him even at this in-house tribunal. Better than trying himself because he'll put his foot in it from nerves. He wants it watertight in case of wrongful dismissal." He thought and jotted down a name for her to take away. "I'll speak to this QC as soon as the holiday is over."

"It'll cost money," she judged by the address.

"Oh yes. It will that."

He got up, thinking her consultation was over, and tried to unwind to the point where he could deliver his own news.

"That's incidental, Watson. Or comes by way of introduction. It transpires that Harris left owing a great many people money, Fergus included. Five thousand pounds."

He almost whistled, admiring style. "Will that ruin him? Or you?"

"No. But Fergus' method of recoupment may. He has a note of guarantee from his mother on the sum and intends to wield that."

"Fair enough. Leave them to slog it out. Though I don't know which one of them is the more idiotic, to lend or to underwrite a loan."

"Quite. But I don't want Fergus to go ahead with what I think he has in mind. You can see, can't you, how pursuing his mother through the courts would take on the status of a holy war to him, avenging his father in some crusading way. But it looks like carnage to the rest of us. I want to pay off Harris' debt, except—"

"You haven't got the money?"

"A small matter of that sort."

As she talked about his avenging motive, Leonie had an image of Fergus as Hamlet. The excessive ratiocination, a man with greater capacity for friendship than for love, both tendencies impaled by the joint crime, death of his father and betrayal by his mother. A man who made all women into Ophelias, rejected for imperfection. Oh, go away, she thought to the casting propensity. He is nothing like.

Watson closed the curtains, wondering why Frances hadn't done it sooner. Most meticulous as a rule about keeping in the heat. "And what makes you think I'll shell out five thousand pounds to stave off someone or other being involved in a nasty legal wrangle, your husband or his mother or your brother-in-law, the only one with whom I have even passing acquaintance, by the way. Three minutes beside a gaming table."

"I know. It's a cheek really. I found myself saying it to Fergus and then wondered if you would."

"You've talked about this?"

"More than we usually do. Your name surfaced."

"So you are asking me for this sum as a substantiation of my good faith in a way that has nothing to do with the loan proper?"

486

Under his ironic tone, she remembered that about money and scroungers he was not indulgent. Begging letters for poor relief were not well received. Straight in the bin. He'd give time and advice to Matthew. A new suite from Harrods or a Cartier diamond if she wanted such a thing, any request in the line of gift would be granted. But hard cash or extortion, no. He was obdurate on levering, just as he hadn't put a penny into Torrisaig under Charlie's stewardship because, double or bust, it was not to his account and he wouldn't subsidise anything that wasn't making its own way. The economist had nothing to spare for sentiment.

"Or," he asked more cruelly, "is this a buy-out clause that eases your own conscience?"

The surface darkened. Water that was nothing, clear, indifferent, suddenly changed and took on the colour of the immediate. Storm threatened.

"I am not bought," she said, "any more than you. Perhaps less so."

"Then why are you trying to implicate me in a suit that already has," he counted off on one hand, "four signatories, not to mention James Geddes' son? Why involve another party? You talk of Fergus' revenge but are you sure you don't want to penalise Moncrieffe because, quite coincidentally, my name appeared among the plaintiffs against Michael Petrie?"

Strange, he had the same instinct as Fergus when it came to family. "No. I don't feel that way. Perhaps I'm appealing for a more general justice because you did the same thing in the same circumstances. Abused the system of trust. Fiddled yourself a bit out of the company's books. You were probably worse than Michael Petrie, and certainly than Matthew, but you came through unblemished and even if you had been found out, you'd have got off with a warning because of who you are. Why should you have all the luck? I'm afraid the democrat in me rebels that the rich get away with misdemeanours and the poor don't."

He had sat down at the Cumberland table to write her out a cheque, colliding with its gate leg. "I am to look on this as a levy to socialism?"

"That's as good as anything. I am a socialist, make no mistake."

"And do I lend or give?"

"I *will* repay."

"With interest?"

"Always."

The circuits of time revolved depositing them back. "You've asked me, Leonie, and so I'll give because you've never asked for much. A fiduciary bond. But there are two preliminaries. My 'fiddling' wasn't criminal but I can see how that may make it worse in your eyes. The Stock Exchange isn't any more assiduous in self-policing than the other professional bodies. Out-and-out rogues it has to banish, but the likeable ones thrive in what is quite a sizeable margin of malpractice. Probably their ingenuity is needed to stop institutions like that from calcifying. Nobody's fit for office. Whatever else, the memoirs always reveal that incapacity."

He started to write the cheque in Fergus' name and had finished the sum in words before she interrupted.

"And the second preliminary?"

"I think you ought to marry me and have done. This situation's becoming unmanageable as well as expensive."

She thought it hardly more appealing than the first proposal she received and was moved to reject it on the same grounds. "I can't run Fergus' house. What makes you think I can run yours? All three of them. The châtelaine, the keeper of the keys? Not me."

He swivelled round, pausing above his signature. "No, you're not equipped to be a wife any more than I am to be a husband. So we'll abandon the terms and say we're two people who enjoy being together and have a go at that instead. It's up to you to decide what happens. You've been wavering for a very long time. Now I am many things, I may even be a charlatan, but not a waverer. I do not abstain. I think you've stood still for long enough. I'm not jostling you. I'm not saying it's marriage or nothing, no whipping, but this indecision is bad for you. And me."

He gave her the bill of exchange and said, "I'll confirm the withdrawal to my bank on Monday so you can present it any time. In case they query it and can't find me."

"Oh, are you leaving again?"

He hesitated to tell her, thinking his grandmother with timing tactful to the minute, would come back with the tea and interrupt them. "This will shock you. It is very bad news indeed." He found these phrases did prepare for the worst. "Charlie had a stroke on Christmas Eve and I've been up there ever since. The doctor told

488

me it was the second stroke he'd had and I suspect the long-term prognosis wasn't good. He was going to have serious disability. But this morning he had another massive brain haemorrhage and died at ten o'clock."

"She knows?" said Leonie after a second, gesturing towards the anticipated step.

"The stroke of course, though I made out it was very minor until I could get up there and see for myself. But not that he died. I couldn't say that to her on the telephone."

She followed the timing of events concurrent with her own. "How dreadful that must be," she said, "for both of your sons to die before you. And you too," she attributed the weariness to its real cause, "you've had a hard time." Journeys, arrangements, decisions all dependent on his momentum. She stood up and put her arms round him pressing him close. "And I've bothered you with all this Petrie business. You should have shown me the door, both of you. Ah Charlie." She remembered she had missed saying good-bye to him at the reception. The two departures, his and Harris', came together with finality. Never again. "Were you with him?"

"Yes. Though it might have been better if I hadn't. You are so utterly helpless."

"What happened?" She stood back and looked into the head that was still adjusting to its own images.

"The patient vomits. The nurse knew what was happening. She'd seen it all before and she was very calm. She told me just to sit by him and keep talking. So I tried. But what can you say? Everything you say is so banal. I told him the greenhouse was all right. I'd been out and watered it and adjusted the thermostat. I think he was still conscious then. It was quick, that was the best of it. Charlie would have loathed being disabled. But it's harder for us to adapt to." He rubbed his eyes, fatigue, disbelief, a surge of sorrow came together.

"Do you want me to stay here with your grandmother?"

"No. She'll be very stoical. She was when my father died."

"You're Lord Moncrieffe," Leonie said, realising the shape of line at last.

"The king is dead. Long live the king. I used to wonder what on earth that meant. It seems ironical when there are so few kingdoms to inherit that I'm not sure I even want mine."

She picked up her coat to go. "What will happen next session?"

"I've got to decide at once about renouncing the title or resigning as MP. If I do, it's another by-election in the spring." Making three, his seat, Quercus' and the Labour back-bencher who died before Christmas, a good cross-section for the media to worm. These microseismic filtrations could bring the government down. "You could stand for Ross and Cromarty yourself," he suggested, "as an Independent."

"Me? It's ten years since I addressed a political meeting and that was only a rabble of students."

"As good a preparation as any. It comes back. Your mother would be pleased. She wouldn't have wasted money on those public speaking lessons after all. Might even canvass for you and pull in the SNP vote. I'll be your agent. Put up your deposit if you like. It would be good timing after *Anna*."

Fergus' hasty words turned into prophecy. "You are joking?"

"No. You've got more political blood than most candidates. Other countries change their actors into politicians or ambassadors. Why not us? We could do with some fire in the House and more women to boost the attendance."

"Not in Wester Ross. They wouldn't come to hear me in a play, far less think I've got some political clout."

"Oh, I'm not so sure. They like celebrities, and freaks. All you need to do is promise to uphold observance of the Sabbath and fight Sunday trading. You don't have to promise to learn Gaelic, even by phonetics." He came across the hall where the floorboards followed the divergent camber of two centuries. "Shall I drive you home?"

"No. I'll walk into Musselburgh then get a taxi. You need to stay here."

"I'm glad you came. Were here at this time."

They looked out of the door into a swirling night. Monday the Old Vic. Next week the Commons. Next month was anybody's guess.

Leonie walked alongside the stone walls of the village gardens until she came to Inveresk House and St Michael's Church behind it with the graveyards, old and new, stretching in a line towards the River Esk. One son buried there. One son at Torrisaig. She wished in a way she hadn't met the old lady, to be haunted by her

490

loss. Whatever Watson thought, and it was the opinion of the childless man, there was no means of reconciliation to the death of offspring because it was the end of the foreseeable future and that dynastic possibility in oneself.

51

Leonie arrived back at the Hermitage from Inveresk in the early evening, sub-zero bitter.

It was only eight o'clock but the house was shut up for the night. The metal-banded door was closed and all the lights, except for the one in Fergus' study, were extinguished. She sent the taxi away and tried her key in the lock but found it wouldn't turn. She rang the bell, but there was no answer and when she rang again she realised it wasn't connecting inside the house. Had the battery gone flat? No, she remembered it was an electric bell. The fuse had been removed from the fuse box, a Petrie device for catching out late revellers. She had been locked out and no mistake.

She had a surge of anger that Fergus should be so isolationist – it would need a diplomatic corps to re-open communications with him – thwarted on what to do next. No bell. The telephone off the hook, or sending out the engaged tone because he worked on the computer. She walked towards the back of the house but the area round the study was sectioned off with a wall and a gate. The light taunted her with its proximity to contact, a wedge of possibility in the darkness of the garden. What would she do anyway if she could get closer to it? Throw gravel chippings like an enamoured groupie to attract attention? Or smash the pane like Muriel and break her way in? She refused to be so undignified as to hoist her leg over a sill like a house thief and her own house too, but began to feel ominously that the shutters were deliberate, locks and bolts proliferating in a mental exclusion zone which Fergus enforced. She might never be allowed inside again. She could knock till Doomsday without getting an answer. 'Who will we associate with?' had been a far sighted question when it transpired that it would not be with each other.

Access to her property denied; access to her child. Her eye went up the castellated front of the building to Andrew's room. Some of this was her share. What was going to happen to it? She had a vivid sight of the child putting his head down for comfort on her lap, touting that noisy duck everywhere he went until the colours wore off the edges of the wood, the moment when he burst into tears most heartfelt because it was most human; pictures that would recur in her imagination but could not sustain it. Fergus might be wise to lock him up. If she had entry, she would be tempted at that moment to steal the boy and fight for the right of custody through the courts, although in this instance she thought possession was not nine-tenths of the law.

The silence was as endemic as the cold, grave-like and repellent to the living instinct. Half an hour of hovering had congealed and Leonie, in spite of the greatcoat, admitted she couldn't hang on indefinitely without petrification herself. Stony, the building frosted over as the street lights picked out mica in the granite. No noise, no music, no voices broke the unfrivolous air. The place was a well so deep it absorbed casual sound and tested the feasibility of the bottomless.

She remembered the cheque, the collection of which had prompted this exclusion and thought it foolish not to deliver it after so many pains. She scrabbled in her bag and found an envelope on which she wrote,

If this eases your decision, use it.

then put the cheque inside and posted it through the letterbox, third party.

She turned to go but, still in the shadow of the porch, wondered where. Locked out on Boxing Day. Each house where she might seek refuge was fraught with its own tension, making her reluctant to reimpose herself at Inveresk or enter the disputes of Grange Loan or knock at Irene Geddes' door. She shied away from more scarifying emotions and headed towards her mother's flat at Morningside where, if not welcome of the traditional sort, there was at least acceptance.

At Inveresk, Watson locked up the house and then went back to the blue-coloured living room. Paper and telephone, the instruments of communication, waited for his input. There was a funeral to arrange, probably on New Year's Eve, and Macleod's duties as co-ordinator fell to him. He started to jot down a list of guests and tasks to perform in separate columns, occasionally relating the two, but this was in part mechanical. His urgent thoughts were interrupted by the import of Leonie's arrival and her message.

The room was snug, its contents protected by a devotion to heritage more comprehensive than insurance policies. It represented a security in every sense, defensible space, the tranquil but also an asset against which the monetary could be raised, a safe house, yes, a safe. He drew himself gratefully inside but with a tremor of fear and of compassion for those outside the walls.

Leonie's narrative had touched him at many points. He grieved for his father's friend and his son, calumniated by the rigmarole of circumstance which forced him into a belated review of Michael Petrie's case. He was as capable as any man of prejudicial glibness and had never doubted that the financier was in some measure guilty. With greater insight, he realised how remorselessly the common law of rumour and report could frame its victim. Justice? No chance. Suspicion was convictive. The story upset the trust he'd placed on the judicial scales.

He was most troubled by the unavoidable comparisons between himself and Harris Petrie. Leonie had been right to turn his confession round and prove his own infringements. He had sat beside that gaming table at that age and, looking back, was hard put to it to say what separated him from Harris. Nothing in integrity, so he fell back on insubstantial luck or an element in these walls, supportive, historic, a standard which elevated him even when he transgressed.

Who goes home? That was a phrase to sober when the wind blew in gusts and leaves ghosted against the window. Not everyone for sure. He had a vision of the younger Petrie, a man in a landscape running and tracked him for some time with his eye across the unprotected space. The runner, the escapee. The lawyer in Moncrieffe condemned while the humanist sympathised with this exiled figure who in legend came to a church door and rang the monks' bell crying 'Sanctuary, sanctuary', because he contained a particle of himself. Where was Harris' safe house? There weren't so many inviolable spots nowadays. The kings' men had turned into technocrats and could apprehend the miscreant three thousand miles away, with Fax dossiers delivered at the press of a button along an international cable.

Moncrieffe was alarmed by this fugitive tendency, didn't admire back-packers or the mental homeless, unlike Leonie, because repeated moving on undercut his version of stability and real progression. The man who couldn't retain money or property seldom managed continuity with people. He foresaw letters sent poste restante, a counterfeit communication under an assumed name. Haz Petrovitch would be anonymous among the displaced persons of Israel or South America, countries with lenient immigration laws that absorbed the code-breakers without an inquisition. To disguise his true identity, Harris would retreat into the patronym in a circuitous reversion, in hiding from himself. Imagine that, being afraid of your own name. Whatever landscape Watson was condemned to run in, it was at least spanned by the signposts of Moncrieffe, wasn't a pathless mapless waste. Family, however stifling, did enclose space.

His thoughts came round to Fergus as they often did. He admired the mathematician more than his own breed of talents because the man was self-made, self-taught and even self-correcting. The autonomous entity inspired. He wished he knew Fergus in person or could at least put a face to the name, although the sainted should be faceless or not drawn in spatial iconography. Not like his siblings, Leonie said, not like anyone which made him, of all the landscape-crossers, the most lonely. It was new territory he explored, going out to the brink of concept and doing the unimaginable of Columbus. Not flat but round, not three but four, dimensions rather than tangible planes. He could move through a perceptual vacuum down the solitary by-ways of the brain. Belief, what belief it needed to set out without firm hope that there was such a thing as destination.

The landscape which was the externalisation of the mind or the achievement altered according to the individual, a parallax. Deserts surrounded Fergus in his view, or the backdrop to a Biblical mythology painting like St John of the Rocks, scribing a monotonous plateau in which the cave-bound hermit contemplated the skull. Aridity for miles around while in the distance Cain wandered homeless on the face of the earth or the other brother Jacob who swindled on birthright was outcast and outlawed.

The two brothers grated in him, partly themselves splintered, thief and thieved from, partly components of Moncrieffe. They invaded the conscience, unappeased by the writing of a cheque since that could not offset the theft of the affections.

Leonie walked down the hill to Morningside in an alternative fear, that her mother's flat would be empty too, with Ellice Barr off to a civic meeting or a party. There were people in the flat, audible from outside, although it wasn't Ellice who opened the door to her but Stuart Ainslie, buffeted on laughter down the corridor. "Oh good," he said, "I wanted to see you about something. Hurry up and get your stuff off." Unceremonious. He followed her into her own room. "Have you been up to the Hermitage?"

"Yes, I couldn't get a reply."

"Here, that's a good coat," he appreciated. "We could use that in the train scenes." He examined its neckline for accuracy of costume detail now that he had started to commute daily to the nineteenth century, between Moscow and St Petersburg. "Fur collar. Hat to match."

"I don't wear fur."

"Well sod you. Society Muscovites did."

The salon disposed itself in ranks, standing, sitting, lying order. To dispel the coldness of the night someone knelt at the log fire and made toast with a long-handled fork, then passed it on to someone else who buttered it on the carpet tablecloth and handed round platefuls. There was a plastic tub of honey circulating somewhere. It reminded of book-bound nursery teas and golden innocence. Sometimes the bread caught alight and sent a singeing round the room. These charred morsels were highly prized by some. Ellice raised a hand to her from a sofa and went on with her conversation.

"Toast?" invited Stuart.

They found a corner. Ellice's chairs seated four people, one in and three against.

"God, Leonie, you're losing your looks."

"I'm just tired and thin. Your preference always was for buxom." She massaged her fingertips back into life.

"No. You're looking astonishingly plain. Get a grip. I want you to look sensuous, not like some incipient version of a bag lady."

He was like one of those doctors who told you to gargle with

496

salted water for a sore throat, efficacious but hardly soothing three hours before the next performance. She ate more, drank a little and started to revive. Stuart had reached the point where he carried a notebook with him if not a full script of the play he was working on, and would dive into this pocket diary to make notes like the most dedicated of scribblers. Leonie took it from him and flicked through. *Anna Karenina* obsessed his mind as much as hers and it was a relief to share the maniac tendency as they turned talkers in code.

"It's a marvellous scene that one when Vronsky comes to Anna's brother's house and looks up over his head and sees her on the landing, lit from behind. Comes and goes away again without declaring himself."

Leonie thought back almost two years and remembered other good nights. "You can't do that scene in a play."

"Ah, agreed. But on television you can. It's almost as intimate as the novel. A hung second. Just visuals. You can do it."

He'd made a list of episodes with the scenes covered in each of the six. By the side were details of clothes and sets. Stuart avoided atmospherics. He loathed films like Polanski's *Macbeth*, all murk and gloom and Pictish dyes. He liked playing to be clean and sparkling and rather hard around the edge, a draughtsman more than a colourist. She picked up his schema from the notes like a sketch for a history painting, annotated with stray ideas that hadn't much to do with paint but everything to do with picture craft.

"Am I always to be in monochrome?" she asked, reading his intention.

"Ah," he rubbed the end of his nose. "I was thinking of giving you a dark blue ballgown. And I imagined one of those beautiful things they used to call morning dresses, a dipped waist," he showed her how, incongruous over trousers, "and in a gorgeous cloth like moleskin. That would have to be grey. Isn't it peculiar how a novel has to be in period costume? Imagine Jane Austen in anything but Regency. It won't go. You get away with Shakespeare and Shaw and Ibsen in modern dress but when you open the curtains on a novel, it's the contemporary scene you see out of the window. The real novel anyway, not those fudged up bits of history or science fiction full of might-have-beens and would-bes. I just can't do *Anna* in modern dress although I'd like to bring her up to date. Too localised. Pity. Even the train is an anachronism, isn't it? What would it be nowadays? Being mowed down by a jumbo jet doesn't have the same glamour somehow. The plot would have to be completely rejigged."

Leonie looked round the room, sifting known from unknown faces in her mother's entourage. There was a rapid turnover among half of the callers; friends of friends came once and moved on, the very young who looked for a niche and decided this heterogeneous mix wasn't it, too argumentative or fluid for comfort, or people who were themselves passing through for a festival or a one-off conference and took away the wrong impression, that this scatter was somehow typical. The rest endured, fellow workers for whatever cause. Archibald was there, struggling for his own political viability. He knew he faced deselection after two electoral defeats. Being the PPC for ten years was a dimension he would miss and so he fought his corner beyond the point of common sense. "Is Alison coming?" Leonie asked, noticing the absence.

Stuart followed her gaze as if he needed to double-check his memory. "No, I don't think so." He answered the immediate and then, perceiving Leonie might mean London and Ontario, added, "She's probably going to do some speaking for the SNP this spring and eventually stand as a local councillor."

"Young for that, surely?" Leonie ascribed local politics to veneration like her mother's or Professor Geddes'.

"Hm. Do her good. Ellice has taken her in hand, training her up. If you did something with Alison she could be a rattling public speaker." Voice down an octave. Sheaf of common sense in her hand, the official party line, not to be deviated from. She might be platform material.

"I hope she gets something out of it. What ward is she thinking of standing for?"

He frowned over the memory search. "I don't know because honestly it bores the pants off me when they get going. I mean I don't mind turning out to mark my box but as for hearing all the background stuff, no ta. By the way," he asked, checking his watch, "why aren't you in the middle of the mad scene on the boards of the Old Vic right now?"

The rest of the room accepted erratic appearances as the norm, either hers or theirs. "Alan Mills gave me leave of absence until Monday evening. But I can't say it's been much of a break."

"Oh, why is that?"

"Haven't you heard about Harris?"

He hadn't and Leonie had to be astonished at the insularity of Petries. Alison and possibly even Muriel didn't know the facts, which were quickly told.

"But there's more than that," he said to the dispirited look which he now saw was more than cold and maigre. "Why has Fergus locked you out? Has the Moncrieffe connection become apparent even to the wilfully blind? Well, don't be such a chump, Leonie. You'd better face up to a lot more publicity than this, and console yourself there's no such thing as a bad press. You live in the public eye and you mix with public figures and this is the bottom line. Add, subtract, result. That Fergus has tumbled to it, or that you've gone and done an Alison and spontaneously told him, doesn't change a thing from the actual situation as it was before. So cheer up and put a bit of weight on." He passed her the calorie-laden toast.

"I fainted after Wednesday's performance," she admitted, going further.

He chewed for a long time, butter mellow, honey sharp and dripping both onto the lapels of his leather jacket before he smeared it beeswax thick. "You're singularly inept, aren't you? Becoming unemployable. You'd better not faint on my set or I'll tear up your Equity card."

"That's more or less what you said last time."

"How do you manage it? Once is careless but twice is crazy."

"That's the way I've always played it. All or nothing. A risky business but otherwise, what is it? Just so much self-indulgence."

"Who knows about it?"

"Nobody. It's been hectic enough for the last few days without that."

"It's good in a way. It fits with the plot." Not hers but his, not real but fictional.

She had to be exasperated by such fanaticism, theatrical, political, religious. "What if I pulled out?" The person asserted her independence from what was imposed on her.

She'd never threatened this before, even indirectly, so he took it to heart. Endanger his script? Not likely. "You will not. You will not pull out. I fought for you to get this part and you're going to play it every line. I'm amazed that you're not down there tonight instead of letting your understudy do a stand-in. She's fine but she's not star quality. It's not professional. The people have paid their money to see you and that's what they should get. The better you are, the more you're obliged to fulfil the quota. Don't forget that or start to indulge yourself in your private life. Suffer away. It's good for the acting but don't on any account quit."

"I'm sick of dying."

"Maybe so. But it is a damned good spectacle. You've not to cheat your public, or yourself for that matter. Why should you give them the satisfaction of saying, She couldn't make it through the final act? No limping off, Leonie, and no understudies. You're going on."

An Amazon he wanted. A woman who would cut her right breast off if it improved the flight of her arrow.

"Is it true what I heard on the grapevine," asked Archibald, catching her attention down a channel of the room, "that Charles Moncrieffe died today?"

The question substantiated Stuart's point. Events twelve hours and a hundred and fifty miles away travelled swiftly when they were attached to an established name. That her corroboration was asked sealed a different form of public knowledge.

"Yes, that's so."

"And what will his nephew do about the seat?"

"I've no idea."

"What's that?" asked Stuart. "Might he resign?"

"Either way," said Ellice, "it's a resignation. You can't sit in both Houses." She reflected that he was no good to anyone as Lord Moncrieffe and hoped he wouldn't give up his power base for a tuppenny-ha'penny title. MP outweighed all other status in her hierarchy. The hereditary gain was void.

Archibald waxed adamant about the value of political experience until someone pointed out that was exactly what Moncrieffe hadn't got.

Leonie was silent in the middle of what became another talking shop. Now that he was in danger of going, each of the political strands in the room annexed Moncrieffe as their own and claimed

500

that if he stayed on in the Commons, he could do their cause some good. Scot, reformer, centrist, one aspect of his tenure at Westminster appealed and felt it would be let down by his resignation though no one had thought he represented anything at all before. Leonie watched as the seats emptied and filled again without too long an interval. Stuart might be right; what they did was more important than who they were.

52

The cold inside the chapel was bitter, eating into the bones. Stone walls conducted the freeze of the air indoors in spite of a wood-burning stove near the pulpit and some massive piping callipered to the wall. It roasted without warming, or the heat rose futile into the raw beams of the roof among the Latinate plaques and some tattered banners, regimental or armorial, that shifted in the currents. Nothing softened the permeated cold of stone.

Even bodies. There were hundreds of bodies. Watson, arriving at the head of the cortège with his grandmother, was scarcely able to take in the rows of faces in the pews. It was a capacity congregation. The villagers spilled over into the churchyard when virtually everyone who had come to the party in September returned now. Charlie had been known and fondly regarded in a dozen cells of Highland life, politician and justiciar, fisherman and gardener and host, so these enclaves sent their representatives to pay their last respects. Watson nodded to heads nodding to him.

There were more extraneous elements present among the mourners. Charlie had been the Moncrieffe of Torrisaig, chieftain of a clan world wide, so in spite of the raw weather and deterring distance a dozen envoys from the Scottish societies in North America and Australia came to the gathering. Watson recognised them because they wore a tartan emblem, like the clan rosette.

He hadn't realised that the funeral, at this unseasonable time of year in the lull between Christmas and Hogmanay, would be a media event until he walked up the main aisle of the church. Fleming had come out of retreat at Chequers and made the long journey north for sentimental reasons. His wife sat between him and the Speaker of the House. They'd all three thought better of the impulse at several points along the way and stamped their feet discreetly to aid circulation. Cameras came to shoot their exit. John Prosser, the reporter from the *Ross-shire Journal* and a dozen other correspondents waited likewise, not for the Prime Minister so much as Watson's decision on whether he would take up Charlie's seat on the cross-benches or disband Moncrieffe and Torrisaig for good.

Friends came to soften the impact of so many outsiders. Quercus, Laidlaw, Simon Dunns heading a league of nationalists and all the Wester Ross folk, the Macleod cousins, both land and political agent, Sandy Govan rowing over from Carse to attend a rite which was ancient and tribal as much as a Christian burial. They were men coming out of the mountains for the chieftain all the more scrupulously because he wasn't theirs; but the days of ceremonial were passing. On this scale, in this way it might never happen again so that the five-hundred-strong congregation came together to salute not only Charles Moncrieffe but their common history.

And the actress. Making an apology to her exasperated director, Leonie flew to Inverness and hired a car to take her to the west arriving with a minute or two to spare before the hearse left the grounds. To curtail argument she joined the Moncrieffes in the first, a breach of protocol and possibly common sense under so many eyes.

"Will you stay?" he asked aside.

"I shouldn't."

Neither would she have taken a place in the family pew if another had been vacant and regretted the imposture. She stood between Watson and his grandmother, a useful bridge when they were both too brittle to unbend towards each other. Proud, they protected themselves from shock or collapse by formality and were rigid in handshake or address.

The service was a cross between presbytery and forum. The minister, peripatetic from Achnasheen to Lochalsh, read a passage from Ecclesiastes, Remember thy Creator, which Charlie was known to be fond of. As simple and incantational as a proverb, it reminded of basic tenets. In the day when the keepers of the house shall tremble, and the strong men shall bow themselves, and the grinders cease because they are few, and those that look out of the window be darkened. That was a message each of them converted into a metaphor for the man they came to mourn and by generality for themselves. They were all grinders, mill and grist sometimes dauntingly out of proportion. The house did tremble, strong men did bow. The moment, while it set at mid-afternoon, contained infinity. Half a thousand people paused in tipping towards the end of a day and an old year to assess their progress, neither smug nor self-righteous. Cold invaded the mind like conscience and left few spots untouched. It gripped.

The peroration was given by Quercus, not the minister. He didn't supplant the official in the pulpit but stood on the dais in front of a lectern, speaking apparently effortlessly and without notes. There were three men he examined in turn: the politician, the practical lawyer, the chief, each one a traditional aspect of Highland lordship. Few were better placed to record Charles Moncrieffe's contribution in the House of Lords or admire the ardour of twenty years spent on the magistrate's bench but it was the landlord that Quercus warmed to.

"Stock," he said. "If there is one word that will serve as an epitaph to Charles Moncrieffe's work it is 'stock'. Livestock, fish stocks, restocking the woods round Torrisaig, plant stock; these separate pursuits of his are a spectrum that define the core concern. Putting back. What we use up we must put back. Charles Moncrieffe was an advocate of conservation long before the word entered the fashionable vocabulary of ecologists. He was mindful of balance and was in all his attitudes the most evenly disposed of men. That is, the swing of his mind came to equilibrium. Neither passive nor excessive, he was capable of that stability because he accepted change. Charlie was always on the lookout for something new, a man of diverse interests, untiring attention to detail and an encyclopaedic knowledge of his subject. Who hasn't been shown round the greenhouses at Torrisaig and been beguiled by those processes of regeneration? The plant genealogist is a man we should pay heed to in our times. It is his intent to develop the new strain from the mutations of the old. He knows nothing flourishes without care and the correct conditions, about which he can afford to be neither haphazard nor negligent. We may not share the aim but we must respect the endeavour. It is a parable for the widest scope of politics, the grafting of modern onto traditional, ways to means, vigorous to outdated but done without needless waste or destruction. Charles Moncrieffe was a man who believed in a tangible future and in small, quite undemonstrative ways built towards his version of it. This ancient seat is the testimony to continuous effort such as his. The paths are laid, the area is planted. Time and inclination do the rest."

Watson listened nine parts convinced. The senator would not demean a man in passing, delivering the innuendo of Mark Antony, but he did omit the salient. A pile of bills, a dwindling manforce were reminders of a harsher national economy than estate management or breeding the ornamental garden variety which wasn't food after all. He felt the words were shaped primarily as a sermon for himself. His time and his inclination were called upon to sustain that planted future. A Conservative peerage, a sound land policy; it was the conservationist's charter, or salvation Tory style. He grimaced at the reversions to type.

Other men got to their feet impromptu and said their piece, witness to kind acts or incidents that lodged in the memory, until the ceremony developed into a spontaneous testimonial which brought the man close again. Far and wide, no one could recall a meanness. The company breathed as one in praise and a subdued sorrow that so few men left no enemies.

The congregation sang The Lord's My Shepherd which, in the church built from the same rubble as the mountain sheiling, was appropriate. There was a Kathleen Ferrier in the choir, sublime in her solo descant although the organ stops, being cold, didn't respond immediately to the fingers of the organist and wheezed a little breathlessly. The psalm moved and expanded like aspiration. Amen was not an end to prayer but its inauguration.

The piper came to the wall of the churchyard where the grave was prepared, the notes of his chanter amplified by wind. Lord Moncrieffe was laid to rest beside Loch Torrisaig and alongside the other lords, father to son for twenty generations. The music was not doleful as much as stirring when piper and bard and harper were the ceremonial entourage of the chieftain, accompanists to every mood from the hearth to the battleground. The crowd, filtering between the headstones which hadn't been allowed to topple, were themselves braced. Only a handful, recognising the plangent notes of 'The flowers of the forest are a' wede away', could connect with the song's historical occasion and found themselves lacking in fortitude.

No one was turned away from the house. The fires had been lit early in the day and the resinous smoke of oak and pine perfumed the chambers. They created a current of people as well as air, with visitors drifting compulsively to hold their hands out to the blaze of logs, admire the firedogs or the mantel carving, and then move round as they were warmed towards the whisky tumblers and jugs of bubbled spring water or tea urns set up like samovars. The place kept on the seethe. People saw each other and were lost again before they had a chance to speak.

"So," said the Prime Minister, drawing his host out of the throng. He was mindful of the hour and a drive back south. Strath Bran didn't inspire him in the dark or the snow although a temporary thaw had set in, clearing the roads. Two security men hovered at the main entrance and he found their restiveness contagious. "What's it to be?"

"How attached you are to the delineations of yes and no."

"A borrowed fondness," said Fleming, remembering the message of refusal to his last invitation. He looked through the window, a square of mottled hand-blown glass that obscured, and was indeed darkened with its outlook. He rubbed the pane to make sure its speckles weren't snow starting to close them in. "It's not too late to change your mind. The offer's open. Whatever you decide, Lords or Commons, we have a place for you. I agree with Quercus. The paths are laid, although mine happen to diverge from the direction of his. I wonder if that will be the last speech we hear from him? Dear oh dear, why do all the good men have to go until we are left with the sedimentary dross?"

This brisk attempt to make a treaty of alliance had echoes of Watson's own declaration to Leonie not many days before at Inveresk, with its fatuous assumption that other people ought to come your way if they are to make intelligible progress and that the floating voter didn't have an in-built resistance to adhering. The facility for changing your mind, or keeping it open, was a precious if deeply a-political idea. He was tempted to borrow Leonie's terms in his reply. I can't run my own House. What makes you think I can help you to run yours? In the end he said, "I feel as though I'd just sustained a massive electoral defeat, although I've probably had a landslide. I can't take it in because the change is so overwhelming. I can't make a rational decision for a few days yet."

"You should by the time Parliament re-opens."

"I know. I will. But not today."

They stood in the smoking room, with the political elements tending to forgather in the male preserve, and Fleming noticed the chess games which hadn't been dismantled. He'd forgotten all about these long-drawn contests of Charlie's. He'd suffered some humiliating checkmates in this room, unable to match Charlie's enthusiasm through to the end game. Early autumn evenings after a day spent on the moor or in the salmon river, sunk in armchairs around a peaty fire, the women circulating together with the port in a drowsy blur where euphoria matched exhaustion. The old days came back vividly, sealed with the polymers of nostalgia. That was the feature of loss which turned the past into an era; its people wouldn't be reassembled again.

Fleming went to collect his wife for the return drive and thought he ought to offer someone a lift in the official car. He was going on to his brother's house in the Borders for New Year and considered taking John Laidlaw, his near neighbour, all the way. Then he remembered the slights of the last Parliamentary year with the Liberals not co-operating over his problems with the post of Solicitor-General, or ready to swell his majority, so he veered away and asked the Speaker if he wanted a lift to Inverness, hoping to influence the direction of the casting vote instead. There was more mileage in that.

As he came back from saying goodbye to his three principal guests, Watson saw Leonie and his grandmother in a window embrasure and was surprised to find he wasn't prompted to go and separate them. Women together were almost a novelty in his experience. If anything, he wanted to eavesdrop and hear how they spoke to each other when they were alone. Kindly? From the far side of the room the gestures were kind, eye to eye, with speech and listening intermarried. They had the affinity of kith as Leonie rose and found the older woman tea and brought people over to speak to her, keeping things quietly on the move round about her without too much drain on energy. Leonie had been more right than he; the death of her son had devastated by its suddenness as much as its fact. Lady Moncrieffe read it as the end of the future. While this provoked him, translated into an additional pressure to decide according to her wishes, Leonie could diffuse the long-term anxiety with talk of the immediate. He heard them stray into areas of the weather, the age of a brass lamp fitment which was skirted

507

with a silk shade, and the fictitious personage of Anna in whom they could dispute vicariously.

Leonie realised that a lift with the Prime Minister was her only chance of catching the last flight to Heathrow, but let it slip.

A group of the long-distance travellers had set out, under the stewarding of the Macleod brothers, to tour the house and Leonie walked along behind them to view the official exhibits and listen to their commentary, Alistair the schoolmaster acting as guide on history, Donald on livestock and geography. She found the objects they revered were pathetically few and crude compared with the interiors of Windsor or Hampton Court or the English stately homes. They were proud of a drinking horn with a silver rim from which the new chieftain had to drink two mutchkins of whisky at his inauguration ceremony. A bit above a pint at one go, no setting down. The thing was itself unexceptional, as rough as the tools and quernstone nearby which had the prehistoric shape of flints. Daily life in the ninth century wasn't far removed from Carse, she thought, primitive and uncosseted.

She looked at the books printed in Gaelic which the chieftain's hereditary pipers and bards had used and wished she had some of the language to decipher its congested diphthongs that read like sighs. Perhaps the summer gatherings and outdoor clansmen recitals were the forerunners of the Mod, the ceilidh of the Gaelic-speaking world much like the Eisteddfod to the Welsh. Singing, dancing, playing, recitation, composition. She didn't know if the festivals were significant or childish. What did gold medals signify to a minority culture when they gave no guarantee of lasting?

Leonie dawdled so long reading the inscriptions that the body of the tour left her behind. It was a copy of the statutes of Iona that gave her pause. In 1611 the chiefs had been placed under a legal constraint to give their children a Lowland education, ostensibly one in English, which confirmed the breakdown of the clan system compounded of the Highland way of life, already under economic threat, and the Gaelic language. That was why the Scottish aristocracy spoke for the most part in faultless southern accents. They had eradicated the provincialism from their speech which eighteenth-century visitors like Johnson and Sterne had laughed at. Brogue in Bond Street. Not on. The banning of the tartan, the confiscation of ancestral lands. How had anything survived? The lessons Leonie learned from her mother had a current use. Scottish Nationalism wasn't the quirk of fanatics. They were serving a preservation order on Torrisaig and like castles.

Watson came into view at the end of a passageway and joined her. "Dusty old stuff, isn't it?"

"It would benefit by some re-arrangement."

"Oh yes, I've no doubt. Son et lumière. Tableaux vivants. I suppose we could make it 3D audio-visual exciting if we really tried. Whose voice on the cassette tape, mine or Donald's?"

"Was Fleming hounding you again?" she wondered, turning back.

"Yes, as I expected. Join the gang. Though he's deluding himself if he thinks a Labour peer can have a glorious future. Can you see one popping up with any credibility in a socialist cabinet? All right for the Conservative image but not the reds. On the other hand it does look effete staying on in the Commons – for the sake of staying on. Perverse."

He stopped and stared out of a window that gave a view down into the valley. It was about six o'clock. Daylight had gone and across the hillside and the loch there were a dozen points of light as men with livestock got ready for the following day's tasks. Pails of meal on kitchen stoves. Bran and hash prepared, a corn store visited in the dark. The crofters went on with the unhurriable, the daily chore of animal dependence.

"I like this place," he said. "I like these people. I want to do my best to hang it all together but you see, don't you, how I could work at it and never make the slightest impression. It's a business nowadays, this type of property. I could put in half a million pounds and still it wouldn't show a profit. I've had enough of doing things badly. Please God let me succeed at something."

Just within earshot, the Macleods were describing the architectural evolution of the house. The word house came along the vaulted walls and interrupted Watson with an echo that was sibilant from repetition. House domestic; House professional. It focused his dilemma not simply between the two Houses of Parliament, but the ancestral home that was entry to the Upper. The family seat in his case was both a residence and a vocation. She understood his dilemma perfectly, torn between her own readings

509

of play house. Fergus was a lucky man, the eremite who needed no external stimulus, sited in one, undivided, monocentred like a spot of gravity that couldn't shift, house singular.

She thought about adding her own news to that momentous day but drew back. She'd maintained that if she ever became pregnant she would keep the child, however fraught the circumstances. That had sprung from a partially feminist defiance. No one was going to take it from her, certainly not a man. The converse, of the father being obsessively involved with his offspring, was something she'd already lived through and it confounded the natural, instinctive response, turning it into his decision. To tell Watson was to unleash a passion, passionate gratitude that in this he had succeeded, passionate arguments for divorce and remarriage, emotions she could hardly face at the end of this day. Life needed a longer distancing from death. Besides, Watson should decide his personal future without bias. Professional first. Domestic later.

"What day is it?" he asked. "I've lost track."

"Thursday."

"And the date?"

"The thirty-first."

"So this is Hogmanay. Great. I'm stuck at Torrisaig and the guests have drunk it dry. What a way to see the New Year in."

"We could always go first-footing round the village."

"No," he considered. "On reflection, I couldn't talk to another soul or face another dram tonight."

"Well then, hush."

"I'll get rid of these laggards and spend an evening stoking the fire instead," and they laughed at the homeliness of the celebration.

53

On New Year's Day there were no newspapers printed in Britain but on the following day, Saturday, Muriel Petrie found herself unreasonably interested in the lead story published in the Scottish daily which she had delivered, a tabloid that veered towards tittle-tattle. So excited was she that she went to the shop at Comiston to look over the piles on the newsagent's counter and bought up half a dozen of the other morning editions on offer.

Then she continued hotfoot on her original errand to see Fergus. The mail had come through the door too, after a day's suspension, and she brought the package with her. A brown envelope with the address typed across the shorter side, smacking of legal matters. Fergus had moved quickly in consulting his solicitor whose letter was enclosed together with a photocopy of the affidavit Harris provided citing their mother as guarantor. High dudgeon. She was in it.

Fergus had had a train of visitors at the Hermitage over the week as it became obvious that his brother's debts left a vortex no one could stop spiralling. He was thoroughly tired of opening the door to strangers who were variously rude, threatening or embarrassingly earnest. He became as expert on the stall as Harris himself, referring callers to the insurance company on whose official business his brother was deemed to be travelling abroad. 'I do not know' turned into an hourly refuge. So Muriel came as no surprise, skidding her tyres against his gravel as Harris had done.

Her greeting was more perfunctory than the double syllable she gave to Leonie a year before. It was nil, his expectation.

Instead, she pushed the envelope towards him. "What is this supposed to be?"

"Supposed to be? Nothing. It *is*, ostensibly."

He turned away from the door and wandered off with nonchalance into the hallway, letting her follow if she wanted. She was snared. She was going to have it out with him but the house delayed her thrust. A year's occupancy by Fergus and his wife had chastened the interior in a way that caught her eye. She envied the capacity to prosper in other people, to make good from nothing and the inexpensive quality of these rooms maddened when she was intent on objects that came at a price. Where had he unearthed that stripped pine cabinet? Her own was not so fine.

"A jumble sale," he answered the stare without benefit of question. "For a fiver. But I wouldn't part with it no matter how much you offered me."

She humped. The Christmas tree too, coming to the end of its twelve days, hadn't shed a needle and was a delectable creation within the limits of homespun, sparkling, simple but above all interesting. Decoration and material fused, more than aesthetic. It was conceptual because it sprung from and satisfied the mind. She couldn't lay her hands on Harris' dismissive remarks because a particle of her saw its restrained beauty. Its philosophy of bargain she admired but still couldn't achieve its rich effect. Such power of selection passed her by. Of all the people who had set eyes on the tree that week she was the most impressed, indeed affected by it, but the least inclined to say so. That phrase she had uttered at random without a basis of solid thought, When all's said and done, Fergus is the most like me, contained a truth. Their aspirations were not dissimilar, great achievers, competitive and single-minded, but the difference was the son had the means and the mother didn't. A primary jealousy divided them. Manifestations of his ability, whether that was progress in his career or in his surroundings, underscored her own penury when it came to the unbuyable.

"Are you coming in then?" was his prompt to her arrestment in the hallway.

"If you've no objections."

"None whatsoever," was the most careless answer he could find.

Fergus went into the kitchen and, remembering that she had in fact poured him liquid refreshment the day he went to Greenbank, he got out two mugs for coffee and started to make it. He was fastidious about coffee and wouldn't use the instant variety, so the process took some time.

His person, precise, immaculate and his reflective speech which

512

rose upwards from trade to profession leaving her behind, galled. Each gesture was correct and comely; the combination of success.

Muriel sat down beside the table and tipped out the contents of the envelope. "I don't know what kind of solicitor it is you've got yourself. He can't even write a decent letter."

"Too rational for you, was it? He's the foremost expert on receivership. But I grant you his epistolary style may be factual rather than embellished with an excess of supposition."

"And this bit of paper," she flicked the photocopy of the guarantee towards him, "is a piece of nonsense."

"My lawyer said it was perfectly sound as evidence."

"It isn't on headed notepaper."

"Perhaps your solicitor couldn't afford a sheet, or thought it was a shady do. That is your current legal representative?" He pointed to an address in a lowly commercial thoroughfare of a man who also advertised himself as Valuer and Estate Agent, a general parcelling of talents.

"Yes but . . . "

The coffee was ready and Fergus poured it. One of the mugs had a hairline crack and as the hot liquid met the weak spot, it split open. Thermal shock seeped coffee towards Muriel's documents which she gathered up ahead of the pool. Methodically, Fergus mopped up the stain on the table top and the differentiated squares of the flooring where it dripped and threw the cup away, starting again.

"Well, did you underwrite Harris' debts or not? That's what it comes down to."

Now this was Muriel's fundamental problem. She didn't know what she'd done. She didn't even know that she didn't know, but covered up all blurring or uncertainty with the assertive. Doubts were weakness and so she didn't harbour them. "I did no such thing."

Fergus leaned across the table and picked up the piece of disputed paper. "I have had your solicitor's signature compared with the notification to start divorce proceedings which you sent out. It matches, according to an expert calligraphist, though you may consider his expertise is also void. Your hand and Harris' are authentic, so the paper isn't really in dispute. Unless you suspect there's forgery involved but in that case, I think the onus is on you

513

to prove that Harris forged your signature. Take him to court over it." He flipped the photocopy back.

"I think you've trumped the whole thing up."

"Be careful," he warned, "of allegations that you can't substantiate because I for one won't forget them." He rose and brought her his accounting book in which the entries were ratified to the total he was due.

She began to be nervous in the face of so much system which scattered her wits further.

"He does owe me that much. You underwrote it. I claim it from you. That is all."

"No, that is not all. This communication doesn't signify one iota. You haven't proved one of your statements. Who's to say it isn't entirely your fabrication?"

"A jury perhaps."

"Try me."

At times, Fergus paused to admire the effects of protective decoy or warning device. The bombardier beetle did the same, making a report like a gun from flexing its joints to scare away large predators. The vulnerable expanded their space in sound or size, adders puffing up, gorillas beating the breast. His mother was a species of verbal sharpshooter. Whip crack away with words to make her big.

And then, just as he was about to take her posture seriously, she lapsed into the maudlin. "How can you hound your brother when he is absent?"

"Not logically, anyway." Fergus remembered the misfortuned were her pets, as long as they kept their troubles at a distance. Harris ensured his reinstatement to favour by putting himself on the wrong side of the law. That would imbue him with the status of victim or underdog, the honest persecuted and as long as someone else was the agent of persecution apart from herself, his plight would evoke every sympathy and even tears, although no help.

"You are a heartless individual," said his mother.

Fergus met in her the same affronts to dignity that Leonie posed. What was it about women and families that made them so rude? He didn't name-call anyone. "Control yourself," he ordered, "and remember where you are. Harris has absconded and, while wishing him no harm, I won't sentimentalise about his actions because

514

they're irresponsible. Don't tell me not to exact my dues, you of all people the most monetarist. Stand still. Face up to reality. My father did. But don't, I implore you, go charging me with words like heartless or hounding. They are unseemly. If you aren't willing to meet my just demands, the law must decide between us."

She wavered, meeting a commensurate willpower, and dipped into alternative logic. "You will remember this is our anniversary."

The time ticked by as he adjusted his mind to her possible meaning. "You mean your wedding anniversary? Well, no, I don't remember it, considering I wasn't there. I don't suppose you've had too many reminders of the fact when you were half way to divorcing Michael when he died."

"I thought you'd chosen the date deliberately."

And so had he at one time. When suspicion was central, accidents borrowed from its animosity.

As she sat, Muriel's eye wandered round the kitchen, poking holes. The house where she had lived for over twenty years threw up some troubling memories. Each room contained a scene, a major scene which erupted again. She didn't go back to the same locations as Alison, the window where she threatened to jump, the fire to gas herself, the door to Michael's room still bearing singe marks under several layers of paint, or the broken windows and cut telephone cord that stuck in Fergus' mind. The done to not the doing she recalled, or maybe the omissions, the not done.

It was not a happy house; Muriel had never thought its prospect settled. Bleak and exposed, it looked out over treetops which filled the garden with leaves and shadows and weren't even theirs. Michael was lazy about the everyday things so that the unturned collected in corners, piling up to mounds. Michael wasn't much good at anything, and certainly no good for her. Repellent somehow sexually. He would try to buy her in the early days, dinner for two, a car if she agreed to sleep with him so many times a week, though he was always loose-worded about his contracts; she could find the loophole if she tried. She thought of her current lover. Some man, although he was trying to get her to set him up in business. Not so free and easy with the loot, she wasn't. Keep the whip hand.

On this instinct, she pulled her bag towards her. She carried large amounts of money on her when furniture transactions were in cash, so didn't like to let the repository wander too far from her person. It lay open, wedged by the paper roll of news not notes.

"Ah yes," she said, reaching down to them. "I'd forgotten these." She put the envelope away and pulled the broadsheets onto the table. Evidence of one sort or another that might affect the outcome. Which shouted loudest, she wondered. Words or pictures, it was debatable.

The funeral of Lord Moncrieffe fell on an empty day in the journalistic calendar and merited full coverage by default. Putting the half-dozen photographs together she could obtain a panoramic exposure of the scene and who had filled it. Some newspapers highlighted the Prime Minister and some the Speaker alongside the nephew and the mother at the graveside, but all of them manoeuvred Leonie Barr into the camera lens. The captions variably fixed her between friend and constant companion. Beside an account of Watson Moncrieffe's genealogy was hers, in stage terms, Hedda Gabler through Lady Macbeth to Anna Karenina, a proof pedigree.

Fergus picked up the sheets and read all about it. Read what his wife had been doing in the last year, where she had been seen by hundreds or by a handful who were still more in the know than he was, it appeared. Its timing expanded many gaps in his ignorance. The story broke.

"Quite an eyeful," declared Muriel who was not without shreds of admiration for front page publicity.

"Scandalmongering," said Fergus, "by gutter press. I'll pay no attention to that."

"He's not even a serious politician," she complained. "He's just a player, or a playboy. So he hadn't risked a genuine career. Knocked about a bit, he has. His wife divorced him for adultery. You may not remember. Quite a cause célèbre at the time."

Her verbal packaging offended, delivered in the same tone as the articles. It provided a commentary on the issue that was trivial or sensational and mirrored, depressingly for him, the reaction of the common mind. All over the country ordinary people would be saying, Oh yes, wasn't he the one who . . . adding inaccurate facts, half-remembered names and situations by which they turned the humdrum into soap opera. Each one of Muriel's sentences he could challenge patiently by extrapolation, but to do so involved taking Moncrieffe's part – he was a serious politician, not a phoney – or his wife's who wouldn't intend putting anyone's career at risk, but the enormity of whole thought deterred him. He had never put his mother right before and couldn't now.

Silence gave consent. She rambled on, reconstructing more and more absurd theories about who had done what and why. He suddenly remembered how she'd gone through a phase of earnest conviction that Michael was a homosexual, of the alternating variety, and misappropriated several incidents to support that idea, married late in life, not up to much etcetera. And Harris, yes. She'd hypothesised that too. Inherited homosexuality: there was a thing now that confounded nature as well as common sense. Again, the only way he could have refuted these accusations was by betrayal, although even if he'd said Harris has girlfriends in abundance, that wouldn't have disproved the notion while it multiplied so grossly in her mind.

The outpouring went on, seeped out and spread to Alison, to that man of hers, to Matthew Geddes who was behind it all and wanted to get his own back. What all? What back? Fergus had a brainwave, a seizure of a kind. The woman was ill, diseased in one cell which happened to be the brain, not full blown certifiable mad but unbalanced. A gardener had once left her employ at the Hermitage muttering 'That woman's aye lossing the heid.' Too true. Her uncontrollable anger had its root in a chaotic mind. He understood at last the cause of mass hysteria; it was the massive power of perverted logic which reason couldn't stem. Perversion was always stronger than normality, evil than good. His own fault had been to take her seriously in the first place or to imagine he could, by persuasion or example, correct the faults of thinking. She had not advanced to the point of self-analysis. Why do I think what I think, was a necessary prelude to correct deduction.

Fergus foresaw many endings, many checks. As she ranted, impugning everybody within a five-mile radius, he was moved to mercy killing, not for her sake but for other people's. How to silence? How to contain? He'd heard of Harris' attempts at throttle which lacked a final courage and was tempted to finish off the business. Lips moved. Words fell out like bullets grazing passers-by, only blanks not lethal, but the noise of ricochet was deafening.

He could do it. Checkmate in one. Into a corner, piece after piece brought up, blow after blow delivered until the moment when squares ran out for her. Position and material would defeat her and she would go down. A victory. An annihilation. Smashed against the walls with no escape. He assessed the possibilities quite coolly, considering those moves most likely to succeed. He was strong enough. Bare hands would do it. Or the kitchen was full of utensils although he thought bloodshed was ugly. Strangulation was the best, on windpipe.

He stood up, stepping outside the effluent of her language. Murder most foul. What would he do afterwards? He anticipated the act clearly and planned ahead to consequences. He would stand trial for her murder in the Court of Session. Guilty reverberated against him with its own enclosure, like an echo. He didn't want to incur that blame, however justifiable, and thought criminal proceedings were a waste of time. Sacrifice his career and his house for her? She wasn't worth it. The positive cancelled out the negative in his motives; life offered a hundred better occupations than sitting in a prison cell. His work and his son restored his wavering sanity.

He folded up the news items and gave them back to her.

"Do you have a telephone?" she asked.

"I've taken it off the hook. I don't want bells going off when I'm trying to work."

"That's as well. Because the phones will be ringing all over the place today."

She was probably right. Torrisaig, Inveresk, the flat in Westminster, Leonie's theatrical agent, the Old Vic. Newsmen following up a lead, teasing out facts relevant or not, so that they could make each day's edition a cliffhanger. Watch this space for developments. How long would it be before he found himself with a journalist on the doorstep, notebook or microphone in hand, eager for his comment, or were deserted husbands not newsworthy nowadays, even when cuckolded by lords?

So much she said.

"Go away," he pleaded. "I don't want to hear you. I don't want to see you. I don't want to know anything about you. Just go away." He led out into the hallway to get rid of her.

"And what about the money?" she tagged on.

He arrived at the point of extremity. He lifted his hands above his head to strike and suddenly aware she sidestepped as the gesture of felling landed in empty space. "I will. If you provoke me more, I will. Go home, old woman, and make your peace with God."

Fergus was angry at himself for having expended so much feeling to give her satisfaction. As she drove away, he locked the door and drew the bolts across from top to bottom. No more callers today. No more callers ever.

54

There was a buzz round Westminster on the first day's sitting after the Christmas recess.

At Normanshaw, Moncrieffe couldn't make headway for the callers who besieged his room. They came to offer condolences and congratulations, hand in hand, but expected confidentiality in return. No one was bold enough to ask Fleming's question, So what's it to be, although the query was implicit in their dawdling. He fobbed them off. 'You will excuse me. I'm finishing a speech for the debate this afternoon. Can we talk tomorrow?'

The visits still gratified. Eminent men came to see him and wish him good luck without being so peremptory as to suggest in which chamber: men from both sides of the House as well as both Houses, the Foreign Secretary, a former Chancellor, a handful of Law Lords stunned by Charles Moncrieffe's demise which in the winter season foreshadowed all endings. These were men who had risen above the enmity that made some of the lower echelons of Westminster politics ugly, with indecorous barging and shoving. They bore home to Watson his old suspicion about the lawmaker in himself; he didn't care what it proposed as long as it was good law. Equally, he didn't care what these men believed in, right, left, centrist, as long as they were good men. Some were not. Some came squatting on his desk in search of titbits, indicative of their general bent, but the preponderance who submitted themselves to the rigours of selection by the electorate, and on a five-year tenure, were honest men. Not exceptionally clever. Any University department had better minds than these but, amongst able practitioners, they served. A fusion of stockbroker and barrister was the norm, like himself. Not exceptionally interesting. They were neither creative nor original, wouldn't have chosen these straits if they were, but were rounded by the British candour, good sense and good humour.

His telephone callers were less courteous. The media men were out in force. Moncrieffe knew all their dodges, the direct and the indirect question set to trap him, the slander to provoke, the impersonation of another spokesman altogether, even of a friend, to wheedle out some indiscretion. The leader of these gossip columnists, who acquired a certain status and even a relationship with his unwilling subjects, parasite to host like the royal paparazzi, because he was good at getting what he wanted and never told a whopping lie although he could spread innuendo to equivalent depth, engaged him in what was quite a genial conversation. No marriage. No divorce. No change. No comment. No thanks. In the end, he asked the Commons switchboard not to put through any more calls to his room for the rest of that day. Switch off was the best reply.

His private life became public again, a stock flotation which everyone could have a share in if they read the press releases. There were photographers installed outside his flat, lying in wait for Leonie. Funny thing, in law your photograph wasn't your own but the property of the person who took it. The use of that image was hardly protected either. He recalled his father handling a case for defamation in which the complainant objected to the use made of his picture in a political leaflet because it implied that he supported that party's policy. He lost.

Quercus came by over the lunch hour, quiet while lesser allies defected to the bar.

"You're making quite a stir." He mused over the headlines. 'Doubt over Lords future' contained a neat little buried pun which was probably accidental because the journalist didn't know where to put the apostrophe. 'The last of Lord Moncrieffe?' was a touch lurid, into novelette as though he were Tarzan and lost in a Commons jungle. 'Scots Lord to go' compressed a subtle dilemma into monosyllabic journalese.

Quercus was unusually irritable. His New Year's resolution had been to give up smoking and half a dozen days on his nerves were frayed. He was more restive than when he had cigars to occupy the hand and eye and felt at a loose end, laying the blame on his resignation from the House which triggered the response of all seniority retirement. He would not be needed in the future. That made him suddenly old, while retreat into Roman literature, long deferred, was instantly less attractive when it was imminent and

521

took the shape of work. The present was the place to live.

"Piffle, isn't it? You'd think editors could find something urgent to give so much newsprint to."

"It's partly the timing," said the older man.

Until Parliament wound itself up, there was little documentary to report, but it was the conjunction with the actress's appearance at Torrisaig which made them headline-hitting stuff, personal and professional coinciding. The story lacked detail or substance but Watson was at least gratified that in the days since the funeral it hadn't deepened, thanks to informed leaks by insiders. His friends, as well as hers in the theatre, stayed true. Its very thinness was an irk, blown out of proportion by his inheritance, trite and meddlesome in purport.

"How is Leonie taking all this?"

"I'm surprised at how equable she is. She simply outstares them, or outwits them and is magnificently aloof." Moncrieffe moved towards admitting that Leonie's problems were northbound, but refrained. That was the misery of public life. In the end you confided in no one because the smallest fact fed speculation.

"I do worry," Quercus continued to make the roll of cigar smoking, empty-handed, "about that little expedition I proposed to see a play in Oxford. I shall be very guarded about theatre-going in the future."

"You needn't. No hard feelings."

The senior digressed into supposition; what would have happened if Watson had gone to Charlie's Savoy dinner after all instead of *Twelfth Night*? The lives of the Independent and the actress were concurrent at so many points it was hard to believe they would have stayed strangers indefinitely. He thought the relationship was inevitable for Moncrieffe, if not with that individual. The man couldn't do the easy thing. There must be an in-built check or bar to simplicitude so that he pitted himself against the impossible adversary, a mountain, a gerrymandered electoral system, conventional morals, villain hero both. The love affair saddened him because he foresaw, unclouded by its passions, the hardships that lay ahead. So many men in British politics had endangered their career for a woman. Parnell and Kitty O'Shea down. A hundred years on, the Victorian hypocrisies were undiminished because the public expected its intercessors to be saints. His major sadness was personal because the life-changing experience, desire and undesirable mixed, had passed him over like office or preferment. Ambition's stakes and dangerous women he had never fluttered on.

"Are you going in this afternoon?" Moncrieffe asked.

"The law and order bill? I don't think so. My pair's away too. And there's a meeting of the 1922 Committee later on which I want to give my mind to."

The clock moved towards three. The minister would still be answering questions. Then the government spokesman would introduce the second reading of the bill, the opposition attack, like court pleaders for and against. Moncrieffe thought he should go in at the beginning of proceedings and gathered up his notes. The two men went out of the block of offices and took the tunnel under Westminster Bridge Road which led directly into the Parliamentary precincts. They could hear the bell on the corner which sounded for taxis, ringing as it always did, day and night superfluous. They went past the policeman on duty who knew them and nodded, and then divided, Moncrieffe to the Commons, Quercus to the library. The journey, paced together a thousand times, became a leave-taking.

There were only a couple of dozen members in the chamber by the time Moncrieffe joined them. They were outnumbered by the press gallery and certainly by the retinue of ushers and policemen guarding this inner sanctum. He cast an eye up at the rows of faces in the strangers' gallery who must be wondering what it was all about. All this build-up for some old duffer droning on about police recruitment standards. Where was the fire? Where was Edmund Burke holding the Commons in his sway for hours at a stretch, compelled by the power of his oratory. Or a Churchill who rumbled like the gathering storm, a danger conductor. Or Sheridan, the playwright turned politician, who had denounced Warren Hastings for the plunder of Oude in a famous speech in 1787. Somebody had offered him £1000 for the copyright and he turned it down because he couldn't be bothered to transcribe his notes. 'The order of nobility is of great use, too . . . in what it prevents. It prevents the rule of wealth – the religion of gold.' Neither condition was feasible two centuries later, quality or principle. Who'd give hard cash for anybody's speech today?

Milton, thou should'st be living at this hour, defender of the Commonwealth, author of the *Areopagitica*, though he might well turn round and argue on behalf of press restraint. The brilliant rhetorician had seldom surfaced in Moncrieffe's tenure and maybe never would again. He had lived into the littleness of politics with members scurrying upstairs like clerks, pencilling out motions and clauses with the punctilio of grammarians, unable to breathe concept into words. Maybe the problem was the prose. All those great orators were also writers. You couldn't speak, self-evidently, without good words. Nor was there any point. The debate was settled beforehand along party lines. They might as well give them proxy votes and let members stay in the constituency. Nowadays persuasion lay in packaging and advertising gimmicks while the power of reason dwindled. Were the mass media to blame? People had forgotten how to listen to an argument and parse the content out of language. They'd gone word-dead. The ear was dulled when it had no eye to supplement the sound. Concentration fell to levels of imbecility, ten minutes at a time between commercial slots. Short and snappy punch lines, the stunt effect of gags. Claptrap ruled O.K.

Boredom, utter boredom he had tolerated for eleven years in the belief that it mattered or that he could, by the example residual in oneself, start a popular movement. After all it was a single voice in the crowd who'd shouted the slogan Liberty, Equality, Fraternity to start with, and went on and on and on shouting it until the phrase was taken up by others and swelled into a rallying cry. Senatus Populusque Romanus indeed, a prayer, a dedication which was unsurpassed. No taxation without representation. That would serve for the minority causes. Four words, that was all it needed to inspire, four words shaped into a banner, a motto on a shield. But for all his championship, Moncrieffe was shy of the challenge. Democracy had no knights.

He got reluctantly to his feet. The enunciators relayed throughout the Palace of Westminster that Moncrieffe was speaking. A trickle of members started back to the debate, thinking they'd give him an audience, show willing. His press coverage had brought incidental benefits. Prosser, who'd staked his resignation against his editor touching the scandal, had a sixth sense. He put his head into the press room below and called, "Get your butts up here. There's a story."

"With your indulgence, Mr Speaker," said Moncrieffe, "and that of the House, I wish to interrupt the course of this debate to make a personal statement."

The Speaker did indulge, a judge who grew restive with tendentious evidence and would give anything for a novelty. The personal statement was rarely deployed as a Parliamentary device and was treated with respect. No one challenged by convention.

Someone told Fleming's PPS and he rang the Prime Minister in his room who came along to hear for himself what he thought would be Moncrieffe's decision. Mentally he prepared a statement for the press to follow the recruitment of one more player to his side.

"The last fortnight has been eventful," said the member for Ross, Cromarty and Skye, "because of the sad and untimely death of Charles Moncrieffe. He has been mourned elsewhere and anyway this was never his place. It has aroused gratuitous comment among certain sections of the press about my likely future in politics. Indeed I believe Ladbroke's have opened a book on whether I renounce my family title or not. Please don't hasten to leave the chamber. They're not good odds."

The Speaker saw he wasn't in for a brief statement and that Fleming had entered the chamber, taking his front bench position ceremoniously. He wouldn't hurry Moncrieffe until the Prime Minister started to look impatient. January afternoons were rum.

"They tell me that a very small number in statistics can be of such trifling significance that it is rounded down to nought. I find myself in the unenviable position of being that zero. I am the last of a vanishing Parliamentary phenomenon, the Independent, and given the hold of party politics, probably the last one ever. Independence isn't a favoured concept at Westminster, as I've discovered, and I'm often reminded of a phrase used about Sidney Webb: he does not take either side and is therefore suspected by both. This might offend if mistrust weren't endemic inside as well as across the party lines. A worse slight is being accused of dilettantism though I've never established what this means. Not voting? Not working? Not attending the House? I exonerate myself from those. Perhaps enjoying myself too much? That's so, but I can assure any intending successors that it's damned hard work being a boulevardier.

"I came to Westminster carrying two tags by which I may be recognised at a distance, in lieu of colour badges. Independence and proportional representation, the forbidden words of British politics. In eleven years I have never heard PR mentioned and certainly not discussed in this chamber. It's like the famous Punch cartoon of truth in Fleet Street, a naked figure hidden behind a mile of print because it is the inadmissable concept. Let in truth and you will have no end of trouble getting rid of the comfortable but embarrassed lies.

"We laugh today about the constituency imbalance before the 1832 Reform Act. Rotten boroughs, bribery at the polling booths, squires who couldn't be challenged and large sections of the new industrial towns which had no franchise. We laugh because we perceive its unfairness or its lack of basic democratic principle which filled the House with men who didn't, by any manipulation of returns, represent their electors, even adult male householders."

Fleming sat on. Let him have his head as long as he did the sensible thing in the end and walked over the floor to the Labour benches.

"The results of the last general election make engrossing reading. Some fourteen million people voted for the present government, eleven and a half for the opposition, leading to an overall disparity of six Parliamentary seats, which is not much above the smallest majority you can have and certainly close to that statistical grey area of a number that has no value. Is this a clear victory? Not when you consider that sixty per cent of the electorate didn't vote for this government and seven million voted positively for other parties, Liberal or the Nationalists, Irish, Welsh, Scottish. And yet the argument is given that proportional representation encourages minority government. We have minority government at this moment. Over half the present MPs, yes, Honourable and Right Honourable Gentlemen within touching distance, however much they may shake their heads, were returned by a minority of their constituents. Parliament never represents the percentage feeling in the country, even for the party forming the government and this 'advantage' is secured at the cost of the smaller parties who may secure no representation whatever in the Commons. Rotten boroughs? Every constituency in Britain is a rotten borough. We offer the electorate a cheat. We offer them a swindle for their pains."

Fleming thought he should demonstrate his disaffection. To be seen to hear was in some ways to endorse. The galleries had filled at both ends, press and strangers', the green upholstered benches swollen as the word leaked out that Moncrieffe was making his personal statement. The Prime Minister considered that turning tail in full view would look cowardly in the reporting. He would sit it out but edited his press handout to 'deepest regret'.

"This Parliamentary system holds a gun to the head of the voter and says, Either, or. It is a form of electoral banditry because it denies the full range of options. It denies a fair hearing to the minority and I say that with some conviction being the minority of one. Minority members in this House enter a form of servitude in which they may work long and earnestly but by no means may acquit themselves of their ambitions to influence, far less direct, events. We twenty-five are sops to the conscience of the nation."

A Tory shadow spokesman became irate and thought he would shout, 'Speech, speech,' to indicate that he considered this a breach of Parliamentary privilege, but a colleague nudged him. If Fleming could take it, so could they. Besides, he might be ready to announce a right-hand exit, in which case they'd have to move up and call him friend.

"There's a wise sentence which you may know," the Independent continued. " 'In each decade, the question is worth reframing: is the British democratic system falling out of balance?' The answer is yes. Our allies, our democratic friends, our EEC colleagues look on these anomalies with disbelief as our unrepresentatives turn up at Brussels and Westminster. Balance is the key word of that sentence. Balance is everything, because it touches on the two priorities of government, legal and fiscal authority. The balance of power is the oldest of political doctrines but we shy away from the notion of consensus like children, frightened by the bogeyman of coalition because we've come to believe there can be no consent without coercion. Understand that I am not against party as such, there is no government or Parliament without party definition, but I've stood outside party boundaries for so long to demonstrate that there are alternatives. I have been asked in, make no mistake. I have been offered inducements, but this only serves

527

to reinforce my conviction that party, as it exists at the moment, is tantamount to self-interest.

"I've interrupted a scheduled debate and although this statement may appear a digression, I do believe law and order and the constitution are inseparable. There are many areas of crisis in Britain in this decade, internal as much as external, and constitutional crisis is high on the list, unacknowledged and for that reason all the more subversive. Law enforcement is breaking down because government has entered disrepute. Defence of the realm is an old fashioned phrase which we might do well to resurrect if by realm we mean integrity, the whole of the United Kingdom, the whole of the people. Divisions are destructive. There isn't a member in this House who isn't tired of factionalism in his party and in his constituency. I make a plea for co-operation, for broad nationalism before party loyalty which is only, at the end of it, a vote for oneself and one's own promotional prospects. We ignore signs of dissent and unrest at our peril."

Fleming listened to an old self. He remembered saying the same a decade or two back. True, oh all true but unrealistic. They all had to harness their own idealism and make it drive. He had heard failed men quip, 'I'd rather people wondered why I hadn't led the party than wonder why I had.' That was a condign judgment on the second-rater, but he fancied Moncrieffe was a rarer breed than the endemic grumbler or spoiler. His impatience was tempered by a genuine regret for talent gone astray and a man who could have risen to senior office and been a party asset.

"The only promotion I am willing to accept is to the Upper House where it will be an honour to sit in the same seat as Charles Moncrieffe, across the lines of party. There's a rather tiresome supposition on the part of MPs that politician is synonymous with member of the Lower House. A point of dialectic but I would beg to remind you of the significant political spokesmen who haven't been through these chamber doors. There is life outside the Commons. There is also life after it. So you have heard the last of me, but only for a week or two."

The effect was marked as the chamber emptied behind his swift exit. His fellows thought it was a remarkable performance, not least from audacity and the fact that he'd managed to get away with it. Men who prided themselves on being good deliverers at the despatch box said it was well spoken, the bursting voice controlled, the gesture never turning into mannerism. For once they listened. They felt they were fortunate if they had sat through the speech that ruffled the equanimity of routine while others who hadn't, invented their attendance, borrowing some reputation from the event.

Timing was on his side, if nothing else. He hit the six o'clock news, and was in time to be interviewed for the later slots. The newspapers whose correspondents had the wisdom to come upstairs when Prosser called and printed the speech in full, sold out of the early morning edition and increased subsequent runs. Hansard printed double. A copy went to the Electoral Reform Society and was filed in a box alongside other advocates of a perfectionist democracy. Cadogan was quoted as saying that the Independent was a Faust who had sacrificed the future for the now. The Labour whip improved on this allusive theme and said he was no Faust but Mephistopheles in a suit. So for a while Moncrieffe considered himself a famous failure.

55

Dear Irene,

Thank you for your letter and for relaying to me what you feel are Fergus' wishes although it does strike me as odd that you should act as intermediary in this way between husband and wife.

I'm sorry there's no immediate news from Matthew's tribunal hearing. 'Suspension awaiting a decision' is such a precarious state of mind to be in that he and all of you have my sympathy, scant comfort I know. I think about you. I wish I could say I pray for you, though I do if prayer without any backing of conviction counts. We didn't pay enough attention to Michael, did we, before or after his trial, and missed drawing wisdom from the event. He said the most salient thing afterwards in prison which the professor passed on to me. *This is not something you recover from. You only start to die more slowly.* Michael had a special quality that we resurrect him by word and deed from oblivion.

As for Fergus, I don't know. You use the phrase about him, He has committed emotional suicide, which I assume isn't accidental and that Fergus has confided as much to you about his father's death as he has to me. That's a relief, that you know, but it doesn't actually resolve the blame that attaches to self-killing, systemic or emotional. It doesn't excuse Fergus' barricades. People shouldn't lock themselves in or lock other people out. It smacks of amour-propre. I abhor keys and all the things that can be operated by keys. I am a keyless person, no car, no house, no property that I'm bristling to put into a safety deposit box. It's the one aspect of religion that I can respect, denial of proprietorial gain. If I can't lay it down or lend it, I don't want the thing.

Is Fergus a moral man? That's a troublesome question. He's not immoral, but is the best of character to stop at a double negative short of more positive endowments? I think a good man wouldn't lock me out peremptorily, wouldn't bar access to my son, wouldn't use you as his crier. What am I to make of these conditions he sets out? He will not bank Moncrieffe's cheque but retains it as evidence against me. I may have a divorce but my son is the forfeit I surrender. Is this humane and reasonable in your opinion?

Maybe it is. Maybe that's why you acted as his scribe but if so, there are several ancillary questions I would ask. Does the professor go along with these proceedings and does my mother, or is this a secret pact you are a mite ashamed of?

I'm grateful to you, Irene, I have to be grateful for the care you've expended on my son, every mouthful of food you've put into him, every patient hour invested. He is to your credit. Making you into my substitute puts us in an odd alignment and I realise that I've entered yet another three-cornered relationship. I don't seem to be able to make simple contracts. I admire simplicity, harmony, reduction to one but can't achieve it.

It's the easiest thing in the world to say I should have stayed at home by my own fireside. I feel your disapproval of me edging this letter, and criticism that I've chosen to do something extraneous to domesticity. But I didn't choose to be dedicated to the theatre. I was chosen. Personal disdain for me is tinged with your attitudes to my profession, which you regard as not important and certainly not hard work. But I am bicellular and I assure you there are people who would condemn me for not utilising this talent more than you do for not staying at home. I may have been too ambitious, so fault me on that instead.

What is to happen then? The conventions require me to choose between these two cells of my make-up, past present, home work, duty love, though Fergus' attitude narrows the options to a divorce from one half on his terms, cruelly and mercilessly applied by the letter. And you can be sure that from time to time, he'll threaten to withdraw from speeding a divorce on the grounds of his religious scruples. You can temper that harshness, Irene. You're suddenly in a position of power over me, have a jurisdiction about whether I am to be allowed to see my son grow up or not because you're the only person to have Fergus' ear. Use your power wisely. I've hardly any rights and a dedicated prosecutor could make a watertight case against me of neglect, absence and adultery. I'm asking you to modify that judgment.

Why should you stir yourself for me again? Because you owe me a favour and only extremity makes me remind you of the obligation. I helped Matthew all I could. If the case goes to court, I am his witness. Think what it will mean to you if the action goes against him. Losing the case is to you exactly the same as it is to me. We are both fighting for our sons not to be locked away, for daylight to be let in, for the current of normal contact to be sustained. I am appealing to you as a mother to assist continuance.

You're undergoing stress the nature of which you never imagined. You've begun to dread the postman. You make a meal and sit down to it and say 'I cannot eat.' You push the plate away and think that you will die. Tiny things become obsessive. A word, a ray of hope, a

531

newspaper article contiguous on your circumstances all palpitate nerves that are daily overstretched. Do you think because I don't show it, I don't know? I appeal to you in basic humanity not to serve on me your own anxieties.

I am going to say something very shocking which I have sensed for a long time and which your letter confirms. You are in love with Fergus. I wouldn't demean either of you by suggesting that a word or gesture has passed, but love it is. Why are the days better when you see him? Why are the hours after you leave him filled with what he said and what he did? You are not a silly, loveless old woman, are already supplied with the stuff of happiness in the form of a husband and a son, but they do not have such composition in their faces as he in his. Love it is, between a virtuous woman and a serious-minded young man twenty-five years her junior. Such aberrant loves come unasked to disrupt the tenor of equanimity, yours and mine. You don't hanker after the unattainable, are sensible and strict but you know you have changed Fergus' life and for the better. What else can love achieve? That is your definition of it and your reward. I know this because I share it and as a woman appeal to you to be compassionate.

You are the peace-maker, but I don't envy you the reconciliation of these sides. Whatever the outcome, whatever your response, you can be sure that I will fight on for the right to have contact with my son. I am not a lier down under adversity. Peace – when ever?

Frances Moncrieffe lowered this letter after she had read it. She had travelled to London in February for Watson's introduction to the House of Lords during the following week. It would be her third such ceremony, husband, son, grandson in turn. She would not see a fourth generation but was assured the visible horizon was not the end.

"Do you mean to send this?" she asked Leonie.

"Why? Don't you think I should?"

"Well," thought the dowager, "I find it best not to write these things down because you have no control over how they will be used. You can see how your husband intends to wield Watson's cheque. I would caution you to be more circumspect. Do not expose your weaker flank."

"I started to reply to her letter in a business-like way but I couldn't ignore what I felt, or her feelings either."

Frances, chiselled through many crises, wondered if these feelings were real, or a defence-mechanism. She wouldn't have written such a letter, but neither could she have written it since she didn't examine her moods to the level of expressing them. Her stoicism gave her the reputation for strength, although in age she wished she had developed the capacity to unbend. "Are you in such pain, both of you?" she asked, disbelieving.

"I think so."

The older woman leaned over and covered Leonie's hand, noticing its delta of blue veins. "Reconcile yourself to it. This pain is energy. When it is the pain of ebb, that's the time to worry." The touch confused. Leonie couldn't remember being touched by another woman and had no gesture to respond to patting. "I'll have a word with Irene myself when I get back," assured the widow.

Surprised, Leonie stopped in the middle of pouring their habitual tea.

"You've forgotten that I know her, and very well. She and James Geddes were quite frequent visitors to Inveresk when Edward was alive." She spanned her mind back over aeons. "I have her measure. Tell me," she inquired, "do they know about our baby?"

"No. If he knew that, Fergus would do everything to humiliate me. Force me to wait the full five years. Make promises and break them to torment me. I have to go along with his conditions because I'm powerless."

"I didn't ask to pry, only to know my ground before I see Irene." Frances turned back to the letter. "These arguments are valid but better spoken. Do you know," she added, "it's a funny thing, but I see Liz from time to time. I found I wanted to know her children. But I couldn't tell Watson that I had spoken to her because he's so very bitter."

"Less so now," said Leonie. The generous interest triggered a subsidiary thought. How would Ellice react to this latest development? Her mother was so involved with Andrew's welfare that she might well sacrifice seeing her second grandchild to safeguard a relationship with the first. Fergus would not like the thought of Ellice effecting a contact between them in the future . . . oh in the long term, years away.

Frances had started to expand into the young woman's friendship, knowing how much she owed her; Leonie had brought her out of mothballs. Insisted on her presence at the formal introduction to the Lords and there was a gracious round of engagements organised in London, a renewal of old acquaintances, a chapel service in the crypt, a dedication, a special invitation from Lord Privy Seal who had been a new boy with her husband. She appreciated how much thought and work had gone into the programme. She was moved to confide a little more, or consult.

"Tell me," she asked, "*did* Michael Petrie commit suicide?"

When she handed her the letter, Leonie had overlooked the point. "It did look that way."

The dowager grieved, her face changing like Watson's under pressure, not slack but stern with self-rebuke. "I concede I did the wrong thing in pursuing him through the courts. I was guided by an avaricious lawyer. No, not avaricious even. Lawyers are like bankers or accountants. They have no will of their own. They make no moral judgments. They simply enact the wishes of their clients. But I achieved nothing by it because there was no money left for creditors. He went to prison, it ruined his family and maybe half a dozen lives thereafter, which was a foolish reparation. I wouldn't do it again. Oh no. It's wise to stop and remember that we set eternity in motion every day."

Leonie moved the third cup out of the way, wondering if Watson would come in time to drink from it. Mid-afternoon, he had promised. She began the waiting game of Parliamentary wives.

The visitor turned to the pile of morning newspapers, all dominated by the headline opinions that Cadogan was going to be ousted from the leadership of the Conservative party. "A good thing too," she concluded. "Good for Watson."

"Why? It doesn't affect him, surely."

"It might. He was never going to join forces with that man. Charles loathed him. But a new leader may put a different emphasis on the party, and acknowledge he needs a broader base if he's to get the Conservatives back to power."

"Do you think Watson would go Tory?" Leonie frowned in dissent.

"I don't think a working pact need be full membership. I was very struck," said the dowager, "by what they said at Charles' funeral, that he was a man without enemies. You know, that's just as true of Watson. It's a useful capacity. A man who can keep his own counsel for a dozen years might well be trusted with the

534

government's. He's not forty yet. Think of the men who haven't entered politics until their middle years. He could make an impression in the Lords. The young hereditary peers are all out earning their living and the experienced life peers are usually senile or the disaffected of their party. It's a clear field for an ambitious man."

"What do you foresee?"

"The Leader of the House of Lords is not an impossibility, and that has cabinet rank. Very occasionally our system does the sensible thing and appoints the best man for the job. Watson's well established on the international scene through his work on electoral reform. A peace-keeping role. Something at the United Nations." She whetted her own appetite for the intrigue. Yes, she would sound out the Lord Privy Seal at dinner.

Leonie had a sharp insight. She remembered Frances had challenged her grandson with the first-night photograph and realised there was a file of cuttings, carefully garnered from all sources, stashed in a cupboard at Inveresk. Yes, they would be meticulously pasted, labelled, pored over and memorised right back to the original try at Edinburgh Pentlands, disgrace or not.

"But he's always been so close to Fleming."

"That's just my point. All to the good. I think it's sound of you to go to Greece at Easter, though you will be careful not to go swimming, won't you? Our current Speaker is esteemed by both sides of the House, and rightly so."

Leonie smiled at the swift transition in her references and got up to disguise it.

"That is where women come in," said Frances, following with her voice. "They nudge in the right direction. Nudge – and fudge if need be." She watched Leonie straighten the room, removing stale tea, easily tidy. "It's time Watson moved from this flat, isn't it? It was convenient as a bachelor pad but the stairs are most unsuitable."

Leonie heard the note of interference and countered quickly. "Oh no. It's inside the division bell, which Watson prizes, and it's become something of an established hostelry. He would want friends to keep dropping in. Besides, they're installing a lift this summer by communal subscription."

Moncrieffe arrived himself, ending speculation. He had been for a final fitting to his tailor and was on edge from standing still so long. "None of the bits of my body seem to match," he complained in dismay. "You are meant to be symmetrical, aren't you?"

The women laughed at his mime of one arm longer than the other. "What do they do to overcome that?"

"Masterful cutting."

"You have twenty suits already," observed his grandmother.

"Quite so. But nothing lugubrious enough for the Lords."

"It's a pity that you wouldn't have Charles' suits altered to fit."

"Or cut in half. There's enough yardage." Watson took two turns about the room and said, "I think I'll take a breath of fresh air," and headed up the staircase to the roof.

Translated, this signified to Leonie that he wanted to talk to her alone, so she moved up the spiral after him. They caught the last of the daylight. No snow had fallen in London over the winter and there had hardly been a frost. The plants on the roof, sheltered by a wall and the parapet, were in premature bud which made the cultivator anxious knowing there were several weeks ahead that could provide a damaging cold snap.

"Why does she irritate me so much?" He gave way to the frustration.

"Because you're irritable. It's got nothing to do with her except that she's your grandmother. Relax and enjoy her."

"She has such a genius for saying the obvious."

"That's not unforgivable when you're over eighty. I like her simplicity. I like her directness. I learn a great deal from her."

"About what?" expressed dubiety.

"Tactics. And you."

They paused from examining the flower tubs and turned together. He couldn't get over it. He simply could not. That he woke up and Leonie was there. That he didn't dream evil thoughts. That he moved into a settled continuity. The mundane terms of the normal were reappraised through her negotiation. He opened the palm of her hand and leaned his face into it, noticing the same veins as his grandmother, pulsing with a force that redirected his. Miraculous; it was the basic miracle that confirmed human faith. His pleasure and his pride in her knew no end.

"Were you filming today?"

"Not till Monday. But I had a meeting with Stuart and the

designer this morning. A day much like yours, really, trying on costumes, that was far from reassuring."

"That's good, though. You needed a few days' rest."

"What have you decided for the summer?"

He broke away and adjusted some protective sacking. There had been a movement for some time in the west Highlands for a festival which could become an annual event if it went well. A small committee which he chaired considered the possibilities. Something to fall shortly after the Braemar Games and to coincide this year with his investiture as the new chieftain. Torrisaig itself was an attractive location, mainland, a good road in, and reasonable accommodation. The landlord of the hotel had pointed out that a tented village, or something of the sort, was needed as a focus for the entertainment and at this Watson balked. Hospitality tents and dinette caravans. It made him squirm. Rather than rent somebody's striped canvas awning, he'd pay to erect a dozen of the A-frame log cabins that were springing up all over the Highlands. Useful now. Useful later. Time-share after all in the Torrisaig forests, with a fishing permit for a stretch of river thrown in during the season. Maybe that was the best way to accommodate democracy.

"The outline estimate is horrifying but I'm assured these frame houses are maintenance-free. They're cedarwood." The Biblical term consoled. "The manufacturers will be responsible for transporting and erecting them, if I want. It's still a huge decision because it changes the nature of the estate."

"Not in essence. You always had cottages for rent. I think it's a workable compromise." She nudged him closer.

He sighed, conceding the advantages. "It would at least mean I could employ Donald's son as an overseer to the holiday village" – he shrank from the contemporary phrase – "and take on a local girl to clean the chalets. That's something, isn't it? Two jobs. We haven't expanded our workforce in that way for thirty years."

His other innovations at Torrisaig were less extreme. He bought a rotavator and had a firm of decorators in. He engaged a book-keeper and asked for monthly statements. He transferred money to a separate number and called it a business account, meaning to keep to a bank reconciliation which an auditor would pass. As he thought his way along the problems, he absent-mindedly tidied the boxes and pruned unwanted growth by nipping out a bud.

The street lighting came on along the Embankment, etiolated by the last brilliance of the afternoon. The traffic underwent a change of momentum, creating a lull before the rush hour proper while, on the Thames, shipping observed its own lanes to discharge cargo and passengers up- or down-river. The daily bustle of the place impressed. People moving in their millions, like molecules, without colliding, made up the atomic day-round energy of the centre. Leonie responded to the chronometry of the city and ticked over towards evening. She gave due weight to this twilight hour and its implicit change, a transitoriness swollen with potential. Her thoughts inevitably turned towards the theatre. There was a personal lull, even when she wasn't due on stage, an hour left empty for self-composure in the congestion of each day.

"By the way, I think you really must learn to drive. I booked lessons for you."

"Must I?" She too was modernised.

He moved downstairs.

Frances had drawn the curtains over the balcony window, and retired discreetly to rest and bathe and change before their dinner engagement. Leonie noticed the letter had been folded and tucked out of sight, like a bad conscience, not to disturb the demeanour of the evening. She and Watson sat over a drink and scanned the dailies, adding more informed substance to their journalistic conjecture about what the future had in store for Cadogan, or themselves. Watson dismissed his grandmother's hypothesis. Once he was stigmatised as a loner, an MP was never trusted in the covens of cabinet.

"You talk as though you were a has-been too."

"Not even that. I never was. What does it matter, anyway, one career? Insiders apart, there aren't many people who could put a name to the Chancellor of the Exchequer before last, far less specify his measures. I'll survive posterity's neglect." He turned his glass against the light.

Leonie listened and heard Big Ben strike the hour in the distance, a summons whether he thought he could ignore its imperative or not.

"Shall we make a move, then?"

Magda Sweetland
Eightsome Reel £2.95

The death of Rhona Rosowicz brings her remaining family to the decaying Edinburgh mansion where she and her daughter Esme had lived a solitary life. Surrounded by people she hardly knows, Esme's behaviour excites, attracts and infuriates her relations as their lives intertwine in the mode of a dance. Esme's growing friendship with her aunt's husband leads to forbidden fruits, and through him she discovers the existence of her Polish father whom she thought long-dead. To escape the scandal, Esme goes to seek her father in Canada. There she meets a handsome RCAF officer and the mistakes of her forefathers begin to repeat themselves.

The Connoisseur £2.95

Innes Hamilton is thirty-five and single, a successful antiques dealer and porcelain expert who commutes first-class to his Edinburgh business from his fine nineteenth-century house overlooking the sea at North Berwick. Innes lives alone, cooks gourmet meals in the evenings, sails his yacht at weekends, and drifts in and out of the occasional affair.

When Jim Stewart, a joiner struggling to provide subsistence for his pregnant wife and five children, moves in next door, Innes fears that the peaceful pattern of his existence will be upset. It is, but not in the way he expects. It is Jim's eldest daughter, Iona, who has a devastating effect on Innes' life.

This second novel by the author of *Eightsome Reel* is a masterpiece of sensuousness and style, a rich story of unfulfilled love and feelings unacknowledged.

'Haunting . . . serious and talented'
ISABEL QUIGLY, FINANCIAL TIMES

All Pan books are available at your local bookshop or newsagent, or can be ordered direct from the publisher. Indicate the number of copies required and fill in the form below.

Send to: **CS Department, Pan Books Ltd., P.O. Box 40, Basingstoke, Hants.   RG21 2YT.**

or phone: 0256 469551 (Ansaphone), quoting title, author and Credit Card number.

Please enclose a remittance* to the value of the cover price plus: 60p for the first book plus 30p per copy for each additional book ordered to a maximum charge of £2.40 to cover postage and packing.

*Payment may be made in sterling by UK personal cheque, postal order, sterling draft or international money order, made payable to Pan Books Ltd.

Alternatively by Barclaycard/Access:

Card No. | | | | | | | | | | | | | | | | | | |

Signature:

Applicable only in the UK and Republic of Ireland.

While every effort is made to keep prices low, it is sometimes necessary to increase prices at short notice. Pan Books reserve the right to show on covers and charge new retail prices which may differ from those advertised in the text or elsewhere.

NAME AND ADDRESS IN BLOCK LETTERS PLEASE:

....

Name ————————————————————————————

Address ————————————————————————————

————————————————————————————

————————————————————————————

————————————————————————————

3/87